a charmed life

jenny b. jones

THOMAS NELSON
Since 1798

NASHVILLE   DALLAS   MEXICO CITY   RIO DE JANEIRO

So Not Happening © 2009 by Jenny B. Jones
I'm So Sure © 2009 by Jenny B. Jones
So Over My Head © 2010 by Jenny B. Jones

Published in Nashville, Tennessee, by Thomas Nelson. Thomas Nelson is a registered trademark of Thomas Nelson, Inc.

Thomas Nelson, Inc., titles may be purchased in bulk for educational, business, fund-raising, or sales promotional use. For information, please email SpecialMarkets@ThomasNelson.com.

Publisher's Note: This novel is a work of fiction. Names, characters, places, and incidents are either products of the author's imagination or used fictitiously. All characters are fictional, and any similarity to people living or dead is purely coincidental.

ISBN: 978-1-40168-688-8

Printed in the United States of America

12 13 14 15 16 17 QG 6 5 4 3 2 1

contents

so not
happening

This book is dedicated to my grandmother, Mildred Jones Griffin. She was my family, but most importantly, she was my friend. She taught me so much, but mostly taught my brother and me that our tails had better be in a pew on Sundays. She is the reason I'm saved. She was Jesus in my life. She was shopping trips, long talks, sugar cookies, outrageous laughter, and chicken and dumplings. Though she had dreams of a red convertible, she helped pay for my college instead and proudly drove a green four-door Ford.

chapter one

One year ago my mom got traded in for a newer model. And that's when my life fell apart.

"Do you, Jillian Leigh Kirkwood . . ."

Standing by my mother's side as she marries the man who is *so* not my dad, I suppress a sigh and try to wiggle my toes in these hideous shoes. The hideous shoes that match my hideous maid-of-honor dress. I like to look at things on the bright side, but the only positive thing about this frock is that I'll never have to wear it again.

". . . take Jacob Ralph Finley . . ."

Ralph? My new stepdad's middle name is Ralph? Okay, do we *need* one more red flag here? My mom is marrying this guy, and I didn't even know his middle name. Did she? I check her face for signs of revulsion, signs of doubt. Signs of "Hey, what am I thinking? I don't want Jacob Ralph Finley to be my daughter's new stepdad."

I see none of these things twinkling in my mom's crystal blue eyes. Only joy. Disgusting, unstoppable joy.

"Does anyone have an objection?" The pastor smiles and scans the small crowd in the Tulsa Fellowship Church. "Let him speak now or forever hold his peace."

Oh my gosh. I totally object! I look to my right and lock eyes with Logan, the older of my two soon-to-be stepbrothers. In the six hours that I have been in Oklahoma preparing for this "blessed" event, Logan and I have not said five words to one another. Like we've mutually agreed to be enemies.

I stare him down.

His eyes laser into mine.

Do we dare?

He gives a slight nod, and my heart triples in beat.

"Then by the powers vested in me before God and the family and friends of—"

"No!"

The church gasps.

I throw my hands over my mouth, wishing the floor would swallow me.

I, Bella Kirkwood, just stopped my own mother's wedding.

And I have *no* idea where to go from here. It's not like I do this every day, okay? Can't say I've stopped a lot of weddings in my sixteen years.

My mom swivels around, her big white dress making crunchy noises. She takes a step closer to me, still flashing her pearly veneers at the small crowd.

"What," she hisses near my ear, "are you doing?"

I glance at Logan, whose red locks hang like a shade over his eyes. He nods again.

"Um ... um ... Mom, I haven't had a chance to talk to you at all this week ..." My voice is a tiny whisper. Sweat beads on my forehead.

"Honey, now is not exactly the best time to share our feelings and catch up."

My eyes dart across the sanctuary, where one hundred and fifty people are perched on the edge of their seats. And it's not because they're anxious for the chicken platters coming their way after the ceremony.

"Mom, the dude's middle name is Ralph."

She leans in, and we're nose to nose. "You just stopped my wedding and *that's* what you wanted to tell me?"

Faint—that's what I'll do next time I need to halt a wedding.

"How well do you know Jake? You only met six months ago."

Some of the heat leaves her expression. "I've known him long enough to know that I love him, Bella. I knew it immediately."

"But what if you're wrong?" I rush on, "I mean, I've only been around him a few times, and I'm not so sure. He could be a serial killer for all we know." I can count on one hand the times I've been around Jake. My mom usually visited him when I was at my dad's.

Her voice is low and hurried. "I understand this isn't easy for you. But our lives have changed. It's going to be an adventure, Bel."

Adventure? You call meeting a man on the Internet and forcing me to move across the country to live with his family an adventure? An *adventure* is swimming with dolphins in the Caribbean. An *adventure* is touring the pyramids in Egypt. Or shopping at the Saks after-Thanksgiving sale with Dad's credit card. This, I do believe, qualifies as a *nightmare!*

"You know I've prayed about this. Jake and I both have. We know this is God's will for us. I need you to trust me, because I've never been more sure about anything in my life."

A single tear glides down Mom's cheek, and I feel my heart constrict. This time last year my life was so normal. So happy. Can I just hit the reverse button and go back?

Slowly I nod. "Okay, Mom." It's kind of hard to argue with "God says this is right." (Though I happen to think He's wrong.)

The preacher clears his throat and lifts a bushy black brow.

"You can continue," I say, knowing I've lost the battle. "She had something in her teeth." Yes, that's the best I've got.

I. Am. An. Idiot.

"And now, by the powers vested in me, I now pronounce you Mr. and Mrs. Jacob Finley. You may kiss your bride."

Nope. Can't watch.

I turn my head as the "Wedding March" starts. Logan walks to my side, and I link my arm in his. Though we're both going to be juniors, he's a head taller than me. It's like we're steptwins. He grabs his six-year-old brother, Robbie, with his other hand, and off we go in time to the music. Robbie throws rose petals all around us, giggling with glee, oblivious to the fact that we just witnessed a ceremony marking the end of life as we know it.

"Good job stopping the wedding." Logan smirks. "Very successful."

I jab my elbow into his side. "At least I tried! You did *nothing*!"

"I just wanted to see if you had it in you. And you don't."

I snarl in his direction as the camera flashes, capturing this day for all eternity.

Last week I was living in Manhattan in a two-story apartment between Sarah Jessica Parker and Katie Couric. I could hop a train to Macy's and Bloomie's. My friends and I could eat dinner at Tao and see who could count the most celebs. I had Broadway in my backyard and Daddy's MasterCard in my wallet.

Then my mom got married.

And I got a new life.

I should've paid that six-year-old to pull the fire alarm.

chapter two

There is nothing like watching your mother dance in the arms of a giant of a man who is *not* your father.

As I pick at my rubbery chicken breast and limp green beans, I stare at Jake. Wearing a goofy grin, he spins my mom to some Michael Bublé tune about how sweet love is. Sweet? I think it's nauseating. Totally hurl-worthy.

I watch my mom's aunt Shirley shimmy her girth under the limbo pole. My mother's parents died before I was born, so there wasn't a lot of family on the bride's side of the chapel.

My phone rings and I slap it open. "Hey."

"Do I hear the chicken dance?" There is absolutely no sincerity in my best friend Mia's voice. "How's the wedding of the New York socialite and the merry widower?"

The ink on my parents' divorce papers is barely dry and my mom hauls me to Oklahoma, over a thousand miles away from my friends, my dad, and my home. And for what? To live with some oaf and his two bratty sons. On a *farm* no less. If I have to slop some hogs, I am on the first plane back to Manhattan.

"Just counting the seconds until they leave for their honeymoon and I fly back to New York." I'm staying with my dad while Mom and Jake rendezvous in Jamaica. Hopefully I can talk Dad into letting me stay. Forever.

"How are the stepbrothers?"

"Mutants, just like last time I met them." I stab a piece of cake with my fork. "I don't trust these people, Mia. Especially Jake. What's that guy got up his sleeve that he would charm *my* mom into marrying him? I Googled the guy, and I found nothing. Don't you find that strange?"

"Er . . . no."

"What if Jake Finley isn't his real name? It could be his alias. He could have a prison record."

"You think he's a—"

"Psychopathic, serial-killing, online predator?" I nod. "Just one of the many possibilities I have to face here."

"I think you're overreacting."

"And I think I know trouble when I see it." I write an advice column for our school Web site, so I deal with problems daily. I know all about catastrophe.

"Oh, Bella . . ."

"My mom just married a total stranger, I will soon live at a zoo, and my new six-year-old stepbrother is dipping his Batman doll in the punch bowl." I drag my hand through my chestnut locks. "Am I the only one who sees the problem here?"

"You can do this. Where's our little optimist?"

"She's in New York. Where her life is." After we hang up, I grab a napkin and blow my nose. Right on the part that says *Jacob and Jillian Finley.*

This all happened so fast. I still don't understand it all. One minute my mom is e-mailing this guy and then six months later, they're married. And I can't call my dad. He doesn't get in from Tahiti until tomorrow morning, in time to pick me up at the airport. Yeah, he's wrapping up another vacation with his latest barely legal girlfriend, whose name I forget. Something like Kippy, Kimmie, or Magenta. I'm serious. The last girl I met—her name was Magenta. With a name like that, you *know* she has to be a stripper. It's her destiny.

So both of my parents are totally messed up right now. One thinks she's found true love. Again. And the other is currently dating through the alphabet.

"Bella!" My mother breaks through the masses, pulling What's-His-Name behind her by the hand. After a group hug, in which Jake stands uncomfortably, still linked to Mom, an awkward silence falls.

I take this opportunity to stare at Jake, taking in his gargantuan form, his outdated ponytail, and the little scar over his right brow. *Do you get that you're ruining my life? If you're an ax murderer, I want you to know I am so on to you. My dad knows tae kwon do, and if you ever raise your voice at me, he will whip out his black belt and go all Jackie Chan on you.*

"Bel, I can't wait until this week is up and we're all back together. We're going to spend some quality time with one another before school starts. Get adjusted." My mom leans into her new husband.

Gonna. Hurl.

"Plus we have to teach Bella here how to milk a cow." Jake winks and everyone laughs. Except me.

Okay, God, I don't know what You're up to, but this is not my idea of a good time. How could You do this to me? How could You rip me from my home and drop me here—in Hicksville? Because, God— Oklahoma? It's not O-K.

chapter three

I'm going to be on *Good Day, New York* this afternoon. What do you think about this jacket? Too Justin Timberlake?"

My dad's Hugo Boss blazer hangs perfectly on his gym-enhanced form. And he knows it.

"I'll be talking about the latest alternatives to Botox, as well as promoting my new retreat packages in Cancún."

And that's a retreat from wrinkles and things that sag. People don't soak up the sun and frolic at the pool when they go to Cancún with my dad, Dr. Kevin Kirkwood. They tell their friends and coworkers they're going on vacation, then come back with a brand-new face. New York doesn't call him the Picasso of Plastic Surgery for nothing.

"Dad, I was hoping we could hang out today. I've barely seen you this week, and in three days I'm an official Oklahoman." A thought that incites my gag reflexes.

"I'm sorry, babe. After the TV gig, I have a coffee date. But then I promise I'll be home."

He grabs a bottle of water out of the kitchen, one I can barely find my way around even still. I've been here every other weekend for the better part of the year, and it's still not home.

My dad is currently dating like he's on *Survivor* and it's an immunity challenge. If dating were an Olympic event, he'd be sporting a neck full of medals and his face would be plastered on the cover of *Sports Illustrated*.

He slides his sunglasses on his face. "Luisa will get your lunch. If you go anywhere, call me."

"Can't we just do lunch? Tavern on the Green? McDonald's?" Anything?

"Look, babe, this is a stressful week for me."

For *you*? "My mother just married a six-foot-five farmer, I have two new brothers preprogrammed to hate me, and I'm rounding out my last week as a resident of New York City." I cross my arms. "Now what were you saying about a stressful week?"

My dad stops long enough to place a hand on my shoulder. "Isabella, I know this is an upsetting time for you. But life can't stay like it was. Your mom and I are over, and she's moved on. I've moved on."

"And by default, I have to?"

"Just think of it as having the best of both worlds. You have fresh air in Oklahoma." *I see that shudder, Dad. I see it!* "And once a month you come back to Manhattan."

"You could've put your foot down. Forced Mom to stay in the state."

My dad smiles, his teeth a perfect white row. "Honey, if you feel like you'd enjoy talking with someone about these negative feelings, I can get you in to see my therapist."

"I could live here." I've only asked a hundred times.

He kisses me on the cheek and rests his hand on my shoulder. "The weeks will fly, and I'll see you next month."

I clench my teeth. "Good luck on your interview." And I leave the kitchen in search of more understanding company.

Like my cat.

I lumber up the stairs to the top floor of the brownstone where my park-view bedroom is tucked away.

"Señor Kirkwood means well, Bella." Luisa, the woman who used to be my nanny, waits for me at the last step, a laundry basket under her ample arm. She follows me into my room.

When my dad moved into this place, he got a professional designer to decorate. Was I consulted about my preferences for my room? Um, that would be a negative. Just like I wasn't consulted about whether I would like to pack up my life, leave everything I love behind, and move to farm country.

I twirl on my heel and crash onto my bed, staring at the ceiling. Where a painting of a group of cherubs glares down at me. They're supposed to look angelic, but to me they look like they're from some gang—fresh out of Compton.

"What's up with him, Luisa?" I sigh. "I just want my old dad back."

"He's a very busy man," she clucks as she places socks in one of my drawers. The drawer with the zebra stripes on it. The decorator obviously had a head injury before taking on my room. Actually the whole house is pretty hideous, but dad says it feeds his creative spirit. I'm not sure creativity is a quality people want in their plastic surgeon.

"I thought this week would be different." I spill my heart out to the woman who is basically now my *dad's* nanny. "I imagined him being grief-stricken that his daughter would be moving across the country, but between work and all his dates, he barely knows I'm here."

Moxie, my Persian, leaps onto my stomach. I pull her close and pet her silky white fur.

Luisa settles herself onto the edge of the bed and smoothes the hair from my face. "I will miss you. Does that count?"

"I'll miss you too. I wish you would come live with us."

She waves a hand. "No. I no live around pigs and cows. I was married once—I know what that's like."

I laugh, even though it saddens me to think of being so far away from the woman who pretty much raised me. But Dad got Luisa in the divorce settlement. There was no detail left unattended in my parents' divorce. Everything was split very neat and tidy.

Everything except me.

~~~~~~~~~

"So, Bella"—my friend Jasmine flips her hair—"are you and Hunter ready to do this long-distance thing?"

I sip my virgin daiquiri and look at the giant Buddha statue across the crowded restaurant. "Sure. Yeah." I nod and smile at my two friends surrounding me at the table. "Definitely."

Mia looks skeptical and Jasmine doesn't meet my eyes.

"Hunter is totally cool with the move." I force a dreamy look into my eyes and turn to Mia. "We'll just take it day by day, you know? With the phone, e-mail, text messages . . . it will be like we're not even apart."

We pay our bill and walk outside into the muggy August evening air, where Mia's driver pulls up in an Escalade. The three of us pile into the back, giggling over nothing in particular.

I smooth my miniskirt then dig through my bag for lip gloss.

"My last time for Club Viva. At least for a while." I sigh, thinking of my fond memories of our favorite teen dance spot.

Thirty minutes later, the Escalade stops at the entrance to Viva's, and we link arms and sashay to the entrance.

"Name?"

I blink at the bouncer. "Richie. It's me." I laugh. "Bella?" *I'm a regular!* I wait for comprehension to settle in.

It doesn't. "Bella?"

"Bella Kirkwood?"

"Oh yeah . . . Bella." Richie scratches his bald head. "I'm sorry, Miss Kirkwood, you're not on the list tonight."

"What? Of course I am! I'm always on the list." I gesture behind me. "We're all on the list." *Dude, we are the list.*

He taps his clipboard and frowns, his forehead wrinkling into folds. "Nope. Sorry. Your friends are here, but you're not. We have a special band performing tonight, and we can only take who's on the sheet here."

I feel the heat of my embarrassment all the way to my toes.

The bouncer runs a meaty finger under his too-tight collar. "Tell you what, I'll make an exception . . . but just this once."

I know I should say thank you, but I'm too busy holding back a good "Do you know who I am?"

"Since you didn't make the cut, I'll have to escort you in myself." Richie unhooks the cording and lets me pass, then stops me. "The back way. Only A-listers go through the front."

I stand rooted to my spot. A-listers? I *am* an A-lister! I'm an A plus! I'm A squared. A times infinity!

He travels fast on long legs, and in my four-inch heels and extra-large attitude, it's everything I can do to keep up. With a fist the size of a Hummer tire, he pounds on the door twice. The pulsing music grows louder as the door swings open.

The back entryway is dark, and I step closer to my escort. We round the corner, then Richie abruptly stops.

"This is the door to the dance floor," he yells over the music. "Knock three times, then go in. Someone will be on the other side to help you find your friends."

I lift my manicured hand and pound three times. I push on the door, but it doesn't budge. Rearing back, I tackle it with my left shoulder, sending it flying on its hinges.

I blink hard as the lights flare to full life.

"Surprise!"

My hands fly to cover my mouth as the room erupts into flashes, cheers, and shouts. The techno song is replaced with "Bye, Bye, Bye."

Banners hang from the back wall. WE'LL MISS YOU, BELLA! and WE LOVE YOU! and BELLA + NYC = FOREVER!

"Oh my gosh!" I shake my head and scan the room, reveling at the sight of a club full of friends. "You guys are the best." Tears pool and I quickly swipe them away as Hunter, my tower of studliness, ambles my way, arms open wide. I fold into him, and we stand under a strobe light, just hanging on and laughing.

I kiss his cheek. "Did you do this?"

He shrugs. "I had a lot of help." Hunter smiles and gestures to Mia, who stands two feet behind us. With a laugh, she leaps to us, moving in for a three-way bear hug.

"How am I ever going to make it without you two?"

"You're not going to." Hunter laces his fingers with mine and pulls me to his side. "Nothing's going to change just because you're moving."

"Totally." Mia's long blonde hair swings as she nods. "We'll miss you while you're away, but we'll just have to make the most of the time you spend here."

The music roars to full volume, and I can feel the bass rumble in my chest. The crowd of my friends fills the dance floor and circles around us. With a final hug to Mia, I pull Hunter along behind me, and I work the room, speaking to every person I pass.

Forty-five minutes later, I've worn out the words *thank you* and my chest hurts from excessive, jubilant hugging.

"Let's get you something to drink." I follow Hunter to the bar area, where he orders my Club Viva usual. "A Sprite with cherry syrup. Three cherries, no stems."

I smile into his beaming face. He leans down, brushes away my bangs, then kisses my forehead. Does it get any better than this boy? He's hot, he's thoughtful, and he throws a good party. What more do I need?

Hunter gets a water for himself, then we walk upstairs to find a table overlooking the dance floor. He pulls out my chair, and I smile at his ever-present politeness. Such the gentleman, that boy.

Hunter is the only guy I've dated. Well, besides Sammy Nugent in the sixth grade, but that was only so he'd share his Oreos with me during children's church. Mr. Perfect and I have been together for two years. Our meeting was like Disney-movie heaven. He was a freshman at Royce Boys Academy, and I was in the same grade at the Hilliard School for Girls. Twice a year, our administration decides to pretend there are boys in the population, so they bring the two schools together for a social. I remember I was dancing with this tall, redheaded kid who had a retainer and watered me like a sprinkler every time he used the letter s. Then with a tap at his shoulder, the boy stopped moving, turned around, and there was Hunter Penbrook.

"Sorry to butt in, but I have to leave soon, and she promised me a dance."

I giggled with relief and curiosity at this handsome ninth grader. Of course, being shut away from boys at my all-girls school, I pretty much giggled anytime someone of the male species was near.

"I don't remember you asking me to dance this evening," I had said, letting this cute stranger take my hand and lead me into a slow dance.

"You didn't. But I thought you looked like you needed saving."

He thought I looked like I needed saving. And with those words, I knew I couldn't let him go. Two years later, here we are. Hunter and Bella.

Together forever.

I hope.

chapter four

Dear Loyal Readers of Ask Miss Hilliard,

As you know, when it is time for the reigning advice queen, Miss Hilliard, to move on, she must pass the torch. It is with great sadness (believe me, you have no idea) that I type my last blog entry as your queen of advice, your royalty of reason. My successor has been chosen, and the new Miss Hilliard will begin next week. So keep those e-mails coming. The new Miss Hilliard has plenty of wisdom to share.

Thank you, my readers, for trusting me with your questions and dilemmas. As I leave our fine school, it seems I have acquired problems of my own. Who does an advice columnist go to for help? Please keep your former friend in your thoughts and prayers as I leave my beloved city and go to a place of complete and utter lack of refinement. I will be living on a farm complete with dirt roads and cows. I have been assured there are no muddy pigs, as we all know from dissection lab last year about my little swine phobia. But, ladies, my situation is dire. This town probably has no fashion. No style. No Starbucks, people! War criminals probably see better conditions.

So Not Happening

> *Think of me fondly and know that your problems filled me
> with joy.*

I shut my laptop and stare out my airplane window. Oklahoma in all its green glory stretches out beneath me.

"Thank you for flying American Airlines. We welcome you to Tulsa. If this is your final destination, you can pick up your baggage . . ."

Welcome to Tulsa. An hour away from my new home in a town called Truman. My stomach clenches at the very idea. I can't shake this feeling that I'll wake up any moment and discover this has all been a bad dream. I'll jump out of bed, find my parents drinking lattes in the living room, and be safely tucked away in our Manhattan apartment. God can do anything, right? Give sight to the blind, heal the lame, raise the dead . . . roll the stone away and resurrect my old life.

Fifteen minutes later I follow the crowd to baggage claim.

And there stands my mom.

Surrounded by my new stepfamily—Jake the Giant and his two mongrel sons.

"Bella!" She rushes to me, arms open wide, and pulls me close. "I've missed you!"

"You too." My face is pressed to her shoulder.

Mom takes a step back, her face beaming. "I can't wait to get you all settled in. We got back from the honeymoon a few days early, so I've been fixing up your room."

"Yeah, as in the room that used to be mine."

I look past my mother's shoulder to find Logan glaring at me like I'm overcooked spinach.

Robbie runs around us, a red Superman cape flying behind him. "Me and Budge are roomies now."

I stare at Logan's back as he walks away. "Remind me again why people call him Budge?"

Mom shrugs. "A nickname from his mother."

I guess it's better than Bubba.

An hour later, Jake's old Tahoe lurches to a stop in the dusty driveway.

"Home sweet home." Mom hugs me for the trillionth time. "I can't wait for you to see your room."

"Oh . . . the waiting has been just as painful for me too." I peel my legs out of the vehicle and step onto the ground.

Right into cow poop. "Ew!" Sick. "How does poop get in the yard?" I run toward a patch of grass and shuffle my feet like they're on fire.

Logan and Robbie laugh as they enter the house.

"Welcome to farm life." Jake chuckles and follows behind his sons.

Yeah, thanks a lot. Glad to be here. Stupid . . . pooping . . . cows.

The wraparound front porch looks like something from a Tim Burton movie—rickety, spooky, and ready to sprout jaws and collapse on someone at any moment.

Mom practically skips ahead of me and flings open the creaking screen door. Clutching my cat in her travel bag, I step inside.

"Isn't it cute?" Mom's smile doesn't quite reach her eyes. "It's going to be a lot of fun decorating. We can do that together."

I stare. Mute. Appalled at the décor around me. I think 1970 came for a visit, threw up, and never left. In the living room to my left is an orange couch, sagging in the middle like it gave up. Yellowed lace curtains hang crookedly over a filmy window.

Over my right shoulder is the dining room. A beaten and battered "wood" table takes up most of the space, piled high with newspapers, books, and random cereal toys. I am drawn to the mess like a moth to a bug zapper. I place Moxie's bag on the hardwood floor and slip into the room. With a ringed finger, I write my name in cursive on the dusty table.

I turn around as Mom stands behind me. "It's not too late to change your mind," I whisper, my eyes boring into hers. "We slip out the back door, we hop a plane, and—"

"Bella." Her hands clench my shoulders. "This is it. Accept it. You're not even trying."

"Trying!" I laugh. "A few months may be all you need to adjust to the idea of a new family and life in this . . . this *frat* house, but I need more time. This home isn't even civilized. I'm afraid to look in my room. Let me guess, gingham curtains and something that resembles an old doily for a comforter?"

"No. Of course not!" Mom blinks. "Maybe a Lord of the Rings bedspread, but it's gone."

"Perfect." My eyes flit across the table and take in the family's collection of junk. A newspaper from last December. Two candy bar wrappers. A stack of wrestling magazines.

Mom pushes me toward the stairs. "We need to get you unpacked."

The stairs creak with every step and lead us to a series of rooms on the second floor.

Mom points out Budge and Robbie's room, then grabs my hand and pulls me to the bedroom at the end of the hall. "This is it." Her hand rests on the knob. "Now before we go in, keep in mind I haven't had a lot of time to do much with it. We'll have to go shopping." She cracks the door, only to pull it shut again. "And another thing . . . you can't compare it to your room at your dad's. Or in our old apartment. It's a smaller space, okay?"

"Just open the door, Mom."

She turns the knob and we both step inside. "What do you think, sweetie?"

I turn a full circle. "I'm . . . I'm speechless."

My closet at my dad's could barely fit in this space. Plain white panels drape from the single window. A simple white duvet covers a twin bed, with pink pillows that used to rest on my plush queen-size bed. On the wall hang pictures of me, my family, and my friends from New York. They all smile back at me in black and white.

"Did you see my surprise?" Robbie, wearing a Superman costume, peeks into the room. He points to the center of the bed, where a homemade card sits propped on a throw pillow.

I force a smile and reach for the card. "I heart my new sister." Aw, that is really sweet. "Thanks, Robbie." I fold him in a tentative hug. "I love it."

"It's printed on post-consumer fiber."

I blink.

"Recycled paper." He rolls his eyes. "The Arctic Ocean could be ice-free by 2050. Every little bit helps."

I look to my mom as Robbie pads out of the room.

"He's a strangely brilliant child," she whispers. "He has an amazing photographic memory. But maybe watches a little too much cable."

Mom unpacks Moxie and places her on my bed. The cat sniffs her surroundings 'til I'm afraid she's going to vacuum the duvet through her nose. "Okay, so I'm going to let you unpack the rest of your stuff. And dinner's in an hour. We're all going to eat together."

I quirk a brow suspiciously. "You cooked?"

"Jake went to get pizza. I have to go clean the dining room table."

"You're going to need more than an hour." *And a forklift. And maybe the* Extreme Makeover: Home Edition *team.*

I sit between my mother and Robbie at dinner. Mom places a chipped plate in front of me, and I can't help but notice that all of the plates seem to be one of a kind. As in, none of them match.

"I'll pray." Jake bows his head and we all follow suit. "Dear Lord, we thank You for this new beginning. For our family. We ask that You bless this food and bless our time as we get to know one another. Amen."

"So, Bella..." Jake takes a slice of pizza and passes it to my mom. "How's the new room?"

"Oh...it's...um...nice." In the same way that pudding is nice. "Budge, I'm sorry you had to give it up for me."

My older stepbrother pops the top on his Coke. "It's not like I had any choice in the matter." If this boy were an animal, he'd be growling right now. "Now I get the joy of doing homework with a six-year-old jumping from bed to bed because he thinks he's a superhero and his ability to fly is going to kick in any minute."

"Budge," Jake warns.

"My new roomie goes to bed at eight, while sometimes I don't even get in from work at the Wiener Palace until eleven, and then I get to step on every Transformer in his collection as I make my way to my bed in the dark."

"That's enough, Son."

Wait—I'm still stuck on Wiener Palace.

"And tomorrow I get to take my computer in because Robbie here erased half my hard drive. Since he thought all my stuff was now his. I'm so *glad* I have a stepsister. Because before my life wasn't complete, but now"—he pushes the hair out of his eyes—"now it is. I'm so glad we're all so *happy*." He slams down his plate and leaves, his chair shrieking across the old floor.

Silence descends on the dining room.

Robbie smacks his lips. "Can I have his pizza?"

~~~~~~~~~~~

When I walk into my room for the night, I find my bed neatly turned down. I grab my favorite oversized t-shirt, a pair of shorts, and some undies and throw my hair into a ponytail. I slip out the door and listen in the hall for any signs of stepbrothers. Confident the area is secure, I tiptoe into the bathroom.

Where I scream my head off. "Get out! Get out! Get out!"

Budge, clad only in his boxers, squeals like a girl. "*You* get out!" He grabs a towel and holds it over his chest like he's hiding a set of Pamela Anderson double Ds.

I stand frozen. My limbs refuse to move, my mouth opening and closing on words that won't form. I'm not used to seeing half-naked guys in my bathroom. Especially of the rotund, 'fro-headed variety.

I regain my breath and jab a finger in his direction. "This is *my* bathroom!"

He laughs. "*Your* bathroom? *Au contraire*, my evil stepsister. This was *my* bathroom, but now it's ours. We'll be sharing it."

"I'm not sharing a bathroom with you. Gross."

"You are. So don't be thinking you're gonna take over with all your little girly soaps." He bumps me as he charges out the door, his hair dripping. "I'm watching you." With two fingers he points from his eyes to mine. And he disappears down the hall.

I close the door, take a seat on the dewy toilet seat, and sigh.

Hello, God? You still up there? I realize You have some big things to deal with: global warming, wars, straightening out Hollywood. But do You even remember me? I'd like to beg You to deliver me from this overflow of ick that has become my life. I would get down on my knees for this prayer, but . . . it's gross. Please help me. I don't think I can take much more of this.

Hours later I swim to the surface of a dream and open my eyes in the dark.

Where am I?

Oh yeah. Truman, Oklahoma. In the world's smallest bedroom.

The hair on my arms prickles, and I sit up. Something's not right.

I hear a noise from downstairs, and my heart leaps into overdrive. I dive for my phone, ready to call for help.

Then headlights bounce off my window, and I jump up and pull the curtains back.

Jake. Pulling out of the driveway. At 4:00 a.m.?

I sigh into the quiet room and lean into the wall. My heart slowly returns to a normal pace as I return to my bed.

Guess he has an early shift at the plant.

Or maybe he's running away.

Wish I'd thought of that.

chapter five

"Bella?"

I drag one heavy eyelid open. "Mmm?"

"It's time to get up for school!"

My head throbs in protest. I flip over and burrow deeper into my blanket, sending Moxie sprawling to the floor. "Go away."

"Get up! Greet the day!" The bed gives way as my mother sits in the remaining space beside me.

"Tell the day I said to buzz off."

"Now you can't go to school with that sour face. Where's your good attitude?"

"In New York."

"I've got breakfast for you in the kitchen."

I wrinkle my nose. "No thanks."

"I didn't cook it. Just some bagels—like back home." Mom smiles and runs her hand across my forehead, pulling the hair from my face. I always wished I had been born with her blonde hair. It fixes in seconds and makes her look all California chic. Instead, I got my dad's chocolate brown hair that, without highlights, is the color equivalent of mud. At least I got her height and long legs. Also, like her, I can't roll my tongue, but so far that hasn't been much of a problem.

After a shower, I lope down the stairs and join Mom in the dining room.

Robbie sits at the table, his elbows planted next to a cereal bowl. "But I like Chocolate Puffies."

"Sorry, sweetie. I threw those out. They're all sugar. For your first day of first grade, you need something special. Like oatmeal!"

"Yuck."

"But I put a raisin happy face on it just for you."

Robbie levels his glass green eyes. "Lady, I could smell that trick before I even got out of bed."

Mom tries again. "Raisins are good for you."

"Look like rabbit turds." He rearranges the red cape around him. Except for the wedding, I've yet to see him without it.

Robbie continues to argue with his new stepmom. His own mother apparently died when he was born, so it's just been the guys here. Living it up in the shag-carpeted bachelor pad.

I slide into a seat and close my eyes. I would think about the fact that Mom just fixed breakfast for the first time in my life, but I'm too wired over school. Today is my first day at Truman High. I'm so not ready. The first day of school is nerve-wracking enough, but being the new girl on day one? Vomit inducing.

I miss Mia and my friends. And Hunter. I've been so busy disinfecting my new room and avoiding Budge and Robbie, I haven't even had time to call him since I got in yesterday. Why is everything happening so fast? It's like my world is spinning, and I'm here hanging by a fingernail. A fingernail in desperate need of a manicure.

Mom places a bagel in front of me, followed by a container of flavored cream cheese. "Just like New York." She waits expectantly. "Eat up."

I pick it up. Doesn't feel like a New York bagel. I sniff it. Doesn't smell like a New York bagel. I crunch into it.

"I don't know what that is, but it's not a bagel."

Mom stands up. "Well, I don't think you're going to pass any street vendors on your way to school, so eat now or forever hold your peace."

Budge walks into the dining room, his large feet dragging. "Hey." He warily takes in the scene before his eyes flit briefly to me. "You ready?"

I blink. "Um . . . no."

"I have a gamers club meeting before school, so hurry up. We're discussing the newest version of Halo, and I can't miss it."

I look at Mom.

"Logan is going to drive you two to school." She pulls her mouth into a smile. "You know I'd love to take you, but Jake and I have to take Robbie. It's his first day of first grade, you understand."

Robbie sticks his finger in his oatmeal. "Parental involvement is directly related to my success as a student." He levels his eyes on me. "I don't think you want to mess with my future."

Ugh. I have got to remind Dad that he was going to buy me a car. I'm one of those weird New Yorkers who actually has a driver's license. Just no car.

"Dude, I'm serious," Budge says. "I have to go. My meeting is very important. We're electing officers."

I take another bite of the cardboard bagel. "I would hate to keep you from your life's work."

"The Halo hierarchy is not something to joke about. It demands respect."

I laugh. "Get over yourself."

"Whatever. The Budge train is leaving. If you want a first-class seat, you get up now. Otherwise . . . it's coach. Something you probably know little about." He stands beside his brother and holds out his fist. Robbie hits it with his own. "Make me proud today, Robmeister. Keep your hands to yourself and remember rule number one above all things."

"Don't discuss politics."

"No, the other one."

Robbie nods. "Don't eat glue." He drops his chin. "It's my weakness."

Budge slams the back door behind him.

I jump up, leaving the rest of my breakfast.

"Have a great day, honey. I'm praying for you. I know it's tough, but you will be a stronger person for it."

I grab my purse and Dooney backpack and follow in the path of my stepbrother.

Outside, the Oklahoma sun shines on the Finleys' small farm. Somewhere in the distance, cows moo and roosters crow. I should find this all peaceful and quaint, but I don't. Gimme some smog and irate taxi drivers any day.

"Are you coming or what?" Budge steps out of an old, dilapidated garage that has seen better days. And those were probably around the World War II era.

I step inside and my breath hitches at the monstrosity before me. "No."

"Get in."

"No way." I shake my head. "There is no power on earth that's going to make me climb into that . . . that . . ."

"Hearse." Budge pats his car, his eyes clouded with love. "Ain't she a beaut?"

"A 'beaut'? *She* used to transport *dead* people, and I am not stepping foot into it. I'd rather walk."

"Driving your prissy self to school was not my idea, so I'm not going to sit here all day and wait for you." He opens the heavy gray door and scoots in. The dead-people mobile starts right up like a Formula One race car.

At the sound of another engine, I turn to see Mom, Jake, and Robbie pulling out of the front driveway. They wave happily, like this instantly complete family. Dust plumes behind the Tahoe.

The hearse cruises by me. "Wait!" I run after Budge's car, my heels punching holes in the yard.

He brakes and cranks his window down. Screamo pours out the car and pounds in my ears. Not only does he have hideous taste in cars, but his musical choices are just as bad. Clearly a sign of mental disturbance.

"You can't just leave me here."

He looks down at my heels and smirks. "Yes, I can. And will. Rich girl, there ain't room enough in my car for you, me, and your overbloated attitude. You can walk to school for all I care."

I sputter. "I don't even know where the school is!"

"Use that nose you've got so stuck in the air—and sniff it out."

And he drives away.

I stand in the driveway, torn. Do I run after him? I'd ruin my dignity. And my Marc Jacobs shoes.

Or do I just walk? Maybe skip school? Forget it all, kick back, and watch some daytime TV?

I rip my cell phone out of my purse and punch in my mom's number. In one long sentence, I fill her in.

"Bella, I can't come and get you. We're still five minutes away from the school, and we can't be late. We have a parent meeting."

A *parent meeting!* Where's *my* parent?

"Why didn't you get in the car with Logan?"

"Do you honestly need an explanation for that question?"

I hear my stepdad talking in the background. "Jake says his farm truck is in the barn. Keys are on a hook in the kitchen. But be careful. You don't have a lot of driving experience."

I sigh and consider bawling for the millionth time since arriving. "Fine. I'll take it."

Mom gives me directions to the school, and we hang up.

Barn. I think I saw one of those.

I smooth down my skirt and head behind the garage, following the sound of cows. My feet are already protesting.

At the fence opening, I maneuver a latch and drag the heavy gate until it's wide open. I teeter across some railing in the ground, losing my footing only once, and just walk.

I head to a grove of trees, and just around the corner is my mecca. A barn. Red, of course, with a paint job so fresh the house would be jealous.

I jump at the bawling of a nearby cow.

Taking three steps back, I hold out my hands. "Stay back. I'm warning you. I have . . . um . . . hair spray and Tic Tacs in this bag, and I'm not afraid to use them."

Big, blinking eyes lazily assess me, but the cow still walks closer. My heart doubles in tempo. Can cows smell fear?

"I'm not afraid of you." I'll psych it out. "I just don't want to hurt you. So for your own good, I'm asking you again to back that thing up." Nothing. "Shoo! Shoo!"

The black-and-white giant marches even closer, and I suck in my breath. New plan—I'll stand still as a statue. No eye contact. No movement. Isn't that what you're supposed to do when accosted by a wild bear?

The hairs on my arms prickle as the cow's heavy, warm breath settles over me like a blanket. Like a nasty, hideous, damp, gross blanket.

The beast smacks its lips.

It's going to eat me!

I give up on my plan to stay mute. "Oh, Jesus. Help me, Jesus. Though I walk through the valley of the shadow of death, I will fear no evil." I'm totally fearing! "Yea, though . . ." I can't think! "Something, something, something . . . uh . . . though you make me to lie down in green pastures."

The animal's expansive, wet nose sniffs me. *Excuse me, but if anyone's the offensive one here, it's you.*

"The Lord is my shepherd, I shall not want—"

Slurp!

My scream pierces the sky.

I just got licked by a giant cow tongue! I swab at my face, breaking my frozen pose. "*Ugh! Ewwww!* You know what, that is enough!" I leap back. "Now you listen to me, you . . . you . . . bovine." I roll my shoulders and straighten my spine. "You are totally violating my space here. I have had a really, really hard morning."

The old thing blinks, and I notice its full, curvy eyelashes. What a waste of a feature.

"Now I am going to just step around you, walk into that barn, and get in a truck. But I'm warning you, if you try to follow me, I will not be responsible for my actions." I lower my voice. "You should probably know . . . I eat burgers. You should *fear* me." *Oh yeah.*

I turn on my heel and sprint away.

The truck, a blue thing born about the same time as the hearse, sits beneath a covered area adjacent to the barn. I swipe at the sweat and cow slobber on my forehead and climb into the cab.

Twisting the key, I offer up a prayer of thanks when it starts. I haven't been behind the wheel since I spent last month with my grandparents in the Hamptons. With shaky hands, I maneuver the truck into the field and wave good-bye to the lone cow. By the time I hit the first paved road in town, I'm singing some classic Beyoncé.

I signal to turn at the final four-way stop. I will not be embarrassed to pull into the parking lot in this truck. I am lucky God provided it. Even though God also provided me with a *jerk* of a stepbrother, making the truck necessary in the first place.

As I lift my foot off the break, the blue truck sputters and chokes. "No, you don't. Come on. Just a few more miles. You can do it." *Break down later.*

I turn left.

And the truck gives up. No more.

With the vehicle's last few breaths, I steer it to the side of the road. Smoke pours out from underneath the hood.

I pound my head on the steering wheel. This can't be my life.

Am I on camera? A reality show, maybe, where they see how much I can take before I crack?

Barely stifling a few choice words, I call my mom again.

No answer.

Swinging the door open, I slide down to the ground, grab my bags . . .

And walk.

"You want a ride?" I jump at a voice as a truck slows down next to me. His bald head sticks out the window.

"No, thanks." Creep. Who trolls down a road and asks girls if they want to get in his truck?

"You Jake Finley's stepdaughter?"

At this I stop. "Maybe."

He looks me over, but the perv factor is pretty low. "I'm a good friend of Jake's. Recognized his truck. I'd be glad to give you a ride to school."

"I'll just walk." I pick up my pace, but he continues to drive along beside me. "I said *thank you*, sir."

"Miss?"

Exasperated, I sigh. "What?"

"You're going the wrong way."

chapter six

~~~~~~

Y ou smell."

This is how the school secretary greets me.

"Thanks." *And your eau de Avon is just a total nasal delight.*

"No, I mean, seriously, hon. You smell."

I toss my backpack on the counter, drape myself over it, and launch into my sob story, emphasizing words like *hearse, attack cow, stalled truck,* and *two-mile hike in heels.*

"You probably want to wash your shoes off. I think you might've stepped in it."

And I'd like to step right back out and fly myself home to Manhattan.

"I've got some wet wipes and soap in the bathroom back here."

I scrub down as much as possible, throw my once perfectly straight hair into a frizzed-out ponytail, and walk back into the office with as much dignity as I can muster.

The thirtysomething secretary smiles and gives me a thumbs-up. "Much better."

"Thank you."

"Now your mama's already registered you and everything, so

I'll just have a student show you to your first class." She snaps her fingers and a sleeping kid in a row of chairs lifts his head. "Josh, take Miss Kirkwood to her first class. It's Mrs. Palmer's room."

With barely a glance in my direction, Josh leads me down a hall, around a corner, and to my first-period class.

He leaves me at the door, and I walk myself in. My already-queasy stomach twists itself into a pretzel knot.

The teacher stops her back-to-school spiel at the front of the room, eyes me, checks her watch, then motions me in.

I hand her my schedule and pray I washed off all the stink.

"Take a seat right over there, please."

Aware of everyone's stare, I follow the direction of her pointing finger, then stop.

Budge.

Right behind the empty seat.

"Um . . ." My voice is a croaking whisper. I check my schedule again, hoping I'm really supposed to be in another room. No such luck.

"Is there a problem?"

Lady, we don't have time to get into all my problems.

My eyes take in Budge, who regards me with nothing less than bored disgust. I limp down the aisle, every blister on my foot tempting me to scream, and settle into the desk.

"Nice walk?" Budge whispers behind me.

"Perfectly enjoyable. I was glad to catch some fresh air." I also caught some bugs in my teeth on that last two miles, but I won't give him the satisfaction of those details.

Fifteen minutes later the bell rings, and I pull the schedule from my purse to check my next destination.

"Can I help you find your class?" I look up from my seat and find a blond guy from two rows over standing near. "I'm Jared Campbell."

I smile, suddenly aware that any lip gloss I had on was probably slobbered off by cow tongue. "I'm Bella. And I would love some help."

His dark eyes glance at my schedule. "Right this way." And we walk down the crowded hall.

"Where are you from?" he asks.

"New York." I feel the ever-present pang of homesickness. "I guess you're a hometown boy?"

He laughs. "Nah, a lot of us are transplants. Many of us have parents who work in Tulsa but don't necessarily want to live there, so here we are. I'm originally from Chicago."

I sidestep a boy wearing saggy pants and a nose ring. "Do you ever get used to it? Is this ever home?"

Jared pats me on the shoulder. "Sure. It takes awhile. I've been here three years, I guess. "

We come to an abrupt halt at room 202.

"Thanks, Jared. I appreciate the help." My first kind soul at Truman High. Well, besides the secretary wielding the baby wipes.

"Why don't you eat lunch with me and my friends? We sit in the corner of the cafeteria next to the vending machines. I'll be looking for you."

A pound or two of weight dissolves from my burdened mind. I have someone to eat lunch with—a total new-kid score.

I leave my second-period art class completely high on paint fumes. Stepping into the ladies' room afterwards, I find a stall and text my mom the location of the truck.

Taking a deep breath, I open the small door and work my way

through the crowd of girls, all of us waiting to look at ourselves in the row of bathroom mirrors.

The girl beside me gasps. "Oh my gosh. Max Azria, right?"

I turn to see she's staring at me.

"Your skirt—Max Azria."

I smile in relief. She's speaking my language. "Yeah. I love his stuff." Though my outfit is now a total wrinkled, wilted mess. "I've had kind of a bad morning. I'm not exactly at my best."

"I'm Emma Daltry. I'm a junior."

"Me too!" I pull out some gloss, finding a spot at a mirror. "I'm new—Bella Kirkwood."

"You must sit with me at lunch. We can talk clothes."

"Oh, I'd love to. But I already have a lunch commitment. Maybe tomorrow?"

"Definitely. I'll see you around." Emma tosses a limp good-bye and flounces out. I guess it was wrong of me to assume everyone here would be wearing Wranglers and cowboy boots.

After chemistry, I move on to something I'm fairly decent at—math. In AP Calculus I'm given a textbook that probably weighs more than Robbie. Mr. Monotone teaches that class, forcing me to count the seconds until the blessed lunch bell finally sounds.

Following the herd, I locate the cafeteria. I wait ten minutes in line for a shriveled-up burrito, then maneuver through the crowd to Jared's table.

"Hey, Bella!"

I smile at the small gift that he remembers my name.

"This is Bella, everybody." Jared proceeds to introduce me to his friends. "And finally, this is Brittany Taylor." The girl beside him gives me the most pitiful excuse for a smile. *She totally needs a French kiss from a cow.*

"Well, hey." Emma, the girl from the bathroom, grabs a seat and sets down her tray. "Bella, right?"

"Yeah. Jared and I have AP English together, so he invited me to join you guys." I'm on the verge of babbling. There's an undercurrent here I can't quite put my finger on. My eyes drift to Brittany again. She stares at me like I still smell of barnyard. Maybe the powder-fresh scent of the baby wipes has worn off.

"So what do you think of your first day so far?" Emma pops a fry in her mouth and leans in.

Oh, how to put this tactfully? "It's fine." *Like eating nails is fine.*

"Bella's from New York." A murmur of appreciation goes round the table at Jared's announcement.

I fill them in on a brief synopsis of my life.

"You went to an all-girls school?" Brittany asks this in the same tone one would say, "You pick your nose?"

I smile. "Yes." *Sister, you do not want to knock my life as a Hilliard Girl. I will recite our pledge, yodel our fight song, and break out the secret handshake if necessary.*

"Has to be a lonely place without any guys around, eh?"

I laugh at Jared. "Not exactly. There's a nearby private school for boys." I feel a pang of guilt for not mentioning Hunter. But these people don't need to know my entire life story yet. "What do you guys do for fun around here?"

Emma sighs prettily. "Not much, I'm afraid. I'm originally from Seattle, and I have yet to adapt to the total lack of things to do in Truman. We go into Tulsa a lot. Shop, eat, hit some hot spots."

I watch the cafeteria crowd as my table enters into a conversation about kids I have yet to meet. I'm living a fashion nightmare. Jeans of every color and style. Shoes that do not match outfits. A blatant disregard for root maintenance. Is this what I'll look like in a year? *You will not suck me in, Truman!*

"So . . . Brittany . . ." Girl who is still staring me down like a rabid schnauzer. "How long have you lived in Truman? Where are you from?"

Emma giggles. "Oh, our Brit's not a transplant. She's an original."

"But we let her hang out with us anyway." Jared nudges Brittany with an elbow. Her face breaks into a reluctant smile.

"Maybe you can help me learn my way around here, then."

Brittany steals a fry off Jared's tray. "Right. Hey, Emma, are we still going shopping Wednesday night?"

"I know! Bella can go shopping with us, right, Brit?" Emma doesn't wait for her answer. "We'll show you Tulsa, then top off the evening at our favorite burger place."

My spirits lift at the magical, therapeutic mention of shopping. "I would love that." *Thank You, God, for giving me friends on day one. Especially friends who appreciate a night out with the credit cards.*

We rush through the rest of lunch, and the gang fills me in on local gossip, pointing out the troublemakers, the shady characters, and the wannabes in the room. I laugh at all their stories and file away the information.

Things learned at Truman High so far:

One, do not get on this group's bad side.

Two, avoid the burritos.

chapter seven

"How was school?" Mom closes her book, *Parenting a Teen Without Being Mean*, when I open the car door.

I shut myself in the Tahoe and dissolve into the seat, tired but grateful to be alone with my mother without the Finley men.

"I arrived a sweaty mess. The school secretary wouldn't let me into my classes until I passed a smell test, and I have English with Budge." I sigh and rest my head on the door. "I'm just a fish out of water here. A Jimmy Choo in a sea of Payless BOGOs."

"We both have to adapt. You think I'm not struggling?" She holds up her book. "I haven't had a six-year-old in the house in a long time. And when I did, I had help."

"I miss Luisa." My nanny would listen to my sad Oklahoma stories, fix me a cup of homemade hot chocolate, and tell me everything would get better. My mom used to be so busy with working out, charity events, and a collection of other random hobbies that I only saw her an hour or so a day. This new version of Mom is kinda freaking me out.

She drives us to the crumbling Victorian I am now forced to call home. The farm truck sits in the front yard, hoisted up on blocks. Two legs stick out from beneath it.

I reach for the door handle. "The day a toilet seat appears on the front porch, I am so gone."

"Give this a chance."

"Hey, guys!" Robbie tears out of the house, barefoot and wearing his usual cape. "Look what I did in school today. Guess what it is."

He holds up a finger-painted blob of red, white, and blue.

"Oh . . ." My mother frowns, clearly searching for words. "Is it a . . . ball?"

"Nope." Strike one for Mom.

"A puppy?"

"Get real, lady."

"A self-portrait?"

"It's a symbolic representation of my patriotic feelings."

I can only nod.

"I watch a lot of CNN." And Robbie pivots on his bare heel and runs back into the house.

"You probably ought to order some more of those books, Mom."

Jake slides himself out from under the rusted blue heap, wipes his sweating head with a handkerchief, and moseys our way. He wraps his trunk-sized arms around my mom and plants one right on her lips.

Ew.

"Did your day get any better, Bella?"

I give him my best plastic smile. "It was lovely. Can't wait to do it again tomorrow."

The screen door opens and smacks shut again, with Robbie squealing and running. "Oh, Daddy! Oh no, Daddy!" He tornadoes in our direction, running right into his dad. "She's gone!" His eyes are huge and serious, his breathing ragged.

"Who's gone, Son?"

"Betsy. She's run away. After all we've been through, she left me."

"Who's Betsy?" Mom asks.

"His cow."

My stomach does a strange flop. "What does Betsy look like?"

Robbie raises his head and pins his eyes on mine. "Like a cow."

"I'm sure she's there. Let's go grab her a little snack, and we'll find her."

Jake and his hysterical son disappear behind the house.

"Don't worry, Bel. This is just part of farm life." Mom wraps her arm around my shoulders and guides me inside. "Why don't you come and talk to me while I start dinner."

"You don't cook, Mom."

"I do now."

An hour later, I'm peeling carrots for Mom's secret recipe when Jake and Robbie return, followed by Budge. Jake hangs his ball cap on a peg in the kitchen, Robbie runs upstairs like his pants are on fire, and Budge lurks in the doorway, his face drawn.

"Did you find Betsy?" Mom stirs at the stove, reading from her cut-out recipe.

"No." Jake's gray eyes land on me. "Did you shut the gate when you drove the truck out this morning?"

I swallow. "No."

Budge sneers. "Didn't you see the cow?"

"Yes, Budge, I did. Not only did I see it, I was totally violated by it, in case anybody cares. I could've been seriously hurt."

My stepbrother laughs and shakes his head. "Afraid she'd lick you to death? That cow wouldn't step on an ant, let alone bother you."

I jerk the peeler over a carrot. "Like I'd know that!" I turn my attention to Jake. "I'm sorry. I was late for school and . . . stressed." *And nobody gave a crap.* "And then the cow wouldn't leave me alone. I've never even *touched* a cow before, and then he, er, she, was all up in my business, and—"

"She's Robbie's pet. He got her from his mama's parents when he was born." The room silences at Jake's statement.

I stare at the pile of orange in the bowl. "I'm sorry. I didn't know. But there was that cattle guard thingy, and—"

Budge smirks. "Cows can jump that."

"How could I know your magic cow could hurdle something *made* to keep her in? Does that make any sense? I mean, what is the purpose of having a cattle guard if it doesn't *guard* the cattle?"

"That's enough," Jake says.

"Your son leaves me stranded here this morning, and *I'm* the one in trouble?"

Jake holds up a hand the size of a tractor wheel. "Nobody said you were in trouble. I'm just trying to piece this all together. If she's been out since this morning . . . well, we'll have to widen our area of search."

Budge looks at me like I have peas for brains. "He means we might not find her. She could be caught in something and hurt by now. Good job."

My cat takes that moment to appear at my ankle and curls herself around it, purring.

Budge sneezes and wipes his eyes. "Get that cat out."

"She can't go outside. She doesn't have any claws." I pick Moxie up and pull her close.

Budge sneezes again and pinches the bridge of his nose.

"Hon, maybe you could take her out of the kitchen." Mom shoots me a warning glance. "Please."

Clutching my cat, my only piece of home, I stomp up the stairs and slam my bedroom door.

I put my iPod earbuds in, fire up my laptop, and log on to the *Ask Miss Hilliard* blog. I need to touch base with normal. Reconnect with real.

Dear Sisters of Hilliard,

Greetings from the heartland!

Miss Hilliard texted me today and said she has been getting lots of queries as to my situation. I am so humbled by your concern. What true friends you all are. And believe me, I could use the support.

I will spare you most of the details, but this morning I was expected to ride to school in a hearse. I refused, of course. Then I was accosted by a wild animal in a field. This beast clearly could've used a session of Mrs. Harbinger's Manners 101.

Next I was forced to drive an old, unreliable truck to school, but of course, it left me stranded on the side of the road, forcing me to walk for miles and practically ruin my heels. And it's not like I can just run downtown and replace them, right? In fact, if these people have a place to shop in this city, I have yet to see it. Unless you need a part for your John Deere.

Ta-ta for now, ladies. I appreciate the thoughts and prayers passed my way. I need them. These are troubled times

we live in—the crisis in the Middle East, the decaying environ-
ment, and me stuck in cow town.

Inhale some smog for me,
Your former Ask Miss Hilliard

Forty-five minutes later, after passing on Mom's attempt at cooking, I throw on my oldest pair of jeans, a t-shirt, and a cute pair of retro rain boots. I hear the "family" in the living room watching *Wheel of Fortune,* so I ease out the back door and walk toward the field.

I make sure to shut the heavy gate behind me this time. "Bet-sy!" My voice scatters some birds. "Bet-sy! Here, cow!"

I continue walking and yelling until my feet and throat are both sore.

Sometime later, I find myself near a pond. And there's Betsy, her black-and-white fur shining as the sun starts to set behind her. She looks up, her dark eyes totally unimpressed with my presence. She continues to drink from the pond.

"Hey, girl." I smile, relieved that I have not single-handedly killed Robbie's pet after all. "Come here." The cow continues to ignore me, as if she is having a private, meditative moment with nature.

"Where've you been?" *And for that matter, where am I?* I glance around at the landscape. Nothing looks familiar.

As I close the distance, I see stickers and prickly things in the cow's tail. "Somebody's been for a walk, eh?" I get close enough to touch her face. "Well, I certainly can't blame you, but time's up. You have to come back with me. I can certainly understand wanting to leave, but if anybody's running away from this place, it's me."

I hold out my hand like I expect her to follow. "Here we go . . . This way. Be a good cow, now." Robbie's pet returns to slurping from the green water. "Bets, can I talk to you—girl to girl? I pretty much made a little boy cry today, and if I don't redeem myself, then I'm in big trouble." I move some distance away and sit down on the bank.

"But maybe today was God's way of getting my attention. The Finleys think I'm just some spoiled society brat. Well, you know what, Bets?" I stand and dust off my jeans. "I'll show them. I will just show them what Bella Kirkwood is made of. And it ain't just Macy's and Prada bags." *I totally just said "ain't."*

"Now . . . how to get us home?" I turn a full circle, eyeing the sun, the trees, some rock piles.

I am so lost.

I sit for what must be hours, hungry, tired, and mad that no one has bothered to come and find me. They probably think I want some alone time. Well, *wrong!*

The sun is almost tucked away when Betsy gets up, moos to the darkening sky, and walks herself past me.

I lift my head from my knees and watch her tail swing in a happy little rhythm. She stops some distance ahead and turns around, as if she's waiting for me.

What do I have to lose?

I stand up, pick off a few leaves . . . then follow a cow all the way home.

<hr />

"I found your cow." I shuck off my boots and walk into the living room, where Robbie sits in my mom's lap.

"You did? Where was she?"

"Just hanging out." Did anyone even realize I was gone?

"I think you're really mean for letting her out."

"Robbie, Bella didn't mean to." Mother smoothes back his red hair. "She and I come from a very big city. We barely even had a yard."

Or a maze of cow dookie to step around.

Robbie glares at me all the way up the stairs as I head toward my room. I grab my cell phone and call Hunter.

"Hey, you! How's my little Oklahoman?"

I start at the beginning and fill him in on every detail. "And then this evening . . ." I sigh. "I had to launch a one-girl search party for a—" A female giggle in the background stops me cold. "Who is that?"

Hunter laughs. "Oh, that's just Mia."

"Mia?" As in my best friend, Mia?

"Yeah, she's helping me with my algebra. Here, she wants to talk to you."

When I get off the phone with Mia, all my worries evaporate like snow in California. It's the same old Mia, same old gossip, same best friend.

The only one who's different is me.

chapter eight

So what do you think of Tulsa?"

I suck on my second Frappuccino, ignoring the brain freeze and relishing the long-lost flavor. It is cruel and unusual punishment to force me to live somewhere without a Starbucks. I mean, come on. I think there might be *three* cities in the world that don't have Starbucks, and Truman is one of them. What are the odds?

"Not bad." In fact, I kind of like the outside shopping center. In Pottery Barn I grab two sets of sheets, a comforter, an armload of throw pillows, and some curtain panels for my room, all centered around an organic Asian theme. Anything beats the garage sale motif of my room now.

I reach for one more pillow. Then drop everything in my arms.

"Let me get that for you." Jared Campbell steps out from an aisle.

"Jared!" Brittany throws her arms around him as he picks up the contents of my new bedroom.

He hands me a package with a lopsided grin. "Your Egyptian cotton sheets, madam."

I smile. "Thank you, sir."

"So the guys and I decided to crash your shopping trip. Are you girls ready for dinner yet?"

I walk to the register with my goods, already envisioning a new paint job for the bedroom.

"Let's take Bella to Sparky's Diner downtown. What do you think, Brit?" Emma asks.

"Yeah, sure."

The cashier gives me the grand total, and I hand over my Visa.

"I'm sorry, but your card has been declined."

I flinch as if she's just insulted my mother. "Excuse me?"

"Do you have another one we could try?"

"Um...sure." I laugh. "I can't imagine what the problem is." And hand her the MasterCard. I smile and roll my eyes at my friends.

"Nope, I'm afraid this one is declined too."

My fragile grip on politeness slips. "That's impossible. Try them again."

"Ma'am, I'm sorry. In fact, I'm going to have to cut them up."

I turn away, unable to watch this horrific display. "Let's go. Something is really wrong. It's got to be their machines. Or maybe my identity has been stolen. Some sixty-five-year-old man in the Philippines is probably posing as me and ordering boxes of frilly underwear online to his heart's content."

"I'm sure it's nothing." Emma pats me on the shoulder.

"Let's go eat. The guys and I are starved." Jared steps in beside me. "I'll buy." He holds up a hand when I open my mouth. "I won't take no for an answer. It will be my welcome-to-Truman gift to you." Jared gives me a quick side-hug. "That's what friends are for, right?"

Sparky's Diner is nothing but a hole-in-the-wall burger joint. And aside from the fact that someone's having to pick up my tab, it's perfect. The walls are covered with black-and-white pictures of Sparky, the owner, and various celebrities who have been here through the years. Sparky and Donald Trump. Sparky and Chuck Norris. Sparky and *NSYNC before Justin left them to bring sexy back.

"Brittany, scoot down a seat so I can sit by Bella." Emma puts her purse down beside me and waits for her friend to move.

Brittany's eyes narrow as she slides across the booth. "So, Bella. Do you have a boyfriend?"

"Yes, in New York." I smile. "Hunter."

"How's the long-distance thing going?" Jared asks, swiping a fry off my plate. A plate he paid for.

"It stinks." But what about this move *doesn't* totally reek? "I left a lot back in Manhattan. I left a school I loved. A huge group of friends. A writing gig as an advice columnist."

"What? How cool," Emma says.

"Yeah, I had an advice blog. Students at Hilliard would write in with their problems, and I would answer them as Miss Hilliard. I still write in some and update my blog fans on my life. Though anymore it consists of entries like, 'Life is awful—just like last week.'"

Brittany lifts a brow. "Truman isn't the place for you?"

"Are you kidding? This is the last place on earth I want to be." I hold up my hands. "I mean, don't get me wrong, it's charming in its own way. I just need the culture and pace of New York, you know? Not to mention I have a demon-possessed stepbrother."

"Budge Finley."

"Yeah." I stare at Brittany. "How did you know?"

"Your stepdad works with mine."

"At the paper plant?"

She nearly chokes on her Coke. "If that's what you want to call it."

My eyes narrow. *Aha.* I knew Jake Finley wasn't on the up-and-up. He left at the crack of dawn *again* this morning, yet he was at the table for breakfast. Something strange is brewing. "What do you mean? They don't make paper at the Summer Fresh factory?"

"Yeah, but that's not all." She laughs. "You'll have to ask your stepdad." She picks up her purse.

"Let's head back to Truman." The group stands up at Jared's command. "Some of us have homework to do."

"Hope you get your credit card situation fixed," Brittany says as we exit. "I'd hate to see you suffer any more than you already have here."

I slam the door and rush through the foyer.

"Wait a minute."

Mom and Jake sit in the darkened living room, the closing credits of *Letterman* on mute.

"Later—I have to call the credit card companies."

"In here. Now."

My foot halts on the first step. I sigh and walk in to join them. "Yes?"

Mom consults her watch. "First of all, you were supposed to be home an hour ago. It's a school night." She waits for my excuse.

I shrug and give her my sweetest smile, a face that has always worked on Mom but would never work on my nanny.

"Jake says when Budge, er, Logan is past curfew, he gets grounded." She holds up her latest parenting guide, *No Means I Love You.* "This book would agree."

Maybe you skipped the chapter where it talks about exceptions for daughters whose lives have been ruined.

Mom gestures to an empty seat and turns on the lamp. "Bella, your credit cards are no good."

"You're telling me! I tried to shop at Pottery Barn tonight and—" I sit up straighter. "Wait a minute. How did you know that?"

"I had your dad cancel them today. I forgot to tell you."

"You *forgot?*"

Mom looks to her husband then back at me. "We're a family now. And we all will live under the same roof, under the same rules. Jake and I want all of you kids to live equally—it's not fair for you to have an unlimited credit card and Logan to have to work at the Wiener Palace for extra money. So any money your father gives you for child support will now be put into a trust fund. And your credit cards are gone."

I stand up. "That's insane." It's like cutting off someone's life support.

"This is our new life, hon."

"Well, I hate *our* new life." I stomp past them and pound up the stairs. "I hate this town! I hate . . ." *Think, think. What else?* "Cows! And those *stupid* roosters that wake me up every morning!" *Stomp, stomp.* "And sheets that don't match!" The walls shake when I shut the bedroom door.

Moxie hops off my bed and greets me, wrapping her white body around my ankles. I pick her up and she purrs into my neck. Outside my window, an overgrown oak tree taps on my window.

Trying my best to ignore it, I sit down at my desk with Moxie. She paws at an imaginary bug as I turn on my Mac.

Dear Hilliard Sisters,

For those of you who pray, I need it. Your former Ask Miss Hilliard is living in the pit of the country. Nobody understands fashion here. They wouldn't know a Marc Jacobs bag if Wal-Mart put them on clearance. The school colors are a hideous green and black. The school parking lot looks like a Ford truck dealership. My stepbrothers are mutants from outer space, the oldest driving a vehicle he purchased at a funeral home's garage sale. The cheerleaders wear bows in their hair like it's 1985. And yesterday someone asked me if my Rock & Republic jeans were a new style from Wrangler!

I could go on and on, ladies. I know you feel my pain, and there is some comfort in that. So this is your former Miss Hilliard . . . asking you for advice. Short of hopping the red-eye back to my beloved NYC, what can I do?

My cat and my memories of Hilliard are all that get me through.

Oh, and my iPod.

And my Wii.

Okay, and my new Chanel bag.

But still. You understand my pain. Keep me in your thoughts during my dark hours of suffering.

That which does not kill us . . . is probably not in Truman, Oklahoma.

Your former Ask Miss Hilliard

chapter nine

Bella, I have a giant favor to ask."
I put down my cereal spoon and glare at my mother. She and I haven't said two words to each other since last night.

"Oh, let me guess, you want me to go out back and get the eggs out of the henhouse?" Do we even have one of those?

Mom takes Robbie's oatmeal out of the microwave, slams it on the table, then all but jumps into the seat next to me. "I've had enough of this." She pushes her blonde bangs out of her eyes. "You think this isn't hard for me too?"

"You signed up for this! I didn't." But I would totally sign up for a stepfamily refund right now.

"All of this is just as new to me. I'm having to learn how to cook, take care of a house by myself, be a mother to two boys, and live on a factory worker's income. This is not easy." Mom's chin quivers, and I see her brave mask slip.

"We don't belong here. We're like two Paris Hiltons stuck on Planet Wal-Mart."

My mother places her hand over mine. "Yes, we do belong here. I do love Jake, and you need to accept that even though this is not a day at the Ritz, we're not going anywhere. Bella, this is all very, very difficult." Lines crinkle on her forehead. "But I need you on my side—not fighting me every step. We're in this together."

"Then why cut off my credit cards and totally humiliate me in front of my new friends? I wanted to *die*. Why leave me carless in my new hometown? I get why your life has to change—you're not connected to Dad anymore. But I am. Surely he can't be supportive of me living this second-rate life."

"Actually, he is."

"He's not! He's just too caught up in his own life to care what's going on in mine." The man has yet to call me. "You know he doesn't have time for any family discussions, so he just agrees with whatever you say. And you're using that to your advantage."

"You are my daughter, and I love you. But being here has made me realize that we led very shallow lives in New York."

"Yes. And I liked it." *I mean no!* I wasn't shallow. I was involved in my church youth group in Manhattan. I did mission work. I was a Big Sister. I took my Little Sis to Barneys every season. I dedicated my time to advising the hurting and downtrodden at Hilliard. *That's* shallow?

"Well, if you're not so wrapped up in material things, you won't mind catching a ride with Logan this morning."

I choke on a bite of Corn Pops. "No way."

"I have a job interview this morning and can't take you to school. Please?"

"I am *not* riding in that death mobile. It's ugly, it's a sign of your stepson's mental imbalance, and it's embarrassing."

Budge chooses that exact moment to raid the fridge. "Too bad you don't have a car."

I toss my hair and snarl. "I'm going to have a fabulous car very soon. Ever heard of a BMW?" If there's any perk to living here at all, it's that I get to drive.

He shuts the door and looks to the ceiling as if deep in thought. "BMW? I hear you're getting something of the used clunker variety like the rest of us *poor* Truman teens."

I suck in air. "What? That's a lie." Daddy promised I could pick out anything I wanted. I have this sporty little black one totally customized online. I turn to Mom. "Would you do something with him?"

"Logan, do mind your own business, please." Mom's eyes drop to her lap. I'm instantly suspicious.

"Mother?"

"Well . . . your dad and I have been talking. And a new car is not in the cards for you right now. It's not fair to the family for you to drive a new sports car and Logan to drive his . . . his . . ."

"Sign of my mental imbalance."

I stand up. "What's not fair is you and Dad pulling the rug out from under me! What's not fair is forcing me to move here and leave everything and everyone I love behind. What's not fair is expecting me to give everything up just because you want me to blend in here. Well, I'm not like Budge and Robbie. My dad doesn't work in a paper factory. He's a plastic surgeon to the stars, and he *promised* me a new car!" Sure, it was his guilt talking, but I'll take it.

"You will live within the same means as everyone else in this family. Anything else just wouldn't be right."

Who cares about everyone else!

I shake my head. "Is there anything more I need to know? Any other grenades you want to lob my way?"

"No, I believe that's it." Mom purses her lips as Jake enters the now-quiet kitchen.

"Something wrong?" he says, and I nearly leap out of my chair and tackle him.

Except that would be like trying to tackle a giant redwood.

I rinse my bowl out in the sink then turn around, a memory surfacing. "Jake, what is it you do at the Summer Fresh paper plant again?"

He coughs. "I'm an assembly line manager of a department."

My brown eyes lock onto his. "Really?" I lean against the counter and cross my arms. "I hear there's more that goes on at that plant than making some wide-ruled. Did you know this, Mom?"

Budge laughs as he unwraps a Pop-Tart. "Dad, didn't you tell her about the military arsenal that's stored there?"

"What do you *really* make there, Jake?" I ask. "My mom and I have a right to know."

"Bella—," my mother warns.

"Something is going on here, and I want the truth. Mom, I believe this could be something illegal. Drugs, smuggling, weapon manufacturing—"

"Dad is chief of operations on the feminine product assembly line." With a smirk, Budge grabs the keys to his hearse then walks out the door.

My world tilts and I grab the counter again.

It's worse than I thought. My stepdad is a cow-raising, truck-driving, chicken-feeding craftsman of maxi-pads.

Life could not get any worse than this.

chapter ten

"Happy fourth hour, Truman Tigers! I'm Bailey O'Connell here to read your morning announcements."

Truman High's morning news show blares to life on the classroom TV.

The perky brunette spouts off the announcements like they're the juiciest Hollywood gossip.

"And that's all you need to know for today, Truman High. But before we sign off, we here at Tiger TV would like to personally welcome our newest students." A PowerPoint follows of the new kids, using their school ID photos. Great. Mine looks like a mug shot. Maybe God will grant me a favor and they'll skip me.

"... And welcome to junior Isabella Kirkwood, who comes from the prestigious Hilliard School for Girls in New York City. Did you know Callie French, lead singer of the Killer Petticoats, is a famous Hilliard alumna?"

People in the class murmur and turn to stare in my direction. I smile bravely.

"And according to a reliable source, Bella is known for her advice-giving skills and has a super-fun blog you'll want to check out on the Hilliard Web site. I can't wait to look at it myself! Get to know this new Truman Tiger. Next we have senior Lance Denton..."

The breath lodges in my throat.

The voice on the TV becomes a buzz in my head.

No.

They can't go to the *Ask Miss Hilliard* blog! They'll read all the horrible things I wrote! I was mad. I was sad. I was hurt. I didn't *exactly* mean all that stuff.

Okay, calm down. What are the odds someone will actually Google Hilliard and locate the blog? Hardly anyone even knows me here. Just Emma, Jared, Brittany, and that group—and they'll probably just agree with it. *Don't freak out. This is not a big deal.*

I take the hall pass and escape to the girls' bathroom. Shutting myself in a stall, I pull up the blog. It won't accept my password! I call Mia, knowing this is lunchtime at Hilliard. She answers on the second ring.

"I'm locked out of the blog. You have *got* to delete my last post to *Ask Miss Hilliard!*"

"No way. That was good stuff. The Pulitzer people ought to be calling you any day now. It was better than anything J. K. Rowling's ever written."

"This is not funny," I hiss. "By some freak twist of fate, everyone at Truman High could be pulling it up after school today. Mia, you have to remove the post. It's easy to do, you just—"

"I know how to do it. I'm just not." She snaps her gum. "Transitioning to a new Miss Hilliard has been hard. My readership took a total dive when you left. But everybody's been reading your entries."

"Oh, really?" *That is so great. I have such loyal friends, and—* "No, wait! Seriously, if these people here read what I said about them—about their town—I am dead. Don't hurt their feelings just for the sake of your blog. I'll send in another post. I'll write something else."

"I came up with this totally cool idea to have the readers write in with their advice to you. You should check it out. There's some really good—"

"Delete it!" *I've created a blogging monster!* "You have to get rid of it. Mia, how can you do this to me? I have to live here. These people will run me out of town if they read it."

"Oh, will they be wearing their cowboy boots when they run? If so, send me a picture to go with the blog."

"Why won't the blog let me on?"

"Because I have full administrative privileges now. There's no need for you to have full access. So from now on, please post your letters where reader comments are."

I close my eyes and lean on the less-than-clean metal divider. "You're not hearing me."

I recap the morning and explain the situation detail by detail.

Mia laughs. "Bella, you're overreacting. Do you really think those people you go to school with are going to read the blog?"

"Yes. No." I groan. "I don't know. Probably not. But just in case—"

"Fine."

My heart returns to beating. "Really? You'll do this for me?"

"Yes. I guess. I'd hate for my best friend to be hog-tied, or whatever it is they'd do to you. I'll do it next hour in the computer lab."

"Great. Thanks. You're the best, Mia."

"That's what friends are for. Oops, there's the bell. Ta-ta. Call me later."

God, please don't let anyone at Truman get to the blog before Mia does. I'll do anything—I'll feed Jake's stupid roosters. I'll teach Mom how to make toast without burning it. I'll play baseball with Robbie. I'll let Betsy lick me in the face. Anything.

I exit the stall.

And come face-to-face with Emma and Brittany.

"Hey, girls." I slip my phone into my purse. "Thanks again for taking me shopping last night. I—"

"We wouldn't know a Marc Jacobs bag if Wal-Mart put them on clearance?" Emma plants herself right in front of me.

"I . . . um . . ." How? Why me?

Brittany scrolls through her iPhone. "Nobody understands fashion here?"

"I didn't mean you guys. Come on, I would never make fun of you all."

"Living in the *pit* of the country?" Emma shakes her head and looks at me like I'm dog vomit. "You know, it's kind of like family. When you're part of the family, you can talk about them. But nobody else can."

"I'm really sorry. I'd had this horrible night—oh, not the shopping. Well, the credit card thing was awful, but that's all because—"

"And I *do* happen to know what a Marc Jacobs bag looks like." Emma holds hers up, a lovely butterscotch number.

"You have to believe me. I wasn't including you in that blog." I push my hand through my hair and force myself to inhale. "Look, I was mad and upset when I wrote all that. My life is totally in the crapper right now. I was lashing out at anything I could. Had I known there was any way someone from Truman would find that blog, I wouldn't have written it. I still don't know how that girl from Tiger TV found out about the Web site."

"It doesn't matter." Brittany's lip curls. "Maybe you should go back to your fancy private school in New York where people know how to dress and talk and act civilized. Sorry we're not good enough for you."

With matching eye rolls, the two swivel on their heels and storm out the bathroom door.

The fluorescent lights hum overhead. I look at myself in the mirror. My face is flushed like I've run a marathon, my eyes wide and panicked. My heart pounds beneath my funky Betsey Johnson t-shirt.

Oh, God. What have I done?

I punch a button to redial Mia. I need a status report. Now.

No answer.

Redial.

Straight to voice mail.

Rounding my shoulders and straightening my spine, I fling open the door and walk down the hall back to class. So two girls know. They have nothing to gain by telling anyone. And the blog should be down by now. *Please, God. Please, God. Please, God.*

When lunch comes, I'm praying for the rapture. A lightning bolt to take me out. A plague of locusts to carry me off.

But the only catastrophic occurrence is that all the school knows.

"I wear Wranglers." The cafeteria lady hands me my fruit plate. "You got a problem with that?"

I swallow. "No, ma'am." I throw out some money and leave the kitchen.

Half the room stares at me. Old conversations stop. New ones begin. The cafeteria is engulfed with talk of my *Ask Miss Hilliard* blog. Groups are gathered around printed-out copies. They pass it around and fan the flames that are destroying my reputation—my life—by the millisecond.

I clutch my fruit and all but run out of the building. I fly by tables and hear my name, taunts, threats, my own words twisted and thrown back at me.

Outside, I keep going until I reach the parking lot. I yank out my phone and call my mom.

"You have to pick me up."

"What's wrong?"

"My life." I sit down between two cars, out of sight. "My life is wrong."

~~~~~~~~~~~~~~~

"What are you doing here?"

My stepdad reaches across the truck and throws open the door. "Climb in. Your mom's got another job interview."

I hesitate, but really, what choice do I have? Go back into the building where the student body is waiting to attack me and use my body for a bonfire, or get a ride home with my non-dad.

I step into the cab and buckle up. My mom working . . . what is this world coming to?

"Are you okay?"

"Oh, fine." *Great. Wonderful. Could not be better if the parking lot swallowed us whole.*

He guides the truck, now running like a new model, onto the road. "Your mom said there was some trouble at school."

I stare out the window at pieces of the town. "Yeah, the fact that I'm enrolled there is trouble."

"You want to talk about it?" Jake doesn't take his eyes off the road.

"Nope."

"I know you're having a hard time adjusting here."

Really? What was your first clue? I thought I was hiding it so well.

"It's like everything I do here is wrong." I can't believe I'm talking to this guy. "You know that story of Midas and everything he touched turned to gold?"

"Yeah."

"Well, I'm the opposite. Everything I touch turns to poop."

Jake laughs, then sobers at my expression. "*Ahem.* I guess I can see what you mean. It will get easier though."

"Your sons hate me."

"They don't hate you. They're just not used to girls in the house. It's a huge change for them too." Jake turns the wheel with one hand, and we're at McDonald's. "You got one of these in New York City?" He gestures toward the golden arches.

"Um, yes."

"Well, they don't serve Häagen-Dazs, but it's not a bad place to get a hot fudge sundae. Do you want yours with or without nuts?"

"Without." I'm maxed out on all things nuts.

He holds the door open for me, and I step inside. The place is nearly empty except for a group of old men in the corner having coffee and reading their papers.

We wait at the front while a pregnant girl who looks younger than me throws fries in the basket.

"You know," Jake says, "the boys haven't seen a female in the house since their mom died six years ago." He shakes his head, and his blond ponytail swipes his shoulders. "And now there are two. They need time to adjust too."

We lock eyes, and my stepdad waits for me to say something. Something profound. Something meaningful in return. Something that reeks of understanding.

"I gotta pee." I disappear into the bathroom, leaving Jake to order.

When I come back out, Jake is filling a large cup with Coke, his phone at his ear.

"Hey . . . um . . . no, I won't be coming in this afternoon. I know, I know. Something's come up." His deep voice drops. "I'll see you when I can see you."

I step in closer, my senses on high alert.

"I know I said I'd be in, but I just . . . can't. I'll explain it later. I need to be with the family right now." He punches his straw in the lid. "Tomorrow. I promise I'll get away. I *will* be there. You're not the only one who has a lot riding on this."

His back is to me and I wait a few seconds before I sidle up next to him, as if I hadn't been there the whole time. "That looks good." I take a hot fudge sundae off his hands. I smile like the world doesn't hate me and I didn't overhear any of that suspicious conversation.

He studies me for a bit before handing me a drink. "Your mom said you like Sprite."

I force another smile. "Very thoughtful of you."

A few minutes later we're back on the road, and I'm inhaling my ice cream like I need it to breathe.

My life just went public for all the town to see.

But now it's time to do a little digging and uncover all of Jake's secrets.

Because something smells rotten in the town of Truman. And it *ain't* the cow pasture.

chapter eleven

Bella, wake up. Your alarm has been going off for forty-five minutes."

I cover my head and whimper. "Go away, Mom."

"Logan's leaving in twenty minutes."

"Tell him to have a swell day at school."

"I can't take you today, so he's your ride." Mom swats my rear and plops down beside me. "Are you ready to talk about this?"

"Two words," I say beneath a blanket. "Life. Over."

"We got a few random calls last night. People shouting horrible things into the phone then hanging up."

"And those are the ones who still like me."

"What exactly did you do?"

"See?" I throw off the covers. "Why is it always my fault? From the moment we've stepped foot onto Truman soil, I'm to blame for everything."

She frowns. "So you didn't do anything?"

"Of course I did. But must we assign blame here?" Sitting up, I stare at my mom with serious eyes. "I'm never going back there. I think I should move back to Manhattan. This isn't working out for me." Or the school-load of people I insulted.

Mother rolls her blue eyes. "Right. I'll give that some thought." She doesn't even try to sound believable. "In the meantime, you're here, so off to school with you."

"But you don't understand. Those people want to—"

"See you downstairs."

If my mother has any small traces of sympathy left, she takes them with her as she leaves. I pull Moxie closer to me and find comfort in her warm fur and rumbling purr.

"All right. Let's do this day." Moxie hops down only to run herself into a chair. I plant my feet on the floor, a total achievement considering everything.

I slip into some faded jeans, a vintage Chanel tuxedo shirt, and black flats. I leave my contacts in their case and reach for my small wire-rimmed glasses, a total package that says, "Though I am semicute, I am hung over with misery."

Downstairs, I find Jake has already left for the day, and Budge and Robbie sit at the kitchen table with my mom. The three of them laugh over some shared joke, and the sound jars my already-pounding head.

I clear my throat. "Hey."

The laughter stops and Budge slashes me with his narrowed gaze. "I gotta go."

"Wait." I fall in behind him. "You have to give me a ride."

He looks me up and down. "I'm a mutant from outer space, remember? I don't *have* to do anything." And he stomps out the back door.

Grabbing my bags, I chase him outside. "Budge, hold up."

For a big boy, he can move quickly. I don't catch up with him until he's in the garage.

I move to the passenger side and fling open the door. "Please stop." He starts the car, but I talk over the loud roar. "Look, I'm sorry. I know you've read the blog." Though Mia assured me last night my posts were deleted, it had been too late. They had already been copied into e-mails and Facebook and permanently branded into people's brains.

"I don't care about your opinion of me. You're nobody to me."

My heart pings a little at that. "You don't know what my life has been like."

"Thank God for that."

"I mean my life now . . . it's hard."

Budge cranks up his radio but yells over it. "I guess we mutants from outer space have it easy." He looks up, his curly hair covering his eyes. "Get out of my car—you know, the car I got at a funeral home's garage sale."

"Budge, I hurt your feelings, and I'm sorry. I was mad when I wrote all that."

"Whatever, Bella. I'm out of here."

He revs the engine, and I dive into the seat, barely shutting the door before he clears the garage.

Budge growls. "This is the last day I take you to school. I don't care about you—couldn't care less if your spoiled butt had to walk every day."

"Thank you." I lay a hand on my racing heart, grateful all my limbs made it into the car with me. "I really appreciate that—"

"Shut up. Just don't even talk." He turns the music up even louder and the bass vibrates the windows.

Ten minutes later Budge pulls over on the side of the road. The radio goes dead. "Get out."

I blink. "What?"

"You're two blocks from school. It's not a long walk."

"Are you kidding me?"

He reaches across me and opens my door. "I don't want anyone to see me with you. Just because you've ruined your reputation doesn't mean you're going to jack up mine."

I open my mouth. Then close it. "But these are two-hundred-dollar shoes."

"Then watch where you step." He points to the road. "Out."

With as much dignity as I can muster, I heave my purse and backpack over my shoulder, slam the hearse door, and get to stepping. "I said I was sorry!" I yell. These people around here do *not* understand the word *forgiveness.*

Two blocks later and I'm standing in the school parking lot.

I stare at the building, unable to move any farther. *God, please help me. I don't even know how to pray in this situation, but I need some holy intervention.*

With the weight of the planet and every other galaxy on my shoulders, I enter the building and head toward the English hall. I keep my gaze on the linoleum floor as I squeeze through the masses of students.

"Hey, rich girl!"

And the verbal game of darts begins.

"Can I get the numbers of your friends at your old school?"

"I got a one-way ticket back to New York for you right here."

I duck into room 104 and take my seat in AP English.

Nobody says anything to me, but there's really no time. As soon as the bell rings, Mrs. Palmer passes out *The Scarlet Letter* and goes into lecture mode.

She gives us a little background on the time period, then the characters. "Hester Prynne was a marked woman. She had committed a huge sin."

The blonde in front of me turns around and glares.

"Hester was an outsider . . ."

Three more students look my way. I feel my cheeks burn.

"She had offended the entire community and was a constant reminder of shame."

So basically Hester and I could be twins. Could the teacher not have chosen something like *Death of a Salesman*? *Huck Finn*?

"She wore a scarlet A on her clothes at all times—A for adulterer."

I turn to the gawking boy on my left. "I don't know what you're staring at, but my similarities with Hester just ended."

When the bell rings, I all but run to art class.

My head snaps up when a shoulder connects with mine.

Brittany Taylor.

"Hey," I say weakly.

Though her mouth doesn't move, the rest of her face says, *Drop dead.*

This is going well. Can't wait to come back next week and do it all again.

When I get to my assigned seat in art, a big glob of wet clay is waiting for me. A girl beside me snickers, but without so much as a flinch, I scoop up the wet mess, throw it away, and clean up the seat.

Mrs. Lee flutters into the room, stands in the center, then spends the next fifteen minutes discussing the joy of drawing an apple. She then places an apple on a table at the front of the room, claps her hands, and says, "Draw what you see!"

There are four of us at my table, and every single student surrounding me knows who I am.

"Hey, you—rich girl."

I keep my eyes on my sketch pad.

"I drive a Ford F-150. You got a problem with that?"

No, in fact, I'd give my entire purse collection for one of those myself.

"She thinks she's something, doesn't she?" Ford boy nudges a tablemate, who joins in the conversation.

"I got a pig farm I'd like to show you, Miss Hoity-Toity." He laughs. "You don't mind a little mud, do you?" He and Ford boy proceed to see who can *oink* the loudest.

"Leave her alone." This from a tall girl with a Lady Tigers t-shirt.

"Students, I need to see you working!" Mrs. Lee circulates through the room, checking for progress. "And cease the barnyard noises." The teacher *tsks* as she nears our group. "Bella, you've drawn a poodle with gigantic teeth. I need to see the fruit. Be the fruit, my dear. Be the fruit."

"Maybe if she had a pair of Wranglers on, it would help." The whole class dissolves into giggles at this random comment.

"Students!" The teacher claps her hands, but the room doesn't quiet. "We need silence for the inspiration to flow! Concentrate!"

"I personally get inspiration from my *big bow*." A student two tables over smirks. "You know, 'cause I'm a cheerleader from the eighties." More laughter. More comments.

I want to curl up beneath the table and cover my ears. I can't take much more of this.

Just as I contemplate the safety issues involved in jumping out the window and making a run for it, Mrs. Lee puts two fingers to her mouth and sends up a whistle that could break glass.

"Stop it!"

The talking comes to a halt.

The dirty looks do not.

The petite teacher surveys the room, taking in every single student. Then she focuses on me. "Come with me. Yes, you."

I pick up my stuff and follow her down the hall.

"Don't take this personally, dear, but the students cannot work with you in the room. You're disturbing the flow of creativity."

She smiles and pats my shoulder, then escorts me into the counselor's office. "Mrs. Kelso, I believe we need a schedule change here."

The counselor, a blonde woman with a mile-high stack of files on her desk, looks up. "Your name?"

"I'm Mrs. Lee."

She sighs. "The student's name, Mrs. Lee."

"I'm Bella Kirkwood."

"Funny you stopped by." The counselor leans back in her chair. "I've had a lot of students in my office since yesterday—very worked up and upset. Seems they all claim the same malady— Bella Kirkwood."

chapter twelve

Sunday morning finds me squished between Budge and Robbie in the backseat of the Tahoe. This is my first taste of the Finley family's church and, irony being what it is lately, of course the church is in the Truman High cafeteria. I'll be so busy reliving last Friday that I won't catch a word of the message.

Or I'll be mesmerized by Robbie's Sunday attire. Surely he will be the only six-year-old wearing spandex pants and a Superman cape complete with inflatable chest.

As soon as Jake stops the vehicle, Budge jumps out and disappears. He probably needs to discuss secret Halo strategies found in the book of Revelation.

While Jake escorts his youngest to children's church, I keep my focus on the floor as Mom and I make our way to a row of seats. Smoothing my skirt, I sit down and open my program.

Then I feel the stare.

My eyes jerk to a man two rows in front of us. Chill bumps skitter across my skin.

The bald man. The one who tried to give me a ride to school.

He turns back around, suddenly immersed in his own program.

"Mom." I nudge her. "I, um . . ." How do you tell your mom that you think her husband is up to something shady? He could be dealing crack. Working for the mafia. Selling half-price panty liners in back alleys. "I think something's going on with Jake."

"He has been a little stressed. But he's been working a lot of overtime lately."

Overtime? You have no idea.

"Something's not right with him," I whisper, glancing at the back of the bald man's head. "I saw him—"

"Didn't think Robbie was going to turn loose of me." Jake steps over me and sinks into the seat by my mom. "He changed his mind when the teacher broke out the Oreos." He smiles at both of us.

I see through you! I know you're hiding something, Mr. Tall and Sneaky.

My stepdad introduces us to a few people nearby. I shake hands like I'm thrilled to be in a church. In a school. In a town that hates me.

We sing a few contemporary choruses, then a middle-aged man in khakis and a plaid shirt walks to the podium.

"Welcome to Truman Bible Church. I'm Pastor Wilkerson, and I'm glad you're here."

Oh, I'm thrilled too.

"Today we're going to finish our series. We've been talking about something really important. Deception."

I hope Jake Finley is paying close attention.

I spend the rest of Sunday talking to Hunter and Mia on the phone. Before I go to bed, my cell rings one more time.

"Hey, kid!"

I lean into my pillows. "Dad?" That voice . . . sounds so familiar. Could it be?

"Who else? How's it going?"

"Terrible."

"Now it can't be that bad. You want to talk *bad*, I had to remove twenty pounds of excess skin from a woman yesterday. Try living with that."

"Yeah, right. My minor issues will never compare to those who undergo the almighty knife. Who valiantly fight the battle of the bulge or wage war on wrinkles."

He sighs. "I hear your sarcasm. You're frowning right now, aren't you? What did I tell you about that?"

If he gives me the whole frowning-uses-more-muscles statistic again, I think I will projectile-vomit through the digital sound waves.

"Tell your dad all about Truman."

I give him the abbreviated rundown, tidying up the blog-leakage story but still giving him the important details.

"People here want to run me out of town." I twirl Moxie's stuffed mouse in front of her face. She only blinks and goes back to growling at her tail. "I was thinking I could move in with you for a while. Maybe try this again next year." Or *never*.

Silence crackles in my ear. "Bella . . . I love you. You know that."

Here we go.

"But my therapist says I'm in a selfish phase, and that's just not a good environment for you—not full-time anyway."

It's good enough for his bimbo-of-the-month club.

"This is a learning experience for you. Your mom called me

Friday, and we both agree that you need to walk through the consequences of your actions."

Walk through the . . . ?

"No, I don't! Yes, I get that posting my rant about Truman for the
whole world to see was stupid. I won't do it again. Lesson learned.
Send me a plane ticket."

"I'm sorry, Bel. I really am. But I'll see you in a few weeks."

"Yeah. Whatever." And I disconnect from my dad.

Just like he's disconnected from my life.

chapter thirteen

When I enter the kitchen Monday morning, Budge is sneezing all over the table.

"Gross. Cover your mouth." Neanderthal.

He lasers me with a glare, then sneezes again, sending Moxie scampering for safer, quieter territory.

"Bless you." Robbie smiles at his brother. "Did you know that saying probably comes from the days of the bubonic plague?"

I glare at Budge. He *is* the plague.

Mom sits down, a nervous look on her face, and rubs my back. At last! I finally get some sympathy around here. "Honey, I have some bad news for you."

I grab the bowl of oatmeal she slides my way and inhale its mapley goodness. "You mean something worse than today I'm going to go to school and be pelted with insults, spit wads, and stray pieces of gravel? I won't have anyone to sit with at lunch, and everyone in class will shun me and egg my car? Oh, wait. I don't have a car."

"Um, yes, there's more."

I drop my spoon.

"Sweetie, Budge is allergic to Moxie."

He sneezes on cue.

"So? He can get some shots or something."

He stands up and takes his bowl to the sink. "Or you get rid of your cat."

I grab my mom's arm. "What? No!"

"I'm really sorry, but he's tolerated the cat for as long as he could. He didn't want to upset you."

Budge stands behind Mom and smiles. He's evil! Evil, I tell you!

"He lives to upset me. You can't make me get rid of Moxie. She's all I have."

"I wouldn't go *that* far," Mom says.

"Well, I would. She and I have been together through thick and thin. And she's special—not just anyone would know that you have to moisten her food. Not just anyone would dig out her toys when she loses them. Not just anyone would know that she needs extra pets when she walks into walls or falls off of staircases. Moxie needs me!"

"Bella, we are part of this family now, and we have to make decisions that benefit everyone."

"Besides," Budge adds, "it's gross to have a cat in the house."

"Oh yeah, because you Finley guys are *really* into hygiene and tidiness. Moxie could get lost in the dust in your room alone."

Budge rears back and blasts another sneeze.

"That's so fake! Look at him—how can you buy into this?"

"Jake will find Moxie a good home, Bel."

I stand up, my chair squawking across the linoleum floor. "Tell him to find me one too." And I race upstairs.

⁓⁓⁓⁓⁓⁓

Knowing I'd rather dance in the front yard topless than ride to school with Budge, Mom drives me herself.

"Have a good day, Bella."

For seconds I stare at her. It's like telling someone on death row to keep her chin up. Closing the door, I walk away.

God, please get me through this day. I'm like Job in the Bible—losing everything. Okay, so, like, everyone he knew died. And I haven't lost any cattle or anything. But still—I got it bad.

I crank up my iPod, bypass my locker, and head straight for English class.

I can do this. I can do this. I can do this.

With room 104 in sight, I pick up my pace.

Mrs. Kelso jumps out of nowhere, stands in the middle of the hall, and blocks my way. "Miss Kirkwood, come with me, please."

"But I need to get to—"

"Now."

The blonde woman leads me to her office and motions to a less-than-plush seat, and I sit. She props a hip on a corner of the desk and looks into my eyes.

"I'd like to pick up where we left off Friday afternoon."

Oh yes please. I'd love to relive every moment of Friday!

"I don't really care that Mrs. Lee thinks you bring bad vibes to her art classroom. But we did schedule too many students in there that hour, so somebody has to go." She raises her brows. "And it's you."

Like I care. Right now dropping out and joining the circus sounds more my thing anyway.

"The question is where to put you." She moves to take her seat behind the massive oak desk. "I got online and read your blog postings—oh yes, they're still out there. Captured for all eternity in numerous places." She taps her acrylic nails together. "It occurred to me that since you like to write, you might do well on the newspaper staff."

"Or I might not." I pick a string from my Betsey Johnson skirt. "I'm not interested, but thanks."

"I really wasn't giving you an option." She returns to her seat and clicks away on her computer. And before I can say, "Homeschooling sounds fun," I'm clutching my newly revised schedule. "I'll meet you after English class to escort you to your new destiny as a journalist."

"I know nothing about writing for a newspaper."

Her passive face breaks into its first smile. "Oh, but you're a smart girl. Let's just hope they don't ask to see any of your previous work."

I suffer through English class, showered with only a handful of slurs. When I wasn't writing my hand to the bone on an essay, I was praying for an Old Testament curse upon Budge's frizzy head.

When the bell rings, I find Mrs. Kelso waiting for me in the hall. "Right this way, please." She stops a few doors down, and we're in an officelike space, with old framed newspapers hanging from the walls, as well as row upon row of awards and certificates. "This is Mr. Holman. He is the paper advisor."

I smile at the white-haired man who shakes my hand. "New student, eh? Can she write?"

"Oh, she's got all sorts of experience. She has a revealing . . . honest approach to her work." Mrs. Kelso sends me a wink. "Now Mr. Holman just oversees the paper. You'll learn the ropes from his editor."

"And that would be me."

I turn around, my eyes widening at the vision in front of me. A vision with hostility flaming in his blue eyes. Mr. Holman might not be familiar with my attack on Truman, but this guy sure is.

"Isabella Kirkwood, I'd like you to meet my editor, Luke Sullivan."

I hold out my hand for Luke to shake, but he ignores it, staring at me like I'm contagious.

"*This* is our new staff member?" He runs a hand through his black hair. "We have a waiting list two pages deep to get on the paper, and *this* is who we get?" Luke shakes his head and huffs. "Unreal. I can't work with this."

"You can, Mr. Sullivan," the counselor says evenly. "And you will. Like all staff members, you will teach Bella the ropes of writing for a newspaper. Are we clear?"

Luke Sullivan walks away as the ten other people in the class openly stare in my direction.

"He cares a lot about this paper." Mr. Holman looks toward his protégé. "It's very important to him. We are an award-winning publication, Miss Kirkwood. I hope you're ready to do everything you can to maintain our standard of excellence."

I smile weakly. The me from last week would say something about Truman's standard of excellence. "You can count on me, sir."

Satisfied that no one is going to tar and feather me today, the counselor leaves. Mr. Holman shows me around the room and introduces me to the other staff members. None of them embraces me in jubilant greeting. Nobody cries tears of joy at my presence.

"Luke here will get you started. Our first edition comes out next week, and the back-to-school issue is an important one." Mr.

Holman pats me on the back, shoots a warning glance at his editor, then leaves us alone.

I stand next to Luke's desk and wait for him to turn around and look me in the eye.

Two minutes pass. I clear my throat.

Sixty more seconds. "Look, Luke—"

"You think you can just waltz in here and play the prima donna?"

I check behind me. Is he seriously talking to me? "Um . . . no."

"I know who you are, and I know about your little gossip column."

"It was an advice column, and I'll thank you not to use the word 'little' like it was nothing. I mean, granted, the last few postings weren't my best work, and I'm sorry about those, but it's time we all get past it and—"

"If you bring even a hint of trash to this paper, I will go to the school board to get rid of you."

"Calm down." I drop my own volume. "What is your deal? You know, you really ought to get some help for your anger issues."

Luke stands to his feet and towers over me. I inhale a light, musky cologne. "The only thing that makes me angry is having to work with some debutante just because the counselor has nowhere else to put you. I have Ivy League schools watching my work, Bella. And when I graduate next year, I don't want to have to go to the community college just because the princess here brought our paper down and I lost all my scholarship opportunities." He takes a step closer until I can smell his Dentyne. "See, my daddy isn't on *E!* on a regular basis and he isn't going to write me a check for college. Do you think you can wrap your little brain around that?"

My cheeks are hotter than a flatiron. "Gee, I don't know. You use such big words." I pout my glossy lips. "They make my head hurt."

"I'm warning you, Kirkwood. One misstep, and I'll see that you're transferred to advanced competitive weightlifting."

I grind my teeth together to keep from totally unleashing on this pompous pig.

"Do you know what the inverted pyramid is?"

I snap my gum. "Um . . . something in Egypt?"

Luke glowers behind his glasses and tosses me a binder. "Read this. It's my tutorial on the basics of journalism. I'll quiz you tomorrow."

"I *can* do this, you know."

"Whatever. Just stay out of my way." He points to a desk. "Go study, rich girl. Writing is more than just cheap shots and a cutely turned phrase or two. You can't buy your status in here. You gotta earn it."

Straightening my spine, I pivot on my heel and walk away. Will I ever live down the Great Humiliation? Everyone thinks I'm some sort of celebutante with nothing in my head but hundred-dollar bills.

"He's intense." A dark-complected girl sits down beside me. "But he's good."

Yeah, good at being perfectly horrible.

"I'm Cheyenne, by the way."

I force a smile. "Bella Kirkwood."

"I know. Good luck—with everything." She glances at Luke's back. "You're gonna need it."

Twenty minutes later, Luke's shadow falls over my binder. I take my sweet time looking up. "Yes?"

He hands me a sheet of paper. "Here's your first assignment."

"Already?" My heart flutters with excitement. "I knew you'd come around. I really am responsible and a hard worker, and I—" My eyes focus on the description on the page. "The cafeteria Dumpster?" I read it again. "A story on the excessive waste at Truman High? You want me to investigate the school trash heap?"

He lifts a coal black brow. "What's the matter, princess? I thought you could handle it."

I'd like to handle *my fist up your nose.* "It will be my pleasure to observe the activity surrounding the Dumpster."

He laughs and it lights up his eyes. "Surrounding the Dumpster? Oh no, Bella. You'll be observing *in* it."

My.

Life.

Stinks.

chapter fourteen

Is there anything lonelier than eating lunch by yourself?
I might as well be the only girl on the planet for all the attention
I'm getting. The embers of anger have died down, and now instead
of battering me with insults, everyone is just flat-out ignoring me.
Looking through me.

I take my yogurt and apple outside and sit under a distant tree,
where the occasional ant scurries by.

My favorite song plays in my pocket, and I reach in and grab my
phone. "Hunter!" I instantly feel better.

"How's my favorite Oklahoman?" His familiar voice has my
lips curving into a smile. I fill him in on the latest. "Can you believe
I have to give Moxie away?" Pain shoots through my heart.

"So you're basically friendless, carless, and catless?"

"And those are the bright spots in my life." I lean back into the
big elm and sigh. "I miss you. I'll be home in a few weeks though.
Not that Dad cares. I think somebody used the cellulite sucker on
his brain."

"Things definitely haven't been the same since you left."

"I know—it's like I took all the cool out of New York, right?" I laugh. "Hunter, tell me what to do. Give me some advice. How do I win these people over?"

"Why would you want to?"

I frown and pick a weed. "Because I live in their town. Go to their school."

"They're obviously beneath you. Get over it. Find some people to hang out with that are more like you. Have some class."

"Hunter, you haven't even met them."

"I read about them on your blog."

Yeah, you and the rest of the northern hemisphere. "I was mad when I wrote that. Angry."

"So they're none of those things you said?"

"Well . . ."

"Exactly. You can do better than that."

"I don't think you understand. Are you hearing yourself? You can't just discount these people because they dress differently or don't know the significance of Forty-second Street."

"All I know is the Truman folks are making you miserable. And I don't like to see my girl unhappy. It makes me unhappy."

Aw. Hunter's mad on my behalf. Isn't that cute? Like a knight in shining armor, he wants to defend me. Slay my dragons.

"Your girl's unhappy because every person in this town wants to torture me—like pluck out my nose hairs or force-feed me pig snouts. I'm not used to *not* having friends." I hear the whine in my voice. "People usually like me, Hunter."

"I know they do."

"But I need *these* people to like me."

"There's my bell. I'll talk to you later, okay? Hang in there. I'll tell Mia you said hi."

"Oh, are you going to be seeing her?"

"Yeah, there's a back-to-school party at Viva's."

My bottom lip pooches out like I'm two. "Have a good time."

"You know it won't be any fun without you."

Right.

We hang up. After I scoop the last bite of yogurt, I rest my head on my knees and send up another S-O-S to God.

All right, Lord—me again.

I need a miracle. Anything—I'll do anything to get back in good graces with everyone I've offended. I can't stand this—being hated. I want to be popular again. And I want to show them who I really am. Please . . . just one miracle?

"You Bella?"

I lift my head so fast it hits tree bark. "Ow." A girl with the body of an Olympic hopeful stands before me, looking none too pleased to be there. "Um . . . yeah." I look around and survey the area. "Are you here to beat me up?"

"Depends. Are you gonna say something stupid?"

"I will sincerely go out of my way not to." And then I see a flash from last Friday. "You're the girl in art class—the one who took up for me. That was really nice of you. I know you didn't—"

"I'm Lindy Miller. Do you mind?" She points to a giant root sticking out next to me and sits down.

"If you're here to tell me off, you probably need to take a number. You might get a turn about mid-December."

She shakes her head and her ponytail bounces with hair the color of an Oklahoma wheat field. "I . . . um . . ." Lindy traces a pattern in the dirt with her Nike running shoe. "I need your help."

I drop my apple. "I'm sorry . . . I didn't hear you right."

Her brow furrows and she stares at me. Hard. "I said I need your help."

I lean in. "Look, if you need money, there's not much I can do for you. I've been cut off like Lindsay Lohan and the booze, you know what I'm saying?" •

Her voice booms. "I don't need your money." She glances behind her, like she's afraid our conversation is being bugged. "I need you to make me more girly."

"Whoa—" I hold up a hand. "Just because my dad is a plastic surgeon—"

She rolls her eyes and huffs. "Forget it. I knew you were a waste of my time." And she jumps up and stomps away.

That girl may be weird, but she also could be my only ray of hope here. I mean, she did actually speak to me.

"Wait!" I run after her. "Stop! Lindy!" At this point I would totally hit my dad up for a boob job for her. Anything. "Please—" I catch up to her and tug on her shirt.

She spins around, her eyes burning hotter than a campfire. "I said forget it."

"No, come on." I brave a smile. "Look, I'm going to be honest with you. I've got no one here. My home life is a disaster, the bathroom walls are filling up with my name and number, and not because I'm a good time. And I can't get a soul to so much as look at me—well, not without flipping me off. The only people left on the planet for me to talk to are in a totally different time zone. Do you understand what I'm telling you?"

"That you're a pathetic loser?"

I bite my lip. "Okay, do you understand what *else* I'm telling you?"

She draws in a deep breath and contemplates the sky. "My problem's name is Matt Sparks."

"Is he harassing you?"

"No." Lindy almost smiles. "I wish. Matt Sparks is the running back for the Truman Tigers. And . . . he's my best friend."

"And you're afraid all his head injuries are affecting your friendship?"

"No." Her hazel eyes drop to the ground. "I . . . Look, it's obvious that you know a thing or two about fashion and crap like that."

"It's true. I know both fashion *and* crap."

"I want you to teach me how to be all girly so Matt will notice me—really notice me."

I study this girl in front of me—her cheeks colored a pink shade of embarrassed, her baggy athletic shorts revealing toned leg muscles, and her school t-shirt hiding who knows what beneath it.

"I don't know . . ." I twist my hair around my finger. "Have you tried just being yourself?"

She snorts. "All my life. It's time for drastic action. Whatever it takes."

"Anything?"

"Except that waxing business."

"And what do I get in return?"

"The satisfaction of helping a sister in trouble?"

I shake my head. "Nah."

"You get friends. I'll need you to hang around me so you can get to know Matt and me better. We're not exactly on the bottom of the social food chain around here, so I think you'll see some benefit to associating with us." She looks across the courtyard at all the students *not* paying attention to me. "Your scandal will blow over eventually. People will forgive you."

"Not likely."

"You just need to . . . I don't know, do something to get back on their good side. Maybe show them you're serious about getting to know them and Truman a bit better."

And if I'm not?

"It's not as if you *really* meant all that stuff you said on the Internet, right?"

"Right." Well, maybe .01 percent right.

"Think about it. But whatever you decide, keep this to yourself. I'm trusting you with this information—I don't know why, but I am. But if you tell anyone about our conversation, I will sic the entire Truman cheerleading squad on you."

I draw a cross over my heart. "I won't say anything."

"If you're up for the challenge, call me." She hands me a piece of paper with her number on it. "See ya, New York." Lindy walks away, her steps quick and efficient. And not an ounce of grace to be found.

The three o'clock bell rings, and I jump out of my seat and am the first in the hall. Still leery of the full-size lockers and my nightmares of being shoved into one, I adjust the weight of my four-hundred-pound backpack and—

"*Oomph!*" Plow right into an argyle sweater. "Sorry."

Luke Sullivan glares down at me, his hands clutching my shoulders. "Going somewhere?"

His eyes cloud, and I notice they're a strange, deep blue. Like spilled ink. "I . . ." *Focus, Bella.* "I'm going home."

"You have an assignment to do. That's an ongoing investigation, and it starts today."

"I think the stinky Dumpster can wait a day. I'm not wearing my 'sit in trash' outfit, but I'll be sure and pack it tomorrow. And get your hands off me."

"Only if you remove yours."

I startle as I realize my palms are splayed across his chest. His surprisingly hard chest. I tuck my hands behind my back, and Luke releases my shoulders, his eyes never leaving mine.

"Luke, seriously, I need a little notice. My mother is waiting in the parking lot, and I have things to do at home." Like lie on the floor and scream until Mom says I can keep Moxie.

"I knew you couldn't do this. You don't have it in you."

"No! I totally have it in me." I have no idea what we're talking about here. "Tomorrow. Really, I'll investigate your Dumpster tomorrow. I think one day won't hurt our foray into the many things I'm sure the cafeteria is covering up." I wince when I hear the mockery seep into my tone.

"Forget it. I'd hate for you to miss a nail appointment or something."

"I don't have a nail appointment!" *You jerk.* "Um, but if I did . . . where would that appointment be?"

He growls low and pivots on his heels. "Consider your assignment revoked."

I'm so sick of everyone's low opinion of me. If it's going to change, I'm going to have to *make* it change. Whatever it takes. *You can do it, Bella. You can do it.* "Fine!"

Luke stops and walks back my way. "What's that?"

I swallow. "I said fine. I'll do it."

"Today. Now."

I force a smile. "Can't wait to get out there. My journalistic fin-gers are just itching to . . . to . . ." My forced enthusiasm falters. "Look, I'll go sit in trash. That's all I can give you right now."

"I want a full report. Dig around in that Dumpster for at least two hours. Got it?"

"And you promise this isn't some way to make me disappear? Some big truck isn't going to show up and scoop me up, right?"

For a millisecond I think I see a flicker of humor in his eyes. But if it was there, it's gone now. Just his cold, assessing stare. "Any trouble you get into will be of your own making."

Oh, I would love to rake that prim and proper smirk off his face. "Yes, sir, Mr. Editor. And maybe if you're nice to me, I'll bring you back a souvenir. Like a petrified burrito or a decomposed hot dog." Because that's all I'm going to find on this pointless errand.

His eyes flicker over me again before he turns around and walks away. *That pompous, arrogant little—*

Outside I find my mom in the parking lot. I slide into the pas-senger seat but leave the door open.

"I've got news," I say.

"Me too. I got a job!" She pulls me into a fierce hug. I close my eyes and drag in her comforting smell. I remember when I was little I would count her hugs like prizes. They were few and far between, unlike Luisa's open arms. Mom was rarely home. And when she was, her ear would be connected to her phone or she'd be taking care of someone else in one of her charity organizations. I always wanted to start a charity for myself. The Where in the World Is My Mom Foundation.

"I'm going to be working at Sugar's Diner downtown."

"*What?*"

"Yeah, I start tomorrow. I'm going to wait tables."

"Mom, you don't even know your way around a kitchen." I stop myself from rolling my eyes. I don't want to hurt her feelings, but this is a disaster in the making. "Wouldn't you like to find something more suited to your skills?"

And then her lower lip trembles. She drops her head to the steering wheel. "I don't have any skills." She sniffs and wipes away a falling tear. "It's so hard."

"Tell me about it."

"Okay." She blows her nose and holds me with a watery gaze. "I married your dad when I was so young. I was in love." She shakes her blonde head. "I dropped out of college to marry him and support him through med school."

"See, you've got work experience. What did you do back then?"

"I mean I supported him emotionally. I kept the apartment pretty—myself pretty. Then your dad's career took off and you came along." She smiles and pats my knee. "And I just forgot about my own dreams. Your dad became this giant personality . . . and I seemed to have lost mine. Bella, I don't even know who I am anymore."

Aha! "Mom, it's okay. We can go back to New York and figure it out. You were confused when you married Jake. I understand."

"Oh no." She closes her eyes, further smearing her mascara. "Marrying Jake was a turning point for me. He encourages me to be . . . me. And now I've got to figure out who that is."

Yes, please hurry. Because I think the real you will want your Manhattan address back.

"I need to figure out what I'm good at. What my interests are." Mom smiles slowly. "I need to get to know my daughter. I've missed out on a lot. But no more, Bella." She swipes at her smudged under-eye area. "You want to know what I decided today?"

"Mom, I don't know if I can take any more of your life changes."

"I'm going back to school!" She giggles. "Isn't it great? Just a few classes next semester, but I'm on the right track. I know it."

I glance at my watch and feel the dread coat my stomach. "I'm really glad for you." Aren't I? "But I've got to go. You're looking at the newest staff member of the *Truman High Tribune*, and my first assignment starts right now. I couldn't get out of it." Or avoid getting *in* it.

My mother straightens and turns the key. "Oh. Well, I was hoping you could help me with dinner tonight. It's my turn to cook, and"—she shrugs—"you know what a disaster that is. Plus I thought it would give us a chance to talk more. But I'm glad to see you making connections already! I told you all that would blow right over."

Yeah, like a dead tree.

I stick a leg out the door and force the rest of my body to follow. "I'll call you when I'm done. Shouldn't be but a few hours." And then a couple *more* hours of showering. My hand hesitates as I shut the door. "Mom . . . I really am proud of you. But promise me you'll keep your eyes and ears open. I really think Jake might be—"

Her cell phone erupts in an obnoxious chime. "Oops, got to take this. Call me when you're done, sweetie."

And my mom drives away. Still oblivious to Jake's deception.

And the fact that her daughter is about to get totally violated by a Dumpster.

chapter fifteen

Assignment Rules: Garbage Exposé

1. *Investigation is confidential and will not be discussed with anyone not on Tribune staff.*
2. *Reporter is to secure the area and make sure no one sees entry into Dumpster.*
3. *Reporter is to stay concealed within Dumpster for a minimum of two hours.*
4. *Reporter is not to do anything but observe and take pictures during this time.*
5. *Anything confiscated during the investigation is the sole property of Truman High School; should anything be kept by reporter, it will be considered stolen property.*

I refold my assignment description from Luke and grab a few necessary items from my backpack. Can you believe those rules? I'm so sure—like I'd *want* to keep anything from the trash. That boy needs to get over himself. Mr. Power Trip.

"Okay, here goes nothing." Throwing my bag on the ground, I

"secure the area" and find the coast is clear. Unfortunately. I walk to the back of the rusted brown Dumpster. And stop. If I get hepatitis or some sort of rash out of this, I will have Luke Sullivan's head on a platter.

Closing my eyes, I take a deep breath. *Ew!* Too deep. Breathe through the mouth.

I grab a milk crate from a nearby stack and set it beside the Dumpster. Right now I think I would rather pluck out my own fingernails than do this.

I plant one foot on the crate.

This is so unfair. The nerve of that guy. You *know* he created this assignment just to smoke me out of the class.

Both feet on the crate.

I'm through being a disappointment to Truman High. If Luke tells me to swim across the Mississippi River in my winter coat with my arms tied behind my back and weighted fins, I will do it.

My hands clutch the top of the metal wall and I peer in.

Truman High is going to see that no matter what they throw at me, I can handle it. I can do anything. I am Bella Kirkwood. I am made of tough stuff—strong resolve, tons of courage, heaps of strength—*sick!* Is that a dead mouse?

With a final look behind me, I stick my heel into a foothold, heave myself up, and hurl my body over the side.

"Yuck!"

And face-plant into a puddle of old spaghetti. My breath coming in gasps, my hands fly to my face and swipe the red stuff off. I think I'm going to be sick. I lift the tail of my top and bury my head in it. There's one shirt ruined. Along with my dignity.

God, I don't know why I've got a front-row seat on this little jour-

ney into humiliation, but whatever You're trying to teach me, I'm here.

And if we could hurry the lesson along, that would be great too.

My feet find the floor, and I find a spot and sit on a trash bag. Time to start opening some of these bags, I guess, because I sure don't see anything suspicious here. Five giant trash bags. A batch of old spaghetti that was stronger than the bag and worked its way to freedom. A few plastic bottles that should've been recycled. And a paint can.

I grab my notebook and jot the items down. Oh yes, I can see the story already. *Cafeteria has perfectly normal, smelly garbage.* Front-page news. Can't wait to have my name attached to that.

Reaching for a bag, I breathe through my mouth and untie it. On second thought, I am *not* digging through that. I don't have gloves. I don't know if my tetanus shot is up to date. And I could get cut on something like glass or metal. Or the cafeteria's rock-hard cookies.

I pry the bag open further and take a few pictures. Maybe I'll get the photos blown up into eight-by-tens and frame them for Luke. Since he's so into trash.

After snapping a few more pics with the digital camera and nothing else to do, I settle onto a bag.

And wait.

Only one hour and forty-seven more minutes.

I pull out my phone and text Mia in New York.

Hunter sez ur going to party 2nite. Make sure he's not slow dancing w/some hot girl. Ha! :) Sorry I haven't called. Fallout from blog has been nuts. U would not believe where I—

"We've got trouble."

My head snaps up at the voice.

Who is that?

Male. Young.

What if he finds me? How will I explain this? Um, just hungry for a little spaghetti and look where I found some!

Another guy answers. "I know who you mean. I'm on it."

"He's on the verge of talking."

"I said I'll take care of it."

"He could blow the cover on ten years of the Brotherhood. We can't risk that. Do you still want to go ahead with the new recruit? Are you sure he's ready?"

Recruit? Ready for what?

"We'll talk to Sparks at the Thursday night party, then decide. Hopefully he'll show. I see no reason to stop now."

Sparks? As in Matt Sparks? That's Lindy's friend.

"Anything to make the coach happy, right?" Silence stretches, and I risk a shallow, quiet breath. "Are you sure you don't want me to handle Reggie?"

A breeze blows and I flinch as something flies up my nose.

I rub my eyes and check out the box next to me. Pepper!

My sinuses constrict. *Oh no.*

I pinch the bridge of my nose. Must. Not. Sneeze.

"No. He's all mine. He needs to learn that we come first. None of us will be talking about last year's mishaps."

I bury my face in my armpit. My eyes water.

Here it comes! Can't. Hold. On. Any. Longer.

"Later, dude."

"Achooo!"

My hands fly to my mouth and I freeze. Who throws away an industrial-sized box of pepper? That is *so* going in my report.

"Did you hear that?"

Silence.

Then feet shuffling. Getting closer to the Dumpster.

My nose burns again. I pinch it and hold my breath. A sneeze is seconds away.

"Hey, somebody's coming. Let's get out of here."

Great idea! Go!

"I'll talk to you tomorrow—with a plan."

Their feet pound the pavement in a hard run.

"Achoo! Achoo!"

"Bella?"

"Achoo!"

"Is that you, Bella?"

I know that voice. The Evil Editor.

I step on my trash bag and hang over the edge of the Dumpster. "Who else would be neck-deep in day-old marinara and used forks?" I glare down at the boy who sets my blood to boiling.

"Are you okay?"

"Yes." *Like you care.* "Why?"

"You seem to have a little . . . uh, something here." He steps forward and brushes my cheek with his knuckles. A featherlight touch. Our eyes lock.

And I fall backward, my trash bag imploding beneath me. "Ugh! I hear you laughing out there, Luke Sullivan!" I brush clinging tea grinds and banana peels off my skirt.

"I'm not laughing."

I peek over again. "Did you get a good look at those two guys?"

He looks behind him. "Who?"

I roll my eyes. *Boys! So unobservant!* "They were just here. You had to have run into them."

"Nope. Didn't see anyone. But I was jotting down some notes on my BlackBerry too."

"Great. So I sit in a giant box of trash and see nothing but an improperly disposed of paint can, yet when a *real* story shows up, you totally miss it."

Luke frowns. "What do you mean?" He holds up a hand for me to grab. "Jump out."

I barely resist a second eye roll. "I'm in a skirt." I motion for him to face the other direction, then with very unladylike grunts and probably a flash of my undies, I crawl out of the dump and back onto terra firma. "Okay, you can turn around now."

His nose wrinkles. "You smell."

"And you're obnoxious. But, Luke, I have a real story. At least a piece of one. These two guys were here and—"

"Save it, Kirkwood."

"What?"

"You are assigned to *this* investigation." He points to the trash. "That's all I want you to cover." He wrinkles his nose. "Maybe not so literally next time."

"But I overheard this conversation and—"

"What was it about?" He grabs the camera out of my hand and slips it in his front pocket.

"Well . . . I don't know. But they were being all secretive. Somebody's got a plan for this hush-hush meeting, and something about the first football game." *Wow. I really do smell.*

"Bella—"

"And they would've talked more but then I snorted a bunch of pepper, which I definitely don't recommend."

"Bella—"

"And I couldn't sneeze, so I was holding it in, and I thought my eyeballs were going to pop out of their sockets, and—"

"Would you be quiet?"

"Oh." I blink. "Were you saying something?"

"You have been assigned a story—"

"An exposé on *trash*?" How can you even call that a story?

"—and you will focus only on your assigned story. So I don't care if someone comes up to you with details of an Orlando Bloom sighting—you will ignore it. You have a long way to go to prove yourself. And this is not a good start."

I open my mouth in helpless outrage. My brain whirs with insults, blistering words, and slurs against his mama. "I am telling you, something is going on at this school. Something related to the game and Matt Sparks—and maybe he's ready, maybe he's not—and they want to stop Reggie from talking about last year." I catch a breath. "What happened last year? Anything? Any sports fiascos?"

"What you probably heard were a few football players discussing game strategy."

"Behind a Dumpster? Luke, this could be big. I smell scandal."

"I smell old cafeteria burritos. Go home, Kirkwood. Don't give this situation another thought. Sort through your notes from this afternoon, and we'll discuss the progress on your research first thing tomorrow in class." And he turns on his perfectly polished leather shoe and walks away. Dismissing me. And my juicy news. As if we're both nothing. Totally insignificant in his little world.

I reach for a crumpled piece of paper in my purse. Checking it, I punch in the numbers on my phone. Voice mail.

"Lindy, this is Bella Kirkwood . . . I'd like to take you up on the offer we discussed today. I'll see you tomorrow at lunch. Can't wait to hang out . . . and meet Matt Sparks."

~~~~~~~

Mom picks me up, and we're both quiet on the way home. She doesn't even ask about my appearance. When she turns on the dirt road, the dry dust swirls around us like a fog.

"Bella, I'm really sorry about Moxie. I know she means a lot to you."

Just everything.

"I want you to know that I placed an ad in the paper. It will start running tomorrow."

I turn my head and look out my passenger window.

"Did you hear me?"

"What do you want me to say, Mom?"

She pauses. "Anything. Tell me what you're thinking."

"I don't think it would change anything."

We pull into the driveway and I jump out, slamming the door behind me. Seems all I do anymore is slam doors.

"Grab a plate!" Jake calls when I enter the house. "Spaghetti's on."

My stomach rolls. "I'll pass." I've seen enough spaghetti for today.

Mom's voice stops me on the stairs. "The whole family is sitting down for dinner together. Wash your hands and take your seat at the table." I turn around, and the set of her jaw tells me she won't be taking no for an answer.

With a long, overdone sigh, I walk past her on the staircase and plop myself into *my* seat at the table. I feel two eyeballs on me. Slowly I face my younger stepbrother.

"What are you staring at?"

His brown eyes narrow. "You look like you've been wrestling in pig slop."

"And you look like you've been eating paste again." I brush a white fleck off his cheek.

"Guilty." He shakes his head. "I try to be strong and resist, but it calls out to me."

"At least you're admitting to your addiction, Robbie."

"People don't understand the burden I carry." He passes me a bowl of salad.

Budge shuffles into the kitchen, glares in my general direction, then sits beside his brother. "You stink."

"Beans for lunch." Robbie rubs his stomach. "Sorry."

"Not you." He punches his thumb toward me. "Her."

"Shut up, Budge."

"You shut up."

"Cat hater."

"Prissy Paris Hilton wannabe."

"Computer techie gamer dork."

"Spoiled brat of a—"

"Enough!" Jake's hand comes down and the whole table shakes. "Now whether you two like it or not, we are a family. And we *will* get along. But I will *not* have you yelling at the dinner table."

Burp!

All heads turn to Robbie.

"Sorry. But this disharmony is affecting my digestive system." He shrugs. "It's very delicate."

"Bella," my mom says. "Would you like to pray for our food?"

"No."

Her lips thin. "Fine. I will."

My mom is going to pray? Until we got to Truman, my mother hadn't even been in a church in nearly three years. I usually went with friends. Sunday became just another day for my parents to work. Well, that's what Dad said he was doing. Work probably went by the name of KiKi or Barbi.

At her amen, food is passed again.

Robbie slathers butter all over his roll. "So how was work today, Dad?"

Jake smiles at his son. "It was fine. We had a machine break down for a few hours, but I fixed it. We had a quota to meet, so it was a sticky situation."

I would think it's always a sticky situation in the maxi-pad business.

After dinner I go upstairs to shower, do my homework, and spend some quality time with my cat. We sit together in the window seat until darkness spills over the sky like black ink.

A breeze blows my hair and shakes the oak limbs outside. Moxie jumps off my lap at the scraping noise.

I study the window screen that looks like it's made of metal floss and has seen better days. With light fingers and a heavy heart, I grab the edge of the screen. It pops out easily, and I place it on the floor. Then, grabbing the Bible on my bedside table and my phone for a light, I climb out onto the roof.

Caution in every step, I work my way to the edge and grab hold of a big thick branch. And I nestle into its crook and sit.

An hour passes before I'm through telling God all the things I'd like Him to fix and come back inside. I set my alarm and nestle into the cool sheets with Moxie purring at my ear.

At 3:55, the buzzing clock blasts me from a dream. I drag myself back to the window seat, my eyes struggling to stay open.

Five minutes later, I watch my stepdad get into his truck. And with the headlights off long enough to get out of the driveway, he steers his truck toward the road.

Jake Finley is up to something.

And I, Bella Kirkwood, intend to find out what it is.

chapter sixteen

Good morning." My mom kisses me on my cheek as I reach in to get a bagel.

"Hey." It's the best I can do. She's *choosing* to separate me and Moxie, so excuse me if I don't exactly feel like blessing her with some kindness. How come the Bible doesn't address this issue? Where's the chapter that deals with parents who throw your pet onto the street? Or daughters who see their stepdads sneak off in the wee hours of the morning?

"Good morning, new sister." Robbie pours more syrup on his Eggo. "Did you know today is National Towel Day?"

"Um . . . no." The collection of facts in this kid's head scares me.

"Well, it is. I thought we could all go around the table and tell why we're thankful for the bath towel."

"Actually, Robbie, I thought we could discuss something else." I wait until Robbie, Budge, and my mother are all looking at me. "Like why Jake snuck out of the house at four this morning."

Mom's eyes widen.

"I'm sorry, Mom. I couldn't keep it to myself any longer. But I watched him sneak out of the house. Your husband is up to some-thing, and we deserve to know what that is."

Her face falls. "Oh, honey . . . I had wanted—"

"Things to be perfect? I know. I'm sorry. But they're not." *Far from it.*

"I had wanted to surprise you." She looks over my shoulder as Jake enters the kitchen through the back door. "Jake, it seems that Bella—"

"I know." I shake my head in disgust. "I saw you leave this morn-ing." *The jig is up, dude.* "I think you owe my mom an explanation." And then we'll be packing our bags and getting out of your way.

And then my stepdad . . . laughs. He laughs! "There's just no getting anything by you, is there?"

"No." Okay, confused here. Now Mom is laughing.

"Come with me." Jake gestures toward the back door. He sees my hesitation. "We'll all go."

The whole family, minus Budge, walks outside.

And there in the driveway, the same dusty path that I watched Jake travel only hours before, sits a lime green VW Bug. With a giant red bow on top.

"Surprise!" My mom squeals and pulls me into her arms. "Isn't it great? Jake found it!"

"Yeah . . . great." I watch him through narrowed eyes. "So this is what you've been working on?"

"I've been a busy guy. We got it last week, but it needed a few repairs." He pats my car. "And a killer stereo system."

Mom pulls me close, her mouth at my ear. "Don't you feel silly now—all that suspicious talk?" She giggles. "You always did have a big imagination."

"These are *all* the notes you have?"

Luke paces in front of me, running a tanned hand through his black hair. The other newspaper staff members are busy writing, but me? I'm getting my daily dose of Luke harassment.

"Um, yes. Frankly, for two hours of swimming through trash bags, rotten food, and old boxes, I thought I did good to come up with *that* much." *Jerk.* "What did you think I was going to find—the secret recipe for the cafeteria meat loaf? The formula for world peace? The whereabouts of Michael Jackson's old nose?"

He stops, lifting his eyes from my notes. "Very funny." He leans in, his arms braced on each side of my chair. "Bella, if you can't take it here, you know where the counselor's office is. She would be glad to change your schedule again."

I blink into his ocean blue eyes. "I sat in trash for you. I think I passed your stupid test, so let's get on with the real stories."

"You've got one." He rises up, crossing his arms over his chest. "Stick to it."

"What are you working on? Maybe I could help?"

He coughs to cover a laugh. "My story is a piece I've been working on for two years. Our advisor is entering it into a national contest. I don't think I need *your* help, but thank you."

Maybe he ought to do a piece on humility, the arrogant little—

"Luke, are we going to talk about the conversation I overheard at the Dumpster yesterday? *That's* the real story here. Not the shameful way the school doesn't recycle."

"If I catch you pursuing anything but the trash article, you're

off the paper. And within a few days, the only electives open will be
Professional Weightlifting and Parenting 101."

"But something *is* going on, and I—"

"No." He thrusts my notes back in my hand. "This conversation
is over."

Your oxford shirt is so over. Ohhh, he makes me *so* mad!

A few hours later, I slip into the cafeteria, my lunch bag under
my arm. I think I saw a little too much in the Dumpster to risk
school food.

I weave through the tables. I catch a few glares, stares, and some
stray insults.

"Hey, Bella."

I sigh with relief when Lindy Miller calls out to me. Part of me
thought she'd stand me up. That I would spend yet another day
here at Truman High without friends. A total loser and loner.

"Bella, this is Matt Sparks." I shake hands with her sandy-
headed BFF, then introduce myself to a few more people at the
table.

"You're the girl who wrote the bad blog about Truman?" Matt
asks.

"Yeah." I continue to stand, not sure I'm welcome here. "It was
a mistake. It was a really bad time for me, and I . . . messed up."

He considers this. "It's going to take awhile for them to warm
up to you." His eyes pan the whole cafeteria. "Not everybody's as
forgiving as Lindy here." He bites into a French fry. "Or me." Then
he smiles.

And I sit down. "So you play football?"

"Yeah, and Lindy here is a beast on the basketball court."

She blushes pink. "I wouldn't say that."

"Oh, I would. She could totally be WNBA material. Hey, Jared."

I turn around, and behind me stands Jared Campbell, the first person who spoke to me at Truman. Before the Great Disaster.

"Hey." His gaze drops to me before focusing on Matt. "Just wanted to remind you to bring your physics notes to practice."

I scrutinize his every word, trying to see if he sounds like either of the two voices I heard yesterday. It's so hard to tell.

"Jared, do you know Bella?" Lindy asks.

"Yeah." His face is a neutral mask. "We've met."

His words contain no heat, and I'm encouraged. "How are . . . things?"

"Fine."

I decide to push my luck and keep talking. "How about that pop quiz in English, huh? I did not see that coming."

"Jared, come on." Brittany Taylor arrives and links her arm into his. If looks could kill, I would be splattered on the wall. "I have a seat for you over here."

He throws up a weak wave, then allows Brittany to escort him away.

I break the awkward silence. "I'd love to see the team practice sometime. I kind of missed out on the whole football thing going to an all-girls school. Maybe Lindy and I could watch you guys today?"

"What?" She chokes on her water. "Why?"

I kick her under the table. "Because we want to support the team." *And your cause, Lindy.* Not to mention, it will give me a chance to watch the football players and see if I can learn anything more about the conversation I overheard. See if I recognize any voices.

"Um, yeah. Watching practice would be . . . fun."

"You girls—anything to watch some sweaty guys, eh?" Matt laughs.

"Well, maybe for me." *Forgive me, Hunter.* "But I think Lindy here has already got her eye set on somebody." I nudge her with my elbow.

"You do?" Matt frowns. "You like somebody and didn't tell me?"

"Uh . . . uh . . ."

"A girl has to keep some of her secrets, right?" My fake smile is bigger than the Oklahoma panhandle. Lindy only stares and nods.

"So Lindy and I thought we saw you at church last Sunday."

My mind reviews last Sunday. I didn't really notice anyone. Well, except the creepy bald guy in front of us. "Really? So you guys go to the Church of the Holy High School?" As soon as it's out of my mouth, I want to stuff it back in.

But Matt only laughs. "Yeah, nothing like coming to school *six* days a week. We should be in our new building sometime next year."

"Is that where your family is going to go to church?" Lindy offers me a fry, and I take it.

"Actually, my stepdad and his kids are from here. Just my mom and I are from New York. Do you know Budge Finley? He's my stepbrother."

"Oh." Matt and Lindy bob their heads. "He's like a computer genius, isn't he?"

Um, he's like a social moron.

"Yeah," Lindy says. "He's on the student team of techies. It's pretty elite—students are trained to fix the school computers and stuff."

"Bella—"

I'm mid-bite as Luke approaches our table. I swipe my hand across my mouth and come back with a mustard-coated finger. Great. Mouth full. Yellow mustache. "Hmmm?" Chew, chew. Swallow.

"I forgot to mention that I'll need you to resume your research today."

"What?" Pieces of sandwich shoot out of my mouth. He motions me over to a nearby wall, out of earshot.

"I am not climbing in that Dumpster again."

"Of course you're not."

That's what I'm talking about. He needs to recognize I have my limits.

"You'll be in the one on the opposite end of campus. Near the gym."

"No! I'm busy. And I think I can still smell myself from yesterday." Even though I spent half the night in the shower to degunkify.

"How are you going to write an article on the contents of school trash if you don't *look* at the school trash?"

Jesus, I'd like to ask for a little restraint. Because I'm about to tell him I think I might be looking at school trash right now.

"Look, I said I would do the article, and I will. But your hounding me at my every step isn't helping."

"I have college recruiters watching our paper. Ivy League."

"Yeah, I think you've mentioned that."

"So get serious about the paper or get lost." He does a perfect heel spin and walks away.

"Wait—" I catch up as he exits the cafeteria. "I need more notice, okay? Believe it or not, there's more to my life than garbage watching. I have to be somewhere after school. I'll do it tomorrow." He looks skeptical. "Seriously."

He exhales loudly and I smell his cinnamon gum. "Is there anything you take seriously, Bella?"

I inch closer to him, closing the distance. "Your lack of faith in me is so encouraging. Tell me, Luke, is this how you treat the rest of the newspaper staff? Is this how you boost morale—by constantly letting them know how little you think of their abilities?" I am *so* channeling Oprah right now.

His eyes darken. "I won't let my paper go down the toilet just because some prissy socialite got stuck in the class. I care too much about my staff and the integrity of the paper."

Have I ever noticed he's like a cross between a preppy Jake Gyllenhaal and that Superman guy from TV? *Wait, did he just say "prissy socialite"?*

"Even though I think this assignment is a total scam to get me to bail, I will dive into every Dumpster in the county if I have to. You're not getting rid of me, so get used to it." Plus I don't want to take that class where you have to take home a computerized baby. I need my beauty sleep, thank you very much.

"You want my faith, Kirkwood, you gotta earn it." And Mr. Dismissive marches down the hall, out of sight. Hunter could so give him some lessons in manners.

After school, I walk across the street with Lindy to the football field. The boys are already in their practice uniforms and in motion. I have no idea how this game of football works, but apparently it involves lots of sweating, grunting, and drinking water like thirsty dogs.

It's kind of hot.

"Lindy, you have to show interest in what Matt does—like his sports." We take a seat midway up on the metal bleachers. "When's the last time you watched him practice?"

"Never. In a few weeks I'll be at practice myself, so that's not really an option."

"Do you go to the games?"

"I'm the water girl."

"Oh." I guess she couldn't get any closer to him on the field if she were a cheerleader. The hot Oklahoma sun beats down on my head, and I swat my limp bangs away. "Hey, I was thinking . . . I'm getting away this weekend to Manhattan . . . Would you want to go?" Nerves spike my stomach. "You don't have to. I totally understand if you'd rather not. You don't know me *that* well and all, and I haven't really—"

"Are you serious?"

I see nothing but excitement in her face. "Yeah, totally. We could get our hair done. Shop. I could show you the sights."

Lindy is speechless for a few seconds. "I would love to. It might take some work talking my dad into it."

"Perfect." I smile. Maybe I'm really making a friend here. "So . . . I was wondering what you could tell me about Truman High. You know, any gossip? Any stories? Any scandals I should know about?" Like something to do with the football team last year?

Lindy swats a bug off her Nike t-shirt. "Can't think of anything."

This is getting me nowhere.

"How did the football team do last year?" I watch Matt throw the football to Jared Campbell.

"We went to the state play-offs. That hadn't happened in a long time. Truman used to be known throughout Oklahoma for our football team. So last year we finally made it to state. We played our archrival, River Bend. The game went into double overtime, but we lost in the last minute."

"What happened?"

"Reggie Lee, our kicker, missed."

As in *the* Reggie? The one the guys at the Dumpster were talking about?

"Between that and some other stuff that happened last year, he's never quite been the same." She points across the field to one of the padded players. "He's a senior this year. He's got recruiters watching him."

Apparently everyone does.

"What do you mean he never got over it? It's just a game."

The head coach blows his whistle and calls for a water break. "That's Coach Lambourn. His son, Coach Dallas, is an assistant." Lindy then does her best to explain the basics of football. The girl is a walking Wikipedia of the sport. About ten seconds into it, my eyes are glazing over and my attention goes elsewhere.

I spy a lone football player heading toward the field house. Reggie Lee.

I interrupt Lindy. "Where's he going?"

"I don't know. Probably to use the bathroom in the locker room." A couple other football players head in his direction.

"I need to grab something out of my car. I'll be right back."

And I make my way down the bleachers, my flats proving to be a good choice today.

I walk toward my Bug, then keep going, following Reggie and the other players at a distance. I have no idea why. I'm kind of new to this investigative reporting stuff, so it's not like I know what I'm doing.

They pass by the field house entry and keep going, walking around to the back of the building.

I stop at the corner and dare a quick peek around.

The tree-sized guy on the left punches Reggie in the shoulder. "Your allegiance is with the team. Are you in or not?"

Reggie bows up. "Back off, man."

"Don't make this hard for us," the other player says.

"Hard for—" Reggie spits on the ground. "You have no idea what it's like to be me—to live with this."

"Can I help you?"

I jerk my head back and flatten myself to the wall. "Um . . ." It's one of the coaches. I read his shirt. Dallas Lambourn. Guy looks young enough to be in high school himself.

Coach Dallas lifts a brow and waits.

"I was just trying to find a bathroom." That's somewhat true. A girl can always use a bathroom.

"Really? Because it looks like you were following my boys here." He gestures behind me, and slowly I turn around.

There stands Reggie Lee and his two teammates. They don't look happy. In fact, I think they have their tackle faces on.

"I'm new here." I smile prettily. "I'm a friend of Lindy Miller's. We're just watching practice. I come from an all-girls school, see, and Lindy was teaching me all about football." *Am I still talking? Why can't I shut up? Stop talking!*

"I don't like anything to distract the team from their practice. Do you understand, Miss—?"

"Yes, I understand completely," I blather, not bothering to fill in the blank with my last name for the good coach. "I'm sorry, I just got a little lost. But hey, Coach, your team looks great." My eyes widen. "Er, not necessarily these three. I didn't mean they're hot and I'm stalking them or anything." One behind me growls. "Not that you're not hot. No, totally fine and all that. Well, the pants might be a little too tight, but I meant the whole team"—I make a swooping gesture toward the field—"looks very professional . . . and, um . . ." I back up slowly. "I'm just going to take my seat with Lindy now. We should actually be going, now that I think about it." I continue retreating. "Good-bye." I wiggle my fingers at Reggie Lee. "Good work." I toss a wave to boy number two. "Go team!" to guy three.

And I speed-walk back to the bleachers. I barely contain a sigh as I resume my seat beside Lindy, who keeps an eye on Matt below.

She tears her focus away from him. "Did you get what you needed?"

I glance back to the field house where Coach Dallas still stands with his players, all eyes on me.

"I'm not sure."

chapter seventeen

I peel Lindy's fingers from my arm as the plane starts its descent. It took Mom and I going over to Lindy's to meet her dad to convince him to allow her to go to New York with me. It's just Lindy and her dad, so he's pretty protective.

"This is only my second flight in my life. Can you believe it?"

I pat her shoulder. "You're doing fine." Oh my gosh. Her fingernails are embedded in my arm. "Not much longer now." My heart does a little somersault at the thought that I will be on home turf in less than thirty minutes. Unless Lindy leaks all the blood from my veins.

"I can't wait to meet your dad," Lindy says, her eyes clutched tightly shut. She's had her eyes closed the entire flight. Even when she went to the bathroom—she just felt her way there. Ran into one drink cart and an old lady. "I think I've seen him on E!, right?"

"Yeah, he's a guest commentator on E! News. Whenever they think a star has had plastic surgery, they call him for his opinion." Though Dad never really rats anyone out.

"Are you excited to see your boyfriend?"

I lean my head into the seat. "Yeah. It's hard to do this long-distance thing." So hard we haven't talked since Monday. "We're both so busy." Hunter with school and sports. And me with . . . um, sitting in Dumpsters and spying on football players.

When the plane touches down, the weight on my shoulders lightens. I'm home. Hello, New York City!

We weave through LaGuardia Airport—as well as you can weave when you have to pull a transfixed Lindy behind you the whole way.

"This airport is so big they have two Chili's!"

"Come on." I pull her around the corner.

And there among the crowd stands my dad. Like I'm seeing him with new eyes, I take a moment to compare him to Jake. Dad is a good six inches shorter—not quite six foot. He wears clothes tailored for his body, unlike my stepdad, who wears whatever flannel shirt he pulls out of the closet. Dad's jeans look worn and faded, yet I know they were hand-picked by a stylist. And Jake's are also worn and faded. From the barn. And hanging out with cows. And feminine products.

"Bella!" Dad throws his arms out wide, and I run into his waiting embrace. He twirls me around in the middle of the airport. "I've missed my girl."

"Missed you too." I inhale his scent, a mix of cologne and shampoo, and smile. Why do things ever have to change?

"Who've we got here?" He sets me down and I introduce Lindy.

"I'm honored to meet you. I've seen you on TV." She stands in awe, like Dad is Brad Pitt or something.

"Why don't we get your bags and go get something to eat?" He throws an arm around both of us.

"At Chili's?" Lindy asks, her eyes wide.

"No. How about some pizza?" And he takes us to Tony's, my favorite pizza place in all of Manhattan.

We three scoot into a booth and give the waiter our drink orders. "So, Bella—" Dad interlocks his fingers. "I, uh, had plans for tonight that I couldn't exactly get out of."

I lower my menu and stare at my dad. "I'm here for two nights, and you're going out?" I feel *so* wanted. "Who is she?"

"Bells, you know I'm glad you're here, honey." He reaches for my hand. "This is not just a date though. It's more like a business appointment. It's important."

Right. Important. Glad you have your priorities straight.

"I'll be out tonight, and then I'm all yours. I thought tomorrow you could take Lindy shopping." He waggles his eyebrows, a sure sign that (a), he feels guilty; and (b), he'll be loaning me his credit card to make up for it. "And then maybe you girls can go to your favorite salon—you've been complaining about a manicure lately. And after you get all beautiful, we'll go out to dinner and catch a show." His eyes twinkle.

"*Wicked?*" I clap my hands in glee as he nods. "Oh, thank you, Daddy!" And I plant a sloppy kiss on his cheek. *Wicked* is just *the* best musical in the history of theater. I've only seen this retelling of *The Wizard of* Oz like ten times. But I love it. I have all the songs memorized.

After dinner, we take a cab to Dad's.

"So everyone in New York City lives like this?" Lindy points to the rows and rows of apartments as we climb out of the cab. "I mean, where are your yards?"

Dad and I laugh, then help our native Oklahoman inside.

"Bella!" Luisa barrels through the living room and wraps me in her strong hug. "Country life suits you." She pinches my cheeks. "Your face has color."

It's probably a rash from the gym Dumpster I was in a few days ago.

I introduce Lindy to my former nanny. Lindy sticks out her hand, but Luisa pulls her into a bear hug too. "I like this one." Luisa clasps Lindy's chin. "This one is nice; I can tell already."

Yeah, Luisa has never quite warmed up to my friends. I don't know why.

"Your friend Mia left a message." Luisa follows Lindy and me upstairs. "She said to meet everyone at the club at nine thirty. That's awful late for my Isabella to go out, yes?"

"No, it's not. I'll be fine." And I cannot *wait* to see everyone. And dance my butt off.

"I changed the sheets on your bed, so it's all ready!" Luisa scurries ahead of us and flings open my bedroom door.

"Augh!" Lindy clasps her heart and freezes in her tracks. "What is *that*?" She points to the mural over the bed. The evil cherubs.

"Don't worry. They won't come down and get you." I don't think.

"And that?" She points to the matching red chairs in the corner.

"Um, they're supposed to be lips." I shrug. "The theme of the room is love. At least that's what my dad's designer said." I say the theme is Designer Smoked Too Much Crack.

"Do my girls need anything?" Luisa turns on the lamp beside the queen-size bed. The lamp in the shape of Shakespeare's head.

"We're just going to get ready and head out for Viva's." I open my suitcase and start pulling out my party clothes. "Dad's got a date." Luisa and I share an eye roll. She mumbles in Spanish all the way out the door. "Get changed, Lindy. It's time to see some New York nightlife."

Her eyes glow with excitement. She wheels her small suitcase into the bathroom. Seriously, she has such restraint. All she came with was this carry-on. Me? I brought my whole Louis Vuitton luggage collection. A girl never knows when she's going to need something!

While Lindy's in the bathroom, I quickly slip into a funky chic dress and some heels and plug in my flatiron for a touch-up. When my phone pings with a text, I giggle at the name of the sender. Hunter.

Can't wait 2 C U. I've got a Sprite w/ur name on it.

He's so sweet. Why can't all guys be as gentlemanly as Hunter? Like Luke the spastic editor.

"Okay." Lindy opens the door. "I guess I'm ready." And steps out, wearing Abercrombie cargos and a plain red t-shirt.

"Um . . . are these your party clothes?" I can hear Mia and the girls already.

"Yeah." Her spine straightens. "What about it?"

I plaster on a smile. "Because we want people like Matt to notice you're a girl."

"Are you saying I don't look like one?"

Tread carefully. "Lindy, you came to me because *you* said you wanted help looking more feminine. If that's going to happen, you can't get offended every time I try to make a suggestion. Tomorrow we'll go shopping"—on Daddy's money, thank You, Lord—"and I'll show you exactly what you need."

"I don't know, Bella."

"It will be fun." I toss my lip gloss back in my purse. "Let's touch

up your makeup"—as in put more on your face besides Chapstick—
"and hit the club."

~~~~~~~~~~~~~~~

I pay the cabdriver and all but drag Lindy to the door of Viva's.
"Come on, you can do this."

"My face looks like a clown."

"You look amazing." And she does. Turns out Lindy has some
enviable hair wrapped up in that ponytail. And lips that would
make Scarlett Johansson jealous.

"Have I mentioned I'm not much of a dancer?"

Clearing the bouncer, I pay our cover and walk in. "Is Matt?"

"Yeah, he's totally got skills."

"Then tonight you'll learn how to dance."

"Bella!" Mia and two friends rush me, squealing my name. We
clutch each other in a group hug and jump up and down.

I cling to Mia like a fabric softener sheet on a sock. "Oh my
gosh. I have missed you guys!" We pull apart, and I introduce them
to Lindy.

"Hi." Mia smiles prettily. "I like your lip gloss. Is it MAC?"

Lindy blinks. "No. It's pink."

The girls dissolve into giggles.

"Come on, Lindy. Let's get something to drink." And I lead her
to the bar area. "Aren't they great?" I ask, pointing to my friends.

"Oh yeah, they're . . . something."

"Bella! What's up?"

"Colton!" I bump knuckles with Hunter's friend. "Just the guy
I was hoping to see. This is my friend Lindy." He holds out his fist
for her. "And this guy right here is the best dancer in the city."

"Oh, go on, girl. Get out of here."

"No, seriously." I pay for our drinks and hand Lindy her Coke. "My friend would like to learn some basic moves. Can you handle that, Colton?"

"Anything for you, Bella. Come on, Lindy. Let's get started."

Her eyes widen like he's offering to push her in front of a moving train.

"If you want Matt, you gotta do the work." I jerk my head toward Colton. "He's the best. Take advantage of the opportunity."

"I'll go easy on you." Colton pulls a hesitant Lindy onto the floor.

And I walk upstairs, sipping my Sprite, the bass of the song sending my head to bobbing. I stand on an open balcony and overlook the dance floor. Colton is laughing at something Lindy said. Her body is stiff and uncomfortable. And so far the girl has no rhythm.

Hands cover my eyes, and a deep laugh rumbles near my ear. "Don't tell my girlfriend, but I was wondering if you'd like to dance."

I giggle and turn around. "Hunter!" I throw my arms around him and just hold on. His hands find my face and he leans down, his lips on mine.

Seconds later we pull apart, but I rest my forehead on his. "Tell me I never have to leave here."

He runs a hand over my hair. "Sorry, Bel. Can't do that. But I wish I could."

I take a step back, keeping his hands in mine. "Why haven't you called me this week?"

"I talked to you Monday." He plays with the hoop in my ear.

I swat his hand away. "That was four days ago, Hunter." I try to keep the hurt out of my voice, but it comes through anyway.

"You know how crazy the first few weeks of school are."

My eyes narrow. "Yeah, I'm sure it's been a very stressful time *for you*." Are you kidding me?

He pulls my chin up with his hand. "We knew this would be hard."

"But we also knew we'd have to try."

"Are you saying I'm not trying?"

I look away and stare at the dance floor. "I don't know what I'm saying."

"Don't tell me you've found yourself a cowboy in Oklahoma."

My lip curls and I return my attention to Hunter. "Don't be small-minded. That's a stupid stereotype."

He steps back and holds his hands up. "Whoa, what is this? I'm just kidding. Somebody sounds a little possessive. Maybe you *do* have another guy."

"Oh yeah, Hunter, I've found someone else. After I sat in a few trash heaps for the paper, then did my new list of chores at the house, and my hours of AP homework, plus the time I've put in helping Lindy, I managed to find a moment or two to cheat on you." My anger could incinerate this whole club. "Do you *want* me to see someone else?"

Hunter just stops. Says nothing.

His eyes fuse with mine. "What's going on with us?" He braves a smile. "Bella and Hunter do not fight."

"I don't know." I shake my head and run a hand through my hair. "This wasn't how I pictured our little reunion."

He tucks a stray lock behind my ear, his hand sliding down my jaw. "I'm sorry I haven't been good about calling. I know you've had a tough few weeks, and I haven't been there for you."

"And I'm sorry I snapped at you."

"Why don't we start over?" The dance floor lights flash in his brown eyes.

He spins me around and his hands cover my eyes.

"Don't tell my girlfriend, but I was wondering if you'd like to dance."

I swivel on my heel and wrap my arms around his neck. "I'd love to dance with you."

chapter eighteen

I 'll see you ladies at dinner, okay?" Dad kisses my cheek and hands me his credit card.

I swear I hear angels singing the "Hallelujah" chorus. Oh, credit card! How I've missed you. Your plasticky goodness. The zipping sound you make when the clerk runs you through a machine. The rattle of a long receipt being spit out by a boutique register.

"Go easy on me today, okay?" He points to his card.

"But, Dad, I haven't shopped in *forever.*" Ever since Mom married Jake and somehow *I* got financially cut off. So unfair.

"You've only been in Oklahoma two weeks."

"But in my heart . . . it's an eternity." I push Lindy out the door before my dad goes back to his idea of curtailing my spending and teaching me a lesson. *Hmph.* Whatever. It's teaching me misery, is all. And causing me to lust in my heart—over other people's clothing.

I step outside onto the front stoop and breathe in the familiar Manhattan air. *Ew.* Maybe I shouldn't breathe too deeply. We are a little smoggy at times.

A yellow cab speeds us away, like a chariot taking me to heaven.

Shopping—oh, I could just burst into song. The closest I've come to shopping lately is squeezing the melons at Wal-Mart with Mom. And that's just indecent, if you ask me.

"Okay, Lindy. Our first stop is Marco Ricci's salon. While Marco's working his magic on your hair, I'll be getting a manicure and a pedi. Then we'll switch." Dad totally called in a favor to have my stylist work us in on such short notice. Marco's usually booked, like, a year in advance. Maybe Dad's giving him a discount on a new nose or something.

"I don't know." Lindy fingers her ponytail. "I kind of like my hair."

"But it's not about what you like. It's about what *Matt* might like." I thought we established this last night when we stayed up 'til 2:00 a.m. talking. I felt like Dr. Phil, coaching Lindy toward a new vision of herself.

The taxi pulls up beside Marco's, and I have to force Lindy out of the car and into the salon.

Lindy plants her feet in the lobby and just takes it all in. The pink walls. The techno music. The ladies in the chairs sipping champagne.

"Um . . . isn't there a Supercuts or a Regis somewhere?"

A squeal has me clutching my ears.

"Profanity! Profanity!" Marco, head to toe in black, scurries from behind the front counter, his beret bobbing on his head. "Who is zees you bring to Marco?"

I swallow. "This is my friend Lindy." I elbow her. She doesn't move. "Greet Marco," I say through gritted teeth.

She tries to shake his hand, but he clutches his hands to his chest.

"Do you know who I am, leetle girl?"

Lindy shakes her head. "N-n-no."

"I am Marco Ricci"—his hand sweeps the room—"hair arteest."

He leans forward, his pinched face inches from hers. "Dream maker." He draws himself up, his spine as straight as a hair pick. "Now would you like to greet Marco again?"

With rounded eyes, Lindy looks to me. And back to Marco. Then she drops herself into an awkward curtsy.

Laughter fills the entry as Marco doubles over and howls. "Zees girl you bring me—she is priceless." He grabs a shaking Lindy by the shoulders. "Kees, kees." And smooches the air beside both cheeks. Then his face sobers. "Oh, we have work to do, no?"

"Yes," I say. "Now you're the expert." I know this man so well. "But I was thinking maybe some blonde highlights. Four or five inches off. Some bangs."

"What?" Lindy squeaks. "Five inches off my hair? Are you crazy?"

"Marco eez crazy about art. And your head eez a canvas vaiting to be painted, no?"

"No." Lindy steps away from Marco. "Nobody's gonna paint my head."

Marco crosses his arms and huffs. "I cannot work with zees."

"You'll have to excuse her. She's very upset." I put my hand over my mouth and lower my voice like Lindy can't hear me. "She desperately wants to impress a boy. They met as young children and have been best friends ever since. But now . . ." I look away with a dreamy gaze. "Her heart has changed, Marco. She loves him, but does he even know the real Lindy exists?"

He shakes his head and clucks his tongue. "Oh no. No, no, zees vill not do." He nods his head once. "I vill do zees for you." Marco pulls Lindy to him. "I vill do zees . . . for love."

"Give her the amoré special on those brows too," I whisper to Marco. And I go in search of a foot bath.

Two hours later, Carmina, the shampoo girl, signals for me to follow her. I clutch my toweled head and join her at Marco's station.

I would let my jaw hit the floor, but there's hair on it. "Lindy . . . you look—"

"Ah, ah, ah." Marco shushes me. "Marco vill now show her vhat she look like. Are you ready?"

Lindy rubs the spot between her eyes. "He tried to rip my flesh off."

He rolls his eyes. "You had caterpillars taking over your face." He looks at me. "Zees one ees tough cookie, no?"

I laugh. "Yeah, she is." I smile down at Lindy, who sits with her back to the mirror. Her face is a mask of calm and nonchalance. But her hands beat a punchy rhythm on her knees.

"Marco geev to you . . ." He whirls her chair around. "My neweest creation!"

Lindy gasps, and her hands fly to her mouth. "Oh." She touches a piece of hair. "My."

"You're hot, Lindy!"

"It doesn't even look like me."

"Of course it does—only better."

"Marco make your true love crazy in ze head. He vill not stop looking at you, no?"

"Matt's going to flip." I hug my new friend. "You look great. The blonde and caramel highlights really make your eyes pop."

Lindy sighs, sending her new bangs flying. "Let's just hope Matt's eyes pop."

We spend the rest of the afternoon shopping. I take Lindy all over Manhattan, from the ritziest boutiques to my favorite discount stores, like H&M on Thirty-fourth Street.

At five o'clock, we wait outside of Bergdorf's for my Dad to pick us up.

"Bella, I just want to thank you." Lindy sets her packages down on the sidewalk. "When I said I wanted help . . . I didn't expect all this."

I take in the revamped Lindy, who now looks nothing like a basketball star. More like a buff runway queen. "I had fun." And I really did. "Well, except for when I had to chase you through the salon during the eyebrow wax." We laugh at the new memory. "But you look amazing."

"I do feel . . . different."

"And that's a good thing, right?"

Her answer is interrupted by the arrival of my dad's Mercedes. We climb into the backseat and smother him with girl talk.

He parks his jet black car then escorts us into Tao, a New York City hot spot sometimes frequented by the Hollywood elite. We sit on the main level by the giant statue of Buddha, which actually is not a very appetizing place to eat some spring rolls. But the whole restaurant is filled with soft shadows, candlelight, and the buzz that is only found in New York. I just want to freeze it and never let it go.

"Luisa tells me you got in late last night," Dad says later, spearing a piece of his sea bass.

I shrug and watch Lindy navigate her way to the bathroom in her new heels. "I guess."

"Your curfew was eleven thirty, was it not?"

"Yes." I feel my cheeks redden. "Can we talk about this later?" I force the corners of my mouth to lift. "It was only forty-five minutes late."

"You were past curfew."

"So were you." I instantly regret my words. Well, regret that I *said* them.

"I'm the parent here."

"Really?" Oh my gosh. This salmon I'm eating . . . It's . . . it's like truth serum! I can't stop myself.

"You and your friend have been shopping all day on my credit card. I think the least I deserve is some respect."

I peep over my shoulder to the table next to us then back to Dad. "I am grateful. But what I wanted this weekend was to spend some time with my father. You've been *occupied* all weekend. I haven't seen you in weeks, and we've barely had a chance to talk. I thought you'd *want* to spend time with me. Instead you booked your schedule and handed me your Visa."

"You know I work long hours."

I nudge the vegetables on my plate with my fork. "You get me once a month. Couldn't you adjust your schedule?"

"Bella, I work very hard at what I do. I have goals. And right now I'm pursuing some opportunities that I've been waiting a very long time for." He rests his hand on mine, and I watch our shadows overlap in the candlelight. "Don't you want a dad who succeeds, a dad who becomes something?"

I slide my plate away, my appetite gone. "I just want a dad, period."

chapter nineteen

T hree-forty-five in the morning.

I sit straight up in bed and slam off the alarm.

Exhaustion drags my eyelids down, but I shake it off. I have work to do. Two and a half hours before I have to be up for school . . . but if my hunch is right, ten more minutes before I have to be out the door—hot on Jake's tail.

I jump out of bed, knocking the cat to the floor. She meows and slinks away. With my phone as a flashlight, I find a pair of black sweats, throw my hair in a ponytail, and lace my feet into some running shoes.

I crouch on the floor and peek over the windowsill.

Seconds later, Jake's giant form appears. He looks back toward the house then climbs into his truck.

In a flash, I grab my car keys and sneak down the stairs like I'm a world-class spy.

In the kitchen, I watch Jake's truck pull out of the driveway, and when it's a distance from the house, I run outside and jump into the Bug. Taking his cue, I leave my headlights off and navigate the car using only the moonlight. Which isn't easy.

I see the outline of his truck ahead as I pull onto the dirt road. I keep a safe distance behind him and hope he doesn't even think to look in his rearview for someone tailing him at four in the morning.

When we hit the first paved road, I hold the brake down, letting him get even farther ahead. Though his lights are on, I leave mine off and pray the illuminated streets will be enough to see by. And keep me hidden.

He turns onto Central Street.

Fifteen seconds later, I do the same.

Three more turns, and we're heading the opposite direction out of town.

He hangs a left at Mohawk Avenue and wheels into an alley, and that's when I stop.

I frown at the landscape around me. I'm not familiar with this area. Kind of industrial looking. Lots of metal buildings. This is definitely *not* the maxi-pad factory.

I park the car a street away and grab my cell phone, my keys, and the best pepper spray New York sells.

I crouch low—why, I don't know—and tiptoe toward the alley Jake disappeared into. Casting a nervous glance behind me, I stop at the corner of the alley and listen. Two buildings line the small street, and music blasts from the door closest to me.

And yelling.

A shiver dances up my spine. I clutch my phone in a shaking hand. Should I punch in 9-1-1 and have it ready just in case? Am I stupid for doing this? What if I open that door . . . and I'm never heard from again? *Lord, please help me. Protect me from anything scary. And if something scary does happen, help me to be strong . . . and not pee my pants.*

I stand there for a few minutes and just listen. And think. And sweat.

I ease my hand out and touch the knob. Inhaling deeply, I twist it, and the door opens easily. The shouts continue from the far recesses of the building. Somewhere in another room.

I step into a garagelike entryway.

No one in sight.

Sticking close to the wall, I follow the voices down a hall.

"This is the last time you cross me!"

I stop. My breath hitches. Jake—that's Jake.

"You can't stop me! No one can!" Evil, menacing laughter echoes through the building, making the hair on my neck rise.

I take three more steps but freeze at the sound of punches thrown, grunts of pain. What if Jake's in trouble? What if Jake *is* the trouble?

My feet have carried me to a set of double doors. He's in there.

His voice booms again. "I can stop you! I don't think you know who you're dealing with."

I sure don't know who I'm dealing with.

I've got to go in.

Somebody falls to the floor. A scuffle. And then a loud, piercing roar.

And I bust through the doors. "Stop!" My camera phone flashes. Crap! I meant to hit SEND. "I'm calling 9-1-1!" *Or taking your picture.* Whatever.

Two men lie tangled in a heap on the floor. Jake has a man pinned to the ground with his legs. Sweat drips from his face.

Jake's eyes are crazed, wild. "What?"

I stomp forward, my legs trembling. "Let him go." My voice squeaks. "I said let him go, Jake."

He stares at the man beneath him. Then back at me.

"I don't know what this man has done to you, but strangling him with your thighs is probably not the answer." I brave a glance at his victim and notice he's naked from the waist up. "I'm onto you, Jake. I've known about your sneaking out for a long time. Secret rendezvous are one thing, but killing someone is *so* not going to go over with my mom." Unless he offs me before I tell her.

Jake releases the guy then jumps to a standing position.

And that's when I notice that he's just wearing pants too. Black spandex. And his foe is in hot pink.

I take a giant step back. "What kind of place is this?" Two guys wearing spandex rolling around on the floor is *not* a healthy sight.

"Bella, I—" He moves toward me.

"No!" I hold out a hand and jump back. "Keep your distance, you—you—spandexy perv! I'm calling Mom. And the police. And . . ." Jerry Springer?

"It's not what you think." Jake swipes a hand through his dripping hair.

"Oh yeah?" I plant a hand on my hip. "So I *didn't* see you entangled with another man, decked out in shiny Lycra, and your legs in places that scream *highly* inappropriate?"

He blinks. "Um . . . okay. That part is right. But let me explain."

"Save it." I spin around, showing him my back, and head for the doors. I can't wait to pack my bags and get out of this town.

"Bella, wait! You have to listen to me."

I glance back. "Why?"

His Adam's apple bobs. "Because . . . because I'm—"

"Captain Iron Jack." A cape appears over Jake's shoulders.

Out from behind him steps that man—the bald guy from church. The one who stopped when the truck broke down.

I wrinkle my nose at Jake. "Are you an exotic dancer?" *Ew!*

"Of course not."

The bald man speaks. "He's a wrestler, that's what he is. And soon to be a professional. I've never trained anyone so talented—even if he is a little late coming into the game."

My head hurts. Can't process it all. "Mom doesn't know." It's not a question.

Jake's eyes briefly flit away. "No. But she knows I get up early and leave."

"And what does she think you're doing, warming up the maxipad maker?"

"She thinks I'm working out. And I am. I'm training."

"But she doesn't know why." She is so going to flip when she hears this. She doesn't know she's married to Hulk Hogan.

"I was going to tell her."

"When? When you were on Pay-Per-View?"

"No. But that would be kinda cool." He shakes his head. "No, I mean of course I was going to tell her. Soon. Bella, this is really hard to explain."

"Well, the visuals have been *quite* lovely so far."

The other two men leave us and retreat to another part of the room.

"I know it's crazy . . . but have you ever wanted something so bad you could taste it?"

Like a one-way ticket out of the heartland?

"Ever since I was a kid, I would watch wrestling on TV and I would think, I want to do that. It's been my dream for as long as I can remember. I wrestled in high school. Then a little bit after that, and things were going really well. But then my family came along, and one day I woke up and I was raising two boys by myself and I didn't have time for silly little dreams."

Silly little *spandex* dreams.

"You've betrayed my mom's trust. There's this huge part of your life that she doesn't even know about."

"I couldn't tell her at first. I had enough trouble with all that online dating business. I sure couldn't say, 'Hey, my name is Jake and when I grow up I want to wrestle.' I just wanted to wait until I had gained some ground with this before I talked to your mother about it. It's just been the last six months that things have taken off."

I run a hand over my face and wonder why I got out of bed this morning. I so need a latte or two right now.

"It's not just a pipe dream, Bella. This is going to work. I have a manager now." Jake gestures to the back where the bald guy rearranges some weights. "Mickey's training me. I've had a few matches, and . . . I think I might actually be good at this."

"You have to tell my mom." *And the sooner you do, the sooner I can get back to Manhattan.* "Like today. This morning." I pull on the door handle and swing it open.

"I'm sorry I've disappointed you."

I just stare at my stepdad. There's just something about looking at a grown man in tights that robs a girl of any words. "I gotta go."

"Don't tell your mom before I get home."

Right.

The drive to the house takes forever, but it's much easier with the rising sun and headlights.

"Mom!" I tear through the kitchen and down the hall. "Mom!"

She sticks her head out of the downstairs bathroom. "What's wrong?" The towel on her head falls to the floor.

"Your husband . . ." My brain is on warp speed, words and thoughts spinning like there's a tornado in my head. "He . . . he's a . . ." I close my eyes at the image. "A pirate."

"What?"

"Jillian?" Mom and I turn toward the sound of Jake bursting through the kitchen. "Jillian?"

"In here!" She picks up her towel and bestows her "disgruntled mom" look on me. "Bella, I am trying to get ready for work—my first day. I don't know what you're trying to pull, but if I'm late, I *will* ground you."

"I am telling you, Mom, the man you married is not who you think he is. You think you know everything about him, but you don't."

Heavy breathing and pounding steps precede Jake's appearance in the hall. "Jillian." He studies her face, then goes to her, his arms manacled to her shoulders. "I have to talk to you."

My mom looks between the two of us—her out-of-breath husband and her ticked-off daughter. "What in the world is going on here?"

"He plays dress-up!"

"I'm a wrestler!"

Our voices overlap and cancel each other out.

Mom shakes her wet head. "What did you say?" I open my mouth, but she stops me. "Jake first."

Um, putting Jake *first* is what got us onto this tragic detour of life.

"Jillian . . ." Sir Spandex takes a slow inhale. "You have to know I would never do anything to hurt you. You believe that, right?"

Her smile is hesitant. "Yes. Of course."

Lemme talk! Me! Me!

"When we met online six months ago, my life changed. Within weeks of our first phone conversation, I *knew* I wanted to spend the rest of my life with you."

And that's fine—if you're on an MTV reality show!

"And I was afraid to do anything that might scare you off."

Like show you his collection of Hulk Hogan pants.

My mom's smile fades and worry tightens her brow. "What are you talking about, Jake?"

"You and I progressed so fast . . ."

Maybe not in dog years.

"And I thought I'd have plenty of time to tell you, but before I knew it, we were making plans, and I just didn't want to do anything to mess it all up. I tried so many times"—Jake looks toward the ceiling like he's trying to will down some holy help—"but I never could find the words to tell you."

My mom steps closer to her husband. "Are you sick?"

"No, no, nothing like that." His laugh contains no humor. "I'm botching this up."

But on the bright side, if you were trying to tell my mom you're dying of brain rot, this would be going really well.

"Jillian, when a man puts off a dream, something he's wanted his whole life—it doesn't just go away. It haunts him, follows him for the rest of his life."

Should I start humming a Josh Groban song here?

"And . . . see, my dream . . . it's like a tree. And then you came along . . . and that tree grew these new branches—"

"Oh, for crying out loud! This morning I caught your husband with his legs wrapped around another man!"

chapter twenty

I walk out into the Monday morning sunshine and shut the door on an explosive argument between the newlyweds.

And find a couple waiting on the front porch, ready to knock.

"Um . . . can I help you?" *If you're selling Avon, now is so not a good time.*

"We're the Petersons."

"Uh-huh." My attention strays to Budge, who pulls his hearse out of the driveway with his brother slumped in the passenger seat.

"We're here to get the cat."

I snap back to focus. "What?"

The wife speaks up. "The Persian cat—we talked to Mrs. Finley about it. We're here to pick the cat up."

"It's for our son," her husband says. "He wants to call him Tigger."

Tigger? They want to take my precious cat, give it to a snotty-nosed kid, and rename it after some ADD character from *Winnie-the-Pooh*?

"I'm sorry, but *she's* spoken for." I'm not totally lying here. I'm speaking for her. And Moxie wouldn't want to go home with these people.

"But Mrs. Finley said—"

"Mrs. Finley is busy right now." Hopefully calling the airport to get two one-way tickets. "But the cat is not available. I'm sorry."

The woman lifts a dark brow. "We'll come back this evening, then."

And I'll be waiting.

I skirt past the pair and escape to my sherbet-colored Bug, for the first time somewhat relieved to be going to school.

I barrel down the dirt road and punch in Hunter's number.

Voice mail.

I try again.

"Hunter, it's me." *You know, your girlfriend.* "Where are you? I tried to call you last night when I got in." I dodge a crater-sized pot-hole. "Anyway, I miss you already . . . and I'm sorry I was so moody this weekend. Some stuff's hit the fan here, so call me."

In English class, I reach into my backpack and dig for *The Scarlet Letter.* When I come back up for air, novel in hand, Budge has parked himself in the seat beside me. "Hey," I mutter.

"I don't know what you're up to, but whatever you pulled this morning has my little brother very upset."

I feel a rubber band snap on my heart. "I'm sorry that Robbie's—"

"Crying," he bites. "My brother was crying all the way to school. He wanted to know why his dad and new *mommy* were yelling. And when I looked in their bedroom, there you were. Right in the mid-dle of it."

I swivel in the seat and face him with my whole body. "What are you getting at? That their argument was somehow *my* fault? That makes a lot of sense, Budge. For your information," I hiss, "*your* dad is the problem here. Why don't you ask him what he did?"

"Why don't you and your mom go back to New York?"

"Why don't you jump off a cliff?"

He draws himself up. "I know why that couple was at the house this morning."

My face sobers.

"They came to get your cat." Now Budge grins. "And let me guess—you didn't let them?"

"So? They can't have my cat."

"We'll see about that."

"Hey, I know! Maybe you can talk to your dad about it in between his shift at Summer Fresh and slamming somebody to the ground in his pirate suit."

Budge's face turns one shade darker than his hair.

"That's right, *step*brother, I know. So apparently this was a cute secret between the Finley men, but I found myself in the neighborhood of a certain gym this morning. It's amazing what people are up to at four in the morning."

"And I bet you couldn't wait to tell your mom."

I roll my eyes. "Her husband plays dress-up. She needed to know."

"You think you're so much better than everyone else." He faces the front as Mrs. Palmer enters the room. "I'm proud of my dad. He was on his way to making it in the big-time until you and your mom showed up."

I snap open my binder. "Anything else you want to blame me for? Global warming? World hunger? Lindsay Lohan's last movie?" I gather my things and move to an empty seat two rows away—but still not far enough from Budge Finley.

In journalism class, I sneak a peek at my phone to see if I have a message from Hunter. Nothing.

"Bella, I need you to outline your article ideas you've been working on. Have that for me in fifteen minutes." Luke paces near my desk. "Looking at your preliminary notes and some of your pictures, I think you have a strong lead for a few articles on the need for recycling."

I push my phone back into my purse and try to look interested.

Luke jots something down in his pocket notebook. Yes, seriously, the boy keeps a fifty-cent notepad in his shirt. If it weren't for the fact that he has the face of that Clark Kent guy from *Smallville*, he would be a full-fledged dork.

His pen stops. "We've been trying to get recycling bins for years, but the board won't go for it—too expensive. Your story could change all that. I want you to go to the library and do some research. And hit the last campus Dumpster after school."

"Can't."

"What?" He rolls up his sleeves, exposing tanned forearms. "I didn't really mean you had an option."

"I told you about giving me notice."

"I tried. I called your phone three times this weekend. I left a message for you to contact me."

Oh. That.

Sounds vaguely familiar. I think I was in a Barneys dressing room when the calls came. Who could blame me for forgetting about it?

"Sorry, Luke, but I have to go straight home after school." I have a cat to save and a room to pack up. And I want to say good-bye to Robbie. "But I was wondering if you know anything about a party Thursday night?"

He blinks at the topic change. "No."

Of course you don't. I'm sure he's too busy reading the *Wall Street Journal* or watching PBS to get party invites. Especially from athletes.

"Bella, I don't really care about your need to get your dance on."

I turn my head before he sees my face split into a wide grin. Somebody's been watching too many *Fresh Prince* reruns.

"But we have a story to do. Trash does not wait on us."

Can't contain my laugh this time.

Luke swings a chair around and straddles it. His face is inches from mine. "The trash will be picked up tomorrow. This is your last chance before your deadline." His smile is far from friendly. "And your last chance before you're out of here. I hear the small engine repair class now has a few openings."

"Are you threatening me?"

"As your editor in chief, I'm saying that if you don't follow through, you're gone."

I stare at the center of his chiseled chin, willing myself not to spill out my whole morning's story and beg him for mercy. But I refuse to grovel. "You . . . are a piece of work, *Chief.*"

By lunchtime I have the whole high school percussion section pounding in my head. Neither my mother nor Hunter has returned my calls. I have to find a way to intercept that cat-stealing couple this afternoon, and I have *another* date with a Dumpster.

"Whoa, you look like somebody just kicked your dog." Lindy slides her tray next to mine. "Bad day?"

I pick through the lettuce in my salad and go straight for the croutons. "One bad day, I could take. It's my entire life that's totally jacked up."

Lindy runs a hand through her highlighted hair. "You should come to Wednesday morning FCA—Fellowship of Christian Athletes. We meet once a week in the library before school."

Duh. "I'm not an athlete." But if being a loser were a competitive sport, there would be a trophy with my name on it.

"You don't have to be an athlete. Matt and I go. Lots of people go. Come on." She opens her Gatorade bottle and tips it back.

"No!" I snatch it back. "Remember what I told you?"

She huffs. "I won't burp when I'm done. I told you I wouldn't share that talent anymore."

"A straw, Lindy. You don't want to mess up your lip liner."

Muttering under her breath, she gets up and walks back to the kitchen area.

Seconds later, Matt Sparks sits down. "Hey, heard you girls had a great time in the Big Apple."

I manage a weak smile. "Yeah, we had lots of fun." And I really did. Lindy might not know a pencil skirt from an A-line, but she didn't bore me for a second. And even though I don't get her sports world, we do have some things in common. We're both closet *High School Musical* fans, neither one of us can stand the smell of green peas, and if sad movies have us reaching for the Kleenex box, it's only because we're laughing so hard.

I bite down on a carrot. "So you haven't seen Lindy yet?"

"Not since Friday. I talked to her a few times, but—" The nugget in Matt's hand plops to the floor. His eyes go round.

I follow the path of his hypnotized gaze, and there stands Lindy.

She looks from me to Matt, chewing her lip. "What's wrong?" Her hands fly to her hair. "Do you hate it? It's too blonde, isn't it? I knew it."

"Um . . ." He clears his throat. "Your hair looks . . . great." His voice is completely without enthusiasm. What's that about?

"It's the skirt, then?" She plops into the seat across from me. "I knew it. I look stupid, don't I?"

Matt says nothing.

I fill in the silence. "I think the skirt really accents her legs. I mean the girl has a sprint runner's calves. You shouldn't hide that."

"No. Er, yeah." Matt's look of shock melts into a frown. "I was just surprised, that's all. You look . . . different."

Lindy's newly shaped brows snap together. "Different?"

"I mean you look . . . nice."

Ouch. "You look nice" is not what a girl who just underwent a major makeover wants to hear. Especially when she's crammed her feet into some fashionable yet pinching flats just for the sake of looking stunning.

"Well, I like my new look. And it's totally me. So get used to it. In fact, I might not have as much time to hang out with you any-more because I'll be, like"—she throws her hand about—"shopping. All the time."

"You?" He finally smiles. "Shopping?"

"Yes." Her nose lifts. "Now that Bella has introduced me to it, I simply can't get enough. I'm going to New York with her next month, too, and I'm counting the days 'til I can return to Marcy's."

"Macy's," I mouth.

"Macy's," she corrects. "Macy's and Blarney's—I love them."

"Are you mad, Lindy?" Matt asks in boy-ignorance.

"Of course not. Why would *I* be mad?" She jabs her straw into the Gatorade and sucks it down like her throat's on fire.

A few tense minutes pass, and finally I can't take the weird quiet any longer. "So, Matt, I heard a rumor about a party Thursday night." My voice is sheer nonchalance. "Are you going?"

Lindy looks up from her tray. "What kind of party?"

I shrug. "I don't know. Maybe it's for the football players?"

"I didn't know anything about that."

"Lindy," Matt says. "It's not a big deal. Some of the guys asked me to one of their get-togethers. It's nothing."

"Are you going?" Her tone is as sharp as a switchblade.

"No . . . Well, maybe."

"Are you crazy?" she bleats. "There's probably alcohol there."

"It's not like that. I'm just going to hang out. Lots of people don't drink. I'm not."

"Yeah, you say that now. But if you've caved in to their pressure to go to their party, then who's to say you won't cave in to their pressure to drink a six-pack or two?"

Matt points a fry at Lindy. "You know me better than that."

"Could we come?"

The two twist their heads and stare at me like I just said I want to be Tom Cruise's next bride.

"I mean, if you're just going for the fun of it, then Lindy and I want to tag along."

"No way," Lindy says.

"Seriously, it would be a great place for me to meet people. And it's time everyone got to know me and see I'm not the spoiled brat they think I am." I nudge my friend's foot with my toe. "And I bet there will be someone of interest there *you* could keep an eye on."

"The guy you like is on the team?"

Lindy's face is a neutral mask. "You never know."

"Come on, Matt." If I find out what the football players are up to, I can totally stuff it in Luke's trash-loving face. "If it's just a casual party and everyone won't be drinking, then it will be fun." If I'm even still here. It will probably take Mom and me a few days to pack, now that I think about it.

"Yeah, if it's no big deal like you said, then what's the problem?"

Matt considers Lindy's words. "Okay. You guys can go. But if things *do* get crazy, we're all three leaving. Deal?"

"Deal. Bella, you might see more than you bargained for."

I smile. "That's exactly what I'm hoping for."

chapter twenty-one

After school, I climb into the cafeteria Dumpster. This would be the fourth one I've sat in, so by now I don't even bother dusting the rust and taco sauce off my pants. I squeeze my hands into a pair of elbow-length rubber gloves and get out the rest of the equipment for my head. I fit Robbie's diving mask over my face and add the final touch of a snorkel.

Before I begin the ridiculous snooping process, I check my phone for any messages. Nothing from Hunter, but a text from Mom.

Meet me at diner after school. Sorry about this morning.

Maybe she packed our stuff and we're leaving straight from her work. Or we're going to eat first, then leave.

A miniscule wave of sadness comes over me. I will miss Lindy. And Matt Sparks. And I'll always wonder what the big secret with the football team was. And if I could've been a good enough writer to break the story. And Robbie. I'll miss that little genius.

Time to start opening bags.

I search through trash, making notes and taking a few pictures, but mostly finding nothing new. Same garbage, different day.

"You sound like an asthmatic Darth Vader."

I jump and find Luke leaning over the edge.

"*Ewwstaymee.*" I spit out my mouthpiece and try again. "You scared me."

"I was about to tell you the same thing." His black hair ruffles in the afternoon wind.

I rip off my headgear. "I find it more bearable if I can't smell the contents of the Dumpster."

And then the weirdest thing happens.

Luke Sullivan actually smiles. "Every reporter has her secrets."

Reporter! He called me a reporter!

"Well, this one is about to climb out. I've been here forty-five minutes and nothing's new. Same expired generic bologna. Same excessive use of Styrofoam. I think my work is done here."

He holds up a hand, and this time, I reach for it.

"Um, Bella, do you want to take off those gloves before you touch me?"

"Are we afraid to get our hands dirty, Chief?"

He pulls me up, and with his hands still wrapped around mine, I jump out. And leap away from him like he's radioactive.

"So did you want anything?" I shield my eyes from the sun and squint in Luke's direction. "Or were you hoping you wouldn't find me here so you could fire me?"

"I check on all my staff. Just wanted to see how your progress was."

And I'm Britney Spears. When will the boy learn to trust me? "See you tomorrow, then. I gotta go." As Luke and I part ways, I feel the day catch up with me. I've been up forever. A hot bath and a nap would be fabulous.

I drive the Bug as fast as the Truman streets will let me. And unlike New York, this town isn't about speed. Creeping along at thirty-five gives me a chance to really look at the city. There are mom-and-pop restaurants I've yet to eat at. A few video stores. A movie theater flashing the titles of two almost-new releases. A tiny library. A water tower with a roaring tiger on it. So different from back home. And I can see so much of the sky here. Nobody's honking. No crazy cabdrivers. People taking their time—not rushing like their life depends on how fast they walk.

The door jangles as I walk into Sugar's Diner.

Everyone turns around as if on cue and yells, "Hey, sugah!"

I hold up a hand in awkward greeting. My eyes search for Mom, but my focus gets lost on Sugar's décor. It's like 1950. Metal and Formica tables. Shiny red bar stools. A jukebox blasting "Hound Dog" in the corner.

And then my mom appears, beelining to a table, doing her best to balance three plates of burgers and a large order of fries. Her pink poodle skirt swishes as she stretches to settle the plates in front of her customer. She spots me and her tired face brightens. Mom says something to her table, then flounces my way.

I watch her customers switch plates and claim their correct orders.

My mom settles onto a bar stool and pats the empty one beside her. "Want a shake? I learned how to make one."

"No, I just want to know what's going on. What time are we leaving?"

She straightens the salt and pepper shakers on the counter. "Leaving?"

"Yeah, as in first class back to Manhattan."

"Bella . . ."

Great. Here we go.

"This isn't how we deal with things—just running away the first chance we get. I packed you a bag, and you and I are spending the night at Dolly's."

"Who?" I follow the direction of Mom's pointing finger, where a woman who could be Pamela Anderson's older sister stands holding seven plates and one tea pitcher. "We don't even know her, Mom."

"I know her."

"I realize you're into quick relationships, but you've only worked with her one day."

"She's offered us a place to stay for the night. I need some time to clear my head."

"What's there to think about? Jake lied to you. I warned you from the beginning that he could be hiding something, that there could be terrible things in his closet." Granted, I didn't think there would be a collection of spandex Onesies in this closet.

Mom takes off her apron and folds it in her lap. "It's complicated. I need time. Jake and I still need to talk—but when we're both calm and levelheaded." She taps my nose and smiles. "Stay here. I have to go wash a few dishes, then I'll clock out."

I twirl myself on the stool a couple of times. Then a couple more.

"You're gonna fly off of there."

I stop. And my world continues to spin. When I'm no longer seeing three of everything, my eyes zone in on Dolly. She leans over the counter and slides a piece of chocolate pie my way.

"You must be Bella. I hear we're going to have ourselves a slumber party tonight."

I take her outstretched fork. "That's what I was just informed."

She throws her platinum blonde head back and laughs. "You *are* an uppity thing."

I gasp, my mouth open and full of pie. "Am not!" *Why does everyone think that?*

"Your mama needs a friend, and that's what she got today. I'm not going to go through your purses and steal the family jewels when you're asleep."

"I didn't think anything of the sort."

And though she doesn't make a sound, her face says she's laughing at me again.

"Kid, not everyone is out to get you in this world."

I smile politely. "Thanks for the pie."

Fifteen minutes later, Mom walks me to my car. "Bella, Dolly's been a waitress all her life. While I'm grateful she's opened up her home to me, I'm sure her house is of modest proportions. If you so much as snarl your nose one time—"

"Mom!" Seriously, am I really *that* much of a brat? "I know how to behave." But would it have been so bad to go to a hotel? Not to mention Mom left my cat back with the Finleys. Alone. Budge will probably give her to the next person who steps on the porch.

"Okay, y'all, let's go!" Dolly pats her big eighties hair as she ducks into her Jeep. "Follow me."

"Your best behavior, Bella." Mom swats my tush then lets herself into Jake's Tahoe.

We caravan through town, weaving through streets, finally winding up on a dirt road. Why are these people so stingy with the asphalt around here? It's not 1880!

Six miles of dust later, we climb a hill. On my left the shoulder gives way to trees. And beyond that a lake. There's a lake in this town and nobody told me? It sparkles bright blue with what's left of the sunlight. In the distance two boats cross paths.

The hill forks, and we veer right.

A sprawling two-story cabin waits for us at the end of the drive.

A tall gate swings open and Dolly's Jeep leads us in.

I shut off the car, grab my backpack, and get out. Tall trees stand guard over a house that could be the centerfold in *Southern Living*. A kidney-shaped pool is tucked into the side yard, surrounded by tall topiaries and shrubs. Flowers cascade out of pots every few paces, and wild blooms line the path to the front door.

They sure pay their waitresses well here in Truman.

After Dolly shows Mom and me to our separate rooms, I force my gawking self to return to the kitchen, where our hostess stands at the island alone, dicing vegetables.

"I hope you like stir-fry."

"Sounds good." Anything would be good actually. It's been a long time since lunch. I run my hand along her granite countertop, checking out some of the pictures she has there on display. Two identical blonde girls look back at me from a black-and-white photo. From their retro garb, I can tell it's not a recent shot. "Are these your girls?"

The knife slices one final time. "The one on the right is Mary Grace." Dolly barely glances up from her cutting board. "She was my quiet one. The one on the left is Cristy. To her, talking was like air—she couldn't get enough of it."

My unspoken question hangs in the air.

"Car wreck. Twenty years ago."

The faint hum of the air conditioner mixes with the call of some distant birds. "I'm sorry."

For lack of anything better to do with the heavy silence, I continue looking at her arrangement of pictures. When my eyes land on the next one, I can't help but grab it, finding a younger version of a familiar face. "You know him?"

She grabs another carrot and studies the image. "Mickey Patrick." *Slice. Slice.* "We were married once."

"How long have you been divorced?"

"Nineteen years, six months, and eight days." She shrugs a shoulder. "But who's counting?"

"I saw him in the gym. Jake said he's working with him."

"So he is."

"Did you tell my mom about the connection? That your ex-husband is training her soon-to-be ex-husband to become a professional wrestler?"

"It's not my place." She points to a cabinet over my head. "Grab some plates. And it's not *your* place to decide whether she stays or goes."

I sniff. "It kind of affects me."

Dolly turns the chicken over, then adds the vegetables. She says nothing more as I watch her work magic on the skillet until the smell all but calls my name. "Fill your plate, Bella, then let's go eat down by the pool."

"Um . . . shouldn't we wait for Mom?"

The doorbell rings, a great chiming number that reverberates through the rafters. Dolly steps out into the living room and calls toward the stairs. "Jillian, you have company!"

The doorbell rings again as Dolly fills her plate and retrieves two forks.

"Aren't you going to get that?"

She pulls open the back door and props it open with a rounded hip. "It's not my place."

"You called Jake, didn't you?"

She winks and steps out into the sun. "Bella, sometimes staying in one's place is just really boring."

Two hours later, I'm drinking Dolly's powerful sweet tea, swirling my toes in the pool, and watching my mother and her husband come out the front door. Hand in hand. Jake leans down and stops her with a kiss.

I don't know what happened in there. I don't know what got settled.

But one thing's for certain—the honeymoon's back on.

~~~~~~~~~

"So you see, Jake just loved me so much that he was afraid of doing anything to push me away."

My eyes burn with exhaustion as I sit on the horrendously vintage couch along with Robbie, who is garbed in a Spiderman costume and petting Moxie. Budge, fresh from his shift at the Wiener Palace, stares out the window and sneezes at perfectly timed intervals. I can't take my eyes off his silky sheikh pants. They're puffier than an eighties prom dress.

"We want you kids to know that we are absolutely committed

to each other and to this family. It's just that when you find some-one like Jillian, you wonder . . . what does she see in me?"

I've been asking myself that on a daily basis.

"But not trusting her with that part of my life was dishonest, and it was wrong of me to keep something so important from Jillian and Bella."

Mom smiles at her husband and wraps her arm around his Goliath waist.

Great. Now Jake is officially out of the spandex closet, and where did that get me? Nowhere. They can't take their eyes off each other. It's disgusting, is what it is.

"*Achoo!*"

"Bella, take your cat to your bedroom. You know the rules." Mom pulls Moxie off Robbie's lap and hands her to me. "And Logan mentioned that Mr. and Mrs. Peterson stopped by this morning to see the cat."

I shoot death-rays at my stepbrother, called Logan only by my mother. "Um . . . yeah, I didn't like them. You can't just give my cat away to anyone." Maybe we should've asked them if they'd have taken Budge instead. "They said they had a little kid. Moxie doesn't like little kids."

As if on cue, she jumps out of my arms and back into Robbie's lap, rubbing her face against his hand.

"Moxie wouldn't have liked *their* kid." My mother just stares at me. "Seriously—they were all wrong. The woman had on mom-jeans and Keds. And the dad . . . Don't even get me started on his tie-and-shirt combo."

"*Achoo!*"

I'm seriously about to let loose on Budge.

Mom sighs. "It's not like Logan is doing it on purpose. You know we have to do this."

"No, we *don't* have to do this." With another evil eye to my stepbrother, I grab Moxie and retreat to my room.

After a quick e-mail to Mia, I walk to my window and struggle until it lifts. Breathing in the fresh air, I smell the promise of rain. Wish it could wash away all my troubles here.

Stepping across the roof, I take a seat on my favorite branch and let myself lean into its strength. With the sticky air around me and a giant half-moon above, I flip through the pages of my Bible, going straight to the topical index.

And for some reason "hideous stepbrother" is nowhere to be found.

chapter twenty-two

I don't know about this, Lindy. I'm so not in the mood for it." She totally knows I have woes that are straight from a soap opera.

"Come on. You'll have fun. Seriously. And maybe some bonding time with God is exactly what you need."

I halt outside the school library door and watch other Truman students file into the Wednesday FCA meeting. They talk, they laugh, they high-five and hug. They know each other.

And I only know three people on this campus. And one of them is Budge the cat-hater and doesn't even count. I miss walking the halls of my school and knowing everyone. I miss Mia and my gang of girls. I miss seeing Hunter anytime I wanted. And God and I haven't been so close lately either. It's like when I moved, I left Him behind too.

"Okay." I pull open the wooden door. "Let's do this."

Lindy leads me toward Matt, who's surrounded by a group of friends. They laugh over some shared joke.

"Hey, guys. I want to introduce you to my new *friend*." Lindy's voice issues a challenge, and I feel my cheeks tingle with pink. "This is Bella Kirkwood."

A tall African-American girl pins me with her dark eyes. "Former author of *Ask Miss Hilliard*? That was some interesting reading."

Jesus may wipe the sin slate clean, but these people sure don't.

"I'm Anna," the girl continues, her face still impassive. "And I bet you're really uncomfortable right now."

Why lie? "Praying for a distraction so I can slip out the door."

And then she laughs, revealing a mouthful of pink-banded braces. "It takes some guts to be here, Bella." She slaps me on the back. "You're in the right place. If you don't find yourself treated right, you let me know. I'll take care of them."

Like an idiot, I smile wordlessly at this Amazon of a girl. She must be close to six feet. "You must be one of Lindy's friends from the basketball team."

She tosses her wavy hair and laughs. "I couldn't hit a basket if it was the size of a pool. I'm the captain of the cheerleading squad."

If we were keeping points based on my ability to impress the good people of Truman, I would be at a negative five hundred.

Lindy jabs Anna with her elbow, her voice hushed. "There's Kelsey." In a blaze of whispers, the group around me watches a blonde girl across the room. She sits in a chair, staring in a zombie-like fashion as her friends chatter on. This Kelsey seriously needs a cheeseburger. She makes Keira Knightley look like a sumo wrestler.

Lindy quietly fills me in. "Kelsey Anderson hasn't been back to school since the end of last year. Her boyfriend, Zach Epps, was a star football player, had a full ride to OU . . . Then he wrapped his car around a tree. He's been on life-support ever since."

"Kelsey fell apart," Matt adds. "They say she goes and sees him at the nursing home in town every day." He shakes his brown head. "It was a really bad year for the team."

"Must've been hard for all the players." I twirl all this information around in my head.

Matt shakes his head. "Zach wasn't our only loss. Last October we also had a teammate commit suicide."

Anna looks over our heads toward Kelsey. "It's like the Tigers are cursed."

"Okay, guys. I'm glad to see everyone." My English teacher, Mrs. Palmer, stands at the front of the room as we all quiet down.

"She's our advisor," Lindy whispers in my ear as we take a seat on the carpeted floor beneath a display of Manga novels.

"Today we have Grant Dawson from Truman Bible Church."

Matt leans in. "He's our youth pastor."

Oh yes. At the Church of the Holy Cafeteria.

Grant takes Mrs. Palmer's place in the center. "Good morning, Truman Tigers!" The crowd cheers in reply, Anna being the loudest. "You know, it's not even close to Christmas, but today I want to talk about Mary—the mother of Jesus. She led such a cool life, she's worth talking about anytime of the year." He opens up his Bible and reads a few passages.

Beside me Lindy picks at her fingernail polish. I slap at her hand. "Stop that," I whisper. "You'll ruin your manicure."

"It's driving me nuts. And so is this t-shirt. It's too tight."

"It's perfect. Shows off all your curves, and it screams 'style.'"

"It screams, 'My chest is trapped and can't get out.'"

I roll my eyes and tune back in to the pastor.

"Did you know Mary was just a teenager when she had Jesus? Can you imagine being handpicked to be the mother of God at your age?" Pastor Grant asks the room.

I can't even remember to floss at my age.

"But see, guys, God uses teenagers—does it all the time. After an angel told Mary about her new future, what did she do?"

Hyperventilate?

He pauses and scans the crowd. "She rejoiced. She got excited. And then she not only obeyed God, but she went and praised God to others. Mary *knew* God was leading her on a totally different path. He was really taking her out of her comfort zone."

I can totally relate. Mary got a manger, and I got Truman.

"But she knew God's plans for her were huge and that it was totally possible the Lord wanted to use her." Pastor Grant runs his fingers through his spiky, highlighted hair. His large eyes are intense, like he's trying to send us a message with mind power alone. "What about you? Has God asked *you* to step out of your comfort zone? To be somewhere you don't want to be for a bigger purpose?"

Does a Dumpster count?

"As you go about this semester, I want you to be praying about God's purpose for you. Guys and girls alike—He might be calling you to a Mary moment. The question is . . . will you be like her—and tell Him yes?" Pastor Grant closes his NIV. "Let's pray."

As I lower my head, I catch a glimpse of familiar black hair a few rows over.

Luke Sullivan.

He's here? Like, he's a Christian? Surely not. I would've sworn he was a minion of Beelzebub. Anybody who makes a girl climb into trash bags cannot be walking in a path of righteousness—can I get an amen? Maybe he's just here for the paper.

I ask him during second hour.

His eyes darken. "What do you mean what was I doing there?"

I spin a pencil in my hand. "Well, you're not an athlete, and I have my doubts that you're a believer."

"That's funny"—he lifts a dark brow—"I would've said the same about you."

Oh, now I'm just offended. "Of course I'm a Christian." How rude.

He shrugs. "Couldn't tell."

I make a strangled noise as my mouth drops. "Right back at you, Chief."

"And for your information, Miss Kirkwood, I *am* an athlete."

"Sudoku is not a contact sport."

He huffs and walks away, his azure eyes piercing. *Oh, he'll have me investigating toilets for that one.*

At lunch I can't seem to quit watching Kelsey Anderson. I know I shouldn't. From the look on her face, she's obviously struggling just to be at school, so I'm sure a cafeteria of people staring at her doesn't help.

"Here are your tickets for the party tomorrow night." Matt passes out a purple piece of paper to me and Lindy.

"We have to have tickets?" Lindy fidgets with the waistband of her skirt until she catches my frown.

"It's a private party. Very exclusive. This is the first year I've gotten an invite. And you can't tell anyone you're going." Matt stuffs his own ticket in his pocket. "We're to meet at the old graveyard on Knotts Hill. From there we're picked up."

"Sounds kind of creepy to me."

"It's going to be fun, Lindy. We'll just go for a little bit, see what it's about, then come home. No worries." But even I'm wondering about meeting in a graveyard. Ick.

"Let's ride together. I'll pick you girls up. Seven?"

The bell rings for fifth hour. I grab my backpack. "Why don't you pick me up last." I send Lindy a secret smile. "I'll need a little extra time to get ready."

I wave a final good-bye, turn around to find a trash can, and find myself nose to chest with Luke.

"You are always in the most inconvenient places," I say to his Abercrombie polo.

"Have a little date tomorrow evening?"

"No." How long has he been standing there?

Then he dismisses the topic like it's already left his oversized brain. "One of our reporters is sick and is going to miss her deadline."

He honestly didn't know I was a Christian. How sad is that? I mean, I don't care what this guy thinks or anything, but I at least don't want to be discounted as a potential believer. I mean, what is it about me that says, "*Soooo* not a Christian"?

"So I'll have it later, right?" Luke pats my shoulder and snaps me back to the present conversation. "Thanks for being a team player."

"Wait—what?"

"Your article on recycling. I want it in my in-box by Thursday at 8:00 p.m."

"I—I can't."

He parks his khaki-covered hip on a table as other students file past us. "Can't or won't?"

"Can't. I'll work on it tonight, but I'm going to need at least the weekend. I'm busy Thursday."

"Busy meeting in the graveyard? Are you really so hard up for entertainment here that you're going to go traipsing over people's final resting places?"

"Yes." *Duh.* "And you were eavesdropping."

"I was merely waiting to get your attention and didn't want to interrupt. We have to have the story, Bella."

"You can't just give me a day's notice."

He steps closer, and I instantly compare his slight stubble to Hunter's always-smooth face. "This is a real working paper we run here. And it's not just a class, but a job. So like a real paper, sometimes we have to pitch in at the last minute to make sure it gets done. If you can't handle that—"

"There's a class called Tire Changing 101 with my name on it?" I poke his chest. Oddly enough, there's muscle there. "Save your threats, Luke. I have gone above and beyond to be a *team player.*" And I totally pull out the quotey fingers here. In his face. "I've done everything— *everything*—you've asked. I've sat in moldy food. I ruined a pair of suede flats. I sunburned my face while digging around in decomposing refuse." My voice rises, though we're inches apart. My breath comes in ragged heaves, and I'm so focused on this one boy that the rest of the cafeteria has faded away. "I will stay up late Friday night and try to finish the piece, and that can either be good enough *or* you can send me to whatever class you want. In fact, I'd be *glad* to be rid of you."

"Would you, now?" His voice is as quiet as mine is loud.

His eyes hold mine for seconds. Minutes.

But I finally step away. "I have to go text my *boyfriend* before class starts."

"Don't you think I hate the fact that our deadline depends on *you*, Bella?" His tone is like a low saxophone and tingles my skin. There's no spite in his words, but I feel their prick all the same. "But irony of all ironies, you *are* our salvation here."

"You do whatever you have to do, Chief. But I'm done with threats and I'm done giving up all I've got for somebody else's sake." My mom, my dad, now this stupid paper.

And I adjust my backpack and push past him. I rush to the bathroom and hole myself in a stall, punching in a text to Hunter.

Why didn't U return my call last nite? Need 2 talk.

I shove the phone back into the pocket of my jeans, open the door, and give myself a final check in the mirror. My face is flushed like I've run the Boston Marathon.

Another stall door opens as I'm blotting my cheeks with powder.

"I think you dropped this."

I lower my compact and watch the person in the mirror.

Kelsey Anderson.

She holds up a purple ticket. "You're going to need it for the Thursday party, right?"

I take it from her pale hands. "Yeah, you must be going too?" I try to coax her with a smile.

She shakes her head, her face as solemn as death. "No."

"Then how did you know about the ticket?"

"My boyfriend had one." Empty eyes meet mine. "The night he hit the tree."

chapter twenty-three

I'm sorry, the cat's not available."

This is the tenth person I've talked to this week and it's only Thursday evening.

"What do you mean not available?"

"I'm going to be honest with you, sir." I clench the phone to my ear. "You don't want the cat. It has a massive shedding problem."

"That's okay. I have other cats. I'm used to it."

"Oh, she can't stand other cats. Last time Moxie was around another cat . . . she ate it." Okay, she bit it. But one could interpret it as a sign of borderline cannibalism.

"Well, I don't know about that. Muffy and Mr. Whisker Britches are gentle souls. They won't take kindly to someone coming in and taking over the herd."

"And take over Moxie will, sir. With her teeth, if you know what I mean. Your Muffy and Mr. Whiskery Bottoms—"

"Whisker Britches—"

"—will not fare well at all. If you value their lives, I would find yourself a different cat, I'm afraid."

"Bella?"

I jump, dropping the phone. Jake.

Hanging up, I square my shoulders and compose my most innocent expression. "Yes?"

"Was that someone calling about the cat?"

"Who, that?" I point to the phone. "Um . . . yes, but they called to say they're no longer interested."

"We've had a lot of people back out on taking Moxie this week."

"Indeed we have." This guy still makes me uncomfortable. I mean he pounds people into the ground for sport. And I want to be around him because . . . ?

He pours a glass of orange juice then hands it to me. "Take a seat."

"Oh, thanks, but I really have to go. Don't want to be late for the get-together tonight."

"Do you want to tell your mom about intercepting the phone calls for Moxie, or should I?"

I toss back the juice and pull out a chair.

"Bella, I'm really sorry the cat has to go. But I know you don't want Budge sick."

"Budge isn't sick. He's totally faking it."

Jake's look is patronizing at best. "He wouldn't do that." If he pats me on the head and calls me a silly little girl, I am so out of here.

"I'm telling you, I seriously doubt your son is allergic to my cat. He just hates me, that's all."

"Budge doesn't hate you." Jake steeples his fingers and inhales deeply. "This has been a tough transition for him too. But nobody wants to see you hurt over your cat. I am sorry. I know she means a lot to you."

Tears cloud my vision. "She's totally my BFF." Yes, that's right, Bella Kirkwood is on the verge of crying here. I don't think I've teared up since I was in diapers. No, I *will* hold it together. "I would do anything to keep her. Anything."

"It's just not going to be possible." His hand settles over mine. Actually, it covers it like a giant's manacle. "I'm sorry. I want you to be happy here, and I know you're not. I've really been praying about this, and—"

"Then pray for me to keep Moxie." I jerk my hand away and explode from the seat. "She's all I have left." And I storm out the kitchen and up to my room, wiping my eyes, my fingers black with melted mascara.

At six forty-five, I check my reflection in the mirror, satisfied with my wavy hair, Fred Segal sundress, and trendy retro sandals. I search under the bed for Moxie to tell her good-bye, but she's not there. Grabbing my purse, I head to the living room to wait for Matt and Lindy.

Halfway down the stairs, I stop.

"So I would make a great home for her. I love animals. The cat I just lost was with me almost twenty years."

I all but fall the rest of the way down. "What's going on here?"

A white-haired woman sits on the couch—Moxie in her queen-sized arms.

Mom stands up. "Bella, this is Marjorie Bisby. She's here to take Moxie."

My throat burns. Words slam-dance on my tongue, desperate for release. "No" is all I can manage.

My mother's arm slips around me. "We've found the best possible home, honey."

"But she's mine." There goes the mascara. Again. "You can't take her away from me. You've taken *everything* else away from me."

Marjorie Bisby's mouth forms an O. She scoots from the middle of the couch to the end—away from me.

"I need her!" I run a hand across my dripping nose. "Does anybody ever stop and care what I need anymore? Nobody cares that I left my home. My boyfriend. My friends. My dad."

"Bella, I do care." Mom tries to hug me to her, but I throw off her embrace. "I love you, but we have the whole family to consider now. I tried to include you in picking where Moxie would go, but you wouldn't have it. It simply came to this." Mom glances at our guest. "And I would never turn her over to someone I thought wouldn't take the best care of her." She stares at the floor. "I'm sorry, but this is it. Moxie will go home with Ms. Bisby. Say good-bye to her, sweetie."

If looks could wound, I wouldn't be the only one moaning in agony here.

With trembling hands, I reach for my cat. I hold her close and listen to her rhythmic purr one more time. Through it all, she's been my constant. Not my boyfriend, not my parents, but a stinkin' cat.

I whisper words to her—mumblings of good-bye, fragments of apologies.

"It's time to give her up." Mom holds out her arms. "Let me have her."

My throat tightens and burns. "You can't change her name. She knows it."

"I won't, dear," the old woman says, her own eyes pooling.

"And she runs into walls. She'll need extra pets when that happens."

"I'll do it."

"And she has a toy mouse that she likes. She likes you to throw it, but"—I sniff loudly—"she won't bring it back to you. And she falls off the bed on a regular basis, so maybe pad the floor with pillows. She's hit her head a lot."

"I promise to take good care of her." The woman stands up from the couch. "I tend to run into walls myself."

That does not comfort me.

"Let her go, Bella." Mom pulls the cat out of my arms just as a car pulls into the drive. Matt and Lindy. I fully release Moxie. Look at her one last time.

Then run out the door.

chapter twenty-four

Snot and parties do *not* go together.

I blow my nose one last time as Matt shifts his truck into park.

"Are you sure you're okay?" Lindy asks for the fifth time.

I just nod my head. Every time I open my mouth, pitiful squeaking sounds are all I can manage.

"We don't have to go tonight." Matt watches the dirt road as headlights approach.

"No." I daub at my eyes. "Let's do this." And then I'll go back home and look for my beating heart somewhere in the yard, where I'm sure I dropped it.

I jump at the knock on Matt's window. He rolls it down.

"Tickets, please." A football player I recognize from the field house sticks his hand into the truck and takes our purple passes. "We need you to get out of the vehicle, and my boy Adam here is going to blindfold you."

Um, excuse me? I know my makeup looks pretty bad right now, but no need to cover up my face.

"We'll help you to our cars then drive you to the secret party location."

Lindy leans over Matt. "I'm not wearing a blindfold, Dante."

"Then this meeting is over. That's the rules." He slaps the hood. "Have a nice night."

"No! Wait! We'll do it." I unbuckle my seat belt and open the door. "Come on, Lindy. Be brave."

She scoots across the seat. "I don't know about this, Bella. We'll be stuck out there with no car, no way home until they bring us back."

"You both know all these guys. I'm sure we can get a ride if we need one. Let's just go and have some fun." I think I deserve fun right now. And a cat.

"Fine," Lindy huffs, then swings her pointing finger between me and Matt. "But if there's any funny business, we are out of there. We walk if we have to. No kegs, no drugs, no streaking."

"No streaking? You could've mentioned that *before* I took the time to shave my legs." I pull her toward Dante and Adam. "Kidding. I'm kidding."

I feel a moment's panic as a black handkerchief falls over my eyes and is tied behind my head.

Dante gently guides me toward a car. "The two girls will ride with me. And Matt will ride with Adam."

Second frisson of panic. *We're being separated?*

When the football player opens his car door, I hear the voices of other girls but don't really recognize them. But I breathe easier that they're giggling and apparently not concerned with their safety. Lindy goes in first. Then me.

Fifteen minutes later my stomach is in my throat as we've weaved through winding roads and whiplash curves. The girl on the other side of Lindy has made choking noises the last five

Jenny B. Jones

minutes, and if she blows chunks on me tonight, I am going to rip off this blindfold and hurt somebody.

I hear the music before we even stop.

"Here we are, ladies. Party central."

A warm breeze hits me as the door is opened. Dante pulls me out by the hand and uncovers my eyes.

I struggle to focus before finally making out an old cabin. "Are we at the lake?"

Dante reaches for Lindy. "I can't tell you anything." He lowers his voice, his dark eyes intense on mine. "If you want to stay, you can't ask any questions."

The car carrying Matt pulls up behind us, and a minute later he joins Lindy and me in the yard.

We follow the pulsing music inside to a large but outdated living room. Outdated as in early nineties. Not as in total antique like the Finleys' taste in décor.

"Hey, Matt! Lindy!" Jared Campbell pushes his way through to us, holding a cup in one hand and a bag of chips in the other. His face dims when he spots me. "Oh . . . hi."

I smile anyway.

He returns his attention to Lindy and Matt. "Grab some food. There're some Cokes and stuff in the kitchen in a cooler. Some harder stuff on the back porch."

"We'll just be sticking with the easy stuff tonight."

Jared pounds his knuckles to Matt's. "I know, dude. Just thought I'd offer."

After grazing in the kitchen for a while, the three of us walk single file back into the living room. The music rattles the windows and shakes the rustic wood paneling.

"You girls want to dance?"

Lindy pales, but I nod. "Yeah. Lead the way."

As Matt clears us a path through our fellow students, I grab Lindy. "This is your chance to show him you can dance."

"I can't dance!"

"Yes, you can. Just remember what Colton taught you in New York." Not that one lesson is enough, but it's a start. Couldn't get any worse than her old way of sliding from foot to foot and snapping her fingers. "Come on, I'll help you. Just follow my lead."

Though I receive a few rude stares from some Truman Tigers who have yet to forgive and forget, most people are too caught up in the music and dancing to care about my past transgressions.

My arms go over my head, and I let the music take over.

Lindy starts out with some basic moves, her arms stiff as broomsticks. But by the end of the second song, she's got it. Well, minus a few obnoxious head bobs.

An hour and a half later, the speakers pour out a slow song. The floor clears a little.

"Do you want to dance?" Matt asks me, nothing but friendship reflecting in those eyes.

"Um . . ." I can nearly taste Lindy's disappointment. "I think I'm going to get another Sprite. But, Lindy, this is your favorite song, isn't it?" I lightly push Matt toward her. "You two should totally dance." I sidestep them and make my way through the swaying masses.

Ten feet away from the kitchen door, I turn back to look at Lindy's progress.

And bump into a solid wall of boy.

"Oh! I'm so—"

Jared glares down at me.

"—sorry." I move to get out of his way, but he steps in front of me and blocks my escape.

"Wait . . . Bella. I . . . um . . . wanted to tell you that I'm sorry."

I lift a questioning brow as a couple bumps into me, totally oblivious to anything but each other and the song. He takes a step out of their way. We both smile.

Jared reaches for my hand. "Come on. We're going to get mowed down if we stand still."

And before I can say, "Let me count the ways my boyfriend Hunter is the best guy in the whole wide world," my arms wrap around his neck, his slide to my waist, and we're moving in perfect tempo.

We dance in silence for a few moments before I am compelled to speak. "So . . . whose house did you say this was?"

He frowns. "I didn't."

"Oh." *That usually works on TV.* "Then whose is it?"

He shrugs. "Doesn't matter."

"Are we still in Truman?"

"Just shut up and dance."

"Wow, if you talk all romantic like that all the time, no wonder you have Brittany falling all over you."

"What?"

He's absolutely clueless. "Um, nothing."

"Bella . . . I just wanted to tell you that I'm sorry for the way you were treated after . . . um . . ."

"The nuclear fallout from my blog going public?"

"Yeah. That. What you said about us wasn't cool, but I don't think anybody wanted you dropped to total pariah status or anything."

My eyes travel the room and land on Brittany Taylor, who looks as if she's trying to wish me away with mind power. "I'm not so sure about that." Her eyes are slits, like those of a snake about to strike. "I know the girls can be mean. But they'll get over it in time. I'd love for you to hang out with us again."

"I . . ." What does that mean? Like a friend or as in he's interested in me? Why are boys so hard to read? "I think it's going to be awhile before Emma and Brittany are ready to talk to me. But I can use all the friends I can get." I tune out the weight of Brittany's stare. "I really appreciate your breaking away from the pack and talking to me."

He opens his mouth to say something just as a large football player appears beside him. Jared and I step apart as the intruder leans down and mumbles low.

At Jared's nod his friend retreats.

"I better go."

"Trouble?" My nosiness kicks into overdrive.

"Nothing serious. Just need to make a sweep of the grounds and make sure nobody's got a lamp shade on their head or is peeing on the petunias. But I meant what I said—or what I was trying to say. I would like to be friends."

I smile broadly. "Friends it is, Jared Campbell." I shoo him away with my hands. "Better go check for lamp shade violations."

Joy flutters in my heart at the sight of Matt and Lindy still dancing, though both look fairly uncomfortable. But we can work with uncomfortable.

Left with no one to hang out with, I decide to return to the kitchen, where I reunite with the Fritos and graze like a grass-starved cow.

Fifteen chips and another Sprite later, my mind drifts back to Moxie. *God, life is so unfair! What could possibly be the purpose of taking away my cat? Punishment? What did I do?*

"I'm onto you, you know."

I freeze mid-bite. Mid-prayer.

Brittany Taylor advances on me like a vulture.

"Hello to you, too, Brittany." There's no way she could know I'm here to sniff out a story.

"You think you can come in here and just move straight to the A-list? It doesn't work like that."

"Yeah, I guess it wouldn't when I have people like you trying to sabotage any efforts at making friends." She flinches. "I *know* it was you who leaked it to Tiger TV about my *Ask Miss Hilliard* blog."

Her pink lip curls. "So?"

"I don't care anymore. The stuff I said was wrong, and I probably needed that little slap in the face to wake me up. Besides . . . I've been at the top of the popularity chain all my life. I didn't realize I had grown bored with it." I pop another chip in my mouth. "Thanks for helping me branch out."

Clutching my can, I flounce past her, onto the back porch and into the darkening night.

Two kegs stand at attention on the deck, but surprisingly nobody is around. Which is odd. Because if there's a spot that never gets lonely at a party, it's next to the keg. Not that I drink. Because I don't. But I've been around it enough.

My mood takes another nosedive as I think of my cat *and* my boyfriend. I texted him a million times to talk to him about tonight's party. It just makes a girl feel good to have her man care where she is—and to at least give her the chance to assure him she only has eyes for him no matter how many tall, buff guys she'll be mingling with. But Hunter never called me, and not only did I not get the privilege of answering twenty questions about the party, all I did get was a text that said "okay." Okay? I tell him I'm going to an event at which there will be alcohol, dancing, and most of the Truman football team, and all he has to say is okay? I think part of me wanted him to ask me not to go. Or at least a "Call me when you get back so you can tell me how you *didn't* make out with anyone." I've already lost Moxie. Am I losing Hunter too? What next, the apocalypse?

My eyes cloud over with tears for the millionth time tonight. I'm like a leaky faucet, and I can't seem to turn it off. Inhaling deeply, I swipe at my face.

Then freeze.

Three shadowed figures at the edge of the property run into the surrounding woods.

Two more follow.

They move silently, stealthily.

Where did they come from?

And where are they going?

Setting my can on the wooden railing, I watch them for another few seconds then descend the steps of the deck and walk toward the woods, following the disappearing shadows.

chapter twenty-five

My heart pounding and my ears peeled like a dog on point, I slow down my steps, careful not to make a sound that the disappearing partygoers can hear. I follow the path of their voices, hanging far behind. We walk deep into the trees, and every ten paces I can't help but sneak a look behind me. I'm officially weirded out.

Just as I'm about to give up because of my really poor shoe choice, they stop.

I'm still too far away to make out the words of their conversation, so I inch forward and move off to their left, seeking cover behind a pair of trees. The moonlight shines down upon them, but I cannot distinguish their faces.

"What's this about, guys?"

Matt! That's Matt Sparks.

"Do you trust us?"

"Dante, just say what you have to say." Matt's voice is weary, cautious.

"You were invited here tonight to become one of us."

"If you're asking me if I think we should all get matching tattoos, the answer is no."

Somebody laughs. "Matt, over ten years ago, a group of football players met after practice. They decided they were sick of losing."

"And?"

"And those players made a pact that they would do whatever it took to see the Tigers become the strongest team in the state. They became more than teammates—they became brothers. And the tighter the team became, the better they played. They were unstoppable."

"What does this have to do with me?"

Good question, Matt. Keep 'em coming.

"Aren't you sick of losing? Don't you want to see us have a winning streak again? Take the state championship?" I recognize one of the voices from the Dumpster.

"Of course I'd like to win, but I'm not following any of this."

"Let's just say that since last year we've been working on our team-building skills. The Brotherhood lives again—with us. Whatever it takes to get to those glory days—that's what we do."

"We think the stronger our bond, the stronger our team becomes. And with strength must come fearlessness. Fear draws us closer. These guys here"—a shoulder is slapped—"these guys are my brothers. I'd die for them. I'd step through fire for them. That's what a real team is."

"What is it you want from me, Dante?"

Get me another name, Matt.

"First of all, what we tell you tonight is private. You discuss it with no one. Do you promise?"

"I don't know. I guess."

One of the football players does not appreciate Matt's casual attitude. "Tonight we are introducing you to the Truman Brotherhood, man. It's all about risking everything—to win. It's about a dare we hope you can't refuse. Because your skills could take us to state this year. Your skills, combined with ours, could get us all a full ride to any college in the state. But we need our strongest players united on this."

"And the coaches are behind this?"

"Oh, Coach knows all about the Brotherhood—and he definitely wants the legacy to continue. The legacy of winning. But we need to know we have your full loyalty, Sparks."

"I don't have to drink any goat's blood or dance naked in the moonlight here, right?"

"This is serious," snaps Dante. "Are you ready to be a warrior?"

"Yeah."

"Care to prove that?"

"How?" Matt asks.

Above me a bird coos in the night. I shiver, even though the air is sticky hot.

"Do you like any extreme sports?"

"Yeah, I like to dirt bike and skateboard. So?"

"Then you're gonna like our idea of an initiation. Are you with us?"

Coo! Coo!

My head jerks up as a bird barrels straight down, its wings mere feet from my face.

I cover my head, open my mouth, and prepare to squeal—

Until a hand closes over my lips.

"What was that?" one of the guys yells.

"Don't move a muscle, Kirkwood," a voice hisses near my ear.

"See if somebody's over there." Someone stomps our way.

I tremble as Luke Sullivan plasters his body to mine. His breath waves over my neck, and his hand still covers my mouth.

Then he cups his free hand and calls into it, making the most perfect shrill cry of a wild bird. He does it again. I hear the footsteps stop.

And as if inspired by God, the bird returns and makes two swoops around the tree, its distressed sounds almost matching Luke's.

"It was just a bird," Matt says.

"We better get back. We've been gone too long. Sparks, you and Dante will go to the house first. The rest of us will follow in a minute."

"We have more to discuss, but we'll be contacting you." My ears perk at a new voice. This one familiar, but too low to really distinguish. "Remember, you know nothing. If any of this leaks, there are consequences. You support the team, or . . . we make sure you get *off* the team."

Matt's response is muffled by shoes crunching on the ground as he and Dante leave, pointing their flashlights on the path.

Satisfied that there's enough noise to move, I turn in Luke's arms and find we're nose to nose. He shakes his head and places his finger on my lips.

Yeah, like I was going to talk at a time like this.

Well, okay, I was. But I was going to be really quiet about it.

I can't make out much of his face, but I can feel his heart beating as spastically as mine.

Finally the rest of the team leaves, but not before shining flashlights near our area of the woods. Luke pulls my head to his chest and covers me with his arms.

The players walk on, their beams hitting trees and bouncing off of Luke's dark clothes.

"You're in pink, for crying out loud," he barks when we're safely alone. "You come out here to spy and you weren't even smart enough to dress inconspicuously."

I rear my head back. "Oh yeah, because wearing camo to the party *wouldn't* have been conspicuous?"

"What were you thinking coming out here by yourself? Do you have any idea what could happen to you?"

"A bird could attack me? My editor could body-slam me into a tree?"

"I saved you. I saved your ungrateful neck."

"I was doing just fine out here on my own. I don't need you or your help."

"Should I review the last five minutes for you? Because I seem to remember saving your completely blown cover."

"You're a pompous, arrogant jerk."

"You're a spoiled, ungrateful prima donna."

"I can't stand you."

"I don't care."

My ragged breathing mingles with his. I feel his biceps bunch under the hands that I've placed on his arms at some point. "Luke?" I whisper.

His head lowers until his mouth rests near my ear. "Yes?"

"Let go of me."

He pushes me away like I'm strapped down with explosives and begins to pace. "You really could've been hurt out here. Those guys are up to something."

"You think?" I lean into the tree and take some deep yoga breaths. "I've been *trying* to tell you that. I *told* you I heard some sort of conspiracy that day at the Dumpster."

"Yeah, but you also inhaled a lot of old burritos that afternoon too."

"Something's up, Luke. Something with the, uh, starting lineup. And now Matt Sparks is getting involved."

"I know. I heard." He clicks on a small flashlight, and I can see the contours of his face.

"How long were you standing there?"

I make out a faint smirk. "The entire time. I followed you from the house. Anybody could've seen you leave, by the way. Remind me to lecture you about discretion later."

"I'm writing myself a note right now." I roll my eyes in the dark. "I didn't know you got an invitation to the party."

"I didn't. I overhead you talking to your friends about it."

"And you *followed* me? Could you get any more pervy?"

The ground crunches as he pivots, and he plants himself in front of me. "You deliberately went against my orders to stay out of this situation. You have a story. This situation is none of your concern."

I jab my finger in his shirt. "You came out here to get information so *you* could get this story, didn't you? Now you're a perv *and* a story stealer. I can't believe you, Luke."

He wraps his hand around my finger. "Keep your voice down," he hisses. "That is not true and you know it. I just crashed the party to see if there *could* be anything to your hunch. I figured I'd be here less then ten minutes—just long enough to ascertain that there was nothing to your idea."

Ascertain? I need a dork dictionary just to keep up with this conversation.

"And just as I was about to leave, I saw you walking into the woods—by yourself." Luke looks at his fist closed over my hand and drops it. "You can't just go walking into a situation—especially at night. In the dark. Alone. Like an idiot."

"Idiot?" I hiss. "This *idiot* has found proof that there's something brewing with the athletes. This *idiot* tried to tell you from the beginning that I had overheard something significant. Maybe I wouldn't have *had* to go off by myself had you believed me in the first place." The bird coos again overhead. "Nice bird distraction, by the way. Somebody's obviously spent a lot of time researching mating calls."

Despite my hot tone, he smiles. "I watch a lot of *Animal Planet*. Look, Bella . . . I'm sorry."

"Do you acknowledge that there's a story here?"

He sighs. "Yes."

"And I can put aside the stupid trash article and work on it?"

"No." He holds up his hands to fend off my verbal attack. "The article is still due first thing. We don't drop one assignment just to work on another. You wrap up your current deadline, and we'll discuss the football situation."

Good enough.

"Bella, this could be huge."

I grin like I've hit the keg a few times myself. "I know."

"What I mean is, you're not experienced. I can't let you work this story. We have a hierarchy at the paper."

"What? No!" I punch his arm. "I'm already neck-deep in it. I let Dante blindfold me and stuff me in a car to be here. I *deserve* this story, Luke."

He runs a hand through his wavy hair. "On one condition."

"I won't share my story with the rest of your staff, Chief."

"Okay. You won't share it with them." He nods then walks away. "You'll share it with me."

chapter twenty-six

"What time did you get in last night?"

As I pour Cheerios into a bowl, I catch the warning in my mom's voice, like she's asking a question she already knows the answer to. "I don't know . . . around midnight."

"You know your curfew is eleven on school nights."

I pull out a chair and sit down. "Sorry. I guess I was so distraught over you giving away my cat that I lost track of time."

Mom puts down her book, *Parenthood Is a Battleground.* "You're grounded."

"What? I said I was sorry."

"That's not good enough, Bella. We have boundaries here— rules."

"Since when do you care about my curfew?" The words fly off my tongue like rocks from a slingshot.

Mom pins on her Sugar's nametag. "I know I've been an absent parent."

Really? And which book did you read that in?

"And I know that I relied on the nanny to do what I should've done myself. And I realize that I spent too much time away from home, taking care of things that might've been important, but weren't as important as my family."

I study my lap and wonder if we could perhaps channel her guilt into the return of my cat.

"But, Bella, if I say be home at eleven, then that's what I mean. I *am* your parent and you will obey me. Now the book I read last week said to start out with small doses of punishment . . ." Mom thinks on this. "So I believe you can forget about going to the game tonight."

"I have to be there for school—an assignment for the paper. I'm not going for the joy of stale popcorn."

She considers this. "Fine. Then cancel whatever you have going on Saturday night. You can babysit Robbie while Jake and I are at a wrestling match in Tulsa."

I swallow a bite of cereal and the ten jokes that immediately pop into my head. I cannot believe she is actually supporting this guy's wrestling dream. How can she not be suspicious of any grown man wanting to wear tights?

My phone rings on my way to school. Hunter.

"Hey." My tone could freeze an Oklahoman pond.

"How's my girl?"

I laugh bitterly. "Your *girl* hasn't heard from you in days."

"I'm sorry. I've been busy."

"With who?"

"Aw, now that's not fair. You know I only have eyes for you."

"Do I?" I swerve past the neighbor's old cow, who seems to spend most of her time in the middle of the dirt road. "You don't return my calls. You ignore my texts. Remember when we said that we'd go above and beyond to make this work? Remember when you said distance wouldn't matter?"

"Hey, back off. I said I had things to do. Do you even care?"

"Of course I—"

"Because every time you *do* call, it's all about you, you, you. *Your* world is ending, *your* cat got taken away. *Your* stepdad's a wrestler. I have problems too. But do you even think to ask me about them?"

"Move it!" I blast my horn. "Stupid pile of feathers."

"Excuse me?"

"No, not you. There's a chicken in the road. Hunter, I'm sorry. I know you have a lot going on. And I apologize if I've been self-absorbed. Why don't you tell me what's been going on with you?"

"You don't really want to listen."

"Yes, I do." Was he always this difficult to have a conversation with?

"Well ... there is this one thing that's been eating at me. Like I can't sleep and I think about it all the time. It's like I can't get out from under the dark cloud."

"I so relate. Go on."

"We're already working on the Autumn Ball with Hilliard, and they want a Victorian theme while we want to totally do the sixties. As president of the student social committee, do you realize what kind of pressure this puts me under? It affects every detail. If we go Victorian, the punch will need to be pink, but if we have a sixties theme ..."

I halfheartedly listen to my boyfriend drone on and on about cucumber sandwiches and the recently established napkin selection committee.

"So you can see it's not just you who's under a lot of stress."

"No," I say, turning into the school parking lot. "I guess my problems barely compare to yours."

"Forget it. You're obviously not in the mood to have a conversation. I remember a time when you used to enjoy listening to me."

Do I really find this part of his life interesting? I worry about my stepbrother smothering me with a pillow in the middle of the night. He worries about whether to leave the crusts on the sandwiches or not.

"Hunter, I'm sorry. I don't want to fight. I know you're stressed."

"Bella . . . you know as activities coordinator, I have to escort a Hilliard girl to the dance. It's a tradition."

"I know." I swing open the door of the Bug and climb out, my skirt waving in the summer breeze. "I wish I could be there for it."

"I don't know who to ask. It has to be someone who will know that it means nothing. Somebody who knows that I'm seeing you."

My pulse quickens at the sight of Dante walking with Matt Sparks into the building. "What did you say? Oh yeah, um, why don't you just ask Mia? You guys will be hanging out anyway."

"Are you sure? That would work out perfectly."

"Yeah, you should call her about that. And tell her to call me. I haven't talked to her in days. Hey, Hunter, I gotta go. Call me later." I drop my phone in my purse and power-walk up the steps and through the doors.

When I'm about three people away from Dante and Matt, I take out my phone again like I have a call. I stick it to my ear and act totally engrossed in a riveting conversation. I'll just imagine Hunter's discussing a balloon and streamer dilemma.

"Dude, I just don't know," Matt says, his voice barely audible.

Dante looks around, and I avert my gaze, as if I'm oblivious to everything but the call.

"I need to know soon. People are counting on us."

"Like what people?"

"Just people, okay? There's nothing more to tell you until—"

I can't hear them. I move closer, my ears straining to—

"Hey!" Suddenly I'm pulled out of the flow and into a class-room. "Luke! What are you doing?"

He grabs my phone, presses it to his ear. "Yeah, Bella's going to have to continue her pathetically fake call later." And snaps it shut.

"Could you get any more amateur?"

"Could you get any more obnoxious?" We're nose to nose.

"You could blow this whole story."

"Oh, the story that wouldn't have happened if it weren't for *amateur* me?"

"You do nothing unless it's cleared through me. You got it, Bella?"

"I know what I'm doing. You're like a rabid bulldog."

"You need to slow this down and follow my lead."

"You need to . . . jump off a cliff." I huff past him, but he catches my arm, blocking my exit. My cheek is inches from his.

I feel his chest rumble with laughter. "Is that really the best you could do?"

"I know. It was weak." I bite my lip on a smile. "I'm just not on my game today. I'll try to have some better insults by second hour."

Something besides contempt glows in his eyes. It holds me in place, and I can't seem to look away.

"Big news," he says, and I struggle to focus. "Reggie Lee got escorted out of early morning football practice—by the police."

"What?"

Luke nods. "They found drugs in his locker at the field. He's been suspended."

Pieces of conversation from that day at the Dumpster float back to me. It has to be connected.

"Bella . . . I have something else I want to tell you." He leans closer.

"Yes?" I breathe.

"I need you to . . ." He pauses, the eyes behind his tortoise frames still fused to mine.

Like there's a magnet pulling me in, I lean closer.

"I need you to be a water girl for the football team."

I blink. Spell broken. "What?"

"Keep it down." He takes a comfortable step away from me. "I thought about it last night. We have to get you on the inside with the football players. Your friend Lindy is a water girl, so have her pull some strings and see if you can't help pass out water or towels or whatever it is you might do."

"That is a dumb idea."

"It beats chasing after some guys into a dark forest."

"Have you ever seen a football player up close? They're . . ." I search my brain for a visual. "Hot and sweaty and they spit a lot."

"I thought you girls liked hot and sweaty."

"From a distance!" *Duh.*

"If you want this story, you have to be willing to do a little undercover reporting—my way."

I blow out a frustrated breath. "I'm about ready to tell you where you can stick *your way.*"

"It's my paper."

"Seriously, are you five?"

Instead of giving a snappy retort, he laughs again and guides me back into the crowded hallway. These flashes of a kinder, gentler

Luke are totally throwing me off. Maybe he really isn't a tool of Satan.

Could it be I won his respect last night?

"Talk to Lindy. I'll see you at the game." And with his hands in his pockets, he saunters down the science hall, confident I'll do his bidding.

~~~~~~~~~

"You want to do *what?*" Lindy fills the water bottles at halftime. I can barely hear her over the marching band's version of "Hang On, Sloopy."

"I said I want to do this." I gesture to the stacks of towels and the coolers. "I want to be a water girl. You know, help the team. And why are you wearing a ball cap tonight? Didn't we agree in New York no more hats and no more ponytails?"

"I'm working, Bella." She heaves a tray of water bottles onto a bench and begins to fill another set.

"Looking hot is a twenty-four-hour job."

She looks up from the cooler. "Wow, that would make a great tattoo. Right on your—"

"I'm serious. You said you wanted help looking more feminine. I don't think I'll find a Tigers t-shirt, a pair of basketball shorts, and a dirty hat in my latest issue of *Teen Vogue.*"

"And look where your doll clothes have gotten me—nowhere. Do you know what he said to me at the party when we were dancing?"

"That you're the sun he wants to orbit for all his days?"

She wipes her own sweat with a towel. "He asked me when this phase of mine would be over. He said it's like hanging out with Malibu Barbie." She laughs ruefully.

"She did always have good shoes." I plod on as Lindy rolls her big eyes. "Don't give up yet. Okay, so maybe we change our strategy. If I'm here on the sidelines with you, then I can help out your cause even more."

She focuses on the remaining minutes of the scoreboard, only halfway listening to me. "How?"

"I can see Matt up close, you know. See what really makes him tick. Notice how he interacts with you in this setting."

"And what do you get out of it?"

"I . . . um . . . get to write an article for the paper. Yeah, I want to write an article on the team's season. You know, their bid for state and all." I would throw in some football jargon here, but I don't know any. I am *so* gonna have to start watching *SportsCenter* like my stepdad. "See how they score with their fumbles and do that thing with the flags."

"You have no idea what you're talking about, do you?"

"That's why I need you! You can teach me what I need to know about the game, and I'll help you down here with the water . . . and with Matt. Perfect!" I hug her close. "Thanks, Lindy!" And though I can't see her face, I know she's rolling her eyes again.

She steps back and shoves a set of towels in my arms. "Here. You can start tonight."

"What?" I gesture to my skirt and patent leather flats. "But I'm not dressed for it. How about next week?"

The football boys trot onto the field and head our way. It would be nice to have a bird's-eye view of their interaction with the coaches. I think at least one of them could be involved in this Brotherhood business. See, this is what happens when you stick a bunch of guys in too-tight pants. It cuts off the oxygen to their brains, and next thing you know they're calling themselves a brotherhood, slapping each other on the butt, and meeting secretly in the woods.

About five minutes into the third quarter, I get into the groove of running water bottles to the guys. I have to dodge lots of towels and spitting, but so far my shoes are still intact. My dignity, not so much. If any of them find it odd that I'm passing out refreshments, no one says anything. They're so focused and intent on the game, I think Jessica Simpson could be handing out Gatorade, and they wouldn't so much as turn in her direction.

The Tigers barely hold it together during the fourth quarter, and we're pushed into overtime. With seconds to go, Dante passes to number twenty-four, who promptly dives for the ball. He lands in a heap of arms and legs. But arises, mere feet from the goal, with nothing in his hands but regret.

And the Truman Tigers lose the first game of the season.

"Here's a towel. Good game. That was some fine . . . um, football stuff." I hand Dante some water. I start to spout off more positivity, but Lindy shakes her head in warning. Okay, shutting up now.

I hand out the last of my water bottles and bend down to pick up the empty ones thrown on the ground. I suppose now would not be a good time to remind the team that I am *not* their maid?

"Our team's unraveling, Matt. You saw it out there tonight. No wins, no college scholarships. Dude, if we keep that up, we won't get recruiters out here to even look at us."

I stay stooped down within earshot of Dante.

Matt pulls his helmet off. "Maybe. I don't know."

"I *do* know. The Brotherhood. That's the answer. We need you in. We need to be a team off the field in order to be a team *on* the field."

"You gotta give me more information, Dante."

"You either trust me or you don't. We're your family, Matt."

Dante stops. "Do you need something?"

From my bent position, I glance up. His steely eyes are fixed on me. "Um . . . just picking up water bottles." I giggle. "Gets a little messy down here." I twirl my hair around a finger. "Sorry about the game." I offer a friendly wink, grab Matt's towel, and walk away.

A few minutes later, after I've helped Lindy pile all the equipment, I grab my notebook and plant myself in front of the first coach I find.

"Coach Dallas, can I have a word with you?" He's definitely the youngest of the coaches. If anyone is more likely to be hanging out with the players, it's him. "I'm Bella Kirkwood with the *Truman High Tribune*. I was wondering if I could ask you a few questions."

His eyes move swiftly to his players as they gather around the head coach. "I really have to go, kid."

"I'll just take a few minutes of your time." I begin my questions, not waiting for permission. "Last year the Tigers were so close to winning state. Does that make you even more intent on capturing the title this season?"

"Uh . . ." The coach struggles to focus on me as his colleague begins yelling at the team in various tones of mad and furious. "Sure, yeah. We really want to make it to state this year. We have a long history of being champs, so we'd like to recapture that."

"And do you think last year's loss of two players has hurt the team morale?"

His expression freezes and he pins me with his full attention. "No. And we didn't lose two players. Zach Epps is still alive to us. Still a part of this team."

"From a nursing home bed?" I continue my barrage. "Were you here last year? What can you tell me about the night Zach was hurt?"

"I've got work to do, Miss Kirkwood. That's all the time I have."

"Coach, I want to drum up some school enthusiasm for the team through a series of articles. I'm just trying to get a little background info."

He sets his jaw. "Last year was my first year. And I know nothing about Zach's incident besides what the paper reported. Why?"

I fire off some mundane questions, trying to sound less intrusive and soothe any suspicions he might have. "What college did you go to?"

"Ole Miss."

"Is that home, then—Mississippi?"

"Of course not. I was a Tiger." He swats a player on the shoulder. "A Truman Tiger." His sleeve rises. And I see a tattoo.

Truman Brotherhood.

"I have to talk to my team now." Coach Dallas walks away, catching up to Dante to talk.

I close my notebook and grab my purse from the ground. Two familiar-looking shoes appear beside mine, and I jump up. "Luke, thank God you're here. Big news."

"Walk with me." He gestures toward the exiting crowd. "You must've worked pretty hard tonight. You have a hair out of place." He reaches out and tucks a wilted strand behind my ear and my mind completely empties. "Can't have my staff looking disheveled. So how did it go? Come up with anything? Did Jared Campbell's brother give you any information?"

"Who?"

"Coach Dallas—that's Jared's stepbrother."

"What? Why didn't anyone tell me this? So Coach Lambourn is Jared's stepdad?" At Luke's nod, I check behind me to make sure no one is tuned in to our conversation as we stroll across the field. "I overheard Dante talking to Matt again, but just more of the same. Still wanting him to join their group. Matt sounds closer to caving in."

"Any ideas on what this Brotherhood is?"

"No. But Dante won't tell Matt everything about it until he commits, so it's a heavily guarded secret."

"One we need to uncover."

"Right." I thrill a little at his use of "we." Like we're a team on this. Like he finally takes me seriously. I grab Luke's arm. "Oh, get this—guess who has a Brotherhood tattoo?"

"Your mom?"

"Coach Dallas—on his upper arm. *And* he was very cagey when I asked him about Zach Epps." I fill him in on my brief interview.

"And your theory?"

I can't believe Luke's asking my opinion. I wonder if he's fevered. He is *not* acting like his usual snarky self. "Um . . ." I try to focus on the issue at hand as we weave through long-faced Tiger fans. "I think it's pretty obvious Coach Dallas wants to reignite that long history of winning he mentioned. In his day, the team was a brilliant success. Maybe he wants to win so bad that he's formed this supergroup of players that he trains really hard and . . ." And here's where my theory dead-ends. "And who knows what else they do."

"It has to be more than additional training if it's so secret."

"Yeah, I guess the players wouldn't need to meet in a dark field to discuss some extra bench presses."

"Keep thinking on it. Maybe pray about it, if you're into that sort of thing."

I stop and an old lady with a giant foam finger rams into me. "What did you just say?"

Luke smiles. "You know—pray or something. A good reporter can't do this alone. We need some help. That's your assignment for tonight—see you later."

He leaves me standing in the center of the field with gaping mouth and whirling brain. The president of the Jerk Club of Truman High just told *me* to pray about it? He's the one who probably has to add "Be nice" to his daily to-do list. Who does he think he is? Like I wouldn't do that? As if I'm such a weak Christian I need that reminder?

Okay, so maybe I needed that reminder. Whatever.

Maybe God and I have been living in different stratospheres lately. It's like I can't get a grip on anything anymore. Nothing is going how it's supposed to. I have an evil stepbrother, my mom married a man who likes to play pirate, my cat is gone, my boyfriend ignores me, and Mia has forgotten I exist. And I'm supposed to find faith in the midst of this *how*? What was it that youth pastor said at FCA? That we should look for our Mary moments? What if I don't want to find mine? Maybe it's in New York, but I'm not there to intercept it.

I glance across the field to see if Lindy's waiting for Matt like I instructed her to. Though I don't see her anywhere, my eyes land on a lone figure in the bleachers. Sitting. Covered up as if it's chilly, yet it's at least ninety steamy degrees this evening.

With legs that seem to move of their own volition, I retrace my steps back toward the stands.

Kelsey Anderson. The girl who was at FCA, the one who dated Zach Epps.

My heart pounding with dread, I continue up the steel stairs and walk toward the girl who sits alone, staring out onto the field like it holds her captive, transfixed. Her pale, haunted face tugs at my conscience. *"He might be calling you to a Mary moment . . ."* No, I totally don't want to talk to her. She's all spacey and weird. I don't even know her!

I stop a few feet beside Kelsey. Clearing my throat, I rest my hand on her shoulder. "Hey, Kelsey."

She jumps. But says nothing.

"I, um, just wondered if you noticed the game was over." *Oh my gosh. I need a script. Why do I say these dumb things?* "I mean, of course you know the game's over since you're all alone out here and all, oh, but not that anything's wrong with being alone. I like to be alone sometimes too. Well, maybe not as alone as I have been in Truman, but in Manhattan I liked nothing better than to be by myself and with some Ben and Jerry's and—"

"Zach would've done anything to have been here tonight." Her fragile voice stops me like a shotgun blast. "He would've done anything for the team."

I take that as an invitation to sit down. "So Zach . . . was he a good player?"

She slowly nods her head. "One of the best. He wanted to go pro." Her lips curve at some memory. "Coach told him he had it in him too."

"And which coach would that be?"

"All of them. They knew Zach was really gonna be something. He was their hope for state. Their star quarterback." Kelsey lapses into silence again.

"Is there someone I can call for you? Do you have some friends you could hang out with tonight?" I can't just leave her here alone.

She shakes her head. "They've kind of moved on, you know?" Her hollow brown eyes finally meet mine. "I know I'm different— I'm not the same. They want to go to parties and shop and laugh. They care about clothes and boys."

Maybe you could introduce me to them?

"But when the person you love the most in the world lies in a nursing home and dies a little every day, none of those things matter."

"No, I don't guess they would." My words sound flat and useless. "Hey . . . um, Kelsey, you mentioned that Zach went to a party the night of the accident. What do you know about that?"

She shrugs and returns her stare to the field. "Just another party with the football guys. Usually he got an invitation for me, but not the last few times he went. Not that night."

"And he always had a ticket, an invitation, to get in?"

She nods. "They would always pick us up somewhere then blindfold us. It was fun at the time. Mysterious."

"Did Zach ever figure out who threw the parties?"

"I don't know."

"Kelsey, was anyone with Zach when he crashed?"

"No, but I should've been."

My hand covers hers. "You can't think that."

She sniffs. "We had gotten into this huge fight. I thought he was cheating on me, going to the parties by himself, without me. When

I'd press him for details, he wouldn't say a word. Just got mad and said I didn't trust him." Tears spill down her cheeks. "Maybe if I had trusted him, he would've let me go to the last parties with him. Maybe I could've saved him."

"Did anyone see the crash? If it was on the night of the party, where were his friends?"

"I have to go." She draws the blanket around her. "I want to go tell Zach about the game tonight."

"Kelsey—" I stand up with her. "Don't you think there are some things that don't add up here?"

She lifts a shoulder and walks past me. "That's life though, isn't it? Bad things happen—things don't make sense. Like Carson Penturf."

"Wait—who's that?"

"Carson played center. Until last fall."

"And then?"

"Then he stepped off a cliff and broke his neck."

"The guy who killed himself last year, right?"

She lifts a thin brow. "That's what they said. I have to go. Visiting hours will be over soon."

"Wait, I just have a few more questions."

"They don't like questions around here, Bella. They'll just call you crazy like they did me. Besides, you can't argue with a police report. Or the football team."

"Is that what you did?"

"I have to go."

And she runs away on toothpick legs, her blanket flying behind her like one of Robbie's capes.

chapter twenty-seven

W e left a list for you. And I'll have my cell phone, but Jake says it gets so loud in the arena that I won't be able to hear it. But remember, no Coke after seven. He needs to be in bed by ten. And I printed off instructions for the Heimlich and CPR, and—"

"Mom," I interrupt. "Seriously, just go. Robbie and I will be fine. I won't let him choke *or* OD on caffeine."

"I know it's only four o'clock, but we've got to be in Tulsa by five." Jake scoops his youngest son into his hulkish arms. "We won't be back until you're asleep, so that's a long time to stir up trouble for Bella. You won't do that, right? You don't want to be banished to the poop deck, do you?"

Robbie giggles. "No, Captain Iron Jack. I'll keep an eye on the ship while yer gone. Arghhh."

Pirate jokes. Perfect. This makes me want to hurl myself off the poop deck.

The doorbell chimes as Mom and her wrestler walk to the foyer.

"Flowers for Bella Kirkwood." Mom closes the door and hands them over to my waiting arms. "Roses. Very nice."

With a big goofy smile on my face, I rip into the card.

I'm sorry for my distance lately. Being without you makes me kind of crazy. Can't wait until we see each other again. Love, Hunter.

"They're from Hunter." I clutch the flowers to my chest then peck my mom on the cheek. "Don't worry about a thing. We'll be fine here. And, Jake, um . . . good luck or break a leg or whatever it is you people say."

Jake grins and pats me on the back. "It's definitely *not* break a leg."

Break a skull? Don't bust a seam? Have a concussion-free evening?

I shut the door behind them as Budge stomps down the stairs. I turn my head so he won't see the giggle that his Aladdin-inspired uniform always sets off.

"What?" he growls. "You think you're too good for the Wiener Palace?"

I swivel to face him. "No, of course not." My eyes narrow in on his name tag. "I can only hope to one day be called a Sultan of Pork."

"Not everybody has a dad who gets rich off of boob jobs."

"Not everybody cares what you think." Immediately I feel bad. I know I shouldn't talk to Budge like that, but he totally pushes my buttons. "Actually . . . Budge, there is something I've been wanting to talk to you about."

He crosses his arms over his velvet vest, wrinkling his puffy sleeves. "You said you didn't care what I thought."

"When it comes to your hot dog career dreams." *And your genie pants.* "But I would like to hear your take on some stuff that happened at Truman High last year."

His face freezes. Then reddens. "What's it to you?"

"You know what I'm going to ask you about, don't you? About the football players?"

"I don't know anything."

"Did you know them? Zach Epps or Carson Penturf?"

"I said I don't know anything." Budge crams on his sultan's hat, a tall silk thing with an enormous ruby sprouting peacock plumes.

I follow him into the kitchen where Robbie sits with a coloring book. "The school isn't *that* big. Just tell me what the talk was when things started going wrong last year."

Budge jerks open the door and it slams against the cabinets. "Things went *wrong?* One guy jumps to his death and another's a permanent vegetable, and you call that things going wrong?"

"Budge, wait. I'm sorry, I just—" *Slam*. The glass panes rattle in the door.

"Everybody knows not to talk to Budge about Zach."

Robbie's words go off like cannons in the kitchen. "What did you say?"

He sticks out his tongue and selects another crayon. "My daddy says there are three things you don't bring up to Budge—my mama, girls, and his friend Zach."

I pull out a chair and sit next to my stepbrother. "So Budge and Zach Epps were friends?"

Robbie rolls his eyes like I'm simple. "Yeah, for like forever. And you can't ask him about it."

"Has Budge ever mentioned Carson Penturf?"

Robbie shades in a puppy's tail with a pink crayon. "Nah."

"Oh." Dead end.

So Zach and Budge were friends? But Budge is . . . Budge. I mean he's all about computers and video games and . . . eating

Twinkies. And Zach must've been a star athlete. A jock. What could they possibly have had in common?

"What are we having for dinner, Robbie?"

He folds his fingers and shoots invisible webs toward a cabinet over my head. "SpaghettiOs."

"Coming right up, little caped crusader."

My phone sings and I press it to my ear. "Hunter! The flowers are amazing." I tap my stepbrother on his caped shoulder. "Why don't you fly off into the living room. I'll make dinner and call you when it's ready."

He nods. "I might have to take a coloring break and go save a few people. Is that okay?"

"Only a few people. You have to be home by the time your dad gets back." I ruffle his red hair, and he scurries out of the room. "So . . . it was a sweet surprise. I loved the card too."

"I've missed you, Bella. When do you come home next?"

"It's going to be a few weeks. Seems like forever." I dig for a can opener in a drawer. After asking Hunter about his day, I update him on the Brotherhood.

"You be careful around all those athletes. I don't want to see you get hurt."

"Oh, you and Luke. I can take care of myself."

"Luke?" Static crackles on the line.

"My editor."

"Is he old and ugly?"

"Um . . . not exactly." He's tall, muscular, and gorgeous. If you like the nerdy, intellectual, rude sort.

"Do I have any reason to be concerned?"

"Of course not!" *Puh-lease.* "He's nothing like you. He's obnoxious. He's insensitive. He treats me like a total idiot. I would rather run my tongue across Jake's cow pasture than date Luke."

"I just wanted to make sure. This long-distance thing really is hard, isn't it, Bel?"

I sigh into the phone. "It's only been a week, but it feels like forever since I've seen you." The microwave dings. "I better go. I'm babysitting Robbie tonight while my stepdad whups up on some grown men."

"Miss ya."

"Miss ya right back." And I slide my phone back into my jeans.

"Robbie! Your gourmet pasta meal is ready!" I walk into the living room, where Superman flies across the television screen. "Robbie?" His coloring books lie open on the floor. I walk to the stairs and call for him again.

No answer.

Running up to his bedroom, I find cars scattered, action figures strewn, and Legos arranged in piles. But no Robbie.

After two minutes of searching and yelling, I race outside, bellowing his name. I check the barn, the old truck, my car, the trees, the pond. Everywhere.

I stand in the center of the pasture next to Betsy the cow, squeeze my eyes shut, and beg God for help. *Please, Jesus. I seriously need a hand here. When I walk in that house, let Robbie be there. If something happens to that kid, I will die—throw myself in front of a tractor and die.*

Fifteen minutes later I collapse onto the couch, hoarse from yelling Robbie's name. My pulse races as I pick up my phone and call my mother.

No answer.

I hit redial until my finger aches.

I text her an urgent message then watch the phone for a reply.

What do I do?

Long moments pass, and fighting the urge to throw up, I press the three dreaded numbers.

9-1-1.

"I need to report a missing child."

By ten o'clock, I've puked twice, talked to the police three times, and tried to call Mom a million times. And nobody at Wiener Palace will pick up the phone.

At 10:05, the picture I gave the police from our mantel flashes on the evening news. The blonde reporter describes his last moments in the house, mentioning the fact that his stepsister was in charge of him for the evening. Great, way to paint me a loser.

I've called Hunter and Mia both, but like everyone else, they don't answer. It's like I'm totally alone in the world tonight.

An hour later, I jump off the couch when headlights shine through the windows. My heart sinks when I see it's Budge. He is going to rip my head off and feed it to the cows for a late-night snack. *Um, hi. Remember your brother? Yeah, I lost him.*

The back door slams, and swallowing back equal parts bile and dread, I meet Budge in the kitchen. "Budge, I lost your brother. I mean he's gone." Snot drips out of my nose like water from a faucet. "I don't know what happened. One minute I was fixing him SpaghettiOs, and I don't know what's in those meatballs, but the next minute the cow and I are walking the fields yelling for him, but he wasn't there. And the police came and one was really short and I kept looking down at him and thinking, 'Wow, he's almost like a midget,' and then they took down all this information, and you just missed him on the news." I wail my last few words.

Budge doesn't even blink. "You lost me at meatballs."

I take deep, shuddering breaths and wipe my eyes. "I said"—I pause as a sob closes my throat—"your brother is—"

The door flings open again and Robbie waddles in dragging his red cape. "S'up?"

"Wh-what?" I point at the six-year-old. "It's Robbie. That's your brother." I rush to Robbie and wrap him in my arms. "Thank You God, thank You God, thank You God."

"Stop squeezing me. Lemme go. You can't kiss superheroes. You're going to suck my powers out!"

"Bella," comes Budge's deep voice. "Step away from the child."

I look up, still clutching my stepbrother. "Where have you been? I've looked for you everywhere. The *police* have looked everywhere."

Robbie shimmies out of my grip. "I went to the Wiener Palace."

"What?" I pin Budge with my evilest glare. "He was with you the whole time? I've been entertaining the Truman PD and watching your brother on the Tulsa news, and *you* had him with you at work? Are you kidding me?" I'm yelling.

"Yeah." Budge picks a piece of lint from his vest. "Good job keeping an eye on my brother."

"But how did you get to Budge's work? Why would you leave and not tell me?"

"I rode my bike. It took a really long time, but I'm pretty strong like my dad. And I *told* you I was going to go save some people."

"I might have to take a coloring break and go save some people."

"I thought you were teasing!"

Robbie frowns and shakes his head. "Being a superhero is not something to joke about. It's my responsibility to the world."

I kneel down to get in his face. "Unless you were there passing out antacids like a Rolaids fairy, I can't imagine why you went to the Wiener Palace."

Robbie scuffs his toe along the linoleum floor. "Budge needed me. You made him sad, and he needed me to cheer him up."

I jerk my head toward Budge. "And you couldn't have called? What kind of crap is that? I've been out of my head with worry."

He shrugs. "Not my fault you couldn't hack ten minutes alone with my brother."

I clench my fists at my side. *Do not punch your fist through his nose.* "You've got issues, you know that, Budge? You're mean, you're thoughtless, and you don't care about anybody but yourself."

The front door opens and closes. Anxious voices call from the living room.

Mom and Jake.

Budge laughs and pushes past me. "Looks to me like *you're* the one with the issues."

chapter twenty-eight

The Holy Church of the Sacred High School has a great choir. It's like watching *Sister Act*. Well, minus the nun outfits. But these people know how to sing some Jesus.

I sit next to Lindy and Matt, opting for some time away from the family. While I didn't really get in trouble last night over Robbie's disappearance, Mom wasn't exactly what I'd call happy with me either.

As I clap along to the up-tempo song, I watch Budge sitting with his friends. He stands with his arms crossed, not singing, looking like he wants to be anywhere but church. Jake totally grounded him for not calling me last night when his brother showed up at the Weiner Palace. And of course, Budge is furious with me. Like it's my fault. If this is the kind of stuff I've missed not having siblings, I can't say I feel deprived.

"What do you say we pick up a pizza and go hang out at the city park?" Matt asks after the service. "Do you want to go?"

"I'm in a dress." I turn to Lindy. "You're in a dress."

"Oh. I guess I'll have to pass. I would hate to muss up my skirt." She flips her hair and her perfume floats between us. "It's Moochie, you know."

I cough. "Gucci."

Matt's face falls. "Come on, Lind. We haven't thrown the football around in forever. You're always too busy doing your nails or worried about messing up your pedicure or something."

Lindy looks to me, waiting for me to throw her a life preserver.

"Maybe a day at the park would be fun. Get a little sun while we eat. Sure, why not?" I link my arm through Lindy's. "Maybe you can do some boy-watching too. A nice day like this—who knows who'll be out there?"

"I'm not going out there so you two can gawk at the guys. Let's just go hang out and have a good time, okay?"

We step into the aisle, and I lean close to Lindy's ear. "He sounds jealous, doesn't he? It's totally working."

Her smile doesn't quite reach her eyes. "I hope he gets the idea soon. I'm sick of dressing like a princess."

"But this is the new you, Lindy. It's not a phase. You've been totally transformed. Lots of girls would kill to have those Chanel shoes you have on right now. You went from looking like a sports warehouse model to a runway model. And he's into it. I've seen him looking at you."

"Yeah, like I'm a psychopathic shopping freak."

"Just trust me." I pat her arm and join my parents.

"Hey, I'm going to the park with—" I choke on the rest of my sentence as I notice a familiar bald man in the family huddle.

"Bella, you remember Mickey." Jake pats his trainer's back.

Yes, how have you been since I broke into your gym and found my stepfather throwing himself on another man?

Mickey takes his eyes off me and focuses on Mom. "Jillian, how's work? Are you adjusting to life at the diner?"

"It's getting better. I never realized what a hard job it was to be a waitress."

Um, probably because you weren't made to be one. My mom used to serve on the boards of directors for charities. Now she's serving anything that comes with fries.

Mickey clasps his hands behind his back, making his chest muscles pop through his oxford shirt. The guy may be pushing fifty, but he could probably take on any member of the Truman football team. "And how is Dolly?" He turns his attention to the floor.

"She's fine, Mickey. Maybe you should come by the diner for a piece of pie someday next week." Mom's face is hopeful.

"I haven't . . . um . . . had any of Sugar's banana cream pie in years."

Mom wraps her small arm around Jake's ox of a trainer. "Sounds like it's been too long. Come in to the diner, Mickey. Things might've changed in there."

Mickey scratches his head. "Oh, did they redecorate?"

"She means Dolly," I blurt. "Not the wallpaper." Boys. They're so dense. "So I'm going to the park with Matt and Lindy, okay?" I give my mom a quick squeeze.

"Why don't you ask Logan to go?" Mom asks as my least favorite Trumanite joins us. She jerks her blonde head toward him. "Bella, wasn't there something you wanted to ask Logan?"

I pry my clenched teeth apart. "Budge, would you like to accompany me and some friends to the park?"

"I'd rather eat hot lava."

"Okay then."

"Bella, go get him." Mom pushes me into the flow of the crowd as my stepbrother walks away.

"Budge, wait." I catch up with him in the school lobby. "Look, you and I have gotten off on the wrong foot, and I'm sorry. Let's—"

"I don't need you, Jillian's attempts to be my mom, or this stupid church. I'm out of here."

"What is your problem?" I catch his arm. "I know losing your best friend had to hurt a lot—still does, I'm sure. But being mad at all of us isn't going to accomplish anything."

"You don't know jack about my life, so butt out." He busts through the lobby doors out into the yellow sunshine, his dark mood like a cloud trailing behind him.

"I'm going to pray for you, Budge," I call out.

At the park I turn off my bad thoughts about Budge and sink my energy into the pepperoni pizza Matt places in the middle of the blanket.

After Lindy leads us in a quick prayer, my mouth closes around my first bite.

And it's everything I can do not to spit it out.

"I see that face." Lindy points her finger. "Do *not* tell us how they make pizza in New York. This is Truman, Bella. Don't be a pizza snob."

"I'm not!" I wipe a string of cheese off my chin. "It's getting better." I chew and smile. "Mmmm." It's like eating cardboard encased in mozzarella. "So, Matt, what did you think of the party Thursday night?" It's the first chance I've really had to talk to him about it.

"It was okay." He stares off toward a giant sandbox inhabited by squealing toddlers.

I so want to just come out and ask him about the Brotherhood, but I can't. I don't know him well enough. And what if he alerted the other guys that I'm onto them? I'd never find out anything else.

"You and the team seem pretty . . . close."

"Yeah, I guess we are."

"It's so crazy," I laugh. "I mean we were there for hours, and I never found out whose house we were at. Do you know whose cabin it was?"

"No. That's the fun of it." Matt wipes his mouth with a napkin.

"Yeah, well, it's not my kind of party," Lindy says. "I don't think we'll be going back. Right, Matt?"

He continues his study of the sandbox.

"Right, Matt?"

"I don't know, Lind. It's good to get away from it all sometimes. None of us drank, so what's the harm?"

Her eyes narrow to slits. "Because we don't *need* to be around that stuff. You've always been adamant about that."

"Lighten up, Lindy. We had a good time."

"Yeah." I nudge her in the ribs. "You said you had a great time dancing. Didn't *you*, Matt?"

His eyes linger on Lindy for a brief second. "You do have some new dance moves I've never seen before. I always thought you hated dancing, but you totally held your own Thursday night."

"Thanks." She bats her curled eyelashes. "Bella introduced me to this guy in New York, and we danced . . . a lot."

I hold my breath, waiting for Matt's reaction.

"I brought a Frisbee. You ladies want to toss it around awhile?"

That's it? No jealousy? No declarations of love?

"I'm game." Lindy forces a smile and jumps up, her skirt swishing around her.

We keep the Frisbee going for a few minutes when my girl radar picks up on something. Yes . . . I'm almost certain . . . I do believe there might be cute boys somewhere close.

"Is that the Truman soccer team?" Just beyond Matt's shoulder a group of guys pile out of cars and onto an adjoining practice field.

"Yeah. They're pretty good. The captain's a little cocky though." Matt spins the Frisbee to Lindy.

A guy balances the soccer ball on his knee. I struggle to bring him into focus, but something tells me—

"Luke Sullivan." And my editor in chief moves closer in our direction and comes into full view. "He's cute." The awestruck words tumble out of my mouth before I can reclaim them. Preppy, uptight Luke has leg muscles any quarterback would envy. And biceps. I had no idea. I just had no idea.

A Frisbee bounces off my forehead. "Ow!"

Lindy laughs. "See something over there you like?"

"What? Me?" I fling the disc and rub my head. "No, of course not! I was . . . um . . . just seeing if anyone of interest for you was over there." This time I catch Lindy's pass. "I know you have your heart set on one guy, but it doesn't hurt to keep your options open." And I release the Frisbee, sending it flying between Matt and Lindy.

They both dive for it, falling into a tangled heap on the grass.

Matt rolls away, shaking with laughter. Lindy jumps up, her skirt stained with green. "Good job, Matt. Look at my outfit." She brushes it with frantic hands. "And my hair."

His freckled face falls. "What's into you lately? It's like you've changed."

"You're just *now* noticing?"

"I'll be glad when this girly phase of yours is over."

"This is me, Matt. This is who I am."

"And I don't like it." His voice rises above the slight breeze.

"I can't stay one of the guys forever."

"I never thought of you as one of the guys!"

"Um, I don't see you burping rap songs in front of any other girls, do you?"

Matt scoops up the Frisbee and the pizza box. "I'm out of here. Let me know if you run into my old friend Lindy. I miss her." He dunks the box in the trash and stomps away.

Lindy's shoulders sag. "This isn't working, Bella."

"Of course it is." I can hardly keep from rubbing my hands together in giddy satisfaction. "Don't you see? He's *finally* noticing you."

"Yeah, noticing that he can't stand me. Fat lot of good *that's* doing."

"Lindy, be patient. He's going to go home, and you are going to invade his every thought. Obviously you've gotten under his skin. If he's unsure about this new you, it's because he's afraid of what he feels." I totally saw this same thing on *Tyra* last week.

"I've got basketball practice in a few hours. I'll see you later."

I watch Lindy go and feel a hitch of nerves. What if I'm not bringing Matt and Lindy together? What if I'm detonating their friendship? But he has to fall for the new Lindy, right? She dresses better, she smells like a girl, and she has killer highlights. Who could resist that?

I stroll across the grass, past a row of swings and an old wooden teeter-totter, lost in thought.

A whistle blows, jarring me from my trance, and I realize I've walked to the soccer field. My eyes locate Luke instantly. He shouts commands to his teammate, then high-fives him. He runs down the field, the chiseled muscles above his knees flexing with every step. The wind sails through his hair, and he pushes the ball toward the goal. I can't help but smile as I see his expression when he sinks the ball in. A grin lights up his face, and his teammates pile around him. Gone is the editor mask. No arrogance. No overblown ego. Out here, he's just a boy.

I reach for my cell and try Hunter.

Right to voice mail. "It's Bella. Remember me, your girlfriend? Give me a call."

A shadow falls across my arm. I look up and Luke smiles.

"Did you come out here to cheer me on?"

"No." Can't. Think. "I was just here with some friends. I'm leaving." I continue my walk, my face red. He'd *better* not think I was checking him out.

"Bella—wait." Luke runs toward me. "Have you found anything else?"

Just my totally buff editor glistening with sweat. "Er, no. You?"

He lifts up a Gatorade bottle and drinks. "Did some research and found out the lake cabin does belong to Coach Dallas."

"How'd you get that information, Detective Sullivan? Did you break into his office? Hack his computer?"

He wipes the moisture from his brow. "Googled the address. Much more legal."

Oh. How unimaginative.

"Now we just have to find out how Carson Penturf's suicide and Zach Epps's wreck are all connected to what I've overheard lately."

"*If* they're connected."

"You know they are, Luke. What does your reporter's gut tell you?" *You know, the one beneath your six-pack abs.*

He slowly nods. "They're related. Just not sure how."

"We have to get more information somehow. And your idea to have me be a glorified waitress at the football games isn't cutting it." Plus I broke a few nails. So not cool.

Luke's tanned fingers tap a rhythm on the bottle as his mind works. "Find out from Matt if there's a party this Thursday night. If so, you have to get an invitation."

"Okay." If my mom will even let me go.

"And why don't you pay Kelsey Anderson a visit?"

"She's hardly ever at school."

"You know where she spends her time, Bella."

I shudder with dread but know the girl could be a source of more information. "I'll go see her tomorrow night."

Across the field the whistle blows again, and Luke's teammates reassemble.

"See you tomorrow. Oh, and, Bella?" He flashes me a wicked grin. "Good luck with your boyfriend."

chapter twenty-nine

Y ou want me to do *what?*"

On Monday I sit beside my mother at Sugar's as Dolly slams down a mug and pours herself a shot of Folgers.

"Cater Jake's party. It will be a fairly small affair at the house." My mom fills a shaker with salt.

Dolly arches an eyebrow. "Who will be there?"

"Jake, some other wrestlers in the amateur circuit, a few select people from the media, and the family."

Dolly juts out a hip and parks her hand on it. "And?"

My mother blinks rapidly, a sure sign she's withholding information. "And a few other random people I've invited. Can't remember who."

"Jillian Finley, I am not going to cook up a spread for the likes of Mickey Patrick."

"I need your help. I don't know how to cook. I can't even manage to squeeze cheese on Triscuits."

"It's true," I say. "She can't."

"It's not that I don't want to help you. It's about . . ."

"Dolly, I think you need to—shoot, there's old man Hodges holding up his coffee cup *again*. That man's going to run my legs off."

Mom bustles away to check on her customer, leaving Dolly, me, and a few questions I'm dying to have answered.

"None of your business."

I blink at Dolly's tone. "What? I didn't say anything."

She smacks her gum and runs a fingernail through her teased hair. "You were going to. I saw it in your eyes."

"Come on, tell me what happened with you and your ex-husband. I mean, if the guy's a jerk, then maybe my stepdad doesn't need to be working with him."

She takes a rag and begins scrubbing the counter with a fury. "He left me, that's what."

"For another woman? Is that what bonded you to my mom so quickly? You know she totally relates to that."

"No, he didn't leave me for another woman. Don't you have somewhere to be?"

"Oh, shoot. I do." I sling my purse over my shoulder. "But we're not through discussing this."

When I pull into the parking spot at Truman Manors nursing home, dread expands in my stomach like a balloon on helium. I turn off the key then rest my head on the steering wheel and offer up a small prayer for fortitude. I do *not* want to go in there. I don't want to see old people in the last stages of their lives. I don't want to inhale the smell that could only belong to a nursing home. And most importantly, I do not want to discuss the football team with Kelsey over Zach's lifeless body.

Five minutes later, I finally talk myself out of the car and into the lobby. On each side of me are seating areas and big-screen TVs. On my right is a glass case that houses ten or so chirping birds. Trapped and on display. Is this supposed to cheer the residents up?

It makes me want to grab a fire extinguisher, bust through the glass, and yell, "Fly away, birds! Go! Go!"

I turn my head from the captive pets and focus on the other side.

And there sits Luke, playing checkers with an elderly man.

"And that's the game! I win again." The man holds out a wrinkled hand and Luke places cash in it. "You want to play another one?"

Luke sees me and stands up. "No, you cleaned me out, Mr. Murphy."

"You can't handle this, can you?"

"Nope." Luke laughs and ambles to my side.

"When you're man enough to face me again, I'll be waiting."

"See you next week, Mr. Murphy." Luke places his hand at the small of my back and leads me through the lobby and past the nurses' station.

"What are you doing here?"

He shrugs an arrogant shoulder. "Waiting on you."

"Really? Because it sounded to me like you're a regular here."

"I don't know what that man's talking about." Luke taps his temple. "He's a bit senile."

I punch his shoulder. "Luke Sullivan, you *do* have a heart."

"Tell anyone and I'll kick you out of the class and send you to—"

"Tire Changing 101?"

I follow him down a hall, passing door after door. Some rooms I have to look away. The residents remind me too much of the trapped birds. Some sit alone in their rooms, empty eyes staring at flashing TV screens. Others yell and call out in barely decipherable words.

"It's not easy being here, is it?" Luke stops before room 202.

I shake my head. "Is this his room?" Unlike the others, this door is closed.

"This is it. Are we ready?"

"You're going with me?"

"Of course." His head tilts and his voice lowers. "You didn't think I'd let you go alone, did you?"

"Because you don't trust me to get the information?"

He opens his mouth, pauses, then starts again. "Let's just do this."

Luke knocks softly, then pushes on the door.

Kelsey sits in a chair shoved next to the bed. The bed where her boyfriend lies, unmoving, with machines pumping and tubes weaving a pattern around him. I swallow hard.

She looks up from her vigil. "Hi, Luke." Her pale eyes dim a little as I step out from behind him.

"I brought you some snacks." Luke reaches into his messenger bag and pulls out some crackers and a bottle of water. "Nurse Betty at the front desk said you've been forgetting to eat lately."

She takes the food and manages a smile. "His color's good today, isn't it? He looks kind of peaceful."

My eyes are drawn to Zach, who looks anything but peaceful.

"Kelsey, I have a favor to ask," Luke says as I sit down in a vacant chair. "I know this is the last thing you want to talk about, but Bella and I have reason to believe that any information you can give us about Zach's wreck would be helpful to something we're working on."

She bites into a cracker. "Are you gonna tell me what this is about?"

Luke sighs. "No."

Seconds pass, the only sound being the push and pull of Zach's ventilator.

Kelsey considers her fingernails for a moment. "Okay." She reaches for her water bottle. "What do you want to know?"

Luke doesn't hesitate. "Why do you think Zach didn't let you go to the last few parties with him?"

She stares at her boyfriend and smoothes a piece of hair from his cheek. "I don't know. I guess I'll never know."

Luke sits on the arm of my chair. "Which players was Zach closest to?"

"That was kind of odd last year. He was always best friends with Budge." She looks directly at me. "Your stepbrother and Zach were inseparable. But during the fall semester Zach and Budge just went their separate ways. Zach started spending more and more time with the team. He mostly hung around Dante and that guy who got suspended this year—"

"Reggie Lee," Luke supplies.

"Yeah . . . Sometimes he hung around Jared Campbell. There were some others."

"These parties—were they at a cabin?"

She shrugs at Luke's question. "A few—they'd change up the location I think."

"Did he ever mention anything unusual going on there?" I ask.

"No. He got really tight-lipped about their get-togethers in the end. Said I would've just been bored, that they were just talking football and planning for the next night's game."

"Why would they drink the night before a game?" I wonder

aloud. "If they are all so obsessed with winning, how stupid is that to wake up on game day with a hangover?"

"Did you see anybody drunk out there?" Luke lifts a dark brow. "I didn't see any signs of people getting hammered. At least not the players."

Kelsey stretches her back and yawns. "I remember the last few parties I went to, Zach would drink a single beer. It was so unlike him. His daddy's a drunk, so Zach couldn't stand alcohol much. And when I'd ask him why he was drinking, he'd say, 'Liquid encouragement,' like he needed bolstering or something."

"Encouragement for what?" Luke asks.

"I don't know."

"You mentioned that you had asked a lot of questions, Kelsey." I lean around Luke and catch the fading scent of his cologne. "What sorts of things didn't add up to you?"

"His car. The fact that he was driving it so fast—and so crazy. That wasn't Zach at all. He loved that Camaro. It was his baby. Washed it every Sunday by hand. He didn't use it like a hot rod. He was always so careful with it."

"It's only natural to want to show off at least once if you have a car like that—see how fast she'll go."

"Not Zach. He was fanatical about that car. Wouldn't let anyone else drive it. He wouldn't have done anything that might've so much as put a scratch on it."

"Accidents happen," I say.

Luke twists around. "But the police report says that some of the players witnessed Zach bragging about his car. Said he wanted to prove what it could do."

"He was at one of those parties. The guys denied it was a party to the police, but that's what it was. Zach hadn't let me go. When the police checked out the scene, everyone had cleared out. Only a few of the guys remained, like they were just hanging out for the evening or something. Reggie told the police that Zach left, tires squealing, his engine roaring. Reggie said they tried to talk him out of it. It was raining that night." She shudders. "So dangerous. And stupid."

I take a deep breath and try to align the facts. "Kelsey, I understand your reservations, but as someone who's not as close to the situation, it kind of all makes sense. It was an unfortunate accident, but it sounds like your boyfriend just overdid it and lost control of the car. What's suspicious about that?"

"Nothing." She runs a hand over her tired face. "But the phone call certainly was."

Luke sits up straighter. "Call?"

Kelsey's hand begins to tremble. "Zach called me from the car—during that joyride. He was panicked, talking nonsense. He kept saying, 'I didn't want to do it. He made me do it. He made me.' Told me he couldn't see a thing, and if he scratched the paint his dad would kill him. Then he said something I'll never forget."

Kelsey sits down on the bed beside her boyfriend. I hold my breath and wait for her to speak.

"He said, 'Stupid coach's son. Trying to make us into something we're not.'" The tears flow freely down her cheeks. "Then I heard it. The crash." Her voice gains in intensity, grows stronger. "You find out what happened. The police wouldn't listen to me. And every time I tried to talk to the players, they'd tell me to let it die. Something isn't right here, Luke. Something happened that night, before the wreck." She chokes on tears.

Luke goes to her and wraps her in his arms. "We'll find out what happened." He rests his head on hers, and his eyes lock with mine. "And I think our Coach Dallas is the guy with all the answers."

chapter thirty

By Wednesday morning, Luke's kinder alter ego is as dead as my MasterCard.

"Absolutely not."

"Why?" I ask him for the tenth time. My temples pound with a stress headache that Tylenol can't touch. The only prescription is Luke getting out of my face. "We need answers."

"You are not going to ask Jared Campbell if he knows his step-brother is evil."

Okay, so it doesn't sound so good coming out of Luke's mouth, but in my head it made a lot of sense. Jared's so nice, so innocently naïve. I really think he'd tell me if he knew Coach Dallas was up to no good.

"What did the coach possibly stand to gain by pressuring Zach to drag race his car?" Luke taps his pencil to his chin.

"Maybe when he was in high school a girl stomped on his heart, cheated on him, and the other guy drove a Camaro. And so he wants to see all of them turned into scrap metal."

"This is not some low-budget horror movie we're working with here."

"It could happen," I mumble.

"Have you talked to your stepbrother? Does he know anything?"

"Budge won't even talk to me about it. For that matter, he won't talk to me, period." Which would be a total gift from the heavens if I didn't need information concerning his former best friend.

"What about Reggie Lee? Kelsey said he gave a statement to the police about Zach on the night of the accident. We need to work on that angle."

"I heard he moved out of town. When are we ever going to see him?"

"He still goes to my church sometimes. We could talk to him Sunday."

"If he's there." I sit on the table and swing my legs, admiring my last new pair of Michael Kors flip-flops. "Sounds like a long shot. We need to be more aggressive than that."

The bell rings, and I hop down.

"Bella, leave the *aggressive* stuff to me."

My heart quirks in my chest. I may not like this guy, but that sounded so hot. "Um . . ." *Focus, focus.* "What?"

His eyes sear through mine. "Your days of taking off alone to trail some guys into the woods are over. No more careless moves. We work together on this or I pull you from the story."

My headache pushes tight on my skull. "I don't need you to watch out for me, Luke. I can take care of myself."

"Yeah, okay, whatever. Think about me saving you in the woods."

Strangely enough, I do. A lot.

"If you go and do something rash, not only will you get hurt or in trouble, but you'll get the paper in trouble."

"Oh, right." My heart sinks a bit. "Wouldn't want you worrying over your paper."

He stands up, planting both palms on the table. "It's not just that—it's . . ."

"Yes?" I lean in.

"The more we find out, the more I'm convinced the people involved in this could be dangerous. It would have to take a lot of intimidation for somebody like Zach Epps to cave in to peer pressure."

At lunch I sit beside Lindy, with a sullen and silent Matt across from us. Neither one of them says a word. The tension is thicker than cafeteria gravy.

"So . . ." I sprinkle sugar into my tea. This stuff grows on a person. "FCA was good this morning, eh? I liked what the speaker said about forgiveness and accepting others as they are."

Matt glares over his sandwich. "I've heard better messages."

"Yeah," Lindy adds. "And the donuts were stale."

"Um, Matt, I was wondering if there was another party this Thursday. I had fun dancing. Meeting people." Not to mention eating Fritos and following people into the woods.

"I'd like to go too."

Eating stops as we stare at Lindy.

"I would. I have a new outfit and there's someone that I want to see it. I think he'll be there." She giggles as she waves to a few guys across the cafeteria.

Oh no. I've created a monster. A flirting, party-going, man-eating monster. While I encouraged this in the beginning, it's not natural for Lindy. It's like asking the football team to wear tutus. Not a good combo.

"Who's this guy you like, Lindy? Just tell me. You used to tell me everything."

She bites into her salad and smiles coyly. "One guy?" She spears a tomato. "I have a few options I'm pursuing, actually. And things are going . . . really well."

Matt looks to me for confirmation. I stretch my cheeks into a stiff smile.

"I'm not going Thursday night, so I guess you'll have to scope out your guys somewhere else."

Lindy cuts him a dirty look. "You're just trying to keep me away from the party."

"Like I care if you're going. You do whatever you want, but I won't be there." He grabs his tray and stomps away.

I grasp a piece of my hair and inspect the ends. "That went well."

"Bella, it's *not* going well. This wasn't part of the plan."

"But he was obviously bothered by the idea of you on the hunt for a boyfriend." Or two. "That's encouraging, right? I really think he's coming around."

She props her chin on her hand. "Then why don't I feel encouraged?"

~~~~~~~~~~

In English Thursday, I slide into the desk behind Jared Campbell and smile, an open invitation to conversation.

A few seconds later he turns around. "This novel is making me miss Hester and *The Scarlet Letter*." He holds up his copy of *Great Expectations*.

I swat his hand and laugh. "I know, instead of *Great Expectations* it should be called *Crappy Letdown*."

He grins and turns all the way around in his seat. "*Great Expectations—of Insomnia.*"

I smile into his eyes, letting mine linger a little longer than a new friend would. "You know what else is a letdown?" I pucker my glossy lips in a pout. "Not getting the chance to dance with you any more. I had a really good time last week."

"Thanks. Me too."

I lean forward on the desk. "It's been so hard adjusting here. But last week at the party I was able to forget all about my worries and just be me, you know?" I wave my hand. "Anyway, I just wanted to thank you for, you know, talking to me again."

"Sorry we didn't get to talk a lot last Thursday." He rests his arm on my desk. "I like to work the crowd to make sure no one's getting too crazy."

"I think that's great. It's really thoughtful of you." My cooing voice sounds obnoxious to my ears. *Forgive me, Hunter.* "Makes a girl feel safe to know someone like you is looking out for . . . her." I giggle.

"I keep an eye on everyone."

"So is it your party?"

He laughs. "It's the *team's* party. It's all for the team. Everything we do is for that win."

"Jared, if you ever find yourself at another get-together and need a dance partner, here's my number." I scribble on a piece of paper and slide it over.

He holds it between both hands then folds it in two. "Actually . . ."

Yes? Come on, big boy.

"I hear there's a party tonight."

"Really?" I'm all innocence.

"I don't usually do this, but if you'd like to go, I could pick you up."

I clap my hands to my chest. "I would *love* to go! But hey, why don't I just meet you there? I have some stuff to do tonight, so I might be a little late. You could give me directions."

"Wow, I'm sorry, Bella. But the location is top secret."

"So it's not at the same cabin? Do you know where it is?" I purr, like I think this is all totally cute.

"Maybe. But if I tell you where it is, I will be toast."

Because your stepbrother would hurt you? Kick you off the team? Maybe Dante would rough you up? Short-sheet your bed? What?

"Then I guess I'll have to meet you somewhere."

He reaches into his pocket and hands me a purple piece of paper. "You'll need this, even if you're with me. Meet me at the old cemetery. Can you be there by eight?"

I pull the ticket out of his fingers, my hand grazing his. "I can't wait."

"Bella, you can't tell anyone about the party. It's top secret, okay?" He lightens his serious tone. "We don't want the entire high school out there."

I tuck the paper into my backpack as the teacher opens her book to start class.

"Today, students, we're going to discuss what Dickens had to say about pretending to be something you're not . . ."

Stupid book.

chapter thirty-one

When Jared takes the blindfold off my eyes, I blink a few times to bring the fuzzy surroundings into focus.

"A campground?"

"An old overflow campsite. Nobody's ever out here." He helps me out of the car and leads me toward the festivities. Music blasts from a CD player, and the rest of the partygoers sit on hay bales around a flaming bonfire. Tiki torches are stuck in the ground every few feet, giving the area a dollar-store tropical theme.

Jared high-fives some of the players. He talks to everyone he passes as if they're his closest friends. He's so kind to people. Looking at him, you'd think he would be all stuck up. I mean, he's got it all—Abercrombie-model good looks, Advanced Placement brains, a position as a starter on the football team. It's going to stink when I eventually reveal my theory that his stepbrother's a total psycho.

"Can I get you something to drink?" Jared's hand presses into my back, and we walk toward a car where a cooler sits in the trunk. I peer inside. All alcohol.

"Um ... nothing for me, thanks."

"Let's keep looking." He takes me to another trunk, reaches into the cooler, and pulls out a Coke. "For the lady."

I thank him with a smile and watch as he grabs one for himself. "I'm not into that stuff either."

But does your stepbrother supply the alcohol for these parties? I want so badly to ask him the questions whirring in my brain. All of Luke's warnings replay in my head.

"I'm glad you brought me tonight." I sigh and gaze into his face. "Whose soiree is this anyway?"

Jared grabs a bag of Ruffles from the trunk, tears it, and holds it open. "It's everyone's party, remember?"

"Is this something you football players throw together?" I can't let this go.

He shrugs. "It's definitely *for* us." Jared's head drops closer to mine. "And anyone special we might want to invite." I giggle but take a step back, putting a little space between us. I can just see me talking to Hunter on the phone tomorrow morning.

"So what did you do last night?"

"Who, me? Oh, went to a party with a guy, flirted with him. Let him think I was interested. How was SportsCenter?"

Another set of headlights shines on the campsite. Jared watches the vehicle until the driver gets out. "Dante's here. I'll be right back." His hand lingers on my shoulder as he passes.

Time to start digging around and asking questions. I grab the Ruffles and turn to find my first interviewee.

And run smack into Britanny Taylor.

"I know what you're up to."

I gasp and a chip lodges in my throat. My cough comes in spasms, and I blink watery eyes.

"Wh-what?"

"You," she spits. "And Jared. I know what you're doing, and I plan to tell him *all* about it."

I clutch the chips to my chest and force myself to take some deep breaths. "What are you talking about, Brittany?"

"He felt bad about how everybody shunned you, and so he's been nice to you out of pity. But you're using it to lure him in."

"Lure him?" What is he, a trout?

"Yeah." Her hateful mouth twists. "So you can get back at *me*. Because you knew I liked him. And now you think you're getting me back for ratting out your *Miss Hilliard* blog. But let me tell you something, Bella. You move in on Jared, and I will come after you with a vengeance. You do not want to mess with me."

Mee-yeow. Is it just me, or are the people in this school just a wee bit violent? Somebody needs to get Truman High some therapy. In large doses.

"Look, Brittany, clearly you've not been to your anger management classes lately, so I can understand why—" I swallow the rest of the words as I look over Brittany's shoulder and see who else gets out of Dante's car.

Matt Sparks.

His face is uncertain, his eyes searching. Then he's swarmed by classmates, teammates, and he perks up. So . . . Matt wasn't planning on coming to the party tonight, huh?

"Are you even listening to me?"

My attention snaps back to the shrew in front of me. "Oh yes. You were threatening me?" My voice is as bland as oatmeal.

Brittany sticks her finger in my face. "Watch yourself, Bella.

Because I'm not going to allow some little rich girl to come in here and take what's mine."

"That's funny—at no point did anyone tell me you and Jared were dating. Because I definitely stay away from the boys who are taken."

She hisses like a venomous snake. "You've been warned." And she slithers away.

That girl is not nice. Let's just hope she stays on her side of the bonfire tonight.

I walk back to the coolers and select another Coke. With dripping can in hand, I approach Matt Sparks. His eyes widen as I stand before him.

"Drink?" I hold it out. He slowly reaches for it.

"I ... uh ..."

"You intended to come to this from the beginning, didn't you?"

His eyes flash. "I don't have to explain anything to you."

"Any particular reason why you didn't want us here tonight, Matt?"

"Why don't you go back home and highlight Lindy's hair or something. She's more your friend now than mine. Maybe I thought it was just time to start branching out and hanging with a new crowd."

I'm torn between furious and hurt. "I'm not trying to bust up your friendship. Lindy—" The truth dances on my tongue, but I force it down. "She cares about you. She misses your friendship."

"I think Lindy and I need some time apart."

"So you can hang out with your new party friends?"

"If you don't approve of them, why are you here?"

I open my mouth. Then shut it. "I'm here with Jared Campbell."

Matt looks over his shoulder then back to me. "Look, just be careful out here, okay?"

"What does that mean?"

He starts to say something then retreats. "I . . . um . . . just, you know, the typical party rules—don't set your drink down, don't go off alone with anyone, don't pee on rattlesnakes."

"Don't pee on rattlesnakes?" I lower my voice even more. "Is that supposed to mean something?"

He speaks directly into my ear. "It means if you squat over a rattler, you'll get two fangs in your butt." Matt leaves me to join some friends.

By ten o'clock, I've danced with just about everyone. Truman seems to be forgetting about the Great Blog Disaster. Well, except for Brittany, but if I never regain her friendship, I think I'll still be able to sleep at night.

Great. I am in sore need of a bathroom. Or I guess in this case, a large tree to go behind. I look for Jared to tell him where I'm going. That way if a wild bear comes and hauls me off, someone will know to look for me.

Not finding my date for the night, I suppress a sigh and walk into a wooded area, my cell phone shining like a weak flashlight. About a hundred paces out, I decide I'm far away from view and pick my tree. Oh, the indignity. For the record, I have *never* peed outside. It's unladylike. It's uncouth. And—ew—apparently I have bad aim!

All finished and anxious to get out of here, I zip my denim shorts and button the top button.

"Are you sure he's going to do it?"

Who is that? I stop at the voice and plaster myself to the back of the tree. I'm probably stepping exactly where I did my business.

"He's here, isn't he?" That's Dante.

"Between the beer and the music, I think everyone's pretty distracted right now. We should be able to slip out in about an hour. Wait for the signal, then meet at the old bridge."

An hour? I have to be home in thirty minutes due to my new, restricted curfew. It took an act of Congress to talk my mom into letting me out of the house tonight.

"He thinks Sparks is the missing link, that we need him in the Brotherhood to make us stronger."

"I don't know, man," Dante says. "This is getting crazy. We can't afford another disaster."

"Look, you know he won't let you out of this. It's too important that the legacy continues. We'll make sure there aren't any more mistakes."

"Mistakes? Dude, accidents happen. People fall. Drivers lose control. We don't have any power over that. And we also can't stand any more bad attention. I'm not going to any more funerals."

"It's his team. We do what he says, Dante. Now either you're in or you're out. But you think long and hard before you leave the Brotherhood. You *know* what happened to Reggie."

"I'm not backing out. You know I'm in this. Just forget it."

Their voices grow weaker as they walk away.

I know one thing for sure.

I have to get home by curfew—so I can sneak right back out, with Luke at my side. We have some late-night spying to do.

chapter thirty-two

Jared pulls over and takes off my blindfold when we hit the town square.

I smile prettily, like it's not the creepiest thing ever to have your eyes covered. "Thanks for taking me back early. My mom's kind of a stickler lately on the curfew." I can't imagine why.

He steers the car back onto the road. "I had a great time with you tonight. I always do."

"Thanks." And I had a good time with him. Jared has an amazing personality. But I feel nothing for the boy.

He puts the car in park when we roll up to the unwelcoming graveyard a few minutes later. I mean, seriously, if you want to impress a girl, do *not* ask to meet her at a cemetery.

"So . . ." His arm rests on the back of my seat. "How's that boyfriend in New York?"

We both laugh. "Very subtle," I say. "Um . . . Hunter and I are finding a long-distance relationship to be harder than we thought."

"Bella—" His eyes grow serious in the dark of the car. "I would love for us to be friends—hang out. But if you get to the point where New York is too far away, there are guys here in Truman who would like the opportunity to date you."

My heart constricts. I wish I liked him like that.

My hand covers his on the gearshift. "Jared, if only I had met you a few years ago. Thank you for your friendship. I didn't intend this, but I've noticed a lot more people are willing to talk to me now that I've been seen with you a few times. And if something changes in my life, I'll let you know. But in the meantime, I still want to do things together." Did that sound suggestive? I mean do things as in go to a movie. Not as in get horizontal on the couch.

"Friends it is." He nods, his gaze sliding across the stones in the graveyard.

"You'll invite me to a party again?" I open my door and step out.

"Next week there will be a ticket for you."

I wait until our vehicles part ways at the downtown four-way stop before I call Luke.

"This better be important—it's late."

"Sorry to disturb your beauty sleep, but I have news." I fill him in on what I heard at the party.

"And what do you want to do about it? You've obviously got something up your sleeve, and I have a feeling it's not good."

I should be offended, but I'm not. "How serious are you about seeing this story through?"

He mumbles something then answers. "What do you want, Bella?"

"Be at my house in ten minutes. Park on the dirt road, turn the lights off, and I'll meet you out there."

"You said you were blindfolded. How do you know where we're going?"

"The GPS on my phone."

He pauses so long I think he's gone back to sleep.

"Luke?"

"Wear something dark this time, Kirkwood." And he disconnects.

~~~~~~~~~~

"You know we're both probably going to get caught and get grounded for life," I say as I shut myself in Luke's 4Runner.

"I'm okay with that."

He takes in my appearance, making sure I'm not clothed in bright pink. Though I was tempted to wear some sequins just to tick him off.

"How do we know where they'll be out there? And what if they see our flashlights?" I'm suddenly panicked by all these details.

He turns onto the highway, leading us toward Byler, the nearest town. "You should have thought of that before you got me out of bed." His eyes cut to me. "But luckily we have some serious moonlight tonight, so that ought to help some. Let's just hope the wild bears don't get us though. The Oklahoma lakes are just crawling with them."

"What?" And then I see his lips quirk. "Oh, you're hilarious."

"Actually, I think I know which bridge they meant. A train runs through the lake area late at night. It crosses an old bridge. It's so rickety, I don't know how it can hold up a train."

Luke drives on for another few minutes before cutting into a field where a dirt road appears.

"How in the world did you know this road was here?"

Luke lifts a dismissive shoulder. "It's a cool place to take girls."

"If you're a serial killer."

Pulling in behind some trees, Luke turns off the engine and faces me. "Are you ready for this?"

His eyes hold me captive. Why is it easier to look directly at someone in the dark? I blink and glance away. "Let's just get it over with."

We spill out of the SUV, and I follow Luke through knee-high weeds for what seems like an eternity.

Somewhere I hear water lapping, and above us a full moon shines down like a Broadway spotlight just for us.

"We'll have to climb this little hill. Are you up for it?"

I know he's looking at my shoes, expecting me to have worn something totally impractical. I shine my flashlight on my black Diesels. "Don't cry if I beat you to the top, Chief."

Ten minutes later, I'm wishing I had packed snacks. And I need a foot rub. "I think people have climbed Mt. Everest in a shorter amount of time."

"Almost there," he whispers. "We need to turn our flashlights off at this point, Bella."

I flip the switch.

"And you're going to have to take my hand."

"Why?" I squeak.

"Because I know my way around here. You don't. So unless you want to fall down the mountain and give away our cover, I'd grab hold."

I stare at his outstretched hand but can't seem to move.

"Suit yourself. See you at the top."

"No, wait!" I run after him, stumbling on a rock, my body propelled right into his. "*Oomph!*" Ignoring my throbbing ankle and my battered pride, I give him my hand. Which he ignores. "Oh, just take it!" I hiss.

With a hint of a smile, he wraps his fingers around mine and pulls me forward.

I'm out of breath and totally disoriented when he finally stops. "Right over there is the bridge." He points about a hundred feet away.

"And there's some of our fearless football players." I watch as their own flashlights illuminate Dante, his friend Adam, a few guys I don't know, and— "Oh my gosh. That's Matt. What is he doing?"

"Looks like he's drinking."

"He doesn't drink."

"Does he jump off bridges?"

I rub my eyes and strain to get a closer look. "Are they tying a bungee cord to the bridge?" In the distance a train sings a warning. My heart triples in beat. "This is his initiation I heard them talking about." I can't believe he caved in to their pressure. Lindy would die if she knew this.

"That train is really close." Luke's voice is a soft breeze near my ear. "They're insane. I still don't get the thought behind this."

"I don't think we ever will. Oh, I can't watch." But yet I'm powerless to look away.

"They're tying his feet to the cord."

It's everything I can do not to call out to Matt. *Please don't do this. Don't do this.*

God, keep him safe. I don't want to watch him crack his head open or see him ripped apart by a train. We have to stop the football team once and for all—before there's another casualty.

The train's whistle grows louder, closer. Its cry seems to bounce off the water and echo.

Matt stands motionless as his teammates move away from him, walking off the bridge.

"Why are they leaving him? Why isn't he moving?" *Go, Matt!* The train's lights come into view. "Why isn't he moving?"

"It's like a game of chicken. He won't jump until the train's right on him." Luke's so close I can feel his heart beat.

"He could be killed."

"That's the point."

I stare transfixed as the train makes its presence known. The whistle blasts into the night. The wheels beat a rhythm on the tracks. Closer. Closer.

I can't breathe.

Can't move.

Jump, Matt.

He watches it. I can't see his face, but surely he's petrified. I'm about to puke, so Matt's got to be at least a little nervous.

The locomotive barrels down the tracks, its urgent whistle a signal of danger, warning.

Almost there.

Closer.

Feet away from him.

It's going to hit him!

And Matt swan dives off the bridge.

Without thinking, I shine my flashlight on the water. Luke grabs me by the arms and rips the light out of my grip. "We have to go. Go!" He pushes me away from the ledge, toward the trail.

"Did they see us?" I'm panting to keep up with his pace. His hand is a vice on mine.

What if I've blown our cover?

Raised voices float on the wind behind us. They're coming. How did they catch up to us so fast? Did they just leave Matt hanging?

"Run faster, Bella!"

"I can't!" Pushing off the ground with my feet, my calves are groaning for rest. I was made for shopping, not running! I struggle to keep my balance on the downward slope.

Luke's grip tightens, and he pulls harder on my arm. Ow. Does he think inflicting pain is going to magically make me go faster?

He zigzags us through a wooded area, different from the way we came. I know it's a matter of time before I trip over something and fall like a girl in a cheesy horror movie. So unoriginal.

"Bella, we've got some distance between us, but it won't be long." Luke's barely out of breath. It's insulting. I'm sweating right through my Soft & Dri.

Though the guys are still a ways back there, it sounds like a herd of elephants stampeding the hill.

"Don't let up until you're in the car. You got that?"

Can't talk. Sucking air.

"Bella, I'm going to need you to trust me to get us out of this. Can you do that?" He doesn't wait for my response. "Go!" he commands as we break through the trees, his 4Runner in sight. I push my remaining energy into sprinting for the door. We jump into the seats, and Luke locks the doors and turns the key. Pushing buttons on his iPod, he suddenly makes a slow country song pour out the speakers.

"What is that?" I say, holding my panting chest. "Pick your music later. Let's get out of here. They're going to be here any minute."

Luke shakes his head, his expression grim. "No time. It's inevitable they'll see this vehicle. So they can't see it tearing out of here."

In the side mirror I spot three of them, their faces shining in the moonlight. They're running right for us. I grab Luke's arm. "Do something! What's your plan?"

He crushes me to him. "This." His mouth hovers over mine. "You said you'd trust me." And his lips cover mine in a kiss. I tense in shock. One muscular arm slides around my back, the other around my head. He deepens the kiss, and I feel myself falling into it. The voices outside grow louder. Their steps, closer. Yet it becomes background noise, a distant thought, as Luke leans into me.

He shifts and frames my face with his hands. I sigh into his kiss and let my fingers thread through his soft, dark hair.

"It's just a couple making out."

"Who is that?"

"Who knows. Let's go. Keep looking."

Seconds, minutes, hours later, Luke pulls away. He rests his forehead on mine and exhales slowly. "They're gone."

My brain spins. My lips tingle. Heart somersaults. "Hmmm? Who?"

He removes his hands and leans back into his seat. With a curious glance at me, he starts the engine. "Thanks for, um . . . playing along. It saved us."

I blink a few times. "Right." I stare at my lap. "Good plan." *Good kisser.*

"We should probably stay here just a few more minutes to throw them off." He changes the song to some upbeat number about a man and his tractor. "So the Brotherhood has initiations." His fingers comb through his hair—the same hair my hands were in seconds ago. "We know these things happen at parties, when everyone else is occupied. What else?"

"Huh? Oh . . . um, we know that . . ." *My editor kisses like a movie star.* "These extreme sports feats probably had something to do with Zach Epps's injury and Carson Penturf's death. And there's a pressure to not only join and participate, but to keep your mouth shut." The fog in my head begins to evaporate. "We've got to talk to Reggie Lee. We could have the power to clear his name."

"You could. You're the one who overheard the conversation in the woods tonight."

Luke puts the car in reverse and pulls us onto the path. We continue the rest of the drive in silence, each lost in our own thoughts. I toss the facts around in my head. They're all in pieces, like a jigsaw puzzle. So close I can see the big picture, but still not enough there to completely connect.

And I realize I haven't thought about Hunter in days. There have been a couple calls this week. Some texts. An e-mail or two. But he's been so wrapped up in his world. And I've been wrapped up in—well, a few minutes ago, my editor.

The car stops on my dirt road. Luke turns, holds me with his stare. "Bella, I . . ." His eyes look as dark as the sky. "I'll, um . . . see you tomorrow."

I nod and fumble for the door handle. "Right." My foot tangles in my purse straps. "Bye." I jump out and run to the porch.

Letting myself in the house, I close the door so quietly even I can't hear it. I tiptoe through the entryway and pass the living room.

A light flares to life.

"Good evening, Bella." Jake sits in his recliner and consults his watch. "Or I guess I should say good morning."

chapter thirty-three

M y alarm goes off, and I shove it to the floor. "Shut. Up." So
tired. I've been asleep less than five hours. The events of last
night play in my fogged head like a bad movie reel. The party, the
bridge, the make-out session with Luke.

Jake's lecture.

I jerk the blankets over my head and try to block out the
images. But I'm right back there. Jake sitting in his chair. His face
blank but his eyes cautious, untrusting.

"Do you want to tell me what you're doing sneaking in and out
of the house?"

"I haven't been drinking. I promise."

"That's not what I asked."

He stared me down with a gaze that he probably reserves for
his toughest opponents.

I shook my head. "I had to go back to the party. It's for the paper."
I held up my hand to stop him. "No, I'm serious. I can't tell you what
it's about, but it's big."

"So's being grounded until you're thirty."

"You could send me back to New York City."

He closed his eyes for a second. "Bella, you know that's not going to happen. Your mother loves you. She wants you right here with her. And whether you care or not, I want you living with our family too."

I twisted my hair around my finger. "I know this looks bad. I just got *ungrounded*, so you *know* I wouldn't do anything to get myself in trouble again so soon." *No, I'd totally wait a few more weeks under normal circumstances.*

"Are you in trouble?"

I considered this. "No. But people are in danger. That's all I can tell you."

"I have to tell your mother."

"You can't!"

"You've put me in a bad position here. Do you realize that?"

"Yes, but—something big's going on at school. People have already gotten hurt. I just need some time. If this situation comes out now, it's over. We've helped no one. Could you wait to tell Mom? Maybe a week or two?" *Or twenty.*

"Sometimes you want to trust a person, but you can't. Right now, you're not in a position to be trusted."

"And you are?" I snapped. "If anybody knows about keeping secrets, I would think you would understand."

"I guess secrets are okay for you but not for the rest of us?"

"Fine, wake Mom up. Let her know what a horrible daughter she has." I walked away, my stomach tied in a triple knot.

His voice stopped me on the first step. "If you know people are in jeopardy, that they could get hurt, you have to tell me what's going on."

I turned back and studied his face over my shoulder. And I felt that pull. That small voice whispering to go against logic and blab it all.

"Jake . . ." I moved back into the light. "I messed up when I first came here. There wasn't a person at Truman High who didn't hate me. But now . . . now I have the chance to change that. I have a purpose for possibly the first time in my life. And I have to follow it. I think . . ." I chewed on my bottom lip and let revelation and acceptance wash over me. "I think I'm in the midst of my purpose here, you know? This is my time. For whatever reason, I've been given a giant task, and I have to see it through. People are counting on me."

My stepdad's silence stretched for an eternity. Finally he nodded. "Okay."

"Okay?"

"I'm going to go against my gut here and trust you—for two weeks. Then we tell your mom and both of us will suffer the consequences."

I would've rushed over and hugged him, but Jake and I—we're not really on hugging terms yet. "Thank you. I know it makes no sense. But you're doing the right thing."

He did not look convinced.

And then four and a half hours later my alarm went off like a tornado siren. I still can't believe he's not going to rat me out. Makes no sense. But then, lately, what does?

Down in the kitchen, Mom reads a parenting magazine while chewing on a piece of toast. Her Sugar's uniform sits stiff and starched on her slender frame.

"What in the world is wrong with you? You look like you've been up all night." She jumps up to pour me a glass of juice.

"Um, nothing. I'm fine. Just didn't get much sleep." I scrutinize every line and movement of her face to see if her husband has spilled the beans.

"Jake said you offered to help with tonight's wrestling party." She wraps her arms around me. "I'm so glad."

"What?" I never agreed to that.

"He told me this morning. Said you two discussed it after I went to bed last night."

My juice hitches in my throat. "Oh. That. Right. Yeah, can't wait to help." He didn't mention there were strings attached to our deal. I have a game I need to go to. Football players to watch. People to stalk!

"Well, this will wake you up." She pulls out the chair next to mine. "I know you've been really upset over losing Moxie."

Still hurts. Thanks for bringing it up.

"So . . ." She shoves a piece of paper across the table. "I got you a ticket to New York. And since you had such a good time with Lindy, I got her one too. You girls leave tomorrow morning."

I hold on to the ticket like it's a Tiffany diamond. "I'm going to New York!" I jump up and down, forgetting my lack of sleep, forgetting my problems. Now I can surprise Hunter at the Autumn Ball. This is perfect. I can see Mia. And Dad.

A plan percolating in my head, I run upstairs to text Mia.

Have big news. Call me later.

"Shrimp puff? Cucumber sandwich? Mini quiche?" I glide through the room, carrying a serving tray of hors d'oeuvres to men who could crush me with one hand.

"Thank you, little darlin'. I love the light hint of oregano on the quiche." This from a man whose wrestler name is Breath of Death. "And I love your t-shirt. If I'm not mistaken, that's a Tory Burch, right?"

I think I've stepped onto another planet. "Yes, it is." I walk away before the six-foot-seven dude starts giving me makeup advice.

About thirty wrestlers and their wives mingle with a few reporters from the local papers, plus a journalist from the Channel 5 news. Mom knows how to throw a party. And how to recruit some PR. She did it all the time for her charities.

"What are they saying about my garlic hummus?" Dolly asks as I enter the kitchen for a reload.

"One guy said it's better than a pile driver, but I have no idea what that means."

She shakes her big blonde head. "Wrestler talk." A shadow of a smile passes her face.

"You miss it, don't you?"

"Of course not. I got so sick of hearing about wrestling back in the day. That's all Mickey did was live, eat, and work wrestling. And now that he's a trainer, it's probably even worse."

"He's been watching you all night."

"Has not." Her cheeks burn a suspicious pink. "Well, if he has, it's because I've had a plate of food in my hands every time he sees me."

"You should go talk to him."

"I'm busy, Bella. Now go push the sausage balls. I made too many."

"How long has it been since you spoke?"

"To the sausage balls?"

"To your ex-husband." I sit down and rest my feet.

She rearranges some perfectly lined up fruit on a tray. "The day he left. We let our lawyers do the talking after that. Not that there was much to say. He walked away and left it all behind. And I mean *all*. Didn't fight for a thing."

Including Dolly, I guess.

"But that was a long time ago. We're different people now with different lives."

"You live in the same town though."

"Big enough to avoid someone." She dusts off her hands on her apron. "Speaking of avoiding someone, if I were you, I wouldn't avoid *that*." She wiggles her brows.

I turn around and there stands Luke, leaning in the doorway, his shoulder resting on a cabinet.

"What are you doing here?" I feel my own face flaming. He and I pretty much ignored each other all day, even in class. It's hard to make out with someone at night then face him in the light of day—when it was all for show.

Dolly takes my tray and heads back out into the sea of over-stuffed men, leaving me and Luke. Together. Alone.

"I was invited. Your mom called to see if the school paper would cover it. I saw the other media. She seems to have covered all her bases."

Now that Mom knows about Jake's wrestling, she's his biggest promoter.

"I talked to Reggie Lee. He's agreed to meet us later tonight if you can get away. He wanted to talk Saturday night, but I thought I heard you tell someone today that you're leaving for New York." His chiseled face is expressionless.

"Thanks. I'm glad you did that—included me. I know you could've met him this weekend on your own."

He smiles. "We're partners."

Awkward! Awkward! Why can't I get over this weird feeling? He doesn't seem to be fazed by it. Maybe he makes out with girls all the time in the name of a good story.

"So are you looking forward to going back home?"

Home. I feel more disconnected from my friends and family in New York than ever. Mia has yet to call. Dad said he'd have to work this weekend. It's like I'm slowly transitioning to Truman. I'm not sure if that's a good thing or not.

"Bella?"

"Oh, home. Yeah, I'm excited to see my dad, my best friend." And just in case Mr. Arrogance thinks I now pine for him, take *this.* "And my boyfriend, of course. I'm surprising him."

Luke has the nerve to continue smiling. "I'm sure everyone will be glad to see you." He pushes away from the cabinet. "I'd better get to work. Hey, pretty cool your stepdad's a wrestler."

"Yeah, about as cool as him making maxi-pads."

Three hours later, there's not a shrimp puff or melon ball left. I don't know about their skills on the mat, but those wrestlers are champion eaters.

"Iron Skull, are you sure you have to go?" my mom asks the final one making his retreat out the front door.

"Oh yeah, Mrs. Finley. That bean dip ought to be kicking in any moment now."

Nice. Maybe he should go by Noxious Gas. Or the Deadly Farter.

"So, Robbie, what did you think about all that?"

I startle at Luke's voice behind me. I thought he had left with the rest of the press.

Robbie scratches his head. "Well, I think tonight we had an

example of mankind laying aside their differences, not to mention their stage makeup, and coming together in unity. It shows that peace is attainable. They are a model to our brothers and sisters in the Middle East."

I pat Robbie on his scruffy head. "He's had a lot of Mountain Dew tonight."

Mickey balances a stack of plates and heads toward the kitchen.

"Excuse me." I leave Luke's company to seek out Dolly, scrubbing down the table in the dining room.

"Um . . . could you give me some help in the kitchen?"

Her hand pauses. "Sure, kid. What do you need?"

I don't answer but walk away, grateful when she follows.

I hear her intake of breath when she sees her ex-husband standing at the sink. He turns around. Frowns.

"Well, hey, Mickey!" My voice is overly bright, even to my own ears. "What a nice guy, doing the dishes. Isn't that nice of him, Dolly?"

Her overshadowed eyes narrow. "Oh, he's a real sweetheart."

Hurt flashes on his face. He turns around and attacks a platter with a scrub brush.

Dolly plants a hand on her curvy hip. "Get out of my kitchen, Mickey."

"I believe it's the Finleys' kitchen. *You* get out."

Her mouth drops. "I'm the caterer tonight. You're just . . . just . . . the—"

"Manager?" He points a sudsy brush at her. "That's never been good enough for you, has it? *I've* never been good enough."

"You leave me out of your inferiority complex. Don't you put that on me. I always supported you."

"As long as I worked eight to five. You wanted me to have a desk job—admit it. You hated my late hours."

"Late hours?" Her voice explodes in the tiny kitchen. "There's a difference in working late now and then and *never* being home for your family."

Just when I expect Mickey to match her volume and snap back with a comment, he closes his mouth. And stares at the floor. The gross linoleum floor.

"I have regrets, Dolly. Don't think I don't."

"Yeah, well, is leaving your family one of them?"

Thunderclouds roll behind his eyes. His expression is so pained, I find myself stepping back toward the door.

"I killed my family."

Dolly's breath hitches. "*I* was your family too. Maybe I needed you." A tear glides down her cheek. "An accident killed our daughters, Mickey. Pulling the plug on our marriage is what I could never forgive you for." She throws down her rag and rushes out, her heels an angry staccato on the floor.

Mickey watches her go. After a moment his troubled eyes rest on me. "I tend to ruin parties." He forces a smile. "I'm not very good at Scrabble either."

"You were driving the car the day your daughters were killed." It's not really a question. But it's also not something I meant to say out loud.

"Yup." He runs a big hand over his stubbly face.

"Don't tell me that's the first time you two have talked about it."

"I kind of disappeared after the accident." The dishwater covers his arms as he returns to cleaning. "I'm not proud of that. I couldn't stand to look at myself, and even worse, I didn't want to see myself through her eyes."

"It was an accident."

He hands me a bowl and a dry towel. "I was driving. I walked away with barely a scratch. My little girls never woke up." His voice is hoarse, raw. He hands me another dish to dry.

"What happened?"

"Ice. It was a bad winter. An eighteen-wheeler lost control, and I swerved to miss him. We spun into the median on the highway." Mickey laughs, a sound as bitter as a rotten grape. "I had a match that weekend. I was mad because Dolly'd been called into a second shift and asked me to watch the girls and not go to the gym. But training came first, and I put them in the car and drove us to Byler so I could get my workout in. So even if my driving didn't kill them, my priorities did."

"That's not true, Mickey." I feel my *Ask Miss Hilliard* instincts kicking in. "You heard Dolly say she doesn't hold you responsible. She forgives you. Maybe it's time to forgive yourself."

He flings the water off his hands. "Nothing's going to bring them back, Bella." Then he looks at me with that expression that says, *Why am I talking to a kid?*

"Mickey, wait—"

But he's gone. I sigh and rub the tension building in the back of my neck.

"Why is it people want to pour their hearts out to you?"

Luke.

"Why is it you like to eavesdrop on my conversations?"

"My reporter's intuition led me here."

"You heard Dolly yelling."

He shrugs. "Something like that." Luke removes my hand from my neck and replaces it with his own. "Got some tension, Counselor Bella?"

My skin tingles at his touch, and I'm reminded of our lip-locking moment. This boy is so maddening. Frustrating. Confusing.

His magic fingers stop, and he turns around.

When I see his face, disappointment swishes in my stomach. He looks totally bored. Not that I like him, but where's the look of burning passion he's unable to contain? Where's the look that says, *Bella, I admire you from afar—your face, your scent, your growing journalistic abilities that could one day rival mine.* Where is that? Instead his face says, *When my hands were on you, I was doing long division in my head.* How dare he look bored!

"Are you ready to meet Reggie Lee? Bella—did you hear me?"

"Huh? Oh yeah, let me grab my purse." I should be packing instead of talking to former football players in secret. I run upstairs to get my bag. My eyes automatically go to my bed, where Moxie should be lying. But she's not.

Outside Luke waits for me in his 4Runner. He doesn't even glance my way as I snap myself into the seat belt. His car smells like his cologne, and I stop myself from breathing too deeply.

"Where are we going?" I ask when Luke turns toward Tulsa.

"We're meeting him at the Cherokee Waffle House."

"Sounds very classy."

Luke shoots down my every attempt at conversation with monosyllable responses until I'm forced to quit talking. Just to be obnoxious, I try to sing along to each tune on the radio. And since it's a country station, I know absolutely none of the songs. So I just make up the words. He ignores me anyway.

The interior of the SUV is illuminated as he pulls into the restaurant's parking lot. Through the glass windows I see tired truckers and mostly old men taking up the seats.

Inside we're greeted by the smell of twenty-four-hour breakfast. And though the interior leaves a lot to be desired, decked out in every Indian whatnot ever made, the food smells heavenly. I didn't have time to eat a single crumb at the party.

I slide into a booth across from Luke and open a sticky menu.

A slender African-American girl stops at our table. She pops a pink bubble. "Are y'all from around here?"

"Truman," Luke answers.

She nods. "So what can I get you?"

My eyes scan the choices. "Belgian waffles with strawberries, please."

For the first time all night, Luke smiles. "Me too." Guess he didn't get to eat either.

We both watch the door for the next hour.

I pick at my last bite of waffle. "He's not coming."

"No. He's not."

We pay and then walk into the muggy night air toward the 4Runner.

"Hey!" The waitress walks out of a side door. She hurries to us. "You're here to meet Reggie, aren't you?"

"Yes. Do you know where he is?" Luke asks.

She looks behind her, as if she's afraid someone's watching. "He couldn't make it."

I step closer to her. "Who are you?"

"His girlfriend. And I think you guys should leave all this alone. Reggie's been through enough. He just wants to move on."

"But what if we could prove that the drugs in his locker weren't his?"

She casts a wary eye at Luke. "It doesn't matter. They'll come after him another way." She shakes her head. "It's over. It's done. He wasn't responsible for Zach Epps's accident."

I startle. "What? Who said he was?"

"I have to go."

"Wait!" Nothing like chasing someone in a parking lot. "Wait!" I catch her at the side door.

"They're like a high school mafia, okay?" Her breathing is ragged, her eyes wild. "You don't know what they'll do. For your own sakes and Reggie's, stay out of this."

"We can't." I read her name tag. "Marissa, one person's dead, one's on life-support. How many more have to be hurt before someone's willing to speak up?"

Her hand pauses on the door handle. "The Brotherhood has its own MySpace page. Only the members can access it. But every initiation is recorded."

This doesn't surprise me. In fact, I should've thought of it. Even serious gangs post videos of their beat-ins, shootings, and initiations. The question is . . . how can we access a MySpace page that's set to private?

"Reggie was racing Zach Epps the night of the accident, wasn't he?"

Her mad stare is the only response.

"Please, you have got to tell Reggie to come forward and talk to the police. Zach lost his life that night."

She wrenches open the door. "He may not be on life-support, but that night . . . Reggie lost his life too."

chapter thirty-four

"I saw you on *E!* last night, Dad. How did the pitch go for the new show?" I lurch forward as my dad slams on his brakes for the zillionth time. New York City traffic—there's nothing like it. I'd rather drive behind a slow tractor in Truman any day over this madness.

He zips into the other lane and honking ensues. "I don't know. Budgets are tight right now. They're not sure if they want to invest in a new show about another high-profile plastic surgeon. I have another meeting with my agent today."

Though she's seen it once, Lindy's nose is pushed against the window like she can't get enough of Manhattan. I know the feeling. It's like a new town every time you see it—even if you live here.

When we get to the house, Luisa crushes me in a hug worthy of a wrestler. "I've missed you, Isabella!" She pulls away, her pudgy hands clasping my face. "Let me look at you. Oh, Oklahoma agrees with you."

"Do I smell homemade chocolate chip cookies?"

"Chips Ahoy! are for losers," Luisa says, ushering the three of us into the kitchen.

"I have to get to my meeting. Here's my credit card." Dad hands over his Visa. "Don't go crazy with it, okay?"

"We do have an Autumn Ball to crash. Might need to buy a dress or two."

He kisses me on the temple. "I'll see you tonight."

An hour later Lindy and I are in shopping nirvana.

Well, I am.

"No, Bella. I don't like the strapless look. Are you sure I can even go to this party?"

"Of course." I throw the pink concoction over the dressing room door anyway. "We're just dropping by. I can't *wait* for the look on Hunter's face when he sees me. Lindy, *why* is this green thing in the try-on stack?"

Her hesitant voice comes from the other side of the door. "I liked it."

"I said no. Green is a color on its way out. You don't want to be *this year*."

"What year do I want to be?"

I hand her another gown. Still so much to learn.

The door creaks, and Lindy steps out into the small hall. I twirl my finger and she spins in front of the mirror.

"I can't wear this." She tugs on the sliding bodice. "I feel naked."

"It's a very conservative dress. Lindy, I know fashion, and that dress is *it*."

She sighs and casts a longing glance at the green dress lumped in the pile. "Green is my favorite color. Matches my eyes."

"But this dress shows off your curves, your toned shoulders. And it's so trendy."

Lindy's gaze meets mine in the full-length mirror. "Are you afraid I'm going to embarrass you? Is that it?"

"No, of course not." Right? I like Lindy for who she is. She simply needs some guidance. "I just think you should leave the clothing decisions to me."

"It's your dad's Visa. Your party." She pulls on her top once more and returns to the dressing room.

Oh, fine. I toss the green frock over. "Try it on."

She squeals, and twenty seconds later she prances before the mirror again, her face beaming.

"How do you feel in that dress?" As if I have to ask.

White teeth sparkle against her tanned complexion. "Comfortable."

"The old green dress it is."

We have lunch at Le Cirque, sitting beneath the big-top light shade hanging from the ceiling. The food is heavenly, but Lindy calls them "snobby" portions. She refuses dessert—the fabulous Le Cirque chocolate—and acts relieved when we leave.

Later that evening, I study my new manicure and wonder how Lindy is getting along upstairs with her makeup. Dad reads through his e-mails beside me.

Luisa enters the kitchen and clears her throat. "Presenting . . . Miss Lindy Miller!"

She sashays into room, almost floating above the marble tile.

The queen has arrived.

The three of us clap for her as she spins, her green dress billowing.

"You girls are going to have a great time." Dad hands me my

clutch from the counter. "Both of you look fabulous. And believe me, I know fabulous."

This is true. He sells it every day.

In the car, Lindy grows quiet beside me. I can feel the nervousness radiating off her like static electricity.

My phone beeps and I check the message. It's from Hunter.

The party is so dull without U. Miss U. Wish U were here.

I laugh and show Lindy. "I can't wait to see him." She doesn't even crack a smile. "Lindy, relax. We're going to have such a good time."

"I love the dress, and I appreciate the hair, the nails. But, Bella, this is your world. Not mine. I'm more of a Yankees-and-hot-dog kind of girl."

"We'll do that next time, okay?" I grab her hand and squeeze. "If Matt could see you now—he'd be speechless. You seriously look hot."

That coaxes her mouth into a smile. "But is it me? Sometimes I look in the mirror—at the highlights, the famous label clothes—and it's like I'm looking at someone else. Like I'm a phony."

"Everyone's got another side to him . . . even your Matt Sparks."

The car stops, and Dad's chauffeur turns around. "We're here, miss."

I pull Lindy out, instructing her all the way on how to depart a vehicle in the most delicate manner. It's like sometimes the girl forgets she's not in basketball shorts. No need to give someone a free peep show, you know?

Music spills out into the lobby of the Broadway Park Hotel. A few of my former teachers greet me, and I introduce Lindy.

Soon old friends swarm, and I lose sight of Lindy in all the chaos.

"How's Oklahoma? Is it hideous?"

"Do you have to shop at Kmart?"

"Have you gone cow tipping?"

"Oh, I can't imagine what you've been going through."

I don't even have time to respond to any of the questions. As soon as I open my mouth to defend my new home, somebody asks something even more ridiculous.

"Lindy?" I shout over the voices. "Lindy!"

I see her hand wave in the back.

"Excuse me—excuse me." She pushes her way through.

"Girls, you remember my good friend Lindy from Truman, right?" Soon Lindy is being peppered with questions.

"Hey," I whisper in her ear. "I'm just going to slip away for a bit and find Hunter. I won't leave you alone for long."

Six songs later, I'm still searching for my boyfriend. Not only are there tons of people here, but at least half of them stop me to catch up.

When I've exhausted every spot in the ballroom, I notice French doors leading outside to a courtyard. The sparkle of tiny white lights strung from the trees lures me outside. I breathe in the night air and look to the sky.

No stars. They must all be in Oklahoma.

I breeze through the courtyard, finding nothing but random couples using the benches to make out.

Time to go back in. Hunter would definitely not be out here.

I stop and catch of flash of something familiar. "Mia?" I can't control my laughter. Mia has a boyfriend and didn't even tell me!

And from the looks of things, it's serious. "Mia!" I'm on limited time here, so I tap my finger on her shoulder, shamelessly interrupting her interlude.

She comes up for air, her face now in the light. "Oh! Bella!" She jumps to cover the object of her affection.

But it's too late.

"Hunter?"

He all but falls off the bench. "Bella, I can explain."

"With the same mouth you used to kiss my best friend?"

He pushes Mia aside and grabs me. "You don't understand. It's been so lonely here without you. And then Mia and I have been working closely on this dance . . . and things just happened. It means nothing though, Bella."

"You're right." My glare could melt a polar ice cap. "It does mean nothing. We're over, Hunter. You never intended to make this work." I turn on Mia. "Neither one of you did. I've done all the calling, all the e-mailing. It took me leaving New York to see how much I really meant to both of you, to see what our relationships were truly made of."

"You didn't make it easy," Hunter says.

"Yes, I can see how rough it's been on you both."

Mia finally finds her tongue. "Every time I did call you, it was Truman this and Truman that. And all about people I didn't know or care about, like that Lindy girl. I mean, seriously, Bella." She crinkles her nose. "You come to see us and you bring *her*. She doesn't fit in with us. And maybe you don't either anymore."

"Of course I fit in here. This is still my home." *Isn't it?* "I walk out in that ballroom and see hundreds of *my* friends. And as for Lindy, she's got more class in her little finger than you've got in your entire *closet*! Just because she doesn't hide behind designer clothes and her daddy's checkbook."

Mia laughs. "Oh, you're a fine one to talk!"

"Um, I think we *were* talking about the fact that my best friend and my boyfriend are cheating on me. So can we get back to the topic at hand, where I was telling you what *skanks* you are?" Voices murmur behind me, and without even looking I can tell there's a crowd gathering. *Good. Bring it.*

Mia stomps closer in her Louboutin heels. "We don't like the new you, Bella." She crosses her arms and looks to Hunter for support. "There. I said it—even if no one else will. You talk about school all the time, you act like our world isn't important, your charity case friend looks like a cabbage in her dress . . . and you have roots."

Giggles erupt behind me. I spin on my heel, only to see Lindy standing there. Tears stream down her cheeks. She shakes her head and runs back into the ballroom.

My fists clench at my sides. "I don't even *know* you people! And if I have changed, I'm glad. Because if the old me acted anything like you, Mia, then thank God He moved me to Oklahoma. I'd rather be real any day than be whatever it is you think *you* are." I take one last glance at my boyfriend. "You can have him, Mia. You two deserve each other." I walk off but throw one final shot over my shoulder. "You should probably know he has a Lifetime fetish. He cries during *Golden Girls*."

I pick up my pace until I'm running through the dance floor, searching frantically for Lindy. The crowd swallows me, and I shove through couple after couple before I break through and locate the exit.

But no Lindy.

I call her phone, but the only response I get is her voice mail. Where could she be? She can't just leave by herself. This is New York, for crying out loud. Not Small Town, Oklahoma.

I question a few adults in the lobby. Two people think they saw a girl in a green dress leave.

I jog to the parking lot and call out her name. No response.

After a brief survey of the rest of the hotel common areas, I give up and call my dad's chauffeur. I can't wait to get out of this place. And far away from my "friends."

The ride home stretches forever as I sit alone in the backseat. I don't even tell the driver good-bye as I tear into the apartment, yelling for my dad.

"He's not here, Miss Bella." Luisa wipes her hands on her apron, her face wrinkled in concern.

"Where is he? Lindy's missing. She just left the party." I shake my head, trying to dislodge the image of her horrified face.

"She's upstairs. Packing. She took a cab."

My sigh of relief could probably be heard from Jersey. "We've had a horrible night." I take the stairs two at a time, a shoe in each hand. "Lindy!"

Out of breath, I shove open my door and find Lindy throwing clothes in a suitcase.

"I hate them," she says.

"Lindy, I'm sorry. They were hideous."

She glances at my ceiling. "I meant them." She points to the demonic cherubs. "They weird me out. I never told you that. But I thought as long as we're all being honest tonight, I'd share."

I sit down on the queen-size bed. My dress fans around me and covers the ghastly comforter. "I'm so sorry. They don't know you,

Lindy. Please tell me you didn't believe a word of what they said."

Tears glisten in her eyes. "You tried to stop me from getting the dress." She runs a hand over the skirt. "I still like it though."

"Of course you do. And it looks great on you."

"They said I looked like a cabbage."

"You most definitely do not resemble any vegetable. They're just jealous. Jealous of your toned biceps. And jealous of our friendship."

"I'm not your charity case though." She unzips her dress as she stomps into the bathroom. She returns in her sweats and a ball cap, then tosses the dress on the bed. "Maybe you can take it back. Otherwise I'll pay you for it. I'll pay for all of it."

"Don't be silly. You're not paying for anything." I laugh and swallow some bitterness. "My dad loves doing that sort of thing—especially when it gets him off the hook for spending time with me."

"Oh, I feel *much* better." She yanks the zipper around her suitcase.

"Please don't do this. Don't go." I hop off the bed and sit next to her bag.

"I have to get out of here. I want to go back home, to Truman. Luisa got me a late flight. I'm not staying here. I can't be around you people any longer."

"I'm not like them. I'm not."

"Are you sure about that?" Lindy closes her eyes for a moment, then her words come out slow and steady. "I may have embarrassed you tonight, but you know what? I embarrassed myself—for trying to be something I'm not." She heaves her suitcase up and charges toward the door. "And I'm done with it."

chapter thirty-five

I've lost my boyfriend. Lost my best friend. Lost Lindy. And the only one worth fighting for is sitting on a bleacher watching the Truman Tigers practice on this Monday afternoon.

"Hey." I sit a few feet away from Lindy, my eyes fixed on the field. "I've been looking everywhere for you." I've spent the entire hour I've been home searching for this girl, praying our friendship isn't over.

"Didn't know I was lost." Her monotone does nothing to inspire hope.

Coach Lambourn blows his whistle. "Jared, snap the ball. Is it really that hard? Do you need to sit on the bench Friday night until you've mastered the fundamentals?"

I wince at Jared's public humiliation. His stepbrother, Coach Dallas, watches the exchange with a smile. Jerk.

Minutes later, the whistle is blown again. "Coach Dallas," the father yells. "Take my starters here and work them over until they're ready to be state champs."

"That's my specialty." Jared's stepbrother escorts them to the other side of the field and shoves Dante forward, and the group begins to jog the perimeter.

I return my attention to Lindy. "I know you're mad at me. And maybe you've decided to totally write me off. But before you do, I have something to say."

"No." She holds up a hand. "Me first. Do you know what I've decided?"

I shield my eyes from the harsh sunlight. "You think a liar like Hunter is bound for a future in politics?"

"No."

"You think I'm the worst thing that's ever happened to Truman?"

"That would be the Miss Truman pageant of 2007. We had our first transvestite in the competition—lots of back hair." She shudders at the memory. "No, I think I'm going back to being me." She reaches down and dusts a speck from her Nike running shoe. "If I have to be someone else to impress Matt Sparks, then I don't want him. I don't want to look in the mirror six months from now and see one of your New York friends staring back at me. I don't want to care whose name is on my shirt label."

I'm guessing it's Adidas.

"I don't want to throw out a perfectly good pair of shoes just because they went out of style two months ago. Or judge someone because they'd rather shop at Payless instead of Prada."

"You're exactly right."

"What?"

"You're right. I tried to make you into one of *them*. And that's not you. Lindy, Matt likes you for who you are, inside and out. I think you should just tell him how you feel and come clean with it. And if he doesn't realize what amazing girlfriend material you are, then it's his loss and he doesn't deserve you. But . . . that doesn't explain why you're out here."

Her eyes return to the field where the boys in the starting lineup look like they could collapse at any minute. "I thought I would catch Matt before practice—talk to him. Tell him how all of this"—she lifts a piece of her highlighted hair—"had been for him. But, Bella, I think I've decided to just leave it alone. More than anything in the last few weeks, I've missed my *friend* Matt. I'm not ready to risk losing him permanently if he doesn't feel the same way."

"Are you sure? I have a few other boy-winning strategies in my repertoire."

A corner of her mouth lifts. "Two days ago you witnessed your boyfriend pawing your best friend. No offense, but your advice isn't worth much right now."

I laugh. "Fair enough."

Though it still smarts. I can't wait until the image of Hunter and Mia disappears from my brain. I've been on a steady diet of Ben and Jerry's ever since. I tried to smuggle it in on the plane today, but security didn't care about my boyfriend cheating on me. They said my contraband pint of Chunky Monkey was a security risk. Like anyone would ever desecrate a holy carton of Ben and Jerry's by sticking a weapon in it. Please.

"Lindy, I'm sorry for trying to change you. I never thought of you as a charity case. Your makeover was fun for me, but I know I got carried away. I don't want you to be like my New York friends." My *ex*-friends. "This weekend I realized how shallow they all are. I can't believe all they care about is shopping and . . . shopping."

"You know that was you about a month ago, right?"

"I wasn't *that* bad."

She bites her lip. "Um, okay."

"Seriously, was I?"

She elbows me in the ribs. "Let's just say you've grown on me."

I giggle in relief. "Still friends?"

"Yeah." She smiles. "I think we are."

Thirty minutes later my butt has fallen asleep. I don't know why I'm still sitting here watching practice. Not sure what I'm looking for.

"Is Coach Lambourn always that rough on Jared?" Seems all he's accomplished with his practice is demolishing his stepson's self-esteem.

"He's hard on all of them, but I think he expects more from Jared."

"It must be hard to grow up in the shadow of his all-star stepbrother."

She shrugs a shoulder. "I guess. He seems okay with it. Jared loves the sport. It's everything to him. We haven't won state since Coach Dallas's day, so I think everybody's just focused on winning right now. It helps the players get scholarships, and it helps the coaches keep their jobs, especially the newer ones."

Yeah, but at what cost? "So you mean if they didn't win this year, some of the coaches might be fired?"

"Yes. It's just how it is. Their jobs depend on winning seasons."

And how far would Coach Dallas go to keep his job *and* restore the Truman Tigers to their former glory?

When practice is over, Jared Campbell finds me sitting on his hood. I hand him a water bottle. "You look like a thirsty boy." Maybe in time I'll like him as more than a friend.

He takes the bottle and scoots next to me on the car. "Could you have picked a hotter seat?"

I consider telling him I prefer my buns toasted, but decide against it. "Rough practice."

He grimaces. "It always is. What are you up to? Didn't see you in school today."

"I was in New York. And I hear you took a bunch of notes today in English. I thought maybe we could hang out and I could catch up on what I missed in class."

"Now?"

"You don't want to?" I need to get into his house and see if he has access to the Brotherhood's MySpace page.

"Well, yeah, but I'm a disgusting, sweaty mess."

He really is.

"I know," I purr. "We can go to your house, and while you clean up, I'll jot down the notes. Then you can fill me in on everything that happened at school today." He looks doubtful. "Don't worry. I won't stay long. I have to babysit my little stepbrother tonight." Surely his password to MySpace is saved. "You'd be doing me a *huge* favor."

"Okay. For you."

"Perfect! I'll follow you." *And maybe your computer will lead me to the proof I need to get Coach Dallas in some very big trouble and end the Brotherhood forever.*

———

"So I'm going to take a quick shower. Help yourself to the fridge. I'll be out before you can dunk your first Oreo."

"Thanks. I really appreciate it. I'd hate to work on an empty stomach."

He saunters down a hall, and I watch him walk into his bedroom. Tapping my fingernails on the table, I try to take some deep breaths and calm my racing heart. I might not find anything on his computer, but I have to make sure.

When I hear the water start, I get up and tiptoe down the same hall. I stand outside his door and listen. After a minute, I decide he has to be safely in the shower. I peek in his bedroom and, seeing no signs of Jared, I push on the door and creep inside.

My eyes home in on an iMac sitting on a corner desk. *Here we go. Steady now. You can do this.*

I click on his Internet icon and wait for it to load. *Hurry! Hurry!*

When Jared bursts into "Friends in Low Places," I stifle a scream, my heart lodged in my throat, until I realize he's still in the shower. And a really terrible singer.

His home page pulls up, and I see the ESPN logo and a list of game scores. My pulse skittering, I check his favorites. Scanning, scanning. Nothing.

I type in "MySpace.com."

"What are you doing?"

I jump like a cat, my hands clutching the chair.

Coach Dallas stands in the doorway. His meanest coach's stare is trained on me, and I can't seem to form a coherent thought.

"I . . . I . . ." *This is bad. This is very bad.* "Your brother is loaning me some notes from class. I was hoping to"—Snap my fingers and disappear. Jump out the window. Ask God for a swarm of locusts—"save some time and use his computer to type them up." I hold up my French-tipped nails. "A girl can ruin a manicure with all that writing we do in AP English."

"Where is my *stepbrother?*"

Oh, do I detect some fraternal sensitivity?

I jerk my thumb toward the bathroom. "You can't hear his *American Idol* audition in there?"

"So you're in his bedroom while he's in the shower?" His lips quirk.

Yeah. Not only am I a snoop, but I'm a perv too. "I wasn't peeking or anything." *Believe me, all I wanted to see of Jared's was his computer.*

"I guess the rules have changed in this house since I lived here."

Coach Dallas relaxes, and I begin to breathe again.

"What are you two doing?" Jared walks out of the bathroom, a towel knotted at his waist. My face floods with heat. Luke would have a coronary if he knew how badly I was bumbling this.

"I'm sorry, I'm in such a hurry with the babysitting thing." I speak to the general space beside Jared. "So I came up here to see if you had a computer. I was hoping I could type your notes. I can do sixty words per minute." I'm rambling! Boy in towel! Look away! "I think I'll wait in the kitchen." Maybe try to drown myself in the sink. Gouge out my eyeballs with a can opener.

"Don't go anywhere." Jared steps behind the door for a split second then reappears in a pair of shorts. "How did you think you were going to type my notes if I hadn't even given them to you yet?"

I giggle like a space cadet. "I heard singing, and I had to follow the sound. It lured me in here, Jared. Like a siren from the *Odyssey*." Or a scratched CD. "And I thought, 'As long as I'm here, I'll check out his computer.'" My face is as sincere as a TV preacher—though what I'm saying makes absolutely no sense. "If you'll just get me the notes, I'll leave you two alone while I copy them the old-fashioned way in the kitchen." *And get the heck out of here.*

"No, that's okay." Jared's eyes flash for a moment, their usual gentleness replaced with something fierce. "Dallas here was just leaving."

"Actually, I wanted to talk to you for a minute, little *brother.*"

I scoot around the desk chair and pass between the two guys. "I'll just get out of your way."

"No, Bella, wait."

I wave a hand and back out the door. "No problem. Finish your talk." I stop halfway down the hall and listen.

"I have a lot riding on this season."

"That makes two of us," comes Jared's angry voice. "Back off, Dallas."

"If the team goes down, we all go down. The school board will terminate all of the staff, and you won't even get to play as a college walk-on, let alone get a scholarship."

"I know that! You think I don't feel the pressure?"

"Dad's been talking about cutting you from the starters. I've held him off, but I can't much longer."

"Nice to know you care."

"This team's important to me. And to Dad."

Jared laughs, his bitterness obvious. "Winning's important to you two. Not me, not the team. *I* care about the team. *I* care about the players. They're not even people to you—just a means to an end. Quit trying to relive your high school days through me."

I replay this in my head, wanting to store it word for word for Luke. Coach Dallas is so our man. Now I just have to get someone to admit it. To confess and hand over the video files. Maybe one more party with Jared, and he'll let me in. He has no reason to protect a stepbrother he doesn't even like. Especially at the cost of his friends.

Two minutes later Coach Dallas sails through the living room. I wave at him from the kitchen table as he slams the front door behind him. Nice guy, that one.

Jared reappears, this time wearing a shirt. "I'm really sorry about that. Dallas and I aren't exactly best friends."

"So I see. It must be hard to live in a family of two coaches."

"He just doesn't get it. He wants everything to be like it was when he was in school—same plays and everything. He thinks he knows what's best for the team, but he doesn't even know us."

"You know, Jared . . . if you ever want to talk, I'm a great listener." *And snooper.* "And I hear I give some pretty good advice." *And this would all be over if we could go to the police together.*

"Thanks." He hands me a stack of papers. "Your notes *and* an invitation to the Thursday night party."

"You're the best." I smile and clutch the ticket like it's gold. "Is it okay if I just borrow the notes tonight? It's getting late, and I really do need to get home for babysitting duty."

"You seem a little more adjusted with your new family."

I think about this. "I guess I am. Except for one stepbrother. All he cares about is making my life miserable."

Jared nods, a faraway look in his eyes. "Then I guess we have that in common."

chapter thirty-six

 No friends over. No parties. No leaving for any reason. And
keep your eye on Robbie at all times."

"He will not so much as tinkle without my presence," I tell my
mom. She and Jake stand on the front porch ready to leave for his
amateur wrestling match.

"I do not pee with an audience." Robbie pulls his cape around
him, his hero's pride totally insulted.

"Emergency numbers are on the fridge."

"Go, Mom. We'll be fine. Superman here will not escape this
time."

"I'm Spiderman tonight."

"What you are is dead meat if you so much as step a foot out of
this house." I shut the door behind our parents.

"I know, Dad's already told me. No CNN for a month if I don't
obey your every command."

"Oh, really?" I walk into the kitchen, Robbie following my
every step. "So if I tell you to clean my toilet with your toothbrush,
you're going to do it?"

"I'll clean it with *somebody's* toothbrush."

I grin and open the freezer door. "Mom said you want pizza for dinner." I pull out pepperoni, his favorite. This kid eats nothing that doesn't come from a box.

Robbie grabs a bag of chips off the counter and pulls out a handful as his brother appears. "Hey, Budge." He shoves the whole mess in his mouth. "Want thom pitha?"

"Nah." He runs his hand over Robbie's head. "I gotta go sell some hot dogs. I'm up for a raise this week."

"That's great." I've decided to try with this guy. Maybe I'll win him over with kindness. "You must be the best thing that's ever happened to the Wiener Palace. The, um . . . Chief Wiener must be so proud of you."

Budge takes a potato chip from Robbie's greasy hands. He chews it as he stares at me. "I heard you went to see Kelsey Anderson."

"Yeah. Nice girl." I cut into the plastic wrap on the pizza.

"She said you asked a lot of questions about the accident. What do you hope to gain by digging into that? You can't bring him back." The edge in his voice makes me put down my scissors.

"No, I can't bring him back, Budge." That would take a miracle, and that's God's department. "But I can expose the truth. If he was pressured into racing his car that night, people need to know. And if there are specific people responsible, then they need to be stopped."

His expression is blank, neutral. But for once he's not looking at me with uncontainable venom. Budge nods his red, frizzy head. "Okay."

"Okay?" I have my stepbrother's approval? "Zach never said anything to you about any of the coaches? The football players? Nothing that would help us out?" I slide the pizza in the oven.

"He just talked about being under a lot of stress. People telling him what to do. But then Zach pretty much stopped talking to me last year. He wouldn't admit it, but I think the players made him cut me out. He only hung out with the team—and Kelsey, of course."

"But even she said he had grown really distant."

"You think you can really get to the bottom of this?"

"I'm going to try." I take a step closer to him. "I could use a prayer or two if you want to help."

The anger slips back over his face. "I'm done with that. Take care of my brother." And he walks out, his sultan pants swishing as he goes.

"Bella, there's someone at the door." Robbie chews on a finger-nail. "He looks mad."

That doesn't narrow it down. Who *haven't* I made mad lately?

"Okay, I'm putting you in charge of watching the pizza. Not much longer, maybe ten minutes, and we'll eat."

Robbie throws himself over a chair, his arms drooping to the floor. "I feel my superpowers draining. I need food."

Walking into the entry, I see Luke's brooding face staring back at me through the screen. With a final glance at Robbie, I step onto the porch. "Hey."

"Hey, yourself."

I see his frigid editor ego has returned. Oh, how I missed him. Like a too-tight bra.

"I got your text. You said you visited with Jared tonight and we needed to talk."

"Yeah, I tried to check his computer to see if I could log on to his MySpace." Without taking a pause to breathe, I fill him in on everything that happened. "And that's when his brother stormed out." I finish, expecting to see Luke beaming with pride over my efforts.

He pushes off from the porch railing and plants himself directly in front of me. "You were told not to do anything alone. I meant that, Bella Kirkwood."

He really needs to work on his "atta girls."

"I'm not in any danger. I went over to get notes from Jared. I was in his room for a little while, no harm done. I was there less than thirty minutes."

"And just enough time for Coach Dallas to *catch* you pulling up MySpace."

"He didn't see that. Just saw me *on* the computer. No harm done."

"You don't know that."

"And you don't know that harm *was* done. Get over yourself, will you? You're just mad because I took the initiative. If you had a better idea for getting into Jared's computer, I didn't hear it."

"Here's a scenario I don't want to hear: you snooping in his bedroom, and Jared in a towel."

His blue eyes are liquid intensity. I have to turn away from them. "Okay, so it doesn't sound like the most wholesome situation. But it's Jared, come on."

"He's a guy with a girl in his bedroom. He's not to be trusted."

I lean in until my nose is inches from his. "What are you, my dad?"

"No, I'm . . . I'm . . ." He crushes his hair with a hand. "I'm your editor. And I'm still in charge of this project."

"It's *my* story."

"Not at this rate. I warned you once, Bella."

"I'm not some underling you can boss around. We don't have time to waste. If I have the means, what's wrong with me taking some initiative and getting some information? The sooner we expose Coach Dallas, the sooner names can be cleared, people can heal, and football players are saved from any more catastrophes."

"You *are* a catastrophe—waiting to happen."

"You're an egotistical ogre!"

"You are not to do anything on this story that isn't cleared through me first. You'll hurt yourself. You'll hurt this story. One mistake, and it's all over. Right now the Brotherhood is too cocky to take it underground completely."

"Well, if anyone knows cocky, it's you."

He closes the small space that separates us. "You're off the story."

"No, I'm not."

"There's no party this week, so we have some time. Stay away from the football players this week. I'm working on a few things, and I don't want your interference. It's important."

"So *you* can operate solo, but *I* can't?" I stomp away from him, pace the length of the porch, then return to face him. "You're just jealous because I have an in with Jared Campbell. You want to be the big dog here because that's how Luke Sullivan operates."

"This is about playing it smart."

"This is about playing by your rules. Well, I'm not in this to stroke your pride, so Thursday, there *is* a party. And I'll be there. And I *will* come away with information that ends it once and for all."

"Who told you there's a party?"

"Jared invited me."

"Then how come nobody's talking about it? There aren't any more initiations left." His forehead furrows deeper. "You're off the story, Bella. Stay away until told otherwise."

I toss his words back to him. "Stay away from *me* until told otherwise."

"Bella!" Robbie's shrill voice calls from inside. "The pizza's burning!"

Luke steps off the porch. "Glad you've got everything under control, then."

My face is a picture of serenity and composure as he leaves. Then I run like mad to the kitchen. The fumes are worse than a New York sewer grate.

"What happened?" Grabbing oven mitts, I place the charred remains on top of the stove. "Five hundred degrees? Did you change the temperature?"

Robbie studies his Spiderman belt. "Maybe. I was hungry though. Starving! I just wanted it to hurry up."

Ugh! I turn on the oven fan, but it does nothing to diminish the black smell. "Find some candles, Robbie." I open windows in the kitchen, then the living room, pressing my nose to the screen to suck in some good air.

Fifteen minutes later, with the sun barely visible, I pray over our peanut butter, jelly, and potato chip sandwiches. Candles glow all around like we're holding a memorial for the dead pizza.

After helping Robbie with some reading homework (I read, he made sound effects), we settle onto the orange couch for *The Incredibles*, a movie he's seen exactly one hundred and four times.

By the time the credits roll, Robbie's drooling on my shoulder. I scoop him up and carry him upstairs. He snuggles into me, bringing a smile to my face. Odd as he is, I do like this kid. When he's twenty-five, he'll probably be the inventor of something to rival Google, he'll be a Jeopardy grand champion, and he'll still wear his Superman underwear. He doesn't even stir when I lay him down on his comforter.

I return downstairs to extinguish all the candles and sandblast the pizza pan. The phone in my pocket beeps. A text. From Hunter.

I'm so sorry. Pls call me. Need 2 talk. We can work thru this. Temporary insanity.

Insane is what I'd have to be if I took him back.

Delete.

Only an hour into my own homework, my eyes grow heavy. I didn't sleep a lot at my dad's. I give in to fatigue, peel back the blankets, and collapse into my bed. I dream of standing on the football field. The Brotherhood is there. They build a giant fire on the fifty-yard line. I want to watch them, but the smoke is too strong. It burns my eyes.

Coach Dallas yells at each player. He blows his whistle. "Run through the bonfire! Show your allegiance to the Brotherhood."

I can feel Matt Sparks's fear from where I am. His pulse accelerates. His skin sweats from the heat.

One by one, the football players run through the flames. They come out unharmed, unscathed.

Then it's Matt's turn. He walks away, only to turn around, get the fire in his sights, and sprint toward his target.

I have to stop him. Some way. Somehow.

"Nooooo!" I burst through the dream, my voice dragging me back to consciousness.

Sitting up, I wipe my hands over my face, my heart pounding in fear.

What is that noise?

Our fire alarm!

That smell.

I shoot out of bed. I have to get to Robbie. Throwing my door open, I'm nearly knocked over by the smoke. The alarm screams. Or maybe it's me. Everything's a blur as I run to his room.

"Robbie!" I yell his name over and over.

"What's going on?" His eyes are wide as tractor wheels. He clutches his sheet to his chin.

"I don't know. We need to get downstairs and go outside though, okay?" I force myself to slow down and talk calmly. We can't both be flipping out. I'm in charge here. There's no one else.

"It's going to be okay." I throw out other useless words of comfort as we hurry down the hall to the stairs.

Robbie points ahead. "The stairs are on fire!"

How in the world could the stairs be on fire? I stand motionless and just watch the flames. Thinking. Praying.

"There's no other way out, Bella!" Tears streak Robbie's face, and he clings to my leg. I pick him up.

"I need you to be very brave, okay?" He nods against my shoulder. "You're my superhero, right? It's time to put those powers to use and save us."

Holding my stepbrother, I run back into my bedroom and grab my phone. "I need you to hold this for me, Robbie. It's a very important job. Can you do that?"

His red head bobs.

I set him down long enough to fling open the window and pop out the screen. "We're going to my secret hiding place, okay? You and I are going to crawl out on a big limb and climb down."

"It's too high." He backs away, but I grab his wrist.

"Robbie"—I bend down to his level—"we have to do this." I hear a loud pop from downstairs. "And we need to hurry."

I don't even wait for his response. "God, help us. God, help us." I recite it like a mantra as I hoist Robbie onto my back and find my balance on the window ledge. "Hang on. Whatever you do, don't let go of me."

I climb out onto the roof, my hands flattened to the shingles so I won't topple over. I scoot closer to the edge where the tree meets the roof, then stand to my feet, grabbing the thickest branch I can find.

"Here we go." I step onto a limb bigger than Jake's arm and test it with my foot. Finding it secure, I put both feet onto it and reach above us for another limb to hold on to.

Stopping every little bit to hoist a slippery Robbie tighter to my back, I walk us around the oak, moving as far away from the roof as possible.

Now. Time to descend.

Please, God. Please, God. Please, God.

Don't let me drop him. Keep my feet steady.

The moon shines on the ground below—the cold, hard, far-away ground. *Look at the branches, not any lower.*

My hair clings to my face in wet strands, and I swish it away. But there's no time. I get us farther down the tree. One limb at a time.

Low enough to brave a look down, I estimate how many more feet until we're safely on land. At least six, maybe seven more branches—

My foot slips.

My world tilts.

And Robbie and I go sailing through the tree. Down, down. I twist and somehow pull him to me, desperate to shield his body from the blows of the limbs.

Falling. Hurting. Crashing.

Land.

My back absorbs most of the hit as I connect full-body with the ground. My head bounces once then is thrown back as the force of Robbie's frame hits me. His elbow, knees, head—every bit of him falls into me.

I struggle to catch my breath as everything in my vision spins. Robbie rolls off of me, shaking out the kinks. Not quite ready to move, I suck in the night air, grateful my stepbrother is safe. Stars swim before my eyes.

"Robbie, my phone. Still got it?" I manage to keep one eye open. Pain shoots through my head.

"Yup."

"Call 9-1-1."

"Last time I called them I got in trouble. They said I couldn't call anymore unless I had a real problem." He mumbles something about giving his goldfish mouth-to-mouth.

"Call them *now*."

He punches in the number with one stubby finger. "Yeah, I have an emergency. My house is on fire." I close my eyes and try to hear the dispatcher on the other end. "My stepsister, Bella, just saved me. But you need to hurry up because I don't want to lose any of my action figures."

I rub my brow bone, the recipient of a mean elbow jab from Robbie. "This night could not get any worse."

"Oh yeah?" He points upward into the tree and giggles.

There, five branches above us, hang my pajama bottoms, swaying in the breeze like a sign of surrender.

And that's how I met the Truman Fire Department.

chapter thirty-seven

I s she gonna die?"

"No, Robbie. She'll just have the black eye for a while." My mother sits on the bed beside me. Mom and Jake came home not too long after the fire trucks showed up last night. After a quick trip to the emergency room, the entire family camped out at Dolly's house.

Robbie squints as he studies my face. "She could get a glass eye. That'd be cool."

"There's nothing wrong with me. You gave me a shiner when we fell out of the tree. Nobody's getting any body parts removed."

But my eye looks hideous. It's a lovely blend of purple, blue, and swollen, and Sephora doesn't sell anything that could cover this up. But the doctor said I was lucky that's all I suffered. I didn't even have a concussion. Just some leaf burns. Some limb lacerations. Bark bruises.

Mom let all of us stay home from school. Budge went with Jake to the house this morning, and Robbie chose to stay with us at Dolly's, not knowing when he would have another opportunity to watch the cartoon channel on her satellite.

We sit in the living room, Robbie inches from the giant TV, while Mom and I lounge on one of Dolly's leather couches.

When Jake and Budge walk into the room, I'm instantly on alert. Jake's eyes dart to me, then to my mother. Budge stands back, looking at no one.

"What's the matter?" Mom asks.

Jake inhales deeply, his frown severe. "The fire chief said the fire was started by a candle left on in the kitchen."

I stop breathing.

"He said it burned until it spread on a plate then caught a nearby towel on fire. It shot right up the wall and eventually caught the stairs behind it."

Mom's face is grave. "Bella, did you burn a candle last night?"

Robbie pipes up. "No, she didn't burn *a* candle. She burned a *lot* of them."

My stomach twists, and I have to fight a wave of nausea. "I snuffed them out—all of them. I know I did." *Didn't I?* It had been a crazy night. A fight with Luke. The pizza burning. Robbie's homework, then mine. What if I *had* forgotten and left one candle burning?

Mom grabs Jake's hand, and he sits on the arm of the couch. I feel like I've committed a crime. And it's them against me. They think I set the fire.

My vision blurs with tears. "I did put out the candle. I know it. At least I'm pretty sure . . ."

"Bella, you could've burned the entire house down." The edge in my mom's voice is like a thousand paper cuts.

I stand up, desperate to get far away from all of them. "I'm telling you, I didn't do it."

"How bad is it?" Mom asks.

Jake studies their joined hands. "Could've been a lot worse. We'll have to redo the back wall of the kitchen, the stairs, part of the ceiling. The important thing is that everyone's okay. Bella, I know I told you this last night, but looking at the house today, I want to say it again. Thank you for your quick thinking. You and Robbie are alive today because you climbed onto that tree." He watches his son, who has gone back to *Scooby-Doo*, totally uninterested in any near-death talk. "You saved my son."

But killed your house.

"What did the insurance guy say?" Mom asks Jake. He shakes his head and speaks to my mom in a hushed whisper.

I take myself into the kitchen, desperate for some aspirin and caffeine. Instead I find Budge.

I jerk one cabinet open then another, searching for a glass.

"Here." He holds out a blue cup. "You know I—"

"Save it," I snap. "Whatever jerk thing you have to say, just keep it to yourself. I know you're mad at the world, and now I've given you one more reason to be miserable—I apparently just burned down part of your house. So I'm sorry we're stuck here for a few weeks. And—"

"I just wanted to say thanks." He clears his throat. Studies his feet.

Shaking my head, I try to reengage my ears, which obviously cannot be working.

"It sucks that we're kicked out of the house for a while, but Dolly does have a killer pool."

"Did you just thank me?"

"Yeah." He stabs his hands into his pockets. "The whole saving-my-brother thing you did was pretty cool." And he walks past me, where I stand in mute shock at his freakish kindness. "Nice eye, by the way. You look like a Cyclops."

Now that's more like it.

~~~~~~~~~~

"Tell me again why you dragged me to football practice?" I sit down beside Lindy on the warm bleacher.

"Your mom said you needed to get out of the house. She's worried about you."

I have spent the whole afternoon in my temporary bedroom, hugging a trash can, afraid I was going to hurl at any moment. Setting a house on fire can do that to a girl.

"Accidents happen, Bella."

My stomach clenches. "Thanks for bringing it up. I love the subject of the fire. I could talk about it *all* day."

"I just mean that it wasn't your fault."

"Apparently it was. I'm the one who lit the match that lit the candle, so therefore, it's my fault. I've tried to think of at least ten other people to blame, such as my cheating liar of an ex-boyfriend or my loser ex-BFF, but logic prevails, and it all points back to me once again. I started the fire."

"But you didn't mean to. That's the important thing. Your parents know that."

"Pretty soon the euphoric feeling that their children are alive and well will wear off, and they will begin to look at me as the arsonist I must be."

But if there's one thing I did get out of this, besides a serious need for a manicure, it's that life is short. And I'm going to take the Brotherhood situation by the horns and talk to Jared. I think I've earned his trust by now. Surely he'll open up to me about what he knows.

My head still throbs, and the shouting of Coach Lambourn and Coach Dallas does nothing to help.

Coach Dallas butts up to Dante, his face inches from his star player's. "When I was in school, we were winners. A state championship was a given. And why? Because we *worked* hard! Because we were a *team*." He moves on to his stepbrother. "Your team makes me sick. You have a heritage here, and you're destroying it game by game. We barely pulled it out last week. Uphold the legacy at all costs." His gaze travels to every starter.

I can't wait to blow the lid on this guy's craziness and send him up the river. To the big house. The pokey. The slammer. If he continues killing off all his players, there won't be anyone left to uphold a football, let alone a stupid legacy.

"Well, look at that."

I follow Lindy's stare and see Luke walking toward us. With Kelsey Anderson.

"Hey, ladies." Luke addresses us both, but he watches me.

"Kelsey, it's good to see you out here. You look great." Lindy lies through her teeth. Kelsey looks like a strong wind could pick her up and deposit her in Arkansas with one gust.

"I ran into Kelsey at the home today and thought some fresh air might be nice," Luke says. "How are you?" He turns his attention toward me as Lindy pulls Kelsey in with some small talk.

"I'm fine." *And still mad, thank you very much.* "Couldn't be better."

He lifts his hands toward my face and eases off my oversized sunglasses. And scowls. "That doesn't look fine. You could've been seriously hurt."

I grab my shades back. "Well, I wasn't."

Luke clasps my wrist and pulls me a few steps away from the girls. "Budge said that the fire department claimed you left a candle burning. He said you swore you snuffed out all the candles."

"I guess I was wrong." And the house is short a few walls to prove it.

Luke casts a glance over his shoulder. He steps closer to me. "What if you're not wrong? What if someone else started the fire?"

"Who, Robbie? I put out the candles *after* he went to bed."

"Not Robbie." A warm breeze blows between us, ruffling Luke's dark hair. "Bella, how hard would it be to get into your house? I'm guessing the windows are fairly old. And if your stepdad is like half the people in this town, the doors probably aren't locked much."

It's true. Jake does not believe in locking doors. Whenever I ask him about it, he just makes a joke about his attack cows.

"But I locked the doors that night. That place is so isolated it kind of creeps me out sometimes."

"Dead bolts?"

"No."

Luke watches the team, his jaw set. "You need to stay away from the football players. No more asking questions. No parties. Nothing."

"No! We've already been through this. I have an in with Jared Campbell, and you know it. There is no reason not to take advantage of that."

"Any of those players could have been in your house last night.

We have to play it safe from this point on. The closer we get to the truth, the more dangerous it could get."

"I have to go to the parties. We have no other options. It's our best resource for information. Unless you want me to enlighten Lindy and see if Matt will tell her anything."

"I said no, Bella." His voice is as hard as an oak tree. "Thursday night I'm going with Kelsey to Zach Epps's house."

"What? Why?"

"We're going to search his bedroom. Check his computer. See if we can find anything at all."

"You weren't at least going to ask me to go?"

He shakes his head. "She trusts me. We've known each other since kindergarten. This is kind of a delicate situation."

"I *knew* you would take over! I knew it. That's what this is about. You want to be the hero here. Spare me your fake concern over my safety, Chief. I'm not backing off this story—and we'll see who gets to the finish line first."

He clutches my arm and pulls me to him, his voice a whisper in my ear. "You're off the article, Bella. You were warned. I can't risk the story." Anger swims in his deep blue eyes. "Or you."

"I'm not your responsibility." I take my arm back. "I don't need your permission *or* your protection."

"Need I remind you of the very first party?"

"And if I need you and your birdcalls again, I'll say the word." My eye throbs like a football's trying to sprout out of the socket. "Good-bye, Luke Sullivan."

"I'll have your new assignment on your desk tomorrow."

"An exposé on the poor quality of toilet paper at Truman High?" And I'll know *exactly* where to stick it.

I say good-bye to Kelsey Anderson and walk toward Lindy's car, hoping she'll get the hint that I'm more than ready to leave.

"Bella!" A sweaty Jared Campbell intercepts me as I reach her Mustang. "Hey." His face is red from the heat, but it doesn't hide his concern. "How are you? I heard about the fire today."

I smile and push my sunglasses farther up my nose. "I'm fine. Really." It is kind of cool how I have people caring about me—the same people who last month wouldn't have minded if the whole house caved in on me.

"I'm so glad." He wipes at his dripping forehead. "We're playing our rival Friday night. You should come."

"I'll be there this week." Even though Luke, spawn of Satan, has removed me from the story, he didn't remove me from manager duty with Lindy. I'm totally going to break this case before he does.

"Are we still on for the party Thursday night? I understand if you don't feel like it."

"No, I definitely feel like it!" Okay, right now I feel like some Ben and Jerry's and an ice pack, but I'm sure I'll be in the mood in a few days.

"I saw you guys talking to Kelsey Anderson." His eyes travel across the field to where she still stands deep in conversation with Luke and Lindy. "What did she have to say?"

"We were just talking about Zach—the night of the accident."

"I don't think that's something we'll ever get over."

I rest my hand on his forearm. Which is also sweaty. "I know it's still tough. It's good that Kelsey's getting out some though, right? She needs a break from her vigil at the nursing home. That place is so depressing."

"You've been there?"

"Yeah, I went with Luke once. Just to visit." *And to dig up some information.* "Do you go?"

He shakes his head. "Can't." He bites his top lip as he thinks on this. "It's hard . . . you know? It's nice that you're spending time with her though."

"Jared—" *Tell me everything you know about the Brotherhood. Where are the videos? Help me stop your stepbrother.* "I, um . . . I'll see you at school tomorrow."

chapter thirty-eight

I think waffles with whipped cream make everything better. The entire family sits at a table at Sugar's. Dolly brings me another round of fresh-squeezed orange juice and pats me on the back. "Honey, you eat up now. It's all-you-can-eat Thursday, so get your money's worth."

"And it's payday too." Mom waves her paycheck in the air. "It's my first full check. Haven't seen one of these things in years." And she looks content. My mom, a Manhattan socialite, sits in a grungy diner perfectly happy with her wrestler husband, grab bag of children, and minimum-wage check. God sure has some strange things up His sleeve. And when I say strange . . . I mean weird.

A bell jingles as the door swings open.

Mickey Patrick walks in. All heads swoop in his direction. And the small-town talk begins. Whispers fly over hotcakes and hash browns.

He waves to a few people, gradually making it to our table. "Hello." His eyes greet all of us. All but Dolly. "Hadn't seen you since the fire, Jake; saw your truck here and just wanted to see for myself that everyone was okay."

Jake's arm settles on the back of my chair. "We're great. Thought we'd have some breakfast together before we all went our separate ways for the day. Sit down and have some coffee."

"Nah." His eyes jump—like he *wants* to look at Dolly. "Saw the house yesterday. Not good, but could be a lot worse."

My stepdad's hand rests on my shoulder, and he gives it a small squeeze. "Nothing that can't be replaced. This is our hero right here."

I nearly choke on my bacon.

"You've got yourself a brave girl all right," Mickey says.

"That we do." Jake nods his blond head. "Couldn't be more proud. And blessed."

Even though I've just inhaled ten pounds of waffles, I suddenly feel a hundred pounds lighter. I'm forgiven. Jake doesn't hate me for nearly burning the house down. No grudge. His words thrill my heart, and it's everything I can do not to jump on this table and belt out a happy tune—*High School Musical*-style.

"Nothing's more important than family. The rest is just stuff." Mickey's gaze aims straight at his ex-wife this time. "Only a fool would forget that."

"You gonna start coming in my diner and spouting off like a fortune cookie on a regular basis?" Dolly pops her gum. "'Cause I don't think my gag reflexes are that strong."

Mickey pulls up a chair and sits himself down. His eyes flash fire. And a challenge. "Maybe." He tucks a napkin into his collar. "Yep, maybe I am."

~~~~~~~~~~

As I sit here in the dark, staring at the rows of gravestones and waiting for Jared to meet me, I picture Luke and what he must be doing right now. He's at Zach Epps's with Kelsey, and they're digging through dresser drawers. Then they move to his computer. Because life is kinder to him, Luke finds a Word file called "Everything You Could Possibly Want to Know About the Brotherhood." He immediately prints it and takes it to the authorities. They are probably minutes away from naming a street after him and declaring it National Luke Sullivan Day.

Tonight I'm ditching Jared and trailing the Brotherhood like paparazzi on Britney Spears. I've got my camera in my purse and fully intend to do whatever it takes to get my own video for the police and pictures for *my* article.

His headlights spotlight my car, and I step out and wave. "I know the drill," I say when he opens his car door, and I hold out my hand for the blindfold.

Jared takes a swig from a giant water bottle. "My car's acting up. Mind if we take yours?"

I quirk an eyebrow. "What? You're going to let me see how to get to the mystery party location?"

He grins and ducks his head. "You know I can't. Rules are rules. But I thought . . . maybe I could drive your car?"

I tap my finger to my lip and consider this. If anything were to happen to the Bug, I would be in the passenger side of Budge's hearse again. Not a comforting thought.

"I promise I'll be careful with it. Come on." He wiggles his fingers for the keys. "You can trust me."

"Fine."

He spins me around and covers my eyes with a red paisley bandanna. This part always creeps me out a bit. Maybe this will be the last party I have to attend. No more rendezvous in cemeteries, blind drives to the lake, or staying out past curfew and getting myself grounded 'til I'm old enough to need Miss Clairol.

"Tell me about Coach Lambourn and Coach Dallas," I say a few minutes down the road. "What's it like playing for your stepdad and his son?"

I hear Jared snort. "Unbearable."

"They seem to put a lot of pressure on the team—especially on you."

"Yeah." He taps his hands on the wheel to the song on the radio, and I think he's not going to elaborate. "My stepdad doesn't even see me. I'm just a means to a win. I'm not even a real person, just a player. We all are."

I throw out some bait. "From watching practice, I get the idea your stepbrother would do *anything* to recapture the former Truman glory. He seems . . ." I pretend to search for a word. "*Desperate* for a win."

"I guess we all are."

Sometime later the car slows then finally stops. Jared continues his tapping on the wheel though the radio is silent.

"Here we are." His sigh drags out. "Sit tight, and I'll be around to get you."

Warm air replaces the air-conditioning as he gets out and opens my door.

"Where's the party music?" Normally you can hear the bass a good thirty seconds away. But tonight it's quiet. "Are you sure there's a party tonight?"

"Yeah." He pulls me out of the passenger seat, his hands gentle on my arms. "No, don't take your blindfold off yet. I, um, have a surprise for you."

"A surprise?" A smile curves my lips. "Interesting." But time consuming! I need to be where the party action is so I can investigate and get some hard evidence. *Before* Luke does.

"Ready? Watch your step." I hear the grass crunch beneath my feet as he leads me forward. "Not much further." A door opens, then light filters through the blindfold. "I'm just going to sit you down here." A chair scrapes the floor, then he's guiding me into it. My hands rest on a table in front of me.

"Uh, Jared, if I break my curfew again, I'll never be let out of the house. The rest of the party crowd will be here soon, right?"

The covering over my eyes falls away, and I blink against the light. The familiar living room of the lake cabin is the first thing to come into focus.

A shiny black handgun is the second.

"You won't be joining the party tonight." Jared Campbell stands in front of me, his trembling hands clutching the pistol.

"Are you insane?" I leap up from my chair, only to be shoved back down. I'm instantly reminded of the sheer strength in this athlete. "Jared, what are you doing? Put that thing down."

"I'm gonna have to ask you to stay right where you are."

My heart shudders to a stop. "Why are you doing this?" So confused. Mind reeling. Have to get out of here.

"You couldn't leave it alone, could you?"

I shake my head, bewildered and dazed. "I have no idea what you're talking about."

"The Brotherhood. I tried to warn you, but you wouldn't take the hint—getting Kelsey Anderson all stirred up again."

Something falls into place in my mind. "The fire. That was you, wasn't it? Did you break into my house?"

He takes a step back, the gun still aimed right at my heart. "I thought maybe it would scare you into going back to New York. I wish it had. I wanted it to. I didn't want it to come to this."

I can't breathe in here. Can't think. "You could've *killed* me. *And my stepbrother.* How could you do that?"

He slams one hand on the table, and I want to bounce out of my skin. "I didn't want to! Don't you understand? Doesn't anybody understand me?"

"I can't understand anything when you've got a gun aimed at me!" I scream back. No, I have to stay calm. He's only growing more agitated. I have to calm us both down. "Tell me what this is about, Jared. I deserve to know." Seeing how I'm going to die for it and all.

"I know you went to Tulsa to meet with Reggie Lee. I know you talked to his girlfriend."

"How could you know that?"

He shrugs. "Brittany Taylor. She may be annoying, but she's useful. She's been following you around for weeks."

Okay, that girl is just evil. "You and your boys planted drugs in Reggie's locker, didn't you?" Empty eyes stare back at me in response. "Why?"

He scrubs a hand over his face. "Because he was going to talk. We'd promised—we'd *all* promised."

"Promised what?"

"That no one would ever know about the Brotherhood. But . . ." His Adam's apple bobs. "Things went wrong last year. It got to Reggie."

"I know about the night Zach Epps had the wreck." Nothing like going out with a lie on your lips.

Sweat bubbles at Jared's temple. "It was a horrible night." He shakes his head. He's there. "We had the initiation for Reggie and Zach all set up. Then the storm came. But there was no turning back—that's our way."

And it's worked so well for you too.

"So Reggie and Zach raced each other." I fill in the blanks. "And Zach lost control."

"We had to keep it quiet. They could never know that we had been there, had been a part of that. We all agreed, just like when we lost Carson Penturf. But Reggie buckled. He came to me at the beginning of school, told me he had to go to the police and come clean. But you can't go against the Brotherhood."

"So you planted the drugs in his locker, knowing it would get him suspended and end any chances of a college scholarship."

"It was a warning. And it worked. He didn't want to risk jail any more than the rest of us."

"And Carson?" I can't peel my eyes away from the gun. "He didn't really commit suicide, did he?"

"We decided his challenge was to climb down a cliff in the dark—no tools, no flashlight. Nothing but his bare hands." His eyes swim with pain. "He was halfway there. Then his foot slipped and he fell."

"What if you had gone and gotten help? What if he could've been saved? Who gave you the right to play God to these people? They were your friends."

"Shut up! You think I don't know that?" His wild eyes scare me.

"Jared, it's not too late to turn back. You've been pressured by Coach Dallas. It's gotten to you. I think we should go to the police—together—and talk to them. Tell them what your stepbrother has driven you to do."

"Dallas?"

"The parties? The initiations? I know this is his lake house."

Jared snorts. "He doesn't even know we use this. He's too busy with his girlfriend in Tulsa and blaming me for every mistake the team makes."

"He forced you to start the Brotherhood again so—so the team would win again like they did when he was in school and he could keep his job."

"I am *so* sick of hearing about his winning streak! Who cares?" he yells. "I've done everything—everything! I've trained, I've watched game films, I've done anything I could think of to make myself better. It's never going to be enough."

My brain clears like I've been doused in ice water. I've been so blind. *It's been Jared all along.* "Your brother knows nothing about your new little boys' club."

"And he's not *going* to know. The Brotherhood will go on as we are—a new breed of players. We will grow closer and stronger."

"And deader!" Okay, that's not a word, but grammar is the least of my concerns. "This is crazy. It has to stop now. All of it. You have to come clean." *And put the gun down while you're at it.*

"I liked you, Bella. I really did."

Did? Past tense?

Walking backwards, he goes to the coffee table, opens a small drawer, and pulls out a pen and paper. He places them in front of me.

"You're going to write."

"For some reason I really don't feel all that inspired at the moment."

He ignores me. "You're going to compose a suicide letter to your mom."

"What?" I squeal. "I would *never* take my own life! Nobody would believe that in a million years. Look, I won't say a word about the Brotherhood." At least not while an unsteady weapon is in my face. "Just drop the gun. This isn't worth it. What's happened so far have been accidents. What you're doing now? Um, yeah, that's called murder. And I don't think your stepdaddy's going to be too happy that his star player has to miss a game because he's in the big house for shooting someone."

"Don't sit there and judge me. You don't know what it's like living with my stepdad and his wonder child."

"And how does asking your friends to bungee jump in front of trains and shooting me fix any of that? Honestly, your little group is the dumbest thing I've ever heard of. Couldn't you get your boys to bond over something a little safer—like a campout or . . . some Guitar Hero?"

Jared wrenches my arm, his face contorted in rage. "Shut up! Nothing is going to get in my way!"

"Okay." I hold up my hands and slowly ease out of his grip and press myself into the back of the chair, wishing I could disappear into it. *God, I need some serious help here. What do I do? If there's a verse on dealing with psychopaths, I seem to have forgotten it. Totally need some guidance right now.*

"I've never been good enough for my stepdad. Can't ever measure up to Dallas. Well, I'm sick of being the loser. Our team's going to state this year. I *will* get a scholarship to play football, and then I'll leave this town and never look back."

I try for a softer approach. "I know it's been rough. I can't imagine what you've gone—"

My phone blasts in my pocket—the song I have programmed for Luke.

"Don't touch it!"

Think! "I . . . It's Luke Sullivan. I've been, um, seeing him."

Jared picks up the phone. "The theme from *Jaws?*"

"Yeah, we're going through a rough patch." I swallow. "This is the time he calls every night, and if I don't get it, he'll send out a search party. He'll know something's wrong." The phone continues to sing, and I feel my chance slipping through my fingers. "My stepdad's a wrestler. Do you really want him tracking me down right now?"

"Turn it on speaker. And get rid of him." He jerks the gun toward my cell. "Tell him you're okay. If you say one word, Bella, I will use this thing."

Please, God. I snap open the phone. "Luke?" I push a button and his voice fills the cabin.

"Where are you? I have some really important news. It wasn't—"

"—Charmin toilet paper in the school bathrooms like we'd thought? I *knew* it." I keep my eyes trained on Jared.

Get rid of him, he mouths. He moves the pistol closer.

"Um, Luke, *sweetie,* we'll talk about the story for the paper later, okay?"

"Bella, are you—"

"In fact, right now I have to let you go because I'm working on the *other* article. But I miss you." *Please find this believable, crazy boy with waving firearm.* "Talk to you soon." I start to disconnect, but Luke's voice stops me.

"Bel, just one more thing. The piece you're writing tonight.

Would that happen to be the bird-calling story or maybe the one about the dangers of making out in SUVs?"

"Hang up," Jared hisses. "Now."

"Bird calling!" My voice is chipper and light. "That's the one."

My lifeline to Luke is lost as Jared rips the phone from my hands and throws it across the room. "That's enough." He gestures to the paper. "Start writing."

"And then you're going to kill me?" Anger begins to replace fear. Who does this guy think he is?

"No, I'm not going to kill you." He reaches into the pockets of his cargo shorts and extracts a plastic bag. "But these pills will."

chapter thirty-nine

I would like to say that when I faced death I had all sorts of deep, inspirational thoughts. That poetry sprang from my lips, and God imparted timeless wisdom into my soul. That I greeted my imminent demise with grace and sweetness.

"Jared, you're a *moron*! Do you realize Fred Flintstone is in this bag? Are you planning on killing me with way too much vitamin C?"

He grabs the ziplock and looks inside. His face flushes red. "I didn't mean to grab those. There are just a few in there. I raided a bunch of medicine cabinets this week." His voice shakes like he's running out of steam.

"At least tell me what I'm taking. Besides a prehistoric multivitamin."

His eye twitches, as if I've offended him. Like I'm really worried about his feelings at this point. "Most are from my parents. The white ones are my mom's migraine pills. Those will make you really sleepy. And that's a good thing." Is he reassuring me or himself? "These purple ones are Dante's acne prescription."

My pulse slows. The roar in my head ebbs.

And some measure of peace fills me—because I don't think this is going to kill me.

Basically I'm going to take a really long nap and wake up with clear skin.

Jared continues to take the pills out and set them on the table. "My stepdad's antidepressants. Those are pretty good for stress."

I should probably eat those first.

"And his blood pressure meds." He sneers and I wonder how I ever thought he was cute. "Maybe if he'd back off on me, his numbers wouldn't be so high."

"I can't imagine him finding any fault with *you*." Hysterical laughter bubbles up like lava.

"Stop it!" He waves the gun like a slippery fish.

"Are these—" I pick up a pill and inspect it close. Then double over in giggles. "Birth control? You took somebody's birth control pills?" And this guy's in AP? "Is there a high risk of pregnancy on the way to the Pearly Gates?"

"I just grabbed stuff, okay?" he shouts. "Clearly I'm not cut out for this."

"No, hey." I touch his arm. "I think you're doing a *swell* job."

"Stop laughing." His hand cracks across my cheek.

My smile disappears and I taste blood.

"Oh, I'm sorry. Bella, I didn't mean to—" He rests the gun on the table, his hands grabbing my face, holding my cheek. "Please forgive me, I—"

I dive for the gun. My hands inches away. I can almost feel the cold metal on my fingertips.

"No!" He pushes me onto the floor, overpowering me with his

strength. When I pull myself back up, the gun is firmly in his grip. "Get back in the chair. You have a letter to write."

"There's still time to back out of this. You don't want to kill me."

"I'm not killing you. You're killing yourself."

"And if I don't take the pills?"

His jaw locks. "I'm responsible for the Brotherhood. Nobody is going to get in my way. Bella, you can either do this the easy way or the painful way. If you don't write the letter and swallow the pills, I will put this gun to your head and pull the trigger."

"And you'll go to prison for the rest of your life."

"No, I won't. I know exactly what I'm doing."

Yet he doesn't look certain at all. He looks scared—mixed with a little psycho. And a dash of nuts.

I must stall him. Surely Luke got my hint that we were at the cabin. And *surely* he went for help. Like Jake. Or the police. Or the National Guard.

"You realize Luke knows, don't you?"

"I suspected." He waves away the idea, like it's not worth discussion. "I'll deal with him later tonight."

"With what? Vitamin E and cough drops?"

Jared points the gun inches from my nose. "Enough talking! Pick up the pen."

It's not so much that I'm scared he'll actually pull the trigger. It's more about being scared of his shaking hands *accidentally* pulling the trigger. I don't want to die with an ugly eye. Even mortician's makeup can't hide this bruising. Nobody will walk past my casket and say, "Oh, doesn't she look natural?" They'll say, "It looks like markers pooped on her face."

"You need to start downing the pills. It will take awhile for them to kick in. Start with the white ones first."

For a full twenty seconds I don't move. I study the room. The distance to the door. The location of the nearest heavy object. The number of steps to the kitchen for a knife.

"Eat them!" Jared pounces on the table, grabs a handful of pills, and forces them into my mouth. I bite his hand, and he yelps. Then smacks my other cheek. "Get them out from under your tongue. Swallow them!"

He cocks the gun.

I force them down and my earlier confidence begins to fade. *God, please help me.*

Jared passes me his water bottle. "The letter should be simple. Make it to your mother. Tell her that you've missed New York so much that you can't go on. You're miserable."

What a coincidence—so are you.

"You miss your dad. Your friends. Your boyfriend." He stops. "You're cheating on your boyfriend with Luke?"

"Yes." My head bobs spastically. "I... um, just love the menfolk. Can't get enough of them." I can't stop nodding. "Love me some boys." And if I *don't* walk out of here alive tonight, they'll know something's up by my mention of Hunter in the letter. Like I'd miss that two-timing sleaze.

He gestures to the paper with his weapon, and I pick up the pen.

Dear Mother,
    This freak of nature is holding a loaded—

Jared rips the paper from the table and shreds it to pieces. He slams down a new piece. "I'm warning you, Bella." He thrusts another handful of pills into my palm. I somehow choke them down.

"How are you getting home?" I ask. "It's not like you can take my car."

His smile is something from a Stephen King novel. "Brittany Taylor."

"Oh." I scrape a film off my tongue with my teeth. "Isn't she sweet."

In between forced servings of meds, I scribble out my first paragraph, telling my mom how much I miss New York and that Truman brought me nothing but pain. Next I include instructions for taking care of my cat and other hints that this letter was forced.

I look up from my work and the room tilts to the left. That's not good. "Have you ever considered medication?"

I close my note, my writing growing sloppier by the letter.

I love you.

And then I add a line in case these really are my last words to my mother.

You were the best mom ever. Be happy with Jake. And tell Dad I love him—and he needs a new decorator.

I lift my pen. "What if these things don't kill me?"

Jared taps the barrel of the shiny gun.

I grab a few more white capsules. "I'm sure these will do me in nicely."

"Sign the note."

"I don't feel so well."

He pops some red tablets past my teeth, leaving my mouth so full I have to breathe through my nose.

God, I'm sorry for everything I've ever done. Forgive me for the way I treated Budge. For not giving Jake a chance. For hating every one of the bimbos my dad brings home.

I'm vaguely aware of tears slipping down my cheeks.

Forgive me for not getting involved in church here. For not being a good friend to Lindy. And for watching Sex and the City reruns.

"I . . ." Why won't my tongue work? "Can't . . . finish."

Jared places the pen in my fingers and picks up my hand. Together we make the first letter of my name.

The room swirls and twirls. Nap. I need to lay my head down. Oh, what pretty lights I see! I want to go to the pretty lights! Here I come! Who's that giggling? Is that me? Oh, I love to giggle!

"Hold the pen still!" Jared roars in my ear. But I don't care! "Finish the letter or I'll—"

A loud crash explodes to my right. The door.

And Luke's there. He's calling out something.

"Bella!"

How nice of him to come and visit. Helleww, Luke!

Look how fast he runs. Like a linebacker. Or is it a quarterback? A quarterliner?

Wait. The gun. Jared's raising the pistol.

Oh. That's not right.

Must. Stop him.

But so tired.

My legs—they're in cement. So heavy.

Focus, Bella. Focus. Move. Eye on the target. God, give me strength.

With all that I have left, I throw my body toward Jared. "Noooo!"

My limp form flops.

Flails.

Falls—right into Jared.

The gun goes off. So loud. Hurts my ears.

Luke dives onto Jared, his fist plowing through my captor's face.

Jared rolls over. He's out.

"Bella!" Luke scoops me in his arms. I hear more giggling. I think it's me. The sound—so far away.

His hands are all over me. *So not appropriate, young man.*

He lifts them to his face. Blood. *Ick, whose blood?*

"Luke . . ." The pretty lights are fading. It's getting dark. "No party tonight."

He pushes the hair from my face. "You saved my life. I came here to rescue you, and you saved my life. We got onto Jared's MySpace page from Zach's computer. Jared filmed every initiation. It was all there. I'm sorry I couldn't get to you in time."

I reach out a hand and pass my fingers over his lips. "You know, you're really not so bad. Hey . . . wanna make out?"

Luke's mouth smiles. His eyes don't. He holds me closer. Tighter. "Maybe later."

A siren. Why do I hear sirens? Maybe there's a parade. I do so love a good parade.

"Hang on, Bella. Please. Stay with me."

"Luke." Can't get my voice above a whisper. "The story—I want back on the story."

"Bella Kirkwood . . . I think you just *became* the story."

The blackness pools all around me. Snuffs out the twinkling lights.

It pulls me down.

And I let it take me away.

chapter forty

The casket is covered in a spray of wildflowers.

The soloist sings "I'll Fly Away." No instruments, just a voice.

There is sadness. Yet also a reluctant peace.

Sun filters through the trees, the light coming through the branches like a band of halos.

Death would have its day.

So life can begin again.

"Hand me a tissue," Budge says, his tie a stiff knot at his throat. "I have something in my eye."

With my good arm, I reach into my purse and pull out a Kleenex. He takes it and gifts me with a rare, small smile.

"Friends and family"—the pastor takes his place in front under the canopy—"we are gathered here today to celebrate the life of a son, a friend, and a football hero. Zachary Epps was this—and so much more."

My left shoulder throbs where Jared Campbell's gun left a bullet. It was just a week ago, but when I close my eyes, I still see it there, fresh and new in my mind. Though parts of it are foggy, like the ambulance ride. Getting my stomach pumped. The surgery to extract the bullet. But I remember the fear. And the chaos.

The preacher finishes and asks if anyone would like to say a few words.

Some of his teammates stand to their feet. Noticeably absent are Dante, Reggie Lee, that Adam guy, and, of course, my favorite kidnapper, Jared, who's looking at the world through some metal bars right now.

Next to speak is Kelsey. She still looks no wider than a pencil, but her voice is mighty and carries to the few hundred gathered. She speaks of love and loss and all that Zach was to her.

"Anyone else?" The preacher scans the crowd as Kelsey sits down. "Let us pray, then."

"I'd like to speak." Beside me Budge stands. I hear him swallow, and I say a quick prayer for him.

"Last year I lost my best friend. He loved his girlfriend, and he loved his family. And he loved that car." The crowd laughs, sharing a memory. "It could have been any of us. He made a mistake and got caught up. But the real Zach Epps would've wanted us to forgive. And live. Because if Zach knew how to do anything, it was live life to the fullest. And to be who we are—not who others want us to be." Budge blinks at moisture in his eyes. "I'll always carry that part of my friend with me. Always."

I can't help but smile as a small group from the Truman band breaks into "Free Bird." Only in Truman. But it fits.

I merge into the line and shake hands with Zach's family. When I get to Kelsey, she pulls me into a hug. "Thank you," she says. "Thank you." Tears flow unchecked, and she waves a hand in front of her face, unable to speak.

I hug her again. I don't need her words. Just the hope that she's going to rejoin the living. And I think she will.

Exiting the canopy, I spot Lindy with some friends, and I walk to them.

"How's the shoulder?" Lindy asks.

It hurts like someone's holding a blowtorch to it. "Not bad."

"Are you taking your pain pills?"

"Nah, something about forcibly puking them up last week makes me not want to down any more." Just the thought makes me want to barf. "I see you're wearing one of the dresses we bought in New York."

Lindy twists a piece of her flatironed hair. "As soon as I get home, it's Nikes and sweats."

"So how's Matt doing?"

"He's grounded for life for one thing."

"Still not ready to declare your undying love and adoration?"

She smiles, her lips a nice shade of Chanel pink. "He needs a good friend. And that's what I'll be." She winks. "For now."

"Bella Kirkwood?"

I turn around at the tap on my shoulder.

"I'm Pam Penturf. Carson's mom." She wrings a tissue in her hands. "I just wanted to thank you for what you did—exposing the truth about the football players." Her voice breaks, and I awkwardly pat her arm. "I couldn't believe my son would kill himself. It's haunted me, you know. I've carried that burden around, thinking what could I have done? How could I not have seen it?" She daubs at her eyes. "I feel like he can rest in peace now—like we all can. Anyway, I just wanted to express my gratitude." I'm wrapped in another hug. "You have no idea what you've done for me." She holds the tissue to her face and hurries away.

I spot Luke standing with another group. His eyes catch mine. He nods toward Mrs. Penturf and smiles.

I ride home with Budge. Even he didn't think driving a hearse to a funeral would be appropriate, so I have the pleasure of seeing him behind the wheel of my cute little Bug.

"Hey, where are you going?" Budge turns into a subdivision instead of heading toward our old dirt road.

"Gotta make a quick detour." He stops the car at a two-story house. "Won't take long." And he bails out of the Bug.

I lightly rub my shoulder, lean my seat back, and close my eyes. Minutes pass.

I jolt awake when my door flings open. Budge stands there. A cat in his arms.

My cat.

"Moxie!" I grab her and hold her close.

"Yeah, she's decided to come live with you again. I . . . um, seem to have been healed of my allergies."

I run my fingers through the cat's silky fur, a suspicious eye on my stepbrother. "Sounds miraculous."

He cracks a smile. "Amen, sister."

chapter forty-one

It's hard to digest a hot dog when you're looking at thirty- and forty-year-old men in spandex. Seriously.

"There's Dad!" Robbie claps his hands then whistles through his teeth at a volume that could shatter eardrums.

"Are you ready for a smackdown? Are you ready for a fight?" The crowd goes wild at the announcer's dramatic spiel. "Tonight in the Tulsa Athletic Arena, we present our regional champion—Captain Iron Jack!"

Our family stands and yells. I lift up a sign with one arm.

"Hold on to your popcorn as he takes on the force from Biloxi—Mississippi Mud!" A man in a hideous poop brown Onesie circles Jake on the stage.

"Did I miss anything?" Luke Sullivan fills the empty seat beside me, and I have to look twice.

"What are *you* doing here?"

My mom reaches over me, waves at her new hero, then returns to yelling for Captain Iron Jack.

"Your mother invited me. Wants me to do another feature in our paper."

"Fabulous," I droll. Images of him crashing through the cabin door and yelling my name flutter through my mind. A faint memory of him holding my hand in the ambulance. Waking up in the hospital and seeing his worried face.

"You know"—he leans in closer—"we haven't really had a chance to talk since everything happened."

Mmm, he smells good tonight. Or maybe I'm high on wrestler sweat fumes. Yes, that's definitely it.

"I just wanted to thank you for, um, you know, saving my life."

I laugh and roll my eyes. "It was the drugs. Had I been thinking clearly . . ."

He opens his ever-present messenger bag and pulls out a paper. "I just submitted this to a national contest—sponsored by Princeton University."

I look at the words. My article on the football scandal. "Are you serious?"

Luke nods his dark head. "It was a great piece, Bella. And when I read it, I learned something about you."

This ought to be good. I cross my arms and wait for the zippy insult. "And that is?"

"You . . . are a writer."

"I'm a—" I blink hard as the words circulate in my brain. Below us Jake twirls Mississippi Mud over his head.

"Writer." Luke's eyes shine brilliant blue in the dimmed lights. "I'm sorry I doubted you. I honestly didn't know you had it in you."

That makes two of us.

"This was your moment, Bella. You went through the fire and came out on the other side. I'm proud to have you on my newspaper staff."

His hand touches mine as I hand the paper back. "Do you say that to all the girls who save your life?"

Luke's laugh is rich and sends happy chill bumps along my skin. "Just you, Kirkwood. Only you."

"And thanks for rescuing me from Jared." My face flushes with heat. "It's not every day a guy breaks down a door for me."

My editor in chief winks. "Don't get used to it."

We watch the rest of the match, cheering and booing at all the right moments.

And life is all about right moments, isn't it?

Okay, so Truman isn't Manhattan. And I'll never get used to stepping around cow pies in the yard. Or being ten minutes late to school because the neighbor had to take his tractor for a ride.

And back in August I had no idea why God would punish me with this place, with this life. But like Luke said, I guess it was my moment. I was meant to be here all along. And who knows where this path will lead? Maybe by this time next month I'll have forgotten all about Macy's and Times Square and love nothing more than a trip to Target and peaceful walks through our pasture with Betsy the licking cow.

Yeah.

That is so not happening.

acknowledgments

Every book is a group effort. I couldn't do it without the help of so many in my life. I would like to thank:

My heavenly Father. I stay tired. I stay stressed. I stay hunched over a keyboard. But I also remain amazed and humbled and awed. Thank You for giving me the opportunity to share the coolness of Christ.

My family for putting up with my end-of-deadline moodiness and outrageous demands for food delivery and for reminding me to brush my hair and shower during the final weeks.

My friends for listening to me gripe about my family harassing me about showering and brushing my teeth.

My students who consistently come up to me and say, "Please put me in your book." It's so sweet. My next series will focus on a girl named KelseyRaynaKarlyKensleeJohnJamieCourtneyAllieSydney SueJayson. Should be a big hit.

All those who follow my blog at jennybjones.com. I appreciate you stopping by to read all about my snow addiction, my cat woes, my inability to turn away from fajitas, and other fascinating items from my thrilling life.

Acknowledgments

My lifelong hero, Carol Burnett. Though you will never read this, you are funny personified and made a huge impact on my life. Though I will always think the role of Annie should've gone to a young unknown named Jennifer Jones, I will forever hold you in the highest regard.

Everyone at Thomas Nelson for giving me a chance—a big chance. I'm so proud to be part of the team.

reading group guide

1. How does pride get in the way of Bella's picture of the "ideal" life? What are the events that humble her? Can you think of a time in your life when you learned a lesson through a humbling event?

2. Bella finds out she has a God-given talent for writing. What are your talents? How could you use your gifts for God? How could Bella? Just for fun, imagine if you could have any talent in the world, what would it be?

3. What would your advice be to Bella so she doesn't date a "Hunter" again?

4. Bella has a hard adjustment to make when she leaves her life in Manhattan for Truman, Oklahoma. What are some things she could have prayed for in order to prepare for that difficult change?

5. Bella does not come from a perfect family. Do you relate to that at all? What are some ways God sometimes challenges us with family issues?

6. Materialism is an idea that pops up a lot in this novel. Even if you're not rich as a rock star, this can be a trap. In what ways was

Bella materialistic? Now look at your own life. Do you have this in common with Bella?

7. Unlike Bella, Hunter is not a Christian. What are the dangers of dating a nonbeliever in your life? How did this not work out for Bella?

8. Bella often rebels against her mother's instruction. Why? Can you relate to this at all? (And who doesn't!)

9. Bella meets her friend Lindy by helping her out. Is it hard for you to meet new friends?

10. Bella found she had drifted away from the Lord. How do you think this happened? What are the reasons we sometimes get inconsistent with our time with God?

11. What kind of a role does our attitude play in being open to new opportunities?

12. One theme for the book is "things are not always what they seem." Can you describe the numerous ways this is evident in the book? What's the danger of taking things at face value?

13. A great verse to go along with Bella's life would be Jeremiah 29:11 which says:

For I know the plans I have for you," declares the LORD, "plans to prosper you and not to harm you, plans to give you hope and a future.

How is this verse relevant to the book, as well as your own life?

i'm so sure

This book is dedicated to my super handsome nephew, Hardy. You are the sweetest, smartest, niftiest boy in the world. And I cannot believe your dad, who used to "accidentally" punch me in the nose and make me his wrestling guinea pig, could have a son as perfect as you. I love you!

chapter one

That dirty rotten cheater.

I lower my binoculars and swap them for a camera. A moment like this needs some megapixel proof. The lens zooms closer and closer on my target. I shove my way farther into the bushes of the Truman City Park and aim toward the old tennis court, where the loser twines himself around a girl who is definitely *not* his girlfriend. Leaning over and balancing on one leg, I angle my body and get the perfect shot. One more close-up to seal the deal.

"Hello, Bella Kirkwood."

With a squeal and a jerk, I topple over and crash into the shrubs.

Spitting dried leaves, I glare at the boy standing over me. "Hey, Chief."

As the sun shines behind him, the editor of the Truman High *Tribune* smiles, and for a moment I forget that I'm sprawled in a small tree with limbs poking me in very uncomfortable places.

Luke Sullivan is delish. Except for his attitude. And his arrogance. And his broodiness. And his genius IQ that makes me feel like I have all the intellect of a gerbil.

"What are you doing?" With his hand on mine, he pulls me upright and I'm catapulted straight into his chest.

"Working." I take a step back. "Mindy Munson hired me to find out if her boyfriend was cheating." I jerk my head toward the couple making up their own game on the court. "I'd say we have a definite love violation here."

"So you're taking pictures of a guy without his permission. Don't you think that's a little creepy? A little unethical?"

I consider the idea. "Not so much."

"This has got to stop. Ever since we busted the football team, people think you're Nancy Drew."

It's true. When you get kidnapped by the leader of a deadly football gang, and said leader tries to permanently erase you from the planet, people think you're the stuff. And when you walk away from the attempted murder with your head still intact, folks start to think you're some sort of sleuthy hero.

Oh, the many perks of almost dying. I've spent the last two months tracking down stolen iPods, cheating boyfriends, a drill team stalker, and one lost bullfrog by the name of Mr. Toady Pants.

Not only does it keep me busy, it keeps me in shoes. Hey, the Prada fairy doesn't visit me like she used to. I do what I must.

"Did you finish the article I assigned?" Now Luke's all business.

"I'm working here. According to my watch the school day has been over for an hour, and believe it or not, I do have a life outside of the paper. What are you doing here anyway? If you're so hard up for female company that you have to follow me around, maybe you should give Mindy Munson a call." I throw a look at her loser boyfriend. "My keen reporter's instinct says she'll be on the market by tonight."

A corner of his mouth twitches; then he tilts his head and pierces me with those ocean blue eyes. "Who says I'm on the market?"

I blink. "Um . . . because I've never seen you with a girl. I realize I'm new to detective work and all, but unless your lady is invisible, she—"

"She's at Harvard." He picks a leaf from my jacket. "Freshman. And no, we don't see much of each other, but she should be in for Christmas."

Why do I suddenly feel like a deflated balloon? "You never mentioned her."

He grins, revealing perfectly straight teeth. "You never asked."

A chilly wind blows, and my chestnut hair reassembles itself into a new formation. Luke reaches out and tucks a wayward strand back into place, his fingers sliding across my ear.

"Get that shot!"

I jump as a flash explodes in my face. As three men surround us, Luke pushes me behind his back.

A squatty man sporting a Donald Trump comb-over steps forward. "Can we get another one of you and your boyfriend?"

I peek around Luke. "*What?* Who are you?" I shove Luke's protective hands away and plant a fist at my hip. "And this isn't my boyfriend." Why am I explaining here?

"Doesn't matter—just move in closer. These will be great promo shots."

"Drop the camera and leave her alone." Luke steps toward the guy. The boy may be tall and wiry, but he's a beast on the soccer field, so he's got some muscles on that frame.

"We just need a few more pics of the girl. Maybe you two could huddle up again?"

I gasp. "We were *not* 'huddled up.'" Though we have kissed once. But it was just to escape the deranged football players. I barely remember it. Just a dim, faded . . . totally hot memory. Donald Trump snaps another picture. "I don't know who you are, but how dare you spy on me and take my picture without my permission!"

Luke quirks a dark brow my way, then returns his stare to Mr. Comb-over. "Who are you?"

The short man shoves his card in Luke's hand. "Marv Noblitz. I work for WWT."

"Who?" No clue what that is.

Luke studies the card. "World Wrestling Television."

Though it's a vague fog swirling in my mind, I feel trouble beginning to take shape. "I think you might be looking for my step-dad." He's known as Captain Iron Jack on the amateur wrestling circuit. But I just call him Stepdaddy Spandex.

"We're looking for the entire family."

A horror movie soundtrack begins to play at full volume in my head. The kind of tune that pounds out right before things get ugly and the fake blood spews. "Look, Mr. Noblitz, Jake's the wrestler. Whatever you're working on, I didn't sign up for it."

"It's a reality show—*Pile Driver of Dreams*." He chuckles. "And you didn't have to sign up—your stepdad did that for you."

"Huh?" My brain tingles with dread.

"Get ready, kid." He pulls out a cigar and sticks it in his mouth. "Hope you're prepared to live your life in front of millions, because we're going to follow you and your family for months. You'll barely take a tinkle that we won't be there with a camera."

I stand there mute. Frozen.

Luke pats me on the back, his face grim. "Looks like Hollywood's knocking on your door."

I sigh and close my eyes. "Yeah, well somebody needs to tell Hollywood Bella Kirkwood is *not* at home."

chapter two

With a camera crew on my tail, I speed through downtown, blaze through some dirt roads, and lose them with a couple of detours near Old Man Peterson's farm. It will buy me at least a few minutes.

I barely put my lime green VW Bug in park before I leap out, oblivious to the biting December chill.

"Mo-*ther!*" Ever since my mom moved us from Manhattan to marry her factory-working, wrestler wannabe, life has been nuts—at best. But *this* is going too far!

"Mom!" Touring the house, I find her, Jake, and my little stepbrother, Robbie, in our newly remodeled kitchen. Laughing. Like life is fine.

Mom cuts into a roll of cookie dough. "Hey, sweetie. We were—" Her knife freezes. "What's wrong?"

Oh, the list. It's too long.

I try to break it down. "Um . . . Jake. Wrestler. Reality show. Surprise. Cameras. Me." Then I just wail.

Mom runs to me and pulls me into a seat. "Calm down, Bella. How do you know about that?"

My mouth drops. "The question is *why* didn't I know sooner?

Like *before* I got all Britney Speared with the camera crew?" Let the record show, I totally had underwear on.

"A few months ago I saw on TV where they were scouting for ten wrestlers for a reality show. So I sent in Jake's application."

Jake's arm slinks around my mom. "We had a one-in-a-million shot of making it."

My laugh is bitter. "With your luck with the odds, I wish you'd bought a lotto ticket instead. Your camera crew should be here any minute."

Jake lets out a shout, then grabs my mom and twirls her around the kitchen. My six-year-old stepbrother takes the opportunity to run circles around them, his Superman cape flying behind. Their whooping happiness makes me want to hurl.

Okay, so maybe most girls would think it would be nifty-cool to have a camera crew in your house and be on TV once a week. But not me. Not when it is centered around your stepfather's attempts at wrestling. The head of our household will be seen shirtless. In spandex. And a pirate costume. He says *aargh*, for crying out loud! I will never be able to hold my head up. And my own dad is going to flip. Though he's been a guest commentator on *E! News* a lot as a plastic surgeon to the stars, he's never been able to get his own show. And now my stepdad gets on TV—just for doing a really good body-slam.

The doorbell rings, and Jake and Mom rush to open it.

Budge, my other stepbrother, takes that moment to come down the steps. In his Wiener Palace sultan uniform, no less. "What's going on?" The feathers on his turban droop.

Budge and I were sworn enemies from day one. But ever since I lifted the lid on the craziness that killed his best friend last fall,

Budge has been extremely nice to me. We talk all the time. Like last week he said, "Hey, moron, can you pass the milk?"

That's some good progress.

"You'd better call the Wiener Palace and tell them you'll be late." I jerk my thumb toward the three men standing in the entryway. "You're not even going to believe this. Your dad's been selected to be on a wrestling reality show. And we're part of the deal. Basically our lives will be on TV for millions to see. No privacy. No control over their manipulative editing. The entire world watching our every move."

Budge shakes his head. "Dude, that is—"

"Humiliating, embarrassing, and intrusive?"

"C*ooool.*" He scratches his red 'fro. "I'm gonna be on TV. Chicks *love* stars. This is gonna be awesome."

Awesomely horrible.

An hour later we're all stuffed into our outdated, 1970s living room. I sit on one end of the orange couch beside a beaming Mom and Jake.

"So I think we've got everything settled. Just have your management look over the contract and give me a call." Mr. Noblitz shakes Jake's giant hand.

"I need to talk to my family first," my stepdad says. "I'll let you know what we decide."

When the door shuts on Mr. Noblitz, Jake gets down to business. "Why don't we pray about this?" He reaches for my mom's hand. She reaches for Robbie's.

Budge and I stare at each other. *Fine.* I clasp his wrist with two of my fingers and bow my head.

At Jake's amen, Mom begins. "This is an amazing opportunity."

My stepdad beams. "Jillian's right. This could take me straight to the top in professional wrestling. But it's going to be an invasion for all of us."

"Who cares?" Budge says. "I'm in."

"Me too!" Robbie squirts invisible Spider-Man webs across the room. Though he leans toward Superman, my stepbrother likes to incorporate all superheroes in his daily routine.

"Bella?" Mom asks.

What else can I say? "I am not totally thrilled about this . . . but okay."

While my mother throws an impromptu party downstairs, I steal away to my room and shut the door on all the madness.

God, I know this is great for Jake's career, but what about me? What could possibly be the purpose in all this? Oh, sure, our family could be a witness to the wrestling community. But couldn't we just send them some tracts?

I fall back onto my bed and stare at the ceiling. My cat Moxie bounds onto my stomach and butts my chin with her face.

My phone rings and I answer without even looking at it. "My life just got flushed down the toilet, Bella speaking."

Familiar laughter fills my ear. "Bel?"

I sit up. *No. Couldn't be.*

He wouldn't dare.

"Bella, you there?"

He did. My rat-fink-cheater ex-boyfriend called me.

"What do you want, Hunter?"

"Don't hang up. I just want to talk."

"So talk."

"Wow. I've missed that sweet voice."

"Hunter, did you need something?"

Seconds of silence. "I miss you." He laughs. "I'm totally blowing this. I . . . just wanted to talk to you again. I miss, um, you know, hanging out. I miss us."

"Really? Every time I miss us, I think about you all kissy-faced with my best friend."

"That was just a moment of insanity. I was lonely when you left New York. Mia and I—we're over. We were never anything to begin with."

"Oh, okay. That makes it all better. Well, thanks for calling and telling me that. Gotta go—"

"Wait!" He sighs into the phone. I picture him in his room, running his hands through his thick hair. "I know I said too much. Look, Bel, I just want to be friends again. You have every right to hate me."

"I don't hate you." *I wish rabid pigs would carry you away, but there's no hate.*

"I have something else to tell you."

Oh, boy.

"I have, um, a disease."

"Ew! Well, that's what you get for being such a male ho."

"Not *that* kind of disease. This is . . . more serious. It's not good."

"What?" Okay, cancel the pigs. "Are you going to be okay?"

"It's treatable. But it's going to be a long haul and nothing is certain. Bel, I just . . . it's really important that I make everything right in my life."

"Hunter, I forgive you. We've gone over this."

"It's not enough."

I close my eyes and breathe. *Fine.* "Whatever you need, Hunter. I'm here."

"I was hoping you'd say that. I'll see you tomorrow."

"Tomorrow?"

"Bella, I'm in Oklahoma."

chapter three

"Happy Tuesday, Truman Tigers! It's time for your morning announcements!"

I tune out the student on the TV and doodle my name in curlicues on my notebook. I should be studying my notes, but I'm busy replaying Hunter's call in my head.

A movement catches my eye outside the door, and I see Lindy Miller, all wide-eyed and spastic hands, gesturing for me to come into the hall. Lindy ducks when Mrs. Palmer glances in her direction.

I make my way to the front of the classroom. "Um, Mrs. Palmer? Can I go blow my nose outside?"

She puts down her pen and frowns. "You can't do that in here?"

"I tend to make goose honks when I blow."

She waves me away and returns her attention to the student news program.

I grab a Kleenex and sail out the door. "What is it?"

Lindy looks like she just missed the game-winning shot. "I . . ." She covers her red face. "It's bad, Bella. It's really bad."

My heart drops to my toes. "Tell me."

"The class president moved today!"

Oh.

"Er, sorry." I pat her on the shoulder. "I didn't know you and Harry Wu Fong were that close."

"No!" she hisses. "Don't you get it? We have, like, three months until prom. The class president is in charge of that. With him gone, the vice president takes his place. And—"

"You're the VP." It all makes sense now. A few months ago, my tomboy friend Lindy got a total makeover. Kicky haircut, golden highlights, waxed brows, new clothes. All to impress her BFF Matt, who still has no idea she wants to be more than friends. Though she rarely wears the makeup I bought her, she still looks great. But she has *no* idea what to do with making anything pretty—like an entire prom. She hates froufrou stuff. Why she's friends with me, I'll never know.

"No, I'm not the VP. Now I'm the stinkin' president!" She wrings hands that can grip a basketball with no problem. "I don't know how to organize a prom. Harry Wu left me his notes, but aside from reserving the Truman Inn banquet room, there's nothing done, and prom is practically tomorrow!"

"Relax, would you? You have plenty of time. And you know I'll help you. Plus, I'm pretty sure you have a prom committee or something, right?"

"I have minions?" She relaxes a little. "This might not be so bad. I totally get to boss people around, don't I? How hard could prom planning be anyway?"

"It will be fine. I organized lots of formal events at Hilliard." That's my old private school in Manhattan. My former best friend, Mia, still goes to school there. This is the same *friend* I caught making out with Hunter not so long ago. I was always willing to share anything with Mia—purses, shoes, a new hat. But my boyfriend's lips? A girl has to draw the line somewhere.

Confident that Lindy is over her panic attack, I return to class. Mrs. Palmer lifts a brow as I pass by. "Took you quite a while."

"Major drainage."

On my way to journalism class, I make a pit stop at the girl's bathroom and touch up my face. It's become a ritual. Reapply gloss, give my hair a shake, and make sure nothing is dangling from my nose. It's not that I care what Luke thinks. Seriously, I don't.

Maybe a little. But I'd never go out with him.

Mr. Holman, the newspaper advisor, intercepts me at the classroom door. "In my office, please."

I trail behind him and find Luke already seated.

And ticked.

His arms are crossed, and he glares at me over his tortoiseshell glasses. His inky black hair is slightly mussed, like he's run frustrated hands through it.

I sit down in the vacant seat beside Luke, while Mr. Holman perches on the corner of his desk. "Bella, you've done some topnotch investigative reporting for the paper."

"Oh." I nod demurely. "Thanks." Take *that* Luke Sullivan!

Mr. Holman casts a furtive glance at Luke then continues. "I'd like to have you writing your own column. We decided that a regular feature on teen life in Truman would be a nice angle. Maybe start with a series on the life of a working student. We think that would be a great idea."

"*We* didn't think so. Mr. Holman did." Luke breathes through his nose like a bull ready to charge. "You've only been on staff since

August. You still need to work on the basics, in my opinion. You're not ready for your own column."

My spine stiffens, and I feel my cheeks flush pink. "I think I can handle it."

Luke rolls his eyes. "This will not be some fluff piece. It's serious. This isn't *Seventeen* magazine. We're a reputable paper. We have—"

"Colleges watching us. I know." Boy, do I know. I hear that mantra in my sleep.

Mr. Holman stands up and wipes at a jelly stain on his shirt. "We'll announce it on the morning news program and give the students an opportunity to e-mail you with their ideas and work stories."

I can't help but smile. "Sounds great. Thank you."

"Mr. Holman?" Another staff member sticks her head in the door. "I need you to check my copy."

He rests his hand on my shoulder. "We'll start this tomorrow. It will be a great addition to the paper. Really liven things up." Mr. Holman walks out of the office and into the small class.

The tension stays behind.

The fluorescent lights hum. The heater blows. The clock ticks.

But Luke Sullivan doesn't move.

I gather my things and rise. "Alrighty then. Just gonna get started on—" Suddenly he's at the doorway, blocking my exit. I catch a hint of his cologne.

"If you were truly interested in being a serious journalist, you would know that you need to stick with the basics and continue building your skills. This isn't like the little advice column you wrote at your old school."

Little? "Since when is helping people *little?*" Ugh, sometimes, this boy. One minute he's got my skin tingling with his charm, and the next he's barking orders like a drill sergeant, and I want to kick his shins. Jerk.

His eyes bore into mine. "I won't cut you any slack on your deadlines."

"Nobody asked you to."

"And you realize you'll need a job. A few of them, in fact. You'll need to make the arrangements and get local businesses to hire you temporarily."

"Yeah, I was totally going to work that angle. I know you're really busy with your Harvard girlfriend, so don't worry about me monopolizing any of your time." Omigosh! Did I just say that? Rewind! Rewind!

His left cheek dimples. "Are you jealous?"

"No, actually I'm sad." I give a slight smile. "For her. I can't imagine what it's like to go out with you. You probably tell her what to order on your dates. Or maybe you woo her by reading aloud from the *Wall Street Journal.*"

"Wouldn't you like to know?" Luke leans over me until there are mere inches between us. "Have fun joining the working class." And he walks out.

"I—I will!" *Take that.*

Okay, if it weren't for the fact that he saved my life last quarter, I'd really let him have it. But no, he simply *had* to show up at just the right moment and rescue me from a homicidal football player intent on killing me. I totally could've handled it myself.

All right, so I was drugged to the point of drooling and on my way to permanent nappy-time, but whatever. I would've figured something out.

Lunch rolls around, and before I can beeline to the caf, I hear my name on the school intercom. *Great. What now?* Maybe the principal wants to talk to me about my ideas to redecorate the building. It's in serious need of a makeover. A little style would help everyone's test scores.

I push through the office door and the secretary greets me. "You've got a visitor."

I turn around and there in a torn vinyl seat is Hunter Penbrook.

For a minute I remember what I first saw in him. His dashing good looks. His impeccable dress. His sense of fun.

But then he cheated on me. And now he's just a picture on my bulletin board for target practice.

He stands up. "Bella, it's good to—"

"What do you want, Hunter?" I grab his hand and lead him outside to the courtyard. I motion for him to sit on a picnic table while I remain standing.

"Thank you for meeting with me."

"Who are you staying with? Why are you here?"

"My dad had some business in Tulsa, so I took the rental car for the day. We're leaving tonight, but I had to talk to you."

"Uh-huh. So tell me about this medical condition you have."

He shakes his head and looks away. "I really don't want to talk about it. They think something is seriously wrong with my stomach, but don't have any clue what it is yet. I've been to the ER a few times. My dad is making them run every test known to man."

"But you could die?"

He shrugs it off. "There are a lot of things uncertain right now. But Bel, I want to make things right in my life." His hand rests on my arm. "I needed to tell you in person that I'm sorry for all the hurt I caused you."

Right now I'm kind of regretting the darts sticking out of his eyes on my bulletin board. "I've forgiven you." Okay, I haven't forgotten it, but when you see your best friend's face mashed to your boyfriend's, it's a little hard. "Maybe you just need to forgive yourself."

His smile is weak. "How do you do that? How do you just forgive somebody for totally devastating you?"

"I wouldn't say devastate."

"I cheated on you with Mia and ripped your heart open—"

"More like a slight snag. A paper cut."

"—and you just forgive me?"

I really want to roll my eyes here. "Yup. It's kind of what you're supposed to do."

Hunter's hand drops away, and he watches the lunch activity around us. Students play basketball. A couple shares a Powerade and some nachos. "I want that. I want what you have, Bel."

I snap to attention. "Well, you can't have it. Your all-access pass to Bella Kirkwood has expired."

He opens his mouth, then closes it, as if struggling for words. "I mean . . . I'd like to understand your faith better." Hunter meets my eyes. "I think I need that in my life."

I've made a lot of mistakes in my relationship with Hunter. One would be dating him in the first place. Hunter is not a Christian. I knew this. Knew I wasn't supposed to go fishing for a boyfriend in unsaved waters. And there might've been some other mess-ups, but if God can wipe my slate clean, why rehash?

"So you're here in Truman because you want me to tell you about Jesus?"

Hunter rubs a hand over his face. "Honestly, I don't know. I just felt compelled to see you. Like I've been led here this week."

"I don't really know what to say."

He tightens his jacket around him. "I know this is all really awkward. Maybe I shouldn't have come. I won't be back...I'm sorry." And he walks away.

Sometimes being a good person is a serious pain.

I run after him. "Hunter, wait." My arm reaches out, clinging to him until he turns around. "Don't go yet."

"I just need a friend, Bella. That's all I'm asking."

I slowly nod. "Okay."

And he enfolds me in a hug.

I allow myself the moment, remembering how I used to love these arms, these hugs. His smell. His strength.

Hunter breaks away, his eyes wide. "What is *that*?"

I follow the direction of his finger and blanch. "Nooo."

There across the street is a two-man camera crew.

"Bella, what is that?"

I give my back to the camera. "*That* is the end of life as I know it."

chapter four

It's hard to have a mature conversation with someone in a spandex onesie.

"I have cameras following me around."

Jake looks up from his choke hold in the middle of the wrestling ring. "We've talked about this. Marv Noblitz told us what to expect."

"Hi, Bella. Good day at school?" This from the man whose head is trapped in the crook of Jake's arm.

"Hey, Squiggy." Squiggy Salducci is actually John Pederson, but that doesn't make for a good name in the ring. His persona is a nerd, complete with high-waisted pants and dork glasses. He calls himself "the intellectual wrestler."

"Jake, I just didn't expect it to be so intrusive."

He laughs as he pins Squiggy to the mat. "If you think that's bad, just wait 'til the crew sets up in the house."

Yeah, I have tried to block those details out. I'm in reality show denial.

"The main focus will be on me, Bella. Don't worry too much about it." Jake releases Squiggy from the floor. "Hey, Luke. Right on time."

Turning around, I find my editor-in-chief approaching. His eyes land on me briefly before turning their full focus on Jake. "Are you ready for the match this weekend?" he asks my stepdad.

"It's the first round of elimination for the show. I think I'm ready." Jake shakes Luke's hand.

"What are you doing here?" I ask.

"Covering the reality show for the local paper. Sometimes I work freelance for them. That way I can run the stories in the Truman High *Tribune* too."

"How convenient. Who called you?"

"Your mom."

Perfect.

"Who's the guy you were talking to at lunch?" he asks.

Oh, just my boyfriend. He goes to Princeton. "An old friend. Jealous?"

Luke smiles. "No. Just needed to know if this was someone of interest for the show."

"I'm headed to the diner. You boys have fun talking." I throw my bag over my shoulder and walk away. "And Jake, if you want a real writer, you know where I live."

I think Sugar's Diner was new sometime when Lincoln was in office and women still wore corsets. Any updates to the Truman establishment were made in the fifties, and things haven't changed since. Pink walls. Jukebox. Red barstools.

When I swing open the door of Sugar's, I find my mom on one of these barstools. She has a cup of coffee in one hand and a pencil in the other. My mother used to be a Manhattan socialite. That was before Dad traded her in for a newer model. She went from the country club in New York to the blue plate special in Truman.

I sidle up beside her. "Whatcha doing?"

"Hey, sweetie." She gives me a side hug and brushes the hair out of my eyes. "Just going over the family budget."

"Yeah, about that. No more off-brand deodorant please. My pits know the difference."

She laughs, but it's short-lived as her face grows serious. "Want a milk shake?"

Anxiety does the rumba in my stomach. "You only offer me a shake when something's wrong. Spill it."

Mom chews on the end of her pencil before tucking it into her blonde ponytail. "Talked to your father today."

That's never good. The two have nothing in common now but me. And Dad only calls Mom when there's something bad he needs to communicate to me but doesn't have the guts to do it himself. Dad is a brilliant plastic surgeon. But when it comes to parenting, he's as effective as a crooked nose job.

She blows on her coffee. "Your dad has run into some financial troubles."

"But he has an accountant."

"Not anymore. Seems she took his money and left for an undisclosed location. Your dad is in pretty hot water with the IRS."

"Didn't he check the accountant's credentials?"

"I think thirty-six–D was all he needed to know." Mom rolls her shoulders and looks me square in the eye. "This means no more under-the-table daddy payouts for you. Your days of visiting him and maxing out his credit card are over."

Mom believes we should *all* live on her and Jake's income, so my child support checks get put into a trust. I think it's the stupidest idea ever. But it hasn't been *that* bad because I do get in some serious shopping when I visit Dad once a month. I had high hopes for some splurging this weekend in Manhattan.

"Bella, you're seventeen. I think you know what this means. It's time to live like other people your age."

"I have to get my purses off eBay?"

"You need to get a job."

"I'm already on it."

My mom just stares.

"Seriously. I got my own regular feature in the *Tribune*, and I have to write a series of articles on the working teenager." I roll my brown eyes. "It should be one swell time."

"A little part-time work won't be so bad. Something to give you some spending money. Besides, it's going to be good for you."

"That's what you said about the Raisin Bran this morning." Ew.

"Logan works." She's referring to my stepbrother, who is also seventeen. Everyone on the planet calls him Budge but my mom.

"I'm not sure where I'll work, but I do know I am *not* serving hot dogs at the Wiener Palace." I have my pride. "But as far as Dad's money issue is concerned, I'm sure he will have this all cleared up soon." And I'll be back in business with the occasional shopping sprees.

Mom stands up and stretches her back. She grabs her order pad and sticks it in her apron. "You can talk to him about that this weekend."

Dolly O'Malley busts through the kitchen doors with an ample hip and an armload of shopping bags. Like my mom, she's a waitress. Unlike my mom, who still drips the occasional coffee and drops a plate a week, Dolly waitresses with as much finesse as a prima ballerina.

"What's in the bags?" I ask.

Dolly's face glows beneath her too-pink blush, and she looks to my mom. "I need your opinion. We know it's a boy, so do I go with a blue crib set?" She holds up a small quilt the color of a robin's egg. "Or maybe something more neutral like yellow?"

"Who's having a baby?" I reach for the yellow comforter as Mom hands me a chocolate-and-banana shake.

Dolly takes a deep breath and grins. "I am!"

I nearly spew ice cream out my nose. "What?" I look back and forth between my mom and her friend. "But you're single . . . and you're, like"—*fifty or something old like that*—"so mature."

Dolly gives her big, blonde hair a toss, a pointless act since it hasn't moved since 1985. "I'm only forty-six."

My mom swats my arm with a towel. "Dolly is adopting. A young woman at church contacted her last month about taking the baby."

"It was such a God thing. I wasn't even considering anything like having any more children." Dolly brushes her hand over a soft baby blanket.

Once upon a time Dolly was married to Mickey Patrick, who happens to be Jake's manager and trainer. Their two young daughters were killed in a car accident a long time ago—with Mickey at the wheel. He moved out not long after that, and let's just say Truman is too small a town for two ex-spouses to avoid each other.

I'm still trying to wrap my mind around someone offering Dolly a baby. "So this woman is pregnant and saw you one day, and thought you were the rightful mother?"

"I used to work with her mother here at Sugar's. The girl's only nineteen. She's got a long way to go before she gets her life together. The father's out of the picture, she's living with her mother, and she has no job. She's in no condition to raise a child."

"Congratulations," I say for lack of anything else. "You'll be a great mom. Hey, you know what else would be great?"

Both women raise their brows, suspicious of my segue.

I plunge on. "It would be supercool if you could get me an after-school job here, Dolly. Maybe you could talk to the manager?"

She cracks her gum. "Sorry, kid. We don't need any help. But I guess I could use some assistance out at my farm."

Dolly's farm is more like a ranch. It's a total mystery to me. She's worked as a waitress for years, yet she has a house and property any movie star would be envious of. She must make some really nice tips.

"Uh. Okay. I go to my dad's this weekend. Can I start next Monday?"

"I'll warn the livestock." She glances over the counter at my ballet flats. "And don't show up in those."

chapter five

~~Having a job can be so stressful for a teen. Last year I babysat for three hours, and I—~~

~~Most Truman High students know what it's like to chase that dollar. This past summer, I sold two pair of my Jimmy Choos to a less fortunate friend and~~

I delete my lame attempts at my first article on teen occupations. What do I know about working? Other than doing a little detective work for some cash, I've never had a job. This is not going to be as easy as I thought.

Luke walks by, and I try to look busy. "Are things not going well?" His face shows zero ounce of concern.

"Things are going fine, thank you very much. I am *loving* the idea of having my own weekly column."

He sits on the edge of the table. "Have you finished the other assignment I gave you? You know, the new weekly assignment doesn't replace the other reporting duties. Just adds to it."

"I'm aware of that." I plaster a smile on my face. "Check your in-box."

He leans a little closer. "You should be happy I sent you on assignment."

"Sending me to the band's oboe concert of Mariah Carey hits is not exactly what I'd call field reporting."

"Oboe players have a story to tell too. Speaking of stories, are you going to be at tonight's wrestling match? I wanted you to get me in to see Jake before it started. I have a few pre-match questions for him."

"I'm leaving for my dad's right after school." I click on the Internet and pretend to search for jobs online.

Luke peeks over my shoulder, blatantly reading my screen. "If you're lucky you'll find a job that utilizes your skills with hair, makeup, and shopping."

I bite back a retort as Mr. Holman approaches. But that *would* be totally cool.

"Just the two I wanted to speak with." He lays a hand on Luke's shoulder. "Luke, I looked over the preliminary notes on the wrestling reality show. I think it's going to be a great piece."

Luke sits straighter. "Thank you, sir."

"But I think we'd be remiss if we didn't take advantage of Bella's insight here. I mean she is *living* this reality show. Why not put her on the story too?"

Fiery blue eyes zero in on me. "I've got it covered, Mr. Holman. I can handle the story. Have I ever let you down?"

"Of course not. I just think we can run companion pieces here. Your take from the outside, and Bella's take from the inside." He slaps Luke on the back. "Okay, good conversation. Let's talk again soon. Bella, can I see you in my office?" Mr. Holman walks away.

You couldn't burn through the tension with a flatiron. I ease out of my seat and squeeze by Luke. "I guess he thinks I'm cut out for more than band recitals." And humming a Mariah tune, I go get the details on my assignment.

At lunch I take my tray and sit next to Lindy Miller and Matt Sparks. My salad tastes like grass, and I look longingly at Matt's cheese fries. The boy plays football and basketball and works out about four hours a day. He could eat a whole vat of cheese sauce if he wanted to.

I pick at a purple thing in my salad. "Did you guys know Luke Sullivan has a girlfriend?"

"Dude, she's hot." This from Matt, who probably thinks anything with boobs is hot.

"Did you know she goes to Harvard?" asks Lindy.

I stab a bite. "Yeah. Seems like I heard that."

"Luke said she's going to be in soon for Christmas break," Matt says.

"Hey, guys." Anna Deason slides her long, chocolate-colored legs into the last remaining seat at the table, her cheerleading skirt fanning around her. "Lindy, when are the nominations open for prom queen? I think this could be my year." Anna is a grade older than us and has been talking about her senior prom since August. Or maybe since kindergarten.

Lindy bites into an apple and shrugs. "I don't know. I, um . . ."

"The race for prom king and queen is not something to put off. It's important to this school. It's a long-held tradition that must be continued." Anna grabs a carrot stick. "Plus my Grandma Ruby's already bought me a dress."

Lindy looks to me for help. I focus on squeezing more ranch on my salad.

"We're having a class meeting next week. We'll get some prom details settled then. We have plenty of money to work with, so you know it's going to be a sweet event." Lindy proudly nods at her first official statement as class president.

"And make sure there's some good food there." Anna scrunches her nose. "None of the pizza roll things like last year. Those things are just nasty."

The entire cafeteria grows quiet, and I lower my fork. Mr. Sutter, the principal, walks down the rows of tables, eyeing every student.

"Uh-oh." Matt frowns. "He never comes in here. Somebody's in some deep dookie."

My pulse speeds as the principal comes closer and closer to where we sit. I scan my brain and review the last month. Does he know I used my cell phone this morning? Is calling Barney's in NYC to hold a pair of shoes really a crime? Because if it is, I would totally suffer detention for it.

Mr. Sutter stops at our table. He eyes every one of us, and I feel my skin grow hot. I might've clogged the toilet yesterday and not told a janitor. Sometimes I use too much toilet paper and don't know when to stop.

"Anna Deason, you need to come with me."

Anna's dark cheeks stain pink. "Why?"

"Because I asked you to, that's why. You have some explaining to do, young lady, and I don't think you want to do it in front of two hundred witnesses."

"Anything you have to say to me, you can say right here. I didn't do anything. I'm a straight-A cocaptain of the cheerleading squad. I don't do bad stuff." Her voice is rising. "I made a thirty-four on my ACT. I'm in select choir. I did *not* do anything wrong."

The principal lowers his voice to a growl. "Miss Deason, right now you are doing something wrong, and that is disobeying my directive. I have asked you nicely to follow me to the office. If you refuse again, my next option is to have you physically removed."

"Lead me there." Anna grabs my arm on her way up. "But I'm taking representation."

"Me?" I squeak.

"I have the right to my own counsel, and you're it."

The principal rolls his eyes and storms ahead.

"Sit down," he orders as we enter his cave-like office. You'd think the top dog of the school would at least get a window. No wonder he's in a bad mood all the time. He never gets to see the sun. He's like a character from *Twilight*.

"Miss Deason, the funds in the junior class account are missing. Would you like to tell me what you know?"

"How should I know? I'm a senior." Anna stands up. "They'd better find them though, because I've been waiting my whole life to be Truman prom queen."

Mr. Sutter drums his knobby fingers on the fake wood desk. "I had a nice long conversation with the president of the Truman National Bank this morning. He informed me that yesterday evening one of our accounts was cleared out to the tune of seven thousand dollars. And do you know where the money showed up?"

Anna and I both shake our heads.

"In a personal account under the name of Anna Deason."

"What?" she gasps. "That's a lie! How would I get the money out of the school account?"

"You did make a thirty-four on your ACT."

"It was luck! So did Brian McPhearson, and he wears his shoes on the wrong feet and drips snot!"

"The money was in your account only a matter of hours before disappearing."

Anna blinks a few times. "Where did it go?"

Mr. Sutter steeples his fingers. "I was hoping you could tell me."

Anna throws her purse on the desk. "You open that bag. I don't have any money in it. I can barely fit two lipsticks and a Summer Fresh pad in there."

Summer Fresh would be the local factory here in Truman. They make feminine products. I happen to be the proud stepdaughter of the maxi-pad line supervisor. Between his spandex tendencies and extensive knowledge of female business, some days I can hardly hold my head up.

"The bank says a girl went through the drive-thru and wrote a seven-thousand-dollar check on your account."

"Well, it wasn't me!"

"She was able to produce a driver's license."

I can't help but chime in. "What bank employee would be dumb enough to hand over seven thousand dollars in the drive-thru?"

Mr. Sutter shifts in his chair. "That's a detail we're also working on. The teller has since been let go. Her supervisor's in some hot water too. Anyway, Miss Deason, where were you at four o'clock yesterday afternoon?"

"I . . . um . . ." She turns tortured brown eyes to me. "I was at the coffee shop."

"Was anyone with you?"

"No. My boyfriend and I had gotten into this big fight, and I just needed to clear my head before I did anything drastic like punch his lights out."

"Or rob a school blind."

"I didn't do it! Somebody is setting me up—because I *have* my driver's license. Maybe the money will show up. It's a bank error! It's the Communists! It's aliens! It's those Scientologists!" Some of Anna's bravado slips, and tears begin to fall down her cheek. "I would never steal money. I don't know how to break into a bank account. You'd have to be a computer wizard for that."

Like Budge. My stepbrother. If I didn't know he worked every Thursday afternoon at the Wiener Palace, I'd have to wonder about his involvement. The dude is a serious genius. Not that you can tell by his grades.

"Is this your signature?"

Mr. Sutter passes a piece of paper across the desk. With trembling hands, Anna looks at a copy of the check from her account. "I didn't sign that."

"But is it your signature?"

Her bottom lip wobbles. "It looks like it." She drops the paper. "I don't understand. Is this some sort of sick joke? Because I am not laughing."

"And neither are we. You should probably clean out your locker, Anna. You might be staying home for a while. As in the rest of the year."

"But I have a game to cheer tonight!"

"And you probably should get that lawyer." Mr. Sutter's face softens just slightly. "This is a serious crime. I want you to think long and hard about this situation. If you have any information, you need to call me as soon as possible. If you're covering for someone, your consequences could be lessened if you just tell us the truth."

"I don't know anything about your money. All I know is that I'm innocent."

Our principal stands on his loafered feet. "Your parents are on their way. I'll just leave you two girls here until they arrive." He exits into the main office.

Anna melts into her seat and clutches my hand. "I didn't do it. You believe me, don't you?"

"Of course." Though it's all very weird. Too weird.

"I knew you would." She exhales a tired breath.

"You still need to get a really good lawyer."

"Lawyer?"

"Yeah, to prove you're innocent."

"I don't need an attorney." She slaps her other hand over mine. "*You're* gonna prove I'm innocent."

chapter six

At LaGuardia airport, I walk into my dad's waiting arms. I inhale his familiar scent and feel that old pang for how things used to be. Before Dad decided to give up family life for a dating marathon. Before Mom turned to the Internet to find her new husband—in Oklahoma. Before I found out my stepdad likes to body-slam people.

"So . . . money troubles?" I broach the topic in the cab, hoping Dad will laugh and tell me it's all a funny joke.

"Things are tight right now, but we'll find my accountant *and* my money. I will make a comeback."

My dad is *the* plastic surgeon in Manhattan. Through hard work, long hours, and the occasional butt implant, he has made quite a name for himself. But the fact that we're riding in a yellow cab instead of being chauffeured by his usual driver makes me wonder if Dad's financial forecast is gloomier than he'd like me to believe.

"Bella, your grandparents are in this weekend for a little visit." Dad doesn't even look at me. He *knows* how I feel about his parents. It's like God went out of his way to *not* give me any semblance of a normal family. My mom's parents died before I was born, but I hear they were amazing people. My dad's parents on the other hand . . . um, amazingly obnoxious. Actually just Grandmother Kirkwood. My grandpa is okay. He can't help his weirdness—he has dementia. This means he's cuckoo in the cranium a majority of the time. "Oh, well. How nice." This is all I can come up with. Last time I saw Grandmother Kirkwood, she eyed my chest and told me if I was lucky, I might get a boob job for next year's graduation. I wanted to tell her it was too bad Dad didn't have a machine that would suck out her horrible personality.

"We're having dinner at the house tonight. Christina is cooking."

I blink in the dark taxi. "Who's Christina? You didn't replace Luisa, did you?" Luisa was my nanny my entire life and pretty much raised me. Now she raises my dad.

He sighs. "I told you about Christina."

"No. You didn't." But Dad forgets a lot of things. Like calling on a regular basis.

"She's a friend—you'll like her. You'll meet her tonight. I think she's cooking some Brazilian food. Your grandmother will hate it." He laughs.

This would be girlfriend number 1,235,984,103 since my parents split. The ladies usually look like they're fresh off the stage of Miss USA and have an IQ slightly higher than a schnauzer.

Inside my room at the brownstone, Luisa waits for me. She hugs me in her ample arms and talks *muy rapido* in Spanglish. "Your father is very taken with this Christina de Luna." Luisa's brown face is impassive, but her voice carries an edge. "She could be the one."

I flop onto my bed and stare straight up at the angry cherubs painted overhead. One of my dad's old girlfriends called herself a decorator and redid his house with every room having a theme. Nothing matches or makes sense. Dad says it's symbolic. I say she must've hated him.

"You must change for dinner. Your grandmother will be rising from her evening nap any moment looking for you." Luisa clucks her tongue and mutters something about an old dragon.

I stay out of the kitchen and avoid meeting my dad's new girl until I go downstairs for dinner. I beg Luisa to join us, but this is bingo night at the Catholic church, and nothing comes between Luisa and her daubers.

"There's my girl." Dad beams at the head of the table. A tall, dark-complected woman stands at his side. Her black hair cascades down her back and stops at her small waist. Her sleeveless shift dress shows off her toned arms. Not only is she beautiful, but she works out. Ick. The worst kind.

"Bella, I feel like I know you already!" The woman comes to my side of the table and intercepts me, kissing the air beside each cheek. I resist the urge to wipe her fake kisses away. "Your father talks of you often," she says with a light accent.

"That's funny." I smile. "He hasn't mentioned you."

Dad pulls her back to his side. "I'm sure you're wrong, Bella. I've mentioned Christina many times." He smiles big, revealing his perfectly white teeth. "And this is Christina's sister, Marisol." Dad gestures to a girl who appears to be close to Robbie's age. "Christina and Marisol's parents died when Marisol was just an infant. Christina raised her all by herself."

Christina's manicured hand lands on my dad's chest. "That is what you do, no? You take care of your family."

He squeezes her tight. "Isn't she amazing?"

"She's something." I greet my grandparents, then pull out a chair and sit down. I don't get too wrapped up in my dad's girl-friends' lives. These ladies are just passing through. Next week he won't even remember Christina's name.

She claps her hands. "Sit, sit, everyone! Marisol and I will bring in the food."

Marisol bounds up with a cheerful grin.

"Such a delicate, graceful girl, that Marisol." Grandmother cuts her eyes at me.

"Like a fawn." I reach for my water glass and take a long drink.

"I used to have an old girlfriend named Fawn," Grandpa says to no one in particular. "She could dance the jitterbug like nobody's business."

Grandmother taps my elbow. "I see farm life has already influenced you."

I remove my arms from the table. "I hang out with cows a lot."

My dad clears his throat, a silent warning.

I try niceness again. "So, Grandmother, how was your flight from Connecticut?"

"It was bumpy, it ran ten minutes behind schedule, and the flight attendant did not have the brand of tomato juice I prefer."

"I hate it when that happens."

Grandmother purses her lips. Well, as much as one can purse with a face that has been nipped and tucked until it's stretched to the point of snapping.

"I used to be a pilot." Grandpa laughs. "Flew right over the president's house one day. Landed in his yard, and he said I had arrived just in time for his daily yoga session." He winks at me and pats my hand. "I can still do a mean downward dog, though your grandmother doesn't like me sticking my butt up in the air, as I'm a bit gassy."

"Here we are!" Christina enters the dining room carrying a big tray of meat. Her sister follows behind and sits right next to Dad. He squeezes her hand, and she beams. I get an icky feeling—like eating too many gummy worms and hanging upside down.

"That looks like roast," Dad says. "I thought you were fixing a Brazilian dish." He addresses the table. "Christina and her sister are from Brazil. As orphans, they were so poor, Christina hitched a ride on a pig truck, then stowed away on a boat to reach America for a better life for her infant sister. That was seven years ago, and now Christina is a talent agent with a prestigious firm."

Oh, boy. Angelina Jolie has *nothing* on this woman's international heroics.

My grandmother daubs at her eyes. My grandfather just stares at the roast.

Christina lays her hand on the back of Dad's chair. "Tonight we are having a traditional English dinner. I wanted to honor your parents' heritage."

My grandmother holds her hands to her heart. "My heritage. Isn't that wonderful?" I think her *father's* father might've been British. So it's not like Grandmother was Queen Elizabeth's best friend or anything. "Are those turnips I see?"

Ew. Seriously? Not touching those. Give me some fries.

"And we have a good horseradish sauce, of course." Christina takes her seat across from Dad.

Marisol grins at my dad. "Uncle Kevin and I made brownies yesterday."

Uncle?

"We sure did, sunshine." He kisses her cheek.

What? That was his pet name for me when I was little. I'm his sunshine!

"Marisol, why don't you and Bella get the other entrees?"

"Of course!" Perky Marisol all but skips back toward the kitchen. After an eyebrow quirk from Dad, I head that way.

"Here are the mashed potatoes. Not everyone can make them as good as I do." Marisol hands them to me. "For dessert we're having custard. I helped make that, too, and it's pretty much perfect."

Whoa. Girl's got an attitude. "The potatoes look great. I may have to pass on the custard." *Custard? A dessert where eggs are the main ingredient?*

Marisol's schoolgirl face slips. "My sister said you lived like a barbarian. Clearly they don't emphasize manners in your new home."

My mouth flies open. "You little—"

"We're going to be a family—the three of us. My sister's going to marry your dad."

I can't help but laugh. "No, she's not, Marisol. You should probably get that idea out of your head right now. I know *Uncle* Kevin is nice, but I wouldn't get too attached."

"They are too getting married! And I'm going to live here and probably take over your bedroom."

"You'll want to redecorate it then." I pat her on her delusional head. "I'm afraid my dad isn't the marrying kind right now, okay? Women like your sister just—"

The little brat swings her arm and knocks the potatoes right out of my hands. With a *splat* they land on the floor. "Don't you dare say anything bad about Christina!"

"I wasn't!" But since she's a lady, that's all the qualifications Christina needs for my dad to not commit to her. "Look, Marisol, I—"

She leaves me in the kitchen. Frozen to the spot. Potatoes on my shoes.

When I get the floor and myself potato-free, I return to the dining room. Marisol sits on my father's lap, bawling on his Armani jacket. He holds her and whispers low. Christina sits on his other side, patting her sister's back. *Oh, puh-lease.*

My dad's angry eyes meet mine. "Marisol didn't want to tell us, but we finally dragged it out of her. Do you want to tell us why she's crying?"

"Because she's a brat?" The words fly out of my mouth like my tongue is a catapult. "I mean *she* threw the potatoes on the floor!"

Grandmother rests her napkin in her lap. "She made them. I highly doubt she would then purposely ruin them."

I glare at a sniffling Marisol. She ought to be on Broadway with that act.

Christina holds up her hands. "Let's just enjoy a pleasant meal, eh? This is not a problem." She forces a smile in my direction.

Marisol jabs a finger in my direction. "Bella called Christina bad names."

"No, I didn't!" All eyes turn to me, waiting for an explanation. "I just, um, set her straight on a few things." I glare at my dad. "Things I will tell you about later."

"Kevin," my grandmother says, her eyebrows never moving from their locked position on her forehead. "Clearly your daughter has been under some unruly influences in Oklahoma." She shudders. "A farm. A wrestler. And who knows what kind of riffraff she's hanging out with in that public school."

"Riffraff? There is *nothing* wrong with my riffraff." What *is* that anyway?

"Apologize to Christina and Marisol." My dad pins me with accusing eyes.

Christina lays a hand on his arm. "It is okay, Kevin. I think you were right—Bella hasn't adjusted to all the changes in her life yet. It's normal for a young girl to act out."

I throw my napkin on the table. "If anyone acted out here, it's your psycho sister. I am seventeen years old. I do *not* throw food or insult my father's house *dates*." Even if they do come with obnoxious little sisters.

Christina stands. "We should leave. Marisol, get your coat."

An eruption of chairs scraping the floor, raised voices, and cries of "please don't go" fill the room like a derailed symphony. I bypass it all and head straight for my room, longing for the comfort of my bed and the evil cherubs.

Slamming my door, I grab my phone and with angry fingers begin a text to Lindy. My phone rings just before I hit Send on a message God would *not* be proud of.

"Hello?"

"Hey, Bel. It's Hunter."

I do a backflop on the bed and just breathe.

"I know you're in town this weekend. I was, um . . . wondering if you'd like to go get some coffee."

I've just had a horrible night with the Saint of Brazil and her possessed sister. Not to mention my dad seems to have a new daughter and didn't even take up for me tonight. The last thing I need is to hang out with Hunter, the guy who I caught tongue dancing with my best friend.

I roll over and grab my coat. "Meet me at Starbucks on the corner of Third and Ninety-Second."

chapter seven

The smell of mocha makes any boy more attractive, right? That's what I tell myself as Hunter opens the door of Starbucks for me. The sharp winter wind ruffles his brown hair, and when he speaks his breath comes out in icy puffs.

"I'm surprised you agreed to meet me." He smiles, the corners of his eyes crinkling, and I feel some of my old resentment melt like whipped cream on a caramel macchiato.

"It's been a night of oddities." I give the barista my order, and before I can reach into my purse, Hunter has paid and tipped the lady.

"How's your dad? I heard about his financial troubles." Something in Hunter's expression stops me from telling him to mind his own business. "My dad had the same accountant. His money situation is pretty questionable right now too."

I take a sip of my mocha. "I had to get a job. On a farm." I think about my grandmother hearing this news and can't suppress a giggle.

Hunter watches me and smiles. "I can't compete with that, but my yearly Christmas trip to Europe got cut down to a mere week."

"Tragic." I wrap both hands around my cup and let the warmth seep through. "How are you feeling?"

Hunter shrugs. "I'm fine. I will be fine."

"Can't you tell me about it?"

"I don't want to burden you. I guess you could pray for me or whatever you do."

"Until a few weeks ago, I stuck pins in my Hunter Penbrook voodoo doll." I bite my top lip on a wicked grin. "I guess I could try some prayer instead. You know, I'm not leaving until Sunday afternoon. You could go to church with me." This was always a sore spot between us. I was into God and church. Hunter was into . . . Hunter.

"Okay."

I nearly spew the Starbucks. "Seriously? You know Sunday isn't Easter or Christmas, right?"

He twists a napkin in his hand. "I'm changing, Bella. I don't know how or why . . . but I am. I know I need something more."

I don't know what to do with this, so I leave it alone.

We finish our drinks, and Hunter insists on riding in the cab to see me back to my house. He walks with me up the steps, and we stop under the light.

"I've missed you." He reaches out and gives my scarf a tug.

"Thanks for the coffee." And before my brain can override, my arms are around him, pulling him into a hug.

Disengage! Disengage!

"See you Sunday." I pull away and rush into the house.

"I want to talk to you." My dad's voice stops me on the stairs. I turn around and find him standing below, his arms crossed.

Here we go. "Look, I didn't do that stuff tonight, Dad. Do you seriously not believe me?" Though I don't want to, I walk down and sit beside him on the first step. "I don't know what that little girl is up to, but she's as crazy as Grandpa."

"Bella, Christina is very important to me."

So were my shoes that got mash-potatoed. "You didn't even take up for me. Her little sister is screaming like a banshee, and you guys act like I had put her in a choke hold." Which I seriously considered at one point.

Dad studies his hands, hands that know precision and don't miss a single detail. "I'm sorry if things were blown out of proportion. It all looked bad from our end."

"If you think your end was bad, you should've been in the kitchen with the little freak."

"I'm going to ask Christina and the little freak to move in with me."

"What?" No! "But you're my dad. Er, I mean . . . that's wrong. You can't live with her. Is money so tight you need a roommate? I can loan you a few bucks." Just please don't move that Brazilian weirdo into this house.

"I really like her, Bella."

"I really like that guy who has the underwear ads on Times Square, but you don't see me asking him to shack up."

"I'm not sure what happened tonight or where the truth is. I don't know that it really matters—"

"It does. I'm your daughter, and you should trust me. No, you should *know* me. I wouldn't antagonize that little girl." Not to mention if my dad really knew me, he'd know I'd come up with something better than Marisol's amateur hour. Throwing potatoes. I'm sure.

"Those two are very important to me," Dad says.

It'll fade. I can speak from experience.

He runs his fingers through his short, spiky hair. "It's been a long night. We'll start again in the morning."

I wait for Dad to tell me he's sorry—that he was wrong.

He walks up the stairs and never looks back.

chapter eight

"Hunter went to church with you this morning?" My mom wheels into our driveway, ending the hour-long drive from the Tulsa airport.

"Yeah, he's been asking me about God and stuff." I tell her what I know about his illness. "He doesn't really talk about his condition, which makes me think it might be bad."

"Well, I think that's great he's interested. I know you don't really want to be around him after everything that happened, but, Bella, you could lead him to the Lord."

A few months ago I wanted to lead him off the Empire State Building. Now, I'm not sure about anything. The Hunter I was with this weekend . . . I liked him.

"Did you see anything fabulous while you were shopping?" Mom asks, that old gleam in her eye. The one that says, *I can spot Chanel couture from twenty paces.*

"Hermès had some of their new spring bags out already."

Her gaze turns dreamy. "I can smell the leather from here." She shakes her head as she turns off the Tahoe. "There have been some changes this weekend."

"Oh, more changes! Just what I wanted." Too much?

"The camera techs rigged up the inside of the house, like the producer talked to us about."

We climb out of the SUV, and I follow Mom inside. There are automated cameras set up everywhere. "This . . . is creepy." My skin tingles with goose bumps. People are watching me somewhere in a control room.

"The bedrooms and bathrooms are camera-free, but sometimes we'll have a real camera crew following us around in the house or in town."

"Perfect." The weight of the weekend sets in, and I climb upstairs to unpack.

When I get to my bedroom, I do a sweep of the area, searching every nook, cranny, and panty drawer for anything that looks like a microphone or camera. I come up with nothing. Thank God for small favors. That's all I need—to be changing bras and find I'm on a webcam in front of millions of viewers.

When my alarm sings the next morning, my eyeballs might as well be stuck together with Krazy Glue. I only travel to my dad's once a month, but that next Monday back at school always kicks my tail.

When I walk by Luke in journalism class, I offer one single crisp word, not sure where we stand. "Hey."

He lifts his chin in greeting and goes back to his conference with Steven Ludecky, our sports reporter.

Thirty minutes later when Luke stands behind me, I recognize his scent before he announces his presence. "Captain Iron Jack did a great job Friday night."

I swivel in my rollie chair. "Glad to hear it."

His eyes never leave the copy on my computer screen. "How was New York?"

"Cold."

He leans down until our faces are level. It's a contact lens day for him, and without the glasses his eyes are even more intense. "Is this how it's going to be? We're back to being enemies again?"

I survey the room, but everyone is busy working on their own stories. "I don't know. You're the boss here. I guess you set the tone."

He pulls out another chair and wheels it forward until we're knee to knee. "I'm sorry for the way I reacted. Sometimes . . . sometimes I get very possessive about this paper."

"*Nooo.*" My face is sheer shock. He is not amused.

"I'm trying to apologize here."

"And for your first time, you're not botching it up *too* much."

"Don't you have anything to say to me?"

How about when you sit this close to me, my heart races like I just finished the Boston Marathon? I still think about our one kiss on that crazy night we were running from football players. Sometimes when I close my eyes, I remember that moment in the cabin when we both could have died, and you pretty much saved me.

"Hung out with my ex-boyfriend this weekend." Did *not* mean to say that. *Bella, thy name is maturity.*

Luke's grin is slow. Sly. "This would be the boyfriend who cheated on you?"

Um, yeah. That would be the one. "So I gotta get back to my e-mails. Lots of work-related thoughts to write about. Job ponderings and occupational musings."

Luke stands up, but not before his lips pause near my ear. "I accept your apology too."

During fourth hour, the secretary announces a required junior class meeting at lunch in the library. When the bell rings to release us from calculus, I head down the hall to the meeting, knowing Lindy will be in a state of panic over having to preside.

Ten minutes later only a third of the class has shown up, and Lindy begins. "As you all know, Harry Wu Fong got accepted into some smart-kid program at Princeton University and is bypassing the rest of his high school years, so that leaves me as your president." A group of athletes cheer. "Unfortunately Fong had not done much in terms of prom planning. I guess he was too busy being a genius." She stops and stares toward the door. We all turn around.

Luke Sullivan walks in—holding hands with some girl. *Harvard* girl.

Lindy continues. "So not only do we need to hustle on making some prom decisions, but Friday we learned someone has wiped out our junior class account. So basically we're broke."

I so relate.

"We need a fund-raiser," someone yells.

"Yes, we do." Lindy chews on her bottom lip. "Does anyone have any suggestions?"

Mikey Sprinkle pushes up his bottle-thick glasses, then holds up a hand. "We could have a car wash and the girls could wear bikinis."

In your dreams, dude.

"We could sell pies." This from the guy in the back of the room who's as wide as a Dodge Ram. "I know I'd buy a few."

Luke's girlfriend is cute. And she looks disgustingly smart. That's a bad combination. I mean, I *knew* she'd be intelligent, but I was hoping she'd look like the butt end of a Doberman.

"Okay, so a bake sale." Lindy writes this down. "Who knows how to bake?"

Everyone just stares at each other. We're teenagers. We know how to eat pies—*not* how they're created.

"We have an idea over here."

I bristle at Luke's voice behind me.

He smiles at his girlfriend and she laughs. "Go ahead, Taylor," he says.

"Last year when I was in high school we did this thing for Valentine's Day. It was called Match-and-Catch. You fill out this personal survey, and it pairs you with your ideal match in this school. Everyone fills out the surveys, but you have to pay to get your results."

Four-foot-nine Will Newman pipes up. "Are you saying I could get a girlfriend out of this?"

"Yes."

Whoops go up all around. "Let's do it!" Dorks and athletes alike high-five and chest-bump.

Whoa, she said you'd get a match. She didn't say you were guaranteed second base.

Lindy whistles through her teeth and brings the meeting back to order. "Thanks so much, Taylor. That's a great idea."

Big deal. She's from Harvard. She's *supposed* to have great ideas.

"We also need to set up a Web site so people can start nominating seniors for prom king and queen. Who can do that?" Lindy asks.

As if on cue, all heads swivel toward Budge Finley, who does *not* look happy to be giving up his chicken nugget time for prom talk.

"I'm busy. I have a gamer's competition coming up next month." He sees our faces void of any sympathy. "December is a hectic month at the Wiener Palace. Wieners are in high demand right before the holidays." He crosses his arms. "Not gonna do it. Final answer."

Lindy looks like she's about ready to cry. "But you're the only one who can do this. Last time we needed a Web page for our class, Zach Dilbert created it and it somehow got hijacked by senior citizen nudists."

Petey Usher shakes his head. "Dude, I saw my grandma on there."

By this time I've made my way over to where Budge sits at a library table. "If you don't do it, I'm going to tell all these people that you have your own loofah and have taken over my cucumber facial scrub."

He sighs. "I can have it ready by Wednesday."

After school I drive my Bug ten minutes out of town to Dolly's sprawling property. Her house looks like a *Southern Living* centerfold, and she has it all decked out for Christmas inside and out.

She swings open the front door before I can touch a finger to the bell. "Let's go. Time's a-ticking. I gotta get back to Sugar's for the dinner crowd." She shoves me off the front porch and toward her Jeep. "Hop in."

"Where are we going?" She pulls back onto her dirt road and

into a field. I hold onto the handle above me as we jostle down the well-worn path.

"I have a little barn back here. Need some work done. I'll introduce you to Clyde, and he'll get you started."

"Started with what?"

Dolly only laughs, a throaty sound that probably sends men's hearts racing, but has me wanting to throw open the door and jump out.

A faint snowflake spits every few seconds as Dolly drives up to her so-called "little" barn.

"Do you keep Donald Trump's horses here or what?" I climb out of the Jeep and just stare, my mouth wide open in awe. Before me is a sprawling horse ranch. Five or six people mill around. There's an enormous barn with stalls. To my left is a giant tracklike area where a man is walking with a bucking pony. Horses are everywhere. And so is the Circle D symbol.

I turn in a full circle. "What is this, Dolly?"

She lifts a shoulder. "A little hobby of mine." Dolly gives me a light tap with her gloved hand. "What, you didn't think I built that house on what Sugar's pays me, did you?"

We walk together toward the man with the wild pony.

"After Mickey left me, I needed something. Everything in my life was gone—my girls, my husband. I sold our two-bedroom house, bought three acres out here, and lived in an RV. After three months of not even getting out of bed, I woke up one day and decided I needed something to do besides smoke and watch *One Life to Live*. I remembered when I was a kid I had a horse. So I bought one. Started working with it. Twenty years, two hundred horses, and a few acres later, I'm now a breeder. Waitressing—just a hobby."

"Are you any good?"

We reach the old man with the pony, and he stops. "Is she any good? Ever heard of Holy Smokes?"

It sounds familiar. "The horse that won the Kentucky Derby?"

"That was Dolly's third Derby horse. This lady here has the magic touch."

Dolly laughs and shakes her head. "This is Clyde Mullins. And he's been with me for fifteen years. Knows a horse farm like you know those fancy shoes. He's going to show you some of the most important jobs of running the place. Clyde, you take it easy on my girl here. I'm out." Leaving me with the white-haired man, she takes off in a loud roar.

"This way, girl."

"Am I going to brush some tails?"

"Nope."

"Dress some ponies?"

"Don't think so."

"File some paperwork?"

Clyde stops at the "little" barn and spits. "You ever seen horse poop?"

I swallow. "Never."

He grins. "You're about to make up for lost time."

chapter nine

God must totally be mad at me.

I scoop up my last batch of horse manure and throw it in the wheelbarrow. I've been breathing through my mouth for the last two hours. During the first hour, I OD'd on the smell and had to put my head between my legs.

"Get the wet shavings now," Clyde calls out as he sticks his head in. "It's gotta be real dry."

"Do you have some potpourri or maybe a nice scented candle for the horse too?" Maybe a Jonas Brothers poster?

He laughs and keeps walking.

Ten minutes later I've swept the floor until my arms ache.

"Don't fill that wheelbarrow up with too much manure at once." Clyde walks by and throws out another helpful tip, and I find myself really tired of his Horse Crap Tutorial.

Swishing the broom across the floor one last time, I decide this is pretty stinking good. Seriously, this horse's bedroom has to be cleaner than mine.

Okay, now to wheel this pile-o-poo out to the manure area. Before today I didn't know people collected manure. I collect vintage Chanel bags, so I guess to each her own.

With gloved hands, I grab onto the wooden handles and drag the wheelbarrow around, pointing it toward the open stall door. *Okay, here goes.* Using all my upper body strength, I lift up on the handles and push it outside. And Clyde didn't think I'd be able to handle a full load.

This thing *is* heavy. Wobbly.

I look ahead the fifty feet it takes to get to the manure pile, and it stretches out before me like another continent.

Clyde ambles by again, his eyes on my progress.

"See?" I raise my chin. "This isn't so bad. Easy! A piece of—" The wheelbarrow pitches to the left. I suck air and lean to the right, pulling with everything I've got. Sweat explodes on my forehead, and my arms burn with the effort to right the wheelbarrow.

I run over a rock, and all control is lost.

The wheelbarrow goes left. The manure flies out in great, steaming globs.

And I fall right into it.

Face first.

I come up gagging and coughing. "Ew! Ew! Gonna die! Call 9-1-1! Get the fire department!"

When I finally clear out my eyes, I see two rough brown work boots.

"I wasn't doubting your muscles there, Wonder Woman." Clyde chuckles and flicks a piece of dirt off his pants. "The wheelbarrow gets unsteady if there's too much weight."

I continue heaving and spitting. "I'm gonna need some help here."

"You sure are." He holds out a shovel. "This ought to do the trick."

By eight o'clock it's dark, I reek like a sewer plant, and my left nostril is clogged with gunk from a horse's butt.

I catch a ride with Clyde to Dolly's house to get my car. He makes me sit in the back so as not to offend his delicate sensibilities. I bail out and watch him make a U and head back to the barn.

I open the Bug trunk and find a towel to throw over my seat. Easing into the car, I twist the ignition key. The engine makes a *thunk, thunk.* I drop my head to the steering wheel and bang it a few good times. This does nothing more than dislodge more dried manure. I give it another go, and the car still won't start. Maybe my smell killed it.

I dig for my phone and call Mom. No answer.

I call Dolly. No answer.

I try Jake, Budge, Lindy, Matt, and a few other friends—even the geek from American History who sends me messages on Facebook that border on sexual harassment.

Nobody is home! Is the whole world gone tonight? Did the rapture come, and I missed it? God thought I stunk too much to let me in?

I close my eyes and let out a whimpery mewl. I have one other person left to call. The last human being on the face of the earth I want to see me like this.

Fifteen minutes later I stare at the opened door of the green 4Runner and think walking back to town doesn't sound so bad. I probably need to burn off a few more calories anyway.

"Get in. I've got the seat lined with trash bags."

I bite back a curse as Luke Sullivan holds the passenger door open. "Thanks for coming. I know you were probably busy." *Talking to your Harvard girlfriend who would* never *be coated head-to-toe in horse business.*

"You smell different tonight. New perfume?" Luke coughs into his hand and turns his head away from me. I don't know if it's to hide his laughter or because he's about to gag.

"Funny. You're hilarious. You should have your own show on Comedy Central."

He shuts me in the SUV, and I hear him laugh it up as he walks around to his side.

I just want to die. To vaporize and disappear.

Even though it's cold enough to ice a pond, we drive with the windows down. I'm too tired and humiliated to even care that I'm freezing. There could be snot dripping out of my working right nostril, and I wouldn't even mind.

Luke stops grinning long enough to break the silence. "Can I ask what you were doing tonight?"

"Working. What does it look like I've been doing?"

"You really don't want me to answer that, little buckaroo." He flips on the heat, careful not to touch me. "You couldn't sling fries like the rest of our classmates?"

"Can you just drive please?" I hear him chuckle again, and it only fans the flames on my temper. "If you tell *anyone* about this, I will . . ." I can't think of a single, legal thing.

"Yes?"

"Tell the world what a horrible kisser you are."

Luke brakes right in the middle of the dirt road and throws it into park. In the dark I see his eyes trained on me. "Bella"—his voice is a gravelly whisper—"right now you are the most disgusting thing I have ever seen. You smell, you look like you got caught in a cattle stampede, and my vehicle will never be the same." He leans over the gearshift. "And if I wasn't so afraid of whatever's coating your lips, I would prove to you what a liar you are."

I stare at his mouth. "Liar?" My word comes out more like a breathy wheeze.

Luke eases forward an inch. "Don't tempt me."

I can hear my own heart beating.

Then he slings it into drive and tears down the road, a slight smile on his arrogant face.

We spend the rest of the trip without talking, and when he's almost to a complete stop in my driveway, I jump out like a stunt guy and all but crash through the front door.

"Your stink is overwhelming my superpower."

I glare at my little stepbrother and slam the door behind me.

Jake looks up from his newspaper in the living room. "Good day at Dolly's?"

"I see that smirk. I see it!" I point a dirty finger, caked with things I don't even want to think about. "Why didn't anyone *tell* me I'd be scooping poop today?"

Mom bounds down the stairs, a camera in hand. She snaps off a shot and smiles. "For your scrapbook."

"Yeah." I waddle toward the steps, leaving a trail of gunk. "Send it to Grandmother."

chapter ten

O n Tuesday I shut my locker and come face-to-face with Anna
Deason.

"What are you doing at school?" I cast a worried glance in every
direction. "They think you're a criminal. Principal Sutter will have
you led out in handcuffs." That would be totally embarrassing. And
you *know* one of those yearbook staffers would be right there with
a camera.

She shakes her glossy dark head. "Nuh-uh. My daddy's not
only on the school board, but he's an attorney. And one mention of
the word *lawsuit* got me back in school until I'm proven guilty.
And right now the teller from the bank who cashed the check is
AWOL."

"The teller is missing?"

"Yeah, gone. Victoria Smith's her name. She'd been at the bank
for about six months. She's a senior here, but her locker's all cleaned
out. The police said she left her mom's house. That's all I know."

"Are the police looking for her?"

"No. They got all the info they need. They have her sworn
statement."

"But her story doesn't add up. Either someone posed as you or she knows the person she cashed the check to wasn't you." And I didn't get a chance to talk to Victoria yet. I have to find her.

"Love how all these people are looking at me like I'm a convict." Anna waves at someone passing by. "Listen, Victoria is not the sharpest eyeliner in the makeup bag, you know what I'm saying? The person who handed over the check might've had a mustache and she would've cashed it."

"Give me her mom's address, and I'll talk to her as soon as I can." Which will be hard to do since I now possess the world's worst job.

"My dad already tried talking to Victoria's mother. She wouldn't tell him anything. She said Victoria's leaving was a family affair and to butt out of it."

Then I guess I'll just have to get the information another way.

After school I call Dolly and tell her that I'll be a little late to the farm. Then with my newly recharged Bug, I drive to the industrial area of town and park in front of Mickey Patrick's gym, where Jake trains every day. That is, when he's not supervising the maxi-pad machine at Summer Fresh.

"Hey, Mickey." I nod to Jake's manager and trainer as I enter the gym.

He looks up from a stack of jump ropes he's untangling. "Jake said your evening at Dolly's kind of stunk." He winks like I don't get his pun.

"Couldn't someone have mentioned that Dolly has a multimillion-dollar horse farm behind her house?"

He lifts a bulky shoulder. "Thought everyone knew." Mickey looks uninterested, but I know it has to be a sore spot—that Dolly totally reinvented her life after he left.

"Hey, when's her baby due? She didn't really have time for details the other day."

"Whose baby?"

"Dolly's."

"What?" Mickey drops a rope. "She's—"

"Adopting, yeah." I watch Mickey's eyes round. "Oops. I assumed I was the last to know."

He runs a hand over his bald head. Mickey looks like a buff, middle-aged version of Mr. Clean. He's built, he's quiet, and he can intimidate the heck out of someone. Like now.

"I'm sorry, Mickey. I didn't know it was a secret or anything."

He looks through me. "I'm sure it isn't a secret. Just shows how out of touch I am." He throws the last jump rope into a pile and walks off, shutting himself in his office.

Jake flings himself from the ropes and smacks into his opponent, Mark Rogers. A two-man camera crew has lights set up and cameras rolling.

I tell myself to ignore the cameras and act natural as I walk toward the ring.

But it doesn't hurt to reapply my lip gloss.

"Dude, you're giving me razor burn. Isn't that a wrestling foul?" Mark rubs his arm.

The two guys laugh and Jake takes to the ropes again. I think wrestling is for boys who never grew up.

I clear my throat and Mark turns, moving out of the way just as Jake flies through the air. He lands a hard belly flop on the mat. "*Oomph!*"

Mark leans over the ring. "S'up, Bella?"

Mark is also a wrestler wannabe. He's pretty new at it, just like he's new at his job on the police force. He's probably been out of the academy a year or so, but ever since I did my own pile driver on some crime, he's been überhelpful.

"Gotta get some Gatorade." Jake climbs out and limps down the hall. The two camera guys follow.

"Whatcha got cooking?" Mark cuts right to it.

"I need an address. Victoria Smith. Where is she?"

"The bank teller in the missing school money case?"

I smile. "That's the one."

"I can't give you that."

"I have some homework to give her." Like twenty questions from me.

Mark zips his lip. "I cannot divulge that information." He wipes some sweat and coughs into his hand. "*Dad's house!*" He coughs again. "Sorry, sinuses."

"That's all you have for me?"

"Sure wish I could give you that address *in Tulsa*, but I can't. I'm a locked box. A sealed envelope. A safe with no key."

"Got it." I smile and hand him his towel. "If you think of anything else you can't tell me, let me know."

I pivot on my heel and run smack into Luke Sullivan.

His arms snake around and hold me steady. "Bella Kirkwood, you're up to something."

I wrench out of his grip. "I am offended. I was just here visiting my stepfather."

Luke crosses his arms and slowly shakes his head.

"Fine." I roll my eyes. "How long have you been standing there?"

"Long enough. I have dibs on a story for the missing junior class funds, so I hope you're not poaching on my territory."

"This isn't about the paper." But if I did solve the money mystery, it wouldn't hurt to write it up in a sweet little article with my name right under the title.

"Are you going to talk to Victoria?" he asks.

"She moved out of her mom's house."

"Answer the question, Bella."

"I've got to get to work."

Luke laughs, the sound rumbling low in his chest. "Call me if you need a ride—to find Victoria, that is."

When I drive my Bug out to Dolly's horse barn, there's a man with a camera waiting. I ignore him and go find Clyde.

"You ready to muck out some more stalls?" He pats down an auburn-colored horse.

I'd rather eat my own socks. "Um . . ."

His laugh rumbles. "Relax, kid. Today I'm going to show you how to groom a horse."

"Like do hair?"

He doesn't smile. "Follow me."

Fifteen minutes later I'm standing next to Sundance Kid and combing her coat. Clyde assured me she was the gentlest of horses, but how do I know what's lurking behind this animal's large, black eyes? Could be an intense desire to karate chop me with a hoof.

I go through the whole grooming routine like Clyde showed me and then pick up a brush to tackle Sundance's tail. I stay to the side of the horse like Clyde demonstrated, working in small sections to ease out any tangles in the hair.

"Sundance, the bad news is you have some serious dead ends. The good news is you've got some great highlights."

Can't seem to get all the tangles. This one piece just will not come out of its knot. "Hang on, girl. I'll get it for you. I'm really good with hair." Need some detangler. I lean down a little closer. "Almost got it. Just a little bit more and—"

The tail lifts and a yellow stream shoots out like a Super Soaker.

I jump back. But not before I'm drenched in horse pee. At the sound of laughter, I look over and see Clyde and the camera guy watching me like it's a spectator sport.

"Hope you enjoyed that." I wring out my hair and wipe my hands on my jeans. "I think I'm going to cut out of here early, if that's okay."

On my way home, I call Dolly and tell her I've got all the info I need on farm life.

"That's okay, sweetie," she says. "It's not for everybody."

chapter eleven

_Budge, your Thursday night gamer meeting is going to have to wait. Jake said the *entire* family has to be home so we can watch the premiere of *Pile Driver of Dreams*." I'm just now getting to the point where I don't roll my eyes every time I say the show's title. It's a huge step in my path to maturity.

Budge readjusts his backpack over his shoulder and bumps knuckles with a passing friend. "So far this reality show crap is lame, man."

"Um, did they get footage of you getting bathed in horse tinkle? I don't think so." Who knows what else they have.

I stop in my tracks at the tap on my shoulder.

"Are you Bella Kirkwood?"

This question always fills me with dread. Especially when asked by a girl in a dog collar who clearly just escaped from a punk rock video. Or prison.

I turn around and hope my eyes are not bugging. "Yes, I guess I am."

"I'm Ruthie McGee. You might have heard of me."

I'm not sure what the right answer is here. "Uh . . . no." The girl in front of me has the most remarkable hair of black and white, like an irate skunk roosted on top of her head. It stands in spikes that defy the laws of gravity.

I look back, thinking Budge took the opportunity to escape, but he stands behind me, frozen. Unable to move, suspended in a trance of hair and black leather.

"I need your help."

My next words take all the courage I've got. "I don't work for free." *Please don't kill me.*

Ruthie chews on a wad of gum, her black-lined eyes narrowed into slits. I take a step backward.

"Fine." She pops a bubble. "I'm willing to pay, but I don't want you to take on any other cases—just mine. And I'll make it worth your while, but only half now. The rest when the mission is accomplished. Here's my problem." She jerks her head toward Budge. "Is he just gonna stand there and eavesdrop?"

My stepbrother's mouth is open so wide, drool is bound to start pooling any second. I nudge him with my elbow.

"Ignore him. He won't repeat anything you say." Plus, I think he's too scared to move.

"I'm running for prom queen."

I process this. "Do you need assistance with your updo?"

She laughs, great rolling barks that come from deep within her throat. Then she sobers. "I need help clearing my good name." She shoves a piece of paper in my face. "This was on my bike when I got out of school yesterday."

"You don't really strike me as the ten-speed type of girl."

"My motorcycle."

"Right." I look the paper over. It has a color picture of Ruthie making out with a guy. I lift a brow in question.

"It's not me."

I check the paper again. "The face is kinda blurry . . . but that is definitely your hair."

"I'm telling you, that isn't me!" Ruthie reaches for her shirt-sleeve, where she's got a small box rolled up. She shakes her head and drops her hand. "No, I'm trying to cut back."

"Marlboros?"

"No." Her face scrunches. "That stuff will kill you. Breath mints. I eat 'em when I'm stressed. I went through twelve boxes just last night."

"There is a pleasant aroma of spearmint about you."

"The picture, Kirkwood. Focus on the picture. That is *not* me. Someone is trying to destroy my good name."

"Why would they do that?"

Her look says *are you stupid?* "Because they're jealous, that's what. I got the bod, the skills, the looks."

And a few tattoos.

"This note was with the picture."

Drop out of the prom queen race or prepare for the consequences.

I study the writing, but can't determine if it's from a male or female hand.

"Ruthie, it's not that bad. I mean, so you're kissing a guy here. Big deal."

"Big deal? This wacko is going to send this to everyone I know. The photo's been doctored, but no one will believe it."

"Who's the guy?"

"My best friend's boyfriend."

"Oh." Not good.

"My daddy's gonna freak."

"I'm sure he'll understand." *With a kid like you, he can't be expecting an angel.*

"Just tell me you'll investigate and find out who's doing this." She stuffs the papers in my purse. "You don't know my dad." And she stomps off in her black spike-heeled boots.

I laugh and look at Budge, who has at least managed to close his mouth. "Daddy must be rougher than she is, if she's scared. Do you know her?"

Budge swallows and nods. "That's the Baptist preacher's daughter."

"She's a nut job."

He dabs at some sweat on his forehead. "I think I love her."

~~~~~~~~~~

After filling out a dozen job applications in town and dropping them off, I return home to the smell of steak.

I say hi to Mickey Patrick, who's perched on a chair in front of the TV. I know he's anxious to see how his star Jake is going to be portrayed tonight.

"Just in time to grab a plate," Mom says as I shuffle into the kitchen. Our kitchen suffered a fire a few months back and got a makeover, and it's the only room that doesn't look like 1975. Mom says we're going to slowly redo the other parts of the house, but so far we haven't even progressed to 1980.

"There's steak on the stove and salad on the table." Jake plops a baked potato on my plate. "Grab something to drink and let's settle in the living room."

We never know when the camera guys are going to be present,

so I'm thankful to see the house is free of them tonight. I count heads and find Budge in the living room already. Mom and Robbie in the kitchen. "Who are the extra plates for?"

"I invited Dolly. She's running late." Her gaze doesn't quite meet mine.

"Who else?"

"Luke Sullivan." Mom smiles and hands me silverware. "He said the paper wanted him to have as much access to us as possible, so I called him."

"Great. Perfect." Maybe he'll bring Miss Harvard. They can talk about super-smart things while we watch footage of Jake in spandex tighties. And if I'm really lucky there'll be footage of me with my head stuck up Sundance's butt while she's soaking me in urinary Mountain Dew.

"Excuse me." Robbie, dressed in his usual garb of a superhero t-shirt and red cape, moves in front of me to grab a baked potato.

"Hey, buddy, you've already got one on your plate."

Nervous green eyes look back at me. "I need to eat to build my strength. These are trying times for a superhero." And he zooms to the living room.

That was strange. The kid usually eats like a bird. But strange is the order of the day with him. It's like he has two personalities—one who believes he can fly. And the other part of him that is brilliant to the point of scary. I mean, when he's not watching Superman cartoons, he's watching the financial network on cable and taking notes.

The doorbell rings as I set my plate on the scarred coffee table.

Mom helps Robbie cut his meat. "Get that please, Bella."

With one dramatic sigh, I fling open the door with a look that's less than hospitable.

Luke smiles. He knows I don't want him here.

"Where's the girlfriend?"

"I'm working, so Taylor wasn't invited." He steps by me and greets the family.

"Luke, we have dinner for you. Bella will show you into the kitchen and get your plate."

Ugh. Seriously, Mom? I know I'm supposed to have a servant's heart, but I think the Bible mentions a few exceptions. Like arrogant, cocky editors. I think it's in Habakkuk. Um, forty-second chapter, two hundredth verse. Might not be in all translations.

Luke follows me into the kitchen. I plop a steak on a plate and let him do the rest.

He stares at the food. "You didn't spit in this, did you? Poison it?"

Hadn't thought of that.

"Any updates on the stolen class funds?"

I yank open the fridge. "What do you want to drink?" Maybe some Ex-Lax?

He moves in and reaches for a water. "You're dodging my question."

"I dunno. No new developments at this point." Unless you count the address for Victoria I got this afternoon from one of her friends.

He gets that look again. The one that makes me think he can see inside my head—and the contents amuse him. "Right." And he walks into the living room, settling in like he's part of our crew.

The only seat left is the space next to Luke on the couch. I consider standing, but I'm working on my maturity. I sit down and scoot so far to the edge away from him, the majority of my butt hangs off.

Dolly pops her head in the front door. "Hey, y'all." She enters the living room, dressed in sweats, Nike running shoes, and her ever-present big hair. She blanches when she sees her ex-husband. "What's he doing here?"

"What do you mean, what am I doing here? What are *you* doing here?" Mickey's cheeks turn pink.

Dolly stomps into the kitchen and returns with food. Jake brings in another chair from the dining room and places it in the space beside Mickey. Dolly stares at all of us, waiting for us to offer our own seats—away from her ex. No one moves.

"Fine." She sits down, her posture so straight it could snap.

As Mom and Jake talk, I hear Mickey mumble to Dolly. "You look nice tonight, by the way."

"I came here straight from the gym thinking it was just going to be a night with the Finleys. My Maybelline's all gone, I smell like sweat, and I just spent an hour in an aerobics class with twenty-year-olds."

His face falls. "I still think you look beautiful."

Oblivious to the Mickey and Dolly soap opera, Jake says a quick blessing and turns on the TV.

A familiar-looking man appears on the screen. He stands in the middle of a wrestling ring.

"*Tonight on* Pile Driver of Dreams, *ten people . . . only one will walk away with the chance to go pro and be a regular on* World Wrestling Television's Friday Night Throw-Down. *America, you will determine their destinies. Every week you get the chance to vote a wrestler off. We bring you live interviews and footage from their homes, getting up close and personal with their families. And we bring you the wrestling matches so you can decide if they've got what it takes to go pro. Ten people dreaming big . . . but is it big enough?"*

Mom's propped on the arm of Jake's recliner. She leans into him and squeezes his muscular arm.

"Careful . . ." Luke whispers. "You're smiling."

I guess I am. "This is a big deal for them." And it hasn't been this big life intrusion I thought it would be. I think the show is so focused on Jake, they pretty much leave the rest of us alone. I hardly ever see the camera crew. I think I expected my life to turn into *The Real World,* but it totally hasn't.

We watch as they do a brief bio on each contestant, showing video of wrestling matches, images of the family and the town each person is from.

The show begins with a guy named William Pearson, aka The Mutilator. In a brief interview, his son talks about what a great dad he is. His boss at Topeka First Federal tears up when he describes William saving the day when an armed robber held up the bank.

Another guy by the name of Sanchez the Snake discusses his mother while doing bicep curls. In the background his ex-wife quietly cries as he talks.

"Yeah, I want to be a wrestler . . . but mostly I want to save my mom. She's in Mexico waiting on a liver transplant. The only thing keeping her alive right now is the hope she has in me."

Oh, boy.

After three more men and two women contestants, Jake's face lights up the TV.

Next, Harvey Runnels, president of Summer Fresh, beams with pride. "In twenty years, this maxi-pad assembly line has never run smoother. Nobody knows feminine protection better than Jake Finley."

"It's true," Budge says from across the room. "Women owe a lot to this man right here." He and Jake do an air high five.

Luke's shoulders give a small jerk, and I know he's laughing inside.

Why can't Jake be a used car salesman like other stepdads I know? The announcer's voice continues to narrate. *"A big man, big dreams, and a small town. But is there more to Jake Finley? Recently married to his online sweetheart, he added a stepdaughter to his family. While Jillian Finley appears to have adapted to Truman life, her daughter seems to cling to the drama of Manhattan."*

The steak becomes a tasteless wad in my mouth. I spit it out into my napkin and zone in to the nightmare unfolding on the television. I scoot closer to Luke to get a better look.

"Suffering a bad breakup when her boyfriend hooked up with her best friend, Bella found solace in the simple life of Truman, Oklahoma. Or did she?"

Video footage rolls of me at Dolly's farm. Me with my head under Sundance's tail, getting sprayed down in horse pee. Me dumping over the wheelbarrow of poop. Me screaming at dumping over the wheelbarrow of poop.

Budge and Robbie laugh until I can hardly hear the TV.

"I had no idea anyone saw that," I mumble. "Especially cameras." And my mom hasn't totally adapted to Oklahoma life either. Yesterday she sat at her computer and stared at a Valentino dress for forty-five minutes.

"Recently Bella Kirkwood's ex-boyfriend has returned to her life. Sources say he could be seriously ill and is searching for forgiveness . . ."

There I am, head-to-head with Hunter at Starbucks in Manhattan.

"... *or is the young couple searching for something more?*"

My dad's front steps. Me wrapped in Hunter's arms. It was such a simple hug, but the photo makes it look like ... so much more.

Beside me I feel Luke stiffen. I steal a glance at his face, but it reveals nothing.

I grab Luke's plate and stand. "This is ridiculous. Those cameras—they're everywhere. I had no idea!" I feel so violated. So exposed. So Lindsay Lohan'd. "This isn't fair. Can't we do something about this?"

Mom slowly shakes her blonde head. "We knew this would be intrusive, Bella. We talked about this. We agreed as a family."

"I thought they'd intrude on *him*." I point to Jake. "My life is one big tabloid now. This is crazy. Everyone knows my business. I feel like an Olsen twin!" I step over Robbie and his cape on the floor and take the plates to the sink.

I have to get out of here. I need some air. Some space.

Some Ben & Jerry's.

chapter twelve

After pulling Mom aside and assuring her I will be home by ten-thirtyish, I sneak out the back door and hop into the Bug. I turn the key. And nothing.

"Come on. I don't have time to charge the battery. You can do it." I pat the car's dash in case she needs a boost of encouragement. I know sometimes I do.

I try a few more times, but the car is deader than my career as a horse groomer.

I jump at the knock on my window. Luke stands there with his arms crossed and that infuriating smile.

"Going somewhere?"

"Nowhere important. Just have to run an errand."

"Would this errand be in Tulsa?"

"Sorry!" I tap on the glass. "Can't hear you! You should probably go back in and take some more notes."

"Car won't start again?"

I roll down the window and feel the frigid December wind whoosh in. "No offense, but you're starting to annoy me."

He casually reclines against the car. "Face it. You need a ride."

"I don't need *anything* from you, Sullivan." I twist the key in vain. "How did you know I was going to Tulsa?"

"I have my ways." He dangles his keys from one finger. "We can stop at the Truman Dairy Barn on our way out of town."

"Like I'd be that weak." I'm sure.

"Double scoops?"

"Let's go."

Luke knocks on the door of apartment 15B. A middle-aged man with three days' worth of stubble answers.

"For the last time, I don't want any Avon."

I turn my head and laugh into my coat. Luke selling Skin-So-Soft. That's a good one.

I nudge Luke out of the way and step into the light. "Mr. Smith?"

"Yeah?"

"We go to Truman High School. We were in the neighborhood and wanted to see Victoria."

"Make it snappy. *CSI* is coming on." He holds the door open. "Victoria! You got company!" He stomps down a small hall and shuts himself in another room.

When Victoria joins us in the living room, she wears a confused face. "Do I know you?"

"Hey, Victoria." I'm not really sure how to begin. "Um . . ."

"We're from Truman High. We work for the paper and wanted to ask you a few questions." Luke takes her elbow and the two settle onto a worn couch. "There's been a lot of rumors about the junior class funds being stolen, and we want to make sure you are accurately portrayed in this story and your side is heard."

I was going to go with "We work with the FBI, and we need information. Don't make us haul you downtown." Whatever.

Luke opens his mouth to fire off the first question, but I jump in ahead of him. Dude is *not* going to steal my case here. "Victoria, we'd like you to go back to that day you cashed the check and tell us about that moment from the time the car pulled up until the time it drove away."

She twists a piece of brown hair around her finger. "I've already told the police all this."

I paste on my kindest smile. "Can you tell us what Anna Deason looked like that day? Can you describe the person who presented the check? The driver?"

Her twirling finger stops. "It's all pretty foggy in my head now. Thanks for stopping by, but—"

Luke rests his hand briefly on Victoria's. "I know you've fielded a lot of questions. I can't imagine how stressful that's been for you."

Victoria's bottom lip puckers as she nods. "I ate a whole jar of peanut butter yesterday."

Hey, nothing wrong with that.

"Did you get a good look at Anna that afternoon?" Luke drapes an arm over the back of the couch.

"I—I thought I did."

"Was it an African-American girl? Can you say that for sure?"

I sit with my mute button on while Luke works his magic.

"Yes, I'm pretty sure. But it's hard to tell with our cameras. We see the driver's side clearly, but the passenger side can be kinda dark."

A small white dog lumbers into the room and rubs against Luke's leg.

"Oh, what a great dog. It's beautiful." Luke pets the wheezing mongrel, who sports random bald spots and looks like it's three barks away from keeling over. "What's your name?"

Victoria giggles and picks up her dog. "This is Maggie."

"Maggie, you're pretty cute. How long have you had the dog?"

I watch Luke turn on the charm and Victoria light up like the Las Vegas strip. I search the floor for a newspaper or magazine. Maybe there's a crossword or something I could do while these two totally ignore me.

"I've had Maggie since I was in first grade. She doesn't have a yard here, so she's mad at me." More giggling. More petting of the geriatric dog.

"Had you been planning on moving in with your dad?" Luke asks.

Victoria's hand stills on the dog. "Um . . . n–no. I guess not. I mean yeah, sorta." She sniffs and blinks out a tear. "It just kind of happened. My boyfriend broke up with me, and the bank fired me. I needed to leave town."

I try to move in with a question, but Luke holds up his hand. His voice is smooth as jazz. "You wanted to leave town or you *had* to leave town? Was anyone pressuring you?"

Victoria stares into Luke's blue sky eyes. The moment hangs there.

"I want my TV back! I'm missing *CSI!*"

She jerks her head as if waking from a trance. "It's my dad's TV night. Thanks for stopping by."

Luke stands and puts his hand on Victoria's back. "If you can think of anything else, please contact me." He gives her a card. "Sometimes stress does funny things. It's not uncommon to take a step back from the event and get a clearer picture. If that happens, if there's something you want to tell us—anything—I'd love to talk to you."

In the parking lot, Luke opens my door for me, and I flop my body into the seat and fume.

"I heard that sigh," he says, as he buckles.

"I'd *love* to talk to you." I clutch his arm. "Oh, Victoria, I *can't imagine* how stressful this has been for you!"

Luke starts the 4Runner. "Well, your interrogation tactics obviously weren't working."

"Her dad watches *CSI*. I thought she'd be used to it!" I roll my eyes until I fear they'll pop out the back side. "And it's a good thing her dad came out because you were seconds away from laying a big, wet sloppy kiss on that mutt."

He turns on a John Mayer CD. "Admit it, you needed my help tonight."

"I need your help like I need mono. Like I need zits on picture day."

A slow piano melody melts from the speakers, and John Mayer sings a husky song about love.

The entire tune finishes before Luke speaks again. "What do you think of Victoria?"

I exhale loudly and watch the barren trees lining the road. "I think she's hiding something."

"Me too." He taps his fingers on the steering wheel in time to the music. "I can ask around and find out who the boyfriend is. Might be useful information."

"Don't bother. I'll find out myself." But I know he's already got a plan brewing in that overly smart brain of his. "Hey, do you know you've made two wrong turns?"

Luke glances in the rearview. "Don't panic, but I think we're being followed." He hangs a stiff right. "Yep, we've definitely got company."

"Is it a cop?" I try to make out the vehicle behind us but can't see anything but headlights. "Maybe we should pull over."

He snorts. "Don't you watch horror movies? That's the *last* thing we want to do."

I say a quick, silent prayer and curl my fingers into the seat. *Lord, it would be supercool if I didn't die tonight.*

"Here it comes." Luke speeds up.

The headlights grow more intense as the car moves closer until it's beside us on the two-lane road.

I turn to get a good look at the vehicle. Four-door sedan. Heavily tinted. Can't see inside.

The car's engine roars, drowning out the sound of my heart pounding.

Time moves in slow motion. One second I'm checking out the car. The next I hear metal on metal, and I'm thrown into the door. The side of my head hits the window.

The sedan pounds into us again. Tires screech. The 4Runner swerves. Luke fights for control of the vehicle as it weaves left and right. A scream works its way up my throat. *Help us, God.*

Luke jerks the steering wheel to the right, and we sail into a ditch. Grass hits the underside of the SUV, and finally we stop—an inch away from a fence post.

The sedan races out of sight.

"Are you okay?" Luke throws off his seat belt. He flips the interior light, and his eyes and hands are all over me. "Bella?"

My body shakes like I'm chilled. My heart is lodged in my throat.

Luke's hands frame my face. "Bella, talk to me. Where are you hurt?" His fingers move across my cheek, my neck, my arms, my—

"Hey!" I slap him away. "Save it for Taylor!"

He leans back some and breathes a sigh full of relief. "So no injuries?"

"There's a distinct possibility I wet my pants."

His lips curl into a small smile. "You're gonna have a bruise here." He touches my forehead with feather-light fingertips.

"What about you?" I ask. "Are you all right? " He had to have felt the brunt of the impact.

Luke nods. "I had the steering wheel to hang on to." His eyes assess me again before he starts up the SUV and slowly backs up and steers us out of the ditch. "Did you see the driver?"

"No. Too dark. Did you ID the car?"

He shakes his head. "I couldn't even tell what color it was. Not a light-colored vehicle. That's all I know. I was just focused on keeping us on the road."

"You did a great job." I slouch deeper into my seat, letting some of the tension go.

His hand reaches out and rubs my arm. "Are you sure you're all right?"

My hand rests over his, and I nod my head. Our eyes meet and hold. I feel my pulse accelerating for reasons having nothing to do with the wreck.

Luke's phone rings, and I'm snapped back to reality. Hero's syndrome. That's all it is. The guy saved us tonight, and I'm just feeling gooshy inside because of it.

Luke checks the display, silences the phone, then rests it on the console. I glance down at the name. *Taylor.*

I look up and find Luke watching me out of the corner of his eye. "I'll call her later."

"She's a cute girl," I say, for lack of anything significant to add. "Hope there's not trouble in nerd paradise."

His laugh is brief. "Not at all. Speaking of paradise, how's your ex? Hunter, is it?"

I chew on my lip and scan my brain for a snappy comeback. A poison dart of a barb. "He's fine." Seeing my life flash before my eyes has somehow robbed me of anything remotely smart. "We've had some great discussions about God lately." Why am I telling him this?

"Do you think God would want you to be romantically involved with someone who cheated on you?"

I eye my purse and envision myself whacking Luke in the head with it. But it would knock him out, and I'm too wired to drive. "I think I read somewhere we were supposed to forgive." My voice is ice. "I could be wrong. Sometimes I get my Bible mixed up with my *Seventeen.*"

"Yeah, there's forgiveness and friendship, then there's stupidity in hooking up with the guy who didn't even respect you enough to be faithful the first time. And with your best friend, right?"

I rub the tender spot on my head. "Thanks for the morality lesson, Mr. Judgmental." Like I'm even considering getting back together with Hunter. At least, I'm mostly not. Pretty much not. More than likely *not* considering it. "Hunter needs a friend right now. And I'm going to be that friend no matter what happened a few months ago."

"I guess it makes for good TV."

"What does *that* mean?"

Luke frowns behind his glasses. "I don't know."

The next ten minutes pass in silence. When I can't take it anymore, I voice the thought that's been running laps in my head. "Are we agreed this wasn't a coincidence?"

I hear Luke's deep exhale. "We'll see what the police have to say."

"But what do you think?"

His gaze is wary. "I think someone wants us to mind our own business."

chapter thirteen

Though my mom wanted to keep me on lockdown this morning, I convinced her I was okay enough to go to school. And with finals next week, I really can't afford to miss a single class.

During lunch I search the parking lot for cars that have some dents and extra paint, but only find one possibility. Call it a gut feeling, but I don't really think Mrs. Brunstickle, the eighty-one-year-old janitor, is our prime suspect.

Grateful my Bug starts, I follow Luke to the police department after school, where we give our statements and file a report.

"Where are you off to?" Luke opens the door to his 4Runner, and it creaks in protest.

"Pancho's Mexican Villa."

He lifts a brow. "Do you have a lead you're not telling me about?"

"No." I feel my cheeks flame. "A job interview." I shut myself in the car before he has a chance to retort.

The owner called and left a message a few hours ago, saying he'd reviewed my application and liked what he saw. I guess listing "I Heart Salsa" as a qualification was a good move.

I park the Bug and take in Pancho's in all of its glory. Thumbing its nose at the principles of architecture and curb appeal, the restaurant is shaped in the form of a sombrero. It sits directly across the street from the Wiener Palace, and word is the competition between the two eateries is fierce.

The door jangles as I enter the building. "Welcome to Pancho's Mexican Villa," three workers call out. They don't look up from whatever it is they're doing, and if they got any less excited, I'd think they were unconscious.

"Um . . . thanks." I approach the one most likely to have a pulse. "I'm here to speak to the owner. Is he here?"

The girl rolls her eyes. "Manny's always here." From beneath her red poncho, she lifts her hand and points to the office. "In there."

"Qué pasa?" a deep voice bellows when I knock on the door.

I ease into the room and blink. "Manny?" I had expected a man of Latin descent. We have a decent-sized Hispanic population in Truman, so surely the owner of the sole Mexican joint in town would *not* look like a lower-class Jersey boy with a beer gut and gold chains.

"Wassup?" He holds out a fist, and I hesitantly bump mine to it. "You must be Bella Kirkwood, right?"

I think I might want to be somebody else. "Er, yes."

"I'm Manny Labowskie. Come on. Let me show you around." He stands up, and I get the full view of the ensemble. Shiny navy running suit, jacket zipped a quarter of the way down. Hairy chest in lieu of a shirt. A thick rope chain hangs around his neck like a memento from a rap star's garage sale. His high-tops squeak as we tour the restaurant.

"Now when people come in the door, you gotta say, 'Welcome to

Pancho's Mexican Villa!'" He scratches his extended belly and grins.
Capped teeth smile back at me. "Go ahead, give it a try."

"Now?"

"Sure!" He lowers his voice to a whisper. "I can tell a lot about a
person by the way they call out the Pancho greeting. Let's hear it."

I nervously scan the room. Besides the workers, there're only
two customers, and luckily I don't know either of them. So far, my
reputation is safe. But as soon as I get my own sombrero and poncho, I can kiss it good-bye.

I cup my hand around my mouth. "Welcome to Pancho's
Mexican Villa." I sound like a ticked-off cheerleader.

Manny slaps me on the back, nearly sending me to the other
side of the room. "Good stuff, Kirkwood. That was sheer poetry.
Now let's visit the kitchen."

I follow him behind the counter. "Shouldn't those guys have
gloves on?" I point to two high schoolers who are elbow deep in
refried beans.

Manny's eyes go all shifty. "Um, right. Definitely. Junior! Chris!
If I see you without gloves again, you're, like, fired. What do I tell
you about the gloves?"

The two guys exchange confused looks. "That we only had to
use them if we saw someone with a health department badge?"

Manny erupts in laughter. "Oh, those kidders. Those nuts." He
smacks one on the back of the head, sending a sombrero into a vat
of salsa.

"Now, Kirkwood, my life's work is to make the best taco in the
whole town of Truman."

Shouldn't be too hard since this is the only place that even
offers tacos.

"We make them good, and we make them fast. You have about ten seconds for each taco."

Yikes. "That's pretty fast."

Manny covers his heart with a big, hairy hand. "Do you believe in the Lord, Kirkwood?"

I nod.

"The town of Truman is my mission field. And I'm reaching the people . . . one taco at a time."

"Touching." I think somebody's eaten too many pinto beans. "You do understand this is temporary and for the Truman High *Tribune*?"

Manny's gold-ringed hand waves away this idea. "People don't stay here long anyway. I'll take what I can get."

Thirty minutes later, I've been shown how to operate the two main assembly lines—the burrito and the taco. I've learned the order of operation and exactly how much of each ingredient should go into the food. I think I've got it.

"Well, what do you think? Are you ready to join the Pancho's Mexican Villa team? We only pay minimum wage, but unlike the Wiener Palace, I can offer you all the chips you can eat."

"I was hoping for a little more."

"Fine. Half off *queso*."

"I'll take it."

"*Muy bien!*" Manny spits on a finger and rubs a spot of dirt off his Nikes. "That means very good. You should probably write that down. You don't know when I'll just bust out the Spanish on you. Now, come with me."

He leads me back to his office and squishes a giant sombrero on my head and drapes me in a poncho marked XL. "Can you start immediately?"

"I guess. I'll need to call my mom." I try to adjust the shapeless poncho, but it's no use. I'm tall, but it still hangs long and offends every fashionable bone in my body.

"I can tell you are just what I need for a very special job. Not anyone can do it, but I trust you with it." He pats his heart again. "I feel like I know you already, and the Lord has spoken to me and said, 'Manno'—that's what he calls me—'Manno, this is just the right person for the job.' Are you ready for that special assignment, Kirkwood?"

I bob my head weakly, knowing doom is about to rear its ugly head.

Manny slides a giant sandwich board over my coat. I readjust my hat and look down. *Pancho's for Your Luncho. Wieners Give You Gas.*

"Clever."

Manny winks. "I know, right?"

Three minutes and seven seconds later, I'm planted by the side of the road, waving a giant taco and wondering what my chances are for an apocalypse.

"Hey!" Budge yells from across the street. "What are you doing?"

"Ruining my odds for ever getting a date!"

He storms over to where I stand guard, his giant Aladdin pants swishing in the brisk wind. "My boss sent me out here. She's warned Manny about that stupid sign."

"I don't think his sign is illegal." Stupid. Humiliating. Possibly a big joke from the dark side, but not illegal.

Budge opens his mouth, then stops. He digs into his silky back pocket and pulls out a phone. "Smile! This baby's totally going on Facebook."

I make a grab for the phone, but the sandwich board slows me down. "You jerk! When I get home, I'm going to—"

I'm interrupted by the rumbling sound of a motorcycle. Budge looks beyond my shoulder, his mouth gaping. "It's—it's her."

I swing around as Ruthie McGee pulls her bike next to us. She kills the engine and whips off her helmet, her spiky hair miraculously bouncing right back into its place.

She reads my sign. "Nice motto. Catchy."

"Is that tobacco in your mouth?" I stare at the wad she's got between her cheek and gum.

"Beef jerky."

"Classy."

"Someone's hacked my MySpace page and sent out all these bad notes about me—complete with pictures. Are you on the job or aren't you?"

It's really hard to have an intelligent conversation with someone when you're wearing a sign about the farting dangers of wieners.

"Look, I've had some developments with another situation. I haven't forgotten about you, Ruthie."

"Someone's out to destroy my reputation. Someone with killer computer skills."

My eyes shift to Budge. "I know someone like that."

"I'm not an evil mastermind. I use my skills for the good." Budge's face softens as he gazes at Ruthie. "I can't imagine anyone hurting you."

She switches her jerky wad to the other cheek. "Really?"

Budge nods. Then nods some more. "T–t–totally. Maybe I could help you?"

"What'd you have in mind?"

"I'd have to take a look at your computer, but we might be able to trace the hacker back to his or her own computer. I get off work at seven."

She turns the key on her bike and revs the engine. "Be at my house at eight." She jabs her gloved finger in his vest. "And don't be late. This is the night I reserve for my flute practice and poetry reading."

Ruthie zooms away, and I don't have to look at Budge to know he's slack-jawed and moon-eyed.

I sigh and straighten my hat. "She could've at least bought a taco."

chapter fourteen

*G*ood morning, Tigers! This is Megan for Tiger TV with your
Monday announcements."

I read over some vocab words in English class, wishing I had
studied more over the weekend. Between church, calculus homework, and a call from Hunter, I just ran out of time.

Hunter is being so incredibly nice. He always was a good boyfriend—well, minus the cheating part. But now he's practically dream
boyfriend material. Like he's a little less self-absorbed, a little more
humble, and . . . I have to admit I like the new Hunter. When I told
him what I had going on at work and school, he actually listened.

"*. . . And don't forget to pick up your Match-and-Catch forms. Junior
class officers will be passing them out in the caf during lunch. To get the
results of your perfect Truman High mate, just pay ten dollars . . .*"

I lean across the row and poke Budge in the shoulder. "Are you
going to do that?"

He huffs, sending his red 'fro bouncing. "Dude, do I have *loser*
written across my forehead?"

"So that's a yes?"

"The day I fill one of those out is the day I wear girl's underwear."

At lunch I go find the Match-and-Catch table, knowing Lindy will be there.

"How's it going?" I ask.

"We're being stampeded. Pass these out." She shoves a stack of forms in my arms. "Don't forget tonight's the FCA ice skating party downtown."

"Yeah, I have to work, so I'll be there pretty late." Tomorrow is dead day—a day to review in every class before finals start Wednesday. So to let off some steam before all the cramming begins, we're having a Christmas party.

"Hey!" Ruthie McGee shoves her way to the front. "Have you seen Budge?"

"No, I—"

Ruthie spots him walking by, grabs him by the collar, and yanks him into the crowd. "Did you find anything out yet?"

Budge blinks a few times. "Um . . . I . . . haven't really found much information for you. I'm still working on it."

She tweaks a form out of my hand. "My boyfriend broke up with me when he saw the incriminating photo. I need a new man." She stares down Budge. "Are you going to fill one out?"

His mouth opens like a fish. "I . . . was just coming here to get one. Bella, give me a Match-and-Catch form."

I pass it to him. "Victoria's Secret makes a nice panty, by the way."

I return from my second night on the job smelling like one big taco. It's saturated my hair, my pores, and permanently stuck up my nose. My fingers hurt from rolling burritos, and my poncho looks like I bathed in salsa. The working world is vicious.

I walk into our living room and find Moxie staring at a wall. She attacks an invisible prey, then walks away purring, her job done. Moxie doesn't do higher-level thinking. We're not real sure that my cat thinks at all.

After I shower off all the greasy gunk, I kiss Mom good-bye and drive downtown to where the ice rink is set up. Though it's nearly nine, the party should still be in full swing.

I hear the Christmas music before I even shut off the car. Carrie Underwood sings about a winter wonderland. I shiver into my coat and find my friends.

"Bella!" Anna intercepts me as I pay for my skates. "Big news."

"You were on *America's Most Wanted* last night?"

Her scowl is filled with attitude. "Real cute. The charges were dropped."

"Are you serious? That's awesome."

"They finally confirmed my alibi."

"How?"

"Your brother took my laptop into the police station and was able to show them I was using the Wi-Fi at the Java Joint."

"You mean Budge?"

"Yeah, I owe that boy. I mean, I knew we could prove I was there, but finding witnesses was going to take a while."

"Who asked him to look at your laptop?"

"It was Luke Sullivan's idea."

"Really?" Why didn't he mention it? "Um, I'm happy for you. I'm glad I didn't go ahead and get you that nail file for Christmas."

"You're really cracking me up tonight, Kirkwood."

I laugh at her sour tone and leave her to join Lindy and Matt.

"Hey, guys." I sit down at a bistro table as Lindy and Matt sip hot chocolate. "How's the rink?"

I peer over the edge to take it all in. Christmas trees stand all over the grounds. Chairs and tables sit under a row of canopies, with tiny white lights twinkling overhead. The oval rink glistens in front of us, and everyone from grandmothers to toddlers spin across the ice.

"Oh. I see Luke and his girlfriend are here." My editor-in-chief skates next to his college girl. A silly stocking cap sits on her head, and her hair sprouts out in two juvenile pigtails.

She looks totally cool. And I want to thoroughly dislike her for it.

"Something wrong?" Lindy follows the trail of my stare.

I force my attention back to the table. "No." I hope this smile is believable. "I'm just impressed with the rink. It's cool the town creates this every winter. I mean, it's no Rockefeller Center, but it's pretty close."

The up-tempo song ends, and a slow one takes its place. Couples filter onto the rink. I see Taylor rise up and kiss Luke on the cheek. They laugh, and he escorts her off the ice.

"You guys should go skate." I nudge Lindy with my knee.

"I don't know." She braves a look at Matt. "Um . . . do you want to?"

He shrugs. "I guess."

"Well, you don't have to sound so excited." She huffs and walks away.

Matt stands up, ready to follow. "What was that about?"

"I don't know," I say innocently. "Maybe you shouldn't sound like you'd rather eat live worms than skate with her."

"We skate together every year. What's the big deal?"

Boys. So dumb, yet so necessary in our world.

Matt joins Lindy on the ice, and after lacing up my skates, I make my way there as well. Sure it's mostly couples, but who cares?

My blades wobble as I step down, but soon I'm steady and gaining speed. I weave through the crowd, the wind catching my hair. Tilting my head back, I fill my lungs with the crisp winter wind. A snowflake falls, then two. I stick out my tongue to catch the next one. After a few minutes, I hold out my arms and skate backwards, and when the speed feels right, I twist my body and pop into a jump.

I turn at the sound of clapping behind me.

"Is this a one-girl show, or can anyone join?"

"Hello, Luke." I face forward again, skating on as if he's not there. I hear his blades slice to catch up. "You're pretty good."

I wave at some friends we pass.

"I said—"

"I heard you."

His brow furrows. "Are you mad at me?"

"Why would I be mad at you?"

"Because you're a girl, and that's what you do."

I know he's just baiting me for a response, so I smile and hum along to the music.

"Do you know there's a guy with a video camera over there?" He points across the rink where a man stands with a lens trained on me.

"Just ignore him. That's what I do."

"Like you're ignoring me?"

I slow my skates. "Look, I've had a hard day of slinging tacos. Why don't you go find your girlfriend and talk to her?"

That annoying smile returns to his face. The one he always gets when I mention Taylor the Genius Girlfriend. "She just left to meet some friends."

I return to ignoring him. Doesn't the Bible say if you don't have anything nice to say, don't say anything at all? No, wait. Not the Bible. My mom? The fortune cookie I ate last week?

"Bella." Luke's hand on my arm stops us both.

Couples swish around us as I study Luke's face. There's something there I can't define.

"I'm not mad at you, Luke. I just wanted some time to skate." I stare up at the sky and let the flakes collect on my lashes. "This makes me miss Manhattan, and I want to soak it all up."

"I saw you talking to Anna."

"You could've told me you were working with Budge and the police."

He runs a hand through his black hair. "This isn't your mystery to solve."

"She asked me to clear her name."

"I should think that car running us off the road would be enough motivation for you to stay out of it."

"What, so you can be in danger, but I can't?"

"You almost got killed the last time you stuck your nose in something here at Truman High."

"Luke Sullivan . . . I think you're worried about me." Now it's my turn for the sly grin.

His face is impassive. "You have a new assignment for the paper. I want you to interview sophomore Tracey Snively. She was student of the month."

"No! You're just trying to weasel me out of the missing funds story. Besides, Tracey Snively is that girl who has like thirty cats. And she smells like yams."

"I'm the editor, and right now we have no missing funds story. And last time I checked, we still had a paper to publish."

"Don't shut me out of this. Anna came to *me* to clear her name. Ruthie came to *me* to get to the bottom of this. Not you."

He pulls us to the side of the rink. "Ruthie McGee? What does she have to do with this?"

"Oh, gee. I'm sorry. But that's something I'm working on all by myself." I bat my lashes. "Can't tell you."

I skate away and rejoin Lindy and Matt. Since they aren't in the throes of one big make-out session, I assume that Lindy didn't declare her true feelings to her BFF, and Matt didn't tell Lindy she's the milk in his Cheerios.

An hour later, much of the crowd has gone home. I say good-bye to my friends, grab my purse, and walk to my car.

The Bug glistens with a diamond frost, and as I stick my key in the door, I notice it's unlocked.

That's funny. I always lock it. No, this isn't the backstreets of New York where they'll strip your car down to the caps, but still, a girl has to be careful.

Suddenly I'm very aware of how alone I am out in the gravel parking lot. Just me and a few cars.

I quickly open the door, and there on the seat is a piece of pink paper. The type is in a jagged font.

Bella,

I'm warning you to mind your own business. I'd hate to see you get caught in the path of what I want. Nothing will stop me—not even you.

A chill snakes down my spine.

And a hand settles on my shoulder.

I scream into the night air and jump straight up, my hands slapping out. "Back off! I know Pilates!"

"Bella." Luke grabs my hands and pins them to his chest. "Bella!"

I melt into him and sigh in relief. "I totally knew it was you. I did." Raising my head, I step back and put some distance between us. "What are you doing out here? I thought you'd left."

His forehead wrinkles. "I was talking to some friends when I saw you walk off by yourself. Thought I'd make sure you got to your car okay." His blue eyes zone in on the note. He takes it from me, and I notice my hands are shaking. So much for acting unaffected.

"How many of these have you received?" His gruff voice is like sandpaper to my nerves.

I snatch the note back. "I'm not feeding you any more information just so you can cut me out and get the story for yourself."

"An answer, Bella."

"Fine." *Why are boys so annoying?* "This is the first. But it's none of your concern."

Luke's fingers latch onto my shoulder again. "*You're* my concern."

I'm pulled in by the intensity of his eyes. He draws me closer to him, and my hands rest on his jacket.

His eyes drop to my lips.

I hold my breath, afraid to move.

Afraid he's going to kiss me.

Terrified he's not.

Beside us a car alarm wails, and we jolt apart.

I pan over Luke's shoulder to see a black-haired man backing away from a Honda, his video camera drooping. "Shoot. I really needed that footage. I don't suppose I can get you two to move in close again?"

We both stare.

"I didn't think so."

chapter fifteen

Mrs. Palmer hasn't even started reviewing for our lit final, and I'm already counting the minutes. Why is it they have to ruin the few days leading up to break with finals? Forcing me to study until my brain oozes out does *not* make me want to break out in some "Deck the Halls." But come Friday, I'll be Manhattan bound and far away from tests and report cards, spending an early Christmas with my dad.

Budge lumbers into English class, his red curly hair shielding half his face. He glances around for a seat, and knowing the only one open is behind me, I wave my hand and pat his desk. With our work schedules, I haven't gotten to talk to him at all. And stepbrother has some explaining to do.

I pounce as soon as he sits down. "Why didn't you tell me you were working with Luke Sullivan?"

Budge picks a piece of lint off his "Frodo for President" t-shirt. "I didn't know I had to report to you."

"I was taking care of clearing Anna's name. And Ruthie's. I don't need Luke's help."

He pulls a pencil from his fro. "I don't do turf wars, but Luke has my loyalty."

I gasp. "He paid you!"

Budge's stubbly jaw drops. "That offends me, Bella. I am wounded to the core. My mind is just reeling. In fact, I might have to look over your shoulder and copy off your final tomorrow just to ease my pain."

I do a partial eye roll.

"*Good morning, Truman High! This is Tiger TV with our last announcements for the semester.*"

"I was in the process of getting witnesses to confirm that Anna was at the coffee shop at the time the check was cashed."

"I'm sorry, Velma. I didn't mean to get in the way of you and the Mystery Machine."

I narrow my eyes. "If you don't help *me* out and keep me in the loop on Ruthie McGee, I'll . . ." Thinking, thinking. "Tell her something that would destroy your reputation forever." I lift my chin. "I know things." Other than the fact that he has one Justin Timberlake CD hidden in his room, I've got nothing.

"Oh, I'm so scared."

Maybe it's the lighting, but I think I see a flicker of doubt.

". . . *The finalists for your senior prom queen are Anna Deason, Felicity Weeks, Ruthie McGee, and Callie Drake. Your prom king candidates are . . .*"

I tune in to the announcements long enough to make a list on my notebook and reread the names.

"*Get online and exercise your American right to vote. Results will be announced at prom in March.*"

"Your girlfriend made the cut."

Budge flushes red. "She's not my girlfriend. And she scares me." His mouth lifts. "I kinda like it."

At lunch I'm supposed to meet cat girl Tracey Sniveley for an interview, but she doesn't show. I fix a salad, buy a water, and walk toward my friends. As soon as I sit, everyone quiets.

I glance at the faces of Anna, Matt, and Lindy. All guilty-looking.

I spy a flash of white. "What's that behind your back there, Anna?"

"This?" It remains out of sight. "Nothing. Just, um, *Sports Illustrated.*"

"Really? Who's on the cover?" Though she's a cheerleader, Anna knows nothing about sports. Even less than I do.

"Uh . . . Tiger Sharapova."

"Hand it over."

With a worried glance at Lindy, Anna puts the magazine in my hand.

"The *Enquirer*?" I read the cover. "The Olsen twins are in secret negotiations with aliens from Mars. Cameron Diaz dates ninety-year-old men. Bella Kirkwood—" *What?* I pull the magazine closer. "Bella Kirkwood: Can This Wrestler's Daughter Juggle Her Two Loves?" And there on the cover is a picture of Hunter with his arms wrapped around me. And another of me standing next to my car, staring into the eyes of Luke Sullivan, his hands on my shoulders.

"It's okay, Bella. It's just a tabloid."

I glare at Matt. "Of *my* life! How can they print this? And why would anybody care?"

"Are you kidding me?" Anna takes back the magazine. "People can't get enough of *Pile Driver of Dreams.* Even my grandma watches it."

"But I'm no celebrity!" What if Luke's seen this? Or his girl-friend? *Okay, calm down.* Nothing's happened between us. No big deal. And do I even care what Hunter thinks? But then again, if he's sick, does he need this kind of stress? I know I don't.

"The pictures . . ." I search for words. "They're not what they look like. I promise. No hanky-panky on my end. I've totally kept my lips to myself." Tragic, but true.

"Heyyyy." I turn at the deep voice. Ruthie McGee sets her tray beside mine. "Nice pics." She elbows me in the ribs. "Juggling two guys. Atta girl!"

"But I'm not!" I take a long drink of Dasani. "Um . . . did you need something? I've got Budge doing his computer magic, so hopefully we'll get to the bottom of who took over your MySpace and sent that picture."

"Well, let me know if you need my help," she says. "I have dis-tant mob connections."

After school I drive to my taco nightmare.

"Um, Manny, my cat kind of chewed a big hole in my sombrero. Do you have another one?" *Please say no. Please say no.*

"You got it, *señorita.*" My boss holds up a meaty finger. "Wait here." He goes back into his office and returns with a hat bigger than the last. "You'll grow into it."

"Only if my head swells," I mumble. I slip on my poncho, flop on the sombrero, and take my place behind the counter.

Two hours later the dinner rush is in full swing.

Two men walk in and I give them the standard greeting. "Wel-come to Pancho's Mexican Villa!" We serve tacos and humiliation.

"I'll have a Nifty Nacho and a Mucho Munchie Burrito. Sam,

what do you want?" The taller of the two steps back to let his friend order.

"You," I hiss. The black-haired guy with the camera. "You work for the show. And you sold the pictures to some *trash* magazine!"

His grin stretches wide. "I got a kid to support. Nice shots though, eh?"

My mouth opens and closes. I filter all the words I *want* to say, but know I shouldn't. "This is my life you're distorting. I have friends, a family. People's feelings are getting hurt." Like mine.

He shrugs. "Who cares? That's the biz, baby. If you were smart, you'd work it. You could have all of America involved in your love triangle. That sells."

"I am *not* for sale. And there is no love triangle."

Chris Stilwell hands me the first order.

"Get used to it, babe," the photographer says. "I'm not going anywhere. And it's okay to be a girl who plays the boys. Keep stringing them along, I say."

Oh!

As if my hand disconnects from my brain, I reach for the salsa and throw it on his shirt. "I am not some cheap skank."

The tall one laughs. "You don't have to be. That's what Photoshop is for."

I turn around, grab the refried bean dispenser. I pull the trigger and bean burrito innards squirt all over my target.

"Dude." Chris twirls two cheese shooters like pistols and hoses the photographers down. "Right on!"

A table of teenagers in the back joins in, throwing *queso* and chips clear across the room.

A woman screams and holds up her tray in defense while her husband grabs three tacos and flings them like grenades.

The air is filled with hamburger meat and other lardy delights. I lunge for the floor and crawl military-style toward Manny's office.

I knock on the door, and it opens. Manny looks side to side, then down. "Did you lose something?"

A tortilla smacks him in the face.

"My job?"

<hr>

Why is it lately when I come home at night, I need to be hosed off?

I guess tonight is the last night for smelling like a nacho platter. I think I got all the research I can from Pancho's. And Manny agreed. I try to focus on something more positive, like getting out of school a day early and leaving for my dad's Friday. I can't wait to get out of town.

With the beans out of my hair, I step out of the shower and into some clean clothes. A little quality time with Robbie will cheer me up before I cram for finals.

My towel still on my head, I walk down the hall to Budge and Robbie's room. Hearing the TV blaring and someone singing, I know Robbie's got to be in there. I knock once and then shove open the door.

My brain shudders as I process the sight before me. Budge screams and flies off the bed. With his bulky body, he shields me from the TV.

"It's not what you think!" His face is white as a tortilla.

"Let me see what you're watching there, stepbrother." I smile.

Whatever it is he's hiding, I have a feeling I'm going to be able to use it.

"Just walk away and pretend like none of this ever happened."

"I heard singing."

His Adam's apple bobs. "Radio. It was the radio."

I glance at the stereo sitting quietly in the corner. "Nah. And the tune . . . it kind of sounded familiar."

Budge closes his eyes. "Leave my room!"

I'm in a scrappy mood tonight, so I do what any stepsister would do. I get a running start, leap into the air, and tackle him. He spins around and around, and I hang on for dear life.

"Aughhhh!" With a battle cry, he flings me across the room, and I land on Robbie's bed.

Where I get a perfect view of the TV. "Hannah Montana!" I dissolve into giggles. "Budge watches *Hannah Montana!*"

"No!" he shouts. "I was just flipping channels!"

I roll off the bed. "It's okay, Budge. I've watched a lot of her too."

He stares back toward the screen. "Really?"

"Yeah, when I was like twelve!" I barely dodge a pillow and run out of the room.

I search the rest of the house and finally find the brother I actually wanted to talk to in the living room. He's sprawled on the floor, tongue stuck out and crayon in hand. An empty bag of chips is nearby.

"Hey, Robbie. Nice picture. What is it?"

He doesn't even look up. "It's a pastel representation of my feelings on the corruption of our legal system."

"Oh." Why can't he draw puppies and smiley faces like other

kindergarteners? "Hey"—I crouch down beside him—"are you feeling okay? You seem a little down lately."

Robbie spins on his stomach, drags his art with him, and faces the other direction. "I'm fine."

"Robbie, what is going on with you? Is it school?"

Robbie's sienna-brown crayon pauses. I watch as his eyes lift to mine and his chin quivers. "I can't tell you." He reaches his small hand into the chip bag, pulls back some crumbs, and licks them off his hand.

"But maybe it's something I could help you with."

"Nobody can help me. Superheroes work alone. We're destined to walk this earth in solitude. If anything's wrong, only I can make it right."

Seriously, the boy watches way too much of those TV shows for smart people. His vocabulary is crazy. I should probably let him take my English final for me.

"You know you can tell me anything, right?"

"I don't want to talk about it." He picks up his crayons and paper, and his feet make slip-slap noises up the stairs.

Hearing my mom talking in her bedroom, I follow her voice while I take the towel off my wet head. She sits on the bed with her cell phone to her ear and waves.

"Dolly, that's great news. Keep us updated, no matter the time."

Mom shuts her phone. "Dolly's about to be a mom! The girl's in labor right now."

"That's awesome." Dolly deserves some happiness.

"Hey, aren't you home from work kind of early?" She leans over and stares at my hair. "What is this?" She picks at my scalp.

I study the red thing in her hand. "Could either be a pepper or a tomato. Hard to tell." I fill her in on my evening of projectile food.

"Bella—"

"I know." I slip off the bed. "It was stupid. But I promise not to shoot beans on my next job."

chapter sixteen

I wake up early the next morning, and before my feet touch the floor, I have a chat with God about parents, boys, and burritos. Seeing I still have plenty of time, I crawl over an unconscious Moxie and go to my desk to catch up on e-mail.

There's one from Dad with a picture of him, Christina, and Marisol at Rockefeller Center. Marisol gazes at my dad like he's king of the world or something. *Delete.*

I click on the next one, which has my own e-mail address as the sender.

> *Dear Bella,*
> *You don't know what you're dealing with. Take my advice and mind your own business. Next time I might not be so nice. You're pretty when you sleep, by the way.*
> *Your friend.*

Chills flitter across my body as I click to open the picture in the attachment.

I clutch my chest. "Oh my gosh!" It's me. Asleep. Someone was in my room last night!

I force myself to take some deep breaths. Okay, this is not funny. I'm totally creeped out. How did this perv get in? And why? I live with a wrestler, for crying out loud. Who would be stupid enough to break into *our* house?

An hour later, Officer Mark leaves the house after getting all the information he could. The kitchen is almost silent, yet the air is heavy with all the unspoken thoughts.

"You are not to go anywhere alone." My stepdad rubs his face with his giant hand. "If you need to go anywhere, you call one of us. You can reach me anytime."

"I'll be fine. How about if I just let you know where I am at all times? I'm sure it's just someone trying to scare me. He's probably harmless." I hope.

"So it's a he, huh?" Budge asks.

I work up my first smile of the day. "This is the work of an idiot, therefore it has to be a guy." Actually, I don't know. I have no idea who it could be.

My mom stands behind me and wraps me in a hug. "Jake will call the security system company today."

"I won't let anything happen to you." His expression darkens. "But you really do need to back off your investigative pursuits. Let someone else handle it."

"Like the police," Mom says as she walks to the fridge. "Robbie, why are there five Twinkies in your lunch sack?" She holds up his black Batman bag. "That's not what I packed last night." She takes them out one by one.

I watch my little stepbrother slide lower in his seat. "I dunno. Guess I thought I'd get hungry."

Jake reaches out and tussles his son's hair. "If you want to be a big, strong man like me, you can't eat all that junk."

"Yeah, you should drink raw-egg smoothies like your dad." I'll take my Pop-Tarts any day. After a family prayer, we all head our separate directions.

"Budge will be following you to school in his car." Mom hands me my purse as I open the door.

"Well, my cool factor just took a nosedive." I kiss her on the cheek and step outside.

"Bella?"

I glance back.

"I know you're not going to let this go, so just promise me you'll be careful. Trouble seems to have a way of following you."

"Me?" I smile, but Mom doesn't return it. "I'll be fine. Maybe just say a prayer for me."

Mom rolls her eyes heavenward. "If I prayed any more for you, I'd have to quit my job at Sugar's. So stay safe or else you'll be spending some extra time with your grandmother." Mom's face is all innocence. "For safety purposes, of course."

Before first hour at school, I close myself in a bathroom stall and take a moment to clear my head. *God, this is so not cool. I need some heavenly pit bulls of protection to guard me. This is something I need to do, but between you and me, this morning I was so scared I nearly peed my Victoria's Secrets.*

"I'm doomed." I hear a voice from the next stall. "I'll go down as the worst president in history. They'll impeach me!"

I know that voice. I stand up on the toilet lid and peep over. "Lindy?"

Sad eyes look straight up. "Oh, hey. Just, um, studying for a final."

Right. "Everything okay over there?"

"Last night I shot a game-winning three-pointer. Why can't being in charge of prom be that easy? No wonder Harry Wu Fong moved away."

"You're doing a great job. We're making a ton of money on the Match-and-Catch fund-raiser. What's the problem?" I haven't turned in my personal interest survey, but I'm going to. Eventually.

"Somehow the reservations for the caterer got cancelled. Where are we going to get food now? They said someone called yesterday and told them we wouldn't be needing their services. And now they're booked up!"

"It's going to be okay, Lindy." Um, not sure how. But it sounds nice. "Did they say who called? Guy, girl? Did you get a name?"

"Oh, so now I'm not only a horrible president, but I'm not smart enough to ask the obvious questions!"

In journalism class, I pull up the threatening e-mail and read it until I've memorized every scary word.

"What do we have here?"

I startle at Luke's voice. "Nothing. Just working." I minimize the screen. "I'm so diligent like that."

"Wow, kinda jumpy this morning." He props a hip at my work-station. "Anything new you'd like to tell me about?"

I try to pull up another file, but my hands can't seem to steady the mouse. "Nope. Can't think of a thing."

"You know, we are supposed to be working on this missing funds story together."

"We've already gone over this. You expect me to keep you in the loop, but you don't return the favor."

"I'm sorry, Bel." His voice is low and sincere. "I haven't been acting fairly."

I study his face. No sarcasm present. "Are you feeling okay today? Running a temp?"

"I've been praying about our situation."

I swallow. "What situation would that be?" *The one where we're in a race to see who can solve the mystery first* or *the one in which I find myself sniffing your Abercrombie-scented air?*

"Us." Luke takes off his glasses. "Circling each other like alley cats whenever we have to work on a story together. I'm the leader of this paper, but I haven't been acting very . . . um, leadery."

"I don't care what Mr. Holman says about you, Luke. I think you have a great vocabulary."

He laughs and the tension between us dissolves like melting icicles. "Look, I know you've probably got some news. And since you're going to be headed out for Christmas break, you can't follow up on your leads. We can either work together and solve this *or* we continue in our stubborn pride and flush it down the toilet."

Toilet. "Before you break out in an inspirational show tune, let me take a wild guess here. Someone overheard Lindy and me talking this morning in the bathroom and came straight to you?"

His grin is nothing less than Big Bad Wolf. "I meant the other stuff too."

"Sure you did." I roll my eyes and give him my shoulder. He totally had me there. And part of me wants to tell him about the e-mail and get a little sympathy. But he'd just take me off the story. And that is *not* going to happen.

"I'll check with the caterer and find out what I can about the phone call. You know if we let that go too long, our chances of getting the caller's number are slim."

He's right. And with a psycho lurker out there, the sooner we get this wrapped up, the better. "Ughhh," I growl. "Fine. But you better keep me updated. Text me over the break. No, actually I want phone calls." I jab my finger into a chest made solid by years of soccer. "Don't let me down."

"*Me* let you down?" He captures my finger. "I'll leave that to your friend Hunter."

I sputter like there's fuzz in my lip gloss. "What is that supposed to mean?"

He drops my hand. "Nothing." He shrugs big. "I just think you should watch yourself around him. Okay, let's review what we know about the stolen money."

Though I go all blinky-eyed at his topic change, I let his cryptic statement go and show him my notes instead.

By the end of the day, my mechanical pencil is out of lead and my brain is devoid of working cells. Finals are straight from the dark side. Not to mention I stared at every single person I came across today, wondering if anyone fit the bill of maniac night stalker.

I blow a kiss to the two camera guys in the car across the street and hop into my Bug. This is Jake's day to train with Mark Rogers, my friend with the Truman PD, and I want to pick his brain.

Swinging open the doors of the gym, I wave at Mickey.

"Hey." He motions me into his office. "I heard what happened last night. I want you to know there are a lot of eyeballs in town watching you." He frowns. "That sounded creepy, didn't it?"

"Little bit."

"You know what I mean. We look out for our own here in Truman." He takes a drink of Gatorade. "Uh . . . so how was school?"

"Fine. My finals are over." I can tell this isn't really what he wants to talk about. "Mom called me at lunch today. She said the baby was born this morning. A healthy boy."

His head lowers in a slow nod. "A boy."

"Dolly's taking him home tomorrow."

Mickey sits up straighter. "Well, I was just asking about school. But I appreciate the update. I . . ." He pauses, and it's like I can feel the words crashing to the surface in his head. "I hope everything goes okay for Dolly. She was meant to be a mom."

And once upon a time, he was a father. "Mickey, I think—"

"I better get back to work." He restacks some papers. "Lots to do before this week's show."

I back out of the office and follow the trail of grunts and yells.

Jake is in full pirate gear today. He has the patch over his eye, tall black boots, and something that's painfully close to a Speedo with a skull and crossbones on the rear.

Mark sees me approach and takes his eyes off his opponent. Jake uses the opportunity to hoist him up and give him a spin.

"Hey, Bella!"

"Hey, Mark," I yell as his feet go swinging by.

My stepdad throws him to the mat and mutters something about making him walk the plank. Stepping back, he breaks character. "How were your last finals?" Jake reaches for a towel from the ropes.

"More fun than a girl has a right to have." And my brain is still mush. "Have you noticed anything off with Robbie lately?"

Jake pats the towel to his face. "Not really. But I've been so busy, I haven't spent as much time with him as I'd like."

"Ah, the price of fame." Mark rolls to a standing position, his hand massaging his back. "I really need to work on my landing."

"I know that look on your face, Bella. I'll take a water break so you can talk to Mark."

I smile at Officer Mark as my stepdad climbs out of the ring. "I think you're making great improvements. You could've totally stopped him from picking you up. I know you like to go easier on Jake because he's older."

Mark crosses his arms. "What do you want to know?"

"Just wanted to check if there'd been any developments on the missing junior class funds."

"No. Your friend Anna was absolved. And Victoria Smith simply made a dumb mistake." Mark sits back into a stretch. "All we know is she saw a guy and girl in the bank drive-thru. We can't even tell what kind of car in the bank's surveillance video. But Bella, until this morning, this case really wasn't on our list of things to be concerned with."

I grab his water bottle from the mat and hand it to him. "What would be a motive for harassing two seniors? And me?"

He shrugs a big shoulder. "Jealousy, a bitter ex-boyfriend, the geek girl who never gets noticed. And no doubt, this person thinks you're getting close to something. I think we can now tie the threats you've received to the night you got run off the road."

"And I just need to find the connection." I pin him with my best serious-girl stare. "What are the chances you'd use me on this case?"

"Less than zero." He takes a drink. "After today's development, you have no business sticking your nose in it."

I smile and dig my car keys out of my purse. "I'm just asking for the sake of the paper. Don't worry about me. I don't have my nose stuck in the case."

Though the rest of my body has plunged right on in.

chapter seventeen

I'm so glad your father suggested I pick you up at the airport," Christina says on Friday as she gives the cabbie directions to the house and settles back into the seat. "He's in a meeting but will be home later."

Her hair is perfectly highlighted, her nails flawlessly manicured, and she has the newest Chloé bag. The one I've been saving for. The one I'm still $1900 away from getting, which is like a million in teen-job dollars.

Christina's hand touches my coat sleeve. "I feel that we got off to a rough start last time you were here."

"Are you living with my dad?" I know the answer. I just want to hear her say it.

She presses her rosy lips together. "Yes. When two adults care about one another—"

"Spare me." *Pull over, driver. I need to puke.* "Will you be celebrating Christmas with us?"

Her smile is as fake as the collagen in her lips. "Yes. Your father thought it would be a nice way for us to spend some more time together." Christina folds her hands in her lap. "Bella, I think you should know that I love your father. So does little Marisol. And we're not going anywhere, so it would be helpful to all of us if you could just accept that."

I stare out the window and watch the snow blanket my city.

The cab lets us out, and I politely refuse Christina's help with my bags. Luisa meets me in the foyer, and I let her smoosh me in a hug. She smells like snickerdoodles and old times.

"How were your finals, *niña?*" Luisa sees my look of stress. "Why don't we get you settled in your room?" She gives me a playful whack on the tush, and we make our way upstairs, leaving Christina alone.

"Tell me she grows on you." I flop on the bed and stare at the psychotic cherubs overhead.

Luisa begins to unpack my suitcase. "Did you bring something nice to wear for Christmas dinner?" She stares at me over the hanger of a dress.

"That bad, huh?" I get up and help her unpack.

"Your grandmother loves her. That is all I say."

That pretty much says it all. Grandmother also likes the idea of boarding school, weak tea, and wearing lots of purple.

"What is this? Bella helping her old Luisa?" My former nanny smiles. "I think Oklahoma has been good for you. I like this new Bella."

We turn at a knock on the door. "Where's my girl?" Dad walks across the pink carpet and pecks me on the cheek. "Good flight?"

Much better than the drive home.

"I guess Christina told you that they're all moved in here. Marisol is visiting friends for the next few days but will be here for Christmas dinner on the twenty-third."

"You know I don't agree with this."

"You always were my little worrier." He tweaks my nose.

Behind him Luisa rolls her dark eyes and files out of the room.

"Tonight I have a dinner meeting with some clients at Tao. It will be outrageously boring, so I invited a friend of yours to keep you company."

They all pretty much stopped talking to me after I found my best friend with my boyfriend. As if I were the guilty party. I don't really have any friends left in Manhattan.

"Who?"

"Well, I ran into Hunter Penbrook at Starbucks the other day. So I invited him."

"Oh." Contemplating this. "Okay." I guess.

A few hours later, Dad, Christina, and I are dropped off in front of Tao. It's a great place to spy some celebs, but as we're led to the table near Buddha, my eyes zoom in on Hunter. He pulls out a chair for me, and I sit.

Dad introduces me to everyone at the table. They nod politely, then jump into business. Hunter and I fade into the background.

"How are you feeling?" I maneuver my chopstick and take a bite of sushi.

"We just ruled out leukemia, so that's a relief," Hunter says.

"That's great."

"Now they're checking on my liver. But enough about that." He smiles. "I have good days and bad."

"And what's today?"

His grin widens, and his eyes sparkle into mine. "Definitely good."

"How is your dad's business?"

Hunter's expression darkens. "He's not faring as well as your dad since the accountant took off with the money. He just can't seem to bounce back."

"I'm sure that doesn't make your health issues any better."

His warm hand covers mine. "I don't want to talk about depressing things tonight. I'm happy to be here—with you."

I'm ten minutes into the main course when I notice the guy in the corner with the small video camera.

"I'm going to slip out," I whisper to Hunter and jerk my chin in the cameraman's direction. "Lately I can't go anywhere without an audience."

"Yeah, I saw the tabloids last week. I hope that didn't bother you."

I try to read Hunter's face. Is he glad the tabloid thought we might be a couple? Or is he smiling because it was kind of funny in a twisted, drama queen sort of way?

Hunter stands up. "Want to grab some coffee?"

I say good-bye to Dad, Christina, and his business associates.

Not wanting to tax Hunter with a walk, I hail a cab to the nearest Starbucks. We walk in and I inhale deeply. I love that smell. If there was a way to safely stick coffee beans up my nose, I would.

Hunter gives our order. "One caramel macchiato and one soy vanilla latte no whip."

"You remembered my favorite drink." There's something nice about a person really knowing the small details that make you who you are. I miss that.

We take our drinks and walk outside into the cool air. It hasn't snowed for hours, yet the sidewalks are still slushy. Times Square looms before us, and I link my arm into Hunter's and lead him that way in a leisurely stroll.

My pocket buzzes. "It's a text from Mom." I pull up the message. "Jake made the cut tonight!" I clap my hands and laugh. "I really hated to miss *Pile Driver of Dreams* tonight, but I recorded it. Have you been watching the show?"

"I'm familiar with some of it." Hunter stops and covers his face with his scarf.

"It's cold, isn't it?" I button up his top coat button. "Are you feeling okay?"

I look over his shoulder and my heart sinks. Mia. She walks toward us, a group of my former friends trailing behind her like faithful troops.

"Hello, Mia." My voice is even. Controlled. Yet I want to scratch her eyes out. "So you've decided to apologize to me?"

"I'm sure." She laughs. "Besides, it looks to me like we're even."

My head bobs with attitude. "I didn't steal *anyone's* boyfriend. Let's get that clear right now."

Mia holds up a hand. "Whatever. When his weird phase wears off, he'll be crawling back to me. And it *will* wear off, Bella." Then she lasers Hunter with her glare. "I don't know what this is all about, but I know you, Hunter. Something's going on. And maybe I won't be there when you snap out of it."

She and her Bratz doll posse saunter down the sidewalk until they're swallowed by the crowds of people on Times Square.

"She is a piece of work." I shake my head and laugh. But Hunter isn't laughing with me. He stands frozen to the spot, staring in the direction of Mia's retreat. "Hey, you okay?"

"Why did you forgive me?"

"Because you asked me to."

"That's all it took? But I don't—didn't deserve it."

A few snowflakes pepper down, and I catch one with my glove. "Nope. You didn't."

"Is this one of those God things again?"

"I guess so."

Hunter wraps an arm around me, and we walk again. "If you weren't a Christian, what would you have done?"

"Kicked you in the giblets."

He rests his head on mine and laughs. "Jesus *does* save."

chapter eighteen

On December twenty-third I bow my head and give thanks to God. As in, *Thank you, Lord, tomorrow I'm going home.*

I have managed to stay out of Christina's way, minus one shopping trip in which she thought she could buy my affection with a new pair of suede boots. It did not work. But when she added the new Burberry coat, I did almost bust out some love poetry on her behalf. Seriously, I'm pretty weak. And the coat is to die for. And I guess Christina's not *that* bad. She seems to care about my dad.

I slip into my dress for Christmas dinner and take a turn in the mirror.

My phone rings, and I skip across the room to get it. Probably Hunter again. We've talked every day that I've been here.

I read the display. *Luke.*

"Do you have news?"

"Hello to you too." His voice sounds good to my ears. "How is Manhattan?"

"Cold. What did you find out?"

"I couldn't get a phone number from the caterer. But they said it was definitely a female who called them and cancelled."

"I guess that's a start. Is that all you dug up?"

"Bella, you should have more faith in me. I'm pretty good at this." I hear the smile in Luke's voice. "Whoever made the call said she was Lindy Miller."

"Why would someone try and sabotage prom?"

"That's the part we'll have to figure out when you get back."

I sigh and slip my feet into some heels. "I can't get back soon enough."

"Missing me that much?"

This makes me grin. "I'm missing Truman, believe it or not." A few months ago I wouldn't have thought it was possible. "I miss my family, my friends." And Luke?

"I saw your picture in a paper today. Looks like you're keeping busy in New York."

"What do you mean?"

Knock! Knock!

Luisa sticks her head in the door. "Time for dinner. The old bird can't wait much longer."

"You fixed turkey?"

She pulls me to my feet. "I was talking about your grandmother."

I press the phone back to my ear. "I'll talk to you later, Luke."

But he's already gone.

I pass the creamed corn and wish for the millionth time that Christina's sister, Marisol, came with a mute button.

"And then I want a new iPod phone. And a MacBook. And this dress I saw at Barney's. And these Prada boots. And tickets to . . ."

Dad catches my eye and winks. He leans down and plants a quick kiss on Marisol's nose.

"Isn't she adorable?" Grandmother beams.

Grandpa's hearing aid whines. "She's giving me gas."

Me too. I mean, first Mom got replaced and now me. *What, am I not cute enough? Not bratty enough?* I think more angry thoughts and chug my water, wishing it was some good Southern iced tea.

When Luisa brings in dessert, a chocolate trifle, it's everything I can do not to jump out of my chair and dive in headfirst.

"Luisa, please stay." My dad stands up. "There's something I'd like to share with the family."

Oh no. No way.

I watch in horror as my dad goes to Christina, bends on one knee, and reaches for her hand.

"Dad, can I talk to you in the kitchen?"

"Not now, Bella." His eyes never leave Christina. "I've made a lot of mistakes in my life. And I've lived a long time as a selfish man. But this lady right"—he holds her hand over his heart—"this special lady here has changed all of that. She's seen me at my lowest, and I hope that she'll join me on my way back to the top."

"Dad, I don't feel so good." A slick sweat explodes on my forehead.

"Later, Bella. Christina, would you do me the honor of becoming my wife?" He slides a ring on her finger.

Little Marisol claps her hands in glee. I want to hurl my fork at her.

Christina lifts her hand up to the light. She laughs and wipes away some tears. "I would be honored to be—"

Blughhhh! I puke in my dessert plate.

"Ew!" Marisol wails and bursts into tears.

"Well, I never!" Grandma holds her napkin over her taut face.

Grandpa pats me on the back. "One time I puked for two days straight. Come to think about it, it was right after I married your grandmother."

My guts feel like they're splitting in two. I'm hot. And cold. And—

"Bella, are you okay?" My dad puts his hand to my head. "Say something."

"Congratulations." And clutching my stomach, I race to the nearest bathroom.

chapter nineteen

Only twice in my life have I wished for death. The first time was in the second grade when Brian Wickham pulled down my skirt in front of the entire Sunday congregation and everyone saw my Care Bear underwear. And the second was last week when somehow I contracted food poisoning and heaved my guts up for a solid day.

Dad repeatedly said he was sorry.

Christina said the salmon dip I'd grazed on before dinner had gone bad.

Grandmother *tsk*ed and said that would teach me to snack before meals.

And I think I said something like, "*Ack! Gag! Barf!*"

After that everyone pretty much left me alone. How was I supposed to know the dip was out so it could be thrown away?

Because I was hugging a toilet when my flight left on Christmas Eve, I couldn't get back to Truman until days later. I missed Christmas with the family, but Mom made everyone rewrap their gifts and have a do-over for my benefit. Robbie loved it, but Budge practiced his twenty-five-variations-on-eye-rolls the entire time. The camera crew filmed every second.

Between Christmas vacation and missing eight days of school for snow, January evaporated like a snowman in Arizona. *Pile Driver of Dreams* exploded into a reality show hit. Everywhere I went people were talking about it. Jake even started getting fan mail. He had some close calls in the show, but is hanging in there. *US* magazine called him a fan favorite in its review.

The snow days also gave our prom wrecker little time to stir up any more trouble. And lots of time to think of new catastrophes for February.

～～～～～～～

"Robbie, make sure you take all your stuff with you from the bus. Don't leave anything behind." Mom Velcros Robbie's lunch sack closed. "It's just Tuesdays and Thursdays. You can handle that, right?" She ruffles his hair and puts a kiss on his sad face before he shuffles to the living room.

Mom now has an early morning class at the Tulsa community college. And Tuesdays and Thursdays are the days Budge and I both have to leave early, me for chemistry tutoring, and Budge for a meeting with his dork gamers, otherwise known as future million-aires whose money will one day make them hot.

Mom rests her hand on my shoulder. "Bad news, Bel. Jake got a good look at your car last night. You need a new alternator."

Perfect. "How much is one of those?"

"More than you've got. So until you save up, you can catch a ride with Budge."

I sigh into my bite of oatmeal. "I'm broke. Christmas wiped me out." And this job-a-thon for the school paper isn't helping. I totally need to clear Ruthie's name and get the rest of her payment. "Mom, don't you ever just miss money? You always act like it's so easy."

"Easy?" She snorts. "Do you know how long it's been since I got a new pair of shoes? Me, who used to attend Fashion Week? I have friends in Manhattan eating lunches that would take my whole week's paycheck. So, no, it's not easy. But I told you it would be an adventure." Her face softens. "And can you imagine life without Jake and your stepbrothers?"

"No." Except when Budge hogs the bathroom.

"I know you've been looking for another job, but you know who's got openings, right?"

I blink. "I'm *not* working at the maxi-pad factory." My dad wouldn't stand for that, would he? "Besides, job hunting is just part of teen life—good material for the column. I'll find something soon." I look toward the stairs and yell. "Let's go, Budge!"

Robbie returns and gives Mom's skirt a tug. "I think I have a fever."

Mom touches his head. "Nope. Feel okay to me."

"I think I have food poisoning like Bella."

I turn to my stepbrother. "Does it feel like a hand is reaching into your stomach and trying to French-braid your intestines?"

"No."

"Then it's not food poisoning." I flatten out some wrinkles in his Superman cape. "Are you sure everything's okay at school?"

"It's fine." He shoves away from the table and grabs his back-pack. "I'm gonna watch TV until the bus gets here." He slinks out of the kitchen and back into the living room.

I stand outside in the backyard as Budge pulls his car out of the garage. Though the initial shock has worn off of having a stepbrother who drives a hearse, it still appalls me to have to ride in it. I mean, *dead* people were in this thing. Their germs are soaked into the steel gray lining of the car. I don't want gross corpse-y germs up my nose!

I get in the car and immediately turn down his screamo. "I need an update on Ruthie McGee."

Budge jumps, his elbow hitting the horn. A foghorn sound follows. "W–what do you mean? There's nothing to talk about. Nothing."

My eyes narrow. "First of all, I *know* you went over to her house Friday night. But I mean what's going on with tracing the anonymous e-mails she's gotten?"

"Dude, I've tried for over a month. I can't crack it. It's like some wizard sent those e-mails." He turns onto David Street, running over a curb. "I have to pick up my friend Newton."

Budge pulls into the drive of a small white house. An old dead Christmas tree sits with the trash at the curb.

Newton Phillips slams out of the front door, yelling back at his mother. "I'll do the dishes when I get home! When I'm rich, you'll be sorry you bossed me around!"

I watch him stomp to the hearse. "Newt's got attitude."

He hops in the back, greets me, then does some secret handshake thing with Budge that only techie dweebs can follow.

Budge looks in his rearview. "Dude, I totally found out how to create a multileveled vortex in that second dimension."

The rest of the ride consists of me humming along to screamo so I don't have to pay attention to gamer talk. By the time we get to school, I want to cut off my own ears and stuff them down Budge's throat.

Walking into journalism later in the morning, my eyes are automatically drawn to Luke, who has his shirtsleeves rolled up and is already in work mode.

"Your interview with sophomore Tracey Snively was riveting stuff," he says as I sit down at my Mac.

I look up from my screen only long enough to glare. "Yeah, your idea to visit her in her home of thirty cats was sheer brilliance. Really gave the article a special edge. Plus I horked up fur for days."

"Well, something has increased our sales." He throws a paper down on my table. "Maybe it's this."

I ignore his sarcastic tone and pick up *Entertainment Weekly*, and there's another picture of me and Hunter from my Christmas visit in New York. It's a close-up of the two of us in front of the Buddha at Tao. This instant celebrity business is so weird.

"Thanks," I snap. "I'll add it to my growing scrapbook." What's his deal? It's not like Hunter's my boyfriend. He's totally not. Actually, I don't know what he is. We've called each other almost every night since Christmas. He seems so different. Changed. And he says he's gone to church a few times by himself.

"Was there something else?" I ask.

"As a matter of fact there is. Why don't we step into Mr. Holman's office for a moment?"

"Fine." I follow him into the empty room. Luke shuts the door. *Uh-oh. This isn't good.*

He rolls up his sleeves, as if taking the time to sort through his thoughts.

"What did I do this time?" I laugh.

But Luke is not smiling as he lifts his head. "When exactly were you planning on telling me that someone broke into your house before Christmas break and e-mailed you another threat?"

"Oh. That."

He closes the small space between us. "I don't even know what to say to you right now."

"Maybe your feelings could best be expressed in show tunes. I know when I get upset, I like to sing some old Broadway favorites."

Luke's left eye twitches. "Number one, we are friends. And friends share things with one another. You couldn't trust me with that information? I had to hear it from Officer Mark."

"I'm not going to ask what you were talking to him about," I snap. "Probably doing your own investigation into our case, so you could take the lead."

"He approached me." Luke's words are short, crisp. "He wanted to make sure I was keeping an eye on you after everything that had happened."

"So you're mad that I made you look foolish in front of him."

Luke pinches the bridge of his nose. "I'm not mad, Bella. I'm furious." He leans down and puts his face level with mine. "If you don't keep me updated on everything that happens, you will be off this paper. Permanently. I don't work with rogue reporters seeking glory and their face on the front page."

"I'm not—"

"I work with team players. Right now, you are a committee of one. And that arrogance is going to get you hurt."

"Arrogance?" *Why, you little pea-brained, chess-playing—*

"I care about everyone on this staff, and that includes you." Luke's voice is calmer. More controlled. It sets my teeth on edge. "From now on, if *anything* out of the ordinary happens, you are to call me immediately. Consider it another assignment." His eyes connect with mine. "And if you don't follow through, it will be your last."

"I am so tired of my life being everyone else's business. What's wrong with keeping one thing to myself?"

He reaches out like he's going to touch me, then drops his hand. "Because the thought of anything happening to you makes me want to tear someone apart."

I swallow.

"Just tell me your solo days are over. *And* you won't be anywhere by yourself. We're working together. It's you. And me."

I fumble for the doorknob, unable to take my eyes off him. "I . . . I have an article to finish." And I run for the safety of my computer.

When I arrive at lunch ten minutes late, I get a good look at our table and realize we've become quite a motley crew. We have Ruthie, the biker chick. Me, the Manhattan transplant. Anna, the ever-enthusiastic cheerleader. Lindy, the stressed-out class president. And Matt, the jock who just sits there and eats his sub sandwich and chips.

"Lindy, are you okay?" My friend is facedown on the table, her salad shoved to the side.

"I was not meant to be a leader. What's Donald Trump's secret?"

I pluck a tomato off her tray. "Bad hair?"

She sits up. "First the banquet hall at Truman Inn. And now . . ."

"Acid rain?"

"It's not funny, Bella. I just got a call from the Truman Inn. They wanted to let me know that when we cancelled the reservation for prom, we lost the five-hundred-dollar deposit."

I open the wrapping on my sandwich. "When was *this* reservation cancelled?"

"About five minutes ago." Lindy holds up her hand to stop my next question. "It was a female who called them. The person pretended to be me. Again."

Matt bites down on a chip. "Did you tell them you still wanted the banquet hall?"

Lindy stares at Matt with her *you idiot* face. "They had a waiting list. So now the Truman Men's Association is having Pedicures and Polish Sausage Night there."

We all take a moment to think about that one.

Ruthie stretches out her arms and then cracks her knuckles. "Well, that makes me want to hit something. Some idiot is ruining my prom."

"I'll be back." Leaving my lunch, I grab my purse and head through the double doors to the courtyard. I call information. "Truman Inn, please."

"Please tell me you aren't making reservations for a romantic getaway."

I swivel around. "Luke." I smile into the winter sun. "I was just checking on something for a friend."

He crosses his arms. "We said we were going to work together. And you're not to be anywhere alone."

"I don't recall ever agreeing to that." I press my ear to the phone and jot down the number.

Luke's hand wraps around my arm. The other reaches for the phone. "I'd be happy to dial."

I roll my eyes. "Fine." And I fill him in on the latest cancellation.

Luke calls the Truman Inn and works his magic. Charm oozes out of his every word. "Write this down." And he reads off a telephone number to me.

When he calls the new number he smiles. "Voice mail."

"Whose?"

"One of your prom queen candidates—Callie Drake."

"Let's go get her." I step forward, only to be snatched back.

"Not so fast. Doesn't this seem wrong to you?"

I stare at Luke's hand on mine. "Oh, I don't know. Doesn't seem too bad. Kinda nice and tingly actually."

"I'm talking about Callie."

Oh. Me too. "I don't even know who she is."

Luke drops my hand. "Before we run to the principal with this, let's do a little surveillance. Unless you have to work after school, that is?"

"Um . . . work? I guess I could squeeze you in."

~~~~~~~~~~~~~~~

I meet Luke at his 4Runner after school.

"I don't have a lot of surveillance experience," he says.

"Me neither. Wait here." I run across the street and through some bushes. I find two of the *Pile Driver of Dreams* camera guys. "I need to follow someone. Gimme some tips." For two minutes I take mental notes of everything they say.

"Good luck!" one yells as I walk back to Luke.

"Well?" He starts the SUV.

"Larry said to park a half a block away and get a good pair of binoculars. Doug said to bring lots of snacks."

"Where are we going to get binoculars?"

I fish through my purse and hold up a small pink pair.

Luke shakes his head. "Why am I not surprised?"

"Nosiness." I smile. "It's my spiritual gift."

"I asked around today, and Callie has a boyfriend. There's a good chance she's at his house. She doesn't work." He hangs a right.

"Nothing wrong with that."

With one hand on the wheel, Luke reaches around his seat and picks up a yearbook. He hands it to me. "Page forty-two. You'll see her picture."

I flip to the page. She's cute. In a natural sort of way. Long hair, no makeup. I thumb through the pages as he drives. "Hey, here's a layout on the Miss Truman High competition. Lookie here." I hold up the spread. "'Girls protest beauty pageant,'" I read. "And there's Callie front and center. Says the protesters claimed it devalued women."

Luke points at the contestants in bathing suits. "I see all sorts of valuables there."

We both laugh, and I smack him with the book. "Maybe our girl Callie wants to be prom queen so she can bring it down. Probably wants to expose it for the ridiculous popularity contest it is."

"Obviously she's working with someone," Luke says as he stares at a house we drive by. "She can't be doing it all alone—running us off the road, magically transferring money, sending untraceable e-mails, harassing you." He pulls onto Main Street. "That was her boyfriend's house. Nobody there."

"Let's move on to her house."

An hour later I've got a crick in my neck, I've eaten all the mints at the bottom of my purse, including the fuzzy ones, and all we've done is watch Callie's silver Focus.

"Let's just talk to her about the call, Luke. I'm tired."

"I'm going to get out and look at her car. Make sure there's no scuff marks on it—in case she's the one who sideswiped us."

I press a button and my chair reclines. "Okay. See you in a bit."

"I need you."

My hand jerks, and my chair sits straight up. "What?"

"I need you to distract Callie while I go check." He opens the car door. "You drive. Pull right up next to her car."

We swap places, and I cruise us to her house. "What will I say?"

"I don't know. You'll think of something."

"Well, it's not like we can talk makeup." I say a little prayer as I hop out of the SUV. *Dear God, please give me guidance in my moment of deceit.*

I look back with dread and Luke motions me on. With a shaky hand, I knock on her front door. Yippy dogs go off like obnoxious, fuzzy alarms.

"Yes?" Callie answers the door.

"Um, Callie? I'm—"

"I know who you are. I've seen you on TV and in the *Enquirer.*"

"Oh." *I've seen your picture too.* "I, uh, am working on a piece for the Truman High *Tribune* and wanted to talk to you about"—*Don't say anything that will tip her off*—"the rumor that they will soon be enforcing a dress code at school."

"They will?"

"Yes." I am *so* uncreative today. "I'm getting some quotes from departing seniors."

"What's the dress code going to be?"

"Er . . ." I watch a kid in a wife-beater sail by on his bike. "Tank tops and skirts. School colors."

"How short are these skirts?"

"Short?" It comes out as a question. "Yes, very short." I point to a spot way above my knee. "They said it will be good for . . . circulation." I look over my shoulder toward her car. I see the faintest hint of a coat. Hurry up, Luke!

"Well, we have an all-male school board. What do you expect?"

"Huh?" I turn back around. "Right! What do you expect?"

"My boyfriend would never allow *me* to wear skimpy clothes. He thinks it takes the focus off my brain and character."

"Uh-huh."

"In fact, he'd probably beat up anyone who even glanced at my legs."

This snaps me to attention. "Oh, is he the jealous sort?"

She smiles like this is cool. "Very. We both just believe in shining with our inner lights and not being judged by outward appearances."

"Yeah, yeah. Lights. Shining. So then how does he feel about your being a contender for prom queen?"

She sighs heavily. "He's not happy. At all. We fight about it a lot." Her voice drops. "But all principles and values aside, sometimes a girl just wants to be the one wearing the tiara, you know? Just once in my life, I want a tiara moment. Does that make sense?"

I smile. "Yeah, it does. I hope your boyfriend comes around."

"I don't know if that's going to happen." Her face darkens. "My friend Felicity Weeks told me that he's been going around *encouraging* people not to vote for me."

"Felicity's one of the other queen candidates, right?"

"Yeah, we're totally BFFs. Joshua—my boyfriend—he doesn't

like Felicity much. He says I need to find some new friends. I just think he's jealous of any time I spend away from him."

I have to ask. "Callie, why are you dating this boy?"

Her brown eyes go all dreamy. "He truly is a great guy. He just has these . . . triggers. But he really does want the best for me."

"Yeah, that sounds really *encouraging.*"

"Looks like *your* boyfriend is ready to go."

I glance back at the 4Runner, and Luke waves from the passenger side. "Uh, thanks for the quotes. And good luck on your run for the tiara."

"Luck?" Callie laughs. "If I get queen, it won't be because of luck."

I say good-bye and hop in the SUV. "Did you find anything on her car?"

"Nothing but a few door dings." Luke stretches and rests his fingers on the top of my headrest.

"Whoever ran us off the road has had plenty of time to repair her vehicle." I tell him everything Callie said.

Luke's brow furrows. "If she wins, it won't be because of luck? At this point, I don't know whether that's inspirational or ominous. Hey, where are you going?"

I pull into the Dairy Barn drive-thru. "I need to talk to the ice cream lady. Last time I was here, she looked very suspicious."

Luke laughs. "I respect your commitment to the job, Kirkwood. You do go above and beyond."

chapter twenty

"So since this Thursday is Valentine's Day"—Lindy shuts her locker and sneaks a glance at Matt—"we're passing out the Match-and-Catch results today at lunch."

Ruthie bites into a Pop-Tart as the first bell rings. "So I can find out who's the best guy in the school for me?"

"Did you fill one out, Matt?"

He looks away from Lindy and shrugs. "Yeah, I mean I guess so. It was for a good cause and all."

"Aren't you the least bit curious who it paired you up with?" she asks.

"I gotta go to science class." He waves absently and joins the downstream flow of the hall.

Callie Drake and her boyfriend walk by. He's got his arm anchored around her neck, and the two are laughing. I zip up my backpack and fall in behind the couple.

"You're going prom dress shopping *again*?" her boyfriend says. "What's the big deal? Pick one out and be done with it."

"I did pick one out—with Felicity. You said it was too revealing. I'm having a hard time finding one with a turtleneck."

I bite my lip on a smile.

"And I don't want you going over to Felicity's anymore. Not while her little boyfriend's there." His voice is angry.

"Him? Are you jealous of him? You are so ridiculous, Joshua. This is out of control."

"I'm not jealous, Callie. He's . . . weird. I don't like him. Why can't you hang out with some new friends?"

I inch up closer, straining to hear.

"There's nothing wrong with—"

"Kirkwood!"

Ugh! I slow down as Ruthie catches up with me.

"What are you doing?"

I bite back a sigh. "Eavesdropping, if you must know."

"You got someone you want me to bug? I can totally set you up. Say the word."

"No!" Tempting though. "No bugs."

"Hey, um, will you tell Budge that my computer has a thingie, and I need him to take a look at it?"

"You got another bad e-mail?"

"No."

"It has a thingie?"

She averts her eyes. "Yeah. On the dooma-flachie. It's broken. It's making it hard to—"

"Print do-hickies and send dealie-whoppers?"

"Exactly."

"Sounds serious. I'll pass that on. But you know, you could talk to him like he's just another boy. He could be interested in you as more than just a computer to fix."

She stiffens. "I didn't say I liked him."

"Right. Okay, I'll pass on the urgent computer request." Sometimes I think she's had one too many piercings.

At lunch I'm called into the office and find I have a huge floral arrangement. I open the card, half expecting to see another scary note.

New York is less without you. But my life is more with your friendship.

> *See you soon,*
> *Hunter*

Aw. Isn't that sweet? I smell the roses and lilies and grin. Plucking one of the blooms, I leave to find Lindy so I can help her pass out the Match-and-Catch forms. She hands me a single envelope.

"What is this? I'm not getting one." I don't have ten extra bucks.

Lindy refuses to take it back. "It's on the house. You've been helping me with all of this, so consider it a thank-you."

"Oh." My fingers tingle to open it. But I can't. I don't want to know. Oh, yes, I do.

"Looks like you don't need Cupid's help."

I set all my stuff on the ground and look up to find Luke. "What are you doing here? Don't tell me *you* paid to get matched. That probably wouldn't thrill your girlfriend."

He lifts and lowers a brow. "Lindy asked me to come and help."

"Oh. Right." I'm an idiot. Why do I always come off sounding like a jealous harpy? I'm not. I'm totally not. I'm sure if his Harvard girl and I got to know each other, I'd love her and want to be her very best friend. We'd probably wear each other's clothes and do each other's hair.

No, actually I want to rip her hair out. She's so stinkin' smart! And pretty! And—

"Luke, here's your Match-and-Catch results." Lindy passes him an envelope.

He stares at it like it's a tarantula. "Um, you can just keep it. I'm really not interested."

"Suit yourself." With a shrug Lindy returns to handing out envelopes and collecting money. "It's in appreciation of the articles you did in the paper on the fund-raiser. It's helped a lot."

"Just take it," I say. "I won't tell Taylor." Oh! There I go again. *God, what is wrong with me?* I've been watching too much *Gossip Girl.* Reading too many snarky books. Maybe I should listen to a bunch of Christian music or watch some *Hannah Montana* with Budge. I know, I'll view *VeggieTales* until the evil is purged out of me, and all that comes out of my mouth is goodness, light, and songs about cucumbers.

Luke just smiles and grabs some Match-and-Catch results to hand out.

"Lindy!" Felicity Weeks shoves her way through the crowd, her blonde curls jiving all over her head. "Guess what! My dad found us a place for prom."

The entire crowd stops and cheers. Two girls burst into tears. Luke and I lock gazes and share an eye roll.

Felicity high-fives a senior. "My dad's rented some huge event canopies. We can have it outside at our house."

"She has a huge home." Luke whispers near my ear. "We could probably have prom in her living room."

Lindy resumes her work. "We can't pay for that. Except for the wad in my hand, we have no money. Zero. Nada."

"But that's the best part. It's free! Daddy's footing the bill. He *wants* to help us."

More *woo-hoos* from our growing audience.

"Felicity, that's awesome." Lindy looks at me. She's beaming, and I can see a load of stress has been relieved.

"Gimme my results." Anna Deason holds out her hand, and I dig through my stack. "This better be good. I want to see if my man's name is on here. Plus, if things don't work out, I'll know who the alternates are."

"Did you hear we have a prom location now?" I ask.

She sniffs. "Whatever. I could've found us another location. I don't know what everyone is so excited about. It's not like she donated a kidney."

Before I can respond, something catches my eye. "Luke, look."

Mr. Sutter stands across the hall with Callie. She's agitated. Red-faced. Her hands move at warp speed.

"Let's take a walk." His hand moves to my back as we migrate to a spot within hearing distance of the principal.

"—but I didn't call the Truman Inn. *Why* would I do that? I'm a senior, for crying out loud. Of *course* I want prom."

"Miss Drake, the inn gave us your phone number. That's where the call came from. They have a record of it."

"Well, they're wrong. Someone probably got into my purse at lunch. I'm in the running for prom queen, Mr. Sutter. Think about it. Why would I do such a thing?"

He crosses his arms. "Last year's Miss Truman High comes to mind."

"Hey, I protested peacefully. I'm not the one who brought the eggs and the squirt guns."

"Unless you can prove someone used your phone, I have no choice but to suspend you for a week."

Mr. Sutter escorts Callie down the hall, and I turn to Luke. "When did you tell the principal?"

"This morning. I talked to some people, and the Miss Truman High wasn't the first pageant Callie protested. I think she's our girl, but we still need to find out who's working with her."

"The boyfriend?"

He nods. "It's definitely something to pursue."

An odd silence falls between us. Like neither one of us wants to move.

"So do you have your prom date?" Luke asks.

I pull a ponytail holder out of my pocket and make a loose knot. "I'm keeping my options open."

Luke tucks a rogue piece of hair behind my ear. "Hunter?"

I struggle to focus beyond the chills on my neck. "What if I do bring Hunter?"

"What if you do?" His face is impassive. "Do you really think that's a good idea?"

"He's changing, Luke. I can tell. He's just . . . different."

"How convenient."

"What is that supposed to mean? What's with all these cryptic comments about Hunter?"

"I just think you should be cautious is all. It wasn't so long ago that you thought he was a total snake."

The crowd around Lindy grows, nudging me and Luke closer.

"Like I said, I've forgiven him."

"Forgiveness doesn't have to mean blind trust."

"Look—" Someone bumps my shoulder, and Luke reaches out to steady me. I stare back into his piercing eyes.

What was I saying?

"Yes?"

"Um . . ." *He has a girlfriend. He has a girlfriend.* "How about you take care of your relationship, and I'll take care of mine."

"I'm just concerned. I would hope by now you consider me a friend."

"I don't get in fights with my friends. My friends don't boss me around."

An arrogant smile tugs at his mouth. "Then what am I?"

I can't read his signal here. Is there an innuendo? A current of something? Is my brain malfunctioning due to lack of lunch?

Luke removes his hands and checks his silver watch. "I have to meet a senior for an interview. Think about what I said."

"Which part?"

But my voice gets lost in the roar of students as he walks away.

When I rejoin Lindy, a cloud of gloom hangs over her brown head. "Hey, why the sad face, madam president? You have one less thing to worry about with Felicity's dad coming through for us."

She hands a classmate the last envelope, then drags her hound dog eyes back to me. "What did your results say?"

"Um, haven't read it yet." Not sure I want to.

"I opened mine. Matt Sparks and I are a match."

"Lindy, that's so totally cool. Do you think he's read his yet?"

"Yeah. Read it and laughed about it. He said, 'Can you believe this thing says we'd be perfect together?'"

"Oh. I'm sorry."

She throws hers in the trash can next to her. "I give up, Bella. I'm done. It's time to start looking for a prom date instead of just hoping Matt will wise up. Do you have any ideas?"

"Um . . . Budge has this brainy friend named Newton."

She nods once. "I'll take him."

chapter twenty-one

I can hear it now.

"How did you spend your Valentine's Day, Bella?"

"At Mickey Patrick's gym with thirty grown men and a roomful of Lycra, watching my stepdad pound someone into the ground. Gosh, who needs a date?"

"Isn't Mason the sweetest thing?" Mom holds Dolly's sleeping son in her arms. "Robbie, can you believe you used to be this small?"

My stepbrother sits between us and nods his head absently.

"How's my little guy doing?" Dolly stops by for the hundredth time in five minutes. "Are you sure you don't mind holding him, Jillian? I've got to bring in ten more cheesecakes, then I can take him."

"I'll help you, Dolly."

The room goes into a shocked silence as Mickey stands by the door.

Dolly lifts her chin a notch. "Fine. They're in the Jeep."

They return carrying handfuls of food, but neither says a word. A few minutes later *Pile Driver of Dreams* starts.

"It's down to five wrestlers, America. Your vote tonight will put one more down for the count. This week we begin announcing the elimina-

tion at the weekly wrestling matches. So cast your votes this evening, and tune back in tomorrow night as we announce who's getting a permanent body-slam."

The show begins to highlight the remaining lady wrestler, and some of us get up to fill our plates. Not surprisingly, most of the men stay planted in front of the TV as they show pieces of Cinnamon's life. Especially those pieces in the leather bustier. Her boobs are like weapons barely contained in her top. Who needs wrestling moves when you could knock someone out with those?

As a favor to Mom, Dolly agreed to cater the event. She has tables set up with a Mexican food theme. Honestly, I haven't so much as touched a nacho since my last night at Pancho's Mexican Villa.

"Just put the cheesecake there." Dolly points to the few empty spots on the tables.

Across the room little Mason whimpers. Then it crescendos into a full-scale wail. Mom stands up and pats his back. "I've tried the bottle. I checked his diaper." Mason's tiny arms flail, and his shaky cry even gets the attention of the guys watching Cinnamon. Mom brings him over to Dolly and places the baby in her arms.

"He's been so fussy all week, and I haven't slept in days. I think he has colic." Dolly says sweet things to Mason in hushed tones.

"Can I try?"

My eyes bug at Mickey's hesitant request.

Dolly starts to wave him off, but the baby doubles his volume. "I guess. But be gentle with him."

"I know, Dolly."

"Well, it's been a long time since either one of us has had a baby to hold." She sucks in her lips like she wants to stop any more words from escaping.

Mickey extends his sinewy arm and places the baby on it like a cradle. He gently rocks Mason, singing a lullaby so low I can't make out the words. The baby peers up at Mickey but continues to yell.

"Maybe you should give him back to me." Dolly holds out her arms.

"No." Mickey continues to rock. "He just wants a different song, don't you, Mason?"

Mickey starts a new tune, and though I still can't hear it, I'm mesmerized by his expressive face. And so is Mason. The baby's volume descends until it's just a whimper. Then nothing. We all stand there and watch as Mickey rocks and sings Mason to sleep within minutes.

"Thank you." Dolly studies Mickey's face for a brief moment, then returns to gazing at her son.

"What was the lullaby you were singing?" I ask as Mickey continues to rock.

"AC/DC."

A cold blast of air filters though the room as I see Lindy, Matt, and Ruthie come through the door. Budge glances their way, then does a double take. He jumps up to the food tables and butts in next to me.

"Did you invite her?"

I ladle out some *queso*. "Who?"

"Ruthie, that's who." His face burns barn red.

"You invited your friends, and I invited mine." I glance at his posse of gamer geeks, who are all but drooling at Cinnamon on the screen. Newt's drink is spilling onto his shirt, and he hasn't even noticed.

"You could've at least warned me." Budge runs a hand over his stubbly face. "I didn't even shave."

I sniff. "You don't smell. Nothing's hanging out of your nose. I'd say that's a pretty good day for you."

Budge looks to Ruthie, who's chatting with my mom. He looks back to me. "I—I . . . Bella, this may come as a huge surprise, but as much as I talk about chicks, I'm actually not very, um, good with them."

"No?"

"Yeah, I know. I really haven't had all that much experience."

"Shocking." I throw on some jalapeños. "Well, here's a tip. Girls do not find talk of vortexes and bump-mapping the least bit romantic."

He shakes his head. "You and your kind are like from another planet. What do I talk about?"

"You've been to her house a few times. What did you talk about then?"

"She did all the talking. I just worked on the computer."

"Talk to her about her bike. Her church. Her . . . addiction to hair products. Just be yourself. Look what you have in common— school, um . . . and school." I wave at Lindy and Matt. "Hey, Budge, does Newt need a date for prom?"

"I guess. Newt said he was waiting for this girl to be his date, but I don't know that it worked out. I do know he's not going without a date."

"Send him over to the food table."

Across the room my mom calls out a greeting as my editor slides through the entryway. "Luke!"

"Your boss is here." Budge snorts and walks back to Newt and his friends.

Luke high-fives and fist-pounds all the guys. He's become a regular, and I can't figure out if I like that or not.

As he walks toward me, I can't help but admire his slightly faded jeans and the steel gray Henley that lightly clings to the muscles beneath.

I mentally shake myself. *Focus on the fajitas.*

"Happy Valentine's Day," he deadpans.

"Yeah, sorry you're here." I hand him a plate. "And not at a candlelit dinner for two."

"This is exactly where I want to be." His frown is slight. "I wouldn't want to miss this."

I feel like our conversation just forked in two different directions. In lieu of a response, I move on down the food table.

Newt chooses that moment to stomp over, his Vans heavy on the concrete. "You wanted to see me?"

"Yeah, Newt, I was wondering if you'd be interested in escorting my friend Lindy to prom." I point in her direction.

"Is she the one in the pink sparkles and mustache?"

"No, *he's* Betty the Bulldozer."

Newt squints behind his glasses. "Does he wrestle in those heels?"

I grab Newt's chin and angle his head toward Lindy.

"Ohh." He nods. "Uh-huh."

That's his only response? How about, thank you. She's *so* much hotter than any other girl I could get on my own. "Are you interested?"

"I don't know. I do want to go to prom . . ."

"What's not to know? Do you already have a prom date?"

"I might have an option."

"Prom's in six weeks. Do you have a date yet or not?"

He scuffs the toe of his shoe. "I guess not."

"Do you have transportation?"

"I should by then. I gotta get my mom's car fixed."

"Tux?"

"I'll get one."

"Lindy has a strict no-hands, no-alochol policy. Can you adhere to that? Raise your right hand and repeat after me: no kissy, no drinkie."

"I got it, Bella."

"And don't you get anywhere near *her* vortex."

With a glowing blush, Newt all but races back to his seat.

Luke coughs to cover a laugh. "What was that about? He looked like he was about to cry."

"Just business."

"Want to go to the basketball game with me on Saturday?"

I drop the ice tongs. "Game? Go? Together?" *Dear God, please anoint me with the power of complete sentences.*

"Yeah, Anna Deason said she tried to call you tonight. She got some threatening e-mails."

I was on the phone with Hunter after school. "E-mails like Ruthie's? Doctored pictures?"

"No, as in telling her that if she doesn't drop out of the prom queen race, she'll be sorry. Two nights ago she was at a game and her shoes got stolen. Could be just coincidence, but I thought we'd go to the game and watch her cheer. Keep an eye out for anything suspicious."

One of the ever-present camera guys darts across the room and trains his lens on me. These guys are like roaches. They're everywhere and impossible to get rid of. I turn around and give him my back. Which puts me right up in Luke's space.

"Yeah, I'd love to go with you. Er, I mean, love to go to the game. But I kind of need a ride."

"Still don't have an alternator?"

"My mom's making me pay for it myself." I see his lips twitch.

"Summer Fresh is looking for part-time help."

"Oh, wouldn't you just *love* for me to be elbow deep in panty liners. Well, no thanks. There is *nothing* that will make me work there."

chapter twenty-two

"You're not going to buy me a prom dress?" I clutch my phone with both hands.

"No, honey. Your mother and I both think you need to learn the value of money."

"But Dad, I do value money. A *lot*."

I hear him laughing. "Get another job, Bella. And save your money. Besides, you have tons of formals from your Hilliard school days."

"Both those are *so* last year, and I have to pay to get my car fixed."

"Christina and Marisol said to tell you hello."

Ugh! Is he even listening to me? Does he even care that I'm wearing last year's dress *and* riding to school in a funeral hearse?

"Christina wants to know how you feel about a summer wedding?"

"Remember how I felt when I got food poisoning and yakked all over dinner? *That's* how I feel."

"Yes, sweetie, your cookies are excellent." He laughs into the phone. "Sorry, Bella, I was talking to Marisol. She made me peanut butter cookies. Isn't that adorable? Now what were you saying?"

"Nothing." *Like it would matter to you and* sweetie. "I have to get ready for the wrestling match in Tulsa. I'll see you soon, Dad. Love you." *God, I seriously need some help dealing with my dad's new life. This is not going well. And I thoroughly dislike that cookie-making little girl.*

I grab my purse and coat and head down the hall. When I hear noises from Budge and Robbie's room, I decide to backtrack and peek in.

Robbie's cape is gone and he's in regular clothes. A flannel shirt replaces a superhero t-shirt. He pushes a button on a remote and a kung-fu guy repeats a move on TV. Robbie attempts a karate chop, then plays it again.

"Whatcha doing, buddy?"

Robbie jumps, hands ready to chop.

"Whoa, don't hurt me." I hold up my arms in surrender.

"I wouldn't hurt you, Bella." He bows like a *sensei.* "I know these hands can be lethal weapons."

I take a seat on his bed. What happened to the Spider-Man sheets? "Where's your cape, Robbie?"

"It's in my closet."

"Why?"

He shrugs and turns his attention back to the TV. "Maybe I want to be a superhero in disguise."

"Why are you watching martial arts movies?"

"Because Dad wouldn't teach me any of his moves."

"And you have to know how to hurt someone *because* . . . ? Robbie, look at me."

He pivots back around but stares a hole in the shaggy carpet.

"Superman and Spider-Man know how to defend themselves. It's part of the job."

"Says who?"

He lifts his head. "Because I—" He shakes his carrot-top head as if erasing the sentence on his tongue. "Because that's what happens in the movies, of course."

I drop to my knees and get eye level. "You'd tell me if anyone was picking on you, right?"

Jake chooses that moment to stick his head in the doorway. "Let's go, guys." He winks at his son. "Daddy's itching to gut-wrench someone tonight."

Used cars. Why can't he sell used cars?

"Are you nervous, Daddy?" Robbie asks, totally disconnecting on our conversation.

"Nah. If I win tonight, I win. If not, that's in God's hands too. It's been a great ride being on the reality show, eh?"

"Oh, it's been a blast." I force a smile. "The camera guys are just like family now." A family of rodents.

Four hours later I've had popcorn, a burger, a candy bar, an extra large Sprite, and six trips to the bathroom. Jake did a great job this evening, and I hope at least for his sake that it's not his last week on *Pile Driver of Dreams*.

"Laaaadddddies and gentlemennnn!" The announcer moves to the center of the ring. "Tonight we have Oklahoma's own Cap-tain! Iron! Jack!"

The entire crowd squints an eye and growls, "Arrrgh."

"Many of you have watched. Many of you have even voted." The screens around the arena change to satellite feeds of the four other contestants in their own venues. "I have the distinct privilege of sharing the results. Will Captain Iron Jack be returning next week to *Pile Driver of Dreams* or is he down for the final count?"

Mom and I scream with the rest of the fans. There has to be at least a couple thousand here.

"The remaining contestants will be in Nevada next Friday night as we move the semifinals to Las Vegas! Our wrestlers will meet *and* compete for the first time!"

"Go Captain Iron Jack!" Budge yells. "Sin City, here I come!"

"Are you ready, Tulsa?" The announcer opens an envelope.

Jake stands in the middle of the ring next to the announcer. Mickey stands below, his hands clasped like he's praying.

"Captain Iron Jack"—the announcer wraps his arm around Jake's shoulders—"I'm afraid I have some bad news for you."

Groans ricochet all over the arena. My heart plummets.

"The bad news is Vegas ain't Oklahoma, but Captain Iron Jack, that's exactly where you're headed! You're going to Vegas, baby!"

The crowd erupts and the four of us jump up and down, screaming. He did it! Jake really did it.

I reach into my purse and grab my phone. "Luke? Jake made it. He's going on to the next round."

He laughs. "That's awesome. Wait just a sec, okay?"

I hear a beep.

"Taylor?"

Ugh. "Nope. Still me. Bella."

"Must've lost her. Tell Jake I'm really happy for him."

I struggle to hear him with the noise around me. "Yeah, I'll do that. Bye."

"Hey, Bella?"

"Yes?"

I hear him breathe deep. "Thanks for calling me."

Silence. "That's what friends do." And I hang up, a little sadder than I was only one minute ago.

chapter twenty-three

B ut I'm really qualified. Nobody knows ice cream better than me."

The owner of the Truman Dairy Barn shakes her white poodle-curl head one last time, and I leave. I've been all over Truman today. *Nobody* is hiring.

I hop in my mom's Tahoe. Times are hard. I need my car fixed and I need a prom dress. And prom shoes. And prom earrings, lipstick, hair, nails, perfume, necklace, and matching handbag. The five dollars in my pocket is *not* going to cover it. I miss my dad's credit card.

This morning in my quiet time I read a devotional about pride. It said that God dislikes it so much, he gives us the cold shoulder. I certainly don't need that. And I know I'm supposed to resist pride, and it's wrong. But I have yet to find anyone in the Bible whose only job option left was cranking out maxi-pads. Who needs a car anyway? I'm doing fine catching rides in the hearse.

Okay, actually, no I'm not. I'm forever thinking I smell formaldehyde. *Fine, God. I'm ready to suck it up and gain some humility. I can't afford you being mad at me. Not with a maniac at large.*

Taylor Swift blasts from my phone, and I pick it up.

"Hey, Hunter."

"What are you doing?"

"Deciding whether I want to give up my car or give up my dignity. I have to get a job, and the only place that's hiring is the factory where Jake works."

"Doesn't he make—"

"Yes!"

Hunter's laugh does not make me feel like turning the car toward the industrial park to Summer Fresh.

"These are desperate times, Hunter. You have no idea."

He laughs again, but this time it's bitter. "Oh, I know more about that than you think. At least you have prom to look forward to."

"I don't know. Maybe I should just skip it until next year. It's going to be really expensive, I don't have a job, and I don't even have a date."

"I'll go with you."

I chuckle. "I'm so sure."

"Seriously. Dad has business in Tulsa in March. I'll just see if he'll postpone it until your prom weekend."

"You'd do that for me?"

Hunter's voice is soft and familiar. "I'd do anything for you."

"And I won't find you outside making out with my best friend under a tree and some twinkly lights?"

"I thought you had forgiven me."

"I have." Forgetting seems to be another matter. "Hunter, I would love it if you'd go to prom with me. It would mean a lot."

"Then it's settled."

I balance the phone between my cheek and shoulder. "So how are you feeling these days?"

"I'm okay." His tone says to drop it.

"Any updates?"

"They've ruled out a few more things. I've got more tests this week. Don't worry about it. You have enough to think about."

"Knowing the doctors can't figure out what's wrong with you and it could possibly be fatal is not something I can just push out of my mind."

"I never said I was dying." I hear him clicking on a keyboard and know this topic has probably lost his attention. "I just said it was severe, and I wouldn't be sure of the outcome. Nothing has changed. But talking to you always makes me feel better. And I know you're praying for me and stuff. It's like sometimes I can feel your faith, you know?"

Being Hunter's friend is so the right thing to do.

As I end my call, I realize in the last few minutes I've driven the Tahoe to Summer Fresh. The entrance to the sprawling concrete building looms before me. If Hunter sees Christ in me, then what would Christ do? Probably move to the next town.

No, he'd suck it up, go in, and fill out an application. *God, give me strength as I walk through this dark, dark valley of life.*

Here goes nothing. I jump out of the SUV, call my overly protective mom to check in, and head toward the Kotex Compound.

"I'd like an application for a job. Part-time."

A gray-headed woman eyes me over the top of her bifocals. "You look familiar."

"I'm Jake Finley's stepdaughter." Throwing around a shift manager's name ought to mean something.

"Nah. That's not it." She opens a drawer and rifles through it.

"Yessiree. Here we go." She pulls out an *Enquirer* and pokes her nail at a picture. "This is you, ain't it? I love this show!"

"Can I just get an application?" I'm not sure if I'm having a moment of maturity or insanity, but it could wear off at any moment.

"I know this is you. Says here you've got two boyfriends."

"I really don't—"

"Says here you solve local crimes."

"It's not like—"

"And you've secretly been dating Prince Harry of England?"

I step a little closer at the clearly doctored picture of me and the prince. Nice. "Just between you and me, it's all true. But if Harry finds out I told, he'd stop buying me diamonds, so let's just keep that one on the DL."

She nods her gray head vigorously. "Look at me—buttoning my lip." She presses her mouth together. "Mmmmmm."

"Great. I knew I could count on you. Um, application please?"

She makes some more muffled sounds and hands me a blank form and a pen.

"Ginger, do you have those accounts ready?" A man lays some manila folders on the receptionist's desk. "Hey, aren't you Jake's kid?"

Behind him Ginger makes fish lips and shakes her head.

"Yes, I'm his stepdaughter. I'm, uh, filling out an application. He said you were hiring."

"Reuben Pierce." We shake hands, then he grabs the form. "You're hired."

"Just like that?" No. That was too quick. "I'm working on a

story on teen jobs for the school paper, so I might not be around too long." *Please tell me that's not acceptable and to go merrily on my way.*

"I can tell a good pad maker when I see one. And we here at Summer Fresh always like to help out Truman High."

Oh. How generous.

"I want to see you here Monday after school. Can you handle that?"

"I'm not sure."

"What's that?"

"I mean, yes. I'll be here." We shake hands again, and I wave good-bye to Ginger, who now is doing the lock-and-key number and pointing to her lips.

Outside, I spy a familiar white van across the street. "Yes!" I yell. "I'm going to make feminine products! Stick *that* on your TV show!" And I peel away.

A couple of hours later, Mom knocks on my bedroom door. "Luke's here, honey."

I save the article I'm working on and skip down the stairs in my jeans, Chucks, and bobbing ponytail.

He sits in the living room and talks to Budge.

"Just gonna grab my coat," I yell and detour into the kitchen where I left it. I wander into a serious heart-to-heart between Jake and Robbie.

"I'm going to ask you one last time, Robbie. Why didn't you finish any of your schoolwork this week?"

As I reach for my jacket on the back of an empty chair, my little stepbrother shrugs. "I dunno."

Jake holds a note with the school letterhead. "Until your teacher calls me with a positive update, no TV."

"But Dad, I *have* to watch my superheroes. And I got some judo DVDs."

"You'll be doing homework, son. No TV this week."

There's a cramp in my heart as little Robbie snivels into his shirtsleeve. What is going on with that kid?

Luke stands up as I enter the living room. "You look nice. Very casual and sporty."

At least he didn't say I look like a good pad maker.

Luke holds an umbrella over my head as we walk outside into a growing rainstorm. As usual, he opens my door and shuts me in. Has Hunter ever opened a car door for me?

"Lindy said to tell you she has your Match-and-Catch envelope. You left it the day we passed out the results," Luke says.

"I've been too busy to even think about it. I guess I'm just hanging in the wind—not knowing who my true love might be."

"Your prom date could be in that envelope."

"Already have one," I blurt without thinking. A full minute of silence ensues. Then another. "You're not going to ask me who it is, are you?"

Luke takes his eyes off the road long enough to look at me with bland eyes. "Let me guess. Hunter called and said *just* the right thing, and you're convinced even more that he's changed, and now he's going to ride up in a white Hummer and escort you to prom."

"Somebody did *not* put on his happy pants today." I stare out the window at a slice of lightning. "I suppose your girlfriend is perfect?"

Luke turns his 4Runner into the gym parking lot and finds a spot. "Have you prayed about jumping back into a relationship with Hunter?"

"Yes." Sorta. Maybe. Pretty much no. "And for your information, Pastor Sullivan, I'm not *jumping* into anything."

We walk into the gym and flash our press passes, which is pretty cool. I feel like a cop on TV when I do that.

I follow Luke to the concession area. "Are we going to interview some people? Take some pictures? Get some quotes?"

"We're getting nachos."

A few minutes later he turns around and hands me cheesy nachos with some canned chili on top. It looks disgusting. And I can't wait to dig in.

"Your Sprite." He extends a bottle, and I'm oddly touched that he remembers these little things, like my favorite drink.

"Luke, do you know what my favorite color is?"

He leads me up the bleachers to find a seat. "Pink. And black." He smiles at my cotton candy–colored scarf.

I settle my food in my lap as we sit. "And on what side do I usually part my hair?"

He focuses straight ahead on the ball game already in progress. "The left. But tonight you've flipped it to the right."

"You do have good reporter skills."

His intense blue eyes leave the court and fix on my face. "What does noticing things about you have to do with me being a good reporter?"

I don't know how long I stare at him, but a blast from the scoreboard snaps me back to the game.

After the junior high game ends, the Lady Tigers take the court, and the cheerleaders line up under the basket. Lindy spots me in the crowd and waves as she sinks a warm-up shot.

"Hey, guys." Matt Sparks climbs the bleachers and sits down

beside me in his team sweats. "Glad you could make it for the games. Bella, good article in the paper about the high cost of prom."

"Thanks." I beam. "Who knew it could be so expensive, right?" But come Monday, I'll be working toward a paycheck. One pad at a time. "Are you taking a date?"

"Nah." Matt looks to the court as the two teams take their places for the tip-off. "I'm sure I'll just hang out with Lindy like usual."

I nearly choke on a chip. "Didn't she tell you? Lindy's going to the prom with Newton Phillips."

Matt blanches. "Who?"

"Newt. He's a friend of—"

"I *know* who he is." Matt's fingers tap the seat. "When did this happen? Is it like a date?"

"Um . . ." What do I say here? "You'll have to talk to Lindy. I didn't mean to spill the beans. I just thought you'd know." *Hope you weren't planning on coordinating your tie with her dress.*

"I need to go stretch." He stands up. "I'll see you guys later."

"That went well." Luke watches him leave.

"How was I supposed to know she hadn't told Matt?" My grin spreads slowly. "His reaction was interesting though, wasn't it? So what about you? Is Taylor coming in for prom?"

He claps when the Tigers score. "She'll be staying at school."

The buzzer sounds for a time-out, and the cheerleaders take center court. I watch Anna smile her peppy smile and lure the crowd into a chant. I scan the audience for anyone even remotely suspicious. Aside from two guys in twin mullets, I see nothing unusual. No one that screams, "I stalk potential prom queens."

"There's Dolly." Luke waves toward the end of the gym, and

Dolly starts walking our way. Baby Mason is held tight to her chest by some sort of sling contraption.

"What are you doing here?" I ask as Dolly sits in the spot Matt vacated.

She lets out a breath, sending her big bangs up even higher. "Mason and I needed to get out of the house for a while." She strokes his sleeping head. "And I have season passes. I love me some basketball. And I figure it's never too soon to introduce a boy to sports, right?"

Mason looks like he's unconscious, so I doubt he'll be absorbing much of the game tonight.

At half-time I'm about to go to the concession stand for some Skittles when the cheerleaders take the court again. They spread across the floor, and music begins to pump out of the speakers. I sit back down to watch the show.

"Wow. They're really good." Dolly pats Mason's back. "They just shot that one girl up like a torpedo."

That one girl is Anna Deason. Though she's incredibly tall, she's slender and light. As a techno mix of a song plays, she and a few other girls do backhand springs across the floor as the other cheerleaders begin to build. The song speeds up, and Anna runs to the center of the formation. Two cheerleaders form a basket with their arms, and Anna is thrown straight into the air as the music crescendos.

My eyes follow her straight toward the ceiling.

The music stops. And the gym goes black.

Shrieks come from all around.

Then a loud thud from the gym floor.

Luke's hand finds mine as I get to my feet. "Don't move."

"But Anna—she could be hurt."

"Must be some storm out there," Dolly says as Mason begins to fuss.

"What's going on?" Did the lightning knock the electricity out?

"Call a doctor!" someone yells from below. Anna. She must be injured. And maybe others, if she fell on them.

Though it feels like an eternity, only two minutes pass before the lights flicker back on. Someone in the press box picks up a mic. "Just the weather, folks. I guess the lightning flipped a breaker. Please stay in your seat until we can get these two young ladies safely out of the gym."

Anna hangs limp over her dad's arms as he carries her out. The cheer coach follows behind, helping another girl hobble toward the exit.

Luke stands. "Let's go check it out."

I trail behind him into the gym lobby. He peruses the anxious crowd that's gathered. "Let's go talk to Hank Gates."

"Ben Gates's dad? Why are we talking to the point guard's father?"

"Because he's the fire chief." Luke slips through a knot of people, then pulls me through, his fingers wrapped around my hand.

He stops in front of a middle-aged guy in a Truman Fire Department cap. We wait until he finishes a conversation with the school superintendent.

"Mr. Gates?" Luke steps forward and engages the man in small talk about the game, his son, and some random current events. "So lightning knocked the lights out, huh?" he finally asks.

"Yep. Looks that way. We've had some wild storms the last few nights, but luckily no damage."

I join the conversation. "Did it just affect the gym?"

He scratches his beard. "Yeah, kind of crazy. It didn't trip any other breakers in the high school but the main gym area. Even the locker rooms had power." He shakes his head. "Mother Nature's just full of mischief tonight."

Luke catches my eye, and I know we share the same thought.

Mother Nature?

Or someone a little more sinister?

chapter twenty-four

H*appy Monday, Truman Tigers! This is Melanie Coulson for Tiger TV with your morning announcements. It's not too late to cast your vote for prom king and queen. Hop online today and . . ."*

Budge sits sideways in his seat, ignoring the TV. "I'm so sick of all this prom stuff."

I dig through my backpack until I find our novel for the month, *Heart of Darkness*, and barely resist the urge to chuck it across the room. More like *Heart of Pukeness*. "Why don't you just ask Ruthie to prom? What's the worst thing that could happen?"

"She'd put me in a choke hold and laugh in my face."

It is possible. "I don't think so. But she is a little untrusting of guys right now. Her last boyfriend dumped her over those doctored pictures."

"What a jerk."

"If you don't ask her, someone else will. What if a biker family moves into town today, and some dude with chaps and a leather vest steals her heart? Do you really want to risk that?"

His head droops. "I could never compete with someone in chaps."

I pat his shoulder. "Seize the day, Budge."

I barely stay awake through the lecture on the novel. When the bell rings to end class, I'm the first one out the door.

"Did you get my message about Anna?" Luke asks, as I sit down at my computer in journalism.

"One broken arm, one concussion, and one surly attitude. Yeah, it was the talk of church yesterday."

I scroll through my e-mails to check for any possible job offers or other miracles.

Wait—what's this?

Bella,

> *You don't listen very well, do you? You have no idea what*
> *I'm capable of. Nobody does . . . but you're about to find out.*

I hit reply to see if the address is legit, but it comes back to me rejected. Big surprise.

"What is that?" Luke hovers over me, and I can smell the clean detergent of his shirt.

"Um . . ." I shut down the screen.

"You just can't get the hang of this sharing stuff, can you?" Luke reaches across and drags the mouse from my hand, pulling up the e-mail. His expression darkens. "A fake e-mail address." He shakes his head. "Why isn't this person coming after me too?"

I pat his arm. "Now's really not the time to get your feelings hurt. Maybe someone will threaten you next week, okay?"

Luke's expression holds me in place. "I don't like you being in danger. And it makes no sense—why just threaten you?" He shoots off a copy of the e-mail to Officer Mark.

I force a smile, despite the fact that I'm more than a little creeped out. "This person probably knows I'm the better sleuth."

Luke doesn't laugh. "In the meantime, you need to still make sure someone's with you at all times. I'm serious, Bella. Go nowhere alone."

~~~~~~~~~~

"All I gotta say is, I *better* get some sympathy votes out of this." At lunch Anna's arm hangs at an angle in a sling. "How's a girl supposed to eat a burrito with one arm?"

"Just lean over it and gnaw."

Ruthie's suggestion has me smiling.

"Hey, Anna." Felicity Weeks stops at our table. "Sorry to hear about your arm. I hope it heals quickly."

"Um. Thanks." Anna tries cutting into her burrito with a plastic fork. "I hear Callie Drake's back today. Word is she's *still* denying calling the hotel."

I watch Felicity's reaction to the mention of her best friend. "Yeah. Oh, speaking of that—Daddy is interviewing two caterers this week."

"Make sure they know how to make those cocktail weenies." Ruthie rubs a napkin over her face. "Man, I love those things."

Felicity wrinkles her nose. "I hardly think either one of them even know what that is."

"We can't afford a caterer right now," Lindy says. "*Especially* a fancy one. Felicity, you can't go making decisions for the junior class like that."

Ruthie jerks her head toward Lindy. "Yeah, *she's* the president."

Felicity claps her hands. "But that's the best part—Daddy's going to pick up the tab!"

Smiles break out across the table. Except for Lindy. "We don't need handouts. I was working on getting the catering donated."

Felicity pats Lindy's back. "I'm sure you're a great class president. But this is my senior prom. I want it to be *perfect*. I've got my dress, my shoes, the photographer, a limo."

"Yeah, too bad you won't have a crown," Anna teases. "Oh, did I say that out loud? Must be the pain meds talking."

As we laugh, Felicity struggles with a smile. "Such the kidder, Anna. Well, I must be off. I have to study for a trigonometry test, and I promised my tutor we'd review. I'll let you know about the caterer."

As she saunters away, Anna frowns. "She took the lead for queen after she got us the new prom location. And now a caterer? That is not even fair. I want that crown. Maybe I can get my uncle to deejay the event. He's Funky Freddie on 105.7 from midnight to four a.m." She glances around the table. "What? Y'all don't know him?"

"Maybe I could ask my third cousin Eugene to deejay." Ruthie fixes one of her hair spikes. "He just got out of prison, so we could probably get him for cheap."

"I'll arrange the music," Lindy says. "Maybe Budge could do it. He was the deejay for one of our student council dances last year."

"Budge?" *My* stepbrother?

Ruthie sighs. "Yeah, as in the boy who was *not* on my Match-and-Catch results."

"Like *those* mean anything." Lindy tears into an apple. "Speaking of that, I still have your results, Bella. You and Luke forgot them in the hall the day I handed them out."

"I don't even want them now." Like I need more confusion in my life. "Ruthie, are those stupid results why you've backed off on chasing Budge?"

"No. I found out some discouraging information. Turns out your stepbrother is not down with JC."

Sometimes conversations with Ruthie McGee remind me of the time I went to Italy, and it took me thirty minutes to communicate I needed a bathroom.

"You know," she says. "He doesn't have a membership card to Club Saved. He doesn't ride the God train. Your stepbrother does not have his passport to the Pearly Gates."

"He's saved." Who would've thought I'd be defending Budge? "He's just struggling right now. But he hasn't skipped church in a couple of months, so don't give up on him."

"So if he wasn't saved, you wouldn't go out with him?" Anna asks.

"Hey, I am a rule follower." She sniffs and runs a finger under her dog collar. "Plus my dad would cut off my hair-bleach allowance."

"I think it's good," Matt chimes in. "We talked about this in FCA just last week."

Last Wednesday at the Fellowship of Christian Athletes meeting, our speaker broke out the Bible and showed us God's big N-O on dating nonbelievers. I can't help but think of Hunter. I dated him *knowing* he wasn't saved. And now what am I doing? Sure, it's just a friendship. But I think Hunter and I both know there could be more simmering beneath the surface.

After school I meet Budge at the hearse, and we pick up Robbie at Truman Elementary down the street.

Robbie steps out of the car rider line and walks toward us, his backpack dragging the ground behind him.

"School is sucking the life out of my little brother," Budge says as Robbie hops in the back and buckles himself in.

I twist around my seat and smile at Robbie. "Good day?"

"Yeah." He doesn't even look at me. "The best. I'd love four more just like it."

I nod to a piece of paper in his hand. "Did you have art? That's a great looking picture of a dog."

"It's Betsy." Robbie's pet cow. "And I already know it's ugly. Billy Simpkins told me so, like, fifty million times."

"What did I tell you to say to Billy Simpkins?" Budge's face is intense as he drives.

"I can't tell him his momma's uglier than anything I could draw. He's a giant. He's a mutant of genetics."

How Robbie even *knows* the word genetics is beyond me. At his age, I think I was still trying to figure out why the left shoe couldn't go on the right foot.

"What grade's this kid in?" I ask.

"Second. For the third time." Robbie leans on the door like the life has left his bones.

"Have you told the teacher?"

"No!" Budge and Robbie yell.

"Dude, that totally breaks man-code." Budge turns on the street that takes us to the industrial park. "If you're a man, you take care of it yourself. Robbie just needs to get some backbone. Outsmart Billy Simpkins."

Robbie says nothing.

I dig into my purse and find my last two dollars. "Stop and get him some ice cream on your way home."

"Um . . . thanks." Budge tosses the money in the console as we pull up to Summer Fresh. "You know when you've been a pad packer here for sixty days, they give you free samples." He grins as I step onto the pavement. "Just something for you to look forward to."

I slam the door.

The ugly building stands before me like my own Billy Simpkins, taunting me and making me feel icky. I do *not* want to go in there. I mutter a quick little prayer and roll back my shoulders. I can do this. But before I go in, I might as well get one thing over with.

I turn around and wave to a distant van. "Yes, I'm *really* going to work here! Get your shot now!" A long telephoto lens sticks out of the window, and I give them a few complimentary poses before running inside.

The gray-headed receptionist gives me a badge, then leads me back to the factory and passes me off to another woman. Her badge reads *Earlene.*

"I'm the assistant line manager for this machine." She pats a big metal contraption. "This here thing is old, but recently rebuilt. It's been a little testy lately, but I think she's fixed." Earlene's hair is so gray it's nearly purple, and I find it hard to focus on her instructions for studying the lavender hue.

"Now, Bella, the feminine napkin will come off that conveyor belt, sticky side up. Your job is to place the adhesive sheet on it and pack it in a box."

Earlene flips a switch, and the conveyer belt lurches and chugs. Within a few seconds pads begin to slowly roll out in a line like little sanitary soldiers. Earlene's Velcro shoes squeak as she leans over the belt and easily puts the slick paper in the right spot.

"Easy stuff, little lady." Her drawn-on brows seem to point to heaven and keep her in a constant expression of surprise. "Now you try."

I step up to the conveyor, snap on some gloves, and repeat Earlene's motions.

"Good job. You just gotta go with the flow." She barks with laughter. "Get it?"

"Yeah." *I need a prom dress. I need a prom dress.*

An hour later I'm listening to my iPod and sticking the thingies on the pads like I was born doing it.

At a tap on my shoulder, I find Earlene. "Guess what?"

I force myself to look away from her mustache. "What?"

"We just got new rush orders, and we need to double our output. I'm going to have to crank up the speed on this baby. Can you handle that?"

"I think so." Considering I could do my calculus homework *and* work the line at this pace, I believe going a little faster would be a welcome change.

With a knobby hand she turns a dial. "Okay, it will speed up gradually so you can adjust. When it gets to double time, it will stay at that constant speed. If you need to stop the conveyor for any reason, push that big red button over there." She points to a glowing circle at the opposite end. "And whatever you do, do *not* let anything touch the floor because it has to be thrown away. *And* it comes out of your paycheck." Earlene's smile reveals overly large dentures. "Are you ready for your break yet?"

"Maybe later." I'd hate to tear myself away from all this fun.

"Okay, but if you get in a *sticky* situation, just holler!" She chortles all the way to the other side of the factory.

I plug my earbud back in and get a rhythm going. Swipe, stick, grab. Swipe, stick, grab. This really isn't that bad. The belt speeds up, and I stand ready with my adhesive papers.

"Are you Bella?"

I throw a pad in a box and pause the iPod. "Yes." Swipe, stick, grab. "I'm Newton Phillips's mom." She holds out her hand. "Janice."

I shake her hand quickly, careful not to miss a beat.

Small eyes blink behind oversized safety goggles, and I have to wonder what part of the plant she works in. "I just wanted to thank you for arranging his prom date. Newt may be brilliant at designing games, but he's not the most socially advanced boy."

I try to compose a look of surprise.

"And I know this Lindy Miller is a good girl, so I'm hoping this is the beginning of a new phase in his life."

"Ms. Phillips, it's just two people going to prom together." I throw some pads in a box. "They're not really dating."

Her smile is slight. "I know. But it's still a move in the right direction for my Newt. He needs to know there's more out there than these fantasy worlds he creates. Good luck with this machine. It can be a little—"

"Sticky. Yes, I know." Doesn't anyone in this building have some original jokes?

Ms. Phillips acts like she's going to hug me, but then seems to think better of it. She leaves me to my work and my music. I mentally take notes for the *Tribune* article. This will definitely provide some comic relief, I guess.

Sometime later it occurs to me that I totally need a tinkle break. I speed to the red button and push it. The conveyor shudders to a stop. I grab my red Chloé bag and scan for a bathroom.

Reeeeeeeek!

I drop my purse at the shrill sound of gears moving. Standing in frozen horror, I watch as the conveyor belt begins to move like a locomotive, gaining in speed and noise. Pads begin to sail out of the chute like bullets from a machine gun.

It comes out of your paycheck . . .

"Noooooo!" I dive for the conveyor, grabbing adhesive papers and sticking them on like I've got four arms. Swipe, stick, grab. Swipe, stick, grab.

Swipe, swipe, stick—

Stick, stick, grab—

No! I can't lose any. But the pads are building into a mound at the base of the conveyor. I rake them upwards with my arm and sit on the belt. I pull up my legs and rest them on the sides, making a wall with my body. There must be no pad casualties!

As if a dam breaks, the pads only come faster and faster. I jump all over the machine, slapping papers with my feet, chin, and hands—everything I've got.

It's too much! It's a tsunami of supermaxis! I'm running out of strength. Out of hands. Out of sticky-on-thingies. Is this what Noah felt like when the rains came?

I've got to work my way back to the red button! I have to stop this deranged machine. It's possessed.

The pads pelt me like an endless hailstorm. Somewhere in my brain the sound of a wailing alarm registers. Maybe it's the ambulance. Maybe I've suffocated in this sea of lady products and I don't even know it. My hands refuse to stop moving though, and I reach out blindly and just keep grabbing. The pads pile all around me until I'm lost beneath them, like a skier trapped under an avalanche.

"Bella? Hellewww? Bella?" A familiar voice. Eula . . . Eunice . . . Earlene!

With my remaining strength I cry. "Save me!"

"Hold on! I'm going to pull the plug!"

Can't. Breathe. Must get out. I have a cat to raise.

I feel the conveyor belt stop beneath me, and the alarm's cry goes silent. My butt's on fire like I've ridden a treadmill on my tush.

"Where are you?" Earlene's hands wade through the pile. "Don't let me grab anything inappropriate. I can't afford a sexual harassment suit."

"Just get me out of here!"

Pads go flying until I finally have a hole to breathe in. Then I can move my arms. And now I see Earlene's face, frozen in shock. Or maybe that's just her brows.

"My stars, little missy. I thought we'd lost you!"

I drag in air in gulping gasps as Earlene begins to rip pads off my body right and left. "Ow. Ouch. Hey!"

"You're covered in them." She snickers. "They're like cockleburs. They're stuck everywhere!" She tears one from my hair. My face. There is no spot on my body that does not have something glued to it. "You look like a maxi-pad mummy."

Earlene can hardly remove the pads for laughing so hard. She lightly touches a few spots on my face and neck. "Little missy, you're going to have what we call around here sticker burn. It will be a little red. A little whelpy. No big deal."

"Makeup will cover it up, right?"

She looks at her shoes. "Uh. Yeah."

"Earlene . . . this was very, um, educational. I think I have

enough information for my article. And this really isn't my thing."
I'm so weak!

"Are you saying this job doesn't make your heart extra-absorbent with happiness?"

I close my eyes and pinch the bridge of my nose.

"Hon, if this place isn't a *super* fit for you, then by all means don't *stick* around."

As Earlene continues her zippy double entendres, I walk away, the sound of her guffaws in my ear. This day could not get any worse.

Out of the corner of my eye I see a guy with a palm-sized video camera trained right on me.

Well. I stand corrected.

Knowing your most embarrassing moment in life will soon be on national television is bad. But knowing it's going to be on YouTube in ten minutes? A *hundred* times worse.

chapter twenty-five

Some girls dream of Jake Gyllenhaal or the boys from *Gossip Girls*. Me? Every night this week, I've had nightmares about drowning in a deluge of feminine protection.

I shut off my alarm this Thursday morning, and Moxie hops onto the floor—promptly tripping over a pair of boots. After my shower, I mosey to the kitchen. Mom sits at the small table, biting into a bagel and turning the page of a textbook.

"How's philosophy?" I kiss her cheek and pour myself a glass of juice.

She sticks the bagel in her mouth and grabs her pencil. "Interesting. I had hoped to find some insight in here on Robbie's strange behavior."

"Like how he TiVo's all of Anderson Cooper's specials on CNN? Or how he's memorized every word of the Superman TV shows, cartoons, and movies?"

"No." Mom scribbles some notes. "I meant his strange behavior *lately*."

"Oh. You've noticed too?"

"He was up before I was this morning. He went to his quiet place. Why don't you go check on him?"

This means he's out in the pasture with Betsy the cow. Betsy's his pet. And she licks me. I don't want Holstein slobber on me this morning.

Mom turns tired eyes to me. "Bel, I was up late last night talking to Dolly. Please help me out here."

"What's up with Dolly?"

Taking a sip of coffee, Mom shakes her blonde head. "She got word yesterday that the baby's father *just* found out about him. He's been stationed in Iraq and had no idea the girl was ever pregnant."

"But Dolly is Mason's mother now. He can't have him back."

"Yes. He can, and he wants his son. Dolly's got a lawyer on it, but with the dad in the picture, this could nullify the adoption. It will probably go to court."

My heart hurts for Dolly. This will make three children she's lost. "I'll go check on Robbie." I go to the back door and grab my coat off a peg. But what I need is a rain slicker or one of those suits like the astronauts wear. Maybe Betsy will keep her tongue to herself today.

With little light, I tromp through the grass and open the metal gate that leads to the pasture. Bundling my coat around me, I walk until I reach the pond. Robbie sits Indian-style with a flashlight, throwing rocks into the water. Betsy lounges beside him.

"Hey, buddy." I sit down. "Kind of a cold morning to be out."

His eyes stay fixed on the pond. "Betsy wanted some company."

The cow looks at me like I'm a giant lollipop. "Robbie, is someone picking on you at school? Has someone hurt you?"

"Nobody's hurt me."

"Well, something's wrong. Please tell me what's going on."

"I'm a big boy, Bella. I have to be strong and take care of myself."

"Says who?"

"Superheroes don't depend on other people. My dad doesn't let anyone get the best of him."

"Yeah, but that's Hollywood. And wrestling . . ." How to put this? "It's not as real as it looks either. Why don't we talk to your dad tonight? You can tell him everything that's going on."

"Nothing's going on, and I don't *need* anyone's help!" He rubs Betsy's wet nose then stands up. "I have to get ready for the bus."

I'm almost sure I see the glisten of a tear as he runs past me and back toward the gate.

Betsy rises as I do. "Oh, no. You stay put—ew!" One French kiss in the face. She bats her big black eyelashes and takes a step closer. And like Robbie, I take off in a sprint.

In journalism class I write a rough draft of another teen job article. I'm calling it "I'd Rather Be Shopping: My Thoughts on Child Labor." I guess I need to interview some other student workers and get some pics of them on the job. I'm so sick of seeing pictures of *me* on the job. Everyone knows about my Summer Fresh disaster by now. As soon as Wednesday it was splashed all over the tabloids. And I'm currently number one on YouTube and Google Video. I knew God was working on my humility, but I didn't know torture would be involved.

Abbie and Tabbie, identical twins and fellow reporters, sit at the computer in front of me. They laugh over something on the Internet, and I double check that it's not me.

Luke makes the rounds to all of his staff and checks everyone's status, answers questions, and offers help. When it's my turn, he doesn't even look at my screen. "Did you find out where Callie Drake's boyfriend was on the night of the basketball game?"

"No. I've been working." To his credit, Luke doesn't even crack a smile. He hasn't made *one* single snarky comment about my run-in with a million maxis.

"The prom queen voting site did have Anna in the lead by a nose." He sits in the empty seat next to me. "Then last week after Felicity came through on the new location, she pulled ahead."

"And after Callie got busted for the phone, *she* plunged to the bottom." I've gotten in the habit of checking it too.

"What do you think—did Callie make the phone call or—"

I finish Luke's sentence. "Did her boyfriend? Luke, I have to be honest. I've asked around a bit and found nothing. I don't know how to approach Callie to find out if her boyfriend has an alibi for Saturday. Everything I've come up with sounds lame."

He smiles. "Think outside the box. What do you know about Callie?"

"Her boyfriend's a jerk. He's the jealous type. He doesn't like her friends, and I overheard him say he wishes she's get some new ones." I ramble off a few more useless facts.

"So ask her to hang out with you."

"Is this an attempt to make sure I'm not alone? How about *you* ask her to hang out." Okay, I know how stupid that sounded. "Fine. I'll work on it." Eventually. I hate awkward situations—which pretty much sums up every minute of my life right now.

"Bump into Callie, tell her you're going to the movies or something Saturday night, and invite her. You're not going to Vegas with your parents, right?"

"I'm going to New York this weekend." While my family whoops it up at the semifinals in Vegas. I feel kind of left out.

"Then Monday night." He stands and gives my shoulder a squeeze. "I have absolute faith in you."

"You're just saying that so you don't have to take care of this yourself."

His grin makes my heart flip. "Maybe I just like to watch you in action."

~~~~~~~~~~~~~~

It's an even larger crowd tonight that gathers at Mickey Patrick's gym for *Pile Driver of Dreams*.

"Take a bite of this chocolate tart and tell me that isn't the flakiest crust you've ever had." The Oklahoma wrestler known as Breath of Death holds out a platter. "My secret is buttermilk and egg whites."

I pop one in my mouth and chew. "Perfect. The crust is airy, yet substantial." I have no idea what I said, but the six-foot-seven Breath of Death claps his hands in giddy joy. If he weren't married, I would seriously wonder about him.

Through the crowd I see Luke slip in through the double doors. He has Ruthie, Matt, and Lindy in tow. I lift a hand in greeting and work my way to the back to talk to my mom.

"Does Dolly need any help?" I ask.

"You might check. Breath of Death handled the desserts tonight, but Dolly insisted on doing the rest. She said it would keep her mind off things."

Tonight's party theme is Western, with beans in a kettle,

barbeque chicken individually wrapped in bandana paper, and all the side items somehow served in cowboy hats. Dolly may be queen of cooking, but my mom knows how to make it all look pretty. I reach past a lasso and sneak a bite of fried potato.

I walk through a group of men making animal noises and taking turns with headlocks, toward Mickey's office. I see Mickey's back and start to ask him where Dolly is.

"Hey—" I immediately swallow the rest of the sentence as Mickey steps to the left, revealing Dolly. The two don't even notice me.

"I just wanted to tell you that I'm here." Mickey runs his finger across Mason's cheek. The baby sighs and nestles deeper in his mother's arms.

I step back a bit so they can't see me.

"Thank you. It will be fine." But Dolly's voice cracks.

"I know a great lawyer in Tulsa. I can make some calls. His firm is the best."

"I don't think that's going to be necessary, Mickey."

"Let me help you."

She shakes her head. "No."

"Dang it, Dolly. Let the past go just long enough to let me help you. When we get this settled, you can go back to hating me."

The silence in the room is a sharp contrast to the noise in the gym.

When Dolly finally speaks, her voice is barely a whisper. "I don't hate you."

"Then don't shut me out of this."

"I've met with Mason's father." She sniffs and rocks her son.

"He's a good man. He served his full term with the army. Fought in Afghanistan. He has supportive parents who are going to help him. Parents who want their grandchild."

Mason squirms in her arms and begins to whimper. Tears well in her eyes as she transfers the baby to her shoulder and pats his back. Mason's crying only intensifies.

Dolly's grin is watery. "Neither one of us can seem to quit crying the past few days."

Mickey reaches for Mason and brings him to his chest. "That's a good boy. Mickey's got you." He hums a low tune and sways. "Go take care of your party, Dolly. Mason's not going anywhere tonight."

Dolly stares at the man who was once her husband. The man she's barely spoken to since the night her girls were killed many years ago.

"What exactly are you doing?" a voice breathes near my ear.

I swallow a yelp and turn away from the office. "Luke!" I hiss. "You scared me to death."

Dolly sails right past us and joins my mom at the food table.

"Budge and Ruthie are talking." Luke jerks his head in their direction. "Well, Ruthie's talking and your stepbrother is just kind of standing there, mouth open like a hooked fish."

"Poor guy. Hey, have you tasted the chocolate tarts? Breath of Death made them."

"Have you ever noticed how giggly that guy is?"

"Have you ever noticed his initials spell BOD?" We laugh, and I notice I've gravitated even closer to Luke.

His smile slips. "Bella, promise me you'll be careful with Hunter."

This is getting old. And confusing. "You tell us to trust our instinct all the time in journalism. I think I know Hunter."

He glances at Breath of Death, who's rearranging the decorations. "Sometimes people just aren't what they seem."

chapter twenty-six

"We're thinking a June wedding. Something small since money's a little tight. No more than five hundred people."

I bite into my steak and try to pretend like I give a poop about Christina's wedding details. I had to listen to them all the way from the airport. I used to bring Lindy with me to Manhattan. But now that Dad has swapped Mr. Chow's for Chili's and is doubling up on nose jobs, it's just me. And them.

"We're going to be bridesmaids." Marisol announces this like she's won the lottery.

"You know, I was in my mom's wedding." I reach for a crusty roll at the dinner table. "Maybe I could pass on this one and just enjoy it like a normal spectator."

Christina's forehead wrinkles. "Kevin?" she whines.

Dad reaches across his dining room table for my hand. "Bella, we want you to be involved. I'm not just marrying Christina, I'm marrying you."

"Ew."

"No!" He shakes his dark head. "What I mean to say is, I'm marrying Marisol. Wait—um, Christina is my bride, but I, er, I mean she and Marisol are a package deal. And you and I are a package deal, and together we're all this big two-for-one special getting married and—"

I hold up my hands. "I think I get the idea." Though my head hurts.

"Yeah, so it will be great. But honey, it is kind of turning into a big wedding." Dad smiles at his fiancée. "Perhaps we could tone it down just a bit." He turns to me. "There are ten other bridesmaids besides you and Marisol."

"I'm the maid of honor," Marisol says with a smirk. As if I'd *want* that title.

"So . . . twelve bridesmaids?" And I battled the dangers of maxipads just so I could buy a prom dress? "Sounds expensive. Dad, do you even have twelve good friends to be your groomsmen?"

He takes a drink of water as Christina answers for him. "Some of my family will be his groomsmen."

"I thought you were an orphan. And your family was all in Brazil."

"Bella!" Dad gives me the *Are you on drugs?* look.

Christina's smile is as fake as the collagen in her lips. "I also have family in the United States. In my culture, we embrace anyone into our family. And we treat them with love and respect. At all times."

I nod my head. "Neato."

"I'm going to ask Luisa to bring in the ice cream for dessert now." Dad brushes off his Armani slacks and stands.

"I'll help you!" Get me out of here. This woman brings out the Sharpay Evans in me.

"No, you stay here and talk."

"I'm not going anywhere, you know," Christina says as Dad is out of earshot. "I've done everything I can think of to be your friend."

You could buy me an alternator. "Christina, I just need some time to adjust. Within the last six months both my mom *and* dad have found me a new stepparent. That's all." *Oh. Plus I don't like you.*

She purses her full lips. "I'm sure you want your father happy. And *I'm* what makes him happy."

I glance at her sister, and she's sitting back with her arms crossed like she's the stinkin' queen of my dining room.

I nearly shout a hallelujah when Dad returns, carrying bowls of ice cream on a tray. Luisa waddles behind him with her famous hot fudge sauce.

"Darling," Christina purrs. "I just had the most marvelous idea! Why don't we take Bella to that therapist we've been seeing?"

"Bananas?" Luisa leans over and cuts some fruit into my bowl.

"I do *not* need a shrink."

Dad's face lights up. "Yes! Brilliant idea, sweetheart. We could all go tomorrow for a group session. Bella, this man works wonders! I've learned things about myself I never knew. Why, did you know I was a midget goat farmer in a past life?"

"Nuts?" Luisa chunks a few on my ice cream and winks a warm brown eye.

"I'll call and make the appointment right now." Dad pulls out his cell, ignoring my string of protests.

"I think I'll take my ice cream upstairs. I want to watch *Pile Driver of Dreams* and work on some other stuff." Like drool over the latest *Vogue* and pray for my dad's midget soul.

I flick on the TV just as the announcer gives a replay of the last episode. I watch the first few contestants as they battle well-known professional wrestlers. Jake is the last to enter the ring. I say a prayer and smile when the camera pans to my mom and stepbrothers. I wish I were there. Sometimes this visitation business barely seems worth it. I spend more time in an airplane than I do with my dad.

By the end of the hour, I feel as jittery as Moxie on catnip.

"The time has come when we must say good-bye to one of our wrestlers. America, you have voted, and tonight we're putting the smackdown on the dreams of . . ."

Please don't be Jake.

"Cinnamon, you're going home." The redheaded lady with cantaloupe boobs buries her face in her hands and cries. I stand on the bed and dance and sing. Before I get to the second verse of my made-up song called "Jake Is Better Than Cinnamon Big Jugs," my phone rings.

"Do you need rescuing from your dad yet?"

"Hunter." I smile. "How did you know?"

"We have a deep connection, Bella. When you hurt, I hurt. When you crave a mocha, I crave a mocha. *And* there's the fact that the last three times you've been to your dad's, you've begged me to get you out of the house."

I fall back onto the bed. "See you in fifteen?"

"I'll be there."

By the time I get to Starbucks, Hunter's already seated with three coffees waiting on the table.

"Are you drinking double tonight?"

He grins. "This one is mine." He taps the smaller one. "The two supersized ones are all yours."

I fill Hunter in on the wedding plans. "My dad is in this weird place right now. I don't think he should just jump into marriage. It wasn't that long ago he was dating every sorority girl in New York state. And now he'll have a child in the house again." The thought of Marisol conjures icky feelings.

Hunter reaches for my hand and twines his fingers with mine. "Things change. We have to roll with it and make the best of the bad."

"I guess. How is your dad's business? Has he been able to recover any since the accountant took off?"

Hunter absently strokes my hand. "My dad will never be the same. I don't think my life will be either."

His sickness. "Hunter, I'm sorry. I know the last few months have been hard on you. And I am rambling on about a stupid wedding." At least I'm healthy. At least my dad's business is still operating.

"Do you have your prom dress yet?"

Speaking of painful subjects. "No. I found this red one at Bergdorf's last month. It's by a new designer named Bliss. She's amazing. It's strapless and red." I sigh. "And heaven." I could totally see myself dancing in it all night long.

We talk a little longer before Hunter offers to see me home. The brakes of the taxi squeak as he stops at my house. Hunter walks me to the door, and for a second I think he's going to hold my hand.

"I'll see you next month for prom," he says under the glow of the porch light.

"Thanks for going." I smile into his face. "And thanks for being my friend again."

His arms wrap around me and he pulls me close, tucking my head under his chin.

"Hunter?"

"Yes?"

"Do you know what my favorite color is?"

"Black." Though he didn't say pink as well, I'll give him partial credit. But every New Yorker lives in black.

"Do you know which side I usually part my hair on?"

He runs his hand over hair that is pulled straight back in a ponytail. "Is this a trick question?"

"Okay, what's my favorite dessert?"

Hunter frames my face in his hands. "Bella, when you're near me, all I see is your face, your eyes. Your smile. I'm sure there are lots of things I don't pick up on, but all I know is when I'm with you"—he presses his lips to my cold nose—"for a little while my world is just right."

chapter twenty-seven

So then the therapist was like, 'Bella, imagine you are a French poodle. Now how would you communicate to your father and Christina?'"

"I hope you didn't say you'd pee on them." Ruthie slaps the lunch table, her belly laugh projecting across the entire cafeteria.

While my forced therapy session with Dr. Moonbeams and Incense wasn't funny Saturday, now that it's Monday and I've got some distance, I'm starting to see the humor.

"And then he lights this candle and asks me to watch the flames and imagine them as my negative feelings eating at my mind." I cover a giggle with my hand. "And then makes me, Dad, and Christina shape our thoughts into Play-Doh."

My laughter dissolves as I spot Luke headed our way.

Anna nudges me with a pointy elbow. "Mmmm. That boy is yum-ee. I would be writing him all *sorts* of articles if he were my editor."

Luke greets everyone but focuses his attention on me. "Can I talk to you?"

He turns on his heel, and I follow him outside into the court-yard. We wind around to the parking lot where Felicity Weeks and

Callie Drake stand next to a black BMW, the very car I had picked out for myself once upon a time. That was before my mom and dad decided I needed to live more Wal-Mart and less Saks.

"My tires are *ruined!*" Tears spill down Felicity's fake-baked cheeks. "Daddy is going to be so ticked! And I do not have time for this right now." She all but hisses at Callie. "I have a voice lesson immediately after school. And a ballet class following that!"

"I'll take you," Callie offers.

"You." Felicity sticks her manicured nail in my direction.

"Me?"

"Yes, you're the little crime-solver around here. Can you find out who did this?"

I stoop to inspect a tire. "Yeah, I can just dust for prints and find out within seconds who slashed your tires."

Felicity blinks twice. "You—you can?"

"No." *I'm not the CIA.* I catch Luke's small eye roll.

"I'm really sorry, Felicity." Callie puts her arm around her friend.

"Don't touch me!" Felicity stiffens and steps away. "You did this. I *know* you did. How could you? We're best friends."

Callie's face registers shock. "What?"

Felicity looks at Luke. "Do you see the pattern? *All* of the prom queen candidates have had something happen to them—Anna and the check, Ruthie and the pictures, and now me and my car. The only one who hasn't had any big catastrophe . . . is Callie."

Luke steps between the two girls. "Now, I don't really think that—"

"You want to win this just so you can turn the prom into some Greenpeacey, feminist liberal circus!" Felicity swipes at stray tears.

"Well, I won't let you. My mother was a Truman prom queen. And my grandmother was a Truman prom queen, and unlike you, *I* respect the title!" Felicity's voice elevates like she's defending her right to breathe.

"Felicity, you *know* I would never do anything like this!" Now Callie's yelling. A small crowd begins to gather around us.

"Know you? Ever since you've been dating Joshua, I barely recognize you." Felicity returns her attention back to me and Luke. "Do I call the police? The principal? The mayor? Who?"

He barely hides a smile. "Yes to the police and principal."

"And the president," I add. This earns me another frown from Luke.

"My Beemer and I will have justice!" Felicity stomps off in patent leather flats.

I watch her sashay into the building. "Please tell me I was never like that."

Luke lifts a dark brow. "You were slightly more tolerable." His wink is slow and chill inspiring. "But you've grown on me."

"Look, I didn't do this. I don't slash tires and steal money." Callie's voice matches her forlorn face.

Luke gives me the eye, like *do something.*

"Um . . . of course you didn't, Callie." I smile encouragingly. "You know what you need?"

"A new best friend?"

Pretty good guess, actually. "What you need is a girls' night out." I nod once. "Yep. A Monday night out with the girls."

"What girls?" she asks.

"Um . . . well, me." Who else can I drag into this? "And . . . Lindy Miller, Anna Deason, and Ruthie McGee."

"I don't know."

I lower my voice so the crowd of students around us can't hear. "Ruthie's harmless. I'll make her leave her nunchucks at home."

"And her pocketknife."

Ruthie would rather saw off her own arm than be without it.

"I'll see what I can do."

"I'm in."

~~~~~~~~~

"You hit my arm one more time, Ruthie, and I'm pushing you out the car door."

I glance in the backseat and wonder again at the stupidity of this plan. I could've just messaged Callie on Facebook.

"Well, excuse me, Anna. I guess you got a total BOGO at the emergency room. You went in for a broken arm and came *out* with a crappy attitude."

"Ladies!" Lindy shoots them both a mom look in the rearview. "Don't make me pull this car over."

"Why are we doing this again?" Ruthie asks. "Don't y'all know there's a new episode of *American Chopper* on tonight?"

"I just want to expand Callie's circle of friends."

Anna leans forward in the seat. "I don't know why. This is the girl who cancelled the caterer, right? And *probably* the banquet hall too. I say if we hang out with anyone, it ought to be Felicity. She's the one who's saving prom."

Lindy turns left onto Main Street and huffs, "I had prom under control before she butted in."

"Let's just show Callie a good time tonight, okay?" I stare down all three girls. "Maybe invite her to church or FCA." Or a few counseling sessions so she'll detox from her boyfriend.

Lindy pulls into the restaurant and turns off the car.

"Here?" Ruthie opens her car door. "You didn't tell me we were eating at the Wiener Palace."

"Is that a problem?" *Please don't break out the brass knuckles hidden in your sock.*

"Problem? I love this place!" She runs on ahead of us.

I swing open the glass door and wave at Callie Drake, who sits in a corner booth. We all squeeze in and join her.

"Welcome to the Wiener Palace. I'm Budge, your sultan of—"

I drop my menu and stare at my stepbrother.

"Bella?" A crimson blush starts at his neck and spreads upward. "Ruthie? W-W-What are you girls doing here?"

Ruthie narrows her eyes to snakelike slits. "I didn't know your stepbrother worked here."

"Oh, yeah." I say brightly. "See those feathers in his hat? You have to earn those. And the bigger the plume, the higher your ranking."

Ruthie's eyes continue up the line of his hat. "You must be like king of wieners or something."

Budge shrugs then looks away. "Some call it a gift."

I bite back a smile. "I'll have the Frankly My Dog, I Don't Give a Chili."

Ruthie only has eyes for Budge. "What do you recommend?"

"I ..."

Please don't say yourself with a side of relish.

"Our special is the Drop It Like It's Hot Dog. It's exceptionally tasty tonight."

She nods her head. "I'll take four of those."

Budge gets the rest of the orders and disappears into the kitchen.

"Ruthie, you could just ask him to the prom, you know," I suggest. "Just as friends, if nothing else. Would that make it easier?"

"Yeah," Lindy agrees. "My prom date isn't a date. He's just a friend of Budge's."

The conversation takes on a life of its own as we wait for our food. Soon Callie is piping in like she's one of us.

"Here are your meals, ladies." Budge balances a tray on one hand and passes out our food. "And here are four hot dogs for you, Ruthie." He takes off his hat and does a sweeping bow in his vest and balloony pants. "Enjoy your stay at the Palace, where everyone is hot, I mean royalty!" His hat slips from his hand, taking flight like a Frisbee. It slices over our table and heads straight for Ruthie's hot dogs.

Splurt! Two hot dogs splatter on her shirt and slide down. Budge grabs napkins in both fists and heads straight toward Ruthie's—

"Hey!" She pushes his hands away, and before I can say *relish*, she has Budge pinned in a headlock.

He swallows hard, sweat beading on his forehead. "I'm sorry," Budge croaks. "Didn't mean to."

She stares down into his reddish purple face. "Bring me another hot dog."

" 'Kay." Without air, his voice is strained, his eyes bulging.

"You're gonna pay for my dry cleaning bill, Budge Finley. You got that? *And* I've decided you're gonna take me to prom. But no funny business. No lip action in the backseat of your hearse, as totally romantic as that would be." She releases his neck, and Budge's gasp for breath nearly sucks in the walls. "My dress is pink by the way."

Budge staggers backward and escapes into the safety of hot dogs and buns behind the counter.

An hour later we've covered nearly every topic imaginable. The conversation is winding down, and my dinner sits like a twenty-pound blob in my stomach.

I decide to get down to business. "So . . . Callie. Your boyfriend seems nice." For a control freak.

She smiles. "He is. We've been going out for about a year. He supports me, he supports my causes, and he's always looking out for me."

Ruthie licks mustard off her hand. "My ex-boyfriend could light a firecracker with his farts."

I think this is probably considered romantic on her planet.

"Don't you hate it when your boyfriend uses your cell phone though?" That didn't sound so lame in my head.

Nobody really says anything. Big help.

I try again. "So what did everyone do this weekend?" I stir the straw in my Sprite.

"I can't remember what I did," Anna drolls. "Oh, wait. I broke my arm. I highly recommend it for some weekend fun."

"What about you, Callie?" *Please take the bait.*

"Joshua was in Tulsa at his dad's all weekend, so I stayed home and babysat my little brother."

Interesting. I prod further. "I'm sure he could hardly eat his lunch when you told him that Felicity blamed you for her slashed tires."

Callie twists a napkin in her hand. "Actually, I didn't get to tell him about it until after school. He stayed home *sick* today."

Quotey fingers. She totally did quotey fingers when she said "sick." Joshua was unaccounted for Saturday night *and* has no alibi for today.

"Did he hang out with anyone at home?" My playful grin is wide—and hopefully believable. "You know, play some Guitar Hero or Halo?"

She shakes her head. "No. Just him. His mom would've killed him if he'd had friends over."

I let this information marinate in my head. I must say, not a bad night out. Mission accomplished.

"This conversation bores me." Ruthie yawns and picks at some chili on her shirt. "Can we talk about *me* some more?"

chapter twenty-eight

On Thursday morning I sit in the kitchen ignoring two camera guys. My head rests on the old table. It's very difficult to eat oatmeal that way. But I'm not giving up.

Budge stomps into the room. "Do you know you have a blob of brown stuff on your nose?"

"My life is in the crapper."

"I think it left a souvenir on your face."

Sitting up, I wipe the oatmeal off my nose and glare. No job. No money. No prom dress. No idea what I'm going to do about Hunter. And I'm still getting to school riding shotgun in a car once used to transport dead people.

"Do you have any openings at the Wiener Palace?" Budge looks at me like I just asked if he'd like to light his computer on fire. "What? You wouldn't even know I was there. I'm a good worker."

"You're a walking catastrophe, is what you are. Every job you've touched has exploded—some literally—in your face."

I stare into camera one. "None of those things were my fault." Okay, maybe a few. But when you find yourself putting antibiotic ointment on your face because a swarm of maxi-pads attacked you, it's easy to get a little depressed.

Mom sweeps into the kitchen in black yoga pants and matching jacket. "Where is your brother, Logan?" She lowers her voice until it's barely audible. "Lately we play this ridiculous game of hide-and-go-seek every morning before school. He hides, and I spend my time looking for him and running late."

I stir my lumpy oatmeal. "I think he hates school."

Budge smirks. "Who doesn't?"

"Doesn't anybody care that something's going on with Robbie?" I whisper, hoping the cameras won't pick it up.

Mom grabs a water and stands behind my chair. "Honey, we've had three meetings with his teacher. We've tried talking to him countless times, but he just says nothing's wrong. I don't know what else to do. I've consulted every parenting book I know."

Before she started her community college classes, Mom read a *lot* of parenting books. She wasn't exactly a major player in my upbringing. But I have to admit, she's doing pretty well in her new role as mother. Except for the fact that she and her husband are totally striking out with Robbie. Something is up with him.

Thirty minutes later, my little brother is accounted for and ready for the bus. And I'm belted into the hearse, my head pounding with the music volume, and hoping my ears don't bleed from the screamo. No wonder teenagers are so violent these days. I know I'd like to hurt someone. Budge swats my hand as I reach for the radio controls. I roll down the window, letting in the March breeze and sharing with all of Truman a little ditty called "Care Bears Wear Beards on Tuesdays."

In journalism, Luke makes his rounds, then sits beside me. "Last week's article on teen jobs was good."

"Thanks. The research has been . . . memorable."

His smile is oddly warm. "I think everything about your life is just crazy right now. It will settle down when the reality show is over. It has to be hard living with constant video cameras and seeing your picture on the cover of tabloids. I saw Budge's picture in *People* last week."

I mentally groan. In that same issue was yet another photo of me and Hunter. This one was from my last visit to New York, and Hunter looks like he's about to kiss my face off.

"Luke, Hunter and I are still just—" Friends.

"None of my business."

What if I want *it to be your business?* "How's Taylor?" I haven't heard him mention his girlfriend in forever.

"She's fine." He drums his fingers on the desk. "Bella, I think we need to talk to Victoria Smith again."

I think about our last visit with the bank teller and cringe. "Are you hoping someone will run us off the road again? Maybe hit the other side?"

"I want to ask her about Callie's boyfriend. Maybe she feels like sharing information now. I've contacted her and arranged a meeting."

"What?" I squeak. "We agreed, Luke. We're a duet. *Not* a solo."

"I didn't hide it from you. Can you ride to Tulsa with me after school?"

I twirl my hair around my finger. "Fine. Pick me up at the house. If there's a chance of being run off the road again and dying in a ditch, I need to change clothes." I don't have good underwear on.

When Budge and I get home, Jake is in the living room with Robbie. The big man paces the floor while Robbie sits like a statue in a chair.

"Do you know how *scared* I was when the teacher called to say you hadn't made it to school yet?"

Budge and I don't even pretend like we're not listening.

"Robbie, you are never, *never* to walk to school. I know you don't like the bus, but unless you can give me a reason you shouldn't ride it, that's our only option right now. Now I'm asking you for the last time, is someone picking on you at school or on the bus?"

I can barely hear his answer. "No."

Jake gets down on his knees, eye level with Robbie. "Son, I don't know what's going on with you, but you know I'd butt drop anyone who tried to hurt you. Please talk to me."

We all lean in, balanced on tippy-toes of hope. Is Robbie going to talk?

He opens his six-year-old mouth. "Nothing's going on at school. No one's picking on me on the bus."

Jake pinches the bridge of his nose and sighs. "Go upstairs. And no TV. You're grounded—again."

As Robbie runs to his room, I notice a hint of red under his shirt.

"His cape." I point to his retreating back.

"I know." Jake flops into a seat. "He doesn't wear it anymore."

"Yes, he does." I glance back at the stairs. "It's under his clothes."

~~~~~~~~~~

Luke and I sit across from Victoria Smith in a Tulsa McDonald's. She eats from the package of fries Luke bought her and keeps one hand on her triple-thick shake. It's like she knows I'm totally lusting after her ice cream.

She looks like she's lost ten pounds and is in need of more than a Happy Meal.

"I don't know what more I could possibly tell you." Her jittery eyes focus on the Playland behind us. "I've told you about the day I cashed the check at least ten times."

"Okay, we won't talk about that anymore." Luke's voice is as soft as puppy fur. "Victoria, do you know Joshua Day?"

"Joshua Day?" She bites on her straw. "Like, the senior from Truman?"

"Yes." I nod.

"No, I don't really know him. Why? What'd he say about me?"

Luke rests his hands on the table and tells Victoria what we know so far. "People are getting hurt at school—the girls running for prom queen. We just don't want to see anything bad happen, and I'm sure you don't either, right?"

"Right." She drawls the word out.

I lean closer to Luke so I can talk. *Ignore his cologne. Don't stare at his jawline.* "We think Joshua might know something about the incidents. Victoria, we would never reveal you as our source, but was he in the car the day you cashed the check? Did he threaten you to be quiet?"

"I—" She sets her shake down with a thud. "I have to pee."

I look at Luke as she leaves. We're, like, nose to nose. I slide down a bit and pretend to wipe some crumbs off my pants.

"You were breathing on my neck."

I glance up. "Was not."

His mouth curves upward. "If you had been any closer, we'd have been PG-13."

"I guess I was just getting into the discussion." My face must be as red as Ronald McDonald's hair. "Sorry."

His finger sweeps across my hand. "I didn't say I didn't like it."

A few minutes later Victoria returns. "I . . . um, have to tell you something."

Luke and I both move to the center of the seat and lean in. If she came back to tell us the toilet paper was scratchy, it's going to be a huge letdown.

Victoria stares at her hands. "I can't say much, but I think you're on the right track with Joshua Day." Her voice seems to gain strength. "You *have* to keep me out of this for my own protection, but Joshua is the one who was behind those calls to cancel the caterer and banquet room. And Joshua . . . he's been harassing the girls."

"Have you been helping him?" I ask.

"No!"

Luke grips his Coke. "Was he the one who transferred the junior class's money into Anna Deason's account?"

"Yes. He's brilliant at computers. He writes all sorts of programs." Her eyes grow distant, as if she's seeing him. "He's great at fantasy. It's reality that he has trouble with. But I love him anyway. Even if he won't stop chasing her and—" Victoria clamps her mouth tight. "I have to go." She jumps out of the seat, doubles back, grabs the shake, and bolts out the door.

We get back to Truman just in time for the opening of *Pile Driver of Dreams*. The crowd has expanded and somehow an even bigger flat screen has appeared.

Dolly sits with Mason in her lap and laughs at something he does. From a distance Mickey watches, his face impassive.

Luke and I grab the two vacant seats next to Lindy and Matt. Not that they notice we're there.

"I just don't see why I have to hear about your prom date from someone else, that's all," Matt says.

"So that's what you've been so pouty about lately?"

"I thought maybe—"

"What?" Lindy barks. "That we'd go together? As friends. Like we *always* do things together—as friends."

"*Best* friends. And I don't even know this Newton guy."

Lindy crosses her arms and jerks her head away. "You can meet him at prom."

"You've been acting weird ever since you got that Match-and-Catch form back," Matt says. "Does it bother you that it paired us together? It's not like I'm your brother or a cousin."

She rolls her eyes. "Aren't you?"

Luke's whisper dances on my neck. "Lindy likes Matt?"

"You're just *now* putting that together?" I *tsk*. "Clearly *I* have the sharper reporter's instinct."

Of course, right now my instinct is saying, *Luke, back up before I get the urge to do something crazy like feel your biceps or run my fingers through your hair.*

With many of Jake's coworkers, friends, and fellow wrestlers, I tune into *Pile Driver of Dreams*. When the show turns to Jake, it shows him at work in the early morning hours. Some footage of him with Budge and Robbie. The family at church last Sunday. And Jake in his pirate garb taking someone to the mat.

"You're on the screen, Bella." Mom grins from across the room. Images flash of me having a one-woman fight with the pad machine.

Me on the front steps with Hunter, staring intensely into his eyes. Mickey's gym erupts into whistles and *ooohs*.

I shake my head and laugh it off. "It's nothing!" I look up and find Luke watching me. He averts his gaze and returns his attention to the TV.

And it *is* nothing with Hunter. Nothing more than friendship.

And I've decided that's all I'm going to let it be.

I think.

chapter twenty-nine

The week passes by so easily, I'm just waiting for the sky to fall. Though lots of March rain, there's no prom queen calamity, and Jake made it through again. Now it's down to just him and Sanchez the Snake. In less than three weeks, the two wrestlers will go head to head. Or spandex to spandex. Wedgie to wedgie.

On this Wednesday morning, I sit Indian-style on the floor of the library at our Fellowship of Christian Athletes meeting. Callie sits beside me, looking a little uncertain.

Today the speaker, a football player from Oklahoma State, spoke on forgiveness and letting things go. It started out kind of boring, but when he started playing the YouTube clips, I began to tune in. And Callie showed up, surprising us all.

". . . And God tells us to forgive as he forgave. You know, Jesus didn't hang on that cross just for you alone and just so you could forget it. We are to be Jesus to others. Are you still holding on to a grudge?"

About ten possibilities pop into my head.

"Are you still withholding forgiveness for someone who deserves it? How's that going for you? Is it accomplishing anything?"

I think of my dad. Maybe I don't like Christina because I'm still hurt he left my mom. Maybe Marisol isn't *totally* awful. I guess I can't show them Christ if I'm catty all the time. And Christina has made an effort with me.

"Think of family . . . friends . . . *former* friends . . ."

Ew. Mia. My BFF who stole Hunter. Okay, so Hunter was just as guilty. And I did forgive him.

I need to call Mia. Tell her it's okay and just let it all go. Or I could talk to her when I go to Manhattan for spring break next week.

And maybe I should forgive Budge for flushing my MAC eye shadow down the toilet last month.

Nah. Let's not go crazy.

After prayer, we're dismissed. I stand up and stretch my arms. "How did you like it?" I ask Callie.

"It was good." Her eyes flit over all the people in the room. "Thanks for asking me. It's like after I got with Joshua, all my friends forgot about me. Except for Felicity." She steps closer. "Bella, you know I didn't do all those things, right? I would never hurt anyone."

"I believe you." And I do. I don't even think she knows about her boyfriend's misdeeds. But she soon will if Luke and I have anything to do with it.

Later in journalism, I stand behind Luke at his workstation. "Did you want to see my final draft?" I ask.

He minimizes an e-mail message, but not before I see his girlfriend's name. "Um . . . yeah." Luke takes my work from my hand. "Bella, this is good," he says after some time. "Just like the job features, every article you've submitted about living with a reality show has been top-notch."

I try to wipe the big goofy grin off my face, but fail.

"I've learned a lot about the wrestling business from reading your work." Luke takes off his glasses. "Learned a lot about you."

"Well . . ." *Inhale. Exhale.* "It's been fun working on this together. I really liked having you around on Thursday and Friday nights." I replay the words in my head. "Er, and everyone else! Yep. Matt. Lindy. Breath of Death. That guy *totally* livens up a party, eh?" *Why am I still talking?*

"I guess since the show is taking a few weeks off before the big finale, our standing date at Mickey's is off."

I swallow. "Yeah." The show will still film the families, but it won't go back on the air until the Thursday night before prom. "Too bad the paper won't send you to Vegas with us for the final show. But then there'd be two of us rushing around like mad Saturday morning trying to get back in time for prom." *He's smiling. What does that mean?*

"There's a class meeting at lunch. Are you going to be there?"

"Yes. Can't wait." *Can't wait for a class meeting? Did I really just say that?*

After calculus I take my rumbling stomach straight to the cafeteria to pick up something to eat. I bump into Anna. "What's your hurry?" I ask.

"Class meeting. Felicity's going so she can make some big announcement. I can't wait to see what it is this time." Anna rolls her eyes. "Maybe her daddy's arranged for horse-drawn carriages for all of us."

"Did you say there's a class meeting?" Ruthie stops. "Will my prom date be there?"

I shrug. "I guess it's possible."

"I'm in. Let's go."

The girls wait for me as I grab a sandwich to go. When I rejoin them at the cafeteria doors, Callie Drake stands next to them along with her boyfriend.

"Oh, and here's Bella," Callie says. "This is my boyfriend, Joshua."

I force a smile. "I feel like I already know you." *Seriously, dude, I mean that.*

"I had a great time at the Wiener Palace last week." Callie looks at all of us expectantly.

"Sorry Felicity's still giving you the cold shoulder," I say. "You can hang out with us anytime." *Just don't bring Psycho Joshua.*

"I'm gonna go get in line. I don't want them to sell out of pizza." Joshua steps away, then turns around. "And Callie, don't be long or I won't hold your place."

She laughs nervously. "He's pretty serious about lunch. I better go."

We say our good-byes and then head to the library for the meeting. Lindy is just calling it to order when I take a seat beside Luke.

"Okay, guys. Next week is spring break, and then . . . prom. We've had a few fund-raisers and now have enough money to pay the deejay and—"

"I have an announcement! Excuse me!" Felicity Weeks makes her way from the back of the room.

From my spot, I see Lindy tense, like she totally wants to tell Felicity to shut her yapper.

"I am here today as a representative of the senior class." Felicity beams like she's found the cure for cancer. "And as you know, I have provided us an alternate location for prom." She stops as a few people hoot in support. "And now I am pleased to tell you that my father has secured the top caterer in Oklahoma, OK Kibbles—all free! My daddy will be picking up the tab as a donation to Truman High."

Half the room cheers in response. The other half just stares, knowing there's more.

"Man, her popularity rating is going to be off the chart," Anna grumbles.

"*And* as a favor to my daddy, Big Cool from KLRC radio has agreed to emcee and deejay the event!"

"Wait!" Lindy yells over the crowd. "Wait! Felicity, you can't step in and take over prom. We have class officers, and we have to vote and—"

"All in favor, say aye!" calls Brady Malone, the secretary.

"Aye!"

The whole room shouts agreement, and Lindy knows it's over. "Fine. Felicity, please give us more details."

Anna raises her hand. "And don't fear because I'm bringing balloons!" She looks around the now silent library. "Fine. I see how you are. You'll have a balloonless prom. That's what you'll have."

After the meeting I spend the rest of my classes thinking about Luke. And thinking about Hunter. Both guys are, like, putting something out there. I don't know what. But Luke has Taylor, and my ship with Hunter has already sailed. Hasn't it? It's just that he's so different. I really like the new version. A lot. But . . . he doesn't make the butterflies bungee in my stomach like Luke does.

After school I hop in the hearse, and in a blaze of shrieking lyrics, Budge takes us to Truman Elementary to pick up Robbie.

"Can you find a ride to tutoring tomorrow morning? I don't have my gamer meeting."

I stare at Budge. "What? Your army of dorks isn't meeting? Did someone die?"

He answers by cranking up his hideous music just as Robbie gets to the hearse.

"Hey, buddy." I ruffle Robbie's hair as he climbs in back. "Did you eat any paste today?"

"Just a little." He shoves some papers into his half-open backpack.

"Did you have art?" Budge asks. "Let's see what you drew. Maybe a symbolic representation of global warming?"

I think of his past artwork. "A picture depicting your feelings on the cruelty of petting zoos?" I wrap my arm around my seat and grab a paper. "Let's see."

"No!" Robbie yells. "Give it back."

"Robbie, it's in two pieces. What happened?" I hold up two halves.

"Nothing."

Budge inspects the paper. "A dog? You painted a dog?"

My older stepbrother and I share a concerned look.

"Maybe it's a metaphor for his need for world peace?"

Budge snaps his fingers. "Yeah, or a symbol of man's inner struggle with—"

"It's a dog." Robbie snatches the paper back and clicks into his seat belt. "Can we just go home?"

"Did someone rip your paper?" I ask.

His short legs kick against his seat as he stares out the window.

Another thought occurs to me, one that makes my heart hurt. "Has someone been making fun of your drawings?" Still no reply.

"If so, Robbie, that's just stupid. You have the best artwork I've ever seen. Like, museum quality."

Budge turns into Sugar's Diner. "Total Smithsonian material."

The car stops and we all pile out. "We'll talk about this later, okay, Robbie?" He ignores me and walks on into the diner.

The three of us sit at the counter on red barstools. I hear a plate clatter to the floor and without looking, know it's my mom.

She scurries by us. "Be with you in a jiffy. I have a chicken-fried steak emergency."

A few minutes later she reappears, her hair wilted to her head. "Shakes all around?"

We all nod. "Crazy day, Mom?"

"Yeah." She looks across the restaurant. "Dolly's had the last few hours off."

I follow the trail of her gaze and find Dolly in a booth, sitting across from a guy who could be her son. Her face is drawn, and even her hair seems deflated.

Mom swipes the counter with a rag. "Mason's dad. This is their third meeting. His parents just left a bit ago."

I can't tear my eyes away from the restrained pain on Dolly's face. "What does her lawyer say?"

"Dolly's already made up her mind." Mom's hand stops midswipe. "She's giving the baby back to his father."

chapter thirty

Webcams are so weird. It's like watching a movie where the sound is a split second off from the film.

"Dad, speak up toward the mic, I can't hear you." I glance in my handheld mirror and feather my lashes with mascara. Running late for school as it was, and then dad *had* to talk to me.

"Bel, I just can't believe it's already Thursday. This week has totally gotten away from me."

"I know. I can't wait to see you Saturday." A whole week in New York.

"Yeah, babe . . . about that. I know you're going to be devastated, but I've cancelled your flight."

"What's that? I don't think I heard you right." I tap my finger on the computer.

"Bel." He sighs big. "This amazing opportunity has come up. Christina has found a cable channel in Brazil that wants to interview me for a TV show. It's what I've always wanted. It would be me and my life and—"

"Butt implants."

"More than that. It's a chance of a lifetime."

"So not only are you cancelling our spring break plans at the last minute, but you could be moving to Brazil?" I lift my laptop and smash it to my face. "Do you see how unhappy I am?"

"Don't do that, honey. A frown today, a wrinkle tomorrow."

"This week was important to me." I hear the catch in my voice and rein it in. "I wanted to spend time with you. Get my dress for prom. See some Broadway shows and be the girl on your arm—like we used to do."

"I know." His pixilated face appears contrite. "I hate that I'm letting you down. Again. It seems like I'm always doing that. But I have to go to Brazil. *E! News* doesn't use me for commentary much anymore, and the offers are fewer and fewer these days. If I'm going to get back on track financially, I have to make some sacrifices. And it will give me an opportunity to meet some of Christina's relatives." His eyes plead with me through the computer screen. "I'll make it up to you—some way, somehow."

"Dad . . ." I take a deep breath. "I've been thinking about some stuff, and I wanted to tell you that I forgive you. For what you did to Mom. And me—for leaving us." His head jerks like I just declared my love for Kmart.

Dad thinks about this. Finally he gives a half smile. "Thanks, Bel. Do you forgive me for bailing on spring break?"

"I'm only doing one pardon a day." *But tomorrow doesn't look so hot for you either.* "Bye, Dad. Have fun." *Without me.*

As long as I'm in the forgiving mood, I might as well call Mia and get it over with. I briefly consider sending her a postcard or e-mail. *No. Suck it up and do it in person.* I pull up her number and hit Send.

"Hey! This is Mia. Please leave a message . . ." Voice mail. Score.

"Mia, it's Bella. I know this is random but, um, just wanted to tell you that I'm sorry for how things went down last fall. I guess you've figured out by now that I've forgiven Hunter, and I wanted you to know . . . I've forgiven you too." I try to think of something else mature or inspirational to say, but come up with nothing. "I hope one day we can be friends again."

Wow. Being responsible sure takes it out of you. This calls for a Pop-Tart.

"Mom, my ride's here! I'm leaving!" I grab a light jacket and head out the front door where Ruthie sits in her mom's Volvo station wagon. I turn my head so she won't see me laugh. If there was ever a girl who did *not* belong behind the wheel of a wagon, it's Ruthie McGee.

"S'up?" she says, squirting ketchup on some Dairy Barn hash browns.

"Wow. Nice pink hair." She turns her head to give me the full effect. "I like it."

She starts the car, licking her fingers. "With spring on the way, I thought I needed a change."

As we drive down the dirt road, the school bus passes us on its way to pick up Robbie. Poor guy. I hate to see him have to get on that thing. I think it petrifies him.

Ruthie sings along to the music, her face scrunched with emotion.

"Celine Dion?" I ask.

"Yeah." She belts out the chorus. "She sure sings some deep crap."

A couple of miles down the road we pass a group of kids huddled together waiting for the bus.

An idea unfolds in my head. "Stop the car." Ruthie brakes and we both jolt forward. "I didn't mean in the middle of the street." Total seat belt burn.

As she turns into a driveway, I fill her in on Robbie's weird behavior. "It's just a hunch, but I think the kid who's harassing him probably rides this bus. So if you'd just let me out, I'm going to get on the bus. Oh, and I'm going to need your hoodie."

Without a word she yanks off her black sweatshirt and passes it over. I pull it down over my head and secure the hood.

A minute later I unbuckle. "Here's the bus. I'll see you back at school."

"Wait!" she yelps, as I climb out the door. "What about calculus tutoring?"

"I'll just skip it today." I hear the engine turn off and look back. "What are you doing?"

"I can't miss this!" She runs to catch up with me.

I wave my arm toward the car parked in someone's driveway. "You're just going to leave the station wagon at this person's house? Blocking the drive?"

"Oh, my mom won't need the car. She'll have my bike to ride." She pushes up the sleeves of her t-shirt. "If we're gonna rough up some little kids, then I totally want in on it."

"Ruthie, I'm not going to rough up any—never mind. Just stand behind me and look mean."

We climb on the bus and walk right past an elderly woman at the wheel. "Good morning, sweeties! It's a great day to do some learnin'!" Granny pulls the door closed with a *whoosh*. I wonder if she can even see me behind glasses that are thicker than my hand.

"Don't stop at the Ford's because they're at Gerald Flatt's," a short kid says in passing.

"Super dooper!" Granny's dentures clickity-clack. "Don't stomp on the Lord just because it's raining cats." She nods and adjusts her hearing aid. "Those are words to live by, little man!"

Oh, wow. Robbie could've been screaming for help every day on this bus, and Granny No Ears would never hear.

With Ruthie following, I make my way to a vacant seat toward the back of the bus, keeping my head down. I spy Robbie four seats up, his head also lowered. I point him out to Ruthie. She gives me a rock-on sign.

Just as I'm about to tell Ruthie her rock-on privileges have been taken away due to her love for "My Heart Will Go On," the bus lurches to a stop again. The door opens and kids spill up the steps and into the aisle. I study the faces. Do any of these kids look like thugs? Who would pick on Robbie anyway? He's the sweetest kid ever. A little weird, but who isn't?

"Oh, yeah, little short one." Ruthie's turned around talking to a middle schooler. "On episode three-hundred-and-twenty-seven, I thought I was gonna pee my pants when Raven got stuck in that tree!"

I swat her shoulder. "Would you turn off the Disney channel and *focus*? Don't draw attention to us."

Two stops later, nobody is even talking to Robbie but the white-haired girl in pigtails sharing his seat. And she looks like she's about to sprout angel wings, not two fists.

Thirty minutes later the bus chugs to a stop at the edge of the elementary school.

"Have a joyous day, sweeties!" The driver opens the door and everyone trickles out.

Shoot. That was a total—wait a minute.

I press my nose to the grimy window and see three kids standing there, arms crossed, scowls in place. They're waiting for someone. I look up the aisle in time to see Robbie file out, his face pasty white.

"Let's go." I bump Ruthie with my hip and nudge her out.

She cracks her knuckles, then her neck. "Lead the way. I got your back."

I slide past her and down the steps. "No weapons, Ruthie. I want to talk to some kids. *Not* get arrested." I hear her sigh.

Robbie walks down the sidewalk toward the school, his backpack hanging low. He doesn't make eye contact with the three boys, just keeps going.

"You owe me money, Red."

The kids look like they might be all of ten. I immediately have the urge to smash their faces in now and ask questions later.

"Red, I'm talking to you. You got my money?"

Robbie sidesteps one, only to run into another. A tall brown-headed kid grabs him by the shoulders. I put my arm on Ruthie to hold her back.

"I want your lunch money, and I want it now."

Robbie stares at the grass. "I—I don't have it. I brought my lunch again."

The kid gives him a small shove. "That's not good enough."

"Maybe you can fly away and get it," another chides. The three laugh heartily as they circle in on Robbie.

"I warned you what would happen if you came to school without my money again."

"And what is it that will happen?" I step forward.

The kid doesn't release Robbie. He looks at me, then Ruthie. "Who wants to know?"

"We do." I smile. "I'm Mary Cline." I flash my driver's license. "I'm with playground security. This here is my partner—"

"Drew Barrymore." Ruthie flexes.

"Right. And Drew and I have gotten quite a few complaints about a group of boys who are such sissies they have to pick on little kids instead of anyone their own size. Would you happen to know where I could find those boys?"

"No." A snot-nosed blond in a flannel shirt spits on the ground. "Why don't you go look for 'em?"

Ruthie and I step closer. I glance at Robbie, who stands there motionless, his mouth a perfect oval.

"Drew Barrymore, I think our search is over, don't you?"

She pops her knuckles again. "I think we've found our sissy boys. Shame too. I was hoping we wouldn't have to get the police involved."

"Wait a minute!" I point to Robbie. "Isn't that the wrestler's son?"

"I think it is, Martha."

I cough. "*Mary.*"

"It is indeed, Mary. I heard that Captain Iron Jack is as mean in real life as he is in the ring. Do you remember what happened to the last bunch who were picking on his kid?"

I whistle low. "Those girls were never heard from again."

I continue to ignore the boys and move closer to Robbie. "Young man, I'm going to have to ask you *not* to do your kung-fu moves on them. I believe we were present for your last tussle, and it took us two weeks to scrape the blood off the sidewalk."

Ruthie shakes her pink head. "Totally ruined the hopscotch area."

"This kid don't know how to fight," Blondie says.

Ruthie and I both chuckle.

"Why do you think we're here?" I ask. "They only alert us when something big's going down. And word on the street was that Robbie here was getting ready to administer some pain."

Brown hair snorts. "Whatever." But his voice isn't quite as strong this time.

"Robbie," Ruthie says. "I would be honored if you would show me your famous dancing tiger block."

Robbie just stares.

"No, no, we can't ask that of him. It's too much." Yikes. What have we gotten into?

"Maybe the peaceful turtle block?" Ruthie does not feel my eyes lasering into her and keeps going. "Or the fiery rat slam. That's a good one."

The boys stare for a moment before dissolving into whoops of laughter. Again.

Robbie lifts wounded eyes to me.

"I would be honored, Robbie, if you would show them your moves on me. I can take the pain." I look at him hard. "Like *now*." I give the smallest of nods.

"I'm not sure . . ." his small voice whispers.

"What a baby."

Come on, Robbie. Read my deceptive, devious mind and work with me!

"Listen, puke-face, we've wasted enough time," pops the tall one. "Double the money tomorrow or we'll take it out on your face."

"*Hiiiiiii-yay!*" Robbie squats into some crazy stance, his green eyes intense on mine. With well-timed grunts, he moves into a series of poses, each one crisp and . . . very believable. This guy has been watching a *lot* of kung fu.

Again I give just a hint of a nod. With a warrior's yell, Robbie charges, his left foot airborne. I take it right in the gut.

"Oomph!" My coat pads the blow, but not before my eyes cross. Purposely I stumble backward groaning with pain. He throws a few *Kung Fu Panda* punches to my side, and I collapse on the ground moaning.

Robbie jumps over my thrashing body. He looms over my face, holds up chopper hands, and I catch his wink.

"*Heeee-yah!*" Pulling a wrestling move from his repertoire, Robbie brings down a hand, and a centimeter before impact, I jerk away as if hit. I wail in agony and look at the boys through slit eyes. It's quite possible they're buying it. At least they're not laughing anymore.

"Oh yeah?" Ruthie stomps forward and roars. "You think you can take me?" She kicks a perfect Tae Bo roundhouse. I see Robbie hesitate . . . then run right for her gut. "Feng shui!" she yells as he attacks.

Robbie lands before her in a cartwheel, pivots, then jabs both elbows into her stomach.

"Aughh!" Ruthie yells. She taps her stomach, sending him a signal. "Hit me again, short one. I can take it."

He clotheslines her neck, and her head bobs roughly to the

right. Ouch. That one was real. She motions to her stomach again—just a small movement.

Robbie faces out toward the boys, then goat kicks Ruthie with everything he's got.

She cries sharply and falls, but not before a red stain oozes through her shirt.

"She's bleeding!" Brown hair boy yells.

"He killed her!" From thug number three.

Robbie freezes as if someone pushed pause on his remote. His eyes are bigger than the tire swings on the playground. His little hands shake.

"We're not worthy to fight you," I croak. "Doctor . . . I need a doctor."

Ruthie lies still, spit dribbling out of her mouth.

While the boys move closer to inspect my friend, I tug on Robbie's pants. "It's okay," I mouth.

He turns on the three bullies. "Next time . . . it's going to be you. I've let you push me just because I didn't want to hurt you. But know this—my dad's a wrestler, I'm a warrior in training, and not only do I land a lethal kick . . . but I eat paste and live to tell about it. If you *ever* pick on me *or* anyone else again, I'll come after you. And I'll be bringing help."

Like something out of a movie, the leader hesitates for only a second before running away. His coconspirators all but trip over their own feet to catch up with him.

Ruthie peels open an eyeball. "They gone?"

I see Robbie instantly relax. "You're okay?"

She laughs and reaches her hand into her shirt, only to produce a squashed ketchup packet. "It was a great day for hash browns."

"But now you're all gross." That's *so* Robbie. He's been problem free for less than a minute and already found something else to worry about.

Ruthie taps the red spot. "For you, I'll wear the stain with honor."

I pull myself upright. "Robbie, you did a great job. I'm proud of you, buddy."

He sniffs his nose, swipes some dirt off his hands, then clutches my waist with all his might. "Bella, you make my whole face smile."

My throat constricts as I wrap my arms around him and squeeze. "I love you, little brother." A tear plops onto my cheek. Right before I'm tackled by Ruthie.

"I love you, too, guys." She snorts into her sleeve. "That was the best!"

"Robbie?" I say with smushed lips. "You'll always be a warrior to me."

"Thanks, Bel," comes his muffled voice.

"But seriously—the paste thing? You've got to give it up. Your breath smells like Elmer's."

chapter thirty-one

After school, I have Budge make a pit stop at Pancho's Mexican Villa. "I'll be right back," I say.

"Can I have a taco?" Robbie starts to bail out too.

"No. They stunt your growth." And I shut the door.

I plow toward the door and fling it open. "Welcome to Pancho's Mexican Villa!" a girl chirps. Her smile is nearly wider than her face.

Wow. "You're new here, aren't you?"

"Yes!" she beams. "First day!"

Tomorrow she'll sound like the other zombies.

I bypass her gleaming counter and hang a right to Manny's office.

At my knock he wrenches it open. "What do you wa—" His hand goes to his largest gold chain. "What can I do for you?"

"Um . . . I just wanted to apologize for losing my cool and starting a food fight."

"How sorry?"

"This much?" I hold out my hands the width of a taco.

Manny chews on a toothpick. "Do you want your job back by chance?"

Let me think about this. "No."

"Look, two kids just quit, and I'm in deep trouble with spring break coming on. You could just work that week for me and then see how it goes."

Well, gee, at one point I had plans to go to Manhattan, but . . . "I could be persuaded."

He smiles, his gold caps gleaming. "I'll up your hourly wage by a dollar."

Not bad, but I have a car to fix now. "Can I have a two hundred–dollar advance?"

His eyes pop. "What?"

"I'll mention Pancho's in my next newspaper article."

"It's a deal. But I'm hiding the refried bean shooter."

"It's probably for the best."

When Budge pulls the car into our driveway, we're singing three-part screamo harmony. Life is pretty good, and Robbie is back to being Robbie.

"I'm off to watch a documentary on the Japanese dung beetle." He skips into the yard, a red cape fluttering behind him.

My phone vibrates in my purse, and I scrounge for it. "Hey, Luke."

"How fast can you get back to school?"

"Five minutes. What's up?"

"Meet me in the school office. And bring Budge with you." The line goes dead.

"Budge, can you take me back to school?"

He rubs a smudge on the hearse. "No way, freak job."

Yes, we are definitely back to normal. "Two words: Hannah. Montana."

"Let's roll."

The twin doors leading into the high school are open, and we walk on through straight to the office.

"Hello?" I call.

"Back here." Luke steps out from the secretary's office. "We have a new development."

Mrs. Norwood sits behind her desk, her face illuminated by the computer screen. "Yes, the grades have definitely been altered. But just for those four."

Luke looks from me to Budge. "This afternoon someone got on the school server and changed some grades. Felicity, Anna, and Ruthie all suddenly had one F each."

"And the fourth person?" I ask.

The secretary taps a few keys. "Let's just say Joshua Day went from academic distress straight to the honor roll."

Budge nods his head. "*Niiice.*"

"Does the grading program tell you what time the grades were changed?" I step over to the computer. Mrs. Norwood's Avon perfume overrides any chances of my sniffing Luke. Plus I think it's killing some of my brain cells.

"Yes." She pulls up another screen. "This person would have to have special access—like administrative codes—to change these grades. Even a teacher's password wouldn't allow for editing a student's grades in all classes."

"What do you need from me?" Budge asks, primed to dig into high-security files.

"All of our tech crew are at a conference." Mrs. Norwood chews on her lip. "I guess I can let you into the grade program. Budge, I need you to tell me who was logged on between one and one thirty."

Luke and I take a seat on the floor. My back rests against the wall in the small office.

"Thanks for calling me." I twirl Budge's car keys in my hand. "I'm glad you didn't leave me out of the fun."

"I think we're about to solve another one." He holds up his hand, and I slap mine to it. "Bella, did I mention Taylor and I broke up?"

A giddy thrill spirals through my body. "When?"

"Christmas."

The thrill swan-dives. "As in December?"

"We're still friends."

"But we're friends too. So why didn't you tell me?"

"I just—"

"We got it!" Budge yells. "Take a look. Check out this list of people who were logged on," Budge says as we gather around him. He reads off a list of twenty names. All teachers. But two secretaries. And one student.

I stare at the name. "Joshua Day."

chapter thirty-two

On Friday morning the parking lot is crackling with spring break energy. Somehow I didn't wake up with it. Maybe it's because my dad dumped me for his Brazilian sugar, and I'm going to be spending every day working in a restaurant known for producing greasy tacos and deadly farts.

Walking up the steps to the school, Mark Rogers, my friend from the Truman police department, intercepts me.

"Hey, Bella."

Behind him two other men in uniform escort Joshua Day, his hands behind his back. "But I didn't do anything! I have no idea what you're talking about! I'm innocent!" Callie runs along behind him, crying as he's stuffed into a squad car.

"You and Luke Sullivan did a great job investigating this case, you know." Mark watches the car drive away. I can hardly hear him over the gathering crowd. "But next time, leave it to the professionals."

"Anything for a prom queen." I scan the parking lot for Luke.

"I'll keep you posted." Mark pats my shoulder and ambles away. A local news reporter follows him. As does a camera guy for *Pile Driver of Dreams*.

I spy Luke talking to Anna, Ruthie, and the gang. Lindy stands awkwardly between Newton and Matt. Luke catches my eye and smiles.

"The Sullivan-Kirkwood team do it again." Anna hugs me to her as I join them.

"And Budge," I add and wave him over.

"My prom date's a smartie." Ruthie high-fives my blushing stepbrother. "Like the smartest computer geek on the planet."

Budge shuffles his feet. "Not *the* smartest. That's Newt."

"So *my* prom date is the smartest computer geek on the planet." Lindy laughs, but sobers when she sees Newt's face. "I meant smartest person. You're totally not a geek."

Newton's left eye twitches.

"Ugh, thank goodness they apprehended him." Felicity joins our circle. "That Joshua was a menace to society. But now we can all go to prom safely."

"Hi, Felicity." Newt brushes the long hair out of his eyes. "You didn't show up for physics tutoring this morning."

Felicity flips her blonde hair and looks at Newton like he's a Payless clearance shoe. "I was busy. I have a lot of prom details to attend to now that it's at my house."

"You could've called," he says.

"Newt, unlike you, I don't have a lot of free time. I'm kind of dealing with some important things right now that someone like *you* wouldn't have a clue about. I'm *sorry* if you cut your stupid gaming schedule short to meet me."

Newt's face is redder than my patent leather bag.

"Do you have a date?"

Felicity laughs at Ruthie's question. "Well, of course I do. My new boyfriend goes to OSU. His daddy's the district attorney in Oklahoma City."

I look at Luke and cross my eyes. Seriously, I was *never* like Felicity. Right?

"I must run off, but don't forget today's the last day the voting results for prom queen will be up on the class Web site. Cast your votes!" Felicity walks away, waving over her shoulder. "Tah-tah!"

"That girl . . ." Anna seethes. "She's totally bought the crown with daddy's money. She's so far ahead, it won't matter how many votes I get between now and prom. Everything she does just makes her votes quadruple. Last week I gave out pencils. No change in the poll. Yesterday I passed out cookies to everyone—all for nothing."

Ruthie nods. "I've been campaigning too. Wednesday I told a girl I hated her shirt."

I frown. "What was that supposed to accomplish?"

"Nothing. But it made *me* feel better."

The first bell rings, and we gradually migrate inside to the lockers. The halls buzz with the news of Joshua's arrest.

Luke stops at my locker. "Are you okay?"

With the news that he's been single for months? "Yeah, why?"

He examines my face. "I don't know. You just seem down. I mean, we just cracked another major case and you weren't even that excited."

"I have to stay here for spring break. I guess I'm just bummed." And I'll be smelling like tacos all week.

"I'm sorry." He leans on the locker beside mine. "I know you were looking forward to seeing Hunter."

I nearly drop my book. "Hunter? No, I wanted to spend the

week with my dad. We had plans." I shut the door, absorbed in one single thought: I hadn't even *thought* about not seeing Hunter. Not only was I not sad about it, but when dad cancelled, Hunter never even crossed my mind.

"Bella?"

"Huh?" I realize he's been talking.

"I asked you if you wanted to get together over break and work on our *Pile Driver of Dreams* articles."

Get together? I stare into his blue eyes. What does that mean? "Um . . . uh . . ."

Luke pushes off with his foot. "It's okay if you don't want to work on break. Not everyone does." He smiles and pats my shoulder. Like Mark Rogers did. Yet different. "I'll talk to you later."

Shoot! Did I just mess up? What if he was asking me out? And all I could say was *uh*. But no. He said it was to work. And this is Luke. The guy keeps his nose to the grindstone. Whatever that means. Why would anyone ever want to put her nose to a grindstone?

After school Budge chauffeurs me, Robbie, and Newt. We drop his friend off first.

"Dude, what is *that*?" Budge puts the hearse in park and bails out. There in front of Newt's garage is a tricked out Honda Civic. "Check out those rims!" Budge runs his hand over the purple paint-job. "Where'd you get this?"

Robbie and I get out and inspect the car.

"Online." Newt smiles with the kind of satisfaction that only comes from having some wheels. "Can't drive it until I get it licensed."

Budge gets behind the wheel. "Where'd you get the Benjamins?"

"Tutoring." Newt points out something on the stereo.

"Tutoring paid for this?" I ask. "That's *gotta* be better than wearing a sombrero."

Budge snorts. "Or getting attacked by a pad machine."

"Nobody asked you."

"Or diving nose first into a wheelbarrow of horse poop."

"Newt, have you ever heard of Hannah Mon—"

"I'm shutting up now."

~~~~~~~~~~~

On our way home, we pass Jake running on the dirt road. A camera crew rides in front of him in a truck bed.

"Dad's really ramped up the training lately." Budge wheels the hearse into the yard.

"I heard him lifting weights at three thirty this morning." Which qualifies as crazy in my book.

Later in my room, I lie sprawled on my bed with Moxie on my stomach. I pick up my phone for the millionth time. No call from Mia. No text. I've forgiven her! She should be sobbing with gratitude.

God, I am so down. Luke's totally thrown me for a loop. Did he not want me to know he'd broken up with Taylor so I wouldn't pursue him? And Hunter's . . . complicated. And Dad totally dumped me. I should be on my way to New York right now. I should be getting ready for shopping, Broadway, and guilting my dad into buying me something. Instead, I'm stuck at home all week working for Manny "Tacos Make the World Go Round" Labowskie.

Knock. Knock.

"Bella?" My mom pokes her head in my room. "Will you come downstairs?"

I roll onto my back and sigh heavily. "Do I have to?"

"I think you want to."

As soon as I hit the kitchen, a guy with a camera jumps out. "Oh!" I yelp. "You little—" Just a few more weeks of this. I compose myself and find a smile. "You little booger." I wag my finger. "You scared me." I turn around and roll my eyes all the way outside.

Following the sound of my mom's voice, I walk into the back-yard. Where Jake sits in my Bug. My beautiful *running* green Bug! The engine purrs like a happy cat.

Clapping my hands in glee, I jump into the passenger side. "Oh, car! I've missed you! But who fixed it?"

"Jake did." Mom holds out my door. "Well, he paid to have it fixed."

I turn to my stepdad. "You did that? For me?"

He shrugs a meaty shoulder, making his neck almost disappear. "It was nothing."

Out of the corner of my eye, I see the camera guy move to get a better angle. "Oh. You did it because of the show." I swallow back a lump of sadness. "Well, whatever the reason, I'm grateful. Thanks." I kiss him on the cheek and go back inside.

"Hey."

I lift my head out of the fridge to see Jake. "Yeah?"

"I wanted to ask you—" He turns on the camera guy. "Could you give us a moment?"

The guy shakes his head. "No way. This is good stuff. Ought to get you a ton of votes."

"I said, *please* go away." Jake draws himself up to his full height. "Now."

The camera guy skitters out.

"Bella, I didn't get your car fixed to make myself look good for the show."

"You didn't?"

"No way."

"Then you got it fixed so I wouldn't have to endure anymore screamo in Budge's car, lose my mind, and possibly hurt innocent people?"

His mouth curls into a grin. "Exactly."

"Thanks. Um . . . I'll pay you back."

"I know you could, but this one's on the house. I would've gotten it fixed sooner, but your mom wouldn't let me."

"Isn't she sweet," I deadpan.

"Thanks for saving Robbie—with those bullies. I should've been more on top of it. I never should've believed him when he said no one was picking on him."

"It's okay. That's what big sisters are for, right?"

"I have something else for you." Jake reaches into his jeans pocket and pulls out an envelope. "I know you're upset that you're not going to be spending time with your dad and doing all your usual Broadway stops."

I put on a brave face. "Oh, who needs to see *Wicked* again? After thirty-seven times, I guess I've got the plot by now."

He hands me the envelope. "Open it."

I peel it open. "Two tickets for the Tulsa Performing Arts Center?" I read the print. "*Wicked*?"

"I was hoping for time number thirty-eight, you'd see it with me. Just you and me—no cameras, I promise."

Tears prick the back of my eyes.

"I know it's not New York. And we won't eat anywhere fancy. Probably just grab a burger at—*oomph!*"

I wrap my arms around this giant of a man. "Thank you! Thank you!"

I blink back the wetness. I do *not* cry. Ever.

Sniff.

Well.

Maybe for *Wicked.*

chapter thirty-three

The alarm on my phone chirps right into my dream just as I'm diving into a sea of Versace dresses. I struggle to stay there as lifeguard Zac Efron waves to me from the shore, but the incessant beeping won't go away. I'm forced to open my eyes.

Monday morning. How is it a school week is so much longer than a vacation week? Though the play in Tulsa with Jake was amazing, the rest of the break was just one burrito after another.

Moxie mewls and covers her eyes with a paw. At least somebody gets to sleep in.

Sitting up, I flick on my lamp and grab my Bible. I pull the ribbon bookmark and open to where I left off yesterday. When I finish, I get out my prayer journal and write a quick letter to God.

"Bella?" My mom taps on my door twenty minutes later. "You awake?"

I put the cap on my pen. "Barely."

"I'm taking Jake to the airport, so you need to make sure Robbie gets ready for school. Don't let him pick out his own socks."

I slide off the bed, grab my robe, and follow her downstairs. Everyone is gathered at the kitchen table.

Last week Jake received word that he had an appearance on *Regis and Kelly* in New York City. I wish I could go with him. I lived there all my life and never went to the show.

Jake cuts a banana for his youngest. "Now Robbie, if anyone gives you a second's worth of trouble, you go straight to the office and have them call me or Jillian. No more secrets, got it?"

Robbie nods his head, his eyes all for the Cheerios in his bowl.

"I'll see you guys in Vegas Thursday." Jake kisses his son on his head, then fist bumps Budge. "This house better still be standing when I get back." He pats my back then heads for the Tahoe with my mom.

At school everyone is just as lethargic as I am.

"Hey, Bella." Lindy intercepts me after English class. "Any word on Joshua Day?"

"Not yet. I'm hoping Luke's heard something," I say. "Is Matt still giving you the cold shoulder?"

She frowns. "He didn't call me once on spring break."

"Maybe his raging jealousy has rendered him mute."

She rolls her eyes. "Nice try."

I hustle down the hallway and into journalism. The class is empty except for one. Luke sits in the chair next to my workstation. A smile crawls up my cheeks, and I'm helpless to stop it. His expression says he's happy to see me, and my stomach wobbles like Nickelodeon slime.

"Mr. Holman wants us to cowrite an article about what led us to Joshua Day."

I set my stuff down. "Good morning to you too."

"If it's good enough, the *Tulsa World* is interested."

I raise my head. "Seriously?"

He nods his dark head. "For real."

I squeal and launch myself into his arms. "Omigosh! That's amazing!" His arms wrap around me just as I realize what I've done. I step back as if I've touched lightning. "Sorry." I clear my throat. "Um . . . you can let go of my hand now."

But he keeps it. "Do you realize what a big deal this could be?"

"You holding my hand?"

His grin is slow. "The paper." He brushes his thumb over my skin then releases me.

I struggle to remain neutral. Unaffected.

"We have to make sure we have every fact straight, so we need to put our heads together and map out the story." He pulls out my chair and motions for me to sit.

"So what's the latest on Joshua?"

"He's still in jail. His family couldn't afford to post bail."

"Callie must be going crazy."

Luke pushes up the sleeves of his Abercrombie henley. "Joshua still insists on his innocence."

"So do most ax murderers."

Since I have the day off from Manny's House of Indigestion, I call Mom after school to see if she wants to run to Tulsa to help me shop for some new heels. I need something to snazz up my old last-year's model of a dress. Though I could get a new dress with my money for bringing Ruthie's harasser to justice and my job advance, I think I'll just save it.

"I can't, Bel. I have to get to Dolly's. The family is coming for the baby. I need to be there with her."

"Today? Now?" But I didn't get to say good-bye to baby Mason. "Can I go?"

Mom's hesitation crackles over the phone. "I don't know . . ."

"Budge can watch Robbie. I'll pick you up at Sugar's." And I disconnect before she has time to argue.

I drive my key-lime-green Bug to the diner. When I swing open the heavy glass door, the overhead bell jingles. And mom stands there waiting just a foot away.

"Let's go." Her mouth is set, her face pinched.

She buckles into my passenger seat as I start the car. "What's with the bag?" I ask.

Mom rests a big plastic bag at her feet. "It's a care package—an entire chocolate pie from Sugar's, smothered chicken fried steak, some Kleenex, a new push-up bra, and a romance novel."

"A bra?"

She shrugs. "Your dad always said perky boobs make everyone feel better."

"He also said thin thighs could bring world peace."

She flings the bra into my backseat. "Good point."

Ten minutes later the Bug eases into the driveway. Mom grabs her bag and we slip into the front door without even knocking.

"Dolly?" Mom calls from the living room, where we tiptoe around suitcases and boxes of Mason's things.

She steps out of the kitchen, Mason in her arms, her eyes red and puffy. "He's been asleep for an hour, but I can't seem to put him down. It's like we're two magnets . . . stuck together." A tear slips down her cheek only to be chased by another.

The doorbell bongs a short melody. All three of us jump.

Dolly's eyes widen and zip to Mom. "He's here." She swallows. "I can't believe this day has come already."

"Are you sure you want to do this?" Mom grips Dolly's shoulders. "We can fight this."

She pats the baby's back. "This is Mason's father—his family." More tears free-fall. "I know I don't go to church and stuff. Haven't stepped foot in one since the girls' funeral. But I do pray. And this is what I'm supposed to do." Her voice breaks on a sob. "It's just so hard."

Mom glances toward the door. "Are you ready for me to let him in?"

Dolly wipes her nose and nods.

Mom pulls open the big oak door. Mason's father stands in the entryway, his parents and attorney behind him.

"Hi, I'm Jonathan." He holds out a hand and Mom shakes it. She puts on her best fake smile and ushers the family in.

The door swings open again, and Mickey Patrick walks in. "Hi. I was . . . um, in the neighborhood."

Dolly keeps her attention on the young father. "These are his things." She gestures to the mountain of boxes. "I did some shopping for him just yesterday. Spring is coming soon, and I wanted him to be ready. There's a really cute Easter outfit in the red suitcase." She sniffs. "You may not want it, of course."

Jonathan stares at his son. "He'll wear it. I'll send you pictures."

"That'd be nice." Dolly's breath shudders in her chest. "The blue bag has his favorite toys. He likes to have his froggy rattle as soon as he wakes up. But that's on the instructions I wrote out for you. Those are in the brown suitcase."

"Yes, ma'am," Jonathan says calmly, like he has all the time in the world. And I guess he does. He now has a lifetime to spend with the son he didn't even know he had. But that still leaves Dolly alone. With a gaping place in her heart.

"And I packed up his crib set and all the décor because he really likes looking at his cowboy things. He loves his horse mobile, so be sure and turn that on for him. Sometimes when he's—"

"Dolly—" Mickey steps from the behind the family and wraps a big arm around his ex-wife. "Let him go, babe."

Her face seizes and she breaks down, clutching the still-sleeping Mason. "I love you, sweet boy." She presses a kiss to each of his cheeks. "You're going to be so happy with your daddy." Her watery words are a struggle to decipher.

Mickey runs a knuckle across the baby's hand. "When he gets fussy, he enjoys a little AC/DC too."

I look at Mom, and she's just as teary eyed as me. This is majorly sad—like *Fox and the Hound* sad. Like *Bambi* sad.

Dolly pulls Mason from her shoulder and kisses him one last time. She whispers words for his ears only, then offers the baby to Jonathan. Slowly. Carefully. Hesitantly. Her arms stretch out to meet his.

Jonathan's face transforms as he holds his son. His parents move to either side of him. He looks to Dolly. "He's going to be my everything."

Though it sounds a little dramatic to me, it seems to be just what she needs to hear. Dolly attempts a smile and nods her weary head.

When the last box is packed away, Jonathan hugs Dolly. "Thank you. God brought Mason to you for a reason. Whatever that is, I'm grateful."

Jonathan holds his sleeping son, and together with his parents, disappears into the van, down the driveway, and out of Dolly's life.

The ride home is a quiet one. No radio. No talking. Just me and my mom silent with our own thoughts.

It occurs to me that something was missing out at Dolly's. "Where was the camera crew? Do they have the day off?"

"I asked them to stay away. This was private." Mom parks the Tahoe in the front of our house. "And it was nice while it lasted." She gestures to two men in the yard, one of them wielding a large camera.

Ignoring the *Pile Driver of Dreams* crew, I follow Mom onto the front porch and almost trip over a large UPS box.

She leans over it. "To Bella Kirkwood."

Fun! "For me?" I pick it up and carry it with me into the house. Too big to be diamonds. To small to be a new Mercedes.

I drop the box on the ugly orange couch in the living room. Peeling off tape with my nails, I lift the flaps. "It's my dress!" I reach in and grab the red strapless piece of art. "It's the one I wanted from Bergdorf's. Is this from Dad?" I didn't even look at the return address.

Mom picks up a small white card from the floor. She reads it, then passes it to me. "Not your dad."

Bella,

Can't wait to see you at prom. I hope this dress is just one of many things that will make the night perfect.

Counting the days until I see you again,
Hunter

I run upstairs, clutching my fabulous new dress. Shutting my bedroom door, I rip off my clothes and ease the dress over my head. I stare into my full-length mirror and peel up the zipper.

It's perfect.

I spin around the room a few times before breaking into a waltz with an invisible partner. Breathless from turning, I collapse onto my bed and call Hunter.

He picks up on the fourth ring. "Hello?"

"Simply amazing."

He laughs. "But enough about me. Tell me how you feel about the dress."

I run my hand over the smooth material. "Oh, Hunter. Thank you. I don't know what to say."

"Don't say anything. I'm just glad to make you happy."

"Happy? I'm delirious! I love the dress. And I love that you did this for me. But Hunter . . . it's so expensive."

"Don't even think about that. Just enjoy it."

I look at the skirt fanning around me. "I will. I don't ever want to take it off." Something beeps in the background. I hear voices in loud conversation. "Where are you?"

"Um . . . at the hospital."

"What?" Here I am gushing about a dress and he's in the hospital. "Are you okay? What's wrong?"

"It's nothing. I came in this morning, and I'll be out in a few hours."

"Please tell me what's going on."

"Bella, forget about it." His voice is weak, but stern. "Just a little flare-up with my stomach. You know the routine—more tests."

"Hunter, I realize this isn't the time. But this weekend we are sitting down, and you are telling me every detail of your health situation. I want to know everything."

He draws a deep breath. "There're are a few other things I want to talk to you about when I see you."

I think of Luke's hand on mine this morning. Then I think of Hunter hugging me the last time we saw each other. Our long talks. This fabulous dress. If Hunter wants to discuss us getting back together . . . I believe I know what my answer will be.

"Hunter, I have something to tell you too."

chapter thirty-four

I know, Lindy. I'm really sorry I can't be there to decorate today and tomorrow. I'm sure you will have plenty of help. I think it's nice that Felicity got the helium for the balloons." I watch the final passengers board the early morning flight to Las Vegas. "No, I don't think she wants everyone to think you're an incompetent, do-nothing class president who doesn't know a streamer from a shrimp roll. Look, I have to go. I'll see you Saturday night."

After a quick call to Hunter to check on his progress, I power off my phone and stick it in my bag.

"The teenage years are difficult and trying ones," Robbie says from across the aisle.

Mom licks her finger and flips a magazine page. "Tell me about it."

In a few minutes the plane taxis down the runway. Then with a lurch that never fails to make my stomach drop, we become one with the clouds, birds, and smog.

Three Sprites, two *Teen Vogues*, and one iPod movie later, we touch down in Vegas. I look over at the boys, and they're head-to-head asleep—Budge with his mouth wide open.

"This is going to be so exciting." Mom lifts Robbie's suitcase from the conveyor at baggage claim.

"Hey, it's Dad!" Robbie scampers away from us and runs straight into Jake's waiting arms. Jake sweeps him high in the air.

"You guys ready to go to the hotel?" With Robbie on his shoulders, Jake wraps an arm around Mom. "It's something else."

Yeah, the WWT hotel. Of all the cool places to stay in Vegas, we have to stay at the one dedicated to wrestling. Why not the ritzy Bellagio? Or the cool one that looks like Paris?

Outside a stretch limo waits for us. Robbie and Budge *ooh* and *ahh*. Even though I've ridden in one many times, I can't help but run my hands over the buttery leather seats.

We all find a window to press our nose to as we drive through town. This Las Vegas place is unreal. It's like we're on a different planet.

The limo glides to a stop at the hotel. We climb out and take in the sight before us.

"It's in the shape of a big wrestling ring." Robbie's head is cranked all the way back to get the full view.

Jake escorts us to the front desk where we're greeted by a staff of men and women in tight Lycra shorts and tank tops.

"Welcome to the WWT hotel," a pert blonde says. "After you get settled in your suite, we hope you'll explore the Spit and Spandex Museum, the Rope Burn Buffet, as well as the Chop Drop Casino. And we also have a virtual gaming room where you can experience a computer generated wrestling match and know the thrill of having a karate chop to the larynx or your arms broken in two."

The guy beside her smiles. "And Clay Aiken will be performing in the Head-Butt Lounge tonight."

None of us move. We all just stare.

"Okay, guys!" Jake hustles us away. "Let's go see your rooms."

We ride the glass elevator to the fifteenth floor. Robbie holds his hands over his head and makes whooshing noises like he's flying. Budge listens to his iPod and openly gawks at all the hot ladies in skimpy uniforms below.

"Here you are." Jake opens our door.

We walk past the bathroom into a living room. On either side of us are two bedrooms. Per *Pile Driver of Dreams* rules, Jake and Mickey each have their own rooms on a private floor, so I pick out a bedroom for me and Mom.

Peeking into the room, my jaw drops at the king-sized bed in the shape of a wrestling ring. Microphones hang over the bed in some sort of freakish attempt to be a chandelier. I think this might be tackier than my bedroom at Dad's.

I check the bathroom. Behind the door hang two velvety robes like a wrestler would wear after a match. The sink is a giant wrestling boot. I reach into my purse and click away with my phone. No one will *ever* believe this place without photographic proof.

When I rejoin the family in the living room, Mickey Patrick sits on the couch, his arm playfully crooked around Robbie's neck. Is it weird that headlocks are an acceptable form of greeting in my family? Dogs sniff each other's butts. Most people handshake. But us? We grab you in ways that make you think your neck is going to snap off.

"Are you nervous?" Mom sits on the opposite couch next to Jake, her hand resting on his knee.

He blows out a long breath. "It's big stuff tonight. For the next two days, we're paired with professional wrestlers from WWT and had just today to plot out a storyline and choreograph the wrestling matches. So this is the big leagues, you know? Tonight's about pleasing the viewing audience for the votes, but tomorrow is about pleasing the judges from WWT."

Jake kisses Mom's cheek. "I hate to duck out so soon, but I have to get back. Lots of work to be done yet."

"I need to go too." Mickey stands up, his gaze averted. "I want to call and check on Dolly."

After dinner we have time to walk the strip before returning to the hotel. Al Gore would *seriously* not be pleased with this town's electricity bill. As night falls, we walk back through the hotel and the clanging casino to the WWT arena.

God, please let Jake win. And keep him safe. It would be really cool if he came through this without anything broken. Like his spine.

An usher guides Mom, Budge, Robbie, and me to our seats near the floor. A camera across the room is trained on us, but I don't care. I'll be through with cameras by next week after the wrap-up show airs. Through with America occasionally seeing my face on TV and in the tabloids. Through living *la vida* Lohan.

Some time later the *Pile Driver of Dreams* host walks to the center of the ring. He wears a tuxedo, and the crowd roars when he's handed a microphone.

"Ladies and gentlemen! Welcome to our two-part finale of *Pile Driver of Dreams*. As you know, our contestants are working with the familiar faces of WWT. Tonight you'll see them in action with the wrestling heroes. After the show, we'll post the numbers, and that's when you call or text your vote."

I don't have unlimited texting, but I think Mom will understand five hundred or so over my limit.

"And tomorrow night the two remaining contestants will go head-to-head for the judges. The scores will be averaged, and we will announce our winner of the WWT contract. Are you ready, America?" The yells and applause of thousands thunder in the arena. "Live from Las Vegas! This . . . is . . . *Pile Driver of Dreams*! Our first contestant will be Captain Iron Jack!"

A door on the center stage opens. Smoke billows out as Jake saunters toward the ring. He poses and works the crowd. As his professional opponent enters the same way, Jake takes the moment to slip through the ropes and step into the ring. Before thousands in the arena and millions at home, he drops to one knee. And bows his head. Oh, my gosh. He's praying. On national television.

I think I'm kinda proud. A good portion of the crowd shouts their approval. I just hope he doesn't split his pants while he's down there. Wouldn't be anything holy about that sight.

I spend the next hour biting my nails. Just another reason to get a manicure before prom. Jake is seriously good, but will it seal a victory? I'm not exactly sure how you measure the quality of a choke hold or a leg squeeze. And his competition, Sanchez the Snake, is the one who dreams of being a professional wrestler just so he can send money to Mexico for his mother's liver transplant. How do you compete with that?

I tried to talk Budge into stepping in front of a bus for some sympathy, but he wouldn't go for it. I guess he doesn't want his dad to win as badly as I thought.

When the show is over, we all walk back to the hotel room with a security escort like our last name is Cyrus. Fans snap Jake's picture and beg him for autographs. It takes us forty-five minutes just to get through the lobby.

On Friday we go to another buffet for breakfast. With such easy access to pancakes, I eat them like I'll never see another.

We spend the rest of the day rotating between sightseeing, finding Robbie when he flies away, and doing interviews for the media in the pressroom, which is the weirdest thing ever.

"Bella," the reporter for *E! News* begins, "all of America has followed you through your public relationships."

"You mean my friendships." Would it be impolite to growl here?

"Has it been hard having your life documented on television while you sorted out your feelings for Luke Sullivan and your ex-boyfriend Hunter Penbrook?"

I feel my face flush with desert heat. What if Luke sees this? "As I have said all along, both of these guys are my friends. I would hate for anyone to make more out of it just for the sake of a story." *Wa-pow!* Take that!

My entire family fields questions like these for hours, as does the family of the remaining contestant. When I walk by one camera fixed on Robbie, I smile as he tells them how his cape helps him save the world on a daily basis.

As Mom finishes up with CBS, I gravitate toward some brownies and snacks on a table.

A woman in airbrushed jeans and a halter top grabs two. "This stuff is crazy, isn't it?"

"I hope you don't mean the brownies," I say. "Because I really need one right now."

She laughs with a Marlboro-laced huskiness. "I mean the months of cameras, the interviews, the gossip magazines."

"Are you Sanchez the Snake's wife?"

She cackles again. "I still can't get used to that name." She wipes her black-lined eyes. "I call him Louie Heine. Though I've certainly called him a snake plenty of times too." She sucks in a fuchsia pink lip. "I'm Frannie, and I am *not* Louie's wife. I'm his *ex*-wife."

"Oh." I crunch my teeth on some nuts. Why do people have to destroy a perfectly good brownie with nuts? "That's too bad about his mom. I hope she gets her liver." Just not with winnings from the show.

She snorts loud enough to turn a few heads. "Right. His dying mom. In Mexico."

Okay, well, her bitterness is putting a downer on my snack time. "I'll see you at the show, Frannie." I stuff some chocolate chip cookies in my purse and walk away. Somewhere there's a buffet calling my name.

Later in the hotel room, after I'm glossed, CHI'd, and sprayed, I join the rest of the superprimped family in the sitting area. We all look ready for our close-up.

Mom has us say a quick prayer for Jake, then we're out the door, walking down the hall on carpet so busy it makes my eyes hurt.

Once again we are escorted to our seats in the WWT arena. Chills break out on my arms as music swells and the host begins his intro.

"Hello, America! We're coming to you from Las Vegas at the World Wrestling Television Hotel, and we are down to the final night. This evening our contestants, Captain Iron Jack and Sanchez the Snake, will have two matches—against each other. We will combine your voting results from last night with the judge's scores at the end of this hour. The winner will walk away from here as the new professional wrestler on the WWT team. Live from Las Vegas . . . it's *Pile Driver of Dreams!*"

The crowd goes wild. Robbie and Budge hold up signs for Jake. I scan the crowd for more just like them.

Giant screens play highlights of the last few months, giving the overview of Jake and Snake's lives.

"Captain Iron Jack gets up before dawn to train, then reports to work at a local factory to help support his wife and three kids. Jillian Finley and Bella Kirkwood, once Manhattan princesses, now live the Wal-Mart life on Jake's income . . ."

Eek. No need to make us sound like we're one paycheck away from living out of the Tahoe.

"Sanchez the Snake works three jobs . . . to pay for his five children . . ."

The person behind me kicks my seat, and automatically I turn around. It's Frannie. Her arms are crossed, her eyes narrow slits. "Pays for his five kids." She does her snorting thing again. "And I'm Reese stinkin' Witherspoon."

I return my attention back to the screen.

"Sanchez the Snake also supports his mother, who will die soon without the money for an organ transplant." They show pictures of Snake's kids and a pitiful shot of his shriveled up mom. The entire arena *awwwwws.*

"*Aw,* my tush!"

This lady is worse than high schoolers in a movie theater. "Frannie"—my voice snaps a little too harshly—"can you keep it down?" I dig into my purse. "I have some cookies if you want them."

"Sorry, kid." She smacks on a big wad of gum. "This whole

thing is about over, and I'm officially at my breaking point." She points toward the screen. "They're making him out to be some stinkin' saint. That man's never paid a dime of child support to my five kids." She blinks rapidly as if holding back tears. "And little Tommy needs..."

I hand her a Kleenex. "Shoes?"

She sniffs. "A Wii."

"But if your ex-husband hasn't paid you in all these years, why are you here?"

"Because I want that money. He owes me." She blows her nose. "But now... my tummy hurts, you know?"

"From all the brownies?"

"No," she whines. "From keeping his secrets."

The heavens open and angels sing above me. "What are you talking about?"

"And tonight he tells me he knows he has it in the bag—and won't be giving his kids their share."

I'm so in her space, I've all but leapt over the seat. "Frannie, what secrets?"

Her dark brown eyes lock onto mine. "Sanchez the *Snake* does *not* have a mother in Mexico. She lives in Scottsdale, Arizona, in a condo on the ninth green."

"But the little old lady? The video footage?"

She waves a hand. "I did some acting in my skinny days—small parts in sci-fi movies. We don't even know that lady. I spent *weeks* Googling to find someone in Mexico who needed an organ or something. I found one other lady, but she was Chinese and spoke clear English."

"So Louie, er, Sanchez the Snake just went and filmed this woman in the hospital?"

"That lady don't speak no English. Apparently neither do any of the reality show crew because nobody's called Louie's bluff." Frannie digs in her purse and pulls out some Maalox. She opens the bottle and chugs it like water. "I ain't proud of this. And I haven't slept in, like, six months since he hatched this plan." She grabs her cheeks and pulls. "And I'm getting wrinkles from the stress."

I glance at my mom and my stepbrothers. The first match has started, and they are so in tune with that, they haven't heard a word of this.

My heart pounds in my chest. "Frannie, wouldn't you feel better if you came clean?"

"I know, right?" She tightens the lid on her Maalox. "I tried to talk to the producer this afternoon, but he told me that Louie had warned him about his 'bitter, delusional ex-wife.' I'm not bitter! I'm furious! And I'm the one who showed Louie all those wrestling moves. Who do you think he's been training with? And those pants he has on? Mine!"

Ew.

I move to the empty seat beside her. "If you want, I could go with you to try and convince them to listen to you again."

"It's no use. The producer kicked me out of his office. He had security tailing me all day."

I stare at the ring where Louie has Jake pinned against the ropes. See, the dirty secret to wrestling is that it's all planned and choreographed. So while the moves are real, your opponent knows exactly what's coming so he can minimize the hurt if possible. Jake is supposed to win the first match and Sanchez the Snake the second, to keep it all fair.

But nothing's fair now! How dare Sanchez the Snake pull the old dying-mother card?

"Security may be following you, but not me. I'll be back." With no time to lose, I don't even bother filling my mom in. I run down the steps and sprint toward the ring.

"Mickey! Mickey!" I stop right in front of Jake's manager. "You have to listen to me. Louie, er, Sanchez the Snake—he's a fraud. His story about his mother—"

With his eyes zoned on the ring, Mickey moves me aside. "Later, Bella."

"No, you have to hear this!"

He walks away, yelling toward the ring at an illegal move.

Augh! *Think, think, think.*

I spy the black-haired camera guy who has followed me around like my own personal paparazzi. "Hey! You!"

"Don't block my camera! Are you nuts?" he yells.

"Crazy camera guy, I have urgent news. Sanchez the Snake—he's no good. He's been playing you guys from the beginning. His mom—"

"Beat it."

I tug on his shirt. "Look, if you don't listen to me—"

"You'll what?" His look is withering. "Shoot me with some more refried beans?"

Sheesh, a girl starts one teensy-weensy food fight. "Dude, the contract the wrestlers signed—that we all signed. It said something about being disqualified for misrepresenting the facts."

"Look, I don't have time for your chitty-chat, but I will tell you that it's too late. We can't do anything about it now. The votes have been tabulated, the judges are set to make a decision after the second match. This is a live show, and we have twenty-five minutes left. It's over."

But this is Jake's dream. He can't lose out to some lying snaky scumbag.

I glance up at Frannie and shake my head. But I'm not going to give up.

Everyone stands and claps as the first match is over. The referee holds up Jake's hand as the winner. After a small break, they begin the second round. I'm losing time here. Where is the producer? I finally spot him behind another camera crew, but he's surrounded by security.

God, what do I do? I need help!

WWWD. What would a wrestler do?

I watch Frannie walk down the steps and stop at the bottom rail. "What do you need me to do?"

I think for a second. "Provide a distraction."

She nods. "Done."

In four-inch heels, Frannie goes running in front of security, screaming wild insults against her ex-husband. Her arms are waving like windmills. I take the opportunity and shoot straight for the ring. I make a flying leap toward the mat, heaving my legs over and rolling until I'm on.

Just as Jake falls right next to me.

"Bella?" His eyes widen like he can't believe what he sees.

"Hey." I smile. "I just thought I'd drop by."

As Jake holds out an arm to shield me, he yanks me up. The ref breaks through, yelling at the top of his lungs.

"What the heck are you doing?" he screams. "Are you insane?"

I feel five thousand faces turn to me. The arena is eerily quiet. Security has dropped Frannie like a dirty diaper and is headed straight toward me.

"Uh . . ." A hundred words pummel in my brain, but none of them will make sentences. Mom stands with Mickey, her face white. I clear my parched throat. "This man is a phony." I point my shaking finger at Sanchez the Snake. "He—he. Mother. Golf. Not. Mexico." Oh, crap! "No, I mean, his liver needs child support!" *Oh, Lord, something has a hold of my tongue and won't let go!*

Jake pulls me to the side and holds up a rope. "You need to leave." A vein throbs at his temple as *boos* come from every direction. I barely dodge a Coke bottle.

Security rushes the ring and climbs up.

"Come with me, ma'am," one says as he grabs my arm.

"Don't hurt her." Jake removes his hand. "She'll go with you."

"No!" I jump back. "I won't! Sanchez the Snake has been lying to you all!" My voice grows in volume and strength. And if I'm not mistaken, I think what I said actually sounded like English. "He pretended to have a dying mother to get the votes. But his mom is alive and well. And he has five kids and has never paid a dime of child support to Frannie." I flail an arm toward his ex-wife below. "She needed the help, so that's why she went along with it. But she couldn't do it anymore and nobody would listen to her." Two beefy guys in black bump Jake out of the way and wrap their hands around my arms like shackles. "Listen to me! There is some lady in Mexico who needs a liver, but Sanchez found her just so he could film—"

The rest of my sentence is drowned out. My eyes are filled with the sight of Sanchez the Snake leaping off the ropes, his body soaring like an eagle. I'm powerless to move as his shadow covers me.

Somewhere I hear Jake's roar. A security guy shrieks like a girl.

And I go down.

Pain and shock register in my back, my head, my face.

Sanchez hits me like a missile, and I'm on the mat, collapsing under his massive weight. My arms. My legs. My head. Pain.

There's a stinky, sweaty man on me.

My eyes roll back in my head. I shudder for breath.

I give into the pushing darkness in my head.

And everything goes black.

chapter thirty-five

I put down the *USA Today* as Mom packs up my things. "The WWT owner was able to find the doctor and get you an early release." She feels my head and winces at the bruises. "I called Hunter and updated him. He'll meet you at prom. But honey, are you sure you're okay? I would feel better if you stayed here today. Maybe even another evening."

The hospital nurse takes away my lunch tray as I down some Tylenol. "No. One night in this place is enough. Plus this gown is scandalous!" I mean, every time I go to the bathroom, everybody sees my business.

Mom pulls a brush through my wild hair. "I don't know *how* you didn't break something. It's a miracle."

Budge tears his attention from the TV. "A miracle *and* Frannie Heine. That was awesome when she did a swan dive for Sanchez right as he was about to land. If he had hit you dead center, we'd be calling your dad for plastic surgery right now."

"That was a brave thing you did, Bella, but stupid. You should've told me what was going on," Mom says.

I run my fingers over my split lip. "I just didn't want Jake to lose—not like that."

Robbie runs around my bed, his cape flapping. "And thanks to you, he won!"

Mom smiles. "Life is going to be very different from now on."

"Great," I droll. "I need some more change in my life. Moving from Manhattan just wasn't enough."

"Bella, please think about—"

"No." I swing my feet over and put on my shoes. "I am *not* missing prom. And neither is Budge."

Jake enters the hospital room and holds the door shut, muffling the sound of cameras snapping outside. He looks at me and winces like my mom.

"Stop doing that! You guys are making me feel like I need to go to prom with a bag over my head."

Budge lifts his brows. "I suggested that months ago."

Jake sits on the edge of my bed. "Good news and bad news. The bad news is since you and Budge missed your flight this morning, I couldn't get you guys on another flight."

I drop my shoe. "Get to the good part."

"The WWT president has scheduled his private jet to fly you and Budge to the Tulsa airport."

"Oh, my gosh. That's awesome!"

He lays a hand on the part of my arm that isn't blue. "*But* the plane doesn't leave until three thirty this afternoon."

The panic I felt when a psychotic wrestler took me out is nothing compared to this. "But that's five thirty Oklahoma time. We'll be late for prom! I wanted the day to get my hair done. To get a pedicure. To at least have time to zip up my dress!"

Mom's eyes grow big. "Do we need to call the doctor?"

"No!" I squeal. I must get control or else they'll strap me to the bed and make me stay here. "I mean, I'm grateful for the ride. If we have time to get ready, then that would be nice. But if not, I guess we'll go as is."

"You could wear your hospital gown," Budge snarks. "Show your best side."

I lunge for my stepbrother. "I'm about to kick your best side—"

Standing at the base of the airplane, I carefully hug Mom.

"I can't believe I'm letting you go. Alone. After something the weight of a refrigerator landed on you." She runs her hand down the back of my head. "I'm going to get the worst-mother-of-the-year award."

I pull away before she drags me back to the car. "I'll be fine. Budge will keep an eye on me."

She rolls her blue eyes. "Actually, Dolly will. She'll be at the house waiting for you to help you get ready. Dolly will also be spending the night, so don't try anything funny like coming in past curfew."

"How about sneaking my date up the trellis to my room?"

Mom's lips form a firm line. "Very funny." She carefully kisses my cheek. "Be careful. And call if you need anything."

Jake tosses Budge the keys to the Tahoe, and we board the plane.

Feeling stressed and nervous over the time crunch, I check my seat belt three times, consulting my watch between each tug. The pilot said it would take us almost three hours to get back home. Then there's the hour-long drive to Truman. Time to change. I guess Budge and I will have to settle for being fashionably late.

My stepbrother reclines his seat. "Ruthie is going to kill me for not showing up on time."

"Does she know you're picking her up in the hearse?"

He adjusts the headrest and closes his eyes. "She told me she was a modern woman and didn't need a man picking her up."

I laugh at the picture in my head. "So she's wearing a dress and riding her motorcycle?"

"You got it."

Hope she has bloomers.

I spend the next two hours watching TV shows on my iPod. Needing to stretch, I get up and grab a Sprite from the refrigerator at the wet bar.

"So is Newt picking up Lindy in his pimped-out Civic?" I hand Budge a Coke.

"Nah," he says. "He's driving his mom's clunker. She won't let him drive his until he pays to get her Chevy fixed."

"Can't be any worse than your death wagon."

He holds up a finger. "*Au contraire.* Lindy will have to climb in on the driver's side because Newt's passenger side is so bashed in."

"I'm sure Lindy will be totally impressed. She'll spend the rest of her life thanking me for this setup."

Budge pops the top on his can. "He told his mom he hit a deer, but there's no stinking way."

The faintest notion tingles in the corner of my mind. "What kind of car does she have? Two-door? Four?"

"Four. It's some sort of grandma sedan."

I lean on the armrest toward Budge. "When did he have the wreck?"

"I don't know. What difference does it make? Sometime before Christmas break, I guess."

My pulse begins to speed. "Like the same time Luke and I were run off the road?"

Budge opens his other eye. "Don't be ridiculous. Newt can barely see to drive at night. Plus he works in the evenings."

"Tutoring?"

"That's after school. Most nights he works as a janitor."

Warning bells ding in my already throbbing head. "Where, Budge?"

"The Truman National Bank."

My mouth falls open. "I think I'm going to puke." My step-brother holds out his barf bag. "Budge, what if Joshua Day had help in all those things he did? Or what if he didn't *do* any of them?" The facts race through my head, and I try to focus and line up every detail like Post-its in my mind. "Whether Joshua was involved or not—Newt was. He *had* to have been."

"That's insane. Newton Phillips is the wimpiest guy I know. He *couldn't* hurt anyone. He's perfectly capable of shutting down the world with his computer, but *not* harming people or threatening anyone." But as Budge says this, his expression shifts. Like the possibility is suddenly not so far-fetched.

"When I was working at Summer Fresh—"

"Is this before or after the maxi-pads attacked you?"

"—I talked to Newt's mom. She said she was glad I had arranged the prom date between him and Lindy because she was worried about what she called his 'fantasy world.'"

"She just meant the games he creates," Budge says.

I grab my stepbrother's arm. "And she said she was glad he was going with Lindy because she was a good girl, and that it was a step in the right direction for him—like he had been messing with some bad stuff. Or bad people." What does this mean? I can't think fast enough! And the gaps—there are too many holes in what I know. "Did Newt date anyone recently?" Did he date anyone—*ever*?

Budge rubs his hand over his stubbly face. "No . . . not really." His eyes close as he thinks. "Wait—he would talk about this girl he tutored. He would always say how hot she was and stuff—how he'd do anything for a girl like her to like him."

"Who was it?"

He sticks a finger in his ear. "Dude, yelling is not going to jog my memory. I don't know. He never told me her name."

"Newt tutored Felicity." The fact explodes in my mind. "It has to be her! He acted weird around her the other day—reminded her she'd skipped tutoring. I've never even seen him *talk* to a girl before that morning."

Budge's eyes grow wide. "All along Newt's been sabotaging the prom queen race."

"And setting up Joshua Day to take the fall." Get me off this plane! I'm seriously about to jump out of my skin. I need a phone. I have to call Lindy and tell her to stay away from Newt!

"Wait a minute." I hold up my watch. "We're descending. What's going on?" We've only been in the air a little over two hours. Did God provide a miracle and speed up time?

The copilot sticks his head out of the cockpit. "Hey, guys. I don't know if they told you, but we're making a pit stop in Denver. We have to drop a small shipment off."

"What?" I shriek. "You can't!"

He smiles. "I heard you guys were excited about some dance." He shakes his head. "Ah, to be young again."

"Um, can you maybe step on the gas a little? You know, break the speed barrier or something?" I force a laugh. "Wouldn't that be so much fun?"

The copilot just grins, then goes back to business.

"I'm on the verge of a screaming freak-out here." I tap my fingers on the armrests.

"Do you think Felicity was in on it?" Budge asks.

I consider the possibility. "I don't know. She was desperate to be prom queen, but her tires got slashed too. Would she do that to her own car? She was leading the race, especially with her dad funding, well, everything."

"If Newt's behind all this, there's no telling what's he's got planned. He's, like, freakishly brilliant. You should call Lindy."

My ears pop as we finally land.

After we roll to a stop, the copilot opens the exit door. "We should be heading back out in thirty."

Thirty whole minutes? "Do you want me to run the package?" I offer. "I'm awfully fast." At least when a psycho-maniac is taking my friend to prom.

The guy gives me another weird look, then exits the plane.

I rip out my cell and call Lindy.

No answer. Just as it goes to voice mail, the line goes silent. I check the bars on my phone. Only one? *Please, God. I need some holy cell reception!*

I try Luke's number.

"Hello?"

My breath releases in a whoosh. "Luke, I have to talk fast—"

"Bella? Hello?"

Are you *kidding* me here? "You have to stop Lindy from going to prom with—"

"Hel*looo*? Hello?" *Click.* Dead line.

I thrash back into my seat. "Try your phone, Budge."

He holds it up. "No reception here."

I pace the short length of the plane until an eternity passes. Finally both pilots are strapped in again, and we're in motion.

"Just an hour and a half," the pilot calls.

I glance at my watch. "We're not going to get to Truman until, like, nine thirty." Rummaging in my purse, I wrap my fingers around a Snickers. This moment calls for chocolate.

"Hey, I'm stressed too." Budge holds out his hand, and I grudgingly give him half. If I've learned nothing else this year, I've learned sacrifice.

He eyes the candy bar. "You gave me the smaller part."

What? I didn't say I was a saint.

My heart stays lodged in my throat during the entire flight. At one point I reach for my phone again, intent on sending Lindy a text.

"You don't want to do a thing like that." The pilot walks toward the wet bar and grabs some pretzels.

"No. I was just . . . um . . . er . . ." Oh, I give up. I toss the phone into my purse.

"Maybe you should do some of that prayer stuff or something." Budge waves a hand around like he's trying to conjure some Jesus.

"You could do it, too, you know."

He turns to look out the window. "I have."

I pray and pray as the plane seems to move at turtle speed. *Please keep Lindy safe. Please let me get in touch with her. Please let Newton split his pants and have to go home.*

For the rest of the way, I divide my time between pleading, praying, and watching the seconds tick. I'm about ready to promise the Lord I'll never say a snarky thing to Budge again when the pilot announces we're landing. Eight fifteen local time. Everyone is at prom by now. What if Newton's hurt Lindy? Or Felicity? Or gone postal on every girl there?

I don't realize I'm holding my breath until the wheels make contact with the runway. When we stop, the pilot lifts a lever and the door whooshes open.

"Thank you. Great flight. You're the best." I heave my suitcase, letting it *thunk* down every step as I pull it behind. "Let's go, Budge!"

I sprint like someone's holding a blowtorch to my butt. My body aches from last night's beating, but I push through it. Budge struggles to keep up. My lungs are burning when we reach the Tahoe. Budge fumbles for the keys.

"Open the car!"

"I'm trying!" he yells. "I can't take this pressure!" His hands shake. His fingers become tangled with one another.

I run to him and latch onto his shoulders. "Pull yourself together, man!"

"I've got them!" Budge holds up the keys like he's found the Holy Grail. "I've got them!"

As he screeches out of the parking lot, I furiously dial Lindy. Straight to voice mail! I try Luke. Same thing! I leave desperate messages.

They're all doing the cha-cha slide, *meanwhile* there's a lunatic among them!

I try one last number.

"You have reached Hunter Penbrook. I can't come to the phone right now. Please leave . . ."

"Hunter, it's me. Call me when you get this. You remember Lindy, right? She's possibly in danger. You have to find her and tell her to stay away from Newt Phillips. Call me!"

Budge drives like a maniac. I check my phone every five seconds. Why isn't Hunter checking his? Shouldn't he be waiting for my call anyway?

"Ruthie's going to kill me when she sees me dressed like this." Budge swats at some chip grease on his jeans.

And my totally amazing dress from Hunter. Wasted. I'm going to my prom wearing my cutoff Abercrombie sweats and hoodie! Can't *wait* to see those pictures.

I hit redial a million times as the miles fly by. I want to shout when I see the Truman city limits sign.

The tires squall as Budge navigates the turns. Felicity's driveway is longer than any street in town. Fancy landscaping lines either side of the path.

Finally I see lights. Cars. Tons of them. Limos. "Park at the front," I say, even though it will block people in.

My head pounding and my side hollow with a dull pain, we run the rest of the way. Through a gate. Straight to the large canopy.

Budge breathes like a rhino. "I'll get Newt."

"And I'll find Lindy."

We throw open the canvas doors and step inside, splitting into two directions. I blink to adjust my eyes to the dim lights. I walk toward the pulsing music.

A hand covers my eyes.

Arms grab my middle.

And I scream.

chapter thirty-six

B ella, it's me!"

My eyes struggle to focus. "Hunter?" I lower my fists and bend at the waist, my bruised ribs begging for rest. As I breathe in and out in my jogging togs, he stands there regal and flawless in his tux.

"Always a trendsetter, aren't you? I think I'm overdressed." He smiles.

"I'll explain later."

"Hey, how are you?" He steps closer, his fingers reaching toward my face. "Let me see what that idiot wrestler did."

I shoo his hand away. "I'm fine." Okay, I'm not. I'm tired, I'm sore, and I really need an ice cream fix. "Hunter, I have to take care of something, but I'll find you in a little bit. We need to talk."

He reaches for my hand. "We definitely need to talk. Bella, I—"

"Not now." I walk backward. "Eat some quiche! Have some punch! Do the Worm!" I put some speed into my steps, my eyes scanning for my friend. "Have you seen Lindy?" Empty, clueless faces stare back at me.

I move to the dance area and weave through the maze of class-mates. "Lindy! Lindy! Anyone seen Lindy Miller?"

This is bad. Very bad.

"Bella?"

I pivot at the deep voice. "Luke!"

His eyes flash fire as he reaches out, his hand sweeping across my cheek much like Hunter's. Yet so not like Hunter's touch. Goose bumps skitter across my skin.

"It looks worse than it is."

His fingers still on my jawbone. "I'd like to tear that man apart."

Oh, any other time I would totally appreciate his macho-protectiveness. But *not now!* "Luke, I need to find Lindy—or Newt Phillips. We were wrong about Joshua Day. Newt was the master-mind behind all of this. We've got to get Lindy away from him. Help me find her."

He doesn't even question me. "Let's go."

"No, we need to split up." I point to the other side. "I'll go that way. Call me when you find either one of them."

"Bella, when this is over, we need to talk."

"Yeah, yeah, get in line." I shoot through a swaying couple and continue my urgent search.

A few minutes later I stand at the back exit of the canopy. No Lindy. No Newt. And I would *kill* for some ibuprofen.

Three girls walk by in a cloud of perfume and giggles. "Don't worry about your lipstick. We'll fix it in the bathroom."

"Wait!" I grab one by her tiny dress strap. "Where are the bathrooms?"

She looks at me like I showed up to prom in sweats or some-thing. "Um . . . in the house. Just follow the Chinese lanterns to the back door."

I butt my way in front of them and zoom out the exit. The path takes me past the pool and some couples making out. I step into the house and into a kitchen the size of our yard.

"Lindy?" I yell her name. Moving down the hall, I find a bathroom and set my fist to the door.

"Just a minute!"

Was that her? "I need to talk to you!" I bang some more. "Hurry up."

The door wrenches open. Ruthie stands there in a pink frothy dress, accented with a black leather spiky belt and dog collar. Combat boots rise to meet her calf-length hem. I sag against the wall and consider giving into hysterics.

"What?" she asks. "Is it my hair? It's too pink tonight, isn't it?" She pats her size XXL updo that's somewhere in the color range of Pepto and Hello Kitty.

With as few words as possible, I fill her in. "Go find Lindy. I'm going to search the house." Ruthie doesn't budge an inch.

I roll my eyes and give her a shove. "Yes, your hair looks fabulous."

With a nod, she disappears.

The kitchen begins to fill with people mingling. Unnoticed, I pass through and follow the gleaming wood floor into a massive living room. Hideous pieces of art hang on every wall. A life-size portrait of Felicity holding a poodle looms above the fireplace.

"Lindy?" I call as I search the first floor. "Lindy Miller!" God, *please-oh-please let me find her.*

Peeking over my shoulder, I make sure I'm alone. Then I open every door I find. Nothing. No one. I climb up the grand staircase, my ribs throbbing with every step.

On rubbery legs, I reach the top and open a door and find a sparsely decorated guest bedroom. Double-checking the closets, I move on to a bathroom that could swallow our living room. The knob on the next room sticks, and gritting with pain, I push 'til it gives.

I'm emptied into a large office. I step inside and—

The door slams behind me. I jump and spin.

"N–Newton." Not good. Not good at all.

His back is pressed to the door, and he looks at me with a wild gleam in his eyes. I've seen that look—on Budge when he's gunning down the enemy on Halo.

"Hey . . . um, have you seen Lindy?" My voice is as high as a ten-year-old boy's. "Nice tie, by the way. Like the tux. And your shoes sure are shiny. How do they do that, huh? I see you didn't wear white socks. That's always a good choice." Oh, my gosh. Am I still talking?

Newt twists the lock on the door, his eyes never leaving mine. "So you figured it out."

"Yes, I was dying to know whether Felicity's dad was a Mac man or preferred the PC." I tap his PC. "I'm more of an Apple loyalist myself." My fake laugh sounds more like a drunken sheep. "Now that I found out, I'll just be going."

"I don't think so."

I drop my act. "Just open the door. Don't be an idiot."

He laughs. "I have an IQ of 170. It's a waste of time to question my intelligence."

Crazy *and* cocky. Perfect. "Why, Newt?"

He looks into the space above my shoulder. "I would've done anything for her."

"Felicity?"

He nods. "When she presented the idea, it was like a gift had just fallen into my lap. Like destiny."

"*She* was with you in the car when you cashed the check at the bank. And you made it appear as if Anna had signed it."

"I'm a good forger. I can copy anyone's signature."

"And the teller—Victoria Smith? Obviously she was in on it."

His grin is predatory. "Let's just say I had some dirt on her she didn't want anyone to know about. And we dated for a bit—before Felicity."

I scan the room for something to use as a weapon. "Why frame Joshua Day? What did he ever do to you?"

"Why, Bella. *You* provided that little detail. Victoria called me from McDonald's that day you met. She mentioned you were hinting about Joshua. Everything had all fallen into place so nicely. This story has simply written itself."

I can't hide my smirk. "Why don't you just ask Felicity out? Why do you care if she gets prom queen? Is it really worth hurting other people?"

"You know nothing about me!" he roars. "I've been in this school since kindergarten and no one ever acts like I even exist! I *love* Felicity. She promised me we'd be together for prom when I had taken care of everything. And I warned you to stay out of this. You're all alike—always in my way."

Hmm. So psycho boy has a small dislike for the female population. "So you did all this—snuck into my house, doctored the photos, transferred the money, got Callie's phone, and—"

"And had Felicity call the caterer, yes. She cared about me." His mouth twists. "As long as she needed me. And by the way"—he shakes a finger at me—"you really should look at getting a new lock for that back door."

I wait a few seconds. Wait for his wave of crazy to ebb. "Then why go to prom with Lindy?"

"To make Felicity jealous."

Somehow I manage to keep a straight face. "And then Felicity broke her promise."

"Like I was a nobody," he snarls. "She never cared about me. And after *all* I did for her. But revenge"—his eyes lock onto mine—"is definitely worth the price of admission."

I force my voice to remain low and calm. "Where is Lindy?"

"When I saw you'd arrived, I sent her on an errand outside. I've been waiting for you, Bella. Because nobody gets the best of me. But now we're through talking." With strength I didn't know he possessed, Newt shoves me and I hit the wood floor, my head barely missing the desk. I am *so* getting a massage after this weekend is over.

He looms over me, his hands fisted. Something shifts in my brain, and my pulse calms. *God, we can do this.*

Last year I survived an entire football team. I've survived an airborne wrestler with nothing to lose. And now *this*? I am *not* letting this dork get the best of me. I scramble to stand.

"Do you see my face, Newt?" Now I'm the one advancing. "I had a little tangle with a man who weighs more than both of us put together. And I *won*." Sort of.

I close the distance and stick my finger in his chest. "Now you're going to let me out of this room or I'm going to tear you apart, limb by stinkin' limb."

His chuckle drips of demented evil. "You know what's cool about being a geek, Bella?"

I tense my muscles, ready to spring. "You always have your Friday nights free?"

"No one really knows anything about you." His leg shoots out in a kick that hits me straight in the ribs. I feel something give and double over, bile rising in my throat. "Like I'm a black belt in *tae kwon do*." He laughs. "I like comic books." He lands a chop to the top of my shoulder, and I sink to my knees. "I've recently learned a lot about explosives." The base of his hand smashes into my temple. "And I'm really great with a computer."

I don't even have time to move as he swings the keyboard like a bat.

Not again.

The floor rises to greet my face.

My eyes cross.

And I'm out.

chapter thirty-seven

I don't feel so well. My mouth tastes like rusted yuck.

Did someone drive a bulldozer into my face? Where am I?

Omigosh.

Lindy! Felicity!

How long have I been lying here?

Ohhhh, Newton Phillips.

I gingerly move one arm. Ow!

Wait—why can't I see? I run my hand over my swollen eyes. I'm blind! *Help me, Jesus, I'm blind!*

The door creaks, and I tense. A shock of pain ricochets through my limbs.

"Bella?"

My mouth hurts to move. "Luke?" I choke back the tears. "I—I can't see. That karate-chopping nerd must've hit my optical nerves and—"

He flips on the light and rushes to me.

"It's a miracle!" I reach for him. "I can see!"

Luke digs into his pocket and calls 9-1-1.

"Why are there two of you? Aw, you're both so cute." I close my eyes again. My head is so fuzzy.

His hands roam over me as he talks.

"Ow ... Ow ... Ow ..."

He snaps his phone shut. "We have to get you to the hospital." Grabbing a Kleenex from the desk, he presses it to my bleeding forehead.

"Story of my life." I clutch his lapel. "Luke, is it too late? How long have I been in here?"

"You've been out of my sight for fifteen minutes."

"Maybe you shouldn't let me out of your sight anymore."

"I don't intend to." He frowns at my wounded face.

Some of the fog dissipates. "Newt—he's going to hurt Felicity. I don't know what his plans are, but they involve explosives. We have to get everyone out of the tent."

"They were winding down the music to announce the prom king and queen when I left."

"Where's Lindy?"

"Budge has her."

I go limp with relief. "We have to go. The police might not get here in time."

Luke scoops me up slowly, as if he's afraid I'll break.

I bite my lip on a yell as I'm lifted into his arms. "When this is over I'm going to have a glass of punch. And a bottle of Tylenol."

His blue eyes sweep over me and rest on my face. "I'm so sorry this happened to you." He runs his hand across my battered cheek, then stalks out the door. Every step down awakens a new ache.

"Wait," I say when we reach the bottom. "I can walk."

"Are you sure?"

Tempting, but yes. Clutching my side, I follow him through the living room and into the empty kitchen. Everyone is outside for the big announcement.

Luke pushes through the crowd in the tent and clears a path. I struggle a few steps behind, as my woozy head jerks from one side to the other looking for Newt. The king and queen candidates form a line at the front of the tent.

The deejay stands on a small stage and pulls a piece of paper from his jacket. "And now, juniors and seniors of Truman High, your prom king is Jackson Feldman . . ."

"We have to get Felicity off the stage!" I yell.

Luke nods and keeps moving toward the front.

"And no prom would be complete without a queen!" the deejay says. "The Tiger prom queen is . . ."

A fake electronic drumroll rattles the tent. The noise escalates as everyone starts to clap.

The deejay holds up the crown. "Felicity Weeks!"

"Bella!" I stop as Lindy grabs my sleeve. "What's going on?"

"We have to get Felicity out of here. Newt's going to hurt her. We need to evacuate the whole place."

Lindy stares toward the stage. "That's not the crown I bought."

The prom king lifts a giant, sparkling tiara over Felicity's head. She sheds big dramatic tears. *Sister, spend an hour in my shoes, and you'll have something to cry about.*

I catch sight of Luke's back. He's headed toward the stage. "Lindy, get out of here. Now."

Pushing past the pain, I rush up the steps to the contestants. Luke stands on the other end of the platform.

I grab the deejay's mic. "We need everyone to clear the tent. Leave immediately!"

Nobody moves. Idiots!

Felicity rips the mic from my hands. "Get off of here, you luna-tic! I've waited my whole life for this."

Her tiara bobbles on her head, and I catch sight of a tiny red flicker. A light. "A bomb!" I scream. "It's on her tiara!"

That does the trick. The floor turns into a stampede. People run in every direction, shooting out exits, diving under tables, and crawling under the plastic walls.

One person stands in the middle. He holds a small device.

"Luke, it's Newt!" I point to our villain.

Infused with adrenaline, I grab Felicity's crown, jump down, and run with it across the empty space. I glance back long enough to see Luke on the ground with Newt. They roll around in a scuffle of punches, kicks, and grunts.

Please God. Save us from the exploding cubic zirconias!

Police sirens wail in the distance. Time moves in slow motion.

"Get rid of that crown!" Luke yells. He punches Newt in the jaw then takes a blow himself.

I see my destination stretch out before me. I can't get there fast enough. Budge steps into my line of vision. "Leave!" I shout. "Go!"

He shakes his shaggy head. "I'm open. Pass it! I'll get it there!"

We both turn at Luke's victorious cry. "I have it!" He holds the detonator. "I've got it!"

Newt writhes on the ground, clutching his stomach. His shak-ing hand reaches into his pocket. I see the shine of metal.

"He has another one!" I cry.

Newt's bony finger presses into the detonator.

"Bella!" Budge calls, arms out.

Grunting like a tennis star, I heave the thing toward him, praying as it sails into the air.

On a yell, Luke charges my way, his body airborne and arcing toward me. I don't even have time to process the hurt as we go down. He turns to take the brunt of the fall, then rolls on top of me, his body shielding mine.

Budge plunges the tiara into the punch fountain. He ballet leaps away, his form a symphony of baggy pants and frizzed-out hair, and rolls under a table, pulling it on top of him.

Kablooom!

A spray of red liquid falls over us like rain. Shards of glass sprinkle everywhere, and I'm pulled tighter to Luke.

Luke rolls off of me and laughs. "We're okay." He pulls me up, picking a piece of glass from his tux. "Are you all right?"

I lick the punch on my hand and taste strawberry. "Yeah, but this totally needs some more sherbet."

He hugs me to him, still laughing. "I thought I was going to wet my pants."

I point to his red-stained trousers. "You sorta did."

Luke pulls away enough to plant a soft kiss on my forehead. "That seriously scared the heck out of me."

"You were amazing." With swollen eyes, I try to bat my lashes. "You're always like, saving me and stuff."

He quirks a brow. "It is getting old." He searches the faces around us. "We've got to get you to a doctor."

A crowd has gathered around us as the tent slowly fills back up. The police filter through, and Budge and Ruthie lead them to Newt, still curled like a snail on the ground.

"Oh, my!" Felicity fans herself with a napkin. "I could've died. You rescued me! I can't wait to tell my daddy about your heroics."

"I'd say you have a lot to tell *daddy*." I gesture to a cop. "Like how you and Newt robbed the class *and* the bank. And how you let Newt keep the money—if he'd sabotage the other queen candidates."

She gasps. "I don't know what you're talking about!" With manicured nails, she gestures to my face. "Clearly you've hit your head a few times."

"Oh, that is *it*!" With arms outstretched, I lunge for the girl.

Luke jumps between us, his mouth in a crooked grin. "I don't think so, Bel."

"No?"

"Nuh-uh," he drolls.

Ignoring my screaming limbs, I rest my hand on Luke's chest, but my glare is for Felicity. "But can't I rough her up just a bit? It would be a humanitarian deed. She needs to know how to defend herself—when she gets to prison."

Felicity blanches.

Luke laughs and wraps an arm around my waist and guides me toward the doors. "Let it go."

A woman in uniform grabs Felicity by the elbow, and I hear her sorry wail all the way outside.

"Omigosh, Bella!" Lindy crushes me in a hug, and my eyes cross. "Are you okay?"

"Easy." Luke pulls me back to him. "Bella's been knocked around a bit."

Matt Sparks stares in the direction of Newt in the patrol car. "I *knew* you shouldn't have gone out with him."

"It wasn't a date, Matt," Lindy protests. "But thanks for dragging me to safety. That was really . . . sweet."

Matt blushes and gives her an awkward side hug. "I just wanted you out of there."

I look at Luke and grin.

"Good catch, *brother*." I ruffle Budge's hair when he walks by. "You saved the night."

He rolls his eyes. "If I'd taken you home in bits and pieces, my dad would've totally killed me. So don't think it was about you."

"Isn't he the best?" Ruthie clutches his arm and sighs. "Oh! Your forehead is bleeding." She digs a tissue out of her cleavage and begins to daub. "My brave champion. If I had known it was going to be like this tonight, I would've brought my favorite knife."

The media covers the area and cameras flash like lightning. Even the familiar two goons from *Pile Driver of Dreams* are in the action.

My policeman friend Mark Rogers breaks into our group. He opens up a kit and commands me to sit on the ground. "Let me take a look at your face. The ambulance will be here shortly."

I let him swab and bandage some bleeding cuts, then beg him to leave. "I'm fine. Really. Go away."

"Only if you promise to have the medics take you in for observation."

Luke rests his hand on my shoulder. "She promises."

"Hey—where's Hunter?" In all the craziness, I totally forgot about him.

Anna Deason saunters by. "If it's the boy I saw you with on that TV show, I think he's over there with that girl."

Standing next to the pool, Hunter faces my direction. A girl has her hand going as she proceeds to gripe him out.

"Hunter!" I call.

The girl turns around, and for the umpteenth time, I'm dizzy. Mia.

I stomp over to them. "What are you doing here?"

"The reality show *paid* me to come out here." Mia snarls at Hunter.

Sure enough, the camera team has moved to a prime spot, their lenses focused right on us.

"What is she talking about, Hunter?"

He opens his mouth, only to snap it shut.

"Tell her," Mia barks.

Hunter's hands reach for me. I shrink away, warning sirens blaring in my ears. "Spill it."

"Bella, I care about you. Please believe that."

"But?"

He moves to touch me again but lets his hand fall. "The show has nothing to do with how I feel about you."

Mia jerks her hand toward the cameras. "Hunter broke up with me when *they* called him."

"What?" And I thought the hits were over. "You were just a prop for the show?"

"It's not like that." His voice is a plea. "Maybe at first, but not later. Not now."

The dark sky tilts, and I struggle to focus. I need to sit down. All these punches, kicks, and body slams are catching up with me. Oh, yeah, and the skanky lies of an ex-boyfriend.

"You don't understand, Bella." He runs a hand through his hair. "They went to my dad first, and everyone was pressuring me. My dad is on the verge of bankruptcy. He needed me."

My laugh is bitter. "Well, I hope you and your big fat check have a lovely flight back to New York."

"I'm sorry I hurt you. Please believe me."

"Believe you?" I laugh. "I can't even *look* at you right now."

Mia squints. "Your eye is pretty swollen."

I turn on her. "And I guess you were here to rub it in?"

She shakes her head. "No. The producer told me to throw a big fit, but I just wanted to warn you. I don't want him back either."

"And what about your disease?" I spit.

Mia snorts. "I'm sure."

"*That* was a lie too?"

Hunter reddens. "I do have a stomach condition. And it is debilitating."

"Irritable bowel syndrome," Mia snaps. "You know, like, when he gets stressed he has the runs."

"For a while they thought it was serious."

I close my eyes at the whine in Hunter's voice. And to think I thought he could've been dying!

"Bella, I'm so sorry. Please forgive me. But I have changed—that wasn't fake. I really did go to church." Hunter plants himself directly in front of me. "Tell me you weren't considering getting back together, and I'll go away without another word."

I look deep into his eyes and will the dizziness to abate. "Hunter, tonight I was going to tell you that I knew without a shadow of a doubt that I wanted nothing more from you than friendship." His face falls. "But you've ruined even that. I need reality—not some hyped-up TV version. Not someone *playing* my friend. Someone who's genuine when all the charm slips away. But I truly do hope you find Jesus one day. So I'll pray for you." I rub my temples and take my last look. "But this friendship is deader than a tiara in a punch bowl."

chapter thirty-eight

"Mom, quit staring at me. I'm not going to shoot lasers out my nose or anything else fabulous."

My mother takes a seat next to my hospital bed. "You have a concussion. The doctor did say to watch you."

"We're never leaving you guys alone again." Jake bounces Robbie to his other knee. "Last night was a close one."

I feel bad the big guy had to cut his Vegas trip short. They took the red-eye and got here this morning. Jake's missing out on lots of promos and interviews. Necessary things for the country's next big wrestling star.

"Yeah, well, you have to leave me alone," Budge says, patting the Band-Aid on his forehead. " 'Cause I'm meeting some friends at the movies tonight."

I lift a sore cheek and smile. "One of those people wouldn't happen to be Ruthie, would it?"

Budge suddenly finds his hands very interesting. "Yeah, her and some people from her church."

"Can we come in?" Dolly sticks her Aqua Net head in the room. Mickey follows her in.

Mom's face is a flashing question mark as she hugs her friend.

"We met in the hall," Dolly whispers. "No big deal." She rests a hip on my bed. "How are you, hon?"

"I'm alive, and none of my friends were blown up. What more could a girl ask for?"

All heads turn at the knock on the door.

I see the flowers first. Then Luke.

"Hey." He smiles and speaks to everyone in the room.

"Let's go get some lunch." Mom stands up and grabs her purse. "I could use something to eat."

"Bring me something back. They tried to feed me mashed peas a while ago. I need a burger." I *deserve* a burger.

Everyone files out, with Robbie trailing behind. He runs to my bed, crawls up, and plants a big one on my cheek. "You're my hero," he says and scampers out.

My eyes grow blurry, and I blink it away. Just fatigue, I'm sure.

Luke wears a dashing smile as he walks to my bedside and brushes the hair away from a bandage. He stares deeply into my eyes, and I wait for his sweet words.

"Kirkwood, you look awful."

Okay. That ain't it.

"Wow, Chief. Words like that just make my insides tingle."

He pulls a chair beside me. "So how are those broken ribs?"

"Bound tighter than a Victorian corset."

"I should've never let you out of my sight," he says.

Now these words I like. "Because you're crazy about me?"

"Because every time I do, you wind up in the hospital." He laughs. "Because the ER doctors know you by name."

"That's not true."

"They probably send you birthday cards."

"No, they don't." Just Christmas greetings.

"We're a pretty good team." Luke holds out his hand. I place mine in his palm.

"We saved the world." I smile into his eyes.

He reaches into his jacket pocket and pulls out an ice cream bar. "For my fellow crime-fighter. It's not from the Truman Dairy Barn, but it was the best I could do."

I unwrap it in one tear. "You're pretty good for me, I guess." I take a bite and sigh. "And face it, my coming on the newspaper staff was the best thing that ever happened to you."

He grabs my hand, drags the ice cream to his mouth, and takes a bite. "Since knowing you, I've been shot at, attacked, and nearly blown apart."

"Is this your way of asking me out?"

"Is it working?"

"I'll go out with you, Luke." I grab my ice cream back. "But just because you *obviously* need protecting."

He laughs. "You are pretty scrappy." His hand disappears into his coat again and pulls out two envelopes. "Recognize these?"

I take another bite. "No."

"Lindy apparently saved our Match-and-Catch results. She thought we might want to look at them." He hands mine over. "Time to see if you're my fated true love."

We both open the white envelopes.

I read the results and smile so big my bruised face hurts. "I'm afraid I must devote the rest of my life to Brian McPhearson. Maybe with my love, he will learn to blow his nose and wear his shoes on the right feet."

Luke nods. "And it looks like I'll be getting to know Tracey Sniveley and her thirty cats."

"I'm sorry. I guess there's just no chance for us." I reach for his hand and give it a friendly squeeze. "But we should totally double-date."

"Let's talk when you don't have a concussion." Luke leans close and presses a kiss on my forehead. "Oh, wait. That's never." And with a wink, he walks out of my room.

Sure. He talks big now.

But one day Luke Sullivan will need saving again.

And I think I'm just the girl for the job.

acknowledgments

As usual, I have a million people to thank. It is with a grateful heart that I acknowledge:

My Facebook friends. I owe you a lot for helping me name and rename (and name and rename) Luke Sullivan. I still don't see why Otis Sprinkledink is such a bad pick. To me it just reeks of hotness.

Editor Jamie Chavez. Book four together and you haven't kicked me to the curb yet! Thank you for your friendship, humor, intimidating intelligence, as well as your juicing tips. Please know I will never drink beets. Never.

Editor Natalie Hanemann. It's been a joy to get to know you and work with you. I can't wait to hang out and talk books even more.

Everyone at Thomas Nelson. To quote Queen Tina, "You're simply the best." It's an honor to be a Nelson author and see what loving care you give your books.

My blog family. Thank you for stopping by three times a week and reading, as if my insanity is entertainment . . . instead of proof I need heavy medication.

Chip MacGregor of MacGregor Literary. For traveling this road with me and for all the funny, encouraging e-mails along the way.

Erin Valentine. I couldn't do any of this without you, and so appreciate your friendship, support, edits, and "you can do it" advice. Are you *sure* you weren't a cheerleader?

Leslie and Kim. For putting up with me during "deadline lockdowns," when I turn into something a little less friendly and a lot more *Nightmare on Elm Street*-ish.

Mom, Kent, Michael, Laura, Hardy, and Katie Beth. I appreciate the love, support, and occasional meals-to-go. (You can't have too much of any of those.)

My readers, whose e-mails make my day. Thank you for giving up hours of your life to read my books, my blog, and the occasional witty line on airport bathroom walls. (Just kidding. I would never do that . . . and admit it.)

My students, who have to put up with a lot as I juggle teaching and writing. Forgive me for the times I stare right through you as a plot enters my head or scribble down your words verbatim because I want to steal them for a book. And I'm sorry for that one review game we did that drew blood. Okay, no. I'm not. That was funny.

The Father, Son, and Holy Ghost. I don't know that anything has stretched me more spiritually than being chained to a keyboard. Thank you for giving me a dream and blessing me indeed. Now as to those extra five pounds I've gained writing . . . we *totally* need to talk about that . . .

reading group guide

1. If *I'm So Sure* was made into a movie, who would you cast as the characters?

2. A reoccurring theme in the book is that things aren't always what they seem. Where was this theme evident?

3. In your own life, have you been in a situation where something or someone didn't match the first impression?

4. Bella Kirkwood really struggles in her relationship with her dad. Is she justified in her bitterness? What advice would you give her?

5. What would the perks be of living your life on a reality show? The drawbacks? Why is America so in love with reality TV?

6. What are some issues Bella has as a result of her parents' divorce? Describe some difficulties of being a child of divorce—either from a personal experience or from what you've seen a friend go through.

7. In what ways do Bella and other characters have a hard time with honesty—either in blatant lying or just not being able to share his/her heart? Why do you think it's so difficult to tell people how we really feel?

8. Bella's made a few mistakes in the boyfriend department. What

advice would you give her? Can you think of a Bible verse that would apply?

9. Bella is learning to rely on family and friends in *I'm So Sure*. Describe the moments she needed them the most.

10. The character of Callie got so obsessed with winning the prom queen contest, she made some really bad decisions. Have you ever gotten so focused on something (one particular friend, a boy, a job, a test) that other things or relationships suffered?

11. How did Bella's "gift" of nosiness lead her into trouble? Do you have a dominant flaw that sometimes lands you in hot water?

12. Bella splits her time between Manhattan and Truman, Oklahoma. What are the perks of each? The downsides? What do you think God is trying to teach Bella with this contrast?

13. What do you believe the title *I'm So Sure* means? When you are making a decision or have a problem, how do you know for certain what the right answer is?

so over
my head

This book is lovingly dedicated to my cute sister-in-law, Laura. She is a ray of sunshine in our family, as well as our missing piece, fitting in just perfectly to complete the picture.

I love you, girl, and am so glad you saw something in my brother. I personally don't get it, as all I ever saw was someone who always stole the front seat as well as my allowance, but whatever. To each her own. May God richly bless you with laughs, love, and cute shoes.

chapter one

If my love life was the knife toss at a circus, I'd have Luke Sullivan speared to the wall with an apple in his mouth.

"Ladies and gentlemen! The Fritz Family welcomes you to the greatest show on earth!" A man in a top hat stands in the center of a giant tent, his curlicue mustache as delicate as his voice is strong. "Prepare to be amazed. Prepare to be wowed. Allow us to entertain you with sights you've never seen, horses whose feats will astound you, and death-defying acrobatics!"

On this first night open to the public, the crowd stands in a swarm of shouts and applause.

I stay seated and jot down some quick notes for the *Truman High Tribune*. Or at least that's what I'm pretending to do. In actuality, it's taking all my energy just to be civil.

"I just don't see why you had to invite her."

From his standing position, Luke glances down. "Are we back to that again?"

"You and I are working on the carnival story. Not Ashley." Ashley Timmons, a new girl who joined the newspaper staff last week, has become my least favorite person on the planet. She's not quite as awful as those on the top of that list—namely the handful of people who've tried to do me bodily harm over the last year. But icky nonetheless. Fresh from Kansas City with her brother, Ashley thinks she is to journalism what Edward Cullen is to vampires. She's disgustingly cute, and worst of all, she's Luke's ex-girlfriend. She moved away for two years, but I can tell she's ready to rekindle anything they used to have. It doesn't take a keen reporter's intuition to see that. Just anyone with at least one working eyeball.

"We've hung out with them all week, Luke."

"I haven't seen Kyle in a long time, and he'll be leaving soon for college." Luke searches my face. "I've included you in everything. Have you felt left out?"

"No." I just want *her* left out. I don't mind the return of his friend Kyle at all. But where Kyle is . . . there you'll find his sister. "Tonight isn't about hanging out with your friend, though. He's not even here. You invited Ashley for the paper."

"You've been ticked at me ever since your last article. But it was weak on verbs and lacked your usual creativity." He sits down and trains those intense eyes on mine.

"Yeah, and then you proceeded to show me some piece of writing wonderment your new recruit produced." Ashley came with glowing recommendations from her former journalism teachers. Everyone on our staff thinks she is, like, the greatest thing to writing since the delete key. Everyone but me.

"You know what your problem is, Bella? Number one, you're jealous and insecure—"

"Of her?" I toss my hair and laugh. "Maybe I just don't like the way she's thrown herself at you from the second she stepped into the classroom. I'm not insecure, but I'm also not stupid."

Luke's mouth twitches. "I meant insecure of your writing abilities. But now that you mention it, you probably are jealous of my talking to her. That would fit."

"Fit what?" A band of clowns ride unicycles in the ring, but I don't even bother to watch.

"It would fit with the Bella Kirkwood pattern." He lifts a dark brow. "You are completely distrusting of the entire male species. I guess one couldn't blame you, given your dad's history *and* your experience with your ex, but I have no desire to get back with an old girlfriend."

"This is outrageous. I do *not* have trust issues with guys! And you know what else?"

"I'm dying to hear more."

"I think you're enjoying all the attention from Ashley." All Luke and I have done lately is fight. While digging into other people's business might be my spiritual gift, I'm beginning to think arguing comes second.

"Ever since we've been together, you've balked at my every comment in journalism. You can't stand to be criticized—even when it's for your own good. And"—his blue eyes flash—"you're just waiting for me to cheat on you like Hunter. You think I don't see that?"

Hunter would be my ex-boyfriend from Manhattan. This past fall I caught him doing the tongue tango with my former best friend Mia. And then not too long ago I considered getting back with him. He swept me up with this new version of Hunter Penbrook, told me he had started going to church, said all the right things, bought me coffee. It's a little hard to resist a cute guy bearing a mocha latte with extra whip, you know? Luckily, at prom two weeks ago, I saw the light and let that rotten fish off my hook.

"I'm not worried about you cheating on me, Luke. I'm tired of you bossing me around and acting all 'I'm in charge.'"

"I *am* in charge. I'm the editor."

"Not of our relationship."

"I'm back!" Ashley chooses that very moment to flounce back to her seat. "I got you a cotton candy." She hands the pink confection to Luke. "Bella, I figured you're like most girls and need to watch your weight, so I didn't get you anything. What'd I miss?"

Luke holds me down with his arm. "Don't even think about it," he whispers.

The crowd *oohs* and *ahhhs* as the Amazing Alfredo begins juggling two long silver swords. I applaud politely when he pulls a third one out of his hat and tosses it into the air with the rest. I'd hate to think where that sword was *really* hiding.

Like a distant relative, the Fritz Family Carnival comes to Truman, Oklahoma, every April and sets up camp on land that, I'm told, goes way back in the Fritz genealogy. They stay at least a month—working on additional routines, training new employees, giving the local elementary teachers a nice afternoon field trip— and don't leave until they can ride out bigger and better than the year before. And while that might be odd, it's nothing compared to the fact that I'm sitting on the bleachers between my boyfriend and a girl who has been openly flirting with him. That chick needs to learn some boundaries.

"Bella, Luke said you might need some help with your article."

He holds up a hand. "I just thought it would be interesting to get our three perspectives. Bella will still handle the interviews."

"It's been so great to work with you again, Luke." Ashley's smile could charm the shirt off Robert Pattinson. "Just like old times, huh?" Her eyes gaze into his. Like I'm not even there. "Kyle's really enjoyed hanging out. Too bad he had a study session tonight."

Luke leans close, his mouth poised near my ear. "Just because we're dating doesn't mean I'm going to slack off on your writing. You're still a staff member. And you *know* I do not boss you around any other time. I have been nothing but respectful to you." He returns his attention to the ring. "Did you write down the fat lady's stats?"

"Of course I did." I scribble something illegible on my paper. No, I didn't get her stats. I'm too busy fighting.

"She's seven hundred and twenty-nine pounds, in case you missed it," Ashley chirps.

"Thanks." *Lord, help me be kind to this girl.*

"You always act like I can't handle the writing assignments," I whisper for Luke's ears only. "I think I have more than proven I can. Not only can I write, but I can crank out some award-winning articles *while* crime solving."

After I moved to Truman, I accidentally became the Nancy Drew of Oklahoma. Now that I'm known for my mystery solving skills, friends and strangers want me to help them out. Just last week I tracked down a stolen iPhone and did a little spying for a suspicious girl who thought her boyfriend Buster was cheating. It's true he hadn't been going to football practice like he said; I found him at Margie Peacock's School of Ballet, lined up on the bar doing pirouettes and high kicks. I hear he makes a heck of a swan in Margie's recital.

"I'm not doubting your writing skills." Luke claps as the magician leaves, and Betty the Bearded Lady bows before starting her performance.

I'm transfixed by the hair on her face, and it suddenly makes me feel a whole lot less self-conscious about the fact that I didn't shave my legs last night. The audience claps in time to the spirited music as the woman's collie jumps through her hula hoop, then dances to the beat on its hind legs.

I shoot a pointed look at his old flame. "Let's talk about this later."

Ashley reaches around me and puts her hand on Luke's knee. "I forgot—I have my latest assignment on my laptop in the car. You told me to spice up my verbs, and I revised it. I wanted you to look at it." She returns to clapping for the Bearded Lady.

"Yes, Luke. She wants you to check out her spicy *verbs.*"

"At least she takes constructive criticism well." His voice is just loud enough for me to hear.

"That girl wants you back. Period."

"I'm not Hunter. And I'm not your dad."

"I have to go interview Betty the Bearded Lady." And I stomp down the bleachers to find her trailer outside. When I glance back, Ashley has scooted down.

And taken my place.

chapter two

The April night air smells of animals, popcorn, and a hint of rain. I feel like a storm is brewing in my head. Luke is such an egotistical jerk sometimes. Is he really so blind he can't see what Ashley's up to?

"Betty?" I knock on the trailer that has the Bearded Lady's face painted on the side. Speaking of gross. If I had a face full of fur I don't believe I'd be going on the road with it. Maybe I should give her the number of a good waxer in Manhattan.

The door swings open and bangs into the metal trailer. "Yeah?"

"Um . . ." *Focus on the eyes. Not on the whiskers.* "I'm Bella Kirkwood. I contacted the owner of the circus about interviewing some of you guys. I'm doing a piece for the—"

"Get in here, you." She pulls me up the short steps and hugs me to her ample bosom. "I haven't been interviewed since 1995, when I accidentally set my face on fire after I had to fill in as the human cannonball." She closes the door and points to a seat. Her collie stands at attention beside her.

Her living quarters are small and dim, but clean. As I take a seat on a gingham cushion at her table, I get a sniff of Pine-Sol and discount store candles.

"Would you like something to eat?" Betty opens a small fridge and extracts a pie that is topped with about two feet of meringue. "I tend to bake on the road. The rest of the crew practices, but it's not like my tricks take much work. Old Peg never fails, do you, girl?" She makes kissy noises toward the dog and places the pie on the table.

As she slices into her creation, I think about hygiene and stray hairs. But this is pie, and I don't want to be rude. I need info for the article, after all.

Betty reaches behind her to grab two forks, and I allow myself to really look at her.

And it's just as bad as I thought.

But beneath the hairy face are kind eyes that twinkle and make me feel instantly welcome. A mouth permanently poised in a smile.

I take my first bite and savor the flavor on my tongue. The woman can bake like a dream.

Pulling out my notebook, I get down to business. "I understand the carnival comes to Truman every year."

"Yes. We normally don't set up the midway while we're here, but Red wanted to. Seems like a waste of money to me, but he doesn't seem concerned with that." She purses her lips. "Pointless."

"It is an unusual setup you guys have. My stepdad says you always spend early spring here in Truman."

"Yep. It's a tradition started by the original Mr. Fritz. We travel through Florida in the winter, then take some time off in April and May to regroup and learn new tricks. It's not always a profitable approach, but this carnival's always been about quality and uniqueness. So it works."

"How long have you been living the circus life?" I ask.

She blots her own mouth, and I can't help but stare at her face again. "About twenty-five years. I'm the oldest one in the show. High school wasn't exactly a good time for me, and I dropped out at sixteen and thought my life was over. Then Old Man Fritz saw me at one of his shows and asked me if I'd like to be a star." Betty chuckles at the memory. "I told him I would indeed like to be a star. I worked for him, then when he retired, I worked for his son." Betty's eyes lose some of their gleam. "Then when Junior Fritz and his wife, Shelly, were tragically killed last year, I stayed on to work for Red Fritz."

"Junior's older brother." I had done my research.

"Yes. He has custody of Junior Fritz's daughter, but she stays with me in my trailer. I'm kind of the carnival mom." She smiles and grabs a picture off the counter. "Cherry is twelve, soon to be thirteen. I took over homeschooling her when her parents died." Betty shakes her head. "That kid means the world to me. I would do anything to protect her."

"I'm sure it can be dangerous sometimes on the road."

Betty laughs, but her eyes dim. "Sometimes it doesn't matter where you go—the trouble seems to pack up and move with you. But nothing's going to happen to Cherry." She settles the frame back in its place. "Not on ol' Betty's watch."

I quickly scribble down her words and try to get her back on track. "Tell me about life with the carnival. Is it just like one big family here?"

Betty absently strokes her dog's ear, sending Peg's dog tags to clanking. "Family? There are some of us who are mighty close. But others"—her hand stills—"you'd rather have as far away from you as possible."

"But I've been watching the show. You guys seem to be having such a good time—like it's one big party."

"Trust me, kid. In the carnival life, things are *not* always what they seem."

Before I can prod further, a knock on the door has Betty standing.

The ringmaster and owner, Red Fritz, pops his head in. "Three minutes 'til the second act. Get a move on."

"I know what time it is." Betty fluffs her hair, turning her back on the man. "I'm doing two appearances in the program tonight, so I have to scoot. Why don't you come back after the show, Miss Kirkwood, and we'll finish this conversation?"

"I think that time would be better spent minding your own business and coming up with a new routine for the dog here. People are getting bored with all that stupid stuff you do," Red says.

"My dog is a crowd pleaser, and you know it."

Red Fritz narrows his eyes. "If your fuzzy face isn't out there on time, it's coming out of your pay. Again." With a parting glance at me, he slams the trailer door.

When Betty turns around, the smile is back in place. "Forget him. Now, let's walk back together, shall we? I have a great story about a clown mishap I can share as we go."

A flash of blonde in the distance catches my attention as I stand in the doorway. "I'll catch up with you later, Betty. I need to check out something in the parking lot."

My feet press into the gravel path, and as Ashley's car becomes more visible, so does its owner. My stomach drops like the floor in the gravity barrel out on the midway.

Under the streetlights, I watch my nemesis wrap her arms around Luke and seal her mouth to his. His hands move to her wrists.

"Working on a new story?" I cross my arms over my chest and feel the fire beneath my skin.

"Bella!" Luke shoves Ashley away. "I—I didn't—"

"Know I was standing here? Obviously."

He steps toward me. "It's not what you think. I wasn't kissing her. I—"

"It's my fault," Ashley purrs. "We got to talking about old times, and I got carried away. Don't blame Luke."

Yeah, she looks real contrite.

Humiliation and hurt battle in my head. "Forget it. I have work to do." I walk away as fast as my shaking legs will move.

"Wait." Luke runs to catch up. His hand clasps my arm. "Bella, hold up."

I round on the boy, my eyes flashing. "And you said it was all in my head—that she wasn't chasing you. Now is my idea so crazy?"

"Ashley didn't mean it."

I blink. "You're taking up for her?"

"No, I—" He sets his jaw and stares at the ground. "This is what you've been waiting for, isn't it? You've just been waiting for me to screw up—like all the other guys in your life."

"Don't turn this on me, Luke. You're the one who had your lips plastered to a girl who is *not* your girlfriend."

"I was pushing her away."

"I can't work with her. I *won't* work with her. I want Ashley off the newspaper staff."

He reaches out again, but drops his hand. "You know I can't do that."

"Then we're through. It's her or me."

"There's no choice here." His voice snaps with electricity. "Ashley's not going to do anything like that again. I'll make sure of it. But she stays on the paper. I can't fire someone for attempted kissing." He steps so close I can't help but breathe in his earthy cologne. "You know I would never cheat on you."

I watch an airplane soar through the night sky. "I need some time."

"For what?"

I bite the inside of my cheek. "Time to figure us out . . . and time to get that image of you two out of my head."

"I know you're mad. You have a right to be. But this boils down to trust—you either trust me or you don't."

I slowly nod and look into the face of the boy I've waited for all year. "I guess right now I don't."

Luke stares past me to the big top. "This is really what you want? Because it seems to me like you're just running scared instead of dealing with what happened—with us."

Pain gives my words a biting edge. "I know it's a big blow to your ego, but I really think a break would do us both some good."

He takes off his glasses and nods. "Good luck with your interview. And your space." Hands stuffed in his khakis, he walks away.

Leaving me standing in the midst of a hundred cars. And one broken heart.

I return to the main tent just as Alfredo the magician is working his way out of some chains. Soon all of them fall, and he's left with nothing but a pair of handcuffs. Finally they, too, drop to the ground, and the audience goes wild. But at the moment the man could completely vanish and I wouldn't be impressed.

"And now, ladies and gentlemen, feast your eyes on the lovely Cherry Fritz, our reigning princess of the trapeze!" Red Fritz waves his arms grandly toward the ceiling as a young girl flies through the air.

Ugh, men. Who needs them? There's my cheater ex, Hunter, and my dad who is planning a wedding even though he's the last person on the planet who needs a wife. And my stepdad? Life majorly changed when he won a professional wrestling reality show. Like having a stepfather who wears spandex on a regular basis isn't stressful enough. Where are the normal guys? I thought Luke was one of them. He's cute in that Clark Kent, Abercrombie sort of way. He's freakishly mature and smart. And he's not just a nerdy brainiac—he's even the captain of his soccer team. I thought I wanted nothing more than to be his girlfriend. Ever since I arrived in Truman this fall, we've been drawn together like two magnets. But tonight his magnetism's pulling in one too many girls.

Feeling absolutely miserable, I sit through the rest of the show. A guy walks on a tightrope. A girl does a handstand on a prancing horse. A small clown gets shot from a cannon. But all I can think about is Luke.

God, what am I supposed to do with all this?

Before I know it, all the lights come up and people are exiting the bleachers. I sit for a while longer and watch the workers go into action sweeping, removing the animals, and clearing the grounds. Finally I gather my purse and head out back to Betty's trailer. A breeze flutters over my skin, and I pick up the pace. Though I would never admit it to Luke, it is a little creepy out here now. Few cars remain in the parking lot, and I wonder at the sense of coming back here alone.

I pass two smaller trailers before coming to Betty's bigger one. The door hangs open, and light spills out.

I knock on the swinging door. "Betty? Hello?"

No answer. I stand on the step and knock louder. "Betty? It's Bella!"

Nothing.

Then my ears twitch at the tiniest of sounds. A distant whimper. An animal. From the back of the trailer.

"Betty?" I step inside just as her collie leaps out. "Peg! Hey, here girl!" I turn back to the trailer.

And feel my stomach drop to the floor.

My scream pierces the air.

Betty the Bearded Lady sits at her table, nose down in her pie.

And one shiny sword in her back.

chapter three

J ust take deep breaths, Bella. Deep breaths."
I don't know how sticking your head between your knees and
staring at your own crotch is supposed to help anything, but here I
am. Trying not to pass out. Trying not to bawl uncontrollably.

Mark Rogers, friend and member of the Truman PD, pats
my back as we sit on the arena bleachers. The rest of the police
force combs through Betty the Bearded Lady's trailer. I've already
answered a hundred questions, and I have a feeling they are just the
tip of the iceberg. *Why me, God? How will I ever get that image out of
my mind? All that blood.*

My breath hitches and Mark does more patting. "Think nice
thoughts." Tonight his voice is as high pitched as a flute. "Go to your
happy place."

"I thought I was *at* one. Then I saw a dead woman." I want this to
be one of those overly realistic dreams you wake up from. The kind
that makes you happy to be awake, realizing it was all just a vivid
dream, and you are safely tucked in bed.

I hear the crunching of a wrapper and raise my eyes. Mark
sticks half a Snickers in his mouth.

"What?" His eyes go wide. "I'm a stress eater. Want some?"

My stomach does acrobatics at the thought of food. "You have
no idea what you're doing here, do you?"

"Not every day I see a bearded lady murdered." He eats the last bite. "Seriously, that is some freaky stuff in there. The only dead body I've ever seen was my Great Uncle Morty. And he was ninety-six, so it wasn't a real shocker that he went, you know? He keeled over at the nursing home square dance. He just did one too many do-si-dos. But still"—he shivers—"he was awfully pale and wrinkly. Kinda cakey looking."

"Thanks for sharing." I cover my face with my hands and rock back and forth. Mark's hand plops on my head. "Stop patting me!"

"Well, pardon me." He sniffs. "It works on my schnauzer."

"Bella?"

At that familiar voice, I stand up. "Luke." He walks past two cops, and I run straight into his arms.

"Shhh." He holds me close, and I breathe in the scent of him. His shampoo, his cologne, the smell of his clothes. Him. "Officer Mark called me."

"Please don't leave me." *Let's forget we broke up. Just for now.*

"I'm not going anywhere." He caresses the back of my head, and I hang on like he's my lifeboat off the *Titanic.* "Your mom and Jake are on their way. It's just going to take them a little bit from Oklahoma City."

My stepdad Jake's on the road a lot with the wrestling circuit, and Mom goes with him whenever he's close. Why couldn't he have been in Philly or Phoenix tonight? Seeing a dead woman definitely qualifies as one of those moments a girl needs her mother.

"She died . . . in her pie." My breath catches. "Why would some-one kill her and let her die in her meringue?"

"I don't know." Luke's voice is calm, reassuring.

"It was good pie too."

"I'm sure it was, Bel."

I sniff on his shoulder. "If I die over pie, I want it to be coconut cream."

"She's a little shocky," Officer Mark says. Like I'm not right here. Like I'm talking crazy. But who, I ask, would want her last breath to be taken nose-deep in raisin pie? Or a meat pie? It would be my luck to go in a big ol' bowl of peas.

Luke steps back, keeping his hands locked with mine. "Do you think you can tell me about it?"

"I'd like to know too." A girl in a sparkly leotard appears, her blonde hair slicked into a ponytail. Though she still wears stage makeup, her face is pale. Her eyes haunted.

"This is Cherry Fritz," Mark says. "She's the owner's niece."

"This was my parents' circus." Watery eyes meet mine. "Betty was my godmother." As she steps closer I can see she doesn't look quite so harsh beneath the makeup. "Do you think she—she . . . suffered?" Cherry's tears inspire some of my own.

"I don't know. It didn't really look that way." Except for the sword the length of my leg sticking out of her back. "She did have dessert, if that's any consolation." Wow. My ability to comfort is just . . . awful.

"Betty didn't have any enemies. I just don't understand. There has to be some mistake." Cherry turns to Officer Mark. "Who would m-murder her?" Tears make tracks down her painted face.

"We'll get to the bottom of it." Mark clears his throat. Probably has a peanut stuck in there.

"Cherry!" The ringmaster explodes through the big top entrance. "Where have you been? We have a killer on the loose, and I couldn't even find you!"

I move closer to Luke as Red Fritz's piercing brown eyes land on me.

"You the one who found her?"

"Um . . ." I swallow past a lump and nod. "Yes."

The seconds stretch as he watches me. I look away, my skin tingling.

"Well, I'm sorry you had to see that." Red stands beside Mark. "We are a family here at the Fritz Family Carnival. And I can't imagine who would do such a vile thing. Surely it can't be one of our own, that much I know."

Officer Mark jots down some notes. "Mr. Fritz, Miss Betty's trailer will obviously be unusable for a while. Will Cherry be staying with you?"

"My son Stewart lives with me in my own trailer, so space has always been too tight for the kid. I've contacted a distant family member in Truman to take Cherry until she can move back into Betty's."

Ew. Like she'll ever *want* to live in the place where her godmother was murdered.

A policeman enters the tent, getting Red Fritz's attention. They speak in hushed tones. Red glances at his niece, then nods.

"What family member, Uncle Red? I can't go stay with a stranger."

A moment later the entry flap opens again and Dolly O'Malley, my mom's best friend, is escorted inside. She nods her head toward the ringmaster. "Red."

He tips his hat. "Looking as lovely as ever."

"How are you doing, Bella?" Dolly hugs me to her. "I can't imagine what kind of night you kids have had." She smiles at Cherry. "My, my. Aren't you the spitting image of your mother. Do you remember me?"

Cherry shrugs. "Kinda."

"Your mama was my second cousin. We used to play together when we were about your age." She brushes a hand over Cherry's hair. "I have a big house and lots of horses. Your Uncle Red thought it would be a fun place for you to hang out for a couple of days." Dolly turns to Officer Mark. "Bella and Cherry will be going home with me. I assume the police are done talking to them?"

"For now, but I'm sure there will be more questions tomorrow."

I follow Dolly and her cousin outside. Though it's April and the night is warm, I shiver a little.

"Wait—what's going on?" Cherry breaks from us and runs toward a police officer. "Stop!"

"The Amazing Alfredo," Luke says, pointing. "It looks like they've cuffed him."

I strain to see him in the dim carnival lights. "Does this mean he—"

"He's been arrested." Officer Mark joins us, staring straight ahead. "It was his sword that pierced Betty's heart. And we have Red's son, Stewart, who claims to have overheard a heated argument within twenty minutes of Bella finding the body. There are some other suspicious details I can't get into, but we're taking him in and waiting on the prints."

The officer pulls a crying Cherry off the magician. "No! He didn't do it!"

Alfredo says something to Cherry, and she steps back, shoulders heaving, and watches the policeman put Alfredo in the car.

"I'm going to get Cherry. We'll meet you at the house, Bella," Dolly says, walking to the girl.

Luke curls an arm around me, pulls me close, and presses a kiss to my temple. "I know you hate people telling you what to do, but try and get some sleep tonight."

"Right." I slide my arms around him until we're locked in a hug. I just need one moment of safety. To breathe in his strength and pretend that all is well. "Thanks for coming back and staying with me."

"That's what ex-boyfriends do."

"Luke?"

"Yes?"

"I have to find out for sure who killed Betty the Bearded Lady."

He sighs into my hair. "I was afraid you were going to say that."

chapter four

The Monday morning alarm goes off, and it's everything I can do not to throw it across the room. My mentally challenged cat, Moxie, peeps open one eyeball, decides she'd rather not get up, and curls into the blanket.* Lucky thing.

I didn't sleep a wink all weekend. Every time I closed my eyes, Betty the hairy dead lady was there. Visions of her eating pie. Visions of her dog jumping through a hoop. But mostly . . . visions of someone plunging that sword into her back. There's only one thing to be said for it all.

I, Bella Kirkwood, will be Betty the Bearded Lady's avenger.

After I have some oatmeal.

I go through the motions of my morning routine and finally walk down the stairs to the kitchen. We live in an old farmhouse that looks like an Oklahoma twister sucked it up, thought better of it, and tossed it right back out. It's rough, it's worn, but it's become home. The interior is not much better. Aside from the kitchen, which got a remodel last fall due to an arsonist's fire, the house is like something out of 1975. But Mom has promised that the reign of shag and wood paneling is almost over now that Jake has made it to the big time in wrestling.

"Hey, honey." My mother stands at the toaster and kisses me as I walk by. "Did you sleep any?"

"Yeah. I'm fine," I lie. I've been on lockdown all weekend, and I have *got* to break out of here and see civilization. If you'd have told me just last year that I'd consider the small town of Truman, Oklahoma, worthy of being called civilization, I would have laughed in your face and then gone shopping with my daddy's credit card. But those days are over. Now it's dirt roads, sweet tea, and the occasional run to Target. The sweet tea I've gotten used to.

"Are you sure you're okay to go to school?" My mom ponytails my long brown hair in her gentle grip. "We could just hang out here at the house."

I sit down at the table, stifling an eye roll. I know she means well.

"I feel a little traumatized myself." My stepbrother Budge reaches for the syrup, his big red 'fro especially buoyant this morning. "Maybe I should stay home with Bella."

"We have a test in junior English, if you recall." I turn determined eyes to my mom. "Can't miss that." Not that I got the chance to study much the last few days. Mom was busy keeping me purposely distracted with her weekend of board games and family movies. "Besides, if I have to play Monopoly or see *Shrek* one more time, somebody is gonna get hurt."

My youngest stepbrother enters the room, wearing a Spider-Man T-shirt and a red cape. "You're just mad because I beat you. All ten times." He taps his head. "It's all about strategy."

"Whatever," I say. "I totally let you win. You're the youngest— that's what we're supposed to do." Robbie is in first grade, and if Harvard knew about him, they'd be recruiting.

Twenty minutes later I climb into my VW Bug and drive to school, grateful for the change of scenery.

~~~~~~~~~

I struggle through a test in English, my mind on facing Luke for the first time at school. With a confidence I don't feel, I sail into the classroom, greet some fellow reporters, and head straight for the safety of my beloved Mac.

Ten minutes into my typing frenzy, a shadow falls over my keyboard.

Luke looms, his blue eyes ever serious. "You don't look like you've slept much."

I stare at the screen as if my own writing is the most engrossing thing ever. "Thanks. Your concern is touching."

"Of course I'm concerned."

"Really? Because practically all of Truman High came to visit me this weekend—but you." Shoot! I was *not* going to say that. I was going to play it cool that he didn't so much as call me after we left the carnival Saturday night. No call. No text. No e-mail.

"We broke up. Remember?"

"Right." I lift my chin a notch. "And I thought we'd still be friends, but maybe you're not mature enough to handle that."

"I heard about all the people stopping by over the weekend, so I didn't want to *smother you*. I know how you hate that."

Nothing like having your words thrown back at you. Like a big spitty paper wad.

"And I didn't know it would bother you to not hear from me." He has the nerve to look smug. "Missing me already?"

"It didn't bother me." I meet his challenging gaze. "My mom was asking about you. That's all." Ugh. I need a scarlet *L* for liar.

Luke sits his Hollister-clad legs on the edge of my work station. "I do have some news that will probably upset you."

"You're stepping down as editor, and Zac Efron is taking your place?"

Luke's eyes narrow a fraction before he continues. "You're being reassigned."

My hands slip off the keyboard. "What did you say?"

"I'm taking over the series on the carnival."

"Um, no, you're not."

He blinks down at me. "Yes. I am."

"But I—"

"I'm the editor, and that's final."

My mouth opens in a sputter. "I . . . but you . . . this can't . . ." I stand from my chair. "I'm going to talk to Mr. Holman." Our advisor will straighten this out.

Luke stops me with a hand on my arm. "I've already discussed it with him. He's in complete agreement."

I put my nose inches away from his. "I cannot believe you would stoop this low." Where's the sensitive guy who came back for me Saturday night? Because this boy right here needs a good, swift kick in the—

"Bella, you're a good writer. We both know that. But you're also reckless and tend to run headfirst into danger."

I glance at his ex-girlfriend, whose blonde hair is disgustingly perfect. "If you assign her to this, so help me—"

"Ashley Timmons has nothing to do with this." His eyes darken. "She has nothing to do with *anything*."

"Didn't look that way in the carnival parking lot."

"Let that go. She and I both have. Ashley's already apologized. She feels terrible."

I'm sure she's doubled over with grief. More like she's planning her next make-out attack.

"I've already finished the first article." I punch my finger in his solid chest. "You can't just rip me off this story."

He grabs my hand, holds it suspended. "Yes. I can. And I just did. We'll run your interview with Betty, but I've e-mailed you the details of your new assignment."

"You are *such*"—I wrench my hand free—"a jerk."

Luke quirks a black brow. "Then I guess I've finally lived up to your low expectations."

I bite my bottom lip to keep from yelling like a banshee. Not that the class would notice. Everyone is writing away and listening to their iPods. Except for one.

Ashley Timmons.

I glower in her direction, and she snaps her attention back to her computer.

"Is this in retaliation for breaking up with you?" My voice is a whisper.

"You know me better than that. This is for your protection—because when you get nosy, you tend to get into near-death situations." He brushes a finger on my forehead. "There's something brewing in there. Admit it."

"Yeah, it's called dislike for my editor and a certain opportunistic reporter."

"We'll revisit this in a few weeks and see if we need to reevaluate." Luke opens his mouth to say something, then changes his mind. "I'll leave you to your new assignment."

My eyes shoot poison darts at his back as he saunters away.

By the time lunch rolls around, I'm in a mood worthy of a category four hurricane.

"He said *what?*" Ruthie McGee cuts into her burrito with the contraband pocketknife she keeps in her boot. Today her hair is a shocking shade of electric blue, teased to Marge Simpson heights and tied off with a camouflage headband.

"Luke took me off the carnival story." My head pounds inside my skull, and I regret not taking my mom up on her idea to stay home.

"Bella, that sounds very thoughtful to me." This from Lindy, the first friend I made at Truman High. She hung out with me in exchange for my giving her a makeover to catch a boy. The makeover and friendship stuck, but Matt Sparks, her best friend and unrequited love, has never treated her as anything more than a sister. "He knows how awful Saturday night was for you—finding that woman . . . um, you know—"

"Nose deep in meringue?" Ruthie crunches on a chip. "Gone to that great Gillette razor in the sky?"

"I mean Luke probably knows how traumatic all that is going to be for you for a while. So I think it's very thoughtful of him to take you off the story." Lindy eyes Matt Sparks, sitting next to her, lost in his burger. "Romantic even."

"And they arrested that Alfredo guy," Ruthie says. "So I guess it's not like you need to go back to the carnival and investigate."

I focus on peeling the label off my water bottle. "Right."

Ruthie gasps, clutching her throat of a hundred necklaces. "I've seen that look before. Like at prom when you and my dream muffin Budge saved us from that psycho who wanted to blow us all up."

"Bella, no." Lindy frowns. "Can't you just lay low for a while? In the short time you've been at Truman, you've almost been killed twice."

"Yeah." I wave off Lindy. "Don't worry about it. I'm sure the police are on top of everything. I just—" I pause as a tall boy stops at our table. He holds out a Gatorade.

"Hey, Lindy." He swallows visibly. "I just wanted to thank you for sharing your water at track practice yesterday." He hands her the bottle. "I wanted to return the favor. I noticed this is your favorite."

Lindy accepts it, a small smile on her face. "Thanks, Bo."

The senior's cheeks pinken. "I'm on my way to check the next practice schedule. Um, in case you'd want to walk with me to the gym."

"Yeah." Lindy laughs and fingers the collar of her T-shirt. "Yeah, I would." Clutching her Gatorade, she follows Bo Blades, THS track star, out of the cafeteria.*

"I'll clean up your tray." Matt picks up Lindy's trash, his movements jerky, his brow furrowed.

Ruthie and I exchange a look.

"Bo is so cute." She sighs. "Not as cute as my Budgie—but still a hot number."

"Especially in those running shorts," I add. "Mee-yeow."

"Lindy had pizza on her shirt again," Matt huffs. "But I guess Bo won't even notice." He stomps away.

I chew on a carrot stick. "Well, that was interesting."

"Indeed. It seems Lindy has an admirer and her BFF is *mucho* jealous. Either that or he just has PMS." Ruthie pats her big hair. "It happens to the best of us."

I see Luke Sullivan enter the cafeteria with Kyle and some of his soccer buddies. Walking by his side is Ashley Timmons. She tips her head back and laughs at something he says. Whatever small appetite I had is now officially gone. He's hanging out with her?

"That girl is too cute," Ruthie says, then catches my expression. "Er, I mean, no. She's *so* unattractive." Her face scrunches in disgust. "I've seen dog butts prettier than her."

"Luke and I have broken up. He can flirt with whoever he wants." Never mind the feeling of a million pinpricks to my heart. I'm sure it's just indigestion. Cafeteria gas.

"So what are we going to do to solve this carnival mystery?"

I blink at Ruthie. "What? *We're* not going to do anything. And besides, like everyone says, it's probably all wrapped up. Just waiting on the sword prints. No mystery."

Ruthie leans over the table, getting closer. "Bella, you're up to something, and I want in on it."

"No."

"Aw, come on! Batman . . . Sherlock Holmes . . . Scooby Doo—do you know what they all have that you don't?"

"Testosterone?"

"Sidekicks!" Ruthie nods her blue head manically. "You need me. I could be the muscles behind the operation, and you'd be the brains. Plus it could be like my graduation present."

"You're a walking arsenal and would probably get us arrested." Why the Baptist preacher's daughter feels the need to carry around brass knuckles and the occasional knife is beyond me.

"Some of the Fritz crew go to my daddy's church every spring when they're in town." She waggles a single eyebrow. "I could get us part-time jobs at the place."

"I'm sure I can get my own job—not that I was thinking of doing that." Item number one on my after-school to-do list: head to the Fritz Family Carnival . . .

"Mr. Fritz might not want to see you around . . . since you bring all that bad mojo and all." Ruthie shrugs. "But my dad could probably talk him into anything."

"I don't bring bad mojo."

"Face it, you got dead girl juju."

"Fine. Talk to your dad."

"About what?" A masculine voice asks.

Luke.

Fabulous.

"You could've told me he was standing there." I swivel to face him. "Did you need something?"

"You wouldn't be making plans to get up close and personal with the Fritz gang, would you?"

"Nope." Ruthie answers for me. "But if she was, I'd be her new sidekick." She picks up her tray and stands up. "I'm probably going to need to get me some business cards. And a logo—I need one of them logos. Maybe a snappy sidekick catchphrase." Still talking to herself, Ruthie walks away to throw out her trash.

Luke slowly shakes his head. "You just can't leave well enough alone, can you?"

"Funny." I shoot a glance toward a watchful Ashley Timmons. "I was about to say the same to you."

chapter five

"N ow we're just going to check on Cherry. That's all. Don't act all weird and suspicious or anything." I hang a left to the Fritz Family Carnival.

Ruthie rolls down the passenger window in my Bug. "Me?" She snorts. "I'm cool. Queen of ice right here."

"Stick close to me and let me do all the talking."

"Duh." She pats a thick book. "That's what assistants do."

"What is that?"

"A manual for sidekicks." She pops her Bubblicious. "Got it off the Internet."

I pull into the gravel parking lot, and we get out. We walk past the Tilty Spin and the Zipper roller coaster.

"That looks awesome." Ruthie points to the twisted tracks of the coaster. "Nothing like being upside down, eh, boss?"

"I'm not your boss." *Or I would've already fired you.* "And you will never see me on one of those things."

Ruthie stops midstride. "Is *somebody* afraid of heights?"

I hold back a shiver as I look at all the rides. "Just when I'm on a ride that looks to be held together by duct tape and rubber bands."

"Ever kissed a boy on a Ferris wheel? It's so romantic." She sighs and looks toward the giant ride in the back of the lot. "Except for that time I puked on Sammy Stutes, which just proves corndogs and the Tilty Spin do *not* go together."

We walk into the big top, and I check out the area. I'm not sure what exactly I'm doing. I guess I'm hoping I'll know it when I see it.

"Can I help you?"

Ruthie and I look to the ceiling. There above us on a platform stands Cherry Fritz, trapeze in hand.

"Actually," I call out, "I just stopped by to check on you. I'm Bella Kirkwood. We met the other night." *You know, the night I found your godmother all dead and stuff.*

She lets the trapeze swing and skitters down the narrow ladder.

"How are you doing?" I ask as she walks to us. "Back to work already?"

She glances up to her trapeze. "I needed to get my mind off things. The show is closed until tomorrow night, but I decided to work on a new stunt with our downtime." Cherry frowns. "Betty wouldn't have approved, but I want to do it."

"Because it's too hard?"

"Almost as hard as the stunt that killed both my parents." For a moment the hollow look returns to her gaze before she shakes it off. "But my uncle says it's what we need to take the circus to the next level. Times are hard. People don't come see us like they used to. He says we have to make this season's show more dynamic."

I look over my shoulder and find Ruthie has vanished. Fabulous. She's either sneaking a free ride on the bumper cars or patting down a suspect.

"How is it working out at Dolly's?"

Cherry smiles. "It's okay. I mean, it was weird at first—we're distantly related and didn't really know each other that well. But she's been amazing. It's been nice to have a home-cooked meal instead of something from one of the food trailers. And Dolly's really easy to talk to."

Dolly has plenty of mother experience. She lost her two young daughters many years ago in a car wreck when she was still married to Mickey, my stepdad's manager. My mom says there's been a big gaping hole in Dolly's heart ever since, so I'm sure she's loving the company at her house.

I startle at the sound of raised voices from the opposite side of the tent.

"I'm through. This place is going under, and I've had it." A man about as tall as my armpit stomps out of a partitioned tent, a clown wig in his fisted hand.

Another guy, who could be his twin, follows close behind. "I can't make a living here. More and more work—and for what? Less pay!"

They bolt through the exit flap, and Cherry shakes her head. "That's our fourth employee to walk today. Where in the world are we going to get two clowns on such short notice?"

The Lord parted the Red Sea for the Israelites. Me? He gives a clown job. "I'll do it."

Cherry blinks. "Are you serious?"

My fake smile wobbles on my face. "Yeah. I'd love the job." *What have I done?* "And my friend Ruthie would too."

"I don't know."

"I'm a great worker." I can't believe I'm having to convince someone that I'd be a worthy *clown*, for crying out loud. "And Ruthie is so dependable and smart."

"Is that her?" Cherry points to a far corner where Ruthie McGee lies prostrate on a magician's table.

A man waves his hands over her. "Abracadabra! Shalla-kazaam! I will now cut you in half, then magically piece you back together."

"Oh boy." Cherry takes off for the couple, and I follow. "Bart!"

He stops, his hand saw held high. Ruthie's eyes go wide as funnel cakes.

"How many times have I asked you not to touch Alfredo's props?" Cherry rips the saw out of Bart's grip. "Especially the sharp ones?"

Ruthie bolts to a seated position. "What? You're not a magician?"

Cherry rolls her eyes as Bart runs away. "He's a mechanic."

"He was going to cut me in half!" Ruthie straightens her biker jacket and sniffs. "I thought something was fishy when he asked me if I had any lug nuts."

"Cherry, I wanted to ask you a few questions about Betty, if you think you're up to it."

She frowns. "I guess."

"You mentioned that Afredo couldn't have killed Betty—"

Her answer comes quickly. "Because he loved her."

"They were a couple? For how long?"

Cherry twirls a piece of her white-blonde hair. "Maybe three months. They had worked together for years, so for them to fall in love was totally out of the blue and unexpected." Her face stretches into a contented smile. "Betty had never been happier. She'd never really had a lot of attention from the guys because—"

"Her man-beard?"

Cherry shoots an annoyed look at Ruthie. "Because she devoted her life to the circus—then to me."

"Did she get along with everyone here?" I ask. "Any enemies? Any fights or disagreements lately?"

She considers this. "No, no one. Well, everyone has the occasional fight with Red, so that's nothing different."

I perk at this. So Betty didn't get along with creepy guy. "What problems could there be between Betty and Red?"

Cherry lifts an eyebrow. "Why do you want to know?"

Ruthie chortles. "Don't you know who this is? She's a famous crime—"

I elbow my friend. "I'm just concerned. If I'm going to be working here and all." I smile at Ruthie. "By the way, how do you feel about red honking noses and rainbow wigs?"

Ruthie pats her blue hair. "That was so last year."

"I'll introduce you to my cousin Stewart." Cherry motions for us to follow. "He's in charge of hiring hourly workers."

She leads us outside to the largest travel trailer on the grounds. This looks like the Hilton on wheels compared to the rest—even Betty's.

After one knock, Cherry swings open the door. "Stewart?" she yells. "I brought you two clowns."

I think I might be offended.

We step up into the trailer. It's much newer than Betty's—large and spacious. The front half is an office of desks and file cabinets. A TV hangs suspended from the ceiling, showing real-time footage of the big-top grounds.

A tall, lanky guy stands up from one of the two desks. He looks like he's a few years older than me, and is just as slender as Red is rotund.

"And what have you brought me today, dear cousin?" He grabs my hand, shakes it, and holds it longer than necessary. "I don't get to see too many beautiful girls on the road." He *tsks*, his beady eyes darting to Cherry. "The carnival really isn't for the pretty."

I draw back my hand. It's everything I can do not to wipe it on my jeans. Ew.

Stewart turns his attention to Ruthie. His smile falters just a bit, but he recovers. "And you"—his eyes trail up to the tippy top of her hair—"also a vision." He tries to capture her hand, but Ruthie deflects.

"You don't want to shake my hand. I just got over a bad case of the runs."

"Stewart, these girls would like a job while we're here in Truman." Cherry's voice takes on a different tone as she talks to her older cousin. The voice my mom uses when reading her grocery list. "We just lost two more clowns—the Bingworth twins. So I thought maybe—"

"Of course, we need the help." Stewart steps closer to me, and prickly chills dance along my arms. "You look familiar."

"Bella is the one who"—Cherry swallows—"found Betty."

Stewart tilts his narrow head, sending his black hair falling over his eyes like a curtain. "How terrible that must've been for you." His sigh sounds loud in the metal trailer. "I'm sure this is the last place you would want to work. And we respect that."

"She wants the job." Cherry softens her face, and I watch in awe as she steps into a new role. Her full lips push into a pout and her head drops. "I just thought with Betty gone, the woman who was like my mother, it would be nice to have some older girls around to talk to." She regards him through her lashes. "That way I won't have to come to you and Uncle Red with my questions about cramps and tampons."

"Okay, okay, okay!" Stewart holds out a hand. "We'll give it a trial period, all right?" I feel Stewart's eyes travel the length of me and resist the urge to shudder. "But I'll be keeping a close eye on you two . . . just to make sure that it's not too much." He sends a slow wink my way. "Especially you—with all you've been through. We wouldn't want to cause you any further unhappiness."

"I'll be fine." It comes out like a squeak. "I'm pretty tough." I nudge Ruthie. "Aren't I?"

My friend nods. "I've seen her kill a rattler with her teeth."

I quickly turn the topic back to our new roles as clowns and get the rundown on the job, which mostly consists of interacting with the audience and assisting the performing clowns. Fifteen minutes later my head is swimming with information, and I feel like going home and taking a good, long shower to rid myself of Stewart Fritz cooties.

"You Truman High students sure are a helpful bunch," Stewart says as we step down from his trailer. "All but one of our positions have been filled now. I think things are looking up for us. And don't forget, Bella—I'll be keeping a special eye on you."

I cough to cover up the retching noise. "See you tomorrow." Pulling Ruthie along, I speed walk away from him.

"Bella," Ruthie says. "The Lord gifted me with the ability to see things in people that others don't. So this information may come as a surprise to you, but Stewart Fritz is one spooky dude."

"Your insight into the human soul is clearly just God-given."

"I know, right?" Ruthie jerks as I pull her to the left. "Where are we going?"

"I want to check out Alfredo's trailer. I noticed they took off the police tape."

"Oh, cool!" Ruthie rubs her hands together. "Are we gonna riffle through some drawers? Dust for any prints the cops might've missed? Set up some hidden cameras?"

"No. *I'm* going in. And you're going to keep watch."

"That's lame. My dynamic duo guidebook says I have to make sure you don't crowd me out of the action."

"Look, I have not said you're my partner yet. So consider this like part of your interview—a test. Did that book tell you that being lookout girl is one of the most crucial steps to being a sidekick?"

Ruthie shuffles a rock with her toe. "No. But I've only read the pages with pictures."

"Well then." I scan the area for anyone who might see us. "Stand outside this trailer while I go in. If you see anyone headed this way, I need you to call out 'good afternoon' really loud, okay?"

Ruthie chews on her lip, blue with a lipstick that complements her hair. "That's not very original. How about I sing a few lines from *The Wizard of Oz?*"

"No."

"And then I could say, 'The monkeys are coming! The monkeys are coming!'"

"Just stick with my plan." I look back over my shoulder as I peel open the door. "Consider this phase one of your test."

"Man, I hate tests. They give me the burps."

The door gives a little squeak as I shut myself inside. *Dear God, if there were a breaking and entering prayer, I would so say it right now.*

The shades are pulled, blocking out the afternoon sun. I slip a tiny flashlight out of my purse and shine it around the trailer. Looks like more than one guy lives here. Each side is split into bunk beds. I take it the stripped bed is Alfredo's. I wave my light around until I see a small chest of drawers on his side. I ease the top drawer open and peer inside. Car magazines, a Snickers, a few pictures. I take one out. Alfredo and a woman. A beardless woman who is definitely not Betty. They're staring into each other's eyes and laughing. Extracting my camera, I snap a shot of the front and back of the picture. My heart races as I listen for sounds outside. I have to hurry. The life of crime is really not my thing.

Moving on to the bottom drawer, I find jeans, T-shirts, socks. Nothing out of the ordinary. I can't imagine having to live with so few belongings. I mean, five T-shirts to your name? If Alfredo is guilty of anything, it's a crime of fashion. I quickly run my fingers over the drawer seams, looking for any sort of hidden compartment. What? It works on TV.

"Somewhere over the rainbow!"

Ruthie's voice from outside jolts me like a cattle prod. I drop my flashlight, and it skitters across the floor, under the far bed. Oh no—I have to get it! I have to hide! My brain scrambles for a rational thought. *Think, Bella! What do I do?*

I must get that flashlight. It was a present from Luke and has my name on it! I leap for the other side of the trailer and throw my hand under the bed, reaching with my fingers.

"The monkeys are coming! The monkeys are coming!"

I hear the door handle being lifted.

Not much farther. Almost got it. I can see the flashlight.

The door groans.

I shoot up to my feet.

Just as Stewart Fritz steps inside.

chapter six

"M iss Kirkwood?"

Fall leaves in Connecticut could not shake harder than I am as I face Stewart Fritz.

He flicks on the lights. "What are you doing?" He takes large steps until he's but a breath away.

"I—I—" I was trespassing and searching through things that didn't belong to me. "I was told there was a bathroom in here." I do a little dip. "It's kind of an emergency. But I couldn't find a thing in the dark." Especially with my flashlight under the bed.

Stewart's small hazel eyes narrow like a snake's. "We have Porta-Potties all over the property."

I toss my hair and laugh. "Oh, silly man! I could never use one of those. And since I'm an employee here now—"

"This is one of the men's trailers you're in."

I look around. "Is it? Why I couldn't tell *what* it was in the pitch black." I giggle some more.

Stewart stares at me as the seconds tick painfully by.

Finally his face breaks into a sly smile. His voice is a low ebb. "Any time you need some help, you ask for me."

Gulp. "Thank you. I tend to get lost often. I'm a little bit airheaded at times."

Stewart rests his hand on my shoulder. "All the more reason for me to keep my eye out for you. I'd hate for you to get hurt out here. The carnival life isn't always as safe as it looks."

"I'll keep that in mind." I try to skirt past him, but his body blocks my way.

"How old are you, Bella?" His eyes dip to my chest.

"Seventeen." If he asks my bra size, I'm knocking him in the teeth.

"I'm twenty-one." His grin reminds me of the Joker in *Batman*. "Do you like older men?"

I take one step around him. "I really have to get back outside. My friend is waiting on me."

"The crazy girl who was yelling outside?"

"Yep. That's the one." I force a smile and take another step. "She's not well today. Her, um, antidiarrheal meds are really messing with her head. She can't be left alone for too long . . . or she could start singing *Rent* any second." What am I saying?

"Sounds serious."

He moves just enough that I make a break for it, sliding past him, hissing as my body has to touch his. Finally I reach the door.

"You want to be careful when you're alone in the dark," he says, as I fumble with the latch.

I shut the door and leap off the steps. Passing Ruthie, I grab her elbow and take off in a jog. "Ew, ew, ew!" Definitely taking a shower when I get home. Extra soap.

"What happened in there, boss?"

"Just keep moving." I shuck off some of the fear as I spot my lime-green Volkswagen. "What happened to the original signal we planned on?"

"I freaked! I think I had test anxiety or something. You're lucky I got 'Somewhere Over the Rainbow' out—the first tune that came to my head was 'I Like Big Butts.'" She shakes her head. "And I cannot lie."

My phone rings before I can unlock my door. Luke Sullivan.

"Yes?" My voice is as calm as a trickling brook.

"Any reason you and Ruthie McGee are sprinting away from the carnival grounds?"

I throw my purse on top of my car, desperate to get a grip on my keys and unlock this thing. Can't seem to make my fingers work. "Um—"

"Let me try."

I jump at the voice behind me.

Luke steps from behind the van next to us. He walks to me, his face tight. Grabbing onto my hand, he gently pulls my fingers apart. He doesn't let go as he clicks my keychain.

Ruthie scrambles inside and buckles herself in. I see her dive to the floorboard for her sidekick guide book.

"Now why don't you tell me what's brought you out here."

"I—"

Luke holds up his free hand. "And be crazy and try the truth."

"I stopped by for a visit." I don't need to explain myself to him.

A Rihanna song pours out of the car as Ruthie rolls the window down. "Tell him about our new job!"

I grit my teeth until my jaw aches. "She's a little out of her mind today."

Ruthie hangs her blue head out the window. "And Bella went snooping in Alfredo's trailer."

I give Luke my haughtiest glare. "I was here to check up on Cherry."

"And that Mr. Creepy Pants caught her!"

"Ruthie, would you study your book and leave the talking to me!" I roll my shoulders, straighten my posture, and face my ex-boyfriend—whose eyebrows are lifted as high as his forehead will allow.

"What do you think you're doing, Bella?" His words are like

sandpaper to my nerves, and he cuts me off before I can reply. "Never mind. We both know exactly why you're here."

I cross my arms over my chest and glare my editor down. "You took me off the story, Chief. But that doesn't mean I can't do my own digging around."

"What was Ruthie talking about? Who caught you snooping?"

I glance at my watch. "I really have to run. Lots to do." *And I need to be somewhere I'm not breathing your cologne.* Breaking up with him was the right thing to do, right?

Luke's hand curls around my arm. "Start talking, Bella."

"I might've gotten lost and found myself in the magician's trailer." I watch Luke's eyes darken. See the flex in his jaw and know he's not going to let this die. "And Red's son walked in." I rush on before Luke interrupts. "But I told him I was looking for a bathroom, so it's no big deal." Minus the pink flashlight with my name on it I left in the trailer. Definitely going to have to go back and find that first chance I get.

"I stood guard!" Ruthie shouts.

Yeah, for all the good *that* did.

"Bella, you were taken off the story for your own good—to protect you."

"I don't need protection. I happen to be excellent at taking care of myself."

Luke's laugh is bitter. "Says the girl who snooped through someone's possessions and then got caught in the process."

"I think the important point here is that I talked my way out of it." Yep, that's the part of the story I personally like.

"And Red Fritz's son bought your story?"

Well, probably not, but it got me out of there. "Luke, it's over. I handled it."

"So I guess the next question is . . . did you find anything?"

"As if I'd tell you!" I'm so sure. "You can't pull me from the story, then expect me to hand over all my information."

Luke inhales slowly and considers the blue sky beyond me. "Just promise me you'll be careful."

"Careful is my middle name."

Ruthie's head appears from the driver's side. "I figured it was something like Myrtle or Helga."

Luke holds me with his eyes. "Take care of yourself, Bella."

Must. Look. Away. Broken up couples do not have long moments of meaningful eye contact!

Say something snarky. Something wickedly intelligent to one-up him.

"Um . . . I gotta pee." I jump into my Bug, banging my head a few times on the steering wheel.

Ruthie smacks her gum. "Everything okay, boss?"

"Nothing a brain transplant wouldn't cure." And I drive the car far away from Luke Sullivan.

~~~~~~~~~

Later that evening the family sits down at the dining room table. We make a circle with our hands as Jake says a prayer over the meal.

"And Lord, please be with me and my family as I begin to travel even more. Give Jillian the strength and wisdom to take care of everything in my absence. Amen."

His absence? What is that about?

I lift my head and gawk at my mom. She folds her napkin in her lap and trails a nail down her water glass. Last year that nail was fully manicured and polished. Now it's neatly trimmed and ink-stained from writing notes for her psych class at the Tulsa Community College.

"What do you mean, 'traveling even more'?" I pass Budge the peas. I do not eat small, green squishy things.*

Jake casts a quick look at Mom. "I have a few more weeks left of training, but after that I'll hit the road full time. I've seen the schedule, and I'll be gone for most of the remaining year."

Robbie lets out a little whimper.

"I knew it would be a lot," Jake says. "I just didn't know it would be almost every day of the year." His mouth spreads into a grin. "When Captain Iron Jack gets more established, I can set my own schedule."

Mom wears the same plastic smile she wore the day she told me my dad was leaving us. This is not good. My dad traded my mom in for a string of bimbos. What's Jake getting? Night after night of spandex wedgies and a stiff neck from the tour bus?

"Budge, you might have to ease up on your hours at the Wiener Palace to help out around here more."

My stepbrother chugs his root beer. "I'm six hundred dogs away from wiener seller of the year. I can't slow down now."

"Maybe I could cut back on my television watching," Robbie says, his face solemn. "I could give up one Superman cartoon and the financial network."

"Nobody's giving up anything." Mom's spine is straighter than a dry spaghetti noodle. "We'll be fine. I'm going to finish up my class at the community college, then take a little break."

"But you've waited your whole life to go back to school."

"It's fine, Bella." She pats my hand. "All things in time. I can pick it back up some other time."

"We'll discuss that later," Jake says. "I do have some good news for you, Jillian."

I don't know if she can take any more.

My stepdad proudly throws his arm around my mom. "You can put in your notice at Sugar's. I'm officially on the payroll. The first check hits this week—and it's a good one."

"Are we rich, Daddy?" Robbie claps his little hands.

Budge grabs a piece of bread. "Can I have a pony?"

"Not rich, kids. But I'm definitely going to be making more than I did at Summer Fresh."

Um, yeah, Summer Fresh would be the factory where Jake previously worked. He made pads. As in lady business. My own father is a plastic surgeon to the rich and famous in Manhattan, so it took quite awhile before I could hold my head up every time I went back to New York City.

"Well, at least we can start updating the house, huh, Bel?"

"Yeah, Mom." I give her my most encouraging face. "It will be fun."

Four hours later I've flossed, moisturized, and read my homework for English—another Charles Dickens novel. It's like Death by Dickens. Lately any time I can't sleep, I just pick up ol' Chuck and next thing I know, I'm drooling on my pillow.

Leaving Moxie snoring on the bed, I walk downstairs to the kitchen to get a bottle of water.

I slip a Dasani out of the fridge, then head back up.

"You could've warned me."

My foot pauses on the third step. I follow my mom's voice through the living room and toward her bedroom. I lean my ear to the partially opened door.

"Jillian, the management just sprang it on me. What did you think this was going to be like? We knew it was a full-time commitment."

"There's a difference in being gone three hundred days of the year and being gone a few days a week."

Ew. Fighting makes my stomach all knotty and squishy. It reminds me of that last year before my dad left.

"This won't last forever. We have to ride it out until things calm down," Jake says.

"Until things calm down? You said that could take years."

"I thought you wanted me to live my dream."

"I do!" Her voice is almost a yell. "But what about mine? At what point did this go from me supporting your dream to you leaving me alone to raise three kids?"

My heart thuds in the following silence.

Finally Jake speaks. "Do you want me to quit? Say the word, and I will."

"Don't make me the bad guy, Jake. Of course I don't want you to quit. What I do want is for this family to be our priority. Find a way to make it work." I hear bare feet on the floor and the rustling of sheets. "I'm sleeping on the couch tonight."

I just get to the living room as my mom opens the bedroom door.

"Bella?" She stands at the end of the small hall, her pillow in her arms.

I freeze, stubbing my toe on the couch. "Ouch!" My breath hisses between my teeth. "Oh, hey, Mom."

"What are you doing?"

"Me? Um . . . just came down to get a bottle of water."

"In the living room?"

"I thought maybe I'd sneak some David Letterman." I shake my finger at her. "But you caught me."

She tilts her head and sighs. "You're a horrible liar."

I get that a lot.

"Good night, Bella." She flops onto the couch and picks up one of her college textbooks.

I walk back toward the staircase but turn back at the first step. "Are we going to be okay?"

"Of course." She flips a page. "It's just going to be a big adjustment. But it should be . . . fun."

"Um, Mom?"

She looks up from her book. "Yes?"

"You're not so hot at lying yourself."

chapter seven

The divorced-parent visitation thing can be a little stressful. Especially when you have an eight-year-old clinging to your dad and sticking her tongue out in five-minute intervals when no adult is looking.

Dad holds open the door to the famous Manhattan restaurant Nobu, and I file in behind his girlfriend and her bratty sister.

"So, Bella, like I was telling you"—my dad pulls out my chair and then sits down—"the show won't air until next year, but it's going to be huge." Huge like his smile. Huge like the hole in my heart every time I'm here, seeing my dad drifting further and further away from me.

Christina, the live-in girlfriend, opens her menu. "Your father is so excited. Our whole family is." She pats her sister's hand.

Ick. A family. After my dad left us, he went on this dating frenzy. At first that bothered me. Then he decided to keep one, and now I long for the rotating door of bimbos. Christina is a talent agent, and currently represents my dad and his dream to bring his plastic surgery skills and advice to the small screen. All he talks about lately—besides their approaching wedding—is his upcoming gig in Brazil. But after his accountant ran off with a ton of his money last year, at least he's not still harping on that.

"So are you going to have to move there?" I take a sip of water and crunch down on a piece of ice.

"Just for six months during filming." Dad surveys me over the top of his menu. "But don't worry, Bel. We don't start shooting until August. And we'll fly you in for some long visits."

"And you and Marisol can play on the beaches of Rio de Janeiro, my homeland." Christina gives her order to the waiter. "Won't that be fun?"

Marisol bats her little eyelashes toward my dad. "I can't wait to get to know Bella better."

"Isn't she precious?" he asks.

Preciously nauseating.

"Bella, I will be running some errands tomorrow." Christina pulls her long, dark hair until it drapes over the other shoulder. "Wedding details, you know. I was wondering if you would be a dear and keep an eye on Marisol."

Beside me Marisol makes little gagging noises. My thoughts exactly. "I guess—"

"I know," Dad says. "Why don't Marisol and I go to the park, and you two girls can do wedding stuff together?" He beams like he just invented a new wrinkle filler. "Christina, you've been talking about how you need some help with the planning."

Her smile is tight. "I meant like an assistant."

"My Isabella is amazing at anything involving style, fashion, and decorating." Dad pats me on the back. It's been so long since I've had a compliment from him, I just run it over and over in my mind, savoring his words.

"I think Bella would be bored and—"

"I can't wait." Anything to get out of monster-sitting. "It will be a fun time." Okay, that was probably too much. But if Christina gets to shop, I know Dad will let me charge a thing or two as well. And there is a new BCBG skirt I'm dying to hang in my closet.

Later I silently eat my lobster salad as the *family* becomes consumed with wedding chatter.

"Roses or calla lilies?"

"Seven bridesmaids or nine?"

"But I don't want Josh Groban to sing for us."

"Don't forget our ballroom lesson next Tuesday."

"Yes, Marisol, I think flowers in your hair."

I push my nearly empty bowl away. "How 'bout those Yankees?" They keep talking amongst themselves. "Anybody seen any plays lately?"

They don't even hear me.

"I found a dead body."

Christina's fork clanks to the floor.

My dad chokes on his water. "What did you say?"

"I, um, found a murdered woman last weekend."

Dad says something that would make my mom flinch. "Why didn't you tell me?"

"You didn't call me this week."

He sits up straighter. "Yes, I did."

"Leaving a message on my phone doesn't count." The words are out before I can pull them back in. I try to soften my tone as I quickly fill him in. Christina holds her hands like muffs over Marisol's ears. Probably a good idea. We don't need any more evil inclinations in that kid's head.

"I had no idea." Dad shakes his head. "I can't imagine."

"That must have been so traumatic for you, Bella. Probably still is." Christina's accent rolls off her tongue. "You should stay at home tomorrow and rest."

"Actually, I've been looking forward to shopping for quite a while." Is she just trying to ditch me so I'll stay at the house and bond with her sister?

"Just what she needs." Dad hands me the dessert menu. "You two will have a great time." He winks. "Just go easy on my friend MasterCard."

The New York sky is dark by the time we finally leave the restaurant. My dad hails a cab, and Marisol and Christina climb in.

"You sit in the back with the girls," he says. "I'll sit up front."

A breeze blows his brown hair, and I remember how handsome I thought he was when I was a little girl. I wanted to grow up and marry a man just like my daddy. He's still as cute as any Brad Pitt or George Clooney, but I don't want to end up hurt like my mom.

"Bella?" He holds the door.

I blink and pull myself out of my gloomy thoughts. "Yeah?"

"I'm sorry I haven't called lately."

I lift a shoulder. "It's okay." But really . . . it's not. It's just not. I want him to *want* to call me. I want him to wonder what his daughter is doing, how the math test went, what bands I'm listening to this week. Know the names of my friends. Know that I broke up with my boyfriend last week, and I'm still a jumbled mess.

On Saturday morning I wake up to the smell of pancakes and sausage. I follow the scent downstairs to the kitchen, where Luisa, my old nanny, stands at the stove.

I throw my hands around her voluminous waist and smack a big kiss on her cheek.

She chuckles and kisses me back. "Hello to you too, *niña*. I hear you are going shopping with Christina today, so I make you big breakfast." She jabs her thumb toward the living room. "That one only eats grapefruit and spinach drinks. That's no way to start a day."

"It's probably how they do it in the homeland." We share a laugh as I grab some orange juice.

"I heard that." The little munchkin lurks in the doorway.

"Good morning, Marisol." Her outfit is clearly high-end, and I think about the Target clothes I've been reduced to. I will not be jealous. I will not be jealous. *God, help me handle this girl*—without *showing her the new wrestling move Jake taught me.*

"Luisa, fix me some eggs," the little girl barks. "And hurry up."

My mouth forms an O. "You do *not* talk to Luisa that way. She's not a servant to be bossed around. She's family." *Real* family.

Marisol curls her pink lip. "You don't tell me what to do. I *live* here. You don't."

I charge toward her, gaining some good momentum, until Luisa steps between us. "Girls, stop." Luisa looks over Marisol's head, her brown eyes pleading with mine. "*Please* just drop it."

"No! She can't talk to you like that."

Luisa awkwardly pats Marisol on her black head. "Why don't you go in the living room and watch TV, eh? I will call when it is done. Will be ready soon."

"Hmph!" Marisol sticks her nose in the air, throws me one of *those* looks, and sashays out of the kitchen.

I just stare at my nanny. "What was—"

"Leave it alone, *mi corazón*. Is none of your business. Your Luisa is fine."

"I'm going to talk to Dad, and he'll—"

"No!" She blocks my exit. "You must not," she whispers. "Things are different here now, Bella. There is a new woman in the house, and things change. I will roll with it." A small smile spreads. "I will—how do you kids say it—be cool?"

"But if you'd just let me talk to Dad."

"No." She shakes her head. "Promise me you will not. Not now."

"Okay." I take a deep breath, and my pulse still beats a wild staccato. "But just for now. I don't know what's going on, but I'm not putting up with anyone treating you like that."

Her nod is brief. Then she waddles back to the stove and fixes my plate.

"Whoa, I can't eat that much," I say as she piles on a mound of food.

"Trust me." Luisa hands me my breakfast. "You're going to need it to keep up your strength."

~~~~~~~

I've been shopping for four hours, and not only have I not had a chance to buy anything, but Christina hasn't stopped once for food, drink, or tinkles. And I'm in desperate need of all three.

I stand in the third wedding boutique as my dad's girlfriend schmoozes with the designer. She tries to impress Enrique with my dad's history on the E! Channel and his famous clientele, and I have to turn away and get the eye roll out of my system.

"Bella, I have two bridesmaid dress possibilities here. Perhaps you should try on the floor samples, and Enrique and I will decide if they work." She pats the little man's bicep.

Christina delicately rests two outrageous frocks on my arms, and I clutch them to me.

"No, no, no." Her head shakes like a bobble. She unlocks the dresses from my grip. "Gently. These are not mere dresses. Enrique's designs are works of art. You would never hold a fine oil painting so tightly."

I chew on my gum to keep from saying something I'll regret, but at this rate, there's not enough Juicy Fruit in the whole state of New York to last me the entire day.

A few minutes later I stare in horror at my reflection in the mirror. I can't seem to make myself open the dressing room door.

"Bella, do you have a dress on yet?" Christina calls from the other side.

"Um . . . I can't seem to find the arm holes."

"There are not any," she says. "You wrap those two boas around your arms and neck. Isn't that genius?"

Genius? It looks like Enrique raided a six-year-old's dress-up stash and hot-glued a bunch of feathers together. I can't be seen in public in this.

"Come on out. We don't have all day." Christina is getting testier the longer we shop.

"If you say so." I ease open the door and step out.

Christina gasps and covers her mouth with both hands.

I see myself in the three-way mirror. "I know, right? It's—"

"Amazing!" She closes her eyes like she just bit into a truffle. "I think my bridesmaids will look stunning in this."

Enrique sniffs, his chest puffing. "It was all the rage at my show in Milan."

It's about to put me in a rage. "I think you should keep looking."

Christina's perfectly shaped brow lifts. "You don't like it?"

A feather piece slips off my shoulder, and I scramble to hold the dress together. "I couldn't even tell which end was up when I was putting it on."

Enrique sputters. "This is art! Who are you to tell me my dress is not anything but superior? I had Madonna contact me just yesterday for a gown fitting." He turns on Christina. "I told Taylor Swift to call back just so I could make this appointment with you. And *this* is how I'm treated?"

"No, Enrique. She didn't mean it." Christina sears me with her eyes.

"Yeah, I'm sorry. The dress is fine." Oh no. Feathers up my nose. "*Ah-ah-achoo!*" Tiny plumes go floating all around the three of us.

"Leave my shop!" Enrique yells. "You have two minutes to get her out of that dress and out of my store!" Remnants of the dress land on his bald head.

Christina pushes me toward the dressing room, hissing hurried instructions.

Ninety seconds later we stand on the corner in front of Enrique's House of Design.

"And stay out! You are forever banned from wearing my creations!" Enrique slams the door and locks it behind us.

"*Achoo!*" I hold a tissue to my nose and a giggle escapes.

"You're laughing?" Christina asks, her hands curled into fists. "I was just publicly humiliated and you're *laughing?*"

I can't help it. I turn my head as the laughter pushes tears out of my eyes.

"I am blacklisted, Bella."

"By a man who decorates with things I could find on the floor of a chicken house?"

Her chin inches higher. "Well, I guess it didn't take long before Oklahoma seeped into your blood. But in upper Manhattan, we care about style and cutting-edge fashion."

I need another piece of gum. "In *Oklahoma* they don't believe in wearing things that require health code inspections and a tetanus shot."

Christina opens her mouth, and I prepare for the verbal thrashing. "You little—" Her phone sings, startling both of us. She takes a deep breath and answers it. "Yes. Uh-huh." Her voice is low, controlled. The opposite of what it was seconds ago. "I see." She glances at me, then back to the ground. "Yes, Mr. Smith. I will check my calendar and get back with you immediately. Give me a few moments."

"Business?" I ask, as she slips her phone back into her purse.

"Yes." She pulls out a ten-dollar bill and presses it into my hand. "Why don't you run over to that coffee shop and get yourself something while I make a few calls. I think you and I need a little cool-down time anyway."

Though I'm mad at Christina, I could weep with relief for the break.

She points to another boutique down the street. "Meet me at that shop in ten minutes."

I all but run to the coffee shop.

God, why do I let that woman get me so riled up? But you know, in my defense, today I'm seeing a totally different side of her. I always knew she wasn't some cuddly, sweet thing. But now she's like Bridezilla . . . on steroids. Maybe I should talk to my dad and suggest a nice Vegas wedding. That feathery concoction would probably fit right in.

A bell chimes overhead as I step inside. I inhale the rich aroma . . . and breathe out the guilt.

The least I could do is go back and ask Christina if she wants anything. Surely even size zero talent agents need food.

I turn right back around and head in the direction I left her. She stands one door down from Enrique's, staring at the opposite end of the street.

I'm just about to call out to her.

Then a yellow taxi pulls up to the curb.

I stop in my tracks as a woman steps out, one long leg at a time. Her giant sunglasses cover her eyes, and a large brimmed hat sits low over her forehead.

Christina looks around, and I duck behind a minivan.

I will be the first to admit I was born with more than my fair share of nosiness. I mean, what's a girl to do? I figure if God gave it to me, then I should use it.

I step into the crowd on the sidewalk and weave my way closer to Christina and her acquaintance. The two talk, their faces intense. Their mannerisms rushed.

Ten feet away from them, a group of teenage girls stands in a huddle and chat. I inch toward them and hover on the outside of their circle. My ears perk at Christina's voice.

"I tried to come alone today. You think I wanted to bring her?"

Oh! How rude! I should have just let her have it and not wasted the gum.

The other woman's voice is so low, I can't even hear it.

"I said I'd work on it, and I am. These things take time. I'll give you the account numbers later."

The woman with the giant shades mutters something, but it's lost in the honking of a car.

Christina throws up her hands. "I haven't been blinded. I know what my job is, and I'll do it. We're partners."

She's a one-woman agenting operation. Partners in what?

"Nobody crosses us and gets away with it."

The girls beside me dissolve into loud giggles, covering up what the stranger says.

"Do you want something?"

I turn and one of the girls stares at me. Like I'm some sort of creepy lurker. Well, okay, I am. But whatever.

"Do I know you?" she asks.

I smile. "Well, you might've seen me and my family on TV recently. We were on a reality show, and—"

"That really wasn't a question." She backs up, her eyes suspicious. "That was code for 'go away.'" She pushes her friends forward. "It's just not safe on the streets anymore. Let's go girls."

"Bella?"

I jump at my name and find Christina behind me. I look around, but the stranger is gone.

"What are you doing?" Her voice has an edge sharper than a stiletto.

"I—I, um, came back to see if you wanted any coffee." I wave my hand toward the group of disappearing girls. "But then I ran into some old friends and stopped." To eavesdrop.

Christina studies me, her mouth in a firm line.

"Did you run into a friend too?" I ask.

Her eyes widen a fraction. So small you had to be looking for it—and I was. "No." Christina licks her glossy red lips. "I did not."

"Oh." Hunger has robbed me of all subtlety, so I push on. "I thought I saw you talking to someone."

Christina glances over her shoulder, in the direction the taxi went, before swiveling her razor eyes back to me. "You are mistaken. The only person I have a need to talk to is your father—to tell him how you've ruined my day."

chapter eight

On Monday morning, my friends sit around me in the courtyard, and I catch them up on my weekend craziness before the
first-hour bell.

"So did you tell your dad what Christina said to you?" Lindy
puts the finishing touches on an English assignment and sticks it
in her bag.

"No. My dad and I really aren't in a good place right now. I didn't
feel like I could talk to him with nothing to go on but my suspicions.
I just had this feeling like I should wait and collect more information first. But I know something is going on."

"I totally would've had to put that woman in her place." Ruthie
leans on my stepbrother Budge, her head on his shoulder, her bouffant hair covering up his smiling face.

"I'm surprised you didn't put her little sister in a choke hold
too," Matt says.

"Luisa asked me not to. But I can't get that out of my mind.
Christina is bad news, and I'm going to get to the bottom of it—the
sooner the better."

"I had a date last night."

All heads swivel to Lindy.

"What?" My voice scares off a nearby bird. "With who? And
why didn't you call me?"

She laughs, her skin turning a light shade of pink. "It was very last-minute. After church, Bo Blades called me and took me out for pizza and ice cream."

Ruthie sits up. "And you spent the rest of the evening staring into each other's eyes and were so caught up, you couldn't so much as text us." Her voice is a sigh.

"Um, no." Lindy's grin is as big as an Oklahoma cornfield. "But after he drove me back home, I called him. And then we just talked for hours."

"About what?" Matt scowls. "What could you possibly have to talk about after hanging out?"

Fire dances in Lindy's eyes. "Lots of things. I could talk to Bo for days and never get bored. Some guys know how to have a conversation with a girl."

Matt snorts. "Whatever. He probably just wanted your homework answers."

"Bo finds me interesting, for your information, Matt Sparks." Lindy gives her best friend her shoulder. "Not that it's any of your business." She turns her excited face back to me. "We're going to run together tonight."

"How romantic." Running. That's right up there with watching documentaries or double-dating with your parents. All definite dating *no's* in my book.

"I don't know about him, Lindy," Matt says. "You should really be on your guard."

"Why?" Lindy barks. "He's on the honor roll. He took us to state in track last year. He plays the guitar in his church. Um, which part of that do you find so shady? Because I must be too caught up in it all to see it."

I watch in fascination as Matt sputters for an answer. He is so jealous. I wonder if he even realizes it. This is perfect.

"Forget it. Have a nice *run*." Matt grabs his backpack and storms toward the double doors.

"Is anyone thinking what I'm thinking?" Ruthie asks, her voice giddy.

My eyes dart to Lindy. "That Matt Sparks is jealous?"

Ruthie frowns. "No, dudes. It's meatloaf day in the caf."

Luke completely ignores me in journalism. Which would be just fine except instead of harassing me, he's giving all his attention to Ashley Timmons.

The man stealer leans over his computer and laughs. "Oh, Luke. You're so funny!"

Behind my monitor, I mimic her girly giggles.

The girl tosses her angelic blonde hair and moves in closer. "You're so smart. That's exactly what my article needed. Thank you!"

Thank you! You're so smart! Ughhh. It's like I need to start taking antinausea medicine before I come to class now.

"Ashley, you're a great writer," Luke says. "You just have a few skills that need some polishing."

"Ohhh." I swear I see her bat her lashes. "Would you work with me? I'd love to get some tips for improving. Your articles are always so perfect."

Luke laughs. "Well, not perfect."

"No." Her hand lands on his bicep. "They totally are."

I'm out of my seat before my brain has time to register that my legs have moved. "For the good of the rest of the staff, could you guys please keep it down?"

Ashley sits up straighter. "We're just working here."

"Really?" I throw her a pert smile. "Is that what you call it?"

"Luke and I were simply talking. He was about to help me with some weak areas."

It's everything I can do not to blast her with a retort on her weak areas. "I need Luke to look over my article, so maybe this one-on-one tutoring could happen later?"

Ashley opens her glossy mouth, but Luke stops her. "It's okay, Ashley. I'll check your copy and prioritize the areas you need to focus on."

I don't miss her look of venom as she saunters back to her work station.

Luke turns the full force of his stormy gaze on me. "Don't you *ever* do that again."

"What? Stop you before you drooled in front of your entire staff?"

He takes a step closer. "Don't ever disrespect me when I'm working with a staff member."

"Since when does flirting fall under the category of work?"

Luke breathes out his nose. "I'm the editor, Bella. And helping my staff improve their writing is what I do. I was not flirting."

I can't stop my laugh. "Whatever."

"Why don't we take this outside?"

"Let's."

I follow him out into the hall where he takes off his glasses and looks down his nose. "I don't bring our personal life into the paper, so I expect you to be professional enough to do the same."

I point between us. "*We* have no personal life, if you remember."

"How could I forget?"

"You're hanging out with her." The words sound pitiful to my ears. Too late to take them back.

"I'm hanging out with her *and* her brother." Hard eyes stare back at me. "Ashley hasn't had time to get reacquainted with anyone yet. I'm strictly being a friend."

"Her methods of getting reacquainted are quite original. Aggressive even." I have got to let this go. I'm annoying myself.

"Obviously you don't have enough to do on the paper, so why don't you copyedit everyone's work for the next week?"

"So I hit a nerve, and to punish me, you're going to put me on grammar duty?"

He shrugs. "One of the joys of being in charge."

"That and flirting with your reporters?"

His head dips low as he plants one hand on the wall over my head. "You are so jealous."

"Nuh-uh." That sounded more mature in my head.

"You know what I think this is all about?"

"That Barbie doll three computers away from me?"

He slowly shakes his head. "It's about the fact that you miss me."

I gaze into his clear blue eyes. "You're right. I do miss you, Luke." I watch his arrogant mouth curve. "Like cramps."

"Still running scared." He pushes off the wall. "That's too bad."

"Or maybe I'm just completely over you." I pat his chest. "It's a bitter pill to swallow. I understand."

Luke's eyes drop to my mouth, then slowly trail back up. "Whatever you need to tell yourself to keep it safe, Bella. You do that." He reaches for the doorknob and glances over his shoulder. "But keep your insecurities out of my paper and don't ever attack one of my staff members again." He winks. "Oh, and better brush up on your commas."

~~~~~~~~~~~

"I don't know if I can do this." I stare into a mirror at my clown garb. I can hear cars pulling up outside the big top.

"It's too late now." Ruthie straightens my big red nose. "The circus is going to start in twenty minutes."

"This might've been my dumbest idea ever."

She fluffs her rainbow wig. "My dumbest idea was when I tried to ride my bicycle down the slide in my backyard."

I laugh. "How long ago was that?"

Ruthie rubs her rear. "Yesterday."

Cherry Fritz pops her head in the door. "You guys ready?" She looks so beautiful in her makeup and glitzy leotard. And here I am in clown paint, shoes made for a giant, and a wig that looks like it suffered a bad encounter with a lightning bolt.

"All you have to do is go into the crowd and meet and greet the little kids." She hands each one of us a bucket of suckers. "And Ruthie, don't throw them like you did when we practiced earlier. We don't want anyone losing an eye."

"Personally I think that would be kinda cool."

At Cherry's worried look, I try to reassure her. "She'll be careful. I'll watch her."

"Your cue to come out of the crowd is when the clown car starts honking. Remember, all you have to do is run down to the center and open the door."

"And we act like we're gonna shut it, but more of those clowns keep coming out." Ruthie acts like it's painful to recall her few instructions.

"Right. And that's it. You'll be great." Cherry gives each of us a brief hug. "Dolly's coming tonight and taking me for a burger afterward. Maybe you guys could come with us."

Raw hope brims in her eyes. How could I possibly say no? "Sounds fun." If I live through tonight and don't kill myself in these shoes. Or die of mortification.

Ten minutes later I'm on the top bleacher talking to a little boy who doesn't know whether to laugh or cry at my hair. "Here you go. Have fun!" I hand him a sucker and make my way down to the bottom row.

My eyes scan the arena, looking for anything unusual or suspicious. Two midgets and a pig in a tutu walk by. I probably need to narrow my definition of suspicious.

"Nice outfit."

I follow the voice to the ground. Luke.

"Though the makeup's a little heavy."

"What do you want, Luke? Or let me guess—you're here to work on *my* story and just stopped by to gloat." I stomp my giant foot. It tangles with the other shoe, and suddenly I'm airborne, headed for the ground. "Whoa!"

Luke steps up, and I land with an *oomph* in his arms.

Face redder than my bulbous nose, I pull my eyes up to his. "Um . . . thanks."

His arms stay locked around me as he lifts me off the bleacher and sets me on the ground.

"Glad to help."

"Hey, hands off the clown." Stewart Fritz stops, just as his dad takes the center of the ring. "You're needed in the sound booth." His eyes leer.

"Me?" I ask.

"No." He jerks his head toward Luke. "This guy." His eyes linger over my form for a moment too long before he walks away, snapping out commands into his headset.

"So I guess he's kind of like the producer?" Luke asks.

"Um . . . you're working here? Since when?"

"Same day you got hired." He shrugs. "I needed something else to fill my time."

"You work for the local paper."

"And now I work here."

I smell a rat. "Yeah, well, just stay out of my way."

He laughs. "Isn't that what the police are always saying to *you*?"

chapter nine

The work of a circus clown is never done.
During intermission, I rush backstage, careful not to trip over my giant shoes. Ruthie and I grab water bottles for those just finishing and pass out props for the next round of performers.

"Serena, I think your hair would look really good with a few strips of magenta," Ruthie tells the lady who does horse tricks. "Maybe tease it up another six inches or so. I have some hairspray that will shellac that stuff right in place. It's like cement."

I brush off her partner's jacket with a lint roller. "So, um ... anyone heard from Alfredo?"

The man's laugh is a mean staccato. "Yeah, right. Like we'd want to talk to the guy who killed Betty."

"But what if he didn't do it?"

He waves my idea away. "Look, kid, his prints are on the sword."

"The forensic results came back?"

"Yeah." He smirks. "Alfredo may be the master of magic, but even he can't make scientific evidence disappear."

"Besides," Serena says with a southern twang. "Alfredo was a dirty crook. He didn't really love Betty. Everyone saw right through him."

"What do you mean?" I ask.

Serena runs her hand over her tight updo. "Betty and Alfredo were the weirdest couple ever. And I'm telling you . . . something wasn't right from the beginning. At first he didn't even act like he liked her. It was like he was forcing himself to date her."

"Life does get lonely out here on the road. And it's not as if there're lots of options for chicks."

Serena smacks her partner. "You got something to say to me?"

He shakes his head. "Nah."

"Maybe you wouldn't get lonely if you'd clean up your messes in the trailer. If I didn't have to follow you around like I was your mother instead of your wife, then I'd have more time to spend with you. Eh?"

"But back to Alfredo and Betty—"

"Ladies and gentlemen!" Red Fritz announces the second half, and Serena and her husband run toward the center of the ring, still arguing over housekeeping.

I glance at Ruthie. "That was strange."

"Nah. Men are slobs. Nothing weird about that. She shouldn't have to put up with socks and tightie-whities on the floor."

"I meant what Serena said about Alfredo not acting as if he liked Betty."

"Not everyone is as kind and sensitive as my Budge."

I think of my stepbrother, who just this morning burped the entire *Star Wars* theme song at the breakfast table. "Yeah, he's just a dream of perfection."

"Did you ever get the flashlight you lost in Alfredo's trailer?"

I inwardly cringe. "No. Someone's always in there." But I've got to get it. Soon.

"Yeah, well, don't cut me out of that. I have a few ideas on how to get inside." Ruthie's eyes glisten. "It involves rope, WD-40, and some mace."

"You forgot one thing in that list."

"What?"

"A warrant for our arrest."

Fifteen minutes later I'm working the crowd and passing out a few balloons as Cherry and two others take to the trapeze. Just looking up there makes my stomach flop.

Feeling prickles of awareness, I look across the arena and find Luke watching me from the control booth. And Stewart Fritz. The two are talking, but both have their eyes trained in my direction. It's not every day a girl gets the attention of two boys. But in this case, one makes me so mad I want to throw him in the middle of one of Jake's wrestling matches. And the other . . . makes me want to douse myself in hand sanitizer.

Red Fritz announces his niece and the trapeze act, and a hush falls over the crowd as they watch them fly through the air.

In his usual garb of top hat and tuxedo jacket, Red walks off the floor and over to the control booth, his large stomach leading the way. He pulls his son aside and whispers near his ear. Luke keeps his eyes on the trapeze, adjusting the lighting and sound controls, but I know that boy. And I know he's doing everything he can to listen in to the father and son's conversation.

Red walks away, exiting out the main entrance. I'm passing out my last balloon when I see Stewart leave the same way.

"Hey, I want my balloon in the shape of a dog."

I pull my eyes from the door and down to the kid below me. "Sorry. That's all I have."

"I want a dog!" he yells.

I yank his balloon back, give it a few twists, and hand it to him again. "There you go." I have to follow Stewart and his dad. Something could be up.

"No!" the kid shrieks. "That looks like a four-leaf clover!"

"Well, then give it to your mom." I pat the little brat on the head. "She obviously needs the luck."

I maneuver my way back down the bleachers. Easier said than

done in a wig that keeps drooping in my eyes and shoes that could knock out an entire row.

The carnival rides flash their rainbow of lights as I step outside. Screams pierce the night as one of the roller coasters swings everyone upside down.

"Two tries for a dollar!" a guy calls out from the basketball toss.

Following a distance behind Stewart, I pass a row of food trailers and inhale the smell of hamburgers.

He hangs a left, disappearing for a moment from view. I keep a nonchalant look about me, as if I'm just taking in the sights and sounds of the carnival. Like it's every day I walk about the carnival grounds in full clown makeup.

When I hear Red Fritz's voice, I stop. The two guys stand talking by the Ferris wheel.

"What do you want?" Red asks. "I gotta close out the show."

I take a step back and hide behind the edge of another game trailer.

"Did you talk to Alfredo?"

"Yeah, I talked to him. Do you think I can't handle him, Stewart? I've got his situation under control. Has anyone seen Betty's stupid dog?"

"She's long gone."

"Well, if you find her, put her to work, then take care of her—permanently. Son, you do your job right, and this could all be yours." Red's voice is barely audible over the rising carnival noise.

I lean out a bit to get a better view.

Stewart laughs, a menacing sound that lifts the hair on the back of my neck. "Whatever it takes. This is a family business, after all. *Our* business."

Red spits on the ground and nods. "Gotta get back. I need to keep my eye on Cherry. She's been acting weird, and I don't trust her."

I gotta go! Move, clown feet. I lift the left, only to be jerked back by the right. I'm stuck! Omigosh. *God, help me!*

Their voices get nearer as I bend over, jerking on my shoe. It's snagged on some sort of canopy pin.

"Maybe I should have a talk with little cousin Cherry."

Oh no, I cannot explain my way out of this one, Jesus. How about a Harry Potter cloak of invisibility right now? Please help me.

I take a giant breath and pull with all my might. Aughhh!

Too late. Two sets of feet appear.

"What do you think you're doing?" Red Fritz demands.

From my stooped position, I lift my eyes. "Um . . . I was just—"

"Waiting for me."

I jerk upright as Luke appears at my back. He sends me a warm smile and curls an arm around my shoulder. "Our first date was at the county fair. And it was on a Ferris wheel just like this that I knew I had found someone special. I thought we'd take a ride tonight and celebrate old times." Luke rushes on before Red can interrupt. "It's my break time."

Oh, he is so full of bull.

And I couldn't be more grateful.

"You shouldn't be walking around out here like this," Stewart says to me. "Alone and all. You never know what might get a pretty thing like you."

"Thanks." Ick.

A short man in a dirty Metallica T-shirt limps over to the Ferris wheel control. "Oh . . . um, hey, boss."

Red Fritz pierces him with an icy glare. "What have I told you about leaving your ride?"

Luke takes the opportunity to drop his keys to the ground. "Oops."

"I know, boss. I, um, had to go to the bathroom real bad and there wasn't anyone around to cover."

Luke yanks on my shoe, and I find freedom. *Thank you, Lord. I totally owe you one.*

Stewart turns his attention back to me as Luke picks up his keys. "How long had you been standing there—waiting?"

"Just got here, Stewart." My voice rises an octave. My heart still thunders like a wild stallion in my chest. "Yep, just found the Ferris wheel."

"I could give you a ride. On the house." The short man attempts a smile for Red. "If that's okay. Then I'll shut it down for the night."

Stewart jerks his head toward Luke. "Is this your boyfriend?"

Luke pulls me to his chest. "It's complicated. We're still working out some kinks." His hand digs into my rib cage. "Right, Bella?"

"Right." Get me out of here. "Just can't seem to stay away from each other." I pat his chest.

"Then by all means, take a romantic spin around a few times." Stewart's eyes have me snuggling even closer to Luke. "I'd hate to get in the way of true love."

"No, that's okay." I look up at the tall ride and swallow. "We're just going to go back to the big top and finish up."

"Nonsense." Red smiles, and I notice a few back teeth missing. "Fire her up, Will. Bella here is the one who found Betty. Stabbed. Dead." His tongue peeks out as he punctuates each word. "I guess the least we can do is give her and her boyfriend a ride."

"He's not really my—"

"Great." Luke pulls me toward the entry ramp. "Thank you." He presses a kiss to my cheek as we walk. "Play along or we both lose our jobs."

"I heard them talking," I say through gritted teeth.

Luke grins and waves to the three carnival workers. "Imagine that. You eavesdropping."

Will runs up ahead of us and holds open the door to the seat. "Hop in."

I freeze in my steps and feel Luke's hand pressed to my back. "Um, maybe we could do this another night. I should get back to the circus."

Luke's tone is pseudo-friendly. "But Red and Stewart are watching us to make sure we get that ride we wanted."

I step one long shoe into the cart and take a deep gulping breath. "Okay. Okay." I can do it. But if this thing stops at the top and dumps me out onto the cold, hard concrete, I'm going to be so mad.

I fumble my way into the seat and plaster my body as close to the wall of the cart as I can get.

Luke throws an arm around me again and pulls me close. "Eyes are watching us," he says under his breath.

The man named Will locks and secures us in, then slaps the cart. "Here we go! You ready? This one goes pretty high!"

"Oh. Great." Why couldn't I have eavesdropped near a kiddie ride? A little choo-choo train would've been nice.

Will runs back to his post and yanks on a lever. The entire ride chugs and shivers.

"Try to look like you're not repulsed by my very presence," Luke says.

"Uh-huh."

"Lean my way."

"I'm good."

He lets out a huffing breath. "Bella, you're—" I watch his face change from frustrated to bemused. "It's not me, is it?"

"Nuh-uh."

I clutch the handlebars until I can feel my nails tear into skin. Luke's chest shakes with his laughter.

"This is not funny," I hiss. "What kind of dumb story was that? We met at the county fair?" We're going up. So not good. I want my mom. And a parachute.

"Are you afraid of heights?"

"No." Just rides that *involve* heights.

"Then why are your eyes closed?"

"I'm praying?"

His laugh is softer this time. "Bella, they're watching us. I don't know why, but they are. I'm pretty sure Stewart Fritz is considering carving out some time in his schedule to stalk you, so if you could help out in any way, that would be great."

"What do you want me to do?" My voice is whinier than Robbie's when he gets a Superman video taken away.

"Just lean in my way."

I pull my shoulder off the wall and put my weight on Luke. He takes my hand in his and holds it tight. "You're shaking."

"Your powers of deduction are red-hot tonight, Chief."

"They're still watching. I don't think they believe you came out here to meet me."

I tuck my head into the space beneath his shoulder and study the fairy tale motif on the ride. "How did you know where I was?" Okay, seriously. We're at the top now. I squeeze my eyes shut again.

"I followed you." His chest rumbles where my ear is pressed. "I knew exactly what you were up to. And if we're not careful, they will too."

"They want Betty's dog for some reason—and not for the show. Red told Stewart to put her to work, then kill her. What kind of people do that?"

"Not nice ones. That's why I don't want you messing around here. Bel, open your eyes. You look like you're a flight risk. Can't you dig down deep and find some acting skills in there? Just get your mind off how high we are."

"Just get my mind off it?" I squeak. "How?"

Luke leans his head down, turning his body slightly. "Remember when we were chased by some football players out at the lake last fall? Remember our plan B?"

My eyes pop open just in time to see Luke's face hover over mine. His smile is slow and lazy.

"Plan B?"

He nods. "Just for the sake of our cover, you understand."

"But we're broken up."

"Break over." His nose brushes mine. "Kiss me like you mean it."

I open my mouth to protest, but his lips capture mine. His arms pull me tight. I'm vaguely aware of Will hooting in the background. I sigh and just give in, letting his warmth surround me. He changes the angle of the kiss, and I follow. My hands work their way up his neck to his face, and all visions of plunging to my death fade away.

Luke pulls back, his eyes searching mine. "Still scared?"

Of him or the Ferris wheel? "Yes."

My heart stutters at his roguish grin. "Then we should continue"—he kisses each cheek—"for the cause."

"For the cause." I thread my fingers through his dark hair, loving the way it curls slightly at the ends.

Luke's head lowers, his mouth a breath away from mine. His eyes roam over my face, my hair . . . the ground below?

"They're gone." He drops me so fast, my head smacks the back of the seat. "Stop the ride, please," he calls.

I sit up straight, mentally counting to five.

"You okay?"

I straighten my wig. "Perfect. You?"

Some of the arrogance leaves his face. "You were a pretty good sport."

"Sometimes we do what has to be done." I sound like my grandmother.

Luke brushes a piece of rainbow fuzz from my cheek. "Admit it, you miss me."

I move in close. Closer. "Luke?"

"Yeah?" He draws out the word, leaning in.

"You have clown lipstick on your face."

chapter ten

Any peace I found in my Wednesday morning quiet time has long since evaporated.

"Luke, I would have never thought to put that sentence there. It makes the article so much better!"

Ashley Timmons sits right next to our editor and coos over every single thing he says like it's the winning number to the Lotto. You know, just because I don't want to date the guy doesn't mean that I want to see other girls throw themselves at him. Especially her. It's so unclassy. I mean, where's her self-respect? Her dignity? Her—okay, if she doesn't take her hands off his shoulder, I'm going to grab that halo of blonde hair and yank until I see roots.

"I think that would be a great idea, Ashley," Luke says, snapping me out of my dismal thoughts. "And I know just the person to help you with it." He swivels in his seat to face me. "Bella? Would you come over here please?"

I watch Ashley's face fall as I approach. "Yes?"

"I was telling Ashley about the carnival, and she wants to do a feature on Cherry Fritz."

"Uh-huh." *How much did you tell her? Did you mention your lips were locked with mine on the Ferris wheel? Because I'd hate to dampen her little crush.*

Luke rolls up his shirt sleeves on forearms tanned from soccer.

"Since you know Cherry better than I do, I want you to introduce Ashley to her tomorrow night before the show."

"Yeah, Bella." Ashley smiles prettily. "I hear you work as a clown. That must be a little embarrassing to have the whole town see you like that."

"Luke didn't seem to mind Monday night." I send him a saucy wink. "I suppose I could introduce you to Cherry. She's kind of a private girl, though. And she's been through a lot lately, so, you know, go easy on her."

Ashley's laugh is light and airy. "That's cute—your advice. I've been working on a newspaper staff for three years and won five national awards." Her smile never falters. "You've been writing for how long?"

Lord, you're going to want to move her out of my way, for the sake of her health and general well-being. "I guess I shot up in the ranks at the *Truman High Tribune* so fast, it seems like I've done it forever. At least that's what our advisor, Mr. Holman, says." *Take that, you she-devil.*

"And before coming to Truman, Bella had a regular gossip column at her old school," Luke says, his face a mask of innocence.

"*Advice* column," I spit out. "And helping hundreds of girls with their problems did prepare me for a lot of things—like writing." I lift a haughty brow. "And learning to read people. I can pretty much size up a person in minutes."

Ashley holds her assignment to her chest. "Luke, I'll see you at my house after school." Her smile is total movie star seductress. "Kyle said to tell you he'd be a little late getting there for your afternoon run."

Oh, and I'll bet you can think of all sorts of things to pass the time. "Speaking of super fun get-togethers," I say to him, "Dolly wanted me to invite you to her house tonight after church. She's having a birthday party for Cherry and wants anyone who can make it to be there." I glance at Journalist Barbie. "But if you have other things to do—"

"I'll be there." His eyes bore into mine. "In fact, Ashley, what are you doing later this evening?"

What is he thinking? "I believe Dolly wants Cherry to be surrounded by friends and family only." And not girls with fangs.

"It would be the perfect place for Ashley to interview Cherry."

"Another great idea!" Ashley claps her hands. "I would love to come. Luke, pick me up at seven fifteen." She gives him a playful punch in the shoulder. "You're going to love my new dress." She saunters away, and I barely resist the urge to stick my finger down my throat and make those mature little gagging noises.

"It's strictly business," he says.

"I didn't say a word." I look down at my editor.

"Just remember—you're the one who broke it off."

Pull yourself together, Bella. "And I meant it. I'm sorry your pride is still so wounded." I pat his back. "It will heal in time. At least that's what all the boys tell me."

Luke stands up to his full six feet. He takes off his glasses, giving me the full effect of his ocean-blue eyes. "All those boys, huh?"

"Right." I nod. "A whole line of them. I could fill a notebook with all the hearts I've left broken."

His grin is tigerlike. "There's been Hunter who, I will remind you, cheated. Oh, and lied to you repeatedly. And then there's been me, who you're afraid will treat you like Hunter. You remember me, right? The guy who kissed you on the Ferris wheel last night?"

I struggle to swim through the spell Luke's weaving and find something coherent to say. "Oh . . ." I swallow. "Yeah?"

"Yep."

No, I will deflect his über-hot words. Time to fight dirty. Time to fight with sass. "Actually, I just remember feeling pukey on that ride." I pause to consider. "Or was it your attempt at a kiss? I believe it was."

"You don't believe that for a second." He leans closer to me. "I know exactly what you do when you're lying. You give yourself away every time."

"I don't have any idea what you're talking about, and it offends me that you would suggest I am anything but the very virtue of honesty." At least fifty percent of the time.

"You twist your hair." He reaches out and stills my hand, my fingers curled around my locks.

I wrench my hand back. "I twirl my hair because you make me nervous—it's hard to act all friendly to you when you're obviously still not over me."

He tosses his dark head back and laughs. "Oh, but don't you wonder, Bella?" The air sizzles around him. "Ashley and I will see you tonight. We can't wait."

After church, I ride to Dolly's with Budge and Ruthie. My mom, who gets starry-eyed anytime there's a party to organize, is already out there, no doubt making sure every detail is just perfect. She's been really distracted lately, so having Cherry's birthday to plan has been just what she needed.

"Youth was awesome tonight, wasn't it?" Ruthie asks from the front of Budge's hearse. Yes, my stepbrother drives a hearse, as in a vehicle formerly used to haul dead folks to their final earthly destination. But it is handy for cramming in lots of people, which we're doing tonight.

I stare out the window and watch a dark, rainy Truman pass by. "It was okay."

"I thought it was interesting too. Dude, why didn't you tell me youth group was so good? I would've gone a long time ago." Budge eyes me in his rearview. "I've totally been missing out on Little Debbies and mochas."

"It's true." Ruthie skips a song on Budge's screamo CD. "Nights we have Oatmeal Cream Pies seem to be especially inspirational. What didn't you like about it, Bel?"

"I don't know. I guess my mind was just on other things. It seemed kind of irrelevant to me."

"Um, it was about trusting God." Ruthie bobs her blue hair to the music. "I think that pretty much covers everyone. Besides, you got some issues."

"I do not."

"Yeah. I knew it from the first time I met you."

"Right back at you." The first time Ruthie introduced herself, she asked me to find out who was passing around pics of her making out with someone who was *not* her boyfriend, and I agreed just so she wouldn't beat me up.

"Nah, I mean for real. You don't trust anyone." Ruthie nudges my stepbrother. "Budgie, did you know Bella's also afraid of carnival rides?"

He sighs and turns into Matt Sparks's driveway. "Add that to the list of her insecurities."

"My—my—what?" I should've walked. Ten miles in the rain wouldn't have been that hard. "You've had your girlfriend a matter of weeks, Budge, so I don't think that makes you any expert. I'm merely a cautious person, as life has taught me that—"

"Dude, I love this song." Budge cranks it up and plays drums on the steering wheel.

"Me too!" And Ruthie sings the chorus to "Lizards: They're Not Just For Breakfast Anymore."

At Budge's honk, Matt runs out of the house. He climbs in the back, next to me.

"Welcome to the Death Mobile," I say. "Let's go pick up Lindy and Bo."

"What?" Matt snaps his seatbelt. "Bo Blades is coming?"

"I heard they went out Friday night—after the track meet." Ruthie wiggles her eyebrows. "They've been seeing each other like a week." She sighs and grabs Budge's arm. "Do you remember our week-a-versary?"

"Do I ever." He pats her knee and stops at a four-way. "I took you to the Dairy Barn for ninety-nine-cent burger night. Seems like it was just yesterday."

"It was last month!" This romance crap is about to make me yak all over myself. "Can we just talk about something else?"

"I agree." Beside me Matt fumes. "People just rush into relationships these days. What happened to being friends and taking things slow?"

"Budgie's pretty much my BFF," Ruthie says. "And believe me, we're taking things slow. Right, poopsie bear?"

He stops in front of Lindy's house. "Sure thing, muffin top. Nothing but first base for us."

Ruthie cranks around in her seat. "No homeruns in this ballgame of love."

"Oh my gosh, stop! Ew!" I shove open my door and jump out so Lindy can get in the seats behind me.

"Hey, guys!" Lindy sails out of her house, pulling a smiling Bo Blades by the hand. "Bye, Dad! And I promise I won't break curfew tonight."

"What?" I hear Matt mutter. "She broke her curfew?"

"Very roomy." Bo stares in wonder at the hearse as he climbs in.

Budge grins. "Just one of the many perks."

"Plus a nice, chemical pine smell." Ruthie inhales. "It's just like I'm in a fake forest."

"Nothing but the best for my girl."

I sink into my seat as we back out, listening to both couples whisper and giggle.

I roll my eyes. "I should have taken my own car."

"I wish you had," Matt mumbles. "I would have paid you to run me over."

I can't help but laugh. "Just ten more minutes and we'll be there." I nudge him with my elbow. "Are you okay?"

"Yeah. Fine. Great." His mouth is grim as he glances back at Lindy, absorbed in her own world with Bo. "I guess I just miss my best friend."

chapter eleven

The sight of Dolly's house never fails to make me smile. As a side-hobby, my mom's friend works at Sugar's Diner downtown by day. But in her off-time she's a champion horse breeder, which has paid for the giant sprawl of a home and her many acres.

"Come on in before you get wet!" Dolly's big eighties bangs blow in the warm breeze as she holds open the door. "Cherry's in the kitchen." Dolly leans close to my ear. "She's a little nervous about not really knowing everyone that well, so anything you can do to perk her up would be appreciated."

"No problem. The food smells good." I follow the scent into the kitchen and give Cherry a side hug. "What are we having?"

"Whatever Mickey Patrick is fixing," she says, gesturing to the back door with a carrot stick. "He's grilling."

My mom stands next to the sink, and I kiss her on the cheek and begin putting ice in cups.

I turn my curious stare to Dolly. She and her ex-husband have been hanging out some in the last few months. Maybe more than I thought. "Mickey's here?"

"Yeah." Dolly shrugs it off. "Now that Jake's made the big time, Mickey's not training as much. He's focusing more on managing."

"I wish Jake could've been here tonight. His plane got delayed in

Kansas City." My mom drops some flowers into a vase, then carries it into the giant dining room.

"Anyway," Dolly says, "I had a problem with the grill, so Mickey came over to help."

I bump my hip into Dolly's. "Lighting your grill—is that what you kids call it these days?"

She laughs and swats me with a towel. "I have to go check on the burgers."

"So, Cherry, are you having a good birthday?" I ask.

Her smile almost meets her eyes. "Yeah. The carnival family gave me a party earlier today. So it's just Dolly and you guys tonight."

"I know you're missing Betty today—and your parents." I hug her again. "I'll introduce you to some people. If you're going to be staying in Truman, you need some friends." Heaven knows I did.

"What I wish I had is Peg."

"Who?"

"Betty's dog." Her eyes tear up. "I just think about her out there alone without me or Betty." She sniffs. "I mean, what if she's hurt? Or hungry? What if someone took her?"

"I'm sure she's okay." I pat her arm and try not to twirl my hair.

"Why hasn't she come back, then?"

I don't know, but it's a good thing she hasn't. How do I tell the girl that her uncle and cousin want to kill her dog? "Are you doing okay out here at Dolly's?"

"Yes." Cherry pours herself a Dr Pepper and takes a long drink. "It's been nice. Dolly's so cool—it's like we've known each other forever. She—she makes me miss my mom. But I also feel bad for imposing on her like this because we *haven't* known each other forever. I'm a distant cousin. She's even taken over my homeschooling. And now she says she's taking a leave of absence from Sugar's."

"The diner is just her social time. Something to do to fill her hours." Dolly makes a small fortune with her horse farm. "Cherry, you know Dolly and Mickey had two girls a long time ago. They were killed in a wreck."

"I didn't know."

I refill her cup. "So you being here—it's not an imposition to her. In fact, I'd say it was God helping her out."

"Why?"

"Because she's been so lonely. I know she loves having you here."

Cherry looks around, then grins. "I have the best bedroom. It's huge! And it's all mine."

I laugh. "And don't forget the pool!"

"You'll have to come over one day and swim with me. When we're not working, that is."

"Um, speaking of work." A thousand questions rush through my mind. "What did you think about Alfredo?"

She shakes her head. "I don't know. I thought I liked him. At first I didn't—at least not for Betty. It was all so sudden, and they just jumped into this relationship. I couldn't believe how fast they moved. But then he really grew on me when I saw how happy Betty was. She told me Alfredo was talking marriage."

"Did you ever hear Alfredo mention it?"

"No. But he seemed to really like her—toward the end. So it was pretty shocking when . . . well, when—"

I finish the thought. "He killed her."

"Yeah. I still can't believe it."

"What if he didn't do it?" I ask, moving closer.

"It was his sword. His fingerprints. People heard them fighting. Still, it doesn't seem like him at all . . . I don't want to believe he did it."

"Had you noticed Betty not getting along with anyone else lately? You mentioned that she didn't exactly see eye to eye with Red."

"Yeah, but that sums up everyone. Nobody gets along with Red."

Cherry sputters on her drink. "Do you think Red did it?"

"No!" I say quickly. "I mean, I don't know. Right now everyone seems kind of suspect to me. I just don't think Alfredo and Betty's story adds up."

"It's true no one trusts Red—or Stewart." Cherry's voice dips to a whisper. "Including me."

"Was there anything special about Betty's dog?"

She shakes her head at my weird question. "Peg was the best. She jumped through hoops and learned all of Betty's routines really quickly. A really smart dog. I guess she knew a lot of commands. Why do you ask?"

"No reason. But if you see anything weird, let me know."

"Bella, I'm thirteen and I work in a circus. All I know is weird."

Cherry and I walk to the living room together, just in time to see the front door swing open and a herd of giants stampede the foyer.

"We heard there was a party here!" Jake breaks through the pack, his eyes landing on my mom. "Thought we'd stop by."

Mom squeals as he picks her up and twirls her around. "What are you doing here?" She looks beyond Jake's shoulder to his friends. "*All* of you."

Jake sets Mom down, his large hands remaining on her shoulders. "I was missing you. There were all these traffic delays due to the weather, and our flight got cancelled. The next one to Dallas was tomorrow morning, so we just got a car and drove here."

Mom laughs as Jake kisses her cheek. "So where is everyone staying?"

Robbie comes bolting through in his red Superman cape and hugs his dad's leg. "With us! Can they stay with us?"

"We shouldn't be too much of a problem, Mrs. Finley. The Truman Inn is booked." A man taller than the doorway holds out a hand. "Vicious Viper—but you can just call me Larry."

The other six men introduce themselves.

"Of course you can stay with us." Mom hugs Jake. "I'd hate to disappoint Robbie."

Jake hoists his son into his arms.

"Daddy, I taped this great documentary we can watch together. It's called *Commodities and Stocks in a Bear Market*."

"Maybe next week, Robbie. I'm only in for tonight, okay?"

"Oh." Robbie's smile melts. "Yeah, okay. I guess Jillian can watch it with me."

Mom sweeps his hair from his eyes. "I'd love to, sweetie." She glances at her husband once more. "I have work to do." And she walks away.

The doorbell rings again, and I run to answer it.

"Luke."

"Hello, Bella." He has the nerve to stand there smiling with Ashley Timmons by his side.

"Sorry we're late," she gushes. "We got to talking and lost track of time."

Shoot me now. I cannot watch her drape herself all over him the entire night. "I hope Luke didn't bore you with his favorite topic of ballet. That boy can talk pirouettes and tutus all night. Or his other favorite pastime—mud wrestling."

"Nice." Luke's jaw is taut as he pulls an uncertain Ashley past me to join the crowd.

"Have a good time now!"

An hour and a half later I'm sitting in a lounge chair by the pool with everyone else. I'm stuffed with cake and amazed at the princess theme my mom threw together at the last minute. There are lily pads floating in the pool, tiny pink lights in every visible shrub, and I can see Cherry's tiara sparkling from here. I'd say the birthday party was a success.

At least for Cherry.

As for me, I've spent the entire evening watching couples—Budge and Ruthie, Lindy and Bo, and now Ashley and Luke. Seriously, if that girl scoots any closer to him, they'll be Siamese twins. Even Mickey Patrick hasn't left Dolly's side. I don't know if they're seeing each other again, but the war seems to be over. I've also been working overtime keeping Ashley away from Cherry. I've intercepted her, like, five times. This is Cherry's birthday. She doesn't need to be hassled by an obnoxious reporter. Unless it's me.

Deciding I'm about ready to call it a night, I gather up some plates and make my way across the yard toward the back door of the kitchen.

"Jake, you saw your son's face."

I stop at my mom's voice. She and Jake stand on the deck, the porch light spilling over her worried features.

"I'm here tonight, aren't I? Instead of sitting in that airport, I came here to be with you and the kids. This is overwhelming to me too. Do you think I like being gone this much?"

"Whether you like it or not doesn't change the fact that this family is suffering. I don't enjoy being the mother *and* father here. How do you think your sons feel when I have to be the disciplinarian? Just like last weekend—Budge stayed up for forty-eight hours straight playing some stupid video game that had just come out. Guess who had to pull the plug on that and be the bad guy?"

"We'll talk about this later."

"When?"

"When I have time to deal with it."

My mom shakes her head. "This family deserves more than visits between layovers. Your *later* might be too late."

chapter twelve

Where else would any fun-loving American teenage girl be on a Friday night? Probably at the mall or the movies. But me? I'm poised over a dunk tank.

"Nobody's knocked you down yet, boss. How awesome is that?" Ruthie tosses a baseball in the air and catches it. "Plus we're getting some extra dough working a few additional hours before the show."

"Yeah, a brilliant idea."

"Dude, I need all the money I can get. I'm graduating next month, you know."

I swing my legs and look on with dread as I see Luke Sullivan getting out of his 4Runner in the parking lot. Of course he would be here early. "And why is it I'm up here instead of you?" I ask my friend.

"Because I have to be all ready for my unicycling debut tonight."

"Your what?" I watch as Luke stops to talk to the roller-coaster operator, making his way closer to us.

Ruthie clutches the ball to her chest. "I just wasn't feeling personally fulfilled with our basic clown work. I needed more. I wanted to feel challenged, alive, and—"

"In the spotlight?"

"I happen to have a gift to share with the world." She stuffs a piece of stray hair back into her wild updo. Gone is the neon blue, replaced with an eye-blinking shade of violet.

"So you're going to ride your unicycle around for a few minutes?"

"Ride it around?" Ruthie harrumphs. "What I do is called art. I will be performing a unicycle ballet I choreographed myself. I call it 'Love Is Squishy.'"

I'm spared the chance to comment as Luke appears. "Hello, ladies."

His casual tone sends Ruthie to chatting. But when he glances at me, I see something lurking beneath that's about as friendly as a derailed coaster.

"Ruthie, will you give me a minute with Bella?" His steel eyes find mine. "I need to talk to her about some homework."

Homework? Not unless the assignment is wringing my neck.

"Sure thing." Ruthie sets the ball down. "I have some important performance preparations to tend to anyway." She takes off in the direction of the nearest funnel cake trailer.

"Dunk tank?" Luke steps closer until he's standing right in front of me. "Anything for the job, huh, Bella?"

"That's your motto—hanging out with Ashley. It's all about the job, right?" I swing my legs, shrug, and study my nails.

Luke reaches through the fence between us and captures a foot. "Want to tell me why you blew off her attempts to talk to Cherry Wednesday night?"

"I don't believe I like your surly tone. So no." I jerk my foot back. "I don't think I do."

"The *Tribune* is still my paper, and I'm still your editor."

"You know, I was going to get that tattooed on my butt, but you say it so many times, I've decided to go with something more original."

A muscle in his jaw ticks. "It's one thing to disrespect me. But it's another to get in the way of one of my staff members' work."

"Disrespect *you?*" I toss my head back and laugh. "If anyone's been disrespected here, buddy, it's me. That girl kisses you, you protest your innocence, but yet you're with her all the time—as *friends.* Then you rip the carnival feature from me—something I was totally wrapped up in—only to hand over part of it to your new girlfriend!"

He lifts his head. "I'm letting her do an interview with Cherry. Not a full-blown series on the Fritz Family Carnival." Luke's voice dips. "And Wednesday night you blocked every attempt Ashley made to speak to Cherry."

"It was the girl's birthday. It wasn't the time or the place to ask her twenty questions about her lonely life as a trapeze performer or how she felt about losing yet another person in her life."

"You know what I think?" He leans onto the chain link fence cage around me, his tan fingers curling around the wire. "I think you're so eaten up with jealousy, you can't even see straight."

"I think you're beating a dead horse. A bloated, maggoty, dead horse. We are clearly so over. So if you want to date—"

"Journalist Barbie." He throws my words back at me with a slow grin.

"If you want to date the stinking queen of England, I don't care. Just don't expect me to do her any favors. Ashley Timmons can figure out her own way to talk to Cherry."

"Number one, while the queen's orthopedic shoes are a huge turn-on, she travels too much to truly be there for me." He picks up a ball and tosses it in one hand. "And number two, I am telling you that you better figure out a way to cool it with Ashley."

"Or?"

He lopes away, his dark jeans slung low over his hips. "Or I'll cool it for you."

I catch the wicked gleam in his eye and go on alert. "Oh no you don't. You wouldn't!"

And with lightning speed, a smiling Luke Sullivan pivots and throws a fastball right toward the bull's-eye.

~~~~~~~~

I stand shivering outside the trailers, cursing Luke Sullivan and thanking God for the millionth time I didn't wear a white shirt today.

Well, maybe my luck just changed. I spy one of Alfredo's old roommates weaving through the trailers, talking to Luigi, one of the ticket takers. It's time to reclaim my flashlight—if it's not too late already.

"Hey, you're Johnny, right?" I call out.

The small man just grunts, but he stops.

"You were really great last night—balancing like you did on that horse. I've never seen anything like that."

His cheeks turn as pink as a cherry limeade.

"I got roped into dunk-tank duty and really came unprepared. I wondered if I could maybe borrow your hair dryer?" I twist my long hair into a rope and water drips onto the ground.

"I guess my roomie has one you can use." He steps toward his trailer when a voice stops us both.

"I don't think that's such a good idea."

I turn around and find Stewart eyeing my wet form.

No! It's a great idea. I have *got* to get back into that trailer.

Stewart runs a hand over his prickly goatee. "If you have to be in anyone's sleeping quarters, I'd prefer it be a member of management's." He crooks a skinny finger. "Follow me. You can dry off in my trailer."

How in the world am I going to get that flashlight back? "Um... okay. But I think I'll run and get Ruthie to keep me company."

"She's rehearsing. Can't bother her now."

Fine. Assuming Red's not in there, this will give me a chance to search the Fritzes' trailer. Praying for protection from sheer creepiness, I follow Stewart to his home on wheels, looking behind me for Ruthie the entire way. But no help comes.

"After you, my lady." He opens the door with one hand and sweeps his other before him like some sort of gallant duke.

I step inside, my nostrils flaring at the smell of stale smoke and burnt microwave popcorn.

"It's not much, but it's home." He brushes past me, taking me through the office space into the living quarters. "Would you like something to drink? A Coke? Water? A beer?"

"I'm seventeen."

Stewart's laugh reminds me of a hyena. "I won't tell if you won't."

"You know, I think my hair's dry enough. And I'll just borrow a towel from one of the ladies."

"No way." He smiles, and I try not to shudder again. "Whatever you want, it's yours."

I wind my purse strap around my hands. In case I need to launch a good swing toward Stewart's head.

"Thanks," I say as he sets a towel and blow dryer on the tiny counter of the bathroom. He moves out, so I can step in. I pick up the beige towel and blot my neck and arms, trying to ignore his lurky presence.

"You have beautiful hair." He stands right there, an arm braced in the doorway. "You know, Bella, circus life can be a lot of fun. I could—"

"Hey, Stewart, you must be really busy." *Being a full-time perv and all.* "Don't let me keep you. I know how important you are around here."

He moves forward until he's blocking the door, crowding out any space left in the bathroom. I reach for a hand mirror. I am the stepdaughter of Captain Iron Jack, wrestling phenomenon, and I know how to use this thing for more than checking my lipstick.

"I know you've got that boyfriend, Bella. But word is you two are having problems." Stewart leans back against the wall, with mere inches between us. "So any time you want to stay after the show and get a few free rides on the Ferris wheel, you let me know. There are all kinds of privileges of dating a carnival manager."

Knock! Knock!

I sag with relief when the door flings open.

"Stewart?" A voice calls.

"Sounds like someone needs you." And it sure isn't me.

I pop my head out to see Luke standing in the office. His eyes flit to me, then to Red Fritz's son.

"There's a problem with one of the horses. The trainer said he needs you immediately."

Stewart's lazy gaze travels back to me. "I'm sorry. I guess we'll have to pick up our conversation later. But you get all nice and pretty in here, and I'll see you after the show." He slides out of the bathroom, his chest puffing as he passes Luke. "Don't you have work to do?"

When Stewart shuts the door behind him, my shoulders all but fall to the floor in relief.

"What in the *heck* do you think you're doing?" Luke demands. "Never be alone with that guy. Are you crazy?"

"He wasn't going to hurt me. Besides, I wanted to peek around in here."

"Oh, I'm sure he has plenty to show you." Luke shoves his fingers through his hair. "When I couldn't find you and someone told me they saw you going in here with Stewart—" He shakes his head. "You have no idea."

"I'm not even speaking to you, so you can just leave now."

"Not without you."

Had he not dunked me in the tank an hour ago, I might've found that hot. "Look, I have things to do here."

"Like what?"

"I have hair to fix and drawers to open." I wave my hand. "So unless you're going to help, get out."

Luke looks back over his shoulder toward the door. "What are we looking for?"

I make quick work of drying my hair, then join Luke in the office, where he sits at a computer.

"See anything?" I open a file drawer and thumb through each one, checking the window for anybody walking by.

"No suspicious e-mails that I can find. Though Red seems to have an online girlfriend."

"I'm sure the top hat is a huge turn-on." I move on to the few folders and files on the desk. Bills. Check stubs. "Wait. What is this?" I flip through a giant-sized checkbook.

"It's Red's pay system. Looks like he still writes his checks by hand."

Curious to see how much Betty was paid, I flip back a month. "That's strange. Betty had been with the circus longer, but Alfredo made quite a bit more."

Luke stands near and peers over my shoulder. "Looks like Alfredo made more than everyone." His hand snakes around me as he runs a finger down the book.

Between Luke's light cologne and the fear of getting caught, my heart beats loudly enough to scare the circus animals. I flip through the pay book backward. "Look—in November Alfredo got paid less than Betty and most of the others. But by December, his check got a major bump."

Luke's voice rumbles near my ear. "Maybe he took on more work."

"What, made more rabbits disappear?" I turn my head and draw in a breath at the closeness of Luke's face. If I just leaned the slightest bit, our lips would be touching. *Omigosh, focus!* "Um ... but December would be about the time Alfredo started seeing Betty."

Luke lifts a brow, seemingly unaffected by being a breath

away from me. Of course, he wouldn't be. He's got Ashley Timmons now.

"Could be just a coincidence." Luke's voice at my ear sends chill bumps down my neck.

"But it might not be."

"You think he was paid off for seeing her?"

I slowly nod. "That was my thought."

He pulls an errant piece of hair away from my cheek. "Any other thoughts in there?"

Just that I'm an idiot to let myself feel this for you. That you draw me in like a sale at Bergdorf's, and I can't stand the thought of you and Ashley. "Nope. That's it."

"You know what I think about?" His voice is as soft as cotton candy.

"That it's a shame girls don't want to talk about the SATs and chess on a date?"

"I think about that night on the Ferris wheel."

"Really?" Ohhh, he's playing dirty. "I don't."

He sighs and smiles, pulling my twirling finger from my hair. "I believe you do. And I think you want a relationship, Bella. But just like that big ol' Ferris wheel—it scares you. And first chance you get, you jump off. It's too easy to believe I cheated on you."

"We really should get out of here."

"Not every guy is out to break your heart."

"They all have." I suck in my bottom lip, knowing I just fell for his bait. "I don't want to talk about this."

"I'm sorry about your dad. I'm sure it hurts to be left out of his life."

"My dad has nothing to do with this."

"Then there's Hunter." Luke takes the payroll book out of my hands. "Total idiot."

"And where do you fit in, Luke Sullivan?" I turn all the way around and look up into his face.

"Right here." He angles his head as his arms go around me. His head lowers, and my eyes flutter closed.

The door flings open, slamming the outside of the trailer. "Hey!" Luke and I jump apart as a pair of hostile eyes take in the scene.

"The time for secrets is over. Tell me why you're here. Now."

chapter thirteen

My tongue freezes at the roof of my mouth. But Luke moves fast. He steps away from me and shoves the payroll book behind his back.

"Hey, Cherry."

Her eyes take in the interior of the trailer. This girl who flies through the air and relies on perfect timing for a living doesn't miss a thing. "I knew you two were up to something."

I finally find my voice. "I came in here to dry off from the dunk tank. Luke followed to check on me. That's all."

"I meant from the very beginning." She closes the door with a slam. "You with all your questions." She gestures at me with her chin. "And this one always prowling and hanging around way after we're closed for the night."

I glance at Luke. "Really?"

He nods proudly. "Yeah."

Cherry stomps her foot and breaks the moment. "I want the truth or I scream my head off for my uncle."

"You don't want to do that." Luke sits down at the edge of the desk. "We're here to help."

"Help yourself to my uncle's checkbook?"

"No." Luke flips it back open and hands it to her. "About the time Alfredo started dating Betty, he began receiving a substantially larger paycheck."

She scans a few pages. "So?"

"Nobody else's pay seemed to go up," I say. "Cherry, everyone we've talked to has commented on how strange Alfredo was with Betty when they first got together. Even you said it. What if he was being paid to date her?"

"That's ridiculous. Anyone could see he loved her. Especially in the last few weeks."

I decide to let go of my best information. "I overheard Red tell Stewart to find Betty's dog. But then . . . Red wants Peg dead. These guys are not to be trusted. He said he had Alfredo's situation under control."

"What? No!" Her face pales beneath her stage makeup. "Uncle Red would never kill Peg."

Luke steps closer to her, as comforting as a big brother. "Bella and I are here to solve Betty's murder. We know you want justice more than anyone."

"But the police say Alfredo did it. I didn't want to believe it, but we can't argue with the evidence. His prints were on the murder weapon."

"Why wouldn't they be?" I ask. "He handled those swords every day. He claims he's innocent—what if he's telling the truth?"

Tears gather in Cherry's kohl-lined eyes. "But my uncle loves me." She rubs her hand over her nose. "I mean, he's never been like a dad or anything. But he took me in when my parents died. He saved me from an orphanage—he's told me about those places."

"And I'm sure he does love you," Luke says so convincingly even I almost believe it. "So we don't want to upset him with anything until we have more evidence, okay?"

"But you think my uncle had something to do with Betty's murder?"

"It's really important we find out." I move toward her and swipe away some dripping mascara on her cheek. "But we need you to act like you know nothing, okay? Can you do that?"

She stares down at the floor, where she makes a figure eight with her shoe. As if she has the weight of the world on her shoulders, she lifts her head. "Uncle Red and Stewart are heading out somewhere after the show tonight. I don't know where. I just heard them talking about looking for something."

Luke's eyes dart my way, but I focus on Cherry. "You can trust us." I pull her into a quick hug. "Everything is going to be okay."

"You promise?"

I stare at the girl who's seen too much sadness in her thirteen years. "I promise."

Thirty minutes after the evening's final performance, I walk out of the tent into the dark night with Ruthie.

"What an evening, huh?" She holds out her arms and spins. "I unicycled like I have never unicycled before. Did you see the finale?"

"It was riveting." All I can think is I hope Cherry doesn't rat me out with her uncle and cousin. I am so toast. This whole thing is.

"Did you see the last part where I fluttered that ribbon behind me? I added that in at the last minute. It was symbolic, you know? I mean, there was a message in there."

"Shakespeare couldn't have said it better." I check my watch. Ten thirty. I'm so tired it might as well be two in the morning. And the night is far from over. "So, I'll see you tomorrow."

As my car comes into view, so does Luke. He sits on the hood, lounged back on his muscular arms. Geeks should not be this devastatingly good-looking.

"What are you doing?" I ask.

"Thought we could hang out." He doesn't move from his lazy recline.

"I'm sure Ashley Timmons is waiting for your call. Besides, I'm just going home."

"Sure you are."

Not once have I ever wished for a crime-solving partner. Not one time.

Ruthie throws a leg over her motorcycle. "You know, maybe it's because it's been a night of emotional expression for me and I'm extra-sensitive, but I'm picking up on some vibes here. Yeah"—she waves a finger between us—"I think you two are up to something. And it ain't no date."

"Good night, Ruthie." I open my car door. "And Luke."

He jumps off the hood and grabs the door. "Not so fast. We're a team."

"A *team* member wouldn't dunk me in a water tank." Every time I think about that, I get ticked. "I'm working solo." I direct my glare at Ruthie too.

She hops off her bike and scurries to my car. Pushing Luke out of the way, she slides into the backseat. "Where are we going?" She bestows Luke with her haughtiest stare. "I am the sidekick, you know, so don't get any ideas about taking my title. I have the book and everything."

A corner of his mouth quirks. "I know a place where we can park the car out of sight and keep an eye out for anyone leaving."

"Oh, espionage!" Ruthie claps her hands. "I love it. Hey, should I have brought my slingshot?"

"No!" Luke and I yell simultaneously.

After texting my mom that I'm going to be hanging out with Ruthie and Luke, I steer the car onto a side road, and we wait.

Ruthie whiles away the time by humming. "Can you guess that tune?"

"Sounds just like the last three." Luke rubs the bridge of his nose.

Ruthie sighs. "Did I tell you the story about the time I stapled the church secretary's skirt to a pew?"

"Yes. And when she stood up to sing 'Just As I Am,' her skirt fell down and she farted. Good story." Ugh, I just want to go to sleep. And get away from Luke. Seriously, the guy almost kissed me tonight. Right? I'm sure he was going to. But why? Maybe now I'm just some challenge to him. I know Ashley sure isn't.

Luke jerks his seat up straight. "There they go—Stewart and Red."

We all watch Red's old Ford F-150 pull out of the carnival parking lot.

"Start the car," Luke says. "But keep the lights off."

"Omigosh. This is so CSI!"

I roll my eyes in the dark at Ruthie, and at the count of ten I put the car in drive.

We follow them through downtown, staying back a comfortable distance. They drive to the city park, and I stop the car across the street.

"What are they doing?" Ruthie whispers.

I reach into my purse and get out my little pink binoculars. "They've got shovels."

"They're stopping at the memorial fountain."

"Probably gonna scoop up some pennies," Ruthie says. "I sneak out here and do that every once in a while myself. You don't get much, but it's a good way to fund a beef jerky and Yoo-Hoo purchase."

"They're digging all right." I hand my binoculars to Luke. "Right next to the fountain."

Thirty minutes later father and son climb back into the truck, armed with nothing but their shovels.

"Whatever they're looking for, they didn't find it." I work out a kink in my neck. "Maybe this is what they wanted the dog for—to find something."

"I totally should've brought snacks." Ruthie pops in her fifth piece of gum. "Some bean dip would really hit the spot."

We all duck down as the truck goes by, its headlights shining through my Bug.

"They're turning down Hall Street." Luke straightens to a seated position. "Let's go."

Over the next hour Red and Stewart stop at a pig farm, the Dairy Barn, and a used car lot. Finding nothing at the water tower, the two guys toss the shovels in the bed of the truck.

"Wait a minute. What's that?" Luke adjusts the binoculars and zooms in. "A piece of paper. They're reading off some sort of instructions or something."

"Maybe it's a treasure map!"

I'm so exhausted I laugh out loud. "Ruthie, this isn't *Pirates of the Caribbean*."

Luke shifts in his seat, his body humming with renewed energy. "She could be right."

I lean on my armrest and yawn. "Buried treasure?"

As we follow the truck back to the carnival grounds, Ruthie voices what we're all three thinking. "Buried *something*."

chapter fourteen

The rest of the weekend flies by, with Ruthie, Luke, and me staking out Red each night after the carnival. Saturday night we followed Red and Stewart out to the lake where they continued their strange digging, but they took Sunday off. I guess even suspicious creepy guys need a day of rest.

"I still don't understand why I'm going to Dad's again." I zip my carry-on as Mom pulls a shirt out of my closet to borrow. "I just saw him two weekends ago."

"We went over this Monday, Bella. And Tuesday." Mom holds the shirt up and studies herself in the mirror. "I want to see Jake's first official show in Los Angeles. He needs my support."

"Why can't Budge and I go? Robbie gets to."

"Because Budge is staying with friends. He's one wiener medal away from Employee of the Month, and I can't take that away from him. Plus, you and Robbie can afford to miss three days of school. Budge can't."

"But I could go with you. Or stay with Ruthie."

"Your father was nice enough to get Ruthie a ticket too, so don't push it." Mom leans over and kisses the top of my head. "I don't like how things have been between you and your dad. This is the perfect opportunity to get in some additional father-daughter time."

"He's just going to foist me off on his fiancée or make me watch the Disney Channel with Marisol." Plus, I need to be here. I could miss something at the carnival. Even though Red and Stewart didn't take any late-night drives with their shovels Monday or Tuesday evening doesn't mean they won't resume them tonight. What if they find something and I'm not there? When I asked Red Fritz for the rest of the week off, he jumped on the idea. Why would he be excited about me leaving town? Because I'm definitely an asset to the circus. My clowning skills are pretty much priceless. Yet he dismissed me for the week as if the show can just carry on without me. I mean, yeah, I might've mistakenly popped a kid with a balloon Saturday night. And maybe that four-year-old *was* crying because I accidentally hit him with my shoe, but that's no reason to be glad I'm gone. What if Red knows I'm onto something? That man is connected to Betty's murder. I'm just not sure how. Or why.

I give my mom the same wounded expression that used to get me what I wanted—from new shoes to jaunts to Paris. I pout my lips. I blink until my brown eyes have a misty sheen. My voice is as sweet as the tea at Sugar's Diner. "Mother, please let me stay in Truman."

By two p.m. I'm standing at the LaGuardia baggage claim with my dad.

"Hey, sweetie." He crushes me in a hug, then I introduce him to Ruthie.

"I don't believe in plastic surgery, sir," she says, handing him her bag. "I'm all about keeping things as natural as the good Lord intended."

As she walks in front of me, I stare at her striped beehive that's a security risk all by itself.

Three hours later Ruthie and I are watching TV in my bedroom.

"Dude, this room is scary." She points toward the trio of cherubs on the ceiling above my bed. "I can hardly watch the movie for thinking any minute one of them is gonna swoop down and stab me with a pitchfork."

"One of my dad's ex-girlfriends decorated the house." That would've been two hundred ladies ago. "Every room has a theme."

Ruthie picks up the lamp in the shape of lips. "What's the theme in here—scary movie props?"

"Love," I sigh. "Anymore, I think it's pretty dead-on. This room gives me nightmares and a stomachache. So do boys."

"Aw, you just gotta find the right guy. Like my Budgie-umpkins."

Before I can totally gag, little Marisol sticks her head in the door. "Guess what?"

The monkeys from The Wizard of Oz *are at the door, and they've come to claim you?* "What?"

"This is going to be my room."

I nearly fall off the bed. "I don't think so! You have your own room down the hall." In the lovely theme of vegetables that are purple.

"But when the baby comes, I'll move into this room."

"Baby? There's no baby." Oh no. My dad can't even keep up with me, let alone another child. I sit down hard on the bed. "Right, Marisol?"

She shrugs a shoulder and sniffs. "Well, there will be one day. I mean, they are getting married soon."

"My dad's already done the baby thing. Me." And I turned out fabulous, thank you very much. "So don't get your hopes up."

"But I heard them talking about it yesterday when they met with Christina's lawyer over the prenup."

How sad is it that an eight-year-old even knows what a prenup is? "So . . ." I pat the space beside me on the bed in invitation for her to sit. She skips into the room, straightens her bow, then takes a seat. "What else do you know about their prenup?" I glance at Ruthie, but she's absorbed in an old Reese Witherspoon movie.

"Nothin' really. After the lawyer lady left, my, um, sister was in a really bad mood."

Hmmm. Maybe it didn't go so well. Good. I hope my dad stuck

it to her and made sure Christina walks away with nothing of his if they divorce. But it's odd only one lawyer was involved. Surely Dad's guy was in on it too.

"I wouldn't set your sights on my bedroom yet." I pat her on her dark head. "Let's get them married first, okay?" Or not.

Marisol's forehead draws into a frown. "They have to get married. She says she's worked too hard for it not to happen."

I blanch. "What do you mean?"

"Marisol!"

The girl perks at her sister's voice. "Christina's home!"

I reach for her. "Marisol, wait—"

She races out the door . . . taking her secrets with her.

Dinner is low-key, with pizza and chips at the dining room table.

"Tomorrow we'll go out for dinner." Dad takes another slice of pepperoni. "Bella, are you going to show Ruthie your city?"

"I thought we'd hit the Statue of Liberty tomorrow. Maybe the NBC studios and Rockefeller." Squeeze in some shopping.

Ruthie chomps on a bite, oblivious to the string of cheese dangling from her chin. "I want to see if I can talk to the guys at *Saturday Night Live*. I have this skit idea they're gonna love. It involves a talking asparagus."

"Kevin, will you cut my pizza into bites?" Marisol slides her plate toward my dad.

"Of course, pumpkin."

"You're the best in the whole wide world."

Like a slo-mo sequence from a horror film, I watch as she leans toward my father. He meets her half way. And they rub noses, giggling. Giggling!

"Aren't they sweet?" Christina asks, like we're in the middle of a Hallmark movie. "She loves him so much." Her smile wobbles for a brief moment. Like a sad memory walked across her mind.

Christina jumps as her phone rings.

"Don't get that." Dad's voice is resigned. "Let it go."

"I can't." She reaches into the pocket of her tailored jacket. "Hello? Oh. Yes, just one moment." She puts her hand over the phone. "I'm just going to take this in the other room." Christina rolls her almond-shaped eyes. "It's a client."

Dad rubs a hand across his deliberately stubbly face. "She's had to work a lot lately. But that's why she's the best. Ruthie, did Bella tell you about the TV show deal Christina got me? It's like *Extreme Makeover*, but in Brazil. And I'm the show's plastic surgeon."

"That's cool, Mr. Kirkwood. I don't watch much Brazilian TV. But sometimes I turn on the Latin soap operas. You should think about getting on one of those." She looks at me and whispers behind her hand, "Kinda weird your dad *and* stepdad have both been on TV. How cool is that?"

"It's the coolest," I deadpan.

"I'm sorry." Christina's heels tap on the dining room floor. "But I have to go. I have a client who's in the middle of a crisis."

"Again?" Dad asks. "This is the third night in a row."

She trails a hand across his shoulders. "I have to be available to my clients whenever they need me. And this particular one is just a little high maintenance."

Dad stands up and brushes the pizza crumbs from his lap. "Then I'll go with you. The girls can watch Marisol."

"No!" Christina checks her gold watch. "I'll be back in no time. Just going to call a cab." She walks away, disappearing into the hall that leads to the master bedroom.

Something is just not right with this chick. I feel the need for a little surveillance. Heaven forbid I go twenty-four hours without tailing someone.

"Wow, I am seriously craving a frappuccino." I kick Ruthie under the table. "Aren't you?"

She pops another pepperoni in her mouth. "Whipped cream gives me gas."

"Starbucks has great water." I stand up and pull her with me. "I'll just grab our purses." I run upstairs like a rabid pit bull is chasing me. When I make it back down, Christina is at the front door.

"I'll see you all in a bit."

"Wait! Ruthie and I are going to grab a coffee. Let's share a cab."

Christina's eyes widen. "No, you two take your own so you can have your girl time."

I move ahead of her and open the door. "We must think green and protect Mother Earth." Not to mention my dad.

"You guys have fun!" Dad yells as we spill onto the sidewalk and into the cab.

My dad's fiancée is quiet during the ride as Ruthie babbles on about things she knows about New York City. "And my mom told me to carry my money in my bra because that would be the last place a robber would look."

"Here you go," Christina says as the taxi pulls up to Starbucks. "Have fun."

We shut the door, and I watch her give instructions to the driver.

"Come on." I pull Ruthie away from the coffee shop door and flag down another cab.

"What are we doing?"

I yank open the door of the yellow sedan. "Follow that cab ahead. But keep at a distance."

Ruthie's eyes widen as she buckles herself in. "Are we tailing Christina?"

I fill Ruthie in on the mystery woman from two weeks ago. "It could be nothing, but my gut says Christina is up to something."

Ruthie rubs her stomach. "My gut says I shouldn't have had that root beer."

My head bobs with every stop and go. Even at night, there's no downtime for New York traffic. It's always rush hour.

"Turn down that street to the right, please," I say to the driver as Christina's cab stops at a hotel a half a block away. I pay the fare and scurry out.

Peeking around the corner of the building, I watch as Christina nods to a doorman, then sails through the revolving doors and enters the Broadway Heights hotel.

"Follow me, but act cool, okay?"

Ruthie and I walk nonchalantly to the door. When I roll on through, I'm emptied into a large lobby with green botanical carpet.

And completely alone.

"Ahhhh!"

With a moan of dread, I turn around. Ruthie runs in circles, banging on the glass. "It won't let me out! Crazy spinning portal! You won't suck me in!"

I stop the glass door and grab my friend by the wrist. "You really have to get out of Truman more often."

"That thing is evil!" She glares back at the offensive entrance. "Evil, I tell you."

I plaster my hand over her mouth and jerk her behind a large potted palm. "Be quiet, would you? Getting us kicked out is kind of counterproductive to following Christina."

Beyond the front desk and across the expansive lobby, my dad's fiancée presses a button for an elevator. With a ding, the doors slide open, and she steps inside. From the glass front, I watch her rise and count the floors.

"Eighth floor." I pull on Ruthie again. "Let's go."

Praying we won't miss Christina, we scurry across the green carpet and get in a waiting elevator.

"Keep your head down just in case she looks over here."

When the door swooshes open, I throw out my arm, stopping

Ruthie's full-speed-ahead departure. "Quietly. Slowly." I point toward the hallway and wave her on.

On tiptoes we walk down the long row of doors with no Christina in sight. When the hall veers right, I follow it, then immediately freeze to a stop.

"Oomph!" Ruthie plows into my back. "A little notice, if you please."

"Shhh!" I point around the corner. "Christina," I whisper.

I watch as she knocks on the door of room 857. "It's me," she calls in her light Brazilian accent.

The door swings open and Christina rushes inside.

"Can I help you?"

Ruthie and I jump as a man carrying a briefcase appears behind us, his face scrunched with suspicion.

"What exactly are you two ladies doing?"

Ruthie goes on the defense. "What are *you* doing? Sneaking up on two teenage girls like that. You ought to be ashamed of yourself."

"Ruthie." I jab her with my elbow. "It's okay. We were just walking through."

"Yeah," she huffs. "Walking through to inspect this place for our dad's pest control company." She leans closer to the guy, dropping her voice. "For some of the bigger jobs where the bugs are more obvious, he sends us to assess the damage." She whistles, her eyebrows going high. "And these here? Freaky big."

The man clutches his briefcase and takes a step back. "You can't be serious."

"This floor seems to be the worst." Ruthie shakes her head mournfully. "You better get in your room and lock the door. My partner and I are on duty for another two hours, so we won't let anything near you. But if you come out"—she lifts her shoulder in a shrug—"we are not responsible for what might happen."

Torn between not buying a word Ruthie said and afraid not to, the man rolls his eyes, dismisses us with a flop of his hand, and walks away. Quickly.

"Nicely done," I say.

"You should probably give me a raise."

"I don't pay you as it is."

"My people will call your people." Ruthie turns her attention back to the hall.

One hour and two sore butts later, the door to mysterious room number 857 creaks open.

"Stick with the plan," says a voice from inside, the accent similar, yet stronger than Christina's.

"She's going to see us," Ruthie whispers, pointing frantically to the door. "Let's go."

I nod in agreement and turn toward the joining hall.

"I don't want to hurt him anymore."

That's Christina! I stop.

Ruthie tugs on my arm. "Come on, Bella. Running out of time here."

Who's "him"? I have to know! What if it's my dad? Or the president? I don't know this woman. She could be planning to take over the world for all I know.

The woman from inside the room speaks again. "We've come too far for you to bail now. You're integral to this plan. And you know you owe me. You owe this family."

"Bella, come *on!*" Ruthie sees I'm not budging. "I'll see you in the lobby."

I wave her on, desperate to hear more of this conversation.

"I'm not backing out," Christina says. "But it's not too late to change our minds. This isn't going to plan."

"And whose fault is that?"

Yeah, whose?

I see Christina drop her head, her gaze focused on the floor. "I have to go."

Oh crap. Here she comes.

My feet beat the floor as I sprint down the hall. I slap the elevator button, but the nearest one is on floor twenty-two. I'll never make it.

I hear the light scuff of Christina's heels on the carpet. Think! Think!

Two wingback chairs sit on either side of the elevators. I aim for the left, then switch and decide on the right. Muttering a prayer, I dive behind it and crouch low, willing myself to breathe quieter. Hoping she can't hear my galloping heartbeat.

She digs through her purse as she waits.

"Darn."

Omigosh. She's dropped her lipstick. If she bends down she'll see my feet.

*Please God, please God, please God. I'm trying to do some good here . . . really. Don't let her see me. I need help. Maybe a miracle. Oh, I know! A guardian angel!**

I see the sheer pink sheen of Christina's nails as her hand nears the floor. Just a millisecond more and I'm outed.

Ring! Ring!

Christina's sigh fills the hall.

Her hand disappears, and I hear her rummage through her purse again. "Hello? Oh, hi, um, Ruthie. Kevin gave you my number? Isn't that nice." She reaches again for the lipstick, her fingers curling around the tube. Completely oblivious to my legs beneath the chair. "Bella's been in the Starbucks bathroom for twenty minutes? Have you checked on her?" The elevator pings and opens. "Sounds like she's having serious stomach problems then. Yes, I'll stop by and get some medicine. See you at the house." And the doors shut, sending the elevator whisking south.

I sag against the chair for a moment before calling Ruthie. "Stomach problems?"

Ruthie laughs on the other end. "It was all I could think of."

"Are you telling me you couldn't come up with anything better than giving me the runs?"

"It worked, didn't it? I watched her come down the elevator."

"Yeah, it worked. Horrible story . . . but strangely enough, perfect timing." I end the call and decide to take the stairs.

Ruthie McGee—my guardian angel of deception.

Maybe she does deserve that raise.

chapter fifteen

On Monday morning I sit at the kitchen table reading the back of the Cinnamon Toast Crunch box and contemplating my life.

Dad was so busy with his TV show preparations, he barely spoke to me. Christina is one big weird mystery I can't seem to unravel—especially when I spend all my time in Truman. And my snooping skills must be getting rusty because I couldn't find a trace of any prenuptial agreement in Dad's office. He's probably keeping it some place I would never suspect. Like his Bible. My dad is not a believer, and I really wish he would get with it. If anybody needs some Jesus, it's him.

My mom shuffles in, still in her robe. She wraps her hair in a ponytail and heads straight for the coffeemaker.

"Running a little slow today?" Normally she's up, dressed, and completely lipsticked way before the rest of us roll out of bed.

She fumbles for a coffee mug and pushes her bangs out of her eyes. "Didn't sleep much last night."

Robbie pads in, his Superman cape over his Spider-Man shirt and jeans. "Did anyone catch that CNN report last night on Middle Eastern politics?"

Mom and I both just stare.

Robbie shrugs and sits down by his bowl. "Your loss." He pours out some cereal, keeping an eye out for the prize.

I help Robbie with the milk. "How was Jake's big show?"

My stepbrother frowns. "He was good. But we didn't get to see him much except from the stadium. Dad's real busy."

Mom pours her coffee and says nothing.

"But he did smash someone's face in."

I ruffle the top of Robbie's head. "I know you must be proud."

He thumbs through some mail on the table, pulling out his *Superheroes in Training* magazine.

"What's this?" I pick up a letter that sticks out. "A note from your advisor at Tulsa Community College? Mom, you didn't get detention or anything, did you?"

Robbie giggles but Mom focuses on adding creamer to her mug. "It's just a reminder about late registration for the next term. No big deal." She grabs the paper and crumples it in one hand, sending it to the trash can in a perfect arc.

"You shouldn't quit school. You love going."

"It's not like I know what I want to major in anyway." She pats me on the back to soften her words. "Maybe next fall."

"My daddy's gonna be superfamous then!"

I glance at Mom, but her face is blank. Is there one area of my life not on the verge of falling apart? Just one?

When I get to journalism second hour, I notice Luke isn't there yet. Disappointment flutters in my chest as I take my seat at my computer. I wanted to grill him on all that happened at the carnival since I've been gone. And that's seriously the only reason I'm sad he's not here. I haven't missed him or anything.

"I talked to Cherry this weekend."

I lift my eyes from my screen and see Ashley walking toward me. Her shorts defy the school dress code. Not that the administration ever does anything about it. But still, it tempts me to make a citizen's arrest for crimes against decency and good fashion.

"Glad you got to talk to her." Which means Ashley went to the carnival. Where Luke was. I blink a few times to block out the vision of them sharing a jumbo popcorn.

Ashley props a hip on the corner of my table. "She really didn't have a lot to say. Did you warn her not to talk to me?"

"No." I type a few sentences on a story outline. "But I do have this little remote in my purse, and occasionally I use it to control her."

Ashley's laugh trumpets the room only to end with a hard glare. "I already apologized to you, so what is your problem?"

"I don't have a problem with you." *As long as you don't talk, move, or breathe.* "You're completely on your own with Cherry. She's young and she's been through a lot. You can't blame her for not wanting to give you the Oprah interview version of her life. Or maybe she didn't talk to you because she didn't warm up to you." *Because it seems like Luke is the only one who can stand next to you and not get frostbit.*

She stands up, one hand to her hip, one hand pointing dangerously close to my face. "Look, things got out of hand that night at the carnival. And your relationship with Luke obviously wasn't strong enough to take it, so I'm not going to take responsibility for one tiny kiss." Her glossy lips curve in a smile. "But now he's single, and I'm single. And since you dumped him and are ridiculously incompatible, there's nothing standing in the way of us going out again."

"Did he say we're incompatible?"

Ashley rolls her eyes. "Luke and I have talked about all sorts of things." She lets the sentence hang, and my mind races with various scenarios of them hanging out, chatting on the phone, texting to their little hearts' content. Just how many times has he LOL'd her?

"I'm kind of busy here." I force a smile. "Was there something specific you wanted?" *Or were you just needing to gloat?*

"I want to do what's best for this paper and for Luke. So let's just all try and get along, okie dokie?"

She is about one *okie dokie* away from me steamrolling her into next week. I stand up and get ready to tell her what to do with her bossy, pseudo-positive attitude. "You know what, Ashley? I think—"

"Good morning, girls." Luke sails through the classroom, his mouth pulled into a grin. "Glad to see you two working together." As he talks, his strong hand latches onto my shoulder and forces me to my seat. "I know how much professionalism means to you both." With a hand at her back, Luke leads Ashley back to her computer, chatting amiably about her current assignment.

I'm halfway through my outline when Luke returns. "You want to tell me why I walked into this room and found you ready to slam Ashley to the mats like Captain Iron Jack just took over your body?"

"That girl is a viper."

"I like her."

Let me just pick this arrow out of my heart. "Clearly."

"I meant as a friend." He sits on the very same spot his little protégé vacated. "She's a good writer, Bella."

"Then tell her to stick to writing and leave me alone."

His mouth curves in a wicked grin. "Can't handle her?"

My eyes narrow on his handsome form. "I don't know what she's like when you two are alone, but with me, she's as friendly as a Manhattan mugger."

His laugh is quiet, but I hear it nonetheless.

"Go away, Luke. I have work to do." I have an article to write for my next column, a future stepmom to investigate, and all sorts of loose ends at the carnival.

He takes the empty seat next to mine and rolls toward me until we're shoulder to shoulder. Looking straight ahead at my computer, his voice is still so close it sends chill bumps dancing down my spine. "If I went away, then I couldn't tell you Red and Stewart went on their treasure hunt every night you were gone."

"Seriously?" I lower my voice. "Keep talking."

He turns his head at an angle, leaning his square chin on his hand. "Unfortunately, that's all I know. They act more agitated every night. And never seem to find anything."

I stare at the ceiling and contemplate this, trying to block out the clean scent of my ex-boyfriend. "Nothing else happened?"

"Surveillance wasn't the same without you."

I look into his piercing blue eyes. "Really?"

"And Ruthie." His wicked grin is back as he gets to his feet. He gives my shoulder another squeeze and walks on by. "See you tonight."

chapter sixteen

"This Bozo wig is giving me a scalp rash." I stick the thing on my head and tuck any loose hair into the elastic band.

"I like mine." Ruthie gives a curlicue a tweak. "I was thinking of wearing it to graduation. It would look better than those stupid hats they pass out. Hey, did you see all the people out there? I think the whole county's here. Obviously they've gotten wind of Ruthie the unicycle wonder." She pops her bowtie, sending it to spin. "Everybody's here but Budge."

"He's a workaholic." I pat her arm. "He'll show up one of these nights."

"I hate the Weiner Palace. It's his real true love. I just can't compete with relish, onions, and pressed pig parts."

"Hey, girls."

"Cherry!" I pull the girl into a loose hug. "How's it going?"

Her nervous eyes dart around the backstage area, looking for eavesdroppers. "It's hard to act natural around Uncle Red and Stewart. Are you *sure* you didn't misunderstand what they said about Peg?"

"Bella's got good ears. And if she said she heard"—Ruthie makes a noise and drags her finger across her throat—"then that's what she heard."

"We'll figure it out." I inject as much confidence in my voice as I can. "Have you overheard anything suspicious lately?"

"Not really."

"Could you try?" The words slip out of my mouth before I can reel them back in. "Er, that is, nobody's closer to those two than you. They won't think anything of you hanging around listening to the occasional conversation."

"I'll see what I can do." She peels back one of the curtains. "Dolly's here."

"She watches you almost every night without fail." I follow the direction of her gaze. "Whoa—and Mickey's with her?"

Cherry nods, the glitter in her hair catching the light. "Yeah, he's been coming over for dinner some. And he was here Thursday and Saturday night. He's cool. And I think Dolly likes him—a lot."

I smile at my own hopefulness. I would give anything to see those two reunited and happy. It's like life's been pulling them back to one another for years.

"Red thinks I should move back into Betty's trailer," Cherry says. "He says he'll move one of the other girls in with me. But I really like it at Dolly's. It's like a home to me." She waves away the idea. "It's stupid to get attached though. By the end of May, we'll be rolling out."

"But I think no matter what, Dolly will always be in your life now."

Cherry bites her lip and smiles. "I think so too."

Ten minutes later I'm passing out balloons to kids and greeting the crowds. "Welcome to the Fritz Family Carnival!" I pat a little boy's head. "Have fun!"

"Clowns are stupid."

I bend to his level. "Clowns are actually a very misunderstood, underappreciated group of individuals who bring joy and gladness to boys and girls of every race, size, and creed." I step up two more bleacher rows. "Disrespectful mutant."

"Bella!"

"Hey, Lindy." I huff out a breath, sending a few multicolored curls flying. "Hi, Bo." My eyes adjust to the sight of my friend holding hands with a boy.

"How's it going, guys?"

"It's awesome." Bo's smile is so big, his cheeks are ready to pop off. "I heard there's a heck of a unicycle ballet. I'm totally stoked for that."

"Yeah." I glance toward the arena floor where Ruthie does leg kicks for her warm up. "Who wouldn't be?"

"Bo"—Lindy pats his knee—"will you go get me some popcorn?"

He jumps to his feet. "Sure. How about a Coke?"

"Sounds good."

"I bet a candy bar would hit the spot too. Be right back!" Her track-star boyfriend nimbly makes his way down the packed bleachers.

"I like him, Lindy. He's such a good guy to you."

She stares toward the door where Bo holds open the flap for a family. "He's perfect. He lets me pick the radio station in the car. He carries my books. Notices my hair. Prays for me."

Shouldn't she be smiling? "You don't sound very happy."

Lindy shakes it off and pulls out a slow grin. "Of course I am. It's exactly what I've always wanted in a guy. I wasn't even looking for him, and he found me."

"I'm glad for you." I think. "Well, duty calls. I have balloons to twist and kids to terrorize." I leave my friend and walk away with an unsettled feeling awhirl in my brain. Just another one to add to the collection.

After another grueling show, I run to the backstage area and take off my makeup with a wipe. Peons like Ruthie and me don't get trailer privileges. We get a mirror tacked up on a tent pole next to a hook for our wigs.

As I walk out, I catch Luke's eye from where he stands at the sound-control table, shutting things down for the night. He gives a curt nod, a signal that we will be doing some undercover surveillance tonight.

The evening air hangs with the strong odor of impending rain. I inhale deeply, loving that heavy smell that will usher in green pastures and sprouting flowers. And hopefully an end to this case. I'm just not convinced the Amazing Alfredo is our guy.

I spot a group of people I have come to know and love, and meander in their direction. Ruthie, still in clown uniform, stands surrounded by Officer Mark, Cherry, Dolly, and Mickey.

"Good job in there." Officer Mark pats Ruthie's polka-dotted shoulder. "When you wheeled out, it was like watching Cirque du Soleil."

Her posture straightens as she considers this. "Well, I don't know who that is, but if they ever need pointers, I guess you could send them to me."

"There's another one of our favorite clowns." Dolly catches sight of me and hugs me tight. "You did great in there too."

"Yeah, I think I only made three little kids cry tonight." A huge improvement from last week.

As Cherry talks with Dolly and Mickey, I pull Officer Mark off to the side. "How's the investigation going?"

He rubs a hand over his badge and shakes his head. "Just once I'd like to be greeted with 'Hi, Officer Mark. How are you?' You don't even pretend to be courteous." He flashes a smile under the carnival lights.

"Any progress? Anything you can share?"

"You know the answer to that. I can't give you anything. But I don't know much anyway. The county's got this one covered. And for all intents and purposes, Alfredo's our man."

"I want to talk to him. Could you arrange that?"

"Only family."

"I'm his circus family."

Mark laughs. "That's just a creepy thought."

"If Alfredo did it, I don't think he acted alone." I share with Mark all I know, leaving out nothing except my prowling through trailers. I still need to go back and try to find my flashlight. That's a loose end I've got to tie up.

"Bella, you know the routine. You stay out of it and let the professionals do their job."

"But I'm on the inside. Your professionals are sitting behind desks thinking they've got their man." I back off when I see his fierce scowl. "Just relay my information to whoever's in charge. I think this case is deceptively simple."

"That's the only kind you stumble onto, isn't it?" He blows out a breath, briefly shifting his eyes to look at something over my shoulder. "I'll pass on your information, but they're really tied up with a series of gang incidents in Tulsa. Your job is done. If you've got a burning in your heart to be a clown, that's your freaky business, but otherwise, I think you better consider retiring from the carnival life."

"And miss all the satisfaction I get from spreading joy and happiness to circusgoers?"

Officer Mark snorts as he steps away. "Butt out, Bella. I mean that."

When I return to the group, I see Luke has joined them. As Dolly talks about homeschooling, Luke doesn't take his eyes off her. But I know he knows I'm there. It's that whole magnet thing. I think we could find each other in a dark tunnel, even if we were on opposite ends. I don't know that I like being that aware of someone.

"I hear Jake had another great night last night," Mickey says, his voice laced with pride. "I'm going to fly out to Seattle and see him next week."

"How's your mom doing?" Dolly asks, her eyes sharp and knowing.

"I guess she's struggling with him being gone so much. Seems to be stressing everyone out." And when I say stress, I mean as in the kind of pressure that can fracture something. Like a marriage. "Jake says he's still trying to find his balance. I hope he finds it soon."

Dolly smiles. "He's a smart guy. I have faith he'll figure it out."

"Sometimes it's easy to take your family for granted," Mickey says, his expression guarded as he looks at Dolly. "And sometimes it takes doing without to see what you had."

At this, the conversation lapses. Around me I hear the sounds of families making their way to vehicles, the roller coaster still zipping, and carnival workers calling for someone to take a chance for a buck.

Dolly wraps her arm around Cherry and kisses the top of her head. "You did so good tonight, girl. Ready to go home?" They head toward the south parking lot.

I turn to Luke and motion for him to follow. "My car's out this way too."

We all walk together and say our good-byes for the evening next to Dolly's Jeep.

She unlocks the vehicle just as Cherry squeals. "Peg!" Cherry points through the crowd, and I see the collie tearing toward her. "Oh my gosh! You came back!" Cherry drops to her knees as the dog pounces, running into her outstretched arms like a lost child. She licks her cheeks, her nose, her chin. Cherry giggles and pulls her closer.

"I can't believe it," Dolly says. "Where in the world has that dog been?"

"It's a miracle." Tears glisten in Cherry's eyes. "Dolly and I said a little prayer for you, Peg, and you came back. It's a miracle, isn't it, Dolly?"

I walk around the Jeep and run my hands through the dog's fur. "Wherever she was, they didn't extend bathing privileges."

"Dolly?"

I feel my blood drain at Red Fritz's scratchy voice. "Go! Distract him!" My whisper comes out in a frenzied rush as I push Cherry toward the other side of the Jeep. Toward Red.

Red's voice grows a bit stronger. "Cherry, it's time you came back home. I know the loss of Betty was a shock, but as we say, the show must go on. Your home is with us."

"She's thriving with me," Dolly says, just as I slink into the back of the Jeep, scooting along the floorboards.

Luke picks up the dog, and she gives a little bark.

"What was that?" Red demands.

Luke shoves the dog at me, then throws back the seat. "Just smashed my finger in the door." I watch Luke shake out his hand as he shuts me inside the Jeep.

Where the dog goes crazy.

"What's going on in that car?" Red asks.

I stick my head up. "Just me! I'm changing clothes!" I make swirly motions with my one hand and hold down Peg's head with the other. "No peeking!" Omigosh. *God, please don't let this dog bark again.*

"We'll talk about this later, Red," Dolly says. "I've got to get Cherry home now. She needs her rest."

"This isn't over, Cherry. You know where you belong. Stewart and me—we're your real family."

My whole body jerks as seconds later the door is flung open.

The first person I see is Luke, staring into the floor. He's surrounded by Dolly, Cherry, and Mickey.

Luke's mouth quirks. "If you smother the dog, Bella, you're the one who'll have to perform mouth-to-mouth."

I look down to see I'm completely rolled on top of Peg, with all four limbs wrapped around her like a vise, both hands clamped on her snout.

"Not a word, Luke Sullivan. Not one word."

chapter seventeen

As I drive to the carnival after school Tuesday, I punch the button on my phone with as much consideration as one would give the command for a nuclear bomb.

"Bella?"

"Hey, Hunter. It's me. I know, surprise, right?" Never thought I'd be calling my ex-boyfriend, pond-sludge sucker that he is. "Yeah, I'm good. Um, there's kind of a reason for my call."

"Missing me?"

Boys. Do they *all* think they're God's gift to the planet?

"No, I do *not* miss you."

"Give it time. You will."

Yeah, like the flu. I turn down my stereo as Hunter Penbrook prattles on about changing, turning his life around, mending his ways. Blah, blah, blah. Heard it all before. Even fell for it once. But never twice.

"Hey, Hunter, I hate to interrupt your dissertation on your virtues, and I think your new vegetarian diet is very noble, by the way, but I need your help."

Silence.

"The last few times I've been to see Dad, things have been pretty weird." I explain my odd Christina moments. "There is definitely something going on there, but I can't be in two places at once. Time is of the essence because Dad's getting married in June. So if Christina's not on the up-and-up, and I strongly suspect she isn't, then I need to get proof of that soon. I can't just go to him with suspicions."

His deep voice fills my ear. "So what do you want me to do about it?"

"Remember the last time you were in Truman—you know, when you were pretending to be someone you weren't because Jake's reality show was paying you?"

His excuses and apologies come in sputters.

"Save it. I do recall, though, that in one of your crying fits one of the things you said was that you'd do anything for me. Remember that, my little dumplin'?"

His sigh blows into the phone. "I didn't cry."

"Okay." I guess now is not the time to bring up his sordid, teary-eyed past. "Well, I need your help."

"Name it."

Nice. If only Luke were this biddable. "I need you to find out who's staying in that hotel room."

"What's in it for me?"

"I'll send you a Christmas card this year."

"You sent me one last year."

"I promise not to stick my tongue out in this one. Can you just help me out here?"

"How's the new boyfriend?"

Um. "Fine."

"That didn't sound fine. Trouble in nerd paradise?"

"Luke is not a nerd." Only *I* can call him that. "He's brilliant, studious, while also being conveniently buff."

"So you two are happy?"

"Every day is another twenty-four hours of bliss."

Hunter laughs. "Bella? Our maids play poker together. I know you broke up with that guy."

"Can you find out who's in room 857 or not? I'm not asking you to save the world here—just do a little snooping around, a little stake-out in front of her door."

"Did I ruin you for anyone else?"

Now it's my turn to laugh. "Yeah, your cheating ways are so hot, I can't bear to be with anyone else now." If I were standing in front of the guy, I'd have to gouge out his eyes just on principle.

"No. I mean you were already leery of trusting anyone. And then I pushed you over the edge with all the crap I pulled." His voice is strangely sincere.

"Twice."

"Twice." More silence. "You know, even after two years of dating, you always did hold back."

"If this is about that night at your parents' lake house, I *told* you I had my boundaries."

"He's not me, but I thought that Luke character was a pretty good guy. You should've seen the way he looked at you at prom. And when he saw you hurt—" Hunter expels a ragged breath. "Never mind. What do I care?"

I pull into my spot at the carnival and turn off the Bug. "Hunter, you're the last person I'm going to take relationship advice from. Are you going to help me or not?"

"I'll do it. Because I really am a better person these days."

"Uh-huh. Well, keep me updated. And . . . thanks."

"Bella? Give the guy a chance. Anybody who's saved your life a couple times can't be all that bad. What are you afraid of?"

The line goes dead, and I sit there with my head on the steering wheel. Hunter Penbrook just went all love-doctor on me. Oh, the irony. It's like taking advice on conservative attire from Britney Spears.

When I walk into the big top, there's a small crowd beneath the trapeze.

"What's going on?" I ask.

Melvin, the fire-eating midget, points toward the ceiling. "Red's making Stewart and Cherry do the Praying Mantis."

"Since when does Stewart know the trapeze?"

"He was raised on it. Trained by Cherry's parents. He just took a few months off to try his hand at managerial duties. But his dad has put him back on as an aerialist starting tonight."

"So what's the Praying Mantis?"

His brown eyes darken. "It's the routine that killed Cherry's parents."

Dolly is gonna freak. "Is it incredibly dangerous?"

Melvin shakes his head. "It's not impossible. That night her parents died, there were equipment malfunctions. And her dad removed the nets—he insisted. He wanted to take the trapeze team to a new level. He thought it would put our carnival up there with the best of them."

I watch Red yell at Cherry and sigh. "And then the Fritz Family Carnival became memorable for all the wrong reasons."

"You got it. But Red wants to change that."

Cherry misses Stewart's outstretched arm.

"You idiot!" Stewart hisses. "Do you need glasses?"

"Pay attention!" Red yells. "This isn't a game."

"I know!" Cherry stands in the nest. "I—we just haven't worked together in a while. Can't Rusty and I do this? He's been my partner since March."

"No." Red curls his mustache between his fingers. "You are both of Fritz blood—circus royalty! It must be you two. Take a ten-minute break." Red claps his hands at Cherry and Stewart like he's a lion tamer.

I do a quick turn when a hand latches onto my shoulder.

"Jumpy today." Luke stands there, an arrogant smile tugging on his lips.

"I was watching Cherry and Stewart." I take a few steps away from the dissipating crowd. "Cherry talked Dolly into taking the dog home, by the way."

"Didn't Dolly want to know why they weren't returning it to Red?"

"Cherry explained it's what Betty would've wanted. Told her she'd heard Red was done with the dog, and his idea of retiring an animal wasn't too pretty. That's all it took for Dolly." I pause. "Luke, um, I need a little favor."

"I'm not going to like this, am I?"

"Would you mind getting my flashlight where I left it?"

"I guess." He shrugs. "Where'd you leave it?"

"In Alfredo's trailer."

"*What?*"

"Shhh!" I clamp my hand over his mouth. "It was an accident."

Luke pries my fingers from his face, keeping my hand hostage. "An accident that you were in there or that you left it?"

"Yes."

"Bella . . ." His growl is scarier than my clown routine. "How did it get in Alfredo's trailer?"

"I might've dropped it a few weeks ago when I was digging around." I rush on to explain. "There hasn't been a single chance to get it. I've tried."

His left eye twitches as he rolls this through his oversized brain. "Would this be the flashlight I got you? With your *name* on it?"

The one that came with a card that said, *Your laugh lights up my day.* "That's the one. And I really want it back."

"You *need* it back, you mean. So they won't know where you've been." He lets my hand fall like he can't stand the connection any longer. "So within weeks of getting my gift, you ditch it in Alfredo the Killer's trailer. I can tell it meant a lot to you."

"That's not fair. For your information, that flashlight did mean a lot to me," I snap. "I thought of you every single time I prowled through someone's belongings."

Luke closes his eyes and stares at the ceiling. "The likelihood of it still being there is slim. I cannot believe you took a chance like that."

"Someone was coming, and I had dropped it. Just find a way to sneak into Alfredo's trailer." I soften my voice. "Please? If you do, I won't insult your favorite blonde reporter one time tomorrow." I pat his chest and give him some more directions. "Be careful, 'kay?"

Ruthie arrives on the scene, cutting off any blistering remark Luke might've had. "Yo, carny dudes. What's up?"

I grab Ruthie by the hand. "Come on. We need to go talk to Stewart while he's on break in his trailer."

"We do?"

"Bella—," Luke warns.

I shoo him away with my hand as I pull Ruthie along. "Godspeed, Luke. May the force be with you. Oh, and also, if you'd provide a distraction for Stewart in about three minutes, that'd be swell." I give Ruthie a hard yank. "Move quickly before he comes after us."

"What's going on, boss?"

"We're going to go talk to Stewart about an idea you have for your unicycle ballet."

"But I don't have an idea."

"You have about ten seconds to get one."

chapter eighteen

Ruthie and I disappear around back, and I take us straight to Stewart's trailer. My hand shakes only slightly when I knock.

"What do you want?"

I pull open the door. "Stew?" I reserve my prettiest voice for only the creepiest of men. "Can we come in?"

His gruff tone changes instantly. "Of course." He swabs his neck with a towel. "I can always make time for two beautiful ladies."

Gag. "Ruthie has a great idea for adding to her unicycle routine. She'd like to describe it for you." I jerk my chin toward Red's son. "Tell him that amazing idea you were sharing with me." *Make something up, Ruthie. Come on.*

"Um, yeah." She clears her throat and forces a dreamy look into her eyes. "Imagine this. I'm decked out in swan feathers . . ."

As she paints her unicycling scenario, I scan the office for any sign of a piece of paper that looks like a much-used list. If I had to put money on it, I'd bet the paper Red and Stewart have been using in their search is a map. And since he's standing here in spandex pants and no shirt—ick!—then it sure isn't on him now. So unless Red has it, it has to be in this trailer somewhere.

". . . And then Melvin the Midget and Wilhemina the Wondrously Tall Woman will come out and serenade me with Celine

Dion's 'My Heart Will Go On.' Then they'll start throwing the rose petals, of course . . ."

I could start with the desk. Then his sleeping quarters. I hate to search through his undie drawer, but if it has to be done . . .

A sharp rapping stops my roaming eye.

Stewart stalks to the door and throws it open. "What?"

Luke peeks through. "Red said to come and get you. Someone's let the horses out, and he needs your help."

Stewart hesitates as he looks at me and Ruthie.

"He said to hurry, Stewart."

Stewart rushes to the back of the trailer and returns with a shirt. "All right, everyone out. I have to go."

"But what about my ideas?" Ruthie calls as we exit onto the grass.

Throwing up a dismissive hand, Stewart runs toward the animal trailers.

I regard Luke with a tiny amount of disdain for his lack of improv. "That was gutsy. Red said the horses were out? Like he's not going to know that's a lie in a second."

"Wasn't a lie. The horses really are loose. Kinda crazy over there." He rocks back on his heels. "By the way—no flashlight."

"Are you kidding me?"

"It's gone." And he's ticked. At me.

Great! Whoever has it knows I was in that trailer.

Luke looks past my shoulder. "Are we going to stand here all day or go back in?"

"Ruthie and I are going in. You stay out here and keep guard." When he starts to protest, I beat him to it. "If Stewart can forgive anyone for being in the trailer, it's us—seeing as how we're girls and all."

Luke clenches his jaw. "Hurry up. And don't leave anything this time."

"Oh, you're funny."

Five minutes later I jump as Luke sticks his head in. "Anything?"

"No!"

"Hurry, Bella. You're driving me crazy." *Slam!*

"There's nothing here, Ruthie. We might as well call it a day. Maybe we'll get another break and try again later."

"Snooping stresses me out. I need a snack." She peels open the small fridge on the counter.

"Get out of there!" I shove it closed. "We have to go."

"I saw chocolate-covered Oreos!" Her eyes twinkle. "Come on. You have to let me have just one. Nobody can walk away from that temptation."

"One. And I'm leaving." I speed walk to the door.

"Who would've thought Stewart was a boxer guy, huh? I had him pegged as more of a—" Ruthie gasps. "Omigosh!"

My hand freezes on the door.

"I found it." She holds up a yellowed piece of paper. "I found a treasure map!"

Brain in overdrive. Heart beating out of my chest. Think! Think! I don't know what to do.

I turn a full circle around the trailer. The printer. I'll make a copy!

"Ruthie, keep an eye on the door." My pulse races, the sound echoing in my head. If we get caught . . . I don't even want to think about it. I slap the paper down on the machine and close the lid. The printer sounds too loud in the silence of the small office.

When someone bangs on the door, Ruthie and I both squeal.

"Hide!" comes Luke's voice from outside.

My eyes flit to the desk. To the sleeping area in the back. Maybe under the dining table?

"Come on. We must have company." I grab Ruthie by the arm and pull her into the bathroom. Shutting the door, I follow her into the cramped shower, where we stand close enough to be PG-13.

"Don't think I usually do this on the first date," Ruthie whispers. "You're an exception."

I hear the trailer door open. Then Stewart's voice. "I don't have time to talk right now."

"But I have some questions about the lighting for Ruthie's ballet," Luke says, his volume raised.

"Look, I have bigger things to deal with than some unicycle act."

Ruthie's mouth drops into an O. I squeeze her arm and shoot her a warning look. *Do not say a word!*

Luke tries again. "If you could come out here and look at the light board—"

"You were told to help with the horses. Now get out there or leave the grounds and don't come back."

I hear Luke expel a harsh breath, then the door slams again, rocking the trailer.

He's gone? Now what? I left the map in the printer. I'm such an idiot! I could've at least grabbed that. We could be stuck in here with a potential killer. My mom is going to be so mad!

I raise my mouth to Ruthie's ear. "Work together. Follow my lead."

I wrench open the bathroom door. "Surprise!"

Stewart jumps straight up, and a string of curses split the air.

I launch into song. "Happy birthday to you! Happy birthday to you!" I clap my hands and walk toward him as Ruthie helps me finish the tune. "Yay!"

I hug Stewart, waving madly with my hands to my friend. *Go get the maps!*

Stewart leans his scrawny self into me and pulls me close. Ew. Ruthie fumbles with the printer as time stretches into an eternity.

Must stall. "Stewart, close your eyes," I purr.

"Oh? Really?"

"Now, no cheating. I'll be mad if you do." I take a step back. "You don't want me angry, do you?" I pucker my lips in a saucy pout.

"No," comes his breathy reply.

"I didn't think so. Because I have a birthday present for you."

"But it's not really my birthday."

He closes his eyes, and I change places with him, turning him away from the office. "I guess I must've heard wrong then." I place my hands on his shoulders and squeeze. I'm totally washing these hands in bleach when I get home. "How about a birthday shoulder massage!"

"Uh . . ." His voice is a deflated balloon. "I guess."

Yeah, that's all you're getting. What was he thinking? Creep.

I let out the breath I'm holding as Ruthie slowly extracts the map and picks up the copy, which disappears down her shirt. I jerk my head toward the refrigerator. *Go!*

"What's all that noise?" Stewart asks.

"That's just Ruthie warming up her hands. She's a whiz at shiatsu. Keep those eyes closed!" As Ruthie moves, I shift Stewart until he's facing the office again. "You have such strong shoulders!" And bony. Almost skeletal in fact. *So* not hot.

I check over my shoulder to see Ruthie in the fridge.

And that's when the trailer door busts open again.

"Dad!"

I drop my hands. "Mr. Fritz!"

"This is treachery! It will *not* be tolerated!" Red's mottled face radiates with fury. It's all over.

"Dad, I—"

Ruthie and I look at each other, and somehow I find my voice. "Mr. Fritz, if you'll let me explain—"

"I'll have his head on a platter!" Red roars.

Stewart stands up uncertainly. "I'll find out who let the horses—"

"Horses?" With wild eyes, Red shakes his head. "I'm talking about Alfredo."

I blink. "Huh?"

"Alfredo DeLucci. He escaped from prison this afternoon." Red's eyes pierce his son. "Seems the magician has vanished into thin air."

chapter nineteen

The birds sing happy morning songs as I get my tired body out of the Bug and join Luke and Ruthie in the school courtyard.

I take a sip from my McDonald's mocha. "Let's see the map."

Ruthie looks at Luke. "Turn around please." She twirls her finger in a circle.

Obviously used to her oddness, he complies without question.

Ruthie sticks her hand way down her shirt, her face scrunched in concentration. "I wanted to keep it protected, so I didn't shower last night. I even slept with my bra on, keeping the map safe. And cushioned."

"Noble of you," Luke says.

She rustles around a bit more before drawing out the paper and holding it up like the Holy Grail. "Perfectly safe . . . if not a little toasty."

I take the map and spread it out on the nearest picnic table. "There's the water tower. The school." I slide my finger across the drawn path. "But . . . where's the end?"

Ruthie straightens her blouse. "Every good treasure map has an X that marks the spot. What kind of loser map is this?"

Luke leans close and peers over my shoulder. "It's not complete. It can't be."

A breeze floats by, carrying his cologne with it. I struggle to focus on anything else but that familiar scent. "So when Red and Stewart were digging all over the place, they were just guessing."

"Then where's the other half?" Ruthie asks. "And who has it?"

~~~~~~~~~~~~~~~~

When Wednesday night arrives, I am in serious need of some church. Our building isn't finished yet, so we meet at Truman High. Like I'm not there enough.

The worship pastor is doing an acoustical jam tonight, and it's just the calm my heart needs. Though I'm sitting next to Lindy and Matt, I focus only on the music, as if I'm the only one in the room. As the pastor sings a spiffed up version of an old hymn, I close my eyes and let the words wash over me, imagining that I'm singing just for Jesus.

When I moved into Jake's house, I would climb out my bedroom window and sit on the roof and just think. And pray. And read my Bible. But I haven't done that in such a long time. God may have blessed me with the gift of crime fighting, but I seemed to have let it take over my life. *Lord, help me to just slow down and find some peace again. I can't solve any mystery or help anyone with all this clutter in my head. Oh, and protect me from crazy carnival people who might've committed a murder or two.*

I watch Dolly sneak into a seat in the back. Cherry sits beside her. I glance across the cafeteria and see Mickey Patrick has noticed her as well. His smile is slow and contented.

After the service we file out into the parking lot. There, sitting on my mom's Tahoe, is Jake, holding a bouquet of flowers. Budge and I lag behind, but Mom and Robbie run right into his outstretched arms. Jake swoops them both up like they weigh no more than a feather each. He swings them around, peppering them with big smacking kisses.

"Let's go eat pizza," Jake says when Budge and I make it to the SUV. "I hopped an earlier flight to get here, and I'm starved." Jake waves at Dolly and Mickey, calling out an invitation to them too.

"Come with us," I say to Matt and Lindy, as they hover nearby. "The three of us haven't hung out in a while."

"That would be fun." Matt twists his class ring. "Lindy?"

"Sure. Like old times."

Thirty minutes later I'm thanking God that the only heavy thinking I have to do tonight is decide between pepperoni or sausage.

"So how were your matches this week, Dad?" Robbie sits on Jake's lap.

"Mostly I trained." Jake takes a giant bite, the cheese stretching from plate to mouth. "But a commentator got sick last night, and I got to sub at the last minute." He turns his megawatt smile on my mom. "It was awesome, Jillian. Most of it's on the teleprompter, but I got to wing it too, you know? They said it went so well, they want me to do some more events."

Mom picks at a breadstick. "So you'll be gone even more?"

The light in Jake's eyes dims. "No, I don't think that's what they mean."

"But you don't know?"

I turn away from the conversation, my own stomach in a knot messier than the emptied appetizer dish in front of me. And that's when I spot Luke sitting in a corner booth with Ashley— her brother nowhere in sight. Like a bad movie close-up, my eyes zoom in on the two. I shove my plate away, having suddenly lost my appetite. I know I broke up with him, so of course he's going to date other girls. But why not a nice girl from Tulsa? Or somewhere farther . . . like Poland?

She laughs over something he says. And my heart breaks. Just a little. He said to trust him—but this does nothing to convince me. What if their kiss at the carnival *did* mean something? I don't want to be someone who gets cheated on—like my mom was before Jake.

God, I have to move on and give up the bitterness. I'm just not going to look over at that table. "So how's the dog?" I ask Cherry, who sits between Dolly and Mickey.

"Peg's going to be okay. Once we got a good look at her, we could see she was in bad shape. She was starving . . . dirty. Who knows where she'd been or how she'd been surviving."

"It's really important you keep her a secret from Red and Stewart," I remind her.

"I know. But they're too wrapped up in the fact that Alfredo is on the loose to even care. Everyone at the carnival is a little jumpy right now."

"Are they afraid he's going to come after them? Maybe kill someone else?" I have to admit I didn't sleep that great last night myself. Kind of spooky having an accused killer out there—whether he did it or not.

"I think everyone's just on edge. But we did finally get a replacement for Alfredo today. The new magician starts tomorrow."

Mickey asks Cherry a question, and my eyes drift back to Luke and Ashley. His back is to me, but she looks like she's having a grand old time. He's probably telling her about his chess club or the vocab flashcards he keeps in his glove compartment. Surely she won't be attracted to that . . . like I was.

My heart seems to beat a little slower tonight. Everyone around me is wrapped up in someone else. Even Matt and Lindy have been talking nonstop.

"I can't believe your time on that half mile at last week's track meet." Matt takes a big drink of Coke. "How does it feel to break the school record by two seconds?"

Lindy laughs. "It was amazing. I wish you had been there."

His mouth curls around his straw. "Me too, Lind."

My phone rings in my purse, and I reach for it. "Hey, Hunter. What have you got for me?" The laughter and conversation at the table are so loud, I can't even hear him. "Hang on. Let me find a quiet spot."

I walk out the front door, the bell jingling as I exit.

"I don't have a lot to tell you."

"Um, not what I wanted to hear." The door behind me opens again, and Luke and Ashley file out. Great. If he kisses her in front of me, it will definitely suck up what little remains of my peaceful, easy feeling from church.

"Yesterday I caught her leaving the hotel. I got a grainy shot of her with my phone. I sent it to your e-mail just now. I couldn't follow her, though, so no idea where she went. But tonight? Bella, I've been standing in this hall for like two hours. Room service came once, but other than that, I haven't seen or heard anything. Well, I thought I spotted that hot chick from *Gossip Girls*, but I'm not sure. This is pointless."

"You can't just give it two hours and call it quits." Luke walks Ashley to her car, and though they stand close, he doesn't touch her. "Have you seen Christina there?"

"I've seen no one."

"What about getting the room next to hers and putting a glass to the door?"

"Does that really work?"

"You should try it and see."

Luke waves as Ashley drives away in a lipstick-red Mustang. No kissing. No hugging. Which means for me—no puking.

"Hunter, please don't give up on this. I know that woman in the hotel room is significant. I can feel it in my gut."

"Maybe you have Irritable Bowel Syndrome like me."

Luke sticks his hands into the pockets of his slouched jeans and walks my way.

"Go home, Hunter. You've done all you can tonight. But promise me you won't give up."

"You know, you're lucky I messed up so big. Otherwise—"

With one finger, I end the call and flip the phone from palm to palm.

"Hello, there." With his azure-blue eyes, Luke looks down where I sit on the sidewalk.

"On a date tonight?" I hope that didn't sound jealous. 'Cause I'm so not jealous. Not at all.

He sits beside me, his shoulder brushing mine. "So what are you doing out here?" he asks.

Okay, avoiding my question. I can take it. "I have Hunter spying on a hotel room in New York. Just getting an update." I glance at my watch. "In fact, I really need to get home to catch his e-mail." I could pull up the picture on my phone, but I want to see it full size. It might be a good lead.

Luke nudges my knee with his. "You seemed down today at school. And tonight you're sitting outside while the rest of your party is in there having fun. And you barely touched your food—that's not like you at all."

"How do you know? You didn't even know I was in there until you got up to leave."

He holds me with his gaze. "I knew the second you walked in the door."

My heart flips like Cherry on the trapeze. "Oh, reporter's instincts and all that?"

"Something like that." Luke's eyes dip to my lips before he regards me once again with concern. "Are you going to tell me what's wrong or not?"

"I don't know," I sigh. "Same stuff. I guess I feel like everything is out of order. Like spinning debris in a tornado—just pieces of stuff floating all around me."

"What kind of tornado trash are we talking here?"

I give a small laugh. "My dad's getting married soon, and so far I'm powerless to stop it. I'm no closer to solving the murder of Betty and—"

"*We're* no closer to solving the murder. You don't think Alfredo escaping is pretty telling—that he did it?"

"No. Maybe he did kill Betty, but Red and Stewart are involved. We both know that."

"What else you got going on in that head?"

I glance back to the restaurant door. "Mom and Jake are . . . in a weird place." *And you've moved on. Instead of pining for me forever like you were supposed to.*

He wraps an arm around me and pulls me to him. "I'm sorry, Bel. I'll pray for you."

I close my eyes and lean into him, pretending for just a second that he's mine and Ashley Timmons doesn't even exist.

"You really want to go home and check your e-mail, don't you?" he asks.

"Yeah."

He stands up and pulls me with him. "Go tell your family. I'll drive you."

In ten seconds I'm buckled into his 4Runner, filling him in on Christina and the Manhattan mystery woman.

"You know, maybe it's nothing. You tend to assume everyone is shady and look for the worst in people."

"That's not true. I just have this intuition." Or an unlucky habit of stumbling onto things I'm not supposed to. Like psychos and dead people.

"Face it, Bella. You don't trust anyone. Like right now, you're probably thinking Jake is going to end up screwing up and sacrificing your family."

It has crossed my mind. "But you have to admit I've been right. A lot."

"Maybe you should let this thing with your dad and Christina go. If he's happy, what's the problem?"

I twist in my seat toward Luke, tucking one leg beneath me. "Haven't you ever just had this *feeling* about someone?"

"Yes." He stops the vehicle in my drive and angles his head my way. "As a matter of fact, I have."

A strange tension hangs in the air as Luke's eyes stay locked with mine. My pulse skitters and begins to race like I ran Lindy's half mile.

"Bella, I—"

"Luke—" Our words overlap. I fumble with the edge of my shirt. "Do you have one of those strong feelings for Ashley?"

"Does it matter?"

A sassy barb immediately comes to mind, but I push the words away and opt for raw honesty instead. "Yes."

"Why?"

I contemplate the beaded necklace hanging down the middle of my shirt.

With a light touch of his fingers, Luke tilts my chin up. "Why does it matter, Bella?"

Why can't I just tell him I like him? That when I'm not think-ing about a dead bearded lady, clown wigs, and a wacko fiancée, I'm consumed with thoughts of him?

He lets his hand fall only to lay it over one of mine. "Until you can explain that, there's never going to be an us. I have no reason to think it's anything more than jealousy."

I can't seem to find my tongue. I know I need to defend myself here—defend us. How can he just give up on pursuing me? The rules are changing right in this car.

He sighs and brushes his thumb over my palm. "You're a com-petitive girl. Is this just a game to you?"

I inhale all the air I can. "I don't know why being with you scares me, but it does."

Luke presses his head to the seat. "I scare *you*?" More chuckling. "That's a good one."

I laugh at his tortured tone. "I'm serious."

"I don't know why I'm explaining this, but Kyle left just before you got there."

"Of course he did." How convenient for Ashley that her brother had to go.

He removes his hand and rests it on the steering wheel. "Until you can trust me and just believe in us, then that's that. Kyle Timmons is a good friend and, frankly, so is Ashley."

"Can't we just—"

"No." In the dark vehicle I see the hard set of his jaw. "When you're ready, we'll talk. But as long as you're afraid of me, I'm not the right person for you."

Those words stab my chest. Who else could be more right for me than this yummy, infuriating boy? Why am I so messed up in the head?

"Are you going to continue seeing Ashley?"

He turns the key, and the 4Runner roars to life. "Good night, Bella."

"If I gave you a reason not to, would you?"

"You and I both know you're not going to do that," Luke says as I open the door. "I've proven I didn't cheat on you."

"Are you kidding? Hanging out with her seems to suggest the opposite."

"You know the truth." He pauses. "You know me."

"I don't know what to believe right now."

"Bella, you chose to let our relationship go, and I respected that. I still do. I'm not going to push anything."

"So I have to be the pusher?"

He nods.

"But if you go dating every cute, blonde reporter, it might be too late."

"Definitely a risk." He puts the SUV in drive. "Now you have to figure out if it's worth it."

chapter twenty

C hocolate-chunk cappuccino ice cream." I pass my money through the window at the Dairy Barn drive-thru and try not to think about my dismal life. My e-mail from Hunter showed a picture of the back of someone's head. Like that did any good. And don't even get me started on Luke. "Better make the ice cream a double, please."* The man slides the glass closed with a nod.

"Did that guy look familiar to you?" Ruthie asks from the passenger side of my Bug.

"Didn't notice him."

"You didn't *notice* him? He was at least seven feet tall." Ruthie flicks off the radio. "What's wrong with you? You've been in a mood all day."

"Nothing. I'm fine." Or will be as soon as I have chocolate.

"You got a double scoop *and* you didn't even notice that man used to work at the carnival."

"Oh." I try to see into the window. "Did he?"

When the giant appears again with my ice cream, Ruthie leans until she's nearly in my lap.

"Lars, what are you doing working here? You're the tall man. Not the ice cream man."

He sticks his order pencil behind his huge ear. "I'm telling you, I've had it with carnival life. I want to be known for more than just being a giant."

I lick the top scoop. "I personally think serving ice cream is an admirable trade."

"You can't quit!" Ruthie yells. "We're your family, and family sticks together."

"Kid, you ain't carny folk. I've only known you for a month."

"But I had just written you into the encore performance for next week."

"Really?" His demeanor softens. "That's so sweet. Nobody's ever included me in a unicycle ballet before." Lars shakes his head, sending his long blond ponytail swishing. "No, you won't tempt me back. There are weird things going on there. Spooky things."

"Like what?" I ask.

He shrugs a shoulder the size of a small country. "I'm just saying things haven't been the same since Betty died and Alfredo went to the big house. Something ain't right on those carnival grounds. And when those trailers pack up and leave, I won't be going with them. I'm staying right here in Truman where there are so many opportunities."

"Like what?" I ask.

"The manager's already told me she'd teach me how to work the deep fryer."

"You gonna make chicken fried steak and onion rings the rest of your life?" Ruthie yells so close to me her blue spike jabs me in the neck. "You have a gift."

Lars sniffs, his blue eyes downcast. "What gift?"

"To entertain the children of the world with your outrageously weird tallness."

"I'm not going back. Fran quit too."

I try to bring this woman to mind. "The lady with the talking pig?"

"Yeah, he also oinks a few Elvis tunes, so it's a pretty big loss."

My ice cream drips onto my hand as the May sun seeps into

my car. "We'll see you later, Lars." In fact, I'll probably be by after tonight's show.

I roll up my window and aim my Bug toward the carnival grounds.

"You had an ice-cream sandwich for lunch," Ruthie says, staring out at a green field.

"So? Maybe I'm calcium deficient."

"Bella, just spill it. You've eaten enough ice cream to make Ben and Jerry name a flavor in your honor. What's wrong?"

I take a large bite and let the light coffee flavor settle into my taste buds. "Luke and I had this weird talk last night. And he basically said if we're ever going to get back together, I will have to do the pursuing." How boringly respectful. I mean, where's his sense of chivalry? His manly leadership?

Ruthie snorts. "Good for him."

"What? Whose side are you on?"

She flips down the visor and glides neon pink lipstick over her lips. "I'm on the side of love, Bella. Love. I just want you guys to be as happy as Budge and I. Every day I say, 'Thank you, Lord, for my Budgey Wudgey.'"

"If you make me yak up my cappuccino chunk, I'm going to stuff your leather riding jacket down your throat."

She applies a top coat of gloss and smacks her lips. "You speak of violent things, but I know it's coming from a place of hurt, so I won't take it personally. You should just go for it with Luke. He's a nice guy."

"He's also demanding, bossy, domineering, and intelligent to the point of being obnoxious."

"You know Luke didn't cheat on you."

"He's still hanging out with Ashley."

"He told you it was nothing more than a friendship."

"It doesn't look like just friendship."

"Lindy dove into the love pool. And look how happy she is."

"Happy? Every time I see her, she looks like her dog just got run over." Except for last night when she was hanging out with Matt again. She laughed and smiled the entire time.

"You got it bad for Luke Sullivan. The sooner you accept that and deal with it, the better. He won't be available forever."

"He was out with Ashley Timmons last night."

Ruthie cracks her knuckles and smiles. "She can be taken care of."

Moments later the sound of yelling greets us as Ruthie and I walk into the big top at the carnival.

"Cherry, you're so stupid! Don't let go of my hand!"

I flinch and look up. "Stewart's such a slimeball."

Ruthie nods. "I got a pair of nunchucks I'd like to introduce him to."

"Focus!" Red yells from the ground. "Cherry, take this seriously."

"I am!" She brushes sweat from her brow. "We've been practicing for three hours. I need a break."

"You've got about two weeks before I expect to see the Praying Mantis." Red glares at his niece. "I won't let you mess this up for my circus."

Even from where I stand below, I can see the hurt flash across Cherry's pale face. What a life she leads. Makes me grateful for my family—crazy though they are.

Red claps his chubby hands. "Back to the beginning. Try it again!"

"No." Cherry climbs onto the ladder and begins to shimmy down. "I'm taking a break."

"Cherry, you hop right back up there this instant! I'm warning you!"

"Or what?" She continues her journey until she reaches the dirt. "You're going to ground me—from work? That's all I do!" She stomps toward her uncle. "Maybe I want what other girls have. Like the chance to have lots of friends, go to dances, and take driver's ed! To sleep in a bed that you don't pull down the highway in a caravan."

"I told you her living with Dolly O'Malley was a mistake," Stewart says as he joins them. "Now little cousin thinks she's better than the rest of us."

"I do not."

Stewart's face pulls into a sneer. "You always have. You think you're privileged or something because of who your parents were."

Ruthie nudges me with an elbow. "This is better than those Latin soap operas I watch. And no subtitles."

"You want to know who my parents were, Stewart?" Cherry's voice packs a punch I've never heard before. "They weren't famous to me. They were kind and loving. And they cared about me. They didn't make me work all day long. And when I did work, it was because I wanted to and because it made them happy. I wasn't just some show dog."

"That's it!" Red pokes his finger in Cherry's face. "When Dolly comes tonight, we are having ourselves a little talk. And you can bet you'll be moving back here—where you belong. I don't know what crazy things that woman has filled your head with, but I will not have you disrespecting me. I took you in when you were an orphan with nowhere to go. Your parents left you nothing because all they cared about was this carnival. But you have a place to stay and food to eat because of me. If it weren't for me you'd be on the streets."

Tears gather like thunderclouds in Cherry's eyes. "My parents loved me!" With a choking sob, she runs away—right past the gathering crowd and out of the big top.

"We better check on her."

Ruthie follows me outside. "Just say the word and I'll get those nunchucks."

I catch sight of Cherry running to the back corner of the carnival grounds. She stops at the Ferris wheel and speaks to the guy cleaning it. He nods and walks to the control box.

"Oh no." I can see where this is headed.

"Want me to talk to Cherry?" Ruthie asks. "I'll jump on with her and you can just, um . . . text some encouraging words from below."

I lift my head toward the heavens and beyond until I find the top cart on the Ferris wheel. Gulp. "No. We'll go together." How is it I can ride a plane once a month with no problems yet can't get on a simple carnival ride without breaking out in hives?

Cherry walks onto the ramp and pulls the front latch of a cart.

"Wait!" I call. "We'll go with you."

The worker frowns and steps in front of us. "Miss, I don't think she wants to be bothered."

"We're her friends," Ruthie says loud enough for Cherry to hear. "And we want to ride too."

We walk to the cart, and I get in, scooting beside Cherry. Ruthie climbs in next, pulling the door closed and squeezing us in like toes in a stiletto.

"What are you doing? Go away." Cherry swipes at the tears spilling down her cheeks. "I want to be alone."

"Too bad." Ruthie gives the man a thumbs-up as he double-checks our door.

My heart squeezes as I look at the pain in Cherry's eyes. "Normally you'd be talking to Betty right now, wouldn't you?"

She sniffs and nods. "Whenever I had a problem, my mom would bring me out to the Ferris wheel, and we'd take a spin. Just the two of us. My grandpa bought this machine for my dad as a wedding present. Every cart is painted in a fairy tale theme. My mom loved it. This Sleeping Beauty one was her favorite." Cherry rubs a finger where elaborate paint swirls rise and fall. "After my parents died, Betty would ride with me in this cart when she knew I wanted to talk. She would have torn into Red today. She wouldn't have let him talk to me like that." Her voice catches. "And now there's no one to take up for me."

I pull her into my arms as best I can, given I'm plastered between the two girls sardine-style.

The Ferris wheel groans, and with a lurch, we're off.

"I'm so sick of being alone," Cherry whispers.

Ruthie leans on me and moves in for a three-way hug. "You're not alone. You've got us."

Cherry's laugh is small. "It's not the same, though. You have no idea what it's like to not have parents. To be an unwanted guest. I'm just a burden to my uncle."

You have no idea what it's like to feel this cart swing and imagine yourself plunging to the ground.

"You've got God too." The words tumble out of my mouth in a rush. "I know it's hard to see that he has a plan in all of this, but he does." Why are my cheeks burning? Why is it so hard to talk about God to people?

"I've gone to church with Dolly. We've prayed." The wind lifts Cherry's hair as we rise. "But how could I buy into that? Where's God in all this? Why was I left by myself? If there is a God, how could he just take my parents?"

I sneak a quick glance at Ruthie. I am so not prepared for this conversation. Why couldn't Cherry ask these questions to someone who knows her Bible a bit better? Or someone who's had lots of practice witnessing. I've had lots of practice shopping. But unless she asks me whether I prefer Gucci or Prada, that is pretty much not going to be worth diddly-squat.

"Um . . . you have to believe that there is a God, and he loves you." Ruthie could pick up the conversation at any moment. She *is* a pastor's daughter. I'm a plastic surgeon's daughter! Ask me about butt implants! But Ruthie's just sitting there leaning on the edge like she can't wait to hear what I have to say next. "Bad things happen. But I know that when we hurt, God hurts. He's not just some big, bad guy up there. He wants us to think of him as a father."

I release Cherry from the hug, and she rests her head back on the seat, staring at the clouds. My stomach rolls as the ride slowly revolves.

"What father would leave his kid stuck with Uncle Red and Stewart? What father would take away both my parents *and* Betty?"

"Cherry, believing in God isn't going to magically fix anything." Don't I wish it would. "And it's hard to trust in something you can't even see, but every day . . . God waits for you to try."

She closes her eyes and rubs her hands over her face. "I just want a life. Is that too much to hope for?"

"No," I say, trying not to glance down as we make another swoop. "And I'm going to pray that you'll have a family and love." I still feel like I'm just spewing words.

"Whatever. Unless you're ordering me up a total life transplant, don't waste your breath." Cherry signals to the carnival worker below, and he throws the lever. When the Ferris wheel stops, Cherry jumps out *over* the cart. No door, no waiting for Ruthie and me to get off. Just shimmies from the seat, leaps off the front, and hits the ground running.

Ruthie reaches into the pocket of her leather pants and gets out her Tic Tacs. "That went really well."

"Are you kidding me?" I set my teeth and count backward from five. "You could have helped me. Instead of letting me just flail in the water."

"I helped." She pops a mint into her mouth.

"Oh really? Tell me one thing of any significance you did."

"Prayed." Ruthie locks her eyes with mine. "I prayed the entire time you were talking." She reaches over and unhooks the door.

"You're quite the doubter, Bella Kirkwood. Anybody ever tell you that?" She hops out, leaving me sitting there.

"Miss, you want another ride?"

I glance at the worker standing by the control box. "No. Thank you."

"You sure?"

"Sir, I think that's about the only thing I am sure of."

chapter twenty-one

Today the weatherman predicted a nice breezy eighty-three degrees with zero chance of precip. As I watch Luke Sullivan walking my way, I think that guy clearly miscalled it. Because I see 100 percent chance of storm.

"What is this?" He slams down a piece of paper next to my mouse.

"Is that my exposé on nerd editors?" *And good morning to you too.* "I should have known it would hurt your feelings." He and I haven't really talked since we, you know, *talked.* I've kind of been avoiding him. It's all so awkward.

"Meet me in Mr. Holman's office. Now."

I definitely should've started this day with coffee. I look back to my computer and type a few more sentences. He can wait. Bossing me around like that. Who does he think he is?

"I would not push me this morning, if I were you," Luke calls out in front of the entire class. Every head in the room pivots from Luke . . . to me. Even our advisor, Mr. Holman, raises a bushy brow as he helps Ashley.

I stand up, smoothing out my funky Betsey Johnson skirt, and with a smile perfectly balanced on my face, I join Luke in the office.

He shuts the door behind us and motions me to a seat.

"I'll just stand, thanks."

"Sit."

Employing Haughty Look Number Four, I lower myself onto the edge of a chair.

He sits in the other one and pulls out the same piece of paper. "Back to our original question, what is this?"

I read the first line and sigh. "It's my column for next week."

"It's about birthday cakes, measles shots, and used books that smell."

"I write from the heart."

He takes off his tortoiseshell glasses and hangs them in the V of his shirt. I'm forced to look directly into his ocean blue eyes.

"This is rambling, lacks voice, and is full of grammatical errors."

"Maybe Ashley can fix it." Omigosh. Did I really just say that? "Or someone else on staff—if you think there's a problem or two."

But it's too late. I see the storm clouds roll out and that familiar arrogance take its place. "You know what I think?"

"You hope sweater vests come back in style?"

Luke wheels his chair closer to mine. "I think your mind's on overload. Between your schedule at the carnival, your family problems, and confusion about us, you can't even concentrate enough to write three cohesive paragraphs."

If I had gotten that morning coffee, I would've just spewed it. "Are you delusional? First of all, I don't work any more than you do." Though I do have the extra burden of clown feet and hair the color of Kool-Aid. "And I hate to burst your gargantuan ego, but I don't sit around all day thinking about you." Well, maybe just a few hours here and there.

"Your column's been weak the last three issues. As of right now, you're taking a break." He places a book in my hands.

"*Reviving the Passion of Nonfiction?*" Sounds thrilling. "Wow, I hate to borrow this from you. I know how you like to read it aloud to all of your dates." I better not have just seen his mouth quirk.

"Take the next week to read and review some work from published pros." His voice softens. "Relax your mind."

The book feels heavy in my hand, and I have to blink to block out the fantasy of braining him with it. "You can't just stop my column. Mr. Holman will never go for that."

Luke stands up, rubbing the back of his neck above his Abercrombie collar. "He will if I'm subbing a new column in its place."

My stomach plummets like the Zipper at the carnival. "Who?"

"Ashley."

Now I'm standing. "I cannot believe you. Let me guess, if I'd go out with you, you'd reconsider? Is this punishment until I come around?"

His look could freeze the Pacific Ocean. "If you think that then you don't know me at all."

"Oh, I know you all right. You're a control freak, and this is just more proof of it. I'm probably the first girl who's ever rejected you."

"The paper is too important. Your column runs on the front page, and lately it's not even worthy to be in it. I expect more from you, and until I see that progress, you're done."

"And you just *randomly* picked her?" I jerk my finger toward the classroom in Ashley's direction.

Luke takes a deep breath, doing that thing he does when he's considering his words and trying to be all uppity editorlike. "Everyone else is already writing all they can and worked to the maximum. But Ashley has yet to completely be integrated into the paper. Not that I have to explain myself to you, but she came to me with a great idea for a feature, and now would be the perfect time to use it, since there will be a big gaping hole where *your* work should go."

I chuckle once and shake my head. "You are so full of it, you know that, Luke Sullivan?"

He leans on the door, his arms crossed. "I'm sorry, Bella. I didn't handle this well. I lost my temper, and I apologize for my tone. But I'm being sincerely honest when I tell you that removing you from the paper for a week or so isn't personal. If anything, it's for your own good. I did it for Trinity Dermott out there last year, and now I'm benching you."

"Was Trinity also an ex-girlfriend?"

His tanned hand clutches the doorknob, yanking it with a twist. "You have your new assignment. Get to it."

"I think—"

"Leave, Bella." He holds the door wide open. "Before you say something else we're both going to regret."

By lunchtime I've printed out all of this month's articles with my name on them, read them a hundred times each, and worked up a seriously hideous headache. Luke is right. My writing has stunk lately. But still . . . to put Ashley Timmons in my place? He had to know that was a low blow. Even if her article last week on test prep anxiety was kind of clever. And funny. And well written. Still!

"Kirkwood, you gonna eat those fries? Can you believe when I got to the front of the line they were all out of meat loaf?" Ruthie steals a handful from my plate. "So I think my unicycle ballet needs a few more figure eights. A little more ribbon waving. Tonight I'm going to get crazy and do purple ribbon instead of pink. It will match my hair."

I stop picking the label off my water bottle long enough to notice Ruthie has once again colored her hair. It looks like Barney held her at gunpoint and took her hair as a hostage. "Very nice."

"Dang right it is." Budge pats Ruthie's teased-out ponytail. "My lady is hot stuff."

"So then he caught the pass and ran right into the goalpost. Knocked him out for five minutes."

Across from me, Lindy laughs at Matt's football practice story. "When is Corey Davis going to suck it up and get his eyes checked?"

"Last week he showed up in his golf shoes. Seriously, the boy needs contacts before Coach sidelines him forever." Matt takes a drink of Gatorade. "Hey, I was going to go sign up to help with the athletic banquet. Want to go talk to Coach and see what they still need?"

"Sure." Lindy stands up and grabs her food tray.

"There you are!" Bo Blades jogs toward her and wraps an arm around her shoulders. "I have a surprise for you in my car. Come on." He takes the tray from Lindy's hands and passes it to Matt. "Take care of this, will you?" Bo pulls Lindy out the cafeteria door, holding her hand like it's a state championship medal.

"Matt?" I watch him just stand there. Motionless. "You okay?"

He sets the tray down on the table. Takes a seat. "Have you ever wanted something, but didn't know for sure you wanted this something . . . until it was too late?"

"I assume you're not talking about the meat loaf."

He props his chin on his hand. "She was my best friend. I didn't want to mess that up. I was afraid if we didn't work out then I would have lost a girlfriend *and* a friend. But now I wonder . . . in playing it safe did I just blow it anyway? I mean, I could've had my chance."

"So you knew she liked you?"

He nods his freckled face. "Yeah. I knew."

"Wow. She did everything to get your attention this year."

"I know. Lindy was the brave one. What's wrong with me that I can't take risks? I can on the field and on the court, but in my personal life—I always play it safe." He glances toward the door. "And look where it's gotten me."

Ruthie steals another fry off my untouched plate. "You could tell her how you feel. I'm a firm believer in honesty."

Budge does a double take. "You told me you had a rare mouth disease for the first two weeks we dated so I wouldn't kiss you."

"I wasn't exactly lying. I was adding to my mystique."

"I had to call my doctor to make sure all my shots were updated."

"Awww . . ." Ruthie throws her arms around Budge. "That's the sweetest thing anyone's ever done for me."

"Matt, maybe you should just tell her how you feel."

He grabs a napkin and folds it over and over. "It's not that easy. I like Lindy a lot—but I don't know. It's kind of scary to think about committing to her in that way." He tosses the napkin down on the table. "Never mind. You wouldn't understand. All that stuff just comes easy to you."

My eyes slide across the room to where Luke sits with his soccer buddies. And Ashley Timmons. "Right. I'm just a natural."

I park by Ruthie's motorcycle on the carnival grounds. I do an automatic scan of the lot just to make sure no escaped killer is skulking about. They seriously need to find Alfredo because I'm sick of having a twenty-four-hour-a-day case of the creeps.

"Hey."

"Oh!" I jump and spin around. "You—you scared me."

The new magician stares at me like he's memorizing my face. "Sorry. I guess you didn't see me behind you."

I look over the parking lot again. Just a second ago there was no one around. Where did he come from?

I nervously lick my lips. "I'm Bella." *And I'd give you my last name, but you look like the type who would Google me, find my house, and come over to show me your knife collection.*

"I'm, uh, Jensen. Artie Jensen." He angles his close-cropped head to the ground and speed walks right past me. "Have a good night."

"You too." Weirdo.

A few hours later I look out from the back curtain. The crowds are getting smaller and smaller every night. Soon the Fritz Family Carnival will be leaving, and if I don't break this case, I'll have nothing to show for it but a deep, abiding hate for honking clown noses and polka-dotted jumpsuits.

The performers meet in the center of the ring and take their final bows. The audience stands up and applauds as Red wishes them a happy evening and safe travel.

As I take off my wig and hang it on the hook, Luke steps into the changing area. "Bella, we need to talk."

I glare him down in the mirror. "I think we've said enough."

Ruthie sits down to pull off her giant clown shoes, not even hiding the fact that she's listening to every word.

"You know we need to discuss this."

"What are we discussing?" Ruthie asks. "I like discussions."

"Go away, Luke." I pull off my bow tie and place it in a plastic crate. "There's nothing more to say. You said my writing sucks, and you put Ashley in my place."

"Oh no, you didn't!" Ruthie slaps her thigh and laughs. "That is some serious drama, boy."

Luke shoots her a silencing glare. "I don't want to fight with you, Bella."

I pick up my purse and sling it over my shoulder. "Then I guess one of us should leave." I sail past him and head out into the arena. *God, why are boys so difficult? One minute I want to kiss him and tell him exactly how I feel, and the next I want to shove my rainbow wig up his nose and pull it out his ear.*

I walk by Cherry, who stands below the trapeze, gazing upward.

"Hey, Bella."

"You did great tonight. You're just amazing up there . . . and the crowd loves you."

Her eyes dim. "My family doesn't."

"Well . . ." I don't know what to say. "Dolly's crazy about you. You know she loves you."

The smile returns. "And Mickey."

"Is he spending a lot of time out at the house?"

Cherry unwraps her ponytail and shakes out her glossy hair. "He's there for dinner every night now. They're still a little nervous around each other, but it's kind of fun to watch."

Lord, I do not want to be in my fifties and still not have this love business figured out.

"Still keeping the dog under wraps?"

She nods. "It's our secret."

"Cherry, um . . ." I check over my shoulder for anyone nearby. "Stewart and Red have been going out late after almost every show and digging." I check for any signs of recognition. All I see staring back at me is cluelessness.

"Digging for what?"

"I was hoping you'd know the answer to that."

"No idea."

"Did Betty ever mention them having to find anything? Maybe they buried something the last time they were here?"

She scans her memory bank. "No. But how do you know they've been searching for something?"

"We've been following them." I catch sight of Luke across the way, sitting in the bleachers as if he's waiting for me. I struggle to rein my thoughts back to this conversation. "And this week I found the map they've been using to search."

Cherry drops her ponytail holder. "How? You didn't break into their trailer again, did you?"

"I might've wandered in there . . . accidentally."

Her fragile hand flutters to her chest. "Bella, Red's never laid a hand on me, but I've seen it in his eyes. And I've seen him be less considerate to others—even his own son. You do not want to mess with him."

A chill flitters up my spine. "We have to figure out what they want."

"I thought you were solving Betty's murder."

"I think it's connected."

"Look out!" I hear Luke's roar before he shoves Cherry out of the way, taking me with her. As we hit the ground, a row of lights crashes around us. Glass sprays everywhere as Luke plasters his body over mine.

"Cherry!" Through the fog in my head, I hear Dolly's voice, distant and loud. "Cherry!"

The volume level rises as workers begin to follow the noise and congregate.

"Bella?" Luke lifts his head from my neck. "Bella, are you okay?"

I shove at his chest to push him off, but find there are two chests. Two Lukes. Two of everything. I lay my head back down. "I can't even handle one of you."

He rolls away and kneels beside me. "Can you hear me?"

"Of course I can." I look up into his eyes so full of concern. "You're always saving me." I roll my eyes and feel pain spike my temple. "It drives me totally nuts."

Luke's laugh is brief. "Obviously you're all right." He holds out a hand, and I take it. He slowly pulls me to a seated position, and my vision aligns into focus.

"What in the heck happened here?" Red stabs an angry finger toward the dirt where a small row of lights rests in pieces. "You've been working on lights, boy. You want to explain this?"

Luke gives my hand a squeeze and stands up. "I don't do rigging. Wouldn't even know how."

"It's Betty's ghost," says Ziggy, one of the clown midgets. "We're cursed."

"We ain't cursed!" Red shouts, throwing his hat to the ground. "It was an accident is all. Accidents happen, for crying out loud!"

"The girls could've been killed." Dolly wraps her arms around Cherry and aims her mama bear stare on Red. "I'm taking Cherry home."

Red's eyes glaze with anger. "I told you last night to bring her stuff back. She's staying here."

"No." Dolly whispers something to Cherry, and with a nod, the girl walks away. "This is no place for her to live right now, and you know it. As long as you're in Truman, she stays with me. And Red, if you want to fight me on this, you bring all you've got. If I got an attorney today, I know the first thing he'd tell the judge is how your niece almost got taken out by your equipment."

Red's eyes flutter and blink. "Now just a minute—she is my flesh and blood. You're just a distant cousin."

"Good night, Red." Dolly turns to me on her way out. "You okay, Bella?"

"Yeah." I feel my body tremble like I'm standing in the Denver snow. "Just another day on the job as a circus clown." I can't even work up a smile for my own lame joke.

Dolly shares a look with Luke. "Are you going to take her home?"

He nods once. "I'll take care of her."

Satisfied, Dolly heads toward the same exit Cherry used to make her escape.

"This ain't over, Dolly!" Red calls. His head rotates as he catches all the onlookers. "What are you people staring at? Get a broom! Get a bucket! Get this mess out of here!"

"Come on." With a hand under my arm, Luke guides me to my feet. "I'll take you home."

"I can drive."

He breathes out a small laugh. "Your stepdad's going to be proud of my body slam."

I cough as my lungs expand back to their normal capacity. "He'll have you fitted in a spandex onesie in no time."

As Luke wraps his arm around me and pulls me close, I snuggle into the safety of his side and try not to think about the fact that I could've been a splatter on the ground. But he saved me. *Thank you, Jesus. Omigosh, thank you, Jesus.*

The night air hits my face, and I suck it through my nose like I'm trying to breathe away the last few minutes.

Luke stops three steps outside the big top, and before I know what he's about, I'm flattened to his chest. "That scared the crap out of me." He presses me to him, lowering his head on top of mine.

I pull my arms around him and rest my cheek to his pounding heart. "But I'm here. Because of you. Thank you."

"Bella, we have to figure this out. I can't take much more of this." His hands caress my back, and I feel some of the trauma ease away.

"I know," I sigh into his shirt. "And I'm glad to know you're still interested in me."

His hands still. He pulls away. "I was talking about Betty's murder. And the map."

"Oh." *Why don't you just slam me on the ground again? It would be easier than this humiliation.* "Totally. Me too."

Luke quirks a brow and pulls my hair away from my twirling finger. "We should probably get your head checked. You took quite a hit."

"I'm fine." It's my achy heart that needs the assistance.

He wraps an arm around me loosely like a brother. Any sizzle that had been there is gone. All the heat blown out like a cheap firecracker.

"Y'all have a good evening."

Luke and I both turn as Artie Jensen throws a cigarette to the ground. He squashes it with his shoe.

"Good night." Luke draws me a little closer and steers me toward the parking lot.

"Be careful out there," Artie calls. "You might not get lucky a second time."

chapter twenty-two

And that's how a bill becomes a law. Isn't that fascinating?" Robbie stares in eagerness at the faces around him. "Any questions?"

"Yeah." I smoosh the chili around on my hotdog. "Will someone pass the relish?"

It's an early dinner on this Saturday night before I go to work at the carnival. Since we're celebrating another rare evening of Captain Iron Jack being home, Mom wanted to dine as a family. Robbie picked Weiner Palace.

"Here's another round of root beers for everyone." Budge bends over to fill our mugs, and a plume from his turban sticks into my dog.

"Budge—please." I gesture to my plate. "You just got chili on your feathers."

He shrugs it off. "That's nothing. Yesterday I dropped it in the toilet."

Okay. I'll just skip the main course and move on to dessert. "Hey, is that Lars back there in the kitchen?" I catch sight of the giant man struggling with a bag of fries.

"Yeah, he started today. I guess the Dairy Barn caught him giving people double dips for the price of a single."

"What a brave, brave man." I don't know if I've ever had this much respect for a person in all my life. "You know, people think it's just ice cream, but to many of us, what he was doing was a ministry."

Robbie takes a bite of hotdog and comes away with most of it on his mouth. "But Bella, that's dishonest."

"That's what addictions do to a person, Robbie." Budge flips me with a hand towel and swishes away in his genie pants.

Mom cuts into her hotdog with a knife like it's prime rib. "I made an A on my philosophy quiz this week."

"Honey, that's great." Jake gives her a loud smooch on the cheek. "What classes are you taking for the summer term?"

She presses a napkin to her lips. "I told you I'm sitting out for a while."

"But we talked about this, Jillian. I want you to keep going. You can't stop now."

"You're right, we *did* talk about this. And the final word was that there was no way I could be a single parent three hundred days a year and go to school." Mom's voice lightens as she forces a smile for Robbie's watchful eyes. "It will be fine. Plenty of time to hit the books."

The tension is thicker than the Weiner Palace chili.

Mom turns her blue eyes to me and changes the subject. "Oh, Bella, I talked to your father. He said for you to be prepared for your bridesmaid dress fitting next weekend. Something about you and little Marisol having matching gowns."

"Can't wait. So Jake, how is wrestling going?" I never get to talk to the guy.

"It's been a challenge, but I like it. Training *and* performing doesn't leave a lot of time."

"And providing commentary," Mom adds.

"It's crazy." Jake's eyes light up. "I never was that good at public speaking, but this commentary stuff is almost more fun than wrestling. Hey, I hear you guys are going to have a watch party for tomorrow night's *Sunday Night Smackdown*."

"Yeah, I guess Dolly's having a big dinner at her house after the evening service at church. Mom's the event planner and Dolly's catering." I put my drink down as Lars walks to our table. He lifts up a hand that could shield an entire town from rain and reads from a page he's holding. "Would you like anything . . . ? Shoot. I can't make out that last word. It got smudged with hotdog grease." He scratches his head. "Now I don't know what I'm supposed to ask you."

I take sympathy on the man who was like the patron saint of ice cream. "I think you wanted to know if we wanted anything else."

He drops his hand and considers this. "Okay. Sounds good. Well, do you?"

"We're good here, thanks," Jake says and returns to his discussion with Mom. Robbie just stares, his head cranked all the way back to take in the man who could've walked out of Jack and the Beanstalk.

"So, Lars, are you missing the carnival?" I ask.

He laughs, a deep belly chortle that nearly shakes the table. "Are you kidding? When I could have all this?" He gestures wide to the restaurant, and it pulls his already-short pouffy sleeves to his elbows.

"I was wondering . . . could you tell me about the night Cherry's parents died?"

Lars winces. "That was a horrible night. Things have never been the same for the carnival." He pulls up a chair and eases into it, the wood creaking in complaint. "It was a stormy night, so we had a smaller crowd. We were in Baton Rouge, stationed in a vacant Wal-Mart parking lot.* Red had only been with us a few years, and I remember he took to the center of the ring and announced Junior and Shelly Fritz. They were going to debut their new routine, the Praying Mantis. It was very risky, but those two"—he whistles and smiles—"they were good. Red had convinced them that this new trapeze act would put Fritz Family Carnival on the map. He said once word got out, people would be coming from miles around to see Mr. and Mrs. Fritz."

"What happened that night?"

"The performance started out so flawless. People were on their feet to get a better look—that's how good they were. Then—" He pauses.

"Yes?"

Lars closes his eyes as if he's stepped back in time. "Just as they were about to do the big finale, lightning blew out the generator. The electricity went out. Junior and Shelly both fell to their deaths. No net."

I replay the facts in my head. "Why wouldn't they use a net? All trapeze artists do."

He shrugs a round shoulder, sending the plumes on his hat to wiggling. "Our fiercest competition has always been an outfit called the Hickman Brothers Circus. They were doing a gig without a net—had some mighty fine aerialists—and were taking our customers. They were always a few steps ahead of us on the tour. So Red convinced Junior that going without a net was the only choice."

"But they were professionals. Experts. Was there any sort of investigation?"

"What are you saying?"

"I don't know." I'm no closer to piecing this all together than I was the day I first stuck on a clown nose. "I'm just trying to get to the truth."

"You think they were murdered? Like maybe the mafia? Some gangs? I saw this show about gangs on HBO once, so I know all about them."

"No, I don't think it's organized crime." But perhaps something just as sinister.

Lars hinges at the waist and leans over. "What about aliens?"

I look into his hazel eyes and can almost see the wide-open space behind them. "I'll let you know."

It's five o'clock when I walk into the big top. I head straight to the back of the tent where all the props are stored and where my small changing area is. I set my purse down on the ground, then reach for the box that contains my clown garb.

And there sits my long-lost flashlight.

I'm paralyzed to the spot as chills explode over my skin.

A hand clamps down on my shoulder, and I turn and scream.

"Shhh!" Luke covers my mouth, his eyes wide. "What are you doing?" he hisses.

I just stare at him, my eyes unseeing, my brain moving at a speed that could cause permanent damage.

"Bella?" His voice is a scratchy whisper. Then his eyes drop to the box. "Oh."

I swallow. "You didn't put it there, did you?"

He shakes his head. "I never found it. I even managed to sneak in Alfredo's trailer one more time." Luke leans down and picks it up, the pink metal gleaming under the dim lights. "It's definitely yours. And I think someone probably wants to send you a message."

I take my flashlight, my fingers sliding across Luke's palm. "They know I was snooping."

"And more than likely are smart enough to know you still are." His forehead wrinkles in a frown. "You okay?"

I inhale deeper, willing my breath to slow down. "Yeah. Just kind of caught me off guard." I quickly fill him in on my conversation with Lars.

Luke's voice is barely audible. "You think Red killed Cherry's parents?"

"Maybe he wanted them out of the way so he'd inherit the carnival."

"But Cherry—?"

"What if she's in danger?"

Luke's eyes widen briefly. "I was so focused on what could've happened to you when the lights fell last night . . ."

My heart does a small cartwheel.

"But what if you were just an innocent bystander, and the lights had been rigged to hit Cherry?" He rubs a hand over his face. "Or someone wants you out of the way because you're getting too close to her . . . and the truth."

"This case creeps me out more than the others have."

"That's why we need to work together." Luke watches me. "Got it?"

"Uh-huh."

His breath comes out in a huff. "Can you at least *try* to sound like you mean it? I'm serious here. No going into trailers by yourself—not even with Ruthie. No being alone with Red or Stewart or anyone from the carnival. We don't know what we're dealing with here, but it's big. And somebody could be out for blood. Not to mention Alfredo is still unaccounted for."

"You're kinda freaking me out."

"I *want* you scared." His hand latches onto my shoulder. "Do you get that? I want you scared enough that you're watching your back and never alone." Luke's hands slide down my arms. "Frightened enough that you'll be safe. Bella, I can't protect you every moment, and it's driving me crazy."

"Nobody asked you to protect me." But strangely enough, for once it sounds kind of nice.

"I think we should talk to Officer Mark. Update him."

"I agree."

Luke's eyes drop back to the flashlight in my hand. "Act like nothing's wrong tonight, okay? Can you do that?"

"Of course." It's becoming my specialty. "I need to go ask for next weekend off. No time like the present to show Red and Stewart that I'm not bothered at all."

"Let's go."

I hesitate for a millisecond before common sense takes over. That and the voice of my mother harping in my head. I follow Luke to the back of the carnival to the trailer area. We get to the edge of Red's just as the door flings open. Luke pulls me around the side, and we flatten to the wall.

"Well, William, this is the finest carnival of its size," comes Red's voice. "We have a long history of entertaining families *and* turning a profit. After we come out of our training season, we're gonna be better than ever."

I peek around the corner and see a short, white-haired man standing on the bottom step of Red's trailer.

"I certainly liked what I saw last night. I believe I'll stick around for this evening's show as well," the stranger says, adjusting his white cowboy hat.

"You do that. My son, Stewart, will make sure you have the best seats in the house. And if you feel so inclined, you can come back to the trailer after the performance and we'll discuss the contract."

The old man laughs. "It's always about money with you, isn't it, Red? Always was."

Cherry's uncle throws his head back and laughs. "William, you know I'd consider selling my soul for a good profit. So you *know* I won't hesitate to sell you the carnival."

Luke and I exchange a shocked stare, and I can't resist looking around the corner again.

"Your price is too rich for me, Red. I don't think I'm ready to sign over that check just yet."

I see Red slap the man on the back. "You just take your time thinking about it. In the end—Red Fritz always gets his way." A leering grin splits his face. "Always."

chapter twenty-three

People may think New York City is weird, but that town's got nothing on Dolly's house when it's packed with wrestlers.

"These little shrimp puffs are divine. Can you taste that tarragon?" Breath of Death pops one in his mouth and closes his eyes as if placing heaven on his tongue. "Dolly is amazing, Mickey. You should never let her go."

Mickey's gaze drifts over the crowd until he finds his ex-wife. "How right you are."

While Mickey still manages Jake's booming career, he's also been bombarded with requests from amateur wrestlers to train them, mostly former opponents of Jake's on the local circuit. I think Breath of Death is going to be his next breakout star—even though outside the ring, he's girlier than I am. Seriously, ten minutes ago he was quizzing me on my Zac Posen sundress.

I weave my way through the mass of people in Dolly's living room and head for her gourmet kitchen, where the food is spread out on two tables. Tonight's theme, courtesy of my mother's handiwork, is the fifties. The tables are draped in material that looks like pink poodle skirts. Vinyl records rest between the plates of food, and a rented jukebox plays "You Ain't Nothing But a Hound Dog." I expect Elvis to pop out any moment.

"Great party." Officer Mark grabs a cucumber and pops it in his mouth. "Wouldn't expect anything less, though. I always love a good Dolly-Jillian throwdown."

"They do work well together." I pour the punch into glasses that look like they're straight from an old time soda fountain. "I hear a lot of this stuff came from Sugar's Diner. Guess there's a ton of junk in storage from all their years."

He winces. "Sugar's is so old there could be dead bodies in storage for all we know."

"Speaking of dead bodies—"

"Bella"—Mark holds up hands of surrender—"don't start. I'm not here as a cop tonight. Just one of Mickey's boys having a nice evening out with the other manly men."

Breath of Death sticks his head between us. "Girl, I just caught a whiff of your perfume, and I *love* it!" He flutters his hand toward his nose. "Burberry, right?" The lummox of a wrestler laughs as he floats away, off to interrupt someone else's conversation.

I pick up my glass, covering my mouth. "You were saying?"

Officer Mark sighs and spoons out some spicy chicken dip. "It's weird that someone that in touch with his feminine side can crush a man's neck with his knees."

"So, Luke and I have been working at the carnival," I begin. "And there's a lot of weird stuff going on."

"Weird?" Mark frowns. "After Alfredo literally threw off his handcuffs and walked away, nothing would surprise me."

"Any leads on him yet?"

"No. Have you heard anything?"

I shake my head. "But there have been some strange occurrences at the carnival grounds." I fill him in, including my encounter with the crashing lights. "Luke and I don't know if it was meant for me or Cherry—or both."

"What makes you think it wasn't just an accident? Circuses

get thrown up really quickly, so quality and safety isn't always a top concern."

"I just know."

"Bella, if you're holding out information from the police, you have to let us know what you've seen and heard."

"But couldn't we share information—you and I? We're good friends—that's what friends do. Share stuff."

"Uh-huh," he smirks. "I'll remember that next time I want to borrow your flatiron and hairspray."

I reach toward a piece of hair sticking up. "Actually you could use a little—"

He slaps my hand away. "But it doesn't work the other way. *You* give us information. The end."

"You've helped me out before."

"*Before* didn't involve a murder."

"Well, actually it did. Both times." Psychotic killers seem to gravitate toward me.

"You know this is different." He adds more to his plate. "So tell me what else you've discovered—not that I approve of your snooping around."

"Last night I overheard Red talking to a potential buyer about the carnival. He's wanting to sell it."

Mark's hand stills on a serving spoon. "I guess the man's entitled to sell his own business. Does anyone else know?"

"I don't think so."

He shrugs and moves down the table. "Still, that's not really anything suspicious."

"I talked to a former employee yesterday who told me about Cherry's parents' death." I fill him in on every detail from Lars.

Mark puts his plate down and gives me his full attention. "Bella"—he chews on his bottom lip as if weighing a decision— "I already know a lot of this. The sale of the carnival is new information, but the rest, I knew." His eyes lock with mine. "Please believe me when I tell you that we have it under control. And also believe it when I say you need to stay out of the way. No more following people and hunting up clues."

"You know Red and Stewart are connected. Why can't you just call them in for questioning and confront them with some of this?"

"This is a delicate situation. And it's being handled as we see fit." Again with the intense eyes. "Can you trust me on this?"

My nosy-meter is off the charts. "What are you not telling me?"

Mark's cell phone vibrates on his hip. After a quick check, he hands me his plate. "Gotta run. But I'm serious about the warning. We know we can't stop you from working at the carnival, but just do your job and go home. Don't socialize with anyone there, don't go into any trailers, nothing." He pats me on the shoulder and gives me his I-know-best look. "You don't want to be responsible for ruining a very delicate investigation, do you?" He turns on his heel and disappears into the crowd, leaving me with a feeling as unsettling as brown guacamole.

I'm on the inside. Doesn't Mark get that? I'm close to Cherry. If I bat my eyes enough, I could probably get anything out of Stewart, and I'm there at the carnival almost every day. I'm the inside girl! What's wrong with *helping* the police?

A half hour later I'm sitting by Cherry and Dolly on one of the couches. Peg the dog rests in Cherry's lap, content to be petted during commercial breaks. Mom watches the *Sunday Night Smackdown* with fluctuating expressions of pride, excitement, and sadness as the camera pans to Jake, who gives a play-by-play of the action.

"He's really good," Dolly says. "Just a natural."

"My dad's the coolest." This from Robbie, who sits on Budge's lap in a leather chaise.

Mickey beams. "That's my Jake."

Actually it's my mom's Jake. But he seems to belong to everyone but her and this family lately.

When my phone sings, I get up and answer it in the dining room. "Hello?"

"Bella, it's me." Luke. The boy with the voice that could melt a Popsicle. "Can you meet me at the school parking lot?"

"Gee, Luke. It's a little late for a make-out session. But I guess I could brush my teeth and be there in ten."

"I'm serious, Bella . . . Actually I'm *dead* serious."

With hasty explanations to the party crowd, I walk out the door and into the steamy evening to my Bug. With my radio cranked up, I'm at the school four songs later.

I step into the passenger seat of Luke's 4Runner and inhale leather, faded cologne, and something else that is solely Luke Sullivan. "What's going on?"

He looks at me for a moment, taking in my spring sundress, then turns the key. "We're going to take a little drive."

"Is this about us?"

He pulls the SUV out and onto the road. "You know my conditions, so this couldn't be about us."

Because I have to be the one to initiate a relationship. Or even the next conversation about it. "Where are we going?"

"The Patton family cemetery."

"Why? Is Ashley going to be waiting there for me with a big ax?" Though it's balmy outside, I suddenly feel like turning the heat on. I'm cold all the way down to my Kate Spade flats. "I've never heard of this place."

"It's a small family-owned graveyard. The family's pretty much died out, so they use it to bury people in town who can't afford plots in the town cemetery." He turns onto Main Street. "I was doing a little surveillance tonight and stumbled upon something. I think

you're going to be very interested. Not that you're dressed for it."
His eyes slide my way again. "You look nice, by the way."

Heart flip-flops. "Thanks. If you had given me some notice, I
could've at least put on some black face paint."

A few minutes later Luke turns off on a dirt road.

"This isn't a cemetery." Creepiness radiating in full force now.

He shuts off the vehicle, reaches in the backseat, and grabs a
flashlight. "Ready?"

"Wait." I rest my hand on his to stop him. "What's going on?"

He hands me a dark running jacket. "We're going to walk down
the road a bit. About a fourth of a mile down is the back side of the
cemetery. We'll camp out in some trees. I brought that jacket for you
just in case you were decked out in sparkles and neon."

"Thanks." I slip my arms into the sleeves and imagine him playing soccer with it on. "Gonna tell me what's going on?"

"Betty the Bearded Lady is buried out here."

"Suddenly I don't really feel like paying my final respects."

"Apparently Red and Stewart do." He opens his door and steps
out. "They started digging her up about an hour ago."

chapter twenty-four

W e're going to see Red and Stewart breaking into Betty's coffin?" Well, here's the one time I wish he would've called Ashley Timmons instead. "And what—we're going to see if they'd like some refreshments?"

Luke locks his vehicle as I hop down. "No, we're going to see what they're looking for." He walks to my side and waits. "Can you handle this?"

"Uh, yeah." I snort. "Totally."

He slings an arm around me as we hit the dirt road. "Then why are you shaking?"

"Fever." I swallow hard and try not to think of Betty's dead corpse. "Probably the flu—just another reason I won't be making out with you tonight."

"Very thoughtful of you." He drops his arm and reaches for my hand instead. "Stick close to me. I know where I'm going."

This moment reminds me of last fall when he and I followed a bloodthirsty group of football boys into the woods at the lake. When they chased us out, we jumped in his 4Runner.

"Bella, I'm going to need you to trust me to get us out of this. Can you do that?"

I could hear the guys gaining on us. I remember yelling, *"Do something! What's your plan?"*

"*This.*" And he leaned in and kissed the life out of me. Fireworks zinged and popped in my head, and I just dove in and went along with it. For survival's sake, of course.

I wonder if he's thinking of that now. Or if he ever does.

"Bella . . . Bella?"

Luke tugs on my hand, and I realize he's been talking. "Um, yes. I agree."

I hear his small laugh. "You're not paying attention. I just asked you if you wanted to go home and snort wet spaghetti noodles up your nose."

I tug his hand right back. "Testing me?"

"Yeah, and you failed." He keeps walking and pulling me along. "I need you to be on your A game tonight. Just in case we have to make an emergency dash back to the car."

And in the dark I see Luke turn his head and look at me. Really look at me. And I know he remembers that night. My cheeks warm, and I smile at him.

"You ready?" he whispers.

For you? For this? To tell you I don't believe you were a willing participant in Ashley's kiss? "I think I might be."

Luke watches me for a suspended moment. For a slip of a second, I think he's going to kiss me. He reaches out a hand . . .

. . . and points beyond me. "Right this way." His attention refocused, he guides me off the road and through some trees. "Watch your step." He shines his flashlight on the ground as we traipse over grass that rises to my bare calves.

A few minutes later he's turned the light off, and I know we're almost there.

"Shhh." He pulls me around a tall pine and points to the left.

I peek around, and there, illuminated in their own spotlight, are Red and Stewart. Both stand with shovels in hand, knee-deep in the wet grass, sending the dirt flying into the air. They really are digging into that grave. If I were Catholic, I'd totally be crossing myself here. This is unholy! It's sacrilegious! It's ... making me glad I slipped my camera into my pocket.

I watch in stunned silence for a few moments as the two plunge their shovels into the earth over and over. If I had any doubts they were capable of anything as vile as murder before, I don't doubt it now.

"Can't you dig any faster?" Red yells, his head barely visible over the ground.

"I'm going as fast as I can. I've been digging thirty minutes longer than you."

My left leg is tingling and numb by the time I hear a shovel hit metal.

"Got it!" Stewart yells. "Not much longer now."

Good. Because I seriously have to pee.

Time creeps in slow motion, and finally the digging stops.

"You do it."

"No. You're older. You knew her better."

Silence. Red mumbles something insulting to his son, then I hear the chill-inducing creak of the lid.

Stewart yelps like a girl.

"Would you shut up?" his dad bellows. "All we need is the cops out here."

"S-S-She looks—"

"Dead?"

Come on. One of you admit you killed her. Say something.

"Check out her neck," Red barks. "Hurry up."

Luke and I glance at one another as whining noises come from Stewart. Oh, to be able to see in that hole. Well, not see Betty. But to spy on those two buffoons—that would be priceless.

"I don't see anything."

"You know you're going to have to check in her blouse."

"It's not here, Dad."

"Check again!"

"Fine . . . oh, sick." Stewart's dry heaving noises have me turning my face into Luke's shoulder. He rests a hand on my head.

"Step back. Can't you do anything? Let me see her." More rustling around and grunting. "Nothing."

"I told you," comes Stewart's wounded voice.

"I don't understand. The map said it was around her heart."

I lift my head from Luke's shoulder, and we share a look. *Around her heart?* What does that mean? And what part of the map are they talking about? That's not on the version we have.

"You're sure that's what it said?" Red asks.

"I saw it, Dad. I saw it with my own eyes before that dog took off with it. But that's all I remember."

That's why they wanted the dog. Because Peg somehow had the other half of the map. But wait . . . if Stewart saw it before the dog ran off . . . I gasp as the thought hits, and Luke plants his hand over my mouth.

Ten minutes later we're shut safely in the SUV, and I give voice to one of the racing thoughts in my head. "Stewart either killed Betty or was in her trailer soon after."

Luke starts the engine. "Did you come up with that before or after you bit my hand?"

"I couldn't breathe."

"Likely story." He backs out of the field and steers us onto the dirt road. "If I have rabies, I'm giving Ashley all your assignments."

At ten o'clock, I'm in my car driving back out to Dolly's. When I wheel into the drive, most of the cars are gone. Budge's hearse is absent. No doubt he took Robbie home to be put to bed. But Mom's Tahoe is still here.

"Did you come back for more cake?" Dolly asks as I enter the living room.

"Um . . . came by to see if you needed any help cleaning up."

A brow lifts toward her teased bangs. "You came all this way to sweep and scrub down some tables?"

"Okay, I really just wanted to talk to Cherry about a few things."

Dolly jerks her head toward the back door. "She's outside feeding the dog. I swear, lately she gives her enough food to feed an entire kennel of Labradors."

I find Cherry by the pool, swishing her legs in the water as Peg rests nearby.

She looks up and smiles. "You're back?"

I ease down beside her on legs stiff from standing up so long. I weigh the contents of my brain, trying to gauge how much to tell her. How do you break it to someone that their parent-figure's grave was broken into?

"Cherry . . . Luke and I saw something pretty disturbing tonight."

"Oh. I didn't know you were still here when Breath of Death sang Clay Aiken during karaoke."

I blink twice. "Okay, though it seems impossible, I witnessed something even more frightening than that." I explain the scene Luke brought me to. I give Cherry a moment to absorb it.

"Why would Stewart and Red do such a horrible thing?" Her face is pale in the dim pool lights.

"They're looking for something. Whatever they've been digging for all over town, they were convinced it was actually *on* Betty." But if one of them killed her, wouldn't he have noticed?

"What do you think they're looking for?"

"I don't know. They said it was 'around her heart.'"

Cherry's feet still. "Look through town. Tear it apart. But the answer you seek. Is circled 'round my heart."

The air in my lungs stops. "What did you say?"

Cherry turns sad eyes to me. "It's the other half of the map."

"H-how could you know that?"

"The dog." She trails her hand down Peg's furry head. "She was gone for an entire day last week. I was crazy with worry, and it's not like I could ask anyone if they had seen her. But she came back to me." She pats Peg's neck, and her ID charm chimes in the breeze. "She's so smart like that."

"And . . . ?"

"And she brought back the other half of the map." Cherry digs into the pocket of her shorts and pulls out a gnarled piece of paper. "It's the rest of it."

I unfold it and read the handwritten script.

Look through town. Tear it apart. But the answer you seek. Is circled 'round my heart.

"It's in Betty's handwriting."

"They didn't find anything tonight."

Cherry nods. "I'm scared, Bella."

"Maybe they'll find this hidden treasure or whatever, and then it will be over."

She lifts her eyes to mine. "That's not when it ends, and you know it."

I take a deep breath. "Then when do you think it's over?"

She stares into the darkness of the pool. "When I'm dead."

chapter twenty-five

I don't work at the carnival again until Tuesday. And by the time the three o'clock bell rings at school, my nerves are as fried as a funnel cake.

So many questions. Who put my flashlight on my clown uniform? Red? Stewart? Both? And if they do know I'm onto them, then why not just come out and say it? Why keep me around?

And as possessive of the carnival as Red is, why would he want to sell it now? Maybe he wants to get an eight-to-five gig in an office and provide a stable home for Cherry. Yeah, right. And I like K-Mart.

And this map? Where's this riddle going to lead us? Ever since Sunday night, that little rhyme of Betty's has been bouncing around in my brain. Circled 'round her heart? Why couldn't she have just said, "Hey, go to the water tower and take five steps. There it is." I mean, seriously, who hides clues in tacky poetry?

I drive straight home to check in with my mom and make myself a PB&J sandwich for work. The first week on the job, I ate dinner every night at the carnival. But a girl can't live on Sprite and hamburgers alone. Though I wouldn't mind trying.

I park the Bug in the back next to Budge's hearse and watch Robbie hop off the porch and do a double roll into the grass.

"Hey, Robbie!" I call. "Are you off to save the world?"

He squats low, his hands in karate chop position. "Yeah. I got secret intel that my cow needs me."

Every kid needs a pet. I have my cat. Lindy has a Lab. Ruthie has a lizard. But Robbie? His is of the bovine variety.

My stepbrother's red cape flutters in the warm breeze. "I have to be on my guard in case there's kryptonite on my path."

"Is that what you're calling cow poop these days?"

With arms outstretched, he flies away to save those in need, those in trouble, those who eat from troughs.

I open the screen door and step into the kitchen. Mom sits at the table, a pencil poised over her notebook. "Studying?"

She looks up and smiles. "Hey, sweetie. Yeah, I have my final Thursday." She pats the seat beside her. "How was your day? You look tired."

Can't imagine why. "Mom, what's going on with you and Jake?"

The pencil *thunks* as she sets it down. "Nothing for you to be worried about. We're just adjusting to his new career."

"You mean *he's* adjusting. We're just . . . here."

Mom's forehead wrinkles, and I wonder if she ever misses her quarterly Botox gifts from Dad. "Bella, basically overnight he went from working in a factory to being a national star. Do you realize by next Christmas they'll have a Captain Iron Jack action figure?"

"Good. If we get one, then he'll always be with us." I wince at the vinegar on my tongue. *Lord, why are nosiness and sass my spiritual gifts? Aren't I supposed to have something like peace, goodness, patience, and all that other sweet stuff?*

Mom shuts her textbook and puts her hand on mine. "I know I brought you to Truman on what seemed like a whim. But I knew marrying Jake was the right thing to do. I still believe that. And even though we didn't sign up for the way things are now, we have to have faith that it's all going to work out."

"I just don't see the end of it, though, Mom. Jake's just getting started. Let's say they retire him in ten years. Can you live like this that long?"

She nibbles on her bottom lip, her eyes on the table. "You and I aren't the only ones who didn't get what we bargained for. Jake spends every night on a bus. He wakes up each day and doesn't remember what town he's in. He misses his family."

"Then why doesn't he quit? Doesn't he feel guilty that you're the one taking care of his sons?" A year ago my mom and I couldn't have had a conversation like this. We barely knew each other. But now . . . we're friends. It's strange. But I like it.

"We're praying about it."

"For how long? When is enough *enough*?"

Mom leans over and curls her arm around me. I smile at the smell of her perfume, a fragrance she's worn all my life. It's just about the only trace of Manhattan left of her.

"Isabella, this is in God's hands. He told Jake and me both to pursue this. He didn't say go for this marriage and this wrestling career—then quit." Her fingernails trail meandering patterns on my back. "I'm going to be honest with you—things couldn't be more wrong. But it's brought me closer to God. Closer to you and the boys. And I know change is coming." She shrugs. "Could be tomorrow, could be next year. But the Lord didn't lead us through all we've been through just to desert us now."

"Mom?"

"Hmm?"

"When that change does come . . . can I have my own credit card again?"

"Bella?"

"Yes?"

"God says no."

Thirty minutes later I'm standing in the big top watching the progress of Stewart and Cherry's new routine. One swing suspends from the center of the trapeze area, and Cherry hangs from the bottom of it as Stewart is braced upside down above her. This new performance has more of a Cirque du Soleil feel to it, and I know it has to be challenging every muscle in her body. I can't imagine having to hold up your own body weight just by clinging to two ropes. And they've added a new element where Stewart will eventually unfurl her from a gigantic sash. It's pretty cool to watch, but I wouldn't want to try it.

"Amazing, aren't they?"

I turn my head as Luke approaches. He looks like he just walked off a Gap commercial, his hair curling at the ends, barely resting on the collar of his gray henley. He stands by my side, and my heart flutters like butterfly wings. I rein it back in and focus above me. "I think the new performance is too much for Cherry. Look at her arms shaking."

"She's determined to pull it off, though. She told me she wants to do this for her parents."

"You know Red wants them to nail this to impress the potential buyer."

Luke nods. "Let's hope that's all he wants out of the act."

"What do you mean?"

Luke's volume drops a notch. "This routine killed Cherry's parents. But you and I know that it might not have been an accident. So what if this is Red's psychotic way of repeating history?"

Chills flare on my skin that have nothing to do with Luke's preppy hotness. "That had crossed my mind. I just wasn't ready to put it out there and say it." It just sounds so evil. "But Stewart would have to be in on it. It's not like Red would kill his own son to get rid of Cherry."

"The question is when."

"And why. Why would he want his niece out of the way so badly?"

Luke watches the two flip until they've changed places on the swing. "Maybe he's jealous of her biceps."

"I know I am."

After the show, I pull off my sweaty clown jumpsuit and place it in the box. My neck is already hurting from looking over my shoulder every five seconds. Stewart and Red both treated me normally tonight. They pretty much ignored me—except for the occasional pervy stare from the younger Fritz. I would love to tell Stewart I would kiss Robbie's cow before I would even *consider* a date with him.

Ruthie, Luke, and I walk outside together, laughing over her unicycle ballet.

"It's not funny," Ruthie huffs. "Whoever had the bright idea to play Snoop Dogg instead of my usual *Phantom of the Opera* needs to be punished." She cracks her knuckles. "And I'm going to have some serious prayer time tonight until the Lord tells me how to go about my pain-inducing revenge."

"I had nothing to do with it. I just run the lights." Luke bites back a smile.

"So are we doing any surveillance?" Ruthie yawns. "These late nights are brutal on my beauty rest. Last night I fell asleep while Budge was telling me about this new game he created. I faded out somewhere between vector sequence and modchips."

I laugh. "I don't think it was your lack of sleep that knocked you out." More like Budge's computer lingo put her in a techie coma.

"We better back off for a while," Luke says, stopping at his 4Runner. "After what Bella and I saw Sunday evening, I don't think there's really any need to follow them. They don't know what they're doing."

Ruthie throws a leather-clad leg over her motorcycle. "I can't believe you guys left me out of that. Breaking into a dead lady's casket? I can't imagine anything cooler."

I can't imagine anything grosser. "We'll call next time."

"See that you do. You shouldn't keep something like that all to yourselves. It just isn't right." She throws up a gloved hand in a wave and zooms away. I stand there and watch her go, aware that she has a cool factor I couldn't achieve even if I had access to every one of my dad's credit cards.

Luke and I stand between our cars. Awkward. Silent.

"So, um . . . I read your latest article." He lifts his eyes from the blur that is Ruthie. "It's better."

I stiffen. "But not good enough?"

"You're distracted is all."

I listen for a hint of power-tripping arrogance, but don't hear it. "It was a perfectly fine piece, Luke."

He leans on his SUV, crossing his arms on his chest. "Nothing perfect about it. And as for fine, you're a better writer than that. I should be reading your work and thinking 'amazing' and 'creatively brilliant.'"

"Maybe you're confusing me with your new girlfriend."

With fire in his eyes, Luke pushes off the vehicle and takes the three steps that separate us. He stares down until I look up. "You have something to say, Kirkwood?"

"No." I don't know why that came out of my mouth. Like Ruthie, I'm just tired.

"I didn't think so." He shakes his head. "Because you're scared."

I draw up my spine. "I don't think *scared* girls watch men dig up graves." I give him the attitude-head-bob. "But maybe I'm wrong."

His smile could charm a snake. "You're scared of what's going on in here." He taps his own heart. "And honesty gives you that little nervous tick. *Real* scares you—admit it."

"I'm getting *real* mad. That doesn't frighten me at all."

Luke's face looms mere inches above mine. "You're jealous of Ashley."

"I am not—"

"You're so crazy about me, you can't think straight."

"Oh my gosh." I force a laugh. "Somebody needs to save you from yourself." Where're Ruthie and her nunchucks when I need them?

"And you're so prideful, you can't even see that your writing still needs work. Lots of work." Luke's voice dips low. "So quit taking it as a personal attack from your ex-boyfriend and consider it from the guy who runs the newspaper and knows what he's talking about."

Our eyes lock and hold. A clash of wills. Of friends. Of old flames.

"You really gotta do something about your split personalities," I breathe.

Luke pulls me to him and crushes his mouth to mine.

"I said I wasn't going to do this," he whispers on a kiss.

"S'okay." I pull him closer, my hands snaking up his back. "Don't mind."

His hands move up to cup my face, to tilt my head, to move his lips over mine again. "Bella?"

"Hmmm?"

I stifle a groan as Luke pulls away.

Still holding my face in one hand, he runs his finger down my nose. Over my cheek. I lean into his palm and just try to breathe. "What?"

"Do you know what this was?" he asks, his mouth near my ear.

"The warm-up?"

"A test."

My cozy smile drops. I step away.

"You're lying to yourself if you think you don't want to be with me."

"I—I"—am so mad—"it was the moonlight. It was the popcorn at nine o'clock."

Luke reaches out and brushes a piece of hair behind my ear.

"Face it—you're totally into your editor." He sighs dramatically. "I hope whatever is keeping us apart is worth it."

I stand there motionless, my tongue glued to the roof of my mouth as Luke climbs into his 4Runner. I should say something. I should yell—or maybe throw a shoe? What would Ruthie do? No. I can't moon him.

In my head fury wars with the theme song from *Pride and Prejudice* as the kiss replays in my head. Again. And again. When I glance back at Luke, I startle to realize he's waiting for me to get in my car and leave.

I give him a small wave. Yep. Going to my car. Unaffected. Absolutely unaffected. I kiss boys every day.

Starting the car.

I was born kissing boys. Boys better than you, Luke Sullivan.

Turning the key.

And that may have been a test for you. But that was just an act for me. Call me Reese Witherspoon because I have Oscar-worthy skills.

I put the car in drive and pull out of the parking lot, my brain on autopilot. His headlights shine behind me as we drive into town. At the four-way stop, I go right. He goes left.

I wheel the car into the school parking lot, put her in park, and indulge in a moment of banging my head against the steering wheel before I go on home.

"Stupid! Stupid! Stupid!" I'm *so* dumb. Why did I let him get the upper hand? Again. I like being in control. Me! This was my game. He can't just flip the rules on me.

Slowly raising my head, I take a few cleansing breaths.

I check myself out in the rearview mirror.

And see a cold-blooded killer in my backseat.

chapter twenty-six

Your brain does crazy things when there's a pistol aimed at your face.

Mine zooms on overload as I consider my options. There's jump out of the car. There's pray for the Rapture. And there's hope for aliens to beam down and suck Alfredo into the mother ship.

"Don't move," Alfredo says, the gun shaking slightly.

"If you shoot me, my mom will rip you in half with her bare hands." How in the world did he get in here? My car was locked— just like his handcuffs when he escaped. Dang, this guy is good. It's like you never see it coming. *Lord, I'd love to get through this alive— without peeing my pants.*

"Put your hands where I can see them. Rest them on the console."

I do as the man says, trying not to gag at the overripe smell coming from the backseat. "You seriously need a shower."

He rolls his eyes. "That's the least of my problems."

"And killing me is going to solve them?"

"I'm not killing you. I just want your attention."

I glance at the cold metal weapon. "You've got it."

"I didn't kill Betty."

"Uh-huh." I had begun to believe that myself, but now?

Alfredo rubs a hand over his bearded face. "I was set up. You have to believe me."

"Are you going to shoot me if I don't?"

He lowers the gun and sighs. "Look, people talk. I know you're like some supersleuth or something. That's why you're working at the carnival, isn't it?"

"How did you get out?"

"Dislocated bones help." The magician looks over his shoulder like a nervous cat. "I can get out of anything. It wasn't as easy as my own trick handcuffs—just two twists and a tug—but it wasn't impossible either."

"Two twists and a tug?"

"Yeah. The carnival cuffs. They're fakes, and if you move your hands right, they pop open."

"Alfredo, I don't know much about the law, but I don't think breaking out of jail is going to do much for your case. Your attorney probably isn't too happy with you right now."

Leaning forward, Alfredo wraps his arm around my passenger seat. The gun dangles loosely in his grimy hand. "I have to prove I'm innocent. Red and Stewart—those guys set me up." His eyes dart outside again. "Hey, could we, like, drive somewhere else? Someone's bound to see me here."

"Look, I've seen enough Oprah. You never agree to drive a guy with a gun somewhere. The second location is always where they find your dead, bloated corpse."

"I'm not a killer!" he shouts.

"If you want to talk, then talk." My voice tremors. This guy is seriously freaking me out. "But I'm not driving us anywhere, so say what you need to say . . . or kill me. Those are your choices." That sounded so much braver than I feel.

Alfredo closes his eyes and rests his head on the seat. "How did this all get so screwed up?" A few moments pass, and I begin to formulate a few escape plans.

"I loved Betty," he says finally. "You have to believe that."

"It doesn't matter what I believe. I hate to break it to you, but it's the judge you'll want to persuade." Seriously, does this guy know nothing about due process?

"You're the only one who can help me, though. My own lawyer thinks I'm guilty."

"Then who killed her?"

His mouth opens and closes on a hesitation. "Red and Stewart."

"What could they possibly hope to gain?" Again, the awkward pause. "I may have a small gift in crime solving, but I'm not a mind reader. Spill it."

"I don't know much. But I do know Betty was afraid of Red. She was anxious to get back to Truman. Said she had stuff to do. Something she had to get."

"Is that what Red and Stewart have been looking for?"

He nods. "Yeah. She had grown to trust me . . . but not that much. So I don't know what she left. Could've been money, incriminating photos, something for Cherry. I just don't know. But she would only tell me that she was the only one who knew about it, and she needed it to save Cherry."

"What does that mean?"

"I said I don't know!" His volume escalates with each word.

"Is this seriously all you have to bring me? I'm supposed to clear your name when you give me nothing more than your statement of innocence? And put that gun on the floorboard, will you? I can't concentrate with you waving that thing around."

"I heard you were bossy." He plops it on the floor without complaint.

"Alfredo, you have to really think about this. Scan your brain for anything weird Red or Stewart have said in the last year or so." An idea flicks to life in my own head. "I saw Red's payroll book. About the time you and Betty started dating, he gave you a raise. What's that about?"

"I loved Betty. I know we were an unlikely couple. Nobody bought it at first, but I loved her with all my heart. We were going to get married and take care of Cherry together."

"And then your sword found its way into Betty's chest."

Alfredo blinks hard, as if trying to push back the pain. "I want justice. Whoever killed my Betty, my fuzzy sweetheart—they must pay."

Ew. "You didn't answer my question. Why the sudden bump in salary?"

His eyes drop to the tan floor mat at his feet. "Times are really bad for the carnival. People started leaving before we even got to Truman, and they were not replaced. So I told Red I would work the job of two men, putting in almost eighty hours a week, and I would only ask for half an additional salary."

I study this man's outline in the glow of the streetlights. "Does Red know what he's looking for?"

"I think so."

"But he doesn't know where—even with the map."

"Map? You have Betty's map?" Alfredo straightens.

"So you know about it?"

"Of its existence, yes. That much Betty told me. You have to let me see it."

I lean back into the door and feel the handle press into my back. "I don't have to do anything." Crazy loon.

"If you let me look at it, it might make sense to me in a way that wouldn't to anyone who wasn't familiar with Betty like I was." His voice drops to a pleading whisper. "Whatever this is, it was important to Betty. And I think it has to do with protecting Cherry. I have to continue Betty's work and see this through. Then ... I can let her go."

"Cherry thinks her life is in jeopardy."

"Then you must share the map with me. It's the only way. I won't let someone else die—not when I can prevent it."

"Where are you staying? How will I get ahold of you?"

"I can't tell you that." He settles back into the seat, slouching low. "But when you're ready to talk, put one of the carnival posters on your dash. I'll find you and leave meeting instructions."

"You've been hanging around the carnival, haven't you? Are you the one who let the horses out and all those other weird things that have everyone so spooked?" He says nothing. "This is illegal. I can't withhold information about a fugitive from the police."

He picks up the gun and moves it from one hand to the other. "Then tell them your life is at stake."

"Is that more blustery bravado?"

"Yes." He nods. "How'd I do?"

"Kinda scary."

"I learned a lot while I was locked up." Alfredo reaches for the handle and pulls. "It really is critical you not tell anyone you saw me. Cherry's life depends on it. I know you wouldn't want her death on your conscience for the rest of your life."

He slips out the door and disappears into the tree-covered lot beside the road. I watch him walk away until he blends into the night.

I have to call the police. Luke. Someone.

I flip on the overhead light and reach for my phone.

But it's gone.

Foiled by the magician.

He breaks out of handcuffs. He busts out of jail. And he steals phones.

Couldn't he just stick with pulling bunnies out of a hat?

chapter twenty-seven

B y Friday morning I'm stressed to the point of snapping. I've
been on edge ever since I found Alfredo in my rearview mirror. When I got out of school the following day, there, in my locked
car, was my cell phone. Just waiting for me, as if it had been there
all along. That Alfredo—it's like he can morph or something. He's
an X-Man.

The rest of the week proved to be uneventful. No more bodies dug up. No more lights crashing at the carnival. And no posters
in my car as a signal to Alfredo. I have yet to tell Cherry about my
encounter. I've never withheld information from the police *or* my
mom before, and I don't want to bring Cherry in on it. At least not
yet. It's bad enough Luke knows. No need to upset anyone else.

"Bella, I still think we should talk to Officer Mark." Luke's voice
is barely audible over the crowd at LaGuardia Airport. I press the
phone closer to my ear.

"We've discussed this a million times."

"No, we've argued a million times. But I don't know that we've
had a calm discussion yet." His voice drips with editor arrogance.
"That's what I'm trying to attempt now, but so far it's a one-man job."

"Hey, I'm sorry, you're breaking up. Lousy reception in this airport." I hold the phone toward Ruthie, and she makes crackly noises.
"Gotta go."

"Wait, Bella—"

"Yes?"

Silence on the other end. "I'm praying you have a good visit with your dad. I hope you find out what you need to know."

Wow. Hard to be snooty to a guy when he talks like that. "Thanks."

"And when you get back, we're telling Cherry everything. And maybe the police."

"Bye." I end the call and throw the phone in my purse.

Ruthie sips her Starbucks. "What did your boyfriend want?"

Why did I bring her with me to New York again? "He's not my boyfriend. And we were just having a small disagreement."

"You two wouldn't have anything to say to one another if you weren't arguing."

"I guess that would leave more time for making out." I smile as Ruthie spews her mocha. "I'm kidding." Mostly.

My purse vibrates with a text. Dad is here. Finally.

"Let's go get our bags and head to the *casa de crazy.*" The teachers had a bunch of meetings today, so school was out and Ruthie and I were able to get an early flight. This gives me more time to get to the bottom of whatever Christina's hiding.

Ruthie walks along beside me, her blue and pink hair catching the stares of the occasional security guard. "So you're going to snoop a little this weekend, and I'm to provide the distractions. Just how is it I'm going to accomplish that?"

"Just be yourself."

In the taxi ride home, Dad updates me on his new highlights, his latest celebrity client, and his TV show developments. He asks few questions about me. It's a conversational rhythm I'm used to.

When we get home, I head straight for the kitchen, hug Luisa, then promptly ask her for any dirt.

"I know nothing. I see nothing. I hear nothing."

I stare my old nanny down. "In other words, you're afraid for your job."

She glances over her shoulder. "You would be to, if you were working for *Señorita* Beelzebub." Luisa makes horns over her head. "And little Marisol is her spitting image. *Querida*, I owe Maria Delgado two hundred big ones from a bad weekend of Texas Hold 'Em, so I must work. I can't give Christina any reason to replace me, you understand?"

"Do you find anything weird about her?"

Luisa hands a cookie to me and Ruthie. "This evening is bingo night at the church, and Father Joseph is the caller. It would take me all day to list what's strange about her, and I'm feeling lucky tonight. So maybe tomorrow we can talk."

She pats me on the behind and waddles away.

"What were you guys gossiping about?" Marisol peeps her head in the door. "Secret stuff?"

Ruthie looks at me and rolls her eyes. "I got three just like her at home. I can take her."

Ruthie and her sisters are the most violent preacher's kids I've ever seen. They could overpower Jake and his wrestling buddies any day. Not a dainty lady among them. It's like they were raised by a pastor *and* a pack of wolves.

"Why don't you show Marisol where the cookies are while I go talk to my dad." I give Ruthie a hard look. *Do not hurt this kid.* Any bloodshed would have a negative effect on the likelihood of my getting Dad's credit cards.

I hear Christina on the phone in the dining room and cruise past her down the hall to Dad's study. Knocking on the mahogany door, I step inside. "Hey, Dad."

He glances up from a phone call and waves me in. "Yeah, I'm really excited too. I know the show will be great. So I've got that list of ideas, and I'll just fax them to you, okay? See you at the wedding. *Até logo.*" Dad hangs up and smiles. "How's my girl?"

"Wow, were you just speaking Portuguese?"

He clasps his hands behind his head and leans back in his desk chair. "I've been seeing a language tutor. When we go to Brazil, I want to be able to communicate with the filming crew."

I settle into a leather wingback chair. "Dad, um, I wanted to talk to you about something."

He wags a finger at me. "You know you can't have that boob job until graduation."

Am I the only girl on the planet whose dad discusses these things like it's as mundane as getting a new sweater at Abercrombie? "No, I don't want to talk about that." Nor do I want anyone taking a knife to the girls, thank you very much. "I know it's none of my business, but I just wanted to talk to you about this prenup you've got with Christina."

His eyes narrow. "How do you know there's a prenup?"

"Marisol. She said you guys met with your attorney."

"Christina's attorney, yes." There's an edge to his voice, but I trod on.

"You didn't each have your own?"

"You know money's tight around here. I'm trying to rebuild my investments and prepare for the move. So we thought we'd save and just have one lawyer draw up the contract. Christina's was cheaper. I really don't see how this is your concern."

My expression is as innocent as a baby's. "Because I love you, and I worry about you. I know money's an issue, and I don't want to see you hurt." *And when you date losers, my inner radar goes off like a microwave timer.*

Dad's mouth grows into a smile. "I understand the accountant situation bothered you, sweetheart. But this time it's under control. I adore Christina and trust her completely. We want the same things. Besides, she didn't exactly walk out ahead of the game in the prenup."

"What do you mean?"

He lowers his voice a notch. "Usually in these deals, you settle on a percentage of your assets. But all she asked for was five hundred grand. Just a flat amount in the event of our divorce." He leans across his desk. "Bella, when the money for this show contract comes in, I'm going to be worth a lot more than that. So don't worry about your old dad. I'm getting a wife I love, and on the off chance it doesn't work out, I have a new career direction *and* my money."

"Uh-huh." Why doesn't this make me feel better? You have to be suspicious of the things that sound too good to be true. "So is there anything in the contract that would make the agreement void? I mean, what if she's cheating on you?"

"Like that's going to happen." He winks. "She's crazy about me. But our attorney advised me to just keep it simple. So no matter the reasons for a split, she gets the money. And I keep everything else. But listen, while I appreciate your concern, nothing is going to go wrong. Christina and I plan on having a long future together."

That's what Mom thought once upon a time too. "Okay." I walk to his side and kiss his stubbly cheek. "I worry about you sometimes. I love you, you know?"

He takes my hand and clasps it in both of his. "I love you too, my Isabella. And when you see me on that TV show, you're going to be so proud of your old dad."

"I am proud of you."

"But this will be even better." He gives my fingers a squeeze. "You'll see. It's going to be amazing."

"Can't things be amazing right here—in Manhattan?" Is it so wrong to want my dad close and not half a world away? Sometimes at night, I picture this fantasy where my dad starts to board the plane to Brazil, then turns around and runs back. He swings me around in his arms and says, "I couldn't leave you. Do you really think I could move so far away and leave my girl behind? You mean more to me than any job offer." And then we hug and laugh. And go shopping.

A shrieking Marisol explodes into the office and pops my fantasy bubble.

"What's wrong?" Dad opens his arms, and the little girl sails right into them as if she was custom made for that place.

"She—she scared me."

Ruthie peeks in her multicolored head. "I have no idea why she's so upset." She walks to my side. "One minute we were talking, and the next she went to freaky town."

"She hasn't spent much time with her big sister lately and is feeling a little down." Dad rubs Marisol's head as she glares at me and Ruthie like a pit bull about to strike. "Come on, let's go find Christina and raid the fridge for some ice cream."

"Okay," she sniffs.

My dad's hand curls around her small one, and I feel something grip in me as well. Right in the heart region. *God, am I ever going to get over this jealousy? It's not just that I'm envious—I'm hurt. Why can't he treat me with half as much care as he shows Marisol?*

The two slide out of the room, and I blink as Marisol sticks out her tongue just before she disappears.

Ruthie clenches her fists. "That little—"

I hold out my arm and block her charge. "Sit down. It's not worth it." I pick up my dad's discarded cell phone and quickly copy down the last number. I might need to call his contact at this Brazilian reality show and ask a few questions. For journalistic purposes, of course.

"Do you know what that little rat said to me in the kitchen?" Ruthie asks.

"She liked your hair?"

"It is looking good today, isn't it?" Ruthie gives it a pat. "No, that little skunk told me that if I didn't give her twenty bucks, she was going to tell your dad that I kicked her in the shins."

"She didn't mention any violence to Dad, so how'd you show her who was boss?"

"I might've accidentally let her see my slingshot." Ruthie shrugs casually. "Sometimes it just slips out of my pocket, you know?"

Later that afternoon I stand in the dressing room of Enrique's House of Design.

"You are lucky I let you back in my shop. You realize that, don't you?" Enrique flips his scarf over his shoulder and grabs his latte from a burger-deprived assistant. "I rescheduled the First Lady just to fit you and your"—Enrique sneers—"stepdaughter in."

Ruthie sits on the edge of her chair. "The first lady? Like Madonna—the first lady of pop? Or Paris Hilton, the first lady of spray tan? Or maybe Dolly Parton, the first lady of cleavage?"

"Silence!" Enrique shoves the latte away and rubs his temples. "Your talking is upsetting the creative vibes in this studio. I meant the President's wife."

"Somebody is snippy," Ruthie whispers toward me, loud enough for all to hear. "Do you think I should offer him some of my Midol?"

"I'll just try on that dress now!" I step in front of the designer with my most angelic smile. "Can't wait to see it . . . again."

"You scoffed at its beauty last time."

"I was young and foolish then."

He nods once. "Very well." He claps his hands, and the skinny assistant reappears. "Get me the Christina De Luna bridesmaid dress."

Ten minutes later I'm sneezing my head off and trying to secure the feather boa straps. *"Achoo!"*

"Come out so Enrique can fit it," Christina calls.

I waddle out in the tight confection. It's literally a pink trash bag with feathers hot-glued everywhere.

"Oh!" My future stepmother gasps when I step outside the

dressing room. "It's heaven, Enrique. I just lose my mind every time I see it."

Ruthie tilts her head to one side, then the other. "I can see why."

"Spin for Enrique," the man says. You have to wonder about people who refer to themselves in third person.

I turn in a half circle, and he grabs the extra material at my waist. "Ow!" I frown at the pins in his fingers. "You stuck me."

"Fashion is pain, darling."

I send a pleading look to Christina, but her eyes go wide in warning.

By the time Enrique finishes, the dress is too tight, I can't move, and I look like a reject from a cross-dresser's garage sale. "It's very tight. Having trouble breathing."

"You are a little blue," Ruthie says. "But it's a nice color for you. Complements your plumage."

"It's perfect as it is." Enrique spins on his heel and faces Christina. "You like?"

She clasps her hands over her heart. "It's a dream. And yes, it's just the right fit."

"Yeah, if your goal is to suffocate me." Which I don't doubt. "But if you expect me to walk in this, it needs to be let out some." Plus, I like my wedding cake. Gotta have room in the dress for that.

"If Enrique says it's fine, then it is." Christina laughs and tosses her black hair. "We would be foolish to argue with a genius, right?"

He chuckles as well, a high-pitched sound that would make a chicken give up her feathers.

"*Achoo!*" Ruthie's sneeze echoes off the walls. "*Ah-ah-ah-choo!*"

"It's her allergies," Christina says, helping Ruthie to her feet. "Nothing more."

"No." My friend points to my dress. "Actually, I think it's that frock of a—"

"We'll just step outside." Christina pushes Ruthie toward the door. "We'll be down at the corner drugstore getting her some decongestant."

"*Achoo!*"

The designer's eyes narrow as they exit.

"I'll change now." I shuffle back to the dressing room, my feet moving inches at a time.

"Do not disturb my pins."

"Wouldn't dream of it."

It takes me fifteen minutes to get the tube of fluff off my body. And I only stick myself six times—if you just count the ones that drew blood.

I sigh with appreciation as I slip into my Rock & Republic jeans and T-shirt. "Here you go." I pass the dress off to the assistant, who takes it with a look of fear. "Don't worry. I'm pretty sure it's dead."

Enrique meets me at the entrance. "Tell Christina the dress will be ready next Wednesday."

"Okay."

"And I will need to know who will be picking this one up. Her or her sister." He clucks his tongue. "When the flower girl's dress was picked up, there was a small security issue. I don't hand my art over to just anyone. How was I to know that woman was family?"

"What do you mean her sister? Marisol is only eight."

He fingers the ends of his scarf. "No. Last week I met the other one."

My brain shudders as if ice water just fell over my head. "What do you mean *the other one?*"

"The tall blonde." Enrique covers his mouth to whisper. "Though it's so obvious she's as real a blonde as Beyoncé. I don't know why she's not in the wedding, but I don't ask. I tell myself, Enrique, you must not butt into your client's business. Did I butt into Brad and Angelina's? No. I am a professional. But sometimes I do have a little talk with Katie Holmes. Not that she listens."

"Oh. Uh-huh. The blonde sister." Thinking . . . thinking . . . "I, um, come to Manhattan so infrequently I don't get to see her and Christina much. Plus, I like to devote most of my time to Marisol." *Dear God, please wait 'til later to strike me down for lying.* "You know, maybe you can help me. I was going to get Christina and her sisters a little wedding present to celebrate the fun day." I rest my hand on his arm like we're old friends. "I bought the most divine jewelry boxes from Tiffany's and want to have them engraved. Do you know how you spell her sister's name?"

"The little one?"

"No. The other one."

"I don't know." He shrugs off my hand. "I was not born to spell. I was born to design. I suppose it is like the car."

"What do you mean?"

Enrique stares at me as if I have cotton candy for brains. "A Mercedes. I would imagine it's spelled the same."

"Mercedes?" That's her sister's name? "Of course. How silly of me." I push open the door and gaze toward the street. "Thank you, Enrique. I have truly been enlightened today."

And now to find out who this Mercedes is.

And arrange a family reunion.

chapter twenty-eight

"Y ou invited *who* over for dinner?"

"I've said it twice already, Bella. Mr. and Mrs. Penbrook and their son, Hunter, are coming over for dinner." Dad unknots his tie and leaves it dangling around his neck. "We've had this Friday night event planned for some time. I couldn't get out of it just because my daughter once dated their son. Jeff and I are still really good friends."

"Great. Just great." I stomp out of the living room and up to my bedroom. I need to find something to wear. What kind of outfit is appropriate for facing your ex after he cheated on you, then duped you on national television? "Hey, Ruthie, do you mind if I accessorize with your brass knuckles tonight?"

I flop next to her on the bed where she watches *Wheel of Fortune.* "That Vanna has such a cake job." She turns up the volume as a contestant buys a vowel. "That's what I want to be when I grow up. Well, either that or a brain surgeon."

"I didn't get a chance to talk to Dad about Christina. She walked in from work just as I was about to broach the subject."

"Bummer. Have you tried texting him?"

I think about this. "You want me to text my father that his fiancée is a lying schemer conducting shady dealings?"

Ruthie rolls her eyes. "Get with the times."

An hour later my old flame, Hunter Penbrook, asks me to pass the peas. I pick up the bowl, only briefly imagining dumping them over his head.

His smile is devilishly cute. "If you drop those in my lap, I will be forced to cause a scene." His hand brushes mine as he takes the bowl, and I realize I don't feel a thing. Nary a flutter nor a tingle. Why is it when Luke touches me, I instantly quiver like Jell-O?

Ruthie holds the dinner crowd's attention with her reenactment of her unicycle routine using salad tongs, the pepper grinder, and two stuffed mushrooms. My dad and Hunter's parents stare in amazement, while Christina studies her nails and Marisol stabs holes in her baked potato.

I take this opportunity to speak to Hunter. "You haven't called in a while. Are you still keeping tabs on that hotel room?"

"As much as I can. I told you I would let you know if I had anything to report."

"I like updates, Hunter. Updates."

"I do not miss your nagging."

I smile into my napkin and wipe my mouth. "I know. I'm too much girl for you. It's no wonder we didn't work."

"I've put in a lot of stalking time for you, so I wouldn't push it."

We share a laugh, and I realize once again, I have forgiven him. When Jesus said to forgive people to infinity, I assumed my ex-boyfriend was the exception. But it's kind of freeing not to be mad or holding a grudge. Besides, I need his cheating eyes on door number 857.

"You're a wily guy. Can't you draw her out of her room?" In a tiny whisper I fill him in on the new Christina development.

"Mercedes?" He chews this over. "I need a last name to get you any information."

"Christina's is De Luna. Try that."

"The woman is a hermit. If she leaves at all, it's while I'm at school."

I slice into my steak. "Maybe you could set up a hidden camera."

"And maybe I could go to jail."

"You'd do that for me?" I set down my utensils. "I'm touched."

"Bella, just give it up."

"How can I?"

"The wedding is June fifteenth. I think your best bet is to simply talk to your dad."

I nearly choke on my bite. "That's funny, I thought you had met the guy." I point toward the end of the table. "Dark-haired fellow. Works 24-7 and forgets I'm alive. He's the chap sitting across from your father."

Hunter glances that way just as the two men share a laugh. "It's good to see my dad happy. I haven't seen that in a long time."

"I'm sorry." I watch Mr. Penbrook high-five my dad as they share a joke. "I know he hasn't ever recovered from the accountant fiasco." My dad and Mr. Penbrook had the same bogus financial guru. Dad has slowly bounced back, since he lost cash and not his practice. But Hunter's father wasn't so lucky. He wasn't in the business of nose jobs and inflatable boobs, and ended up losing almost everything.

"It's okay. Things are turning around. He and my mom actually went on a date together last weekend. For a while I didn't think they were going to make it."

I know how that feels. "I'll bet you being out of the house and spying on that hotel room gives your parents even more alone time."

Hunter laughs. "You're about as smooth as a rattlesnake. But I'll get back to my Peeping Tom duties this week."

"Not just anyone would stalk a lady for me, Hunter." I pat his arm. "And I appreciate it. You're a good guy."

His eyes grow serious. "Really?"

"Yeah. And to thank you, I'm going to set you up with this girl I know named Ashley Timmons . . ."

On Saturday, Ruthie and I wake up late to find muffins on the kitchen counter with a note from Dad. The house is empty.

I pour myself a glass of juice. "Dad had to go in to work for a bit, and Christina took Marisol to dance lessons."

"That kid neeths politeness wessons," Ruthie says around a full mouth of muffin. "She has no mannerth."

Says the girl who just spit out two blueberries. "I think we should get ready and pay my dad a visit. We have business to do."

"Whoa." Ruthie swallows her giant bite. "I don't have any business with a plastic surgeon. I don't want anything plucked, sucked, or tucked."

"We're just going to talk. I didn't get a chance to speak to him last night about that designer saying Christina had a sister."

"Maybe her sister's a member of a terrorist network, and Christina's only trying to protect your family. Or maybe her sister is a communist, and she and Christina have a plan for world domination . . . one plastic surgeon at a time."

I roll my eyes and take another swig of juice. "And this is why I'm the crime solver and you're the sidekick."

After a twenty-minute taxi ride, Ruthie and I climb out of the cab and take the elevator to my dad's clinic.

Walking into the lobby, I greet the twin receptionists. "Hi, Kim. Hi, Leslie." I have never been able to tell them apart, but Dad swears he can. He also swears they speak English, but I think their sole qualification is hotness.

"You go see your dad?" one asks.

The other shakes her bleach blonde head. "He very busy. Important client."

I smile at the two standing in front of a water fountain backdrop. "Good thing I'm his daughter and he *always* has time for me." I grab

Ruthie by the hand and lead her down the hall. "Walk quickly. Dad said they both have their black belts, so I don't want to push my luck."

Ruthie snorts. "Like I'm afraid of a black belt. Dude, I got street cred."

"Yeah, Main Street in Truman. I'm sure they're shaking in their push-up bras."

I zip us around a corner and power walk down the next hall. At the last door on the right, I rap my hand in a hearty knock. "It's me, Dad."

"Bella?" I hear him inside, getting up from his desk. The door opens a crack. "This better be an emergency. I'm with a client."

"Oh, it's a crisis all right."

His frown is not encouraging. "Like the crisis last year when you needed me to choose which shoes I thought looked the best with your skirt?"

"You should be glad I value your opinion." I try to peek in to see if his client is famous, but he stands in my way.

"Go to the nearest waiting room and hang out there. I'll get you when I'm through with my patient."

"Is it anyone I know?" I whisper.

He leans close. "Yes."

"Gonna tell me who it is?"

"Not on your life." Dad smiles and pats me on the shoulder. "But she was nominated for an Oscar last year."

Half an hour later Ruthie and I are back in his office, the surgery-requiring actress long gone. Dad is really crafty at protecting his clients' identity. I can't say it's a quality I respect about him.

"So tell me what brought you all the way to my office." Dad sits behind his desk and steeples his fingers. "I know it has to be something important or you'd be shopping right now."

"A girl can only shop so much," Ruthie says, eyeing the objects on his desk.

"Yes, I know." Dad grins at my friend. "And my daughter can shop *so much*, I sometimes think I need a second job."

Ruthie lifts a big rubber squishy ball. "What do you call this? A weight?"

I share a smile with my dad. "I call it a D cup."

"Ew." Ruthie drops it back to its resting place.

"State your business, Bella. I don't like to work late on Saturdays."

Oh, how to proceed? How do you tell your dad that his future wife is up to something? That you don't think he truly knows the real Christina? "Um . . . well . . . I have been having some weird moments with Christina the last few times I've been here."

Dad's leather chair squeaks as he lounges back. "Honey, you know she's been stressed with the wedding plans, her job, not to mention retooling my career with this TV show. The Brazil deal is a risk, and we're both staying pretty keyed up."

"A few weeks ago we were trying on dresses. And she told me she was going to call some clients and sent me to get a coffee. I came back early and saw her not on the phone. But talking to . . . some woman."

Dad's face is as bland as oatmeal. "Are you kidding me with this?"

"They were arguing. The woman had obviously come to meet her and talk. And Christina kept telling her that she wouldn't back out, that she would go through with their plan. Dad, I know it sounds crazy, but I just have this feeling."

"You're a teenager. It's called hormones."

"You got that right." Ruthie harrumphs. "Last week they took over my face in a zit attack."

"Okay, so yesterday I'm back at the same dress shop." Where I was again violated by chicken feathers and Enrique's assault on fashion. "And the designer asked me about Christina's sister. And he didn't mean Marisol. He said her blonde sister Mercedes had picked up a dress."

Dad leans an elbow on the shiny black desk and rubs the bridge of his nose. "You're giving me a stress headache. And stress headaches lead to crow's feet."

Oh, quit being such a girl! "Would you please listen to me?"

His hand drops with a slap to the desk. "I am. And I don't like what I'm hearing."

"Then can you explain any of this?"

"Bella, what is there to explain? I have no idea what you're talking about, but I'm sure it's all a big misunderstanding. We all know about that overactive, suspicious imagination of yours."

Beside me Ruthie bites her lip to cover a smile. That traitor.

"How do you explain her sister?"

"I'm sure Enrique was mistaken." Impatience flows with Dad's every word. "Marisol is her only sister, her only family. When Marisol was only a baby, Christina—"

"Yes, brought her from Brazil all by herself." On the back of a donkey. Or swimming the ocean with only a piece of driftwood. Or holding on to the wings of a swarm of migrating butterflies. "And do you really think it's in your best interest that your own attorney wasn't involved in your prenup?"

"That's none of your business." Dad stands up. "Actually none of this is. I believe you need to get back home. Now."

I jump to my feet and step toward the desk. "Dad, I know something's wrong here, and you're too blinded by Latin love to see it."

"Do you need me to call you a cab?"

A clock ticks on his desk as we fall into silence. Staring each other down like two enemies about to draw pistols. Instead of a father. And his daughter.

"I know this adjustment has been hard on you." The angles of Dad's face soften. "But you need to accept it once and for all that your mother is married and has moved on. And I'm going to be married. Your mom and I will never be together."

"Is that what you think this is about? Some juvenile wish for my parents to be together? I love my life in Truman." My words are pointed arrows, and I let them fire. "I can't imagine going back to how things were. I have two parents there who love me and are involved in my life."

"That's enough, Bella."

"Jake calls me from the road. Just to talk to me. My *step*dad calls me more than my own father. And Mom makes me breakfast and goes to my school events. We have family game night and go to church together. And you think I want what we used to have?" I shake my head as a tear drips to my cheek. "I could never settle for second-rate parenting again. I have a real family now, and I deserve that. I deserve people who love me on a full-time basis."

He swallows and blinks. "You know I love you."

"On your terms." Now my nose is dripping. I'm totally snot-crying. "And you know what, Dad? It's not good enough anymore. I've been trying to get your attention for years. And I'm sick of it. I happen to be a great daughter. And I've changed this year, and you haven't even noticed. You know why? Because you never even knew me in the first place." I sniff and pick up my purse. "Let's go, Ruthie."

"Isabella, you stop right there."

But I keep walking. I'm done with this conversation. And done with trying to win my father's love.

chapter twenty-nine

S ome people have their prayer closets. I have my prayer Volkswagen.*

I sit in my Bug Monday after school, my head on the steering wheel, and just spill my heart out to God.

Lord, my life pretty much stinks. Like week-old beans. Like Budge's shoes. Like the cafeteria on sauerkraut day. I left my dad's with nothing resolved. I don't know anything more about Christina and her mystery sister. I thought Marisol would cough up the details, but she played ignorant when I quizzed her two days ago. And Dad and I aren't even speaking. I just knew he would tell me how sorry he was. Nope. Nor did he act like he even cared a bit about all the info I dug up on his fiancée. He trusts her more than me, and she's totally shady! I need help, God. I need strength and wisdom and ice cream and sprinkles—

Tap! Tap!

I jump at the rapping on my passenger window.

Luke frowns down at me from the other side of the car. "Open up."

"Go away."

"You've been a hag all day."

"Take your sweet talk somewhere else." My cheeks burn with the embarrassment of just being caught whining to Jesus about my life. Most girls could've at least made it out of the school parking lot.

Luke leans his arms on the car and presses his forehead to the window. The breeze plays with his dark hair. "Talk to me, Bella."

I start the car. "Gotta go."

"Open this door or you'll be driving through Truman with a new hood ornament."

This image brings a small smile to my face.

"You have five seconds to unlock this door, or else I call your mother and tell her about your current pursuit of a murderer."

Click!

"Much better," Luke says as he slides in.

The car instantly smells like him, which only serves to muddle my head even more. "I don't have time for boys," I mumble.

"Bella, I've been thinking."

"You want to put me back on my weekly feature for the newspaper?"

"Not yet." He picks up a CD resting between us. "Been listening to some John Mayer?"

Luke and I have little in common. But one thing we do share is our closet love of all things Mayer. Seriously, I hear that piano and husky voice, and I melt on contact. Luke said it didn't have *quite* the same effect on him.

I snatch the CD back. "I have things to do, so I'll see you at the carnival."

He twists in the seat until his back is pressed to the door. "I want to know what's going on with you. You had at least three good opportunities to snip back at Ashley today in journalism, and you didn't take a single one."

I run my finger over the bumps and plains of the steering wheel. "Bad weekend with my dad." I tell him about Mercedes. "And when I confronted my dad with all this fishy stuff about his fiancée, he just blew me off. He is such a jerk."

"Jerk's a bad word? And here all this time I thought it was just your endearment for me."

"Do you know what I'd do if I were still living in Manhattan?"

His voice is as low as Mayer's. "Tell me."

"I'd go to a spa and just spend the whole day getting pampered and forget about all my troubles."

"I'll never understand the appeal of mud baths."

"I want my dad to pick me, you know? Just once I want to be his priority. I want to be able to look back on our relationship and know that I was well and truly loved."

"I like you."

I roll my eyes. "You don't count."

"You've made that abundantly clear."

"I mean nobody can replace my dad. Not even Jake."

"What about God?"

"He tends to forget to send me birthday cards," I quip. "It's just not the same. Yeah, I get he's the father of all fathers. But I want Kevin Kirkwood to man up and treat me right. I want to be . . . enough."

Luke pulls my hand until I'm leaning on him. "You are enough." He kisses the top of my head and wraps an arm around me. "Your dad has to be a selfish moron to not want to spend time with you."

"And to not listen to my voice of reason."

Luke's chest rumbles in a laugh. "That too. Maybe you could try talking to him again. Don't overload him with all your Christina stuff. Just tell him how *you* feel about the two of you."

"Honesty is so hard. Why can't people just say what they want?"

"I ask myself that question all the time."

I raise my head. Luke's fingers filter through the hair at my temple.

His eyes drop to my lips. "I'm not going to kiss you again, so don't even look at me like that."

"But you want to."

"But I'm not."

I lean in a centimeter.

"Move back, or you'll be the first girl I've ever elbowed in the ribs."

"Why?"

"Because I don't believe in hitting girls."

I smile. "No, why won't you kiss me?"

He removes his arm. "Because you're worked up about your dad. You're hurt and confused. If you kissed me, it wouldn't be about you and me. It would be about me being . . . an ice cream substitute."

"The honor couldn't get much higher."

He pats my knee like he's my grandpa. "Want to pray?"

"I'd rather make out."

Luke reaches for my hand again and none-too-gently tilts my head 'til it's bowed. "God, I pray for healing for Bella and for her relationship with her dad. I pray she would see that no matter what happens in her family, you truly are all the father she needs. Give her the strength and the courage to give all her pain to you. Help her see that not all guys are going to hurt her or leave her. Help her to trust the men you have put in her life. God, I pray that—"

"Lord, I ask that Luke realize I am a fabulous writer and let me have my column back. If this is dating retaliation, help him to get over it. I know the pain of not being able to have me right now is like a dagger to his black heart. And I—" Luke squeezes my hand 'til I shut up.

"Jesus, give Bella and me the wisdom to figure out our . . . friendship."

"And—" I get the hand squeeze again, so I let him continue.

"Give us the wisdom to deal with the carnival issue the best way. Help us to act with integrity and do what's right. And protect us."

Okay, let's wrap it up. "In Jesus' name, amen."

His thumb strokes across my hand. "Amen."

"I've been thinking about something." I watch my hand in

his and wonder if he knows he's still holding on. "This integrity business..."

"Yeah?"

"You want me to go to the police about Alfredo, don't you?" I ask.

"I'd sleep a lot better knowing we weren't doing anything illegal. Not to mention the thought of a guy charged with murder showing up in your car doesn't exactly give me nice, peaceful dreams."

Like a good facial, it finally sinks in. Luke cares about me. He genuinely cares about me. Not because my dad goes to parties with Hollywood elite. Not because my mom ruled Manhattan society. And not because I have a closet full of Prada, Gucci, and Zac Posen. He's been telling me this all along, and I just couldn't hear it. But my heart is still such a work in progress. I've come miles since moving to Truman, and I don't mean the frequent flyer kind. But it's still so scary. To be with someone and just be yourself. It's like going to Wal-Mart without makeup. Do I dare?

"Bella?"

"Mmmm?"

"Let's go talk to the police."

Way to rain on my warm, giddy moment. Men. They're so un-romantic. "Fine. But Luke?"

"Yeah?"

"You're a cute boy... but you're no Rocky Road."

chapter thirty

"You did *what*?"

"Shhh!" I hold a shaking finger to my lips. "Keep it down, would you, Cherry?"

"But why would you tell the police about Alfredo?"

I want to say, "Sister, do you even *know* how hard that was?" Officer Mark was furious I had waited so long. Actually, furious doesn't quite touch it. I thought he was going to go all *Terminator* at the Truman PD.

"Withholding that information is a crime," Luke says. "And the police need all the help they can get to solve this case."

"But they think they already have their man—Alfredo." Cherry paces three steps in the big top, then returns. "And what's the harm that he's out? He didn't hurt you. And he didn't kill Betty. Alfredo says Red and Stewart did."

Luke crosses his arms. "What do you mean 'he says'?"

Cherry hesitates. "When I got to visit him in jail a few weeks ago. He told me everything he knew. And he said Red and Stewart had set him up."

"Has Alfredo approached you?" Why the sudden change in Alfredo's defense? This girl is not on the up-and-up. "Have you seen him since he escaped?"

"No!" Her eyes dart all around, then she lowers her tone. "I just know in my heart he's innocent. You weren't there. For the last six months Betty raised me. And I saw her fall in love with Alfredo. And he loved her. I've realized he couldn't fake that."

"Actually, he could."

"Bella," Luke warns.

Well, he could. Guys are like master fronters. "Cherry, when Alfredo and I had our little *meeting*, he seemed very interested in the map."

"Of course he would be. Betty told him it existed. Just not where it was."

"Are you sure you don't know where the map leads?" Luke asks.

"No. If I did, I'd be searching myself. Did Alfredo tell you why he wants to see it?"

Luke looks at me and nods.

"Yes." How to soften this? "He, um, said that you were in danger. That Betty was protecting you from something, and the map was somehow the answer to making sure you were safe."

Cherry's mascara-coated eyes widen. "You've known this for almost a week, and you didn't tell me?"

"I wouldn't feel left out," Luke mutters.

"Okay, so I'm not good at sharing information. I'm a bit of an evidence hog. And, Luke, if you don't quit rolling your eyes . . ." I focus my attention back on Cherry. "I don't think Alfredo is telling us everything he knows. I'm . . . I'm turning him over to the police tonight."

"Why?" Her voice is childlike. Desperate. "How?"

"Alfredo told me when I was ready to discuss the map, I needed to leave a carnival poster on my dash, and he'd contact me with directions to meet. So I'm going to put a flyer in my car tonight and wait for him to find me."

"I hate that part."

I turn on Luke. "Officer Mark said it was the only way."

"You know the drill." Intense eyes stare at me from behind his glasses. "Don't go anywhere alone, let me know where you are at all times, don't—"

"Luke, you drive me nuts."

He lifts a brow. "I think I proved that in the car when we almost—"

"Okay!" I cut him off. "Anyway, I'm not asking your permission, Cherry. I'm just updating you. This is your life we're talking about here, and I thought you should know. You need to be on guard too. If you see *any* sign of Alfredo or anything suspicious, you have to tell us. Or the police. Officer Mark is going to have a uniformed cop here every night and day."

Cherry bites her lip and looks in the distance at the carnival crew getting ready for the big show. "I was wrong to believe the police report and think Alfredo killed Betty. I don't care if his prints were the only ones on that sword, you're about to put an innocent man back in prison when he clearly escaped to solve Betty's murder . . . and keep me alive." She walks away on her muscular aerialist's legs.

"That went well." What have I done? Did I make the wrong decision? "Why is she suddenly so sure Alfredo didn't do it? What's changed?"

"You know you had to talk to the police," Luke says. "Let God handle the rest."

One hour and two snow cones later, I stand in the back and watch a white-gloved Ruthie juggle softballs as she turns circles on her unicycle. The crowd claps to the beat of Michael Jackson's "Bad." Only Ruthie.

I'm pulled away from the sight as Frank, the horse trainer, approaches. "You're Bella, right?"

"Yes."

"Note for you."

I open the folded notebook paper and scan the message. Ice explodes in my veins.

I know who you are. And I know what you're doing here.
Mind your own business, and I might let you live.
In the meantime . . .
I'll be sharpening my blade.

"Wait!" I run after Frank. "Who gave this to you?"

He shrugs nonchalantly. "I don't know. Some townie kid."

"What does that mean?"

"A customer. Some kid. Said a guy handed it to him and paid him with a buck."

"What did the guy look like? Was he skinny? Tall? Did he look like Alfredo? Maybe like Red?"

"I don't know! Who cares?"

"Can you find the kid again?"

"I'm up in five minutes. And I couldn't care less who sent you the love note."

"This is not a love note. It's—" A threat on my life. Visions of Betty race through my head. "Please. It's important."

"I wasn't even paying attention. I was messing with one of the horses out back. Couldn't pick the kid out of a two-man lineup."

I watch Frank disappear as my pulse escalates beneath clammy skin.

"Everything okay here?"

With a yelp I do a one-eighty and find the new magician standing right behind me. "Hey—" What's his name? "Um, Artie."

"Relax. It's just me." His face is void of all emotion, just like his monotone voice. "Everything okay here?"

"Did you send me a note?" What if it's him? I've had a weird feeling about this man from the get-go.

"Note?"

Does this guy ever speak in sentences consisting of more than three words? "Yes, a note. Did you send a note by way of a kid?"

"Get a scary message?"

"How did you know it was scary?"

Artie's eyes meander to the paper in my hand. "All your screamin' has me thinkin' in that direction." He spits on the ground. "Could be wrong. Can I look at it?"

With lightning speed, I throw my hand behind my back. "Nothing to see. Don't—don't worry about it." *I'll do enough for both of us.*

"Somebody threaten you?" he drawls. "I could help."

Oh, I'll just bet you could.

"Artie!" Red breaks through the curtain, his face as bright as his name. "You're up in thirty seconds. Get out there, you lazy mutt!"

"Yessir." Alfredo's replacement strolls toward Red, but before he disappears into the big top crowd, he turns around, his eyes as hard as bullets. "You be careful and watch your back. Anything could happen here."

My body convulses in a shiver, and I fight back the urge to ralph all over my clown shoes. Big inhale ... big exhale ... big inhale ...

Officer Mark told me I had to tell my mom if anything else happened. But I can't. If someone's targeting me, then I'm close to the truth. And the sooner this is over, the sooner Cherry will be safe. And the right killer, whether it's Alfredo or a Fritz, will be behind bars.

I have to find Frank again. He could tell me who was around him with the horses. And perhaps *that* person could identify the kid who brought the note. The note that spells out my scary, sharpy, pokey death.

Ruthie steps behind the curtain, clutching a handful of roses. "How was I? I felt a little off tonight, like my emotional intensity wasn't quite there. But look at all this." She jerks her chin toward her multicolored bouquet. "My people love me."

"Great. Yeah." Wonderful. Cherry and I could both be dead soon. "Maybe you could throw your pretty flowers on my cold casket."

"Jealous much?" Ruthie snaps a bud from its stem and tucks it above her ear. "I mean, I knew you were envious of my mad figure-eight skills, but I didn't know it ran *this* deep."

I shove the threatening note in her face. "Read it."

"'I know who you are. And I know what—'"

"Silently."

Her lips move as her eyes scan over every word. "This is not good. In fact, I'd say it pretty much stinks."

"I need to talk to Frank, the guy who does the horse tricks. I'll be back."

"No way you're going alone. I don't want Luke mad at me." She grabs a water bottle and follows me through the back exit.

The generators hum and sputter as we make our way through the menagerie of people, trailers, and animals. I head toward the horse area.

I spot Frank's wife, Serena, brushing a horse the color of a cloud. "Have you seen your husband?"

Her head shoots up with a frown. "Why do you want to know?"

Ruthie steps forward. "He was asking me about unicycling."

"Oh really?"

"Yeah. I get a lot of requests for tips and instructional tutoring. I'm sure you know how that goes."

Serena sniffs and ignores us.

"Frank said he wants me to create a routine for you—a special love song."

Her grooming stills. "He said that?"

Ruthie nods. "He told me nothing could express his deep, burning love like a unicycle ballet."

She runs her hand down the horse's flank, then continues her brushstrokes. "It's his break, so I'd check the Ferris wheel. He's probably smoking with Kent, the guy who runs the machine."

"Thanks," Ruthie says and drags me by the hand. "Snap out of it. You're weirding me out." As we walk, she reaches into her deep clown pocket and pulls out her phone.

"Now is not the time to text a love note to Budge!" We hang a left at the carousel.

"I'm not," she barks. "I only do that on the minutes that end in an eight. And right now"—she consults her leather-strapped watch— "it's only nine twenty-two. So let's hurry this up. I thought of a new poem for my Budgy-wudgy-poo."

My urge to barf just returned.

"If you must know, I'm texting Luke."

I stop midstride. "He has you watching me, doesn't he?"

Ruthie finishes her message and drops her phone back in her suit. "Luke means business about keeping you safe." She does hubba-hubba eyebrows. "And about you in general. Come on."

I focus on the Ferris wheel and watch it come closer, spinning happy people in perfectly timed revolutions. They sit up there and watch the world, completely unaware that death could be lurking beneath them.

"Let's take the back way." Ruthie snakes behind the trailers and game booths, giving us a view that's like turning over a piece of embroidery, revealing the knots and guts of the carnival.

"Kent, I don't care how cute the ladies are!"

Ruthie and I stop at Red's bellow.

"I want you to take a ticket from each and every person. There are no free rides here! If I get one more report of this, you can find yourself a new job." From fifteen feet away, I watch Red point his stubby finger in the carny's face as Stewart stands by him and smirks. "Am I perfectly clear?"

"Yes, Mr. Fritz. No more free rides, I promise."

"I'll be watching you," Stewart says. Could this note be from Stewart? Is he watching me too?

"Is there a problem, gentlemen?"

"William!" Red's chameleon face changes to a look of pleasure as he sees his potential buyer. "I'd heard you were going to stop in tonight." The ringleader laughs. "Did you come by just to bring me a nice, big check?"

The man adjusts his cowboy hat. "I'm still weighing my options, Red."

"Well, you said you'd have an answer by tomorrow afternoon. So let's talk about those options, shall we?"

Red motions toward the trailer near us.

My heart lurches, and I hunt for a place to get out of sight. But not too far out of hearing distance. "Ruthie, over here."

We scutter behind the duck hunt game, resting against the cool metal of the building.

"Jonas, why don't you take your break now," Red suggests a little too nicely.

"But, Mr. Fritz, I just took one."

"Take it again."

I peek around and see the game attendant slip out of his box and walk away.

"Have a seat, William." Red gestures to one of the three wooden stools in front of the gun stations. "Now, what are you thinking, friend? Are you ready for all this to be yours?"

The old man takes off his beige hat and rests it on the low counter. "She is a beautiful operation. Seeing it in action sure helps. Some problems, but nothing a little TLC couldn't fix, I suppose."

Red twirls the end of a mustache curl. "A little TLC . . . and maybe five thousand dollars knocked off my asking price?"

"Oooh-wee!" William slaps his knee. "You sure do know how to make it hard to resist. But I still need some more time. It's between this carnival and the Mulligan family circus in Pittsburg. They have a heck of a trapeze show. It's like a Vegas act." The man looks meaningfully at Red. "Drawing a mighty big crowd, I hear."

Stewart speaks up. "So are we." He glances at his dad. "Me and my cousin Cherry have been packing them in since we amped up our own performance. And if you come back next Monday, you'll see what we've been working on all month for our big finale—before we start the tour in Kansas."

"Yes, William," Red says. "It's an aerial routine that you've never seen the likes of. Challenging. In fact, the level of difficulty is so great, it killed the former owners." Red lowers his head. "My own brother and sister-in-law, God rest their souls. But we're reviving it, and we will pull it off."

"I don't know." William returns his hat to his round head. "Next Monday, you say?"

"We're running two shows that night to celebrate our fiftieth anniversary and last night in Truman. First one runs at six. You won't want to miss it." Red digs into his pocket and pulls out two tickets. "I got some reserved seats just for you."

The man takes the tickets and smiles. "I guess I'll see you next Monday night then."

Red slaps him on the back. "And bring that checkbook."

The guys share a few more laughs, then Williams takes his leave. Ruthie and I exchange a look, and I shrug. I don't know what's going on. But it's weird.

I peek my head out again, only to jump back. Red and Stewart are still there, with Stewart facing my way.

"You gonna be ready for next Monday, son?"

"I told you I was."

"This is more than a performance. Got a lot on the line here."

"I said I was ready. I won't mess this up."

"You only got one shot," Red says.

One shot at the aerial routine? One shot at what?

"We go through with the plan just like we talked about. No backing out and no mistakes." Red's tone makes goose bumps sprout on my arms.

"You told William last week I was part of the package."

"I told him you were a powerful part of the Fritz empire. Let him think what he wants. We'll be long gone with a few million in our pockets by the time he realizes you're not in the deal. Can you handle two performances Monday night?"

"I'll be ready."

"I have big plans for the second one."

Ruthie and I stare at one another in a frozen tableau. *What does that mean?*

"It still bugs me that we didn't find Betty's hiding spot. That map doesn't lead anywhere—like a decoy. It's the riddle that holds the key."

Red laughs. "We got a buyer, Stewart. We don't need it! When you're driving your new sports car, I promise you, it won't bother you nearly as much." His cackling grows louder.

"I guess."

"Well, I know. I can already smell freedom, and it's worth every price."

Stools shuffle, and I hold my breath as I hear the sounds of Red and Stewart leaving. *Don't walk around this way.*

Seconds stretch.

Then only the noises of the carnival.

"They're gone," Ruthie whispers.

"Let's get out of here. I need to talk to Officer Mark."

"And plant that carnival poster in your car."

On quivering legs, I walk beside Ruthie around the game booth to the front side.

"Whew." Ruthie sucks in the night air. "That was pretty close. I was so scared Red and Stewart were going to cut through the back way to the big top and see us."

"Yeah, me—"

Something catches my eye, and I do a double take at the food booth in front of us.

Artie Jensen.

He stands across the way, holding a Snickers. And staring. His magician's eyes float down the grassy aisle to Stewart and Red in the distance. Then meander back to us.

He knows we were eavesdropping.

"Ladies." He holds up his candy bar in a salute. "Nice night for a walk, isn't it?" He pierces me with his deep brown eyes, and I swallow back fear. "You never know what you might stumble upon."

chapter thirty-one

"You're moving up the wedding? You cannot be serious, Dad."

"Bella, I didn't call you to get more attitude. I called so you would have time to adjust to the idea and get your travel plans in order."

I slip into some red flats for Wednesday night church. "Don't you see what's going on here?" It sure isn't an apology. When I saw his number on my phone, I just knew he had called to tell me how sorry he was. "Christina knows I'm onto her. She knows the truth is getting ready to unwind right in front of her eyes like a big tangled ball of yarn." Okay, bad metaphor, but I'm exhausted. I haven't exactly been sleeping much these days. "Did you confront her?"

His sigh is impatient, as if he's barely tolerating me. "I asked her about her sister, yes."

"And what did she say?"

"That Enrique was mistaken. Mercedes is just her close friend, but in order to get the designer to let her pick it up, she had to tell him Mercedes is her sister."

"And you *fell* for that?" I'm so sure! "And what about the mystery woman who's staying in that hotel?"

"Also Mercedes. Look, Bella, this friend of hers has fallen on some really hard times, and Christina's paying her to run errands and do odd jobs."

"How convenient."

"Listen, young lady, you may not like Christina, but you will respect her. She's going to be my wife this Saturday—and your stepmother."

Gag. "Did you tell her about the conversation I overheard? What's this plan she has to stick with?"

"Again, she's helping Mercedes out. Not that I need to explain any of this to you."

"Yeah, I guess my own father isn't my business."

"That's not fair, and you know—"

"I'll see you this Friday. And I'm bringing a friend."

"Fine. And Bella?"

I plop down on my bed and drag Moxie into my lap. Her gentle purr does nothing to calm me. "What?"

"If you have any plans of ruining this wedding, you should just stay home."

"Is that what you want me to do—not even come?"

"Of course not." I hear Dad inhale and let out a ragged breath. "Whether you believe it or not, I love you. You're my daughter, and I want you there with me. I want to see you in all your feathery glory next to Christina and Marisol."

Mom yells from downstairs.

"I have to go. I have church."

"See you Friday?"

I run my finger over Moxie's jingley collar. "I'll be there."

"And no funny business?"

"No." My heart wilts in my chest. "I think you've got that covered all by yourself."

~~~~~~~~~

On the way to church, I ride in Budge's Death-Mobile. His hearse follows Mom, Robbie, and a newly returned Jake in their Tahoe.

"When did Dad roll in?" Budge yells over his screamo music.

"About thirty minutes before you got in from work."

He turns down the volume, apparently not finding the song "Road Kill Pizza with a Side of Cattle Prods" conducive to conversation. "Did you hear them fighting?"

"Yeah." How could I *not* hear it? "I somehow found my ear pressed against their bedroom door."

Budge sends me a sideways glance. "That happens. Kind of like I happened to find myself in front of the vent in the laundry room."

"The one that's connected to their room. Nice." I nod in appreciation. "Did Robbie notice?" It kills me to think of that little guy watching his new family falling apart before his eyes.

"No, I made him go feed his cow."

"What are we going to do?"

Budge swerves on the dirt road, barely missing one of Mr. Patton's ducks. "I've, uh ... I've been praying about it."

I shake my head to try and dislodge the ear clog. "That's funny. I thought you just said—"

"I prayed about it, okay?"

"It's okay to admit that." I smile at his defensive tone. "You've really come a long way since you started dating Ruthie."

"She's all right." A grin spreads across his ruddy face. "A little psycho, but I dig her."

He does more than dig her, and we both know it. "I'm really worried about Mom and Jake. It's not working, Budge. Mom's mad all the time. Jake's never home. And the more successful he gets, the worse it will be."

"So you like it here in Truman?"

I pull my eyes from the road and face my stepbrother. "I'm about to weird you out, so brace yourself."

"Nuh-uh. Don't do it. Do *not* say—"

"I love you."

"Oh, man! Dude."

I start to giggle. "I love you and Robbie. And his stupid cow. And our rundown farm house. And your dad."

"I'm gonna have to pull off the side of the road and hurl."

"And I love our family dinners. I miss those, you know?"

"*What* have I done to deserve this moment?"

I plod on, talking right over his protests. "I'd even miss fighting over the bathroom. And this nasty hearse that at one time I was too good to even look at."

Budge laughs at the memory. "You were so stuck-up."

"And you were such a tool."

Silence hangs in the car as we stare at the back of our parents' Tahoe.

"I don't want to lose our family either," Budge says. "Robbie needs all of us. Together."

"Right. For Robbie's sake." We all need our family. "So what are we going to do about it?"

"That is so you, Evil Stepsister-O-Mine." Budge shakes a finger in my face. "You try to fix everything. But we're not going to do a thing."

"We have to. We can't just sit back and watch our family crumble in the name of spandex and body slams."

"Sitting back is exactly what we're going to do." He pauses, his mouth seeming to try to push out a difficult thought. "I, um . . . I know it's going to work out."

"What is this, Budge the Disney version?"

"No. I mean . . . I don't know, Bella." He shoves a chubby hand through his oversized 'fro. "I've just really been talking to God about this, and . . . I have a peace about it. Don't ask me how, but I know this is going to be okay."

"Have you been snorting mustard at the Weiner Palace again?"

Budge rolls down his window and lets the spring breeze inside.

"Yeah, it's nuts. I mean, what do I know? Up until recently I've been the church dropout. But I cannot shake this feeling."

I study his serious face. *God, it's like this trust issue keeps jumping up like a carp and slapping me in the face. Even Budge seems to be getting it. Why can't I?*

"Forget it." Budge jerks a hard left with the wheel. "It was stupid."

I let his words hang there for a moment before answering. "No. It's not." I take a cleansing breath and pray for a boost of faith. A Red Bull of belief. "If you say you have a peace about it, then that's that. God has obviously spoken to you." *Why can't the Big Guy say these things to me?* "Thanks for telling me." *A trust lesson from Budge Afro Finley. What is the world coming to?*

He cranks up the radio, and we sing—or yell—the rest of the way to church.

I push open the heavy door of the car and set my foot onto the parking lot. "Oh, and Budge?"

"Yeah?" He grabs his Bible from the back.

"You know you'd, like, donate a kidney if I needed one."

"You're right. I would."

I smile in triumph. The dude loves me.

"But only if I got a big, fat check."

Wanting a little distance from the frosty exhaust between Mom and Jake, I find Lindy and Matt and sit beside them. Matt's in the middle of a story that has my friend howling with laughter. They don't even stop to say hi to me. Just keep on talking. Keep on laughing.

"This seat taken?"

I look up to find Luke. He obviously got his hair cut after school, as it doesn't curl around his neck, but stands up in a deceptively messy pattern. Nothing accidentally messy about this boy.

"What are you doing here?"

He settles in beside me, his arm sliding against mine on the seat rest. "I didn't feel like driving all the way out to my church tonight. With all that's been going on, I'm kind of tired."

I narrow my eyes and scrutinize every twitch of his face. "You're checking up on me, aren't you?" Luke's church isn't *that* far out of town.

"Can a guy not visit a church without there being an ulterior motive?"

I point right at his button-down oxford. "Not you." But being next to him does give me some comfort. Even though I put the carnival poster on my dash Monday night, Alfredo hasn't contacted me yet. I'm still waiting. And stressing.

He settles his Bible in his lap and focuses toward the front. "Matt and Lindy seem to be getting along well."

"Don't change the subject." But I glance to my left. "Yeah, they are. I'm glad they didn't let their friendship get too off track." I turn back. "Romance can do that."

His eyes sear into mine. "Right. Good thing they played it safe and didn't end up dating." He looks over my head. "Clearly they got just what they wanted."

Bo Blades walks in and goes immediately to Lindy. Matt closes his mouth on the rest of his story as Bo hugs his girlfriend.

"Would you mind scooting down a seat?" Bo asks a blank-faced Matt.

"Here." I jump up. "We will." I give Lindy an encouraging grin. "No problem." But her happy face has disappeared. In its place is a sham of a smile that barely lifts her lips.

"I wanted to surprise you." Bo leans down and kisses Lindy's cheek. "I thought we could hang out after church."

"Yeah. That'd be great."

"There's a picnic packed for us in my truck. I brought all your favorite food—even homemade chocolate chip cookies."

She lets him take her hand. "Those are my favorites. You're so thoughtful to do that."

"I guess Matt never had a chance," Luke whispers. "Bo seems to be everything Lindy wants."

I shoot him a look that could melt ice cream. "You have something to say?"

"Just seems that the only one happy over there by you is Bo."

I refuse to humor him by looking at Matt and Lindy. But honestly, I don't need to. I know the gloom I'm going to find. Isn't there anyone I know who's content these days?

Luke yawns beside me. "I've always found playing it safe to be such a bore."

"Welcome!" the pastor says, taking the mic. "Tonight I want to talk about Noah and the ark. Ask yourself this: would you have had the faith to get on that boat? Or would you have gone down the drain like everyone else?"

Oh, come on. Could we not have a more comfortable topic? Like tithing? . . . Or adultery?

After church, the family gathers together at the Dairy Barn. I skip dinner and go straight for a double fudge sundae.

"Watched you on TV last Sunday night, Jake." I spear a banana and swirl it in some chocolate. "I like the new jazzed-up pirate costume."

"Thanks." Jake rests his arm around my mom's chair. "It's a little hard to wrestle with the eye patch, but it's specially created so I can actually see out of it."

"Hey, there's Officer Mark!" Robbie waves toward the door, a french fry dangling out his mouth. "Over here!"

Oh poop. I slink down in my seat and keep my eyes locked on my dessert.

"Jake, good to see you." The blue of Mark's uniform matches the navy of the dated restaurant curtains. "Jillian, I miss talking to you over coffee at Sugar's. It's just not the same without you and Dolly."

"I'm really busy with the kids." Mom's smile is as fake as the blonde streaks in her hair. "But I get lonesome for the diner crowd sometimes."

Probably gets more lonesome for her husband. And someone to talk to who's old enough to vote.

"Dolly seems to really be taking to that Fritz girl. I see them in town all the time." Mark steals a fry from Robbie's plate, sending my stepbrother into giggles.

"Mickey too," Jake says. "Any time I talk to him, that dominates the conversation. He loves that girl."

"It's a blessing Cherry came along." Mom hands Robbie an ignored chicken nugget from his plate. "It's drawn Mickey and Dolly together like nothing else could have. They go to church together, they eat dinner together, they go to the park. They've become a very tight family." I hear the teaspoon of jealousy mixed in her voice.

"Is that Bella over there?"

I don't miss Mark's sarcastic tone, so I also don't bother to look up.

"Bella, why are you hiding behind a menu?" Mom asks.

"Um . . ." Slowly I lower it. "I don't think this sundae is going to be nearly enough. Just checking out the milk shake options."

Mark ambles toward my seat. "Has Bella told you about the latest happenings at the carnival?" A table of blank faces stare back at the officer. "That's funny. I asked her to make sure you guys were in the loop since some *dangerous* incidents have transpired."

Mom blanches. "Dangerous? What are you talking about?"

"It's nothing." Mark's hand rests near my dish, and I give it a light jab with my fork. "Truly nothing."

"Dolly might've mentioned some weird stuff going on," Mother says. "But I didn't think it involved you."

"Oh, it always involves Bella Kirkwood." Mark smiles down at me. "Am I right?"

All I want is some peace and privacy to meddle into other people's business.

"Why don't you fill us in?" Jake levels me with a stare used to take down giants. "I seem to have missed something while I've been gone." He glances at Mom. "Maybe too much."

"Our little private eye here has been investigating a murder at the Fritz carnival."

My mom gasps. "I thought that magician did it."

"I don't think he did." I catch myself. "But I'm not investigating it really. I'm just, you know, hanging out and absorbing the atmosphere of the place. I might've *accidentally* run into a few suspicious facts."

"She also might've run into a set of lights that fell from the sky."

"Do you mind?" I hiss at Officer Mark.

"You said that was an accident. So this is why you insisted on working there." Mom shakes her head, and I can almost see the steam coming out her ears. "What else?"

"Um, I think Mark has to go now. Yep, Lars is yelling at you from the counter. Your order's—"

"Your daughter went to her car last week and found Alfredo, the accused murderer, in her backseat."

"Good heavens." Mom shoves her plate away. "I think I'm going to be ill. *How* could you not tell us?"

Jake stares down his friend. "Why didn't you tell me?"

"Bella assured me she would be speaking with you about it." He grins down at me. "I should've known. Nancy Drew here kind of likes to work solo."

Mark gives my parents the unabridged version of a story I'd title "Reasons Bella Kirkwood Will Be Grounded 'Til She's Fifty."

"That's it." Mom slams her napkin down on the table. "I've been so busy with everything that I haven't kept a good eye on you kids. Is there anything *else* I need to know?" Her eyes linger on Budge and Robbie.

Robbie bows his head. "I ate some glue last week. And when the teacher sent a note home . . . I ate that too."

Budge's cheeks dimple in a grin. "Guess that makes me the angel of the family."

"You are not returning to work there, Bella," Jake says.

Mom swoops her head toward her husband. "Don't tell her what to do. You've been a parent for five minutes this month. *I'll* tell her how it's gonna be." Mom clears her throat and straightens her posture. "Bella . . . you will not be returning to work there."

"What? I have to! You don't understand."

"I know all I need to know," Mom says. "And my decision is final."

"When will she ever learn?" Budge clucks his tongue. "Maybe you should send her to military school."

And maybe I should shove this banana up your nose. "Cherry's life could be in danger. And I am the perfect person to have on the inside."

"Apparently your life is in danger. And I will not even debate this with you." Mom shoves another nugget toward Robbie's hand. "We'll discuss it at home."

"Y'all have a lovely evening." Officer Mark has the audacity to wink at me as he walks away.

Mom steeples her fingers and leans on her hands. "Anything else I need to hear, Bella?"

I think about the threatening letter Frank brought me. "Uh . . ."

"Spill it," she barks.

"I guess it's time you finally knew . . ." I suck in a breath and just let the truth pour out. "Budge watches Hannah Montana."

chapter thirty-two

I've sat behind that potted tree for weeks, Bella. I'm done. I'm through."

I stir the whipped cream in my mocha and look across the table at Hunter on the day before my father's wedding. The hustle and bustle of Manhattan carries on outside the Starbucks window as parts of my life grind to a shattering halt.

"The wedding is tomorrow afternoon. Just accept it and let it go. This fixation isn't good for you."

Beside me Ruthie blows bubbles with her straw. "You can't second-guess her hunches. They're always right." She nods at me with confidence. "The sidekick guidebook says I'm to defend you in the face of doubters."

"Thanks." I guess. "Hunter... okay, fine. It's over. You're right, I need to move past this and accept the fact that my dad is marrying someone else, and I'm sure there's a perfectly good explanation for all the weird stuff I've witnessed."

Hunter shakes his head, his expression grim. "That was too easy. You're up to something, aren't you?"

"Are you kidding me? I'm already grounded for eternity in one time zone." I brush my finger over a wrinkle on the napkin. "I can be mature about this."

Hunter snorts. "Oh, this is gonna be bad."

On Saturday morning I awaken with morning breath, a hanker-
ing for Luisa's waffles, and a renewed determination to nuke this
wedding.

"Now don't forget." My dad takes a snicker-doodle out of the
cookie jar. "I need you dressed and at the church by noon." He
picks his TAG Heuer watch off the kitchen counter. "You slept late
enough."

"I wanted to be refreshed for your big day." I bat my eyes and
draw my big fluffy robe tighter. "Didn't want to have bags for the
pictures, you know."

"You missed the bridesmaids' breakfast for Christina."

"I couldn't leave Ruthie. She'd feel left out." I elbow my friend.

"Yeah," she sputters into her chocolate milk. "I'm allergic to,
um, quiche. I break out in a rash. Makes my butt itch."

Dad looks to me, but I only shrug. "Bella, don't let me down,
okay?" After a pause, he walks to me, bends down, and presses a kiss
to my cheek. "I do love you. You know that, right?"

I stare into eyes just like mine. "I'm working on it."

He acts as if he's going to say more, but straightens instead.
"I have to go. I have some last-minute details to take care of, then
I'm getting dressed at the church. Oh, and you and Ruthie will
ride home with your grandparents. They'll stay here with you and
Marisol tonight."

"Luisa will be enough of a chaperone for us." Seriously, on top
of everything else, I cannot take twenty-four hours with my grandmother. She makes pit bulls look like lapdogs.

"No deal. Luisa's leaving after the ceremony to go on a church
retreat."

"Where to?"

He slings his tux bag over his shoulder. "Caesars Palace. Vegas."

I watch him walk out of the kitchen and listen for the click of the front door. "Let's go."

Ruthie and I slide out of our robes, revealing our clothes for the wedding. I glance at my friend's skintight leather pants.

"What? I wanted to match your dress."

"Can you even breathe in those things?"

Ruthie frowns at her pants. "I guess it's a good thing I left the matching bedazzled bustier at home."

I grab my purse from its hiding place in the cabinet. Locating my phone, I call a cab. "Let's go wait on the front steps."

We get to the foyer, my hand on the door, when Luisa stops me. "Wait a minute."

I pivot and plaster innocence all over my face. "Yes?"

"The wedding isn't for another hour and a half. Where are you going?"

"We're off to save the world," Ruthie says.

Luisa looks to me for confirmation. I finally nod.

"Okay, then." She rolls her dark eyes at my dress. "But don't wrinkle that thing. I do windows, but I do *not* do feathers." She waddles away, muttering under her breath in Spanish.

When the yellow cab pulls up to the sidewalk, we rush inside. "Broadway Heights hotel. And there's a twenty-dollar tip in it if you can get us there in twenty minutes."

I was handing over a crisp Andrew Jackson in fifteen.

"So what's the plan?" Ruthie asks as we step inside the lobby of the hotel.

I stand in the middle of the vast space and just look around. I have no idea what I'm doing. Reaching into my purse, I feel around until my fingers touch my camera, my mace, and my Orbitz gum. All potential tools for detonating a wedding.

Ruthie taps her spiky boot. "You do have a plan, don't you?"

I consider this. "Yes."

"Oh, man. You don't." She covers her eyes with her hand. "The book warned me of times like these. When all your superpowers would go to your head."

I make a mental note to introduce this book to a blowtorch. "We'll figure it out when we get up to Mercedes' room. I just need to get in there so I can talk to her."

"And what are you going to say?"

"Would you quit asking these questions?" These questions that make . . . sense!

We ride the elevator to the eighth floor in silence. I chew on a glossy nail.

"You're kinda molting." Ruthie points toward some stray feathers on the floor.

"I don't have time to worry about this dress right now." I tug on a plumey strap and try to hold it in place. "We need to get in, force the truth out of her, and get out in time to stop the biggest disaster of my dad's life." Otherwise it will be the biggest disaster of mine.

"I still think we could've gone with my idea to hang Marisol up by her toes until she hurled up the truth."

I did give that one some serious consideration. But so far my questioning of that kid has gotten me nowhere. She's a locked box.

The elevator dings and comes to a whooshing stop. My breakfast jumps on my stomach like a trampoline.

"We could pull the fire alarm." Ruthie steps out and scans the walls of the hallway. "Pull it, and she'll come running. You can tackle her and—"

"Get arrested?" I guess that would give me a great excuse for missing the wedding. "I can't think." I'm so stressed! *God, I know I've got some dubious behavior going on here, but I checked my Bible last night. And there's nothing in there about causing a big stir to drive out a mysterious lady in hopes of stopping your father's nuptials. For a* second I thought I had found something in that chapter on animal sacrifices . . . but no.

"I'll be back." Ruthie turns back toward the glass elevator.

"Wait!" I lower my voice. "Where are you going?"

"Just hang on to your feathers. I'll be right back."

This could be bad. Very bad. "Nothing illegal. And keep your clothes on!" I don't know why I needed to add that. But this is Ruthie. Anything is possible.

As she disappears behind the gold double doors, I walk down the hall and find the potted tree Hunter must've spent a good deal of time with. Easing down in the tight dress, I park it on the floor. And wait. And wait.

This must've been what Hunter felt like. No wonder he was so whiny. Ten minutes and my butt's already numb.

In the distance I hear the elevator ting again. "Bella?" comes a stage whisper. "Bella!"

I jump up, rub my tush, and peek my head around the corner of the hall. Sighing with relief, I see Ruthie. And then I see the cart. "What in the world are you doing?"

She is wearing a white smock, a billowy chef's hat, and is pushing a metal food cart. "Getting you into that room."

"How did you get that stuff?"

She moves her head in a jerky shake. "Don't ask. Just climb on."

I glance at the covered serving dishes on top. "Maybe we should pull the fire alarm."

Ruthie lifts the white cloth draped over the cart. "Get under here. Sit on the bottom, and I'll cover you up. When I push you inside the room, you can jump out and talk to her."

I guess it doesn't matter if we pull the fire alarm or not. Either way, I will not survive this day without being hauled away in cuffs. But desperate times call for . . . mug shots.

"Okay. Let's do this." I slip under the tablecloth and with a few tries, finally get situated good enough to be covered up. "Oh my gosh. I'm like a pretzel in here." I'm so going to need a massage after this. And a really strong latte.

"My name is going to be Mavis," Ruthie says above me. "Mavis Durbinkle, the food service girl."

"Whatever gets you by."

"Mavis has had such a hard life. She needs this job."

I pull up a foot by its pink heel. "Write your autobiography later, Mavis. I have a wedding to stop."

My world goes black as Ruthie flops the white material over me and the cart. I hear her inhale big . . . then she puts us into motion. Oh shoot. Oh shoot. Oh shoot. Moment number 1,981,642 my mom would not be proud of.

My butt bounces with every rotation of the wheel, and the dishes clank a clumsy tune above my head.

Knock! Knock! "Room service," Ruthie drawls.

"Nice country accent," I whisper.

"Thank yew, sugah."

The door opens, and a loud *thunk* tells me it caught on the safety latch.

"Yes?"

I swallow hard and pray none of my feathers are showing.

"Room service, ma'am. Just fer yew."

"I did not order room service."

"It was sent up. Compliments of someone who said you'd need a little pick-me-up right about now."

Nice job, Ms. Durbinkle.

"I—I don't know. Who sent this?"

"The woman just said you'd know, and that she would talk to yew later. She popped her sweet li'l head in this mornin' and gave us the order. Dark-headed lady. Real nice." Ruthie stretches the syllables out like Laffy Taffy. "I think we have some chocolate goodies in here." My friend taps a serving dish, and I can feel it vibrate all the way to my Jimmy Choos.

"Okay . . . I guess come on in."

Ruthie pushes the cart, and it bounces over the carpet. "Oh, I see yer packin' up here. Are you leavin' us?"

"Yes."

"I hope it's nothin' we did wrong. We here at the . . . um, the . . ."

The Broadway Heights! It's the Broadway Heights!

"The *hotel* wants to make sure all our customers are happy as a pig in the mud. At least that's what my ex-boyfriend would say." A beat of silence. "Before he left me for another girl. But she was a hunter and a fisher like him. And Ezekial never could get past the fact that I couldn't skin my own possums."

Shoot me now.

Achoo! Ah-ah-choo!

Oh no. Mercedes sneezes three more times. It's my feathers!

"That's strange. *Achoo!* I had the hotel take away all the down pillows, but—*achoo!*—I seem to be—*achoo!*"

"Um, here we go. Here's some—oops! That's pea soup. That ain't right. I specifically asked for chocolate cheesecake."

"I'm afraid you're going to have to leave." Mercedes makes a whirling noise in her throat. "I seem to be allergic to you."

"No!" Ruthie cries. "It's not me. But I gotta serve yew some dessert now. Let's just uncover this other dish right here." Ruthie sticks her foot under the cloth and shakes it. It makes contact with my knee.

"Ow!" I slap a hand over my mouth. I have to move. I have to bail out of here and confront this Mercedes woman.

"I must insist you leave. I'm to catch a plane in a few—*achoo!*—hours to leave the country."

"Oh, I've always wanted to travel." More kicks beneath the cart. "Where are yew goin'?"

"None of your business."

"I've never been there."

"Please take the cart and leave at once!" The woman sneezes again. And again. "I'm calling management if you don't walk out of here right now."

"Yeah? Well, not before you see this!"

Light explodes in my eyes as Ruthie flings the cloth away. The tall woman's eyes go wide. She mutters a curse and reaches for the bedside phone.

"Stop!" I yell. "Stop. I won't hurt you." I move closer.

She doubles over and launches into a sneezing fit. "Get. Out."

"I know who you are."

"I don't care!" Her face is turning purple.

This isn't going well. I probably should've thought this out more. I figured she'd see me, see the dress, and know I was part of the wedding party, then fall at my feet, confessing the truth.

Ruthie lunges for the phone, but the woman knocks her hand aside. "Get away!" she screams.

"Mercedes, I just want to talk to you." I spy three framed photos across the room. The one in the middle is of her, Christina, and a younger Marisol. Surrounded by pictures of others I'm assuming are family.

"I don't know who you mean." Her left eye is swelling shut. It's not pretty. "But you have broken into my room, and I am calling the police."

Ruthie makes another try for the phone, but the woman throws herself on Ruthie and digs in her long nails.

"Ow!" My friend howls in pain. "I knew I should've brought my brass knuckles!"

I jump into the fray, only to trip over the train of my dress. Stupid feathers!

In a move worthy of any professional wrestler, Mercedes

clotheslines me with an arm, and down I go. She grabs the phone receiver and punches a button. "I need security. Room 857. Now."

From my position on the floor, I see her other eye taking on a gargoyle quality as well. Praying she can't see me, I race back to the cart, dig into my purse for the camera, and snap off some shots. But who would ever recognize this swollen creature?

"Come on!" Ruthie yanks hard on my arm and drags me toward the door. "Sprint like an Olympian!"

We run like mad to the stairwell. My heels dig into the carpet, and my feet cry out for mercy. *Please don't let us get caught! Please don't let us get caught!*

I lose a shoe at the fifth floor. "We need to separate!" I yell, kicking off the other heel. "They're going to be looking for two girls together. I'm going to get off at the fourth floor and ride the elevator. You go to the bottom floor and go through the kitchen. I'll meet you at the coffee shop half a block down. I won't leave until you show up." I wheeze out more instructions.

"Bella?" Ruthie calls as I pull open the fourth-story door.

My chest heaves. "Yeah?"

"I will never forget this."

"I know. I'm sorry, Ruthie."

Her face splits into a grin. "Are you kidding me? This is the best graduation present ever!"

"Remind me of that when we're wearing stripes." I shoot through the door and run down a series of halls until I reach an elevator.

It's all I can do not to shout a hallelujah when the elevator pings open and I step inside with a group of Asian tourists. When we hit the lobby, I shuffle close to them, completely invading their personal space until I'm emptied onto the street.

Freedom! Yes!

My dress straps long gone, I hold up the bodice with one hand

and use the other to propel me down the street. At the sight of Manhattan Mocha, I slow down and sag against the building.

Thirty-one minutes later I sit at a bistro table inside and drum my fingers on a cup. Where is Ruthie? What if she got caught? What if the police have her? What kind of friend am I that I even dragged her into this twisted mess?

I lower my head to the table and bang it twice. "I'm the worst friend ever. I'm the worst—"

"If you get a bruise on your schnoz, that is *not* going to look good for the wedding pics."

I lift my head in a rush. "Ruthie!" Throwing my arms around my friend, I hug her close. "You made it! Thank God. You're the best sidekick ever!"

"Dude!" She goes limp in my arms. "Back off, okay? I don't even let Budge get *that* handsy."

"I'm so glad you made it. I was freaking out."

"When I went down to the kitchen, they wanted me to unload the dishwasher." She shrugs and straddles a seat. "I thought it was the least I could do."

I rest my head in my hands. "The wedding's in thirty minutes, and I've got nothing. I could try and show those pictures to my dad or people who know Christina, but who would even recognize that woman with her face all swollen?"

"Seriously. That chick looked like a bloated up shar-pei."

"It's over. I have to admit defeat and let the wedding go on. It was a half-baked plan anyway."

"The guide book said you'd have times of self-doubt." Ruthie reaches into her shirt and pulls out a frame. "Maybe you can show your dad this."

I snatch the picture and stare at Christina and her smiling family. "Aw, Ruthie. You're the best."

"Even without my slingshot."

Failure spirals in my gut. "But what does this really prove? Let's face it. I got nothing."

Ruthie takes the frame, unlatches the back, and hands me the photo. "Check it out."

I flip it over and read. *Marisol, Christina, and Sadie Vasquez.* "Omigosh." I dig through my handbag with frenzied hands until I find my phone. With trembling fingers, I pull up my ex-boyfriend's number. "Hunter?" I suck in a shaky breath. "I need you to meet me at my dad's wedding. Make sure your father is there . . . I think I just found their money-stealing accountant."

chapter thirty-three

S adie Vasquez. Of course. It was staring me in the face the whole time.

"Can't you drive faster?" I yell to the cabbie.

"And roll up your window." Ruthie sputters and spits. "It's like a wind tunnel of feathers back here."

I press the phone more firmly to my ear. "Hunter, Christina De Luna is actually Christina Vasquez, sister of Mercedes."

"Sadie Vasquez." His words are as sharp as knife points. "The psycho who took my dad and yours for millions."

I grab Ruthie's wrist and check her giant alligator skin watch. "You have to stall the wedding. I'll never make it on time."

"What do you want *me* to do?"

"I don't know! But think of something." We come to a stop at yet another red light. Are there no green lights in this town? "I'm going to call my dad and tell him to wait, but I don't know if he's going to buy it. You find him and tell him you've talked to me, and I'm on my way."

"Got it. I'll wait for you inside the chapel."

The minutes tick by, and at one o'clock, when we're stopped yet again, I order the driver to pull over. "We're getting out here." I shove some cash in his hand. "Gonna have to run the rest of the way."

"Follow me!" I yell to Ruthie and take off down an alley on my bare feet. Three blocks later my phone rings again. "What?"

"Bella, it's no good," Hunter says. "Your dad won't even listen to me. He said he figured you wouldn't show up, and he wasn't going to wait. Something about Christina told him she knew you had made alternate plans for the day. I've been escorted out of the church."

"*Un*-believable!" Oh, my lungs are about to explode. And don't even get me started on my feet. "Go talk to him again. Tell him what I know. Tell him about Sadie."

"I tried. There's some big Brazilian goon guarding his door now. Says he's a friend of Christina's and the best man. He kicked me out and won't let me back into his changing room."

Without so much as a good-bye, I end the call and punch in my dad's number. Voice mail. I hit redial again and again. My own father won't take a call from me. How do you like that?

As I pound the dirt-encrusted pavement, I glance at Ruthie. She runs beside me like a track star. Even pace. Bouffant hair defying the laws of gravity and hair spray. Not so much as breaking a sweat.

"It's just around this corner." I think. Five blocks later I know I'm lost. *God, please help me. I need to get to my dad!*

I screech to a halt as a woman passes by, pushing a stroller of twins. "Hey!"

She casts a worried look and keeps going.

"Ma'am! Please stop, I need help."

She turns around. "Your dress is beyond help."

"I know that's right." Ruthie studies my torn frock, now minus the two bottom layers. I look like a flapper who got caught in a tornado of geese.

"Do you know where St. Augustine's Chapel is?"

The short brunette lifts a hand to block out the sun. "Yeah. It's two blocks north. Then turn and go four blocks east, and at the Y, head south."

North, east, south? Is she kidding me? "I need landmarks. Turn

at the red bud tree by the fire station, hang a left at the playground.
I do not speak this directional jibbity jab!"

Ruthie grabs me by the arm and offers the woman a sympa-
thetic look. "Don't worry, ma'am. She just got cut from the Miss
Manhattan Poultry model search, and she's feeling a little crazy. I
plan on slapping her at the next street." My friend yanks me across
the road and returns to running. "I can get us there."

"You don't know New York!" I scream over the passing cars.

She picks up the pace. "No, but I was a boy scout once, and I can
tie a square knot, start a fire with gum wrappers, and know the difference between north and south."

I hold the pain at my side. "Um . . . a *boy* scout?"

"What they didn't know didn't hurt them."

So on faith and Ruthie's internal compass, I follow my friend
through the streets of the city that never sleeps. And judging
from the sludge on my feet, the city that needs to work on its
sanitation.

"There it is!" Ruthie calls many moments later. "I see it!"

Relief duels with sadness. We're here . . . but it's twenty past
one. The wedding was to be a short ceremony. And I'm sure with
Christina tipped off now, the service was cut down even more.

Just as we approach the small yard in front of the church, I
notice an olive-skinned man standing in front of the antique entry
doors. He looks like a member of a Brazilian mafia.

"Ruthie . . . that guy's waiting for me. I know it. I'm going to need
you to provide a distraction while I find another way in."

She gives him the once-over. "I can take him. I've watched a lot
of wrestling lately."

Oh, Lord help us. "Just use your wits. Not your muscles. Or that
slingshot tucked into the back of your pants."

"You can see it?"

"That and your panty line."

"That guy is kind of big." She swallows hard. "Isn't he?"

I pull her behind a nearby shrub. "Oh no." I shake my head. "No, you don't. You are not wimping out on me now. You, Ruthie McGee, are my sidekick. And I have never needed you more than I need you now. Do you understand me?"

She nods—slowly at first, then more certain. "I understand."

"You can do it. I believe in you."

"I sure wish I had that book."

"You don't need that stupid thing." I tap her temple. "Everything you need is right here. And in your heart. The truth is, you're all I've got here. But you know what?" I look into the heavily lined eyes of a girl who has become my closest friend. "I wouldn't trust this moment to anyone else. I'm glad you're here with me." I can't resist a slap to her butt. "Now go get 'em, partner."

She clutches her chest with a gasp. "Partner? Really?"

"Of course. Who wants to be a sidekick when you can be a dynamic duo?"

Ruthie lets out a happy sigh. "McGee and Kirkwood—mystery solvers."

Let's not go crazy. "Um, that's Kirkwood and McGee." I give her a playful shove and run toward the back of the chapel.

But not before I hear my partner in action.

"No way!" she squeals. "It's Brad Pitt! Oh my gawwwsh—I loved you in *Twilight*! Can I have your autograph?"

Limping like a peg-legged pirate, I jog around the brick building. Pink-dyed sweat trickles inside my strapless bra. I find a metal door and yank with all my might. Nothing. Locked.

At the back of the church, yet another door. Sealed tight as one of my dad's eyelifts. With clenched fists I beat the entrance, but no one answers.

"Are you kidding me?" I yell.

"You always were a drama queen."

I spin around, tripping on a remnant of the skirt. "Hunter! Why aren't you in there stopping this?" I'm too late!

"Because I knew you'd want the pleasure. Need a boost?" He points upward. Above us hangs a folded fire escape, leading to a window. "The bodyguard wouldn't let me near any of the other exits. He's sure not going to let you in." He squats low and holds out a hand. "May I?"

"I just want to tell you that I had a lot more dress on when I started."

My ex-boyfriend casts a doubtful look at my outfit. "I'm not judging."

I step onto his thigh and swing my other foot over his head until I'm sitting on his shoulders. With rubber knees I rise until I'm standing. "Don't even consider dropping me." He walks us beneath the window. "And don't even *think* about looking up what's left of my skirt."

"Wouldn't dare."

Hunter wraps his hands around my wobbly calves, and I reach my arms overhead. I feel the warm metal of the ladder and pull it down. "Look out below," I call as it grows toward the ground. I leave the safety of Hunter's perch and jump onto the rungs.

"Good luck," Hunter calls.

I shimmy up the rest of the way and push the partially opened window with dirt-streaked hands. Throwing a leg over, I crawl inside. Running out of the room, my feet slap all the way down a dim hallway as wedding music comes to a crescendo. The ceremony must be over. They're probably walking arm in arm down the aisle together as man and wife now.

"Dad!" I bellow. "Dad!" Must get to him.

I whisk down some steps, only tripping on one. "Dad! Wait!"

The stairs empty me into the small lobby. Smack into the burly man.

"Going somewhere?"

I look up at the beast. "You have to let me in there. That's my dad."

"I know all about you. Christina told me you'd try and stop the wedding." He shakes his bulldog head and smiles. A gold tooth winks back. "Not going to happen."

"Oh yeah?" Ruthie leaps out of nowhere, her slingshot poised. "Take this!" She fires away at the brute, pelting him with one rock after another. "Go, Bella! Go!"

I jump around the shrieking thug and yank open the sanctuary doors. "Noooo!"

Two hundred heads swivel my way. Whispers skitter across the aisles.

My dad stands at the end of the church, his hand over Christina's.

It isn't too late! They're not married yet! *Thank you, Jesus! I sooo owe you one! Or fifty. Okay, a million.* "You have to stop!" My voice echoes in the rafters as I speed toward my dad. "Christina isn't who you think she is."

"Get on with the ceremony," she hisses to the preacher. "I warned you his daughter might try and sabotage this."

I stop before them, and the balding minister nods my way. "It's true. She did."

"Bella, this is madness. I waited for you. You said you were coming, and I wanted to believe it." Dad takes in my disheveled state, his mouth tight in fury. "I held this ceremony off for twenty minutes hoping my only daughter would come through for me. And this— *this* is what I get?"

"You don't understand, I—"

"Christina was right. She said you'd try and ruin this day, and I didn't believe her."

"Of course she said that." I glare the woman down. "She's a liar!"

Gasps bounce all around the room.

"Bella, you need to leave." Dad lowers his voice. "Now."

"Listen to me. This woman"—I jerk my finger toward his waiting bride—"is the sister of Sadie Vasquez, your former accountant. Sadie, also known as Mercedes, is the woman who was staying at the hotel all this time. She's the woman I saw your fiancée plotting with. They're going to take your money—again."

Dad's brown eyes travel back and forth from me to Christina. "This can't be true."

"Believe it." I hold up my photo. "Check out this photo."

He squints and holds the phone close. "It looks like the face of a rhino."

"It's her sister!"

"Bella, I don't know, I—"

Ruthie takes that moment to charge through the doors. "Wait!" She plows right down the aisle. "I have proof!" She squeals to a stop, and with a heaving chest, pulls the framed photo out of her shirt.

"How does she do that?" Dad mutters.

I shake my head. "I don't know. It's like a Mary Poppins bag down there." I shove the picture into his hands. "Does this woman look familiar? It's Sadie. And you"—I growl at the woman who would've been my stepmother—"are her sister."

Marisol latches onto Christina's leg and begins to cry.

"I love you, Kevin," Christina says. "Please believe me. I love you."

I pull the picture from the black frame and show my father the names on the back. "She lied to you. This whole time, it was all a lie."

The evidence dangles in Dad's hand. "What about our future? What about the show in Brazil? Was that just a lie too, Christina?"

She shakes her head, her eyes brimming with tears. "Yes. At first. But I could've made it happen—somehow."

"But that wasn't the plan you and Mercedes had, was it?" I challenge as the pieces fall into place. "You had Dad sign that ridiculously generous prenup where you got a lump sum. An amount that would've been chump change to a guy who thought he had a multi-million dollar television deal."

Dad's eyes could freeze dragon fire. "You were going to leave me before the final round of contract negotiations were finalized, weren't you? Trump up some excuse for a quickie divorce?"

Christina throws herself on my father, her hands clutching his shoulders. "I didn't mean to fall in love with you." She rubs a mani-cured hand over her wet cheek. "You had that careless fling with my sister and just discarded her."

I glare at my dad. "You had an affair with your accountant?" No wonder she took all his money.

Christina continues. "Mercedes got away with your money, but it wasn't enough for her. She became obsessed. Desperate. Nothing I could say would reach her and her broken heart." She sniffs loudly. "I feared daily she would take her own life. One day . . . I promised her I would do whatever it took to avenge her honor."

What is this—honor-code according to *Sex and the City*?

"We formulated a plan. And I was to marry you, convince you there was a show."

"She knew where my weak spot was." Dad drops his head and pushes Christina's hands away. "Seduce my ego first, right?"

I glance back at the wedding crowd. They sit motionless on the edge of the pews, taking in every morsel of this living soap opera.

"I didn't plan on falling in love with you." Christina's voice is a weak whisper. "But I did. Do you have any idea how this has killed me?"

Ruthie cracks her knuckles. "Wanna brainstorm some ways we could make that happen?"

"You don't love my dad. Stealing his money isn't love."

Christina lifts pitiful eyes to my father. "I do care for you, Kevin. We could still work this out." Her voice lowers to a whisper. "Please don't send me to the police."

"You were actually going to go through with it." Dad glances down at a weeping Marisol. "Was it worth it? How could you do this to your little sister?"

"She's not her little sister."

Everyone pivots toward the doors. Mercedes Vasquez saunters down the narrow aisle. People rotate as she passes by, turning like dominos.

"You're supposed to be on a plane," Christina hisses.

"I couldn't leave without you." She ambles forward and joins our awkward grouping. Her wild eyes cut to me. "Nice dress, by the way."

"More of your sister's good taste." Even a crazy woman recognizes this frock is hideous.

Dad's laugh is ripe with disbelief. "What are you doing here, Sadie?"

"Mommy!" Marisol runs to Mercedes and clings to her pant leg.

"Mommy?" the church crowd echoes.

"That's right. This is my daughter—Christina's *niece*. If Marisol was Christina's sister, you wouldn't go looking for any long-lost relatives." She shakes her bleached-blonde head. "I knew this was over. First of all, I knew my sister couldn't pull it off." She stumbles to Dad and stabs him in the chest with a pointy nail. "And since your bratty kid here"—she tips her chin toward me—"messed everything up, I wanted to at least be here to see your face when you realized the woman you loved didn't love you."

"Don't say anything more, Mercedes," Christina pleads with her watery eyes. "It's time to go."

"I called the police fifteen minutes ago," Ruthie says. "I don't think you can get too far."

Dad runs a hand over his mouth like he's trying to wipe away a sour taste. "My own daughter tried to tell me. And I wouldn't listen to her." He looks at me with an unspoken apology. "What an idiot I've been."

Cant argue with you there, Pops.

Dad reaches out and brushes his fingers through Marisol's hair. "So you wanted revenge—fine. But how could you do something so heinous to this little girl? Who's going to take care of her when her mother and aunt are behind bars?"

Marisol turns her face to her mom's waist and lets out a wail that pierces my heart. Even brats don't deserve this.

Mercedes laughs as police sirens call in the distance. "I'll get off. We both will. It's a crime of passion. Who would ever lock me away after the horrible way you treated me, Kevin?" She pats her daughter awkwardly on the back. "And besides—her father can take care of her."

"Shut up, Mercedes," Christina warns. "Don't say another word until we talk to lawyers."

Dad's eyes widen as his tanned face turns the color of the white church walls. "No. I don't believe it."

Craziness shines in Mercedes' dark eyes. "Oh, did I forget to tell you?"

My father shakes his head. "That's not even possible."

The skin at the back of my sweaty neck tingles. "What? Dad, what's she talking about?" I don't feel so good.

Dad's tortured eyes flit from me to Marisol.

"That's right, Kevin." Mercedes cackles and pushes her daughter forward. "Marisol, dear . . . say hello to your father."

chapter thirty-four

A t two a.m. I tiptoe downstairs, dragging my hand down the banister with each slow step. I'm sure there are conversations that every parent must have with his child that he dreads. The period talk. The alcohol lesson. The sex lecture. But they have to be nothing compared to the "Why Did You Have a Fling with Your Accountant and Have a Love Child" talk I must give now. Parents have no idea the burden of being a kid.

I check the living room for my dad, but find nobody but my grandfather snoring on the couch. An infomercial blasts from the TV, and noticing my grandfather's credit card in his hand, I hope he didn't just order the Sand Away Hair Remover.

Detouring through the kitchen, the floor is cold on my bare feet. I stick my hand into the cookie jar and extract two snicker-doodles. This chat requires reinforcement. Snagging a Sprite from the fridge, I plod on to the office. Still no dad. Between talks with his attorneys and the police, I haven't seen him since I left the church.

After completely searching the house, I ease the back door open, and that's where I find my father. Sitting in a metal chair on his tiny inch of grass, staring at the dark sky.

Slumped down in the seat, elbows on the armrests, he reclines back, still garbed in his crisp tuxedo shirt with the sleeves rolled to his forearms. Reminds me of the way Luke wears his button-downs.

But that's pretty much where the similarities end. This flawed man before me is hurting . . . damaged . . . and in need of an instructional manual more than Ruthie could ever be.

"Hey." My voice sounds harsh in the quiet evening air. "We missed you at dinner." I hand him a cookie.

Dad lifts his head. "You mean your grandmother drove you nuts, and you wish I had been there to intercede."

"Something like that." The woman lectured me on the improper etiquette of busting up a wedding. For two hours.

I sit down on the grass and contemplate the polka dots on my pajama pants.

"Ruthie asleep?" Dad asks.

"Yeah, she went a few rounds with Grandfather on Rock Band, and it totally wore her out."

"Your grandpa can't remember anything beyond 1966. How could he play that?"

"He has a surprisingly good grasp of everything Metallica ever did."

Minutes trickle by as I pick at some grass and try to think of something to say. Do I go with the blunt truth and say, "Hey, you royally jacked up. Again." Or maybe something deep and inspirational like, "The Bible says you can be lifted up on eagles' wings. Yeah, Dad, even you."

I inhale and decide to give it a go. "I—"

"Isabella—"

Our voices trip over each other, and my dad holds up a hand. "Me first." He pulls himself up in the chair and leans forward, resting his hands on his knees. "Bel, I messed up. I don't even know where to begin."

"You could try the beginning."

He nods. "Sadie—or I should say Mercedes—had been my accountant for years. She came highly recommended about nine years ago. We instantly clicked, and eventually one thing led to another."

"Like Marisol." Mercedes was in jail tonight, but Christina, who had confessed to being a small part of the embezzling crime, was out on bail and in a nearby hotel with Marisol. It still weirds me out to think I could have a half-sister. Does this mean I have to take her bra shopping when she's twelve? She'll probably strangle me with it.

"Marisol cannot be mine."

"But you've known her long enough."

"Not in that way. We began seeing each other about three years ago. You've got to believe me." He pushes his fingers through his hair. "Things got really awkward with Mercedes, and I ended it. It didn't go well. She went a little nuts."

"Well, obviously she matured. Because now she's full-on psycho," I say. "Did Mom ever know about Mercedes?"

"She suspected. But she was suspicious of every woman I met."

"Can't imagine why."

Instead of calling me on my disrespect, Dad nods. "And look where it got me. I've really done it this time."

"But why would Marisol stay with Christina?"

"I think that was Christina's choice. Probably knew Marisol wasn't safe with Sadie. I mean, did you see the woman?"

I take a bite of snicker-doodle. "She looked like Lord Voldemort's sister."

"As the police were cuffing the ladies, Christina told me Sadie has been getting steadily more unbalanced. She begged me to protect Marisol. Aside from the man I thought was my best man and television producer, Marisol has no family in America." He sends me a wary look. "I'm going to keep her."

"Marisol's not a puppy."

"No, but she's going to need a home. At least until Christina gets her stuff straightened out. I don't think she'll do much time. But Sadie—who knows."

I can't help the anger that spurts to life. "Do you seriously think you can take care of a kid? By yourself?"

"I've got Luisa."

The old bitterness bubbles up and threatens to spill over like a volcano. "So you're just going to let the nanny raise her. Like you and Mom did with me."

Dad straightens his spine. "I know I've messed up with you. Obviously your mom has made changes in the right direction. I can tell you two are closer." He sighs and looks at the ground. "But I'm still this huge failure to you. Right?"

This is probably the part where I rush to him, throw my arms around his neck, and say, "Gosh, Daddy, no! Don't say that about yourself."

"You're the best plastic surgeon on the planet." I twirl my finger around a dandelion and smile wistfully. "I remember sometimes I used to come visit at the office, and watching those famous people stroll in and out would be like stepping into a fairy tale. And they were all there to see my dad."

"But?"

"But then you never came home. You lived at that office. And when you were home, you just avoided me. And I thought when I moved to Oklahoma things would change. I thought you would change. How could you stand to let me go, Dad?" My throat thickens.

"I had to, Isabella." Dad slips out of his chair and sits on his knees in front of me, the tails of his shirt dragging the ground. "Your mother needed you, and you had this whole life waiting for you."

My bangs fall into my eyes, and I push them back. "And then I thought when I would come for my monthly visit to Manhattan that you would drop everything to spend time with me. I mean, to see your daughter forty-eight hours a month, who wouldn't make the most of it?"

"But not me," he says heavily. "I was too busy working."

I lift my head and look my dad directly in the eye. "You don't know what to do with me, do you? When I'm here—you don't know how to just be my dad."

"I guess you're right." His laugh is wrapped in bitterness. "Frankly, Bella, you scare me. I looked up one day and you were this young woman—a young lady I didn't even recognize."

"Because you didn't bother to get to know me. And now you're going to take on Marisol like you get to start over or something. You've got a daughter—me."

He rests his surgeon's hands on my leg. "I know my slate is far from clean with you. And you may not believe me, but I want to work on that. I don't think Marisol is my chance for a redo." Dad grimaces. "If you think I'm scared of you, you have no idea what I feel for that little tyrant."

"And now she's going to be your tyrant?"

"Maybe." He pats my knee. "But so are you. And I want to change, Bella. I do. For us. I want to be a better man. Maybe that's why I feel so strongly about taking care of Marisol. I know I have to change—for your sake. And mine. I've missed out on so much."

"Yes." Flashes of my life spin through my mind. Ballet recitals, first dance, skinned knees, my first short story Luisa hung on the refrigerator. "You have missed out on a lot. And that makes me sad. And mad."

"I don't want to be left out of one more thing. I don't want this rift between us to be how it is forever, you know?" Dad reaches out his ringless hand and closes it over mine. "Tell me what to do, and I'll do it. Because, baby, I have no idea."

A tear falls from my eye, and I brush it away with my knuckle. "I'm the kid, Dad. It's time you figured out how this parenting stuff works. Because I sure don't know."

He gives a weak smile. "You're right a lot, you know?"

"Maybe you could tell Mom that."

Dad pulls me to him and envelopes me in his strong arms. "I want my daughter." He smoothes my hair and presses a kiss to my temple. "I know I want my daughter."

More stupid tears fall and dampen my face. Must've been that Hallmark commercial I saw earlier. Because I am *so* not a crier. "Love is a risk, isn't it, Dad?" I think of all the breakups in my life, my family. And I think of Luke.

"It's worth it, though. You're worth it. I love you, Isabella Kirkwood."

Nose drips. "Right back at you."

"I'm going to figure this dad stuff out. I promise."

"Hey, Dad?"

"Yeah?"

"I hear credit cards are a great way to show affection."

<hr>

Later, as I push open my bedroom door, I'm greeted by the buzz-saw noises coming from Ruthie's open mouth. The stress of the day caught up with my crime-busting partner.

Or those pants finally cut off her circulation and she simply passed out.

I plop on the bed and stare at the ceiling, where the evil cherubs stand poised in their painted glory, ready to swoop down and attack. I feel so worn down. So drained. *God, everything is changing. Again. I'm not sure I'm ready for all this. A new dad. Maybe a new sister. I seriously need some Ben and Jerry's.*

I reach across the bed and grab my phone from the nightstand. It's ridiculously late, but I punch in the number anyway. Some moments just call for a comforting voice.

"Only a total idiot would call me at this hour."

I laugh at Luke's tired greeting. "Sorry to wake you."

"It's after two in the morning."

Luke sighs on the other end, and I hear the rustle of covers. "How did the wedding go? I texted you a few times, but you didn't respond. I took that as a sign you were being physically restrained somewhere in a padded cell."

I laugh again. "You make me smile, Luke Sullivan."

Three seconds of silence pass. "What's wrong, Bella?"

"I can't call and just be nice to you?"

"I'm sorry about the wedding. Did they leave on their honeymoon?"

I fluff a pillow under my head and let the sham cool my cheek. "One of these days you're going to learn not to doubt me."

"You stopped the wedding?"

"Yeah, you should've been there. It was a masterpiece of epically horrible proportions." I spend the next fifteen minutes filling him in on my day, not sparing any wacko detail.

"I can't believe it."

I grin into the phone. "Maybe you should put a little more trust in me."

"I don't think my trust in you has ever really been our problem."

I flush at his serious tone. "You have to admit I have good instincts."

"Except at relationships," he says. "And then . . . they suck."

The air hangs suspended in my chest. "I . . . I—"

"I'm through waiting, Bella. When you get back Sunday, I'm coming to your house. And you and I are going to have a big long talk. And I'm not leaving until you tell me exactly what you want."

"Okay." Sure. Yeah, I can do that. The thought of it gives me a strange barfy feeling, but surely that will pass. With ice cream.

"I didn't kiss Ashley Timmons. And you know that."

I let this go.

"Bella?"

"Hmm?"

"I'm glad I'm the one you called."

My heavy eyelids begin to flutter to my cheeks. "Actually, I went through the whole list of boys from the junior class. You were just the first one to pick up."

"Go to sleep." I can hear the smile in his voice. "You're beat."

I yawn. "Luke?"

"Hmm?"

"Thanks. I can always count on you."

"Never forget it."

chapter thirty-five

"What happened to coming home early Sunday?" Luke slides into the vacant seat beside mine in journalism on Monday. "Remember the talk we were going to have?"

I save my document and give him my attention. "The conversation you demanded?"

He doesn't budge. "That would be the one."

"Want to talk about it now?"

"Of course not. This is hardly the time or place."

But I saw that hesitation.

I let my brow rise just to the point of being flirty. "Afraid Ashley Timmons will get mad?"

Luke opens his mouth to speak, then glances across the room at his star reporter and occasional friendly companion who's not even bothering to hide the fact that she's eavesdropping. "I'll call you after the carnival performance tonight."

"Oh, I'll be there."

He slants his arrogant head. "Your mother forbade you to go."

I hold up a newly manicured finger. "She barred me from work-ing at the carnival."

"And then she grounded you. You can't just slip out."

"It's a special night for Cherry. I'll talk Mom into it. The whole family's going." Well, minus Jake. He's taping a performance for

World Wrestling Television in Oklahoma City. He's apparently going head-to-head with some guy called Chainsaw. My stepdad said it's a promotion, so I guess the scarier the names, the higher up you are. When he's in a match with someone named Throat Slasher, I'll know he's really arrived.

"I don't think you should be at the carnival," Luke says. "It's not safe. Alfredo is still out there somewhere, and who knows what Red and Stewart have in mind for you."

"And it's safe for you?"

"Don't start that sexist routine with me."

"Um, I'm pretty sure *you* started it. You don't think you're in danger? They know we're friends and probably conspirators."

Attitude flashes in his eyes. "Nobody's flung stage lights on me yet."

I lean forward and drop my voice. "That could've been just for Cherry—if it was even intentional."

"We both know it was intentional. And I'm asking you not to go tonight."

"And I'm telling you no."

We stare each other down until my eyes burn from lack of blinking.

"Fine," he says finally. "Do what you want. I know you're going to anyway." He tosses a piece of paper on my desk. "Have a new article ready for your column next week."

"I'm back on?"

"Yes."

I stand up and clap my hands together. "Thank you, Luke. You won't regret this!"

"Don't even think of hugging me right now."

I step back. "Wouldn't dream of being so unprofessional, Chief." I wink and lean toward his ear. "I'll save that for later."

Plopping back down at my work station, I begin brainstorming ideas for my next column. Maybe I'll focus on seniors and the different graduation festivities. Or maybe I'll write about summer vacation plans.

I stop my mental list as a shadow looms over me. I see her reflection in my monitor and don't bother looking up. "Did you need something, Ashley?"

"Yeah, I, uh, just wanted to say Luke made me read some of the archived papers. And . . . you're a good writer."

Now this jerks my head upright. Ashley studies a spot on her shoe, and I notice her cheeks are tinged a nice, telling pink.

"Wow. Thanks."

"Didn't see that coming, did you?" She flips her long, blonde hair.

"No." I give her the closest thing to a real smile I can muster. "But thank you."

"I read all those articles on mysteries you've solved—the football boys' fraternity and the prom fiasco."* Ashley pulls her eyes from the ground and stares me in the face. "It was solid writing, Bella. And it was also good teamwork between you and Luke."

This thought brings a genuine grin to my face. "Yes, it was. We work well together." When we're not fighting.

"I picked up some writing pointers from your work." Her mouth hardens. "So now that I've got that nicety out of the way, I want to tell you that I'm going to give one hundred percent to pursuing your front page space *and* your ex-boyfriend."

I bring myself to my full height on my Stuart Weitzman heels. "Maybe you should go back and reread those pieces of mine. Because while you may have taken some notes on the mechanics, you obviously missed some common themes." I tick them off on my fingers. "One, I don't ever give up. So I may have been off my game for a few weeks, but I'm back now with all sorts of ideas—ideas that don't include you keeping my space as a regular feature columnist. And two, I don't believe in letting opportunities get away. So I'll be the one getting back with my ex. Not you. I'll be taking care of the final details this evening." I give her a condescending pout. "But I don't mind the competition, really. Keeps me on my toes. And reminds Luke that everything he wants is right here."

Ashley shakes her head slowly. "That's not what he said last night on the phone."

I narrow my eyes, and she catches my flicker of doubt.

"He said he's tired of your little games, Bella. So just prepare yourself. Your boyfriend's moved on. I wouldn't even waste your time talking to him tonight." Her voice drops to a whisper. "I'd hate to see a strong girl like you embarrass herself and beg." She pats me on the shoulder and walks on. "Just looking out for a fellow reporter."

~~~~~~~~~~

Ruthie slides her cafeteria tray beside mine. "I feel so wrung out today."

Lindy bites down on a fry and sighs. "Me too."

And me three. Life is stressful. What would make me feel better is solving this mystery. And some new shoes.

"It's like I pour everything I am, my heart and my soul, into my unicycle ballet. And then there's not much left of me. The carnival is a soul sucker." She shoves her food away. "You know something is wrong when you can't even enjoy some high-quality meatloaf."

Matt lifts his head from his AP History homework. "You got Female Athlete of the Year at last week's athletic banquet, Lindy. I thought you'd be on top of the world."

She shrugs. "Yeah. I am." She says this with as much conviction as one would say *I love being grounded.*

"We haven't gotten pizza and gone to the park in a while. How about hanging out after school?" Matt asks. "You know, like the old days."

"That would be fun. I . . . um, just have to check my plans."

"With Bo." Matt rolls his eyes. "Didn't know he was in charge of your life and had to approve your schedule."

"I have a boyfriend now and things have changed."

Matt blinks away hurt, letting anger take over. "Fine. Whatever."

Speaking of the Track Star Romeo, Bo Blades walks to our table, his new Nike Airs a perfect match to his running pants. "Hey, Lindy." He squeezes her shoulder and sits down. "The Tulsa Oilers are doing a special benefit game this Friday." Bo holds up two tickets. "I thought you might want to go."

Lindy's smile wobbles. "I do love hockey."

"I know. I remembered you said that once. So when I heard it announced on the radio, I thought of you."

"You're always thinking of me. It's the perfect date."

"So I'll pick you up at five?" Bo laughs. "Well, maybe I better come by earlier. Last weekend your dad and I talked so long, we almost missed our movie. Dude, your dad is so awesome."

"Yeah." Lindy stares at her lap. "He thinks you're the best."

Bo squeezes her hand and stands. "I'll see you later. I promised a friend I'd pray with him before his sixth-hour test. I'll call you tonight. But not until after your *SportsCenter*, right?" He hums as he leaves.

"Bo, I can't!" Lindy jumps to her feet.

We all drop our plastic utensils.

He turns back to our table, still smiling. "What's wrong? You can't go to the hockey game?" He shrugs. "That's okay, Lindy. Maybe your dad and a friend can take our tickets. We can do whatever you want Friday night."

"I know." She bites her lip and steps forward.

Matt, Ruthie, and I lean closer.

"I . . . er . . ." Lindy wrings her hands, then lets the words just spew. "Bo, you're too perfect!"

He blinks twice. "Excuse me?"

Yeah, *huh?*

"You know all my favorite songs, my father adores you, you're the best Christian guy ever, you hold my doors open, and you know my every interest and dislike—sometimes even before I do."

"And that's a problem? Tell me what to do, and I'll fix it."

"That's just it. I know you would." Lindy folds and unfolds the hem of her T-shirt. "You're so perfect that I feel like *I* have to be perfect. And I'm not. I can't be myself around you."

Bo frowns. "I don't know what you mean."

"Did you know I always spill food on my shirts? Always. But when I'm with you, I feel like I have to watch my every bite. And I usually just stop eating after a few minutes because I'm so nervous."

"I didn't—"

"And you're so good to everyone, it makes me feel like I have to be on my best behavior all the time. But you know what? I get in bad moods sometimes."

"I'm sure everyone does."

"Not you, Bo. You're always happy. And it makes me uncomfortable. And you know what else? Your clothes are never wrinkled. Do you iron everything you wear? Even your T-shirts?"

"I guess I think it's important to look nice at all times."

"And you've never made me watch a stupid shoot-'em-up movie."

"I don't understand. I know you don't like that kind of stuff, so of course I would never do that."

Lindy's smile grows. "You're an amazing guy. But you're not *my* amazing guy. I can't be myself around you. I need someone as flawed as I am. Someone who also gets pizza on his shirts and occasionally makes me watch a stupid action flick because that's what *he* likes."

Bo rests his hand on Lindy's shoulder. "What are you saying here?"

"That you're pretty close to perfect. But that makes you perfectly wrong for me. I think you're an awesome guy. I do. But I've kind of lost myself in all of this. And it's time to get back to being me."

He casts a self-conscious glance at our table. We don't even pretend to look elsewhere. "Are you sure about this?" he whispers.

Lindy nods and pats his hand. "Go find your dream girl, Bo."

"Still friends?"

She laughs. "I knew you'd say that."

He drops his grip. "Let me guess, because I always say the right thing?"

"Because you're you."

"Um . . . do you think your dad would want to go with me to the game?"

"Definitely. I may have broken up with you—but he hasn't."

Bo gives Lindy his best reassuring grin, then walks away. Out of her life.

Lindy sits back down, and her sigh of relief could blow the ketchup off Ruthie's meatloaf.

"That was some good lunchtime entertainment," Ruthie says. "I give it four stars out of five. There wasn't any blood, or else I'd totally bump up the score."

I shoot Lindy a curious look. "I didn't see that coming."

She picks up her water and takes a drink. "I didn't either. But dang if that didn't feel good. Oh, and Matt, my schedule seems to be clear today for an after-school date at the park."

Matt's eyes go wide. "Date?"

"Yes. I'm asking you out."

My head jerks in a double take. "Who are you and what have you done with my friend Lindy?"

She only has eyes for Matt. "I am never more myself than when I'm hanging out with you, and I've missed you lately. I've missed us. And I realize you've never felt anything but friendship for me, but you need to know that I'm sick of pretending to be someone I'm not. And who I am"—Lindy straightens her back, squares her shoulders—"is a girl finally telling you how I feel."

"I—I, um . . ." Matt's face is as red as cherry Kool-Aid. "I . . . don't know what to say."

"Oh." Lindy's face falls. "Okay, yeah, sure." She picks up her tray. "I gotta go." With the speed that's earned her many a track medal, she leaves the table and heads toward the exit doors.

"You're just a chicken." Ruthie cracks her knuckles. "And if you don't go get her right now, I'm gonna tuck your head so far up your—"

"Wait!" Matt jumps up. "Lindy, wait!"

Ruthie and I follow him, as he runs to catch up with our friend in the hall.

"Lindy!"

She stops and slowly spins around. "What?"

Matt's lips struggle to form the words. "Um . . ." He stares at the white ceiling tiles over her head. "Would . . . would you like to go to the park today? On, um, a date?"

Lindy studies his face for a moment before she breaks into a wide grin. "Okay."

His head bobs once. "Then okay. I will, uh, see you there after, um, school."

"Don't forget the pizza."

His smile grows steadier. "No, I won't forget." He watches her walk away. "Oh, and Lindy?"

She turns.

"You have burrito on your shirt."

chapter thirty-six

"No, Bella. Absolutely not."

"But, Mom!" I pace the kitchen, torn between wanting to yell or stuff my face with Oreos. "I have to see Cherry's last performance."

My mother crosses her arms and gives me the stern look she's been cultivating for almost a year. "You should've thought of that before you left me out of so many details in your life."

"Those were trifling details though. I thought they would just bore you."

"Then I'm glad we've got this cleared up. So *next* time an accused murderer breaks into your car or someone tries to kill you with carnival equipment, you will know to clue me in."

"Right." I nod once. "I'll definitely do that. Let me just get my purse, and I'll go with you to the carnival."

Mom wags a finger. "Nuh-uh. You can stay home and clean the house."

Sometimes I really miss my old tuned-out Mom who I had wrapped around my finger. Those stupid parenting books. I think the first order of business in cleaning will be flushing those things down the toilet.

Mom snaps her fingers. "Oh, I almost forgot. Dolly and Mickey have been at the carnival grounds all afternoon keeping an eye on Cherry. I need you to go over to Dolly's and let Cherry's dog out."

"I can go all the way out there, but I can't go down the road to the carnival?"

"I've already checked in your car—there's no one hiding out. You go straight to Dolly's and right back." My mother plants a kiss on my cheek. "I mean it, Bel. If I see you at tonight's show, I will ground you for life. You'll be fifty and still won't be allowed to date."

"But—"

"No buts. Dolly is taking her new video camera, so she'll get it all."

"Are we ready to go?" Robbie does two swoops around the kitchen, his red Superman cape flapping behind him. "I didn't get my name on the board all week, so I get a funnel cake. And the rides close extra early tonight, so we have to hurry."

"Get in the Tahoe, Robbie. Budge will meet us there." Mom picks up her keys and gives me a final warning stare. "I'm serious. If you disobey me on this, there will be heavy consequences unlike any you've ever seen—including a long summer at your dad's."

"Ugh. Say no more. Like I want to be there right now." Just because Dad and I are on the mend doesn't mean that I want to spend too much time in Manhattan right now. Dad called this morning, and Marisol's already moved back in with him—indefinitely. Talk about a recipe for a nightmare.

Barely resisting the urge to throw myself on the floor and scream *No fair!* I watch Mom and Robbie pull out of the shrub-lined driveway and turn onto the dirt road.

Might as well get the dog task over with. Grabbing my own car keys—plus three more cookies—I slip out the back door and into my Bug.

My phone beeps, and I check the text. It's from Luke.

You + Me = Later.

I'm ready for our big talk. I think. And though I didn't get to speak with him the rest of the day, I'm pretty sure Ashley Timmons was just blowing smoke. Some girls and their insecurities. I mean, she's so full of it. Right?

As I buckle my seat belt and do my fifth check in the backseat for any unwanted passengers, I feel another wave of anger over how tonight has turned out. I can't believe everyone in town will be at the carnival, and I won't. After all those long hours in clown shoes and honky noses! And for what? To get grounded and locked away while the rest of the world is watching Cherry and Stewart. And probably while Luke is solving the mystery. By himself. Without me . . . and hopefully without a certain blonde reporter.

Ten minutes later I stop the Bug in Dolly's driveway. Using Mom's key, I unlock Dolly's massive front door and slip inside. The setting sun bounces off the large windows in the living room, making me want to flick on the TV and curl up on the overstuffed couch. I bypass the warm, inviting space and call for the dog.

"Peg! Here, Peg!"

Thuds resound overhead as the dog scrambles through the rooms above, then down the stairs.

"Hey, girl." I stand at the end of the long staircase. Peg lands next to me with a leap and instantly goes to sniffing. "Um, kind of intrusive there. Watch the nose. Watch the nose!" I would never sniff her butt. She could at least return the courtesy.

I reach down and run my hand over her furry head. "You ready to go out? Come on."

Peg's ears perk at that command, and her feet *clickity-clack* on the hardwood floor as I open the back door. "Okay, girl. Do your thing, and make it snappy."

Ten minutes later the dog has not returned, so I step outside. "Peg!"

I walk the grounds of Dolly's massive yard, calling Peg's name and searching high and low. Nothing. I even look over the side of the pool to make sure she's not floating face down, doing the eternal doggy paddle. But aside from some stray leaves, the pool is empty.

Where is that dog? This animal is all that Cherry has left of Betty the Bearded Lady. If I've misplaced Betty's only child, I will never get ungrounded.

And that's when it hits me.

Look through town. Tear it apart. But the answer you seek. Is circled 'round my heart.

That's it.

I know the answer to the riddle.

chapter thirty-seven

eg! The answer has to be with that dog! Aside from Cherry,
there was nothing more important to Betty.

Reaching into my pocket, I pull out my phone and call Ruthie.
She answers on the third ring.

"This better be important. We're about to start, and I haven't
done my pre-unicycle deep-breathing exercises yet."

"Ruthie, I need to talk to Cherry. Now."

"Fine. I'll get her. But some people need to recognize there's
more than one star to this show . . ."

I continue yelling for the dog, but there's no sign of the furry
beast.

Finally I hear Cherry's voice. "Yes?"

"This is urgent. I think I know the answer to the riddle, but I
need to find Peg. I'm over here at Dolly's, and I let her outside. But
that was almost fifteen minutes ago. Where would she be?"

The background noise of the carnival almost overpowers her
voice. "I don't know. Probably out at the barn. She loves the horses."

"The barn's like a few miles away!" I'm not in the mood for a
long walk.

"Yeah, you'll have to drive out there. She won't come back on
her own, though. That's why you use the leash by the door."

"Oh. Right." Well, excuse me. Any dog that is intelligent

enough to work for a circus ought to be able to figure out how to pee and return home by herself. "I'll go out to the horse stables then. Thanks."

"Wait—Bella. You said you have the answer?"

"I think the answer is around Peg's neck. She's the missing piece in all of this. I'm going to check out her collar."

"Let me know what you find . . . and be careful out there."

Hopping back into the Bug, I beat it down the dirt road and turn into the field that leads to the horse stables.

The foreman drives my way in his beat-up Ford, and I roll down my window. "Have you seen Peg—the dog?"

He leans out his truck and spits on the green grass below. "Yup. Seen her around here nosing 'round my horses. Get her on back home, would ya? And close the gate when you leave the property. We're all checking out for the night. Going to the big top to see Cherry."

Who isn't? Oh . . . me.

I search in every building until my feet ache. My patent-leather flats are not dog-hunting shoes. Sticking my head in the last stall, I grin with relief. "Peg!" The dog runs from the side of a chestnut mare and sniffs my hand. A smart girl probably would've brought treats. Now how am I going to coax her into my car?

"Hey, Peg. It's time to go back home now, okay? You've had your big walk." And hopefully a big tinkle. "Let me see this collar here." I go to my knees in front of the dog. She sticks her nose in my hand as I try to wrangle with her tags. "What does this say here?"

"Thanks for the tip."

My head shoots up, and I'm on my feet. "Alfredo." I eye the magician with cold dread. "Wh-what are you doing here?" My hand slips into my pocket.

"Don't even think about going for the phone. In fact"—his arm shoots out and grabs my hand—"these ought to keep you from doing anything stupid." Alfredo wrenches my arms behind my back and slaps handcuffs on my wrists.

"What are you doing? Are you nuts?" My pulse escalates until it pounds in my ears. "Let me go."

"I don't think so." Leaning down, he coos to the dog. "What do we have here? So the answer's on the dog's collar. My Betty—she had a heart of gold, but she wasn't the smartest rabbit in the hat." His beady eyes narrow as he flips over the dog's name tag. "Nothing here! Just the dog's stupid name." He looks up at me with wild eyes. "It's a name tag. Cherry said you knew the answer was on the dog's collar."

"She called you after I talked to her, didn't she?" How does a runaway convict have a cell phone?

"Cherry knows I only want what's best for her. She trusts me—whether she should or not. She told me you were gonna turn me in."

"So that's why you haven't contacted me."

"This could've played out much differently."

"Have you been staying out here?" I remember Dolly saying Cherry had been feeding the dog—a lot. "Cherry's been bringing you food, hasn't she? She's known you were here the whole time. You've forced her to break the law."

"Shut up!" Alfredo blasts. "I only want what's best for her and—"

He freezes like a statue as a truck rumbles outside. I take advantage of the moment and scream like I'm on fire. "Help! I'm in here, I—*oomph!*" My words are lost as Alfredo plasters his hand to my mouth.

"Be quiet. This doesn't have to be like this, so cooperate, would you?"

I torque my head and glare. Like I'm going to let him just do—I shudder—*whatever* to me without a fight.

"Alfredo?" A familiar voice calls. "Alfredo?"

"In here!" my captor yells, causing the horse beside us to stir. "I got company."

Red Fritz steps into the dimming light of the stable. "You." His voice is as menacing as one of the villains on Robbie's cartoons. "This kid's been a problem from the moment Stewart hired her." He steps closer to me and runs a gloved finger down my cheek. "And then when I put him in charge of getting rid of you, he couldn't do that right either. You got her locked up good?"

I thrash against Alfredo, but he only drags me closer to him, ignoring the kick of my legs. "She's not going anywhere." He turns to me and drops his hand. "If you know anything about this dog's collar, you better tell me now."

"It's just a name. I thought there would be a map there on the back or something." I shrug with as much casualness as I can fake. "Guess I was wrong. But you do know the police are up-to-date on all of this, right?" I watch Red's eyes widen. "They know I was in contact with Alfredo, that my life was threatened, and that Cherry's in danger."

Red stoops down and grabs the dog's collar. "This is what I was called out here for? I got a fill-in covering the last half of the first show, and you drag me out here to read Betty's mutt's tags?" He peers closer. "Who would call an animal Peg Aurora Smith anyway? What's wrong with names like Spot or Fido?" He shoves the dog aside. "Waste of time."

"What do we do now?" Alfredo asks.

Red spears me with his beady eyes. "You know what to do. The girl goes with us. I got business to take care of during the second act." He smiles and pats his pocket. "I just sold the carnival two hours ago. So now I have a show to wrap up, a niece to kill off, and my own little disappearing act to complete."

Fear roars through my head like a New York subway. "What are you going to do to Cherry?"

"Wouldn't you like to know, you nosy little brat! You've been in my way ever since you went digging through Alfredo's trailer. Yeah,

I'm the one who so kindly returned your flashlight. But you still didn't take the hint to butt out." Red blows cigar smoke in my face, and I blink against the burn. "Let's just say there will be a tragic accident during Cherry's second performance." He tsks his tongue. "And she will finally get that family she's been dreaming of—when she's reunited with her parents in heaven." Red holds his large stomach and laughs.

"Cherry's parents didn't die in an accident, did they?" As if I have to ask.

"It's taken awhile, but I've finally gotten what should've been mine all along." Red jabs his pudgy thumb in his chest. "I was the oldest. I should've been the one to inherit the carnival—not my brother."

I send a look of desperation to Alfredo. "Are you seriously going to stand by and let this happen?"

"Red's cutting me in on the deal." A wicked glint lights Alfredo's eye. "It's been me and him the whole time. He paid me to get Betty off his back."

"By killing her?" I charge.

"By dating her."

"Speaking of good shows!" Red claps Alfredo on the back. "Now that was an Oscar-worthy performance. Imagine—that woman ever thinking a man would be interested in her." His face sobers. "Take care of the kid and be in my trailer fifteen minutes before the final show is over."

Fear slides across my skin. "If you're going to kill me, you might as well tell me what you've been looking for."

Red laughs. "Doesn't matter now. I got the carnival sold, the check in my pocket, and soon I'll be a grieving uncle. Everything else can just stay buried." He waves a white hand over my head. "On second thought, bring the girl with us. We don't have the time or the resources to deal with her here." He moves his leering grin close to my face. "Don't worry. It will be painless—mostly. Just like Betty, I've found if I want someone killed well, I have to do it myself."

My brain shudders. That slimy, creepy, curly-mustached freak. *God, please help me. I'm too young and fashionable to die!*

Alfredo tightens his hold on my arms as Red motions him on. "Let's go."

"Peg Aurora Smith. Stupid name for a stupid dog." Red hops into his truck.

"Anything you want to tell me?" Alfredo stares at me with focused intensity.

"Nope."

"I had a feeling you wouldn't make this easy." His frown is sharp. "It'll only hurt for a bit."

I thrash against him as he pulls out a taser. "No!"

Violent heat pours through my body as I scream and drop to the ground.

The electricity stops and I grasp for breath.

"Now you got anything to say?"

I close my eyes and turn my head in answer.

Red's face splits into a smile as he hands the magician a roll of silver duct tape. "You two meet me in the truck."

My leg connects with Alfredo's knee but he holds up the taser. "You don't want to do that." He picks me up like a sack of feed and hoists me over his shoulder.

My mind races with options for escape.

And I think of the dog.

Because she's been the answer all along.

chapter thirty-eight

I stare at the floorboard of Red's truck and pray like my life depends on it. 'Cause, um, I'm pretty sure it does.

I have to get out of here! If only I could reach my phone. My body jerks as I force myself to breathe through my nose, slow and deep. *Don't panic. Do not panic, Bella.*

The vehicle comes to a rough stop, and the engine shudders into silence. "Get her out and bring her to the haunted house," Red says. "I've already missed more of the show than I meant to. Let's make this quick, because I sure can't miss my niece's Praying Mantis."

The door swings open and Alfred's hands pull me by my arms. "Nice ride, princess?" He heaves my body into his arms and over his shoulder, pinning my legs down with his iron grip, my bound ankles making my attempts at kicking pitiful and pointless.

The dark of the night covers us as the two men walk toward the haunted house. The eerie quiet of the closed rides does nothing to comfort me. *God, please rescue me. Save me from a really painful death. I have a cat to raise!*

I'm jostled onto Alfredo's bony shoulder as he climbs the steps into the dim spook house. My eyes search all around for anyone to help me. I scream behind my tape, but it goes nowhere.

"Throw her inside. Shackle her to that rail."

Alfredo does as Red commands. He drops me on the floor, and pain rockets through my body. He jerks my hands overhead and in two swift motions locks my cuffs to a rail. I donkey kick him with my duct taped legs, but he barely stumbles.

"Is she secure?"

Alfredo's nod is grave. "Don't you think this is clumsy—leaving her to die like this? You know they'll see the cuffs first thing."

"Who cares?" Red glances out the door. "We'll be long gone with a big check to share. If anyone knows how to stay out of sight, it's you." He throws down his cigar. "Are you sure she's secure?"

Alfredo's eyes laser into mine. "Two twists and a tug couldn't even get her out of these babies."

Tears flow unchecked down my face. No, I'm not a crier, but if there ever was a reason for it, surely this is it. And to die here of all places. Home of the worst job I've ever had. Well, aside from Pancho's Mexican Villa. And scooping poop at Dolly's. And getting attacked by the maxi-pad machine at the Summer Fresh factory. But, no, this *has* to be the worst. Because none of those other jobs resulted in my death.

"Light her up." Red runs his fingers down the curve of his mustache. "Don't worry, girl. Once the smoke gets to going good, it'll knock you out. You won't feel a thing."

I flop like a fish, yanking on the cuffs, screaming behind my gag. *Help me! Someone help me!* Panic fills my chest as I struggle to breathe.

"There's enough plywood on this thing to make one heck of a bonfire." Red checks his watch. "Ten minutes until Cherry's routine. Get to it."

Alfredo's wide eyes bore into mine again. Like he's trying to send me some sort of message, but I don't know what. Forgive him? Yeah, right. I'll consider that when my body is melting like a s'more.

The magician slams the door, and I'm thrown into darkness.

Seconds later, I hear something slide through the handle. I'm toast. Literally. *God, please.*

With ears attuned to every sound, I listen as the men work outside, my body jerking with every noise. Finally . . . silence.

Silence is not good. Silence means the fire has started. And I'm minutes away from the end. Why didn't I tell Luke how I felt about him? Why didn't I tell my mom I loved her today? Or call my dad. Or punch Budge in the arm. And Robbie—I'll miss that little guy and all his superhero fantasies.

Tears continue to drop on my cheeks, and I wonder if I could cry enough to douse out some flames.

I scream behind the tape as smoke filters its way into the trailer. *Please, someone see the smoke and call for help. It's my only hope.*

Smoke billows through the cracks of the haunted house, and a full minute passes until I see a flame lick the wall. I pull on the cuffs with all I've got.

Right this moment Cherry is getting ready to fall to her death. And there's nothing I can do to stop it.

And I'm about to burn up in a carnival attraction dedicated to horror. The irony does not escape me.

God, just let it be quick. I want to pass out from smoke inhalation just like Red said. That is possible, right? He wasn't just lying? Because I don't know if I can believe a word out of his fat, lying mouth.

I close my eyes against the smoke and hang my head. So many things I wanted to do still. Tell Jake he needs to fight for my mom. Let Luke know I'm over the moon for him, that I don't want to go another day without being the girlfriend of the bossiest, most arrogant boy on campus. I wanted to go to college and write for a university newspaper. Get married. Meet Prince Harry. Maybe marry Prince Harry and redecorate Buckingham Palace.*

The smoke. It's getting to me. I have to think. There has to be a way out of here. Now can't be my time. Not like this. *Lord, what do you want me to do?*

Why was Alfredo staring at me so hard? What was he trying to tell me? Think! I cough into my shoulder and recall every word that came out of that dirty crook's mouth.

Two twists and a tug couldn't even get her out of these babies.

Of course! The handcuffs. He was letting me know the cuffs are his magician's props.

I get to my knees and turn my head against the flow of the smoke. Flames eat at the wall and climb higher. Closer.

I twist the cuffs once. Twice.

And pull.

My hands snap loose of the restraints, and I nearly collapse on the floor. *Thank you, God!* Quickly, I rip off the tape from my mouth. My heart pounding, I feel for the seam at my ankles, as one anxious second passes into another. "Yes!" Finally, my fingernail snags the end of the tape, and I give it a pull, unwrapping my legs. "Help! Help me! I'm trapped!" Covering my mouth with my T-shirt, I pound on the wall in front of me.

I quickly look to the entrance, but the door is fully engulfed. No time to lose. Must get out.

Reaching into my back pocket, I rip out my phone. I punch in Luke's number. No answer.

"Luke, I'm trapped in the haunted house! Please come get me. Cherry's in trouble. Do not let her take the trapeze." *And get me! Find me! Rescue me.*

Now to call 9-1-1. A board pops overhead, and with a shout, I jump out of the way.

And drop my phone.

The roof is going to cave. I can't stop to find the phone. I just have to get out.

Using my hands, I fumble along the walls and try to locate a door. I know there's at least one more. People go into the haunted house, so they have to come out. I hope.

Splinters tear into my fingers as I grope along the rough wooden surface, moving along fast enough to stay ahead of the flames. But I know it could go at any time.

"Help me! Someone!" I scream some more then cover my mouth. The smoke—it's too much. Recalling Mrs. Bryant's ninth-grade health class, I stoop as low as I can to the ground, still searching for a door. I push past the light-headedness and keep moving.

"Bella?"

I freeze. Did I just hear my name? *Please, God!*

"Here I am!" I wheeze and cough. "In here!"

"Bella!"

Just gonna sit down for a second and close my eyes. So sleepy. Feeling oozy. Head spinning. Eyes sting. Throat raw.

Air flows over me, and I hear my name again. "Bella! Can you hear me?"

Then arms lift me up and cradle me close. Is this what dying feels like?

"Bella, hang on."

I nearly choke on the fresh air as it hits my lungs. I'm gently rested on the ground, and suddenly Luke's face looms near and aims close. Mouth open.

"Wait!" My lungs spasm as I wheeze. I push his face away and just move the breath in and out. I'm alive!

Luke sighs big and drops his head to mine. "You're okay. Thank God you're okay." He says this over and over.

"Luke?"

He doesn't move. "Yes?"

"Get off."

He lifts me to him and pulls close. "Some girls will do anything to avoid mouth-to-mouth."

I wrap my arms around him and just hold tight, letting the night air cleanse my mind and lungs. "Omigosh!" I shove him away and ease into a sitting position. "We have to save Cherry! Did you tell them not to let her go on?"

He frowns. "No, I heard the first part of your message and just ran out."

"We have to go." I stumble to my feet, and he helps me to stand. "Stewart's going to drop Cherry tonight. Red wants her dead. I heard the whole thing."

He looks back to the fully engulfed trailer. "I could kill someone myself right now."

"Save it for later. We have to go."

I take a step and pitch toward the ground. Luke pulls me up and plasters me to his side. "Are you sure you can make it?"

I just nod and keep up the desperate pace.

"What if we're too late?" My voice shakes.

"Cherry and Stewart were just going up when I left."

God, please let us get there in time.

I could cry with relief when I see the big top come into view. I keep praying as we draw closer and burst inside.

The fuzziness gone from my brain, I stare toward the center ring. "*Noooo!*" I grab Luke's hand, and we run toward the middle. Our voices drown in the sea of cheers from the crowd.

Cherry and Stewart suspend from an oversized swing from the ceiling. He hangs upside down by his feet and lowers Cherry by a giant red sash.

She glides down.

Down.

Down. It's too fast!

"Stop!" I yell, and it's as if time stands still. Can't get there fast enough. In the corner of my eye, I see a blur as Luke races ahead of me, arms extended.

Must get to Cherry.

Her body unrolls from the sash.

And empties toward the floor.

"Noooo!" The scream rips from my throat as I watch my friend pitch toward the ground headfirst.

Too late. Can't get there in time. Luke will never make it.

The entire room gasps, the crowd coming to its feet. Not part of the show.

Cherry's shriek pierces my ears, and I stare in sick horror as death waits to swoop in and capture this innocent girl.

Two uniformed cops fly ahead of Luke, arms outstretched.

The audience gasps again, and I have to shake my head to clear my vision. Is that ... Artie Jensen with them?

Cherry torpedoes right into one of the officers, and the two slam to the ground, the red sash billowing over them like crepe paper.

I kick it into gear and race toward them. "Cherry!" She lies motionless on the man, her eyes glazed slits.

"Don't touch her!" Artie holds out a hand, then bends down to Cherry. "Can you hear me? Cherry, are you okay?"

She nods vacantly. "I don't know. My arm—it hurts."

The crowd of carnies pushes in, desperate to get closer. The audience stands in a hushed tableau.

"Back off!" Artie yells. "Get back now." He aims his head straight to the swing. "And, Stewart Fritz, I need you to know you're under arrest."

I blink at the man who fifteen minutes earlier would've been pulling bunnies out of a hat. "What?"

Artie Jensen holds up a badge. "I'm Detective Denny Whillock, Payne County PD. You have the right to remain silent."

The man finishes reading a hanging Stewart his rights, then gets to business running his hands over the unconscious officer, checking his pulse, behind his eyelids. Gone is the creepy magician. In his place stands a loud, brash cop. Unreal. He was in on it the whole time. I was working with the fuzz and didn't even know it! Awesome.

"Cherry, are you okay?" I drop down to the ground next to her. "Just stay right here." I spy Dolly and Mickey running across the arena. "Help's coming. Don't move."

Dolly and Mickey surround Cherry. "An ambulance is on the way," Mickey says, gingerly touching Cherry's limbs for broken bones. "Stay put."

Luke stands beside me and places his hand on my back. "They can check you out too."

"I'm fine." I smile up at him. "I think my hero got to me just in time. Want to go with me to make my statement?"

He laughs and clasps my hand in his. "Don't I always?"

I flash him my first smile all night. "It's like our standing date. You, me, and the Truman PD."

The detective formerly known as Artie Johnson fires off instructions into his phone as he sits with the downed officer. "I think he'll be fine. Took a pretty good hit. Probably got some broken ribs."

"That scared me to death." Mickey squats next to Dolly and Cherry. He wraps his arms around his ex-wife. "I thought I was going to die when I realized I couldn't get to you in time, Cherry."

Her smile is small. "It's okay. Everything's fine."

"No, it's not. And it hasn't been for some time." His scowl is fierce as his eyes sweep Dolly and Cherry. "Let's change that."

Dolly caresses Cherry's hand. "What are you talking about, Mickey?"

"I mean tonight—when Cherry was falling." He swallows hard. "For a second I thought I had lost it all again." He blinks back moisture in his eyes. "But I didn't. And I'm not going to let my family go again." He pulls Dolly closer to him. "You two are my family. We were meant to be together and nothing can stop that. I love you guys so much."

Dolly's voice is tear-clogged. "I love you too."

"I mean it, Dolly. This is it. The three of us—forever."

Dolly grins down at Cherry. "Can you handle that?"

Cherry nods and gives a weak smile. "I could probably handle it better with some Tylenol."

The paramedics surge through the growing crowd and place a stretcher next to Cherry and her hero.

Luke signals to one of the EMTs as he holds me close. "Don't look now, but here comes your mom." His hand rubs my shoulders. "She looks a little stressed."

I turn my head into his shoulder and smile. "I think I just got grounded—again."

chapter thirty-nine

I sit on the back of the ambulance getting the "Bella Special." This checkup routine is nothing new. Is my head cracked? How many fingers do I see? Does anything need stitches?

When Officer Mark passes by with Alfredo in cuffs, I push the EMT out of the way and jump down. "Wait!" Ruthie follows close behind.

Mark stops. "You did it again." His smile is reluctant. "I'm impressed, as usual, but mad that it had to go this far. You never stop, do you, Bella?"

I glance at Alfredo. "I didn't really solve anything this time. Just got in the right people's way, I guess."

"I would have come back for you," Alfredo says. "I would. But I had to save Cherry."

"You were never worthy to watch my unicycle ballet," Ruthie growls. "I should've shown you all the cool tricks *I* know with my switchblade collection."

"I couldn't figure you out." I step closer to Alfredo. "One minute you were harmless and the next, I was being shackled in a burning trailer."

"It all just went wrong. I didn't mean for you to get hurt."

"You were in cahoots with the man who killed your fiancée."

Alfredo shakes his dark head. "I loved her. Sure, I was paid to date her at first—and keep her out of Red's way. But I fell for Betty. And I did this all for her. She wanted Cherry protected at all costs, and I promised her I'd take care of that. I—I just didn't know how. I thought if I made Red believe we were working together, I could get close enough to get Cherry out of there. Take care of her."

"Your parenting skills leave something to be desired," Mark says.

"And then Red set you up for murder." The weird, jagged pieces of the puzzle begin to ease into place.

"Took me awhile to catch on to that," Alfredo says. "Red was telling me he had it under control and wouldn't let me hang. When I figured he was double-crossing me, I came up with the escape plan and decided to pull one over him—and get Cherry." Alfredo gives me that focused stare again. "You know how the dog's connected, don't you?"

I nod slowly. "Yes. I do."

"Take care of Cherry for me."

I glance to where she lies on a stretcher, surrounded by her new family and a detective. "She'll be well taken care of. You can cross that off your worry list—and focus on surviving prison."

Officer Mark laughs. "A guy who can do magic tricks? Oh, I have a feeling Alfredo here will be very popular with the fellas." He pushes Alfredo forward, and the two walk toward a flashing car.

Luke returns to my side. "Are you ready to put some closure on this?"

"Am I ever."

～～～～～～

Hours later I stand next to the Ferris wheel with a small crowd of my family and friends, including Cherry, who insisted on being present, even with her broken arm and black eye.

"That's the seat." I point up to the third cart. A carnival worker pulls the lever, letting the wheel turn until the cart comes near.

"How did you know?" Cherry asks, pulling the safety bar open and stepping up.

"Peg's tag. Her middle name is Aurora."

"Who gives dogs middle names?" Ruthie asks.

"People who love their pets," I say. "Or people who want to leave a clue about where something's hidden. When I read the dog's tag, I remembered you saying the Sleeping Beauty seat was your mom's favorite on the ride."

"And Aurora was Sleeping Beauty's name in the story," Luke adds. "Pretty smart thinking."

I smile at his compliment. "Thanks."

"Allow me." Mickey steps in beside Cherry and tugs on the back of the seat until it gives. "Seems to be a panel here of some sort."

Ruthie fishes in her top. "Need this?" She pulls out a screwdriver. "What? You'd be surprised how often that thing comes in handy."

Mickey shoves the screwdriver under the small panel and pops it off. "What do we have here?" He sticks his hand in the back of the seat then pulls it back out. "It's a key."

I read the tag. "Number 308." I look up at Mickey. "Lock box?"

"Only one way to find out."

I peek at my watch. "It's after ten."

Ruthie takes a pin out of her ratted hairdo. "Say the word, and I'll get us inside any bank in Truman." She holds up a hand. "Security systems are still a little dicey for me, but doors? No problem."

Mickey laughs and clasps the key tight. "I was thinking we'd just ask someone to let us in."

My friend snorts. "Amateur."

~~~~~~~~

After an unsuccessful trip to Missouri Savings and Loan, we caravan to the only other bank in town.

"Looks like one of our lock box keys all right." Joel Dean, the president of Truman National Bank, leads us into the vault. "This is a very unusual situation, and I'm not exactly following protocol here, but the records show Shelly and Junior Fritz do have a box paid through the rest of the year."

Cherry does a half circle in the stuffy room. "It could be a letter from my mom, something special of Betty's—anything."

Ruthie comes alongside Cherry. "I want you to know if it's money, I won't ask for a cut. Even though I am now officially Bella's partner, and since she solved this mystery, technically I did too."

"We'll both put our keys in the locks." Mr. Dean motions for Cherry to join him. "There we go. Just slip in your key."

I'm as nervous as a girl taking a pop quiz after a snow day. What could be in there that was worth killing for?

In the silent room, the click of the lock echoes off the walls. Mr. Dean slides out the metal box and places it on a nearby table. "Be my guest."

"Go ahead, sweetie," Mickey says, his arm around Dolly.

With a trembling hand, Cherry lifts the lid and peers inside. "It's an envelope."

Ruthie sighs. "Probably just a greeting card." She leans close and whispers in my ear. "I hope it's one of those singing ones. Those things are cool."

Cherry peels the envelope open and pulls out a piece of paper. Her eyes scan the document for what seems like an eternity. Finally, with wide eyes, she gasps and lets the paper fall to the ground.

Dolly swoops in to pick it up. "Well, if that don't beat all. It's a will. From Cherry's parents, naming her as beneficiary of their estate, which is the Fritz Family Carnival." She holds the paper to her chest. "You own the circus, Cherry."

"That's why Red wanted you gone," I say. "He wanted to sell it and keep the money himself."

"And make sure you weren't around to contest it," Luke adds.

"He thought he had the perfect plan. And Betty knew it was here. She must've created the map to throw him off the scent."

Ruthie shakes her head in misery. "I can't believe I donated my artistic talents to those slimebags."

Mickey grabs the will and reads it over. "So I guess the sale of the carnival is null and void now, since Red wasn't ever the rightful owner. Cherry, what do you want to do? It is your legacy."

Cherry pulls out a chair at the small table. "I want a family, not a full-time job. It was important to my parents, but that's when we were together. I just want to stay here with you and Dolly."

"And Peg," Ruthie pipes in. "Don't forget the dog."

"And to think." My brain swells with the possibilities. "If Peg hadn't have come back, we would never have known any of this."

"Betty had a heart of gold." Cherry smiles at the thought. "But she wasn't especially creative."

"I guess it worked out like God intended." Dolly goes to her young cousin and wraps her arms around her. "He was in this the whole time."

"Crazy as it sounds"—Cherry's eyes find mine—"I do believe you're right. Because suddenly everything that seemed so wrong . . . feels just right."

chapter forty

When girls are silent, everyone knows we're mad—or up to something. But when guys play the quiet game, it's just a big mystery. It could be anything from *I'm ticked* to *I need a cheeseburger.*

"You haven't said two words since we left the bank." I stare across the dark SUV at Luke, watching the way the city lights play on his skin.

He drives right by the carnival parking lot where my car waits, but he keeps going.

"Um . . . if you're planning on running away with me, I should warn you I have a psychotic friend with lethal talents."

Luke continues driving until he reaches the city park. Pulling into a spot, he kills the engine, walks around to my door, and holds it open. "Let's talk."

I step outside and notice he doesn't offer me his hand. "Okay." What does this mean? Was Ashley Timmons right? Did Luke reach his expiration point for how much of my waffling he could take? Can't a girl change her mind? Can't a girl play hard to get? It works in the movies!

Luke gestures to the swings. "Take a seat."

I lower myself into a seat that cups my butt in ways that remind me I'm no longer six. "Luke, I've been wanting to tell you that I—"

"Bella"—he paces the dirt mound in front of me—"I can't take this anymore. You obviously don't want a relationship from me, aside from friendship, and I've come to realize despite all your flirting, that's your final answer."

"But I've been flirting because I—"

"If you don't trust me by now, after all we've been through, then there's nothing I can say or do to help you or change your mind. You have to work this stuff out on your own. But I won't be waiting for you when you get it together." He drags his fingers through his hair and continues wearing a trail in the ground. "I realize you've seen a lot of crap and guys have let you down. But I've more than proven myself. I thought at some point you could just follow your heart and see what we had. But now I know you're just not ready. And I'm backing off, okay?" He stops abruptly and drags in a deep breath. "I don't know what I am to you . . . but it's not your boyfriend."

I watch a star fall in the sky beyond his shoulder. Leaning back, I push off with my feet and swinging once, I jump out right in front of Luke.

"You're always talking." I shove his shoulder. "Always telling me how it is. Well, do you want to know how *I* think it is?"

His Adam's apple bobs. "I don't think so."

"I think you're the most amazing guy ever." I watch him try to control his look of shock. "You're one of my best friends. You make me laugh, you're scary smart, and I always know you have my back. And Mr. Editor, more than anything, I want to be your girlfriend. And maybe I will be looking over my shoulder and waiting for something bad to happen between us, but that's just going to take some time." I step forward until we're nearly nose to nose, and I clasp his hands in mine. "I'm crazy about you, Luke Sullivan. Tell me you're still into me. Because if you've decided I'm too much trouble, I fully intend to sic Ruthie and her slingshot on you."

His lopsided grin has my heart tripping. "I'm still going to be bossy in journalism."

I roll my eyes. "Tell me something I don't know." Pivoting on my heel, I walk back to the swing and sit down.

Luke follows. He wraps his hand around the chains and bends down, his lips a breath away from mine. "I thought I had lost you tonight."

I search his face. "We've suffered through maniac football players and that tiny explosion at prom. What's a little smoke and flames?"

"Are you sure this isn't just hero's syndrome? I save you and you get all gushy?"

I can't help but laugh. "I never gush. But I also don't share. No more hanging out with just Ashley and her brother. It's not that I don't trust you. But that girl is on the prowl."

He nods. "Done. I'll only hang out with one Timmons—Kyle."

"Are you positive Ashley is out of the picture?"

"She was never even an option. I'm afraid you're it for me. It's kind of like a disease. I call it the plague of Bella."

"You say the most romantic things, Chief."

"I am a writer."

I cover one of his hands with mine. "You might break my heart."

"It's possible." With gentle fingers, Luke caresses my jaw. "But I'm sure gonna try not to."

Luke pulls on the swing until his lips are a feather-light brush against mine. I slip my arms around his neck and curl my fingers in his hair. With his careful touch, I block out thoughts of evil and death. Memories of the haunted house burn away like ashes as I stand up and crush my mouth to his.

He rains small kisses on the side of my lips, my forehead, and my cheek . . . then pulls my head to his chest and strokes my hair.

"Luke?"

"Hmmm?"

"How are we going to handle dating and the newspaper?"

He rubs the tension at the base of my neck. "I tell you what to do and you'll ignore me."

"So . . . like normal?"

"Yeah."

"Sounds good."

~~~~~~~~~

Nothing like an attempt on your life to extend your school-night curfew. When I walk into my living room, it's almost midnight. And the whole family is there.

Including Jake.

"Bella, good heavens." The big guy rushes to me and nearly chokes me in his hug. "I came as soon as I heard."

"Um, Jake?" I step away. "Why are you still in your pirate uniform?" I stare at his gold vest and black stretchy pants.

He shakes his head. "I was getting ready to go against Chainsaw when Mickey called. I rented a car and drove like a maniac. Are you okay?"

"I'm fine." I'm more than fine. I'm Luke Sullivan's girlfriend! And I'm happy. "You didn't need to drive all the way back just for me. We handled it."

"That's what I tried to tell him." Mom sits on the couch with her feet curled beneath her. Robbie lies in her lap, passed out and wrapped in his cape.

"Close one tonight, sis." Budge wiggles his bushy brows. "I almost got my bedroom back."

"You can bet your Wiener Palace flair I wouldn't give in that easy."

"I'm sorry." Jake clamps his arm around my shoulders. "I should've been here."

I lean into him. "Hey, relax. We understand."

Jake angles his head toward Mom. "No, there's no excuse, and I've worn out your patience in understanding . . . I quit tonight."

"What?" Mom lurches to her feet, accidentally dumping Robbie to the floor.

"Ow! Hey, what gives?" The little guy rubs his head.

"On the long ride back to Truman, I had a lot of time to think. And I'm sick of living without my family." Jake kisses me on the head. "I almost lost one of you tonight"—he frowns at me—"again."

I shrug. "Narrowly escaping death does seem to be one of my pastimes."

"Jake, you can't just quit the WWT." Mom moves beside us, and the wrinkle between her brows would have Dad breaking out the Botox. "This is your dream. You've worked too hard."

"For what?" Jake throws up his hands. "To leave you alone to raise our family? I need to be here—for you, for the boys, and for Bella."

Mom slants her eyes my way. "Keeping up with her does seem to be a full-time job."

"Jillian, I want my family back. This isn't a decision I've just made in the heat of the moment. I've been thinking about it for a while now, and I know this is the right thing to do."

I step aside as my mother curls her arm around her husband. "Are you sure? What will you do, Jake?"

Budge groans and flops onto the couch with his brother. "Dad, you can't go back to the pad factory."

"If that's what it takes. I'll do whatever I need to do to support this family and be at home with the ones I love."

"I think we should all join hands and sing a song now," Robbie says. "Maybe a nice inspirational Josh Groban number?"

"Dude, my gag reflexes are already being pushed to the limit." Budge reaches for his Coke on the coffee table.

"Are you sure about this?" Mom asks.

"Looking at all your faces, I've never been more certain of anything in my life."

"Aw." She gives Jake a quick kiss on the lips. "Group hug! Come on!"

Robbie, Budge, and I reluctantly make our way to our parents, piling arms and hands until we're one big wad of family.

"I love you, guys," Jake says.

"Love you!"

"Love you too!"

"Ditto."

We stay like that for a long while until my heart overflows, my arms ache, and . . . my eyes burn.

"Budge . . . did you fart?"

"Oops."

Ah, family.

They may be crazy, but I'll take them—the good, the bad . . . and the stinky.

chapter forty-one

"Ruthie looks great in her graduation cap and gown," Luke says beside me, fanning the both of us with a program in the heat of the evening.

I watch my friend walk across the stage on the football field. The principal hands Ruthie her diploma, and she grins wide for the photographic moment. She shifts down the line to the superintendant, who frowns, then moves Ruthie's tassel to the other side.

"Her hat is pretty clever." Budge snaps a picture on my other side.

"And totally Ruthie." Only Ruthie McGee would forego the graduation beanie and wear her motorcycle helmet. "But I like how her hair is in school colors."

Luke intertwines my fingers with his and leans over to Budge. "Has she decided what she's going to do yet?"

"Yeah. She had lots of offers, but she took the full ride from Tulsa University."

I blink. "That's funny. I thought you just said—"

Budge grins. "I did. My Ruthie-poo is one humble genius. Turns out she pretty much set the curve on the ACT last year. And of course, every college wants her for her unicycling ballet skills."

"Of course." I laugh and clap for my friend as she leaves the stage.

"Did you see the paper today?" I ask Budge.

"Yeah, great article, you two. Pretty cool to get published on the front page of the *Tulsa World*. Wouldn't you know Stewart would end up singing like Justin Timberlake in tight undies? And to think, Cherry's parents had entrusted Betty with the key to the will. They all knew Red was bad news."

"And Alfredo," Luke adds. "I guess we'll never know if he really did fall in love with Betty."

"I think he did." Even though the jerk nearly killed me, I still believe there's a good heart in there somewhere. And love just found him unexpectedly.

It happens to the best of us.

I lean into Luke's side and stare at the clouds lazily rolling along overhead. Truman, Oklahoma—who would've thought this would be home sweet home? Jake will start his new job next week as a commentator for World Wrestling Television. The show was furious that he left, but when my story hit the press, and the world knew why Jake left his match that night, America fell in love with my wrestling stepdad. And soon WWT was calling and begging him to come back. And he did. On his terms.

Dolly proposed to Mickey last night at Sugar's diner over a piece of lemon chiffon pie. That's right—*Dolly* proposed. Mickey and Cherry said yes.

And then there's me.

I don't know what will happen with my dad. We're talking more now, but it's still awkward. Seventeen years is a long time to know someone—but not really know them. So we're working it out. And now that he's the temporary parent of an eight-year-old, he needs my support. Actually he needs the support of the entire National Guard, but so far they haven't returned his calls.

And I'm just taking it day by day—my relationship with Luke, my attempts to get a raise in my allowance for that new Chloe dress, and my new decision to keep my nose out of other people's business. It's just too risky! After all, God has given me a lot to live for.

The graduates toss their hats in the air, and my eyes nearly bug out of my head when I see Ruthie's helmet take out a science teacher on its descent.

I curl my arm around Luke's waist and walk toward the seniors to hug some friends.

"Excuse me."

I turn at the tap on my shoulder and smile. "Yes?"

A teenage girl steps close. "I've heard all about you, and I think I have your next job for you."

"Oh no." My laugh is a tinkling bell on the wind. "I'm out of the business."

The girl doesn't move. "I think my boyfriend is cheating on me, and I want you to investigate."

Luke's smile is slightly indulgent. "She's retired."

"Yeah, I can't help you." I'm walking the straight and narrow path.

"Oh." Her face falls. "That's too bad. My aunt is a buyer for Gucci, and I was going to pay you in purses."

I eye her shiny green bag with appreciation. "Well . . . we could at least talk about a down payment."

To some, God gives the gift of encouragement, of teaching, maybe of mercy. But to me? Nosiness.

And I've never been one to turn a gift away.

acknowledgments

If I had to write a book by myself, I'd still be scratching incoherent sentences in a one-subject notebook. It takes a lot of people to throw these things together, and I'm grateful for every soul who had a part.

It is with huge amounts of gratitude that I thank:

Natalie Hanemann, my fabulous editor at Thomas Nelson. Thank you so much for all you've taught me and for putting up with all my crazy e-mails and ramblings. And for understanding my pain and heartache over any video with Jillian Michaels' name on it. But we are gonna be so toned this time next year. (Okay, you will. I have too much of a dependent relationship with Ben and Jerry's. But I'll cheer you on from afar.)

Jamie Chavez, another amazing editor. I'm so lucky to work with this dynamic duo, and Jamie, I appreciate the friendship, the travel advice, and for pointing out all the dumb mistakes I make in every book. Like how there aren't three days in a weekend. But you have to admit—it's a nice idea.

My family. Things always get crazy during deadline crunch time, and I'm so glad you haven't locked all your doors and windows so I'd move on to another family. Thank you for embracing the inevitable fact that you are stuck with me. And that I require lots of chicken and steak dinners.

Acknowledgments

My friends. For still talking to me after I turn into Deadline Medusa. Y'all are the best. Thank you for the laughs, the movie nights, and all our traveling adventures. And for tolerating my airplane takeoff/landing freak outs. It's not that I'm scared. I'm just dramatically concerned.

Chip MacGregor, the best agent and Ameri-Scotsman on the planet. Your zippy one-liners make my day, and your career advice is top-notch. I can't imagine entrusting these big dreams to anyone else. Thanks for believing in me. (Hum Josh Groban as you read this paragraph for maximum effectiveness.)

Erin Valentine, once again you have been such a huge source of help and support. Thank you for prereading the sloppy drafts, even when they make no sense and require a PhD in crazy to even read through them. I couldn't do this without you.

The sales and fiction staff at Thomas Nelson. Thank you for everything you do, and for making the job of writing books so worthwhile. I love you guys!

My blog family at jennybjones.com. You guys are the most awesome Web family ever, and I love hanging out with you every week. You seriously brighten my days.

My readers, the most amazing people on the planet. A handful of years into this writing life, and I still cannot figure out why anyone would read my little stories. Voodoo? Trance? Brainwashing? I dunno, but please don't find the antidote. I'm grateful to every one of you and pray for you often. Thank you for being a part of the ministry of fiction. Pass it on.

Jeff Spivey, funeral director extraordinaire and former classmate. Thank you for answering my questions about burials without even blinking an eye. I don't know how I can repay you for the information on digging up bodies, but if you figure out its favor equivalent, give me a shout.

Tony Humphrey, a hero of a fireman and medic. I appreciate

the help with answering my questions. Thanks for lending me your expertise. And for not laughing at my crazy inquiries. Or turning me over to the police . . .

Ken "Bubba" Whillock, of the Arkansas State Police, for all the procedure assistance. That taser info might come in especially handy. Thank you for keeping Arkansas and Bella Kirkwood safe.

Joel Dean, king of all things techie. I'm so thankful for your help through this series and for putting up with my dumb computer questions. I appreciate your time, patience, and for keeping your eye rolls to yourself.

Finally, a huge acknowledgment to God. Every book takes me on a spiritual theme. I intend it for the characters, but somehow I get pulled in along for the ride. I'm so grateful for all You're teaching me and the countless ways You're blessing me. God is good. All the time. (Pass that on too.)

reading group guide

1. What do you think the title means?
2. After Luke's ex-girlfriend returned to Truman High, Bella didn't handle it very well. What would you have done in her situation?
3. In a carnival or circus, things are often not what they seem. Where else was this true in the book?
4. What's some advice you'd give to a friend who's struggling with a parent's remarriage? What would God want her to know?
5. When Jake gets his dream job as a pro wrestler, things didn't quite turn out like he or the family thought. How so? Describe a time when getting what you wanted wasn't quite all you thought it would be.
6. Bella ultimately forgives Hunter, her cheating ex-boyfriend, and resumes a friendship with him. Was this the right thing to do or should she have stayed away from him?
7. Communicating in families is often hard. Why do you think Bella's dad wouldn't listen to her warnings about Christina? Why do parents sometimes not "hear" you?
8. If God sat down and had coffee with Bella, what would he tell her she needed to work on?
9. How has Bella and Budge's relationship grown?
10. What tips would you give Bella's dad for repairing his relationship with his daughter? Where would he even start?
11. 1 Corinthians 1:9 promises us that God is faithful. In what ways do you see this in the book? Where have you seen this in your own life?

Grief brought Finley to Ireland.

She is on her way to Ireland to follow the travel journal of her late brother,
hoping the place he felt closest to God will bring her peace.
But a Hollywood heart-throb and the pressures of school leads
her to a new and dangerous vice.
She finds more questions than answers, but she holds out hope that . . .

Love will lead her home.

there you'll find me

jenny b. jones

An Excerpt from *There You'll Find Me*

Prologue

Sometimes I think about when I was little, and my older brothers would take me out to fly kites.

"Give it some slack!" Will would yell.

It was almost painful to watch, that kite of mine.

Tethered to the string in my hand. Dancing in the sky all alone.

My breath caught in my throat, my pulse beating wild and crazy in my chest. My heart soaring with every dip and turn of the kite, as if I were flying along, instead of standing with my two feet on the ground, squinting against the sun to see the dance.

What if it fell?

What if the breeze took it away?

I counted the seconds until I could reel it back in.

I was that kite.

Fragile against the wind. Soaring one minute. Spiraling straight down the next. Just looking for something to hold me up.

Before I spun out of control and flew away.

Disappearing from sight.

Chapter One

I'm on my way to Ireland! I've pretty much lost a whole night's sleep on the plane, but who cares? Great things are waiting for me. I know it.

—Travel Journal of Will Sinclair, Abbeyglen, Ireland

"M iss?"

I pulled out an earbud as the flight attendant leaned over me. "Yes?"

"We have a few seats available in first class. Would you like to have one of them?"

Seats like recliners, meals that didn't taste like burned Lean Cuisines, and no guy in front of me leaned back 'til he was in my lap? "Yes, please."

I grabbed my backpack and followed the woman through the narrow aisle, dodging two ladies on their way to the bathroom.

Five more hours of the flight to Shannon, Ireland. I couldn't get there fast enough. But a cushy seat would surely help pass the time.

"Here we go." She smiled widely, and her eyes brimmed with an excessive amount of enthusiasm for a good deed she surely did every day.

Thanking the flight attendant, I slipped into the seat, the leather crunching beneath me, and set my backpack at my feet.

"Have fun," she said.

Have fun?

I glanced at the guy beside me. He leaned against the wall, his head propped into his hand, a Colts hat covering his head and shielding his eyes from view. From the stillness of his body, he had to be asleep.

I settled in, pulled out my travel pillow, zipped up my hoodie, and burrowed. Reaching for the newspaper, I opened to the second page, where the article from the front left off.

. . . The latest bombing in Iraq has been claimed by terrorist Hassan Al Farran, ringleader of the al Qaeda cell thought to be responsible for the deadly blast in Afghanistan that killed a schoolhouse of children, as well as CNN correspondent and humanitarian Will Sinclair, son of hotel magnate Marcus Sinclair. On the Most Wanted list, Al Farran is number four in command in the Taliban and continues to elude capture.

As the familiar churning began in my stomach, I took a few deep breaths. One day the pain wouldn't be as fresh as if the loss of my brother had just happened. Instead of two years ago. My counselor said I should've been past the anger stage. But I wasn't.

But on October twentieth, perhaps I would be.

I continued to read the article, but it provided no new information, and soon the words swam and blurred until I finally had to close my eyes and rest for just a bit in the dimmed lights of the plane.

֍

"The captain has turned on the Fasten Seat Belt sign. Please remain in your seats and refrain from moving about the cabin."

Somewhere in the fog of my sleepy brain, the flight attendant's voice registered, but I couldn't seem to pull myself to the surface. So tired. And warm. And comfy.

"Sir, your friend needs to put her seat belt on."

"As much as I like a lovely girl leaning on my shoulder," a lilting voice whispered near my ear, "I think you might want to listen to the flight attendant."

My head lifted with a jerk as the plane shuddered. "What?" *Where am I? What time is it?*

The boy beside me laughed, and after I blinked a few times, I saw him more clearly.

Snapping myself in, my cheeks warmed. "Was I just—"

"Sleeping on me?" He nodded his head, his blond hair peeping out from his cap. "Yeah."

"And did I—"

"Drool?" His voice carried a hint of Ireland. "Not much."

Gray eyes. Chiseled cheekbones. A grin that revealed a dimple. A voice low enough to send chills along my aching neck. A smile that would send most teen girls into a squealing fit of adoration and hyperventilation.

"Oh my gosh—"

"Shhh." He pressed one finger to his lips. "Don't say a word. I've gotten this far without being bothered."

"Beckett Rush."

He flashed that million-dollar grin again. The one that earned this nineteen-year-old the lead role as the darkly romantic Steele Markov in a franchise of films such as *Vampire Boarding School* and *Friday Night Bites*.

"If you stay mum about this, I'll give you an autograph." He leaned close. "But you should know I've given up signing body parts."

I blinked twice, my mouth open in an O.

"I know, it's shocking," he said. "I guess the flight attendant thought she was doing you a favor sitting you next to me, but—"

"I don't want your autograph," I finally managed.

Beckett tilted his head and flashed those gunmetal grays. "Okay. One picture. But later. After we land, and I've had my breakfast."

"I don't want your picture either." I scooted away from his seat. "The last thing I want, Mr. Hollywood Party Boy, is to be photographed with you, where it will surely land in some trash magazine. As if I need any more of *that*."

His frown was the first genuine facial expression I'd witnessed. No doubt, Beckett Rush was not used to anything but fawning and fainting from teenage girls. *And* their mothers.

"Have we met?" he asked.

"No." Digging into my backpack, I pulled out a magazine and flipped past the glossy cover. None of the girls looked like me. They were all rail thin, unlike my size nine. Scrawny legs, where my own were muscular from years of cheerleading. And their hair displayed artful compositions of chaos and grace, while my long, dark locks were stuffed into a messy bun on top of my head after an endless day of travel.

"Are you sure, so?"

"Quite." Returning the magazine to my bag, I retrieved the sheet music I'd been working on for weeks. My audition piece.

"Because now that I get a good look at you, you seem familiar."

I swiped my fingers through my brunette bangs until they offered a little coverage. "I have one of those faces."

"And you've certainly a strong dislike of me." I could feel his eyes study me as I reread the first eight measures. "As if I've done something to you."

"You have not."

"Then—"

"It's your type," I said, without looking up. "I know your type."

"Well now, that's interesting."

His cologne filtered my way and clung to my shirt where I'd fallen asleep against him. I probably had crease marks on my face from his shoulder. How embarrassing.

"Did you have a good nap, then?"

Boys like him were only after one thing. And I was done with him and his entire species. "Fine. Thank you."

"Since we've established who I am . . ." He lifted a blond brow when I didn't respond. "The next line is where you tell me your name. I think if you're going to drool on me, we should at least be on a first-name basis."

I sighed and looked toward the window where I saw nothing but dark sky.

"You look like a Myrtle to me," he said to himself. "Maybe a Mavis. But I could be wrong."

"Finley." I tried to rearrange my mussed hair with my fingers. "Finley Sinclair."

Silence. Then his eyes widened. "Of the hotel fame?"

Here we go. "My dad might own a hotel or two."

"One or two *thousand*." And then new understanding dawned. "You've had quite a year. I think I saw you on the cover of *People* some months back. 'Hotel heiress sneaks into club and parties the night away.'"

"That was last spring." And I had worked my tail off making amends, getting away from what my dad had called my crazy season. Thank goodness any small amount of notoriety I had did not extend to foreign countries. I would start over with a clean slate. "The article was grossly exaggerated, and I'm sorry I took a photo op away from you. But don't worry, your Wild Child title is safe. I don't want it." Not anymore, though you couldn't tell it from my list of escapades last year. And I was done associating with people like Beckett, or my ex-boyfriend, who just wanted to have a good time and didn't care about the costs.

I didn't miss the flash of Beckett's eyes before his amiable mask returned. "Since you're not a member of my fan club, let's talk about something else," he said. "A safer topic perhaps. What brings you to Ireland?"

Years of manners drilled into me made it impossible to totally ignore him. But I wished I were still asleep, blissfully unaware of the choppy skies or whom I was sitting next to. "I'm going to Abbeyglen. Foreign exchange program." And I was two weeks overdue. Instead of leaving last month like I was supposed to, I had opted for an orchestra camp instead. Now I would arrive mere days before school began.

My body jolted as we hit another air pocket.

"So your parents wanted you out of the country."

"It was my choice, actually. My brother Will came here for his senior year and I wanted to do the same. I hope to see every place he went." I thought of his travel journal in my backpack, sandwiched between a romance novel and *Seventeen*. And Will's violin, stowed in the front of the plane, the one I would use to get into the New York Conservatory. I'd stay in Abbeyglen through March, then go back to Charleston and graduate with my class. Just enough time to soak up the culture, buy my parents some souvenirs, and totally change my life.

Beckett put his elbow on my armrest and leaned my way. "I'm sorry about your brother."

"How did you know about Will?"

"What happened to him got the whole world's attention. I've already read two scripts based on your brother's life."

Anger had a stranglehold on my throat, and I considered pulling down one of those masks until the black spots went away. "Will's life was more than some Hollywood opportunity." How dare they commercialize the event that ripped my family in two? I'd seen enough of the real video footage to last me the rest of my days.

"I know that must've been hard."

"Thank you," I finally said. "Life can be hard. In the real world." What did Mr. Vampire know of difficulties? He lived in a magical palace where girls threw him rose petals and their never-ending loyalty. His movies' opening-night revenues could build a hundred of the schools in Afghanistan my brother had worked so hard for.

His smile was a slow lift of the lips. "Just a piece of advice. You might want to brush up on your people skills if you're going to make it in Abbeyglen. The Irish are some of the nicest folks on earth, to be sure. They won't take kindly to your surly attitude and sullen looks." Beckett's eyes took a lazy stroll over my face. "Pretty though those looks might be."

The boy was unreal. "Does that seriously work on girls?"

"Yes." He scratched his chin as he contemplated this. "Yes, it does."

I delicately cleared my throat and studied my nails. "Did absolutely nothing for me."

"Interesting. I guess there's a first time for everything." He shrugged. "So you don't care to sit by me. And you don't want my autograph. What is it you do want, Finley Sinclair?"

Some peace. Some healing. To hear God's voice again.

I wanted to find my brother's Ireland. To put it into song.

And I wanted my heart back.

"I'll know it when I find it." I looked past Beckett and into the night sky. "Or when it finds me."

The only thing scarier than living
on the edge is stepping off it.

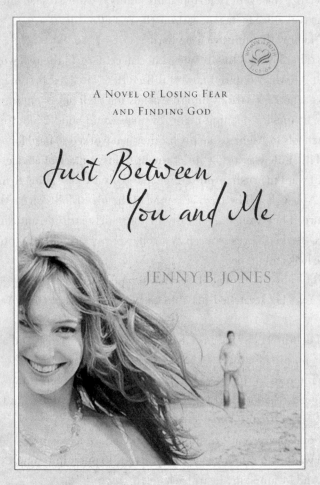

A NOVEL OF LOSING FEAR
AND FINDING GOD

*Just Between
You and Me*

JENNY B. JONES

A Carol Award-winning novel

THOMAS NELSON
Since 1798